MÖNKEY KING
AND THE WORLD OF MYTHS

THE MONSTER AND THE MAZE

MAPLE LAM

putnam

G. P. PUTNAM'S SONS

APR -- 2024

JKJC

G. P. PUTNAM'S SONS
AN IMPRINT OF PENGUIN RANDOM HOUSE LLC, NEW YORK

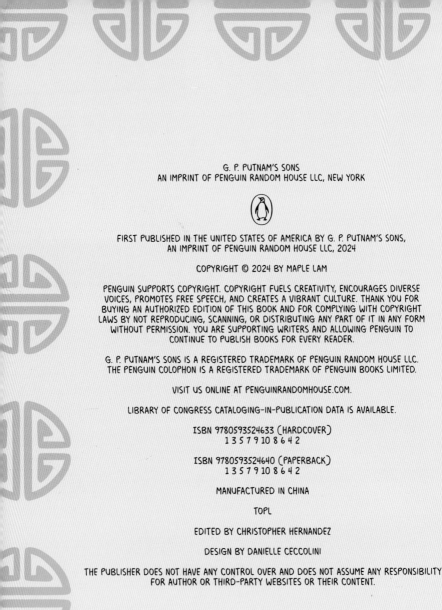

FIRST PUBLISHED IN THE UNITED STATES OF AMERICA BY G. P. PUTNAM'S SONS,
AN IMPRINT OF PENGUIN RANDOM HOUSE LLC, 2024

VISIT US ONLINE AT PENGUINRANDOMHOUSE.COM.

LIBRARY OF CONGRESS CATALOGING-IN-PUBLICATION DATA IS AVAILABLE.

ISBN 9780593524633 (HARDCOVER)
1 3 5 7 9 10 8 6 4 2

ISBN 9780593524640 (PAPERBACK)
1 3 5 7 9 10 8 6 4 2

MANUFACTURED IN CHINA

TOPL

EDITED BY CHRISTOPHER HERNANDEZ

DESIGN BY DANIELLE CECCOLINI

TO MOM AND DAD

THANK YOU FOR KINDLING MY INTEREST
IN MYTHOLOGY, HISTORY, AND ART.

I LOVE YOU.

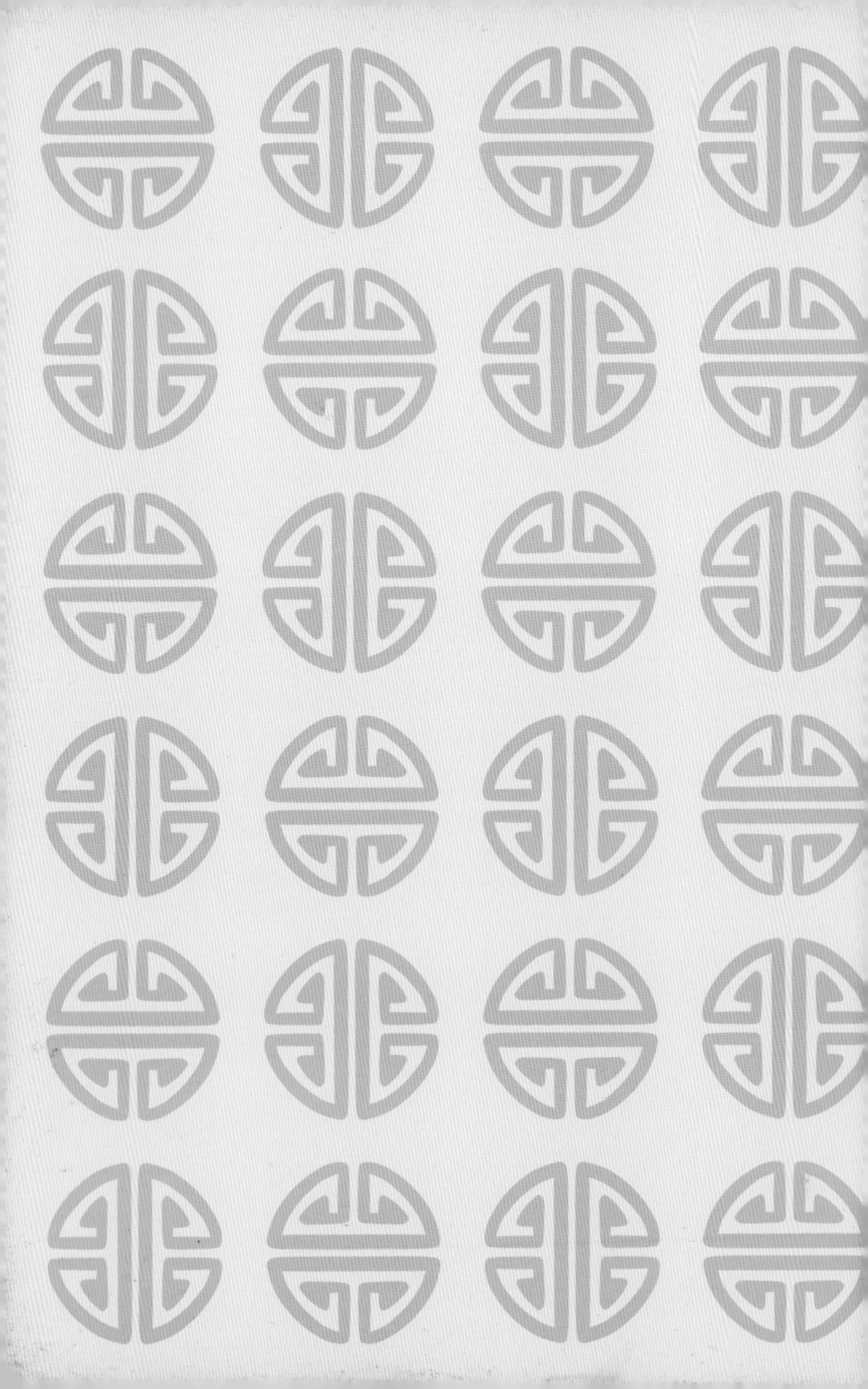

PROLOGUE THE MONKEY FROM A ROCK

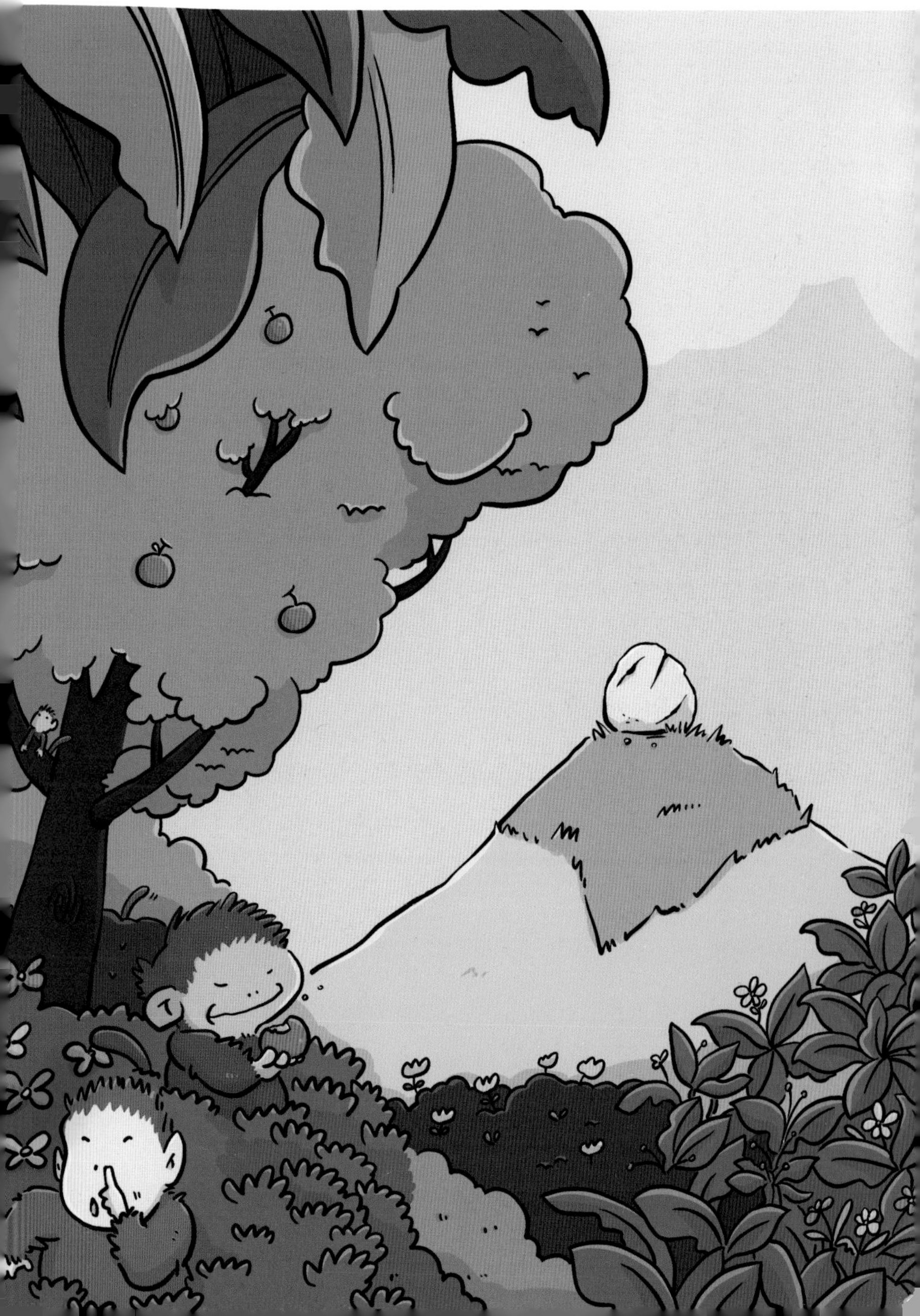

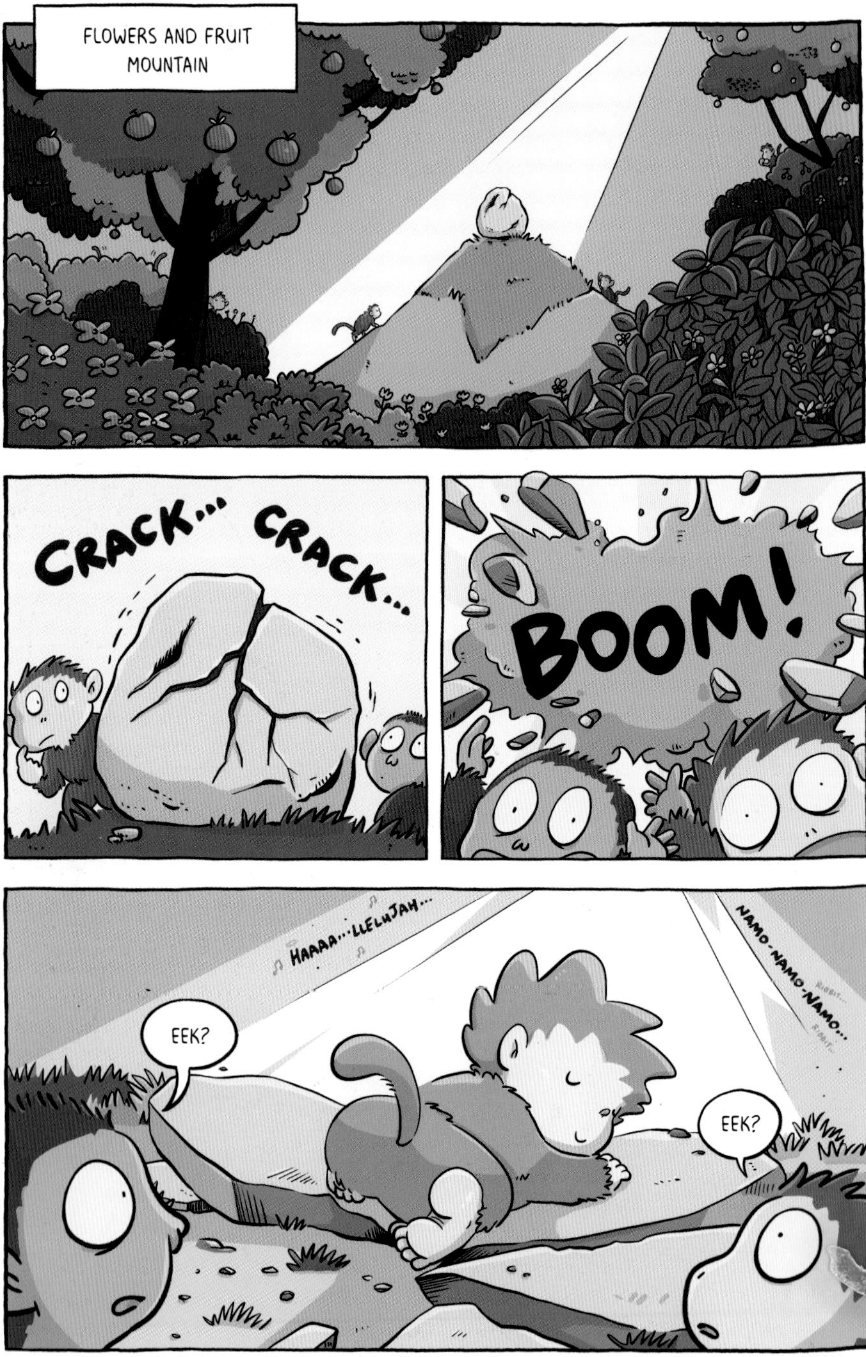
FLOWERS AND FRUIT MOUNTAIN
CRACK... CRACK...
BOOM!
HAAAA...LLELUJAH...
NAMO-NAMO-NAMO...
RIBBIT...
RIBBIT...
EEK?
EEK?

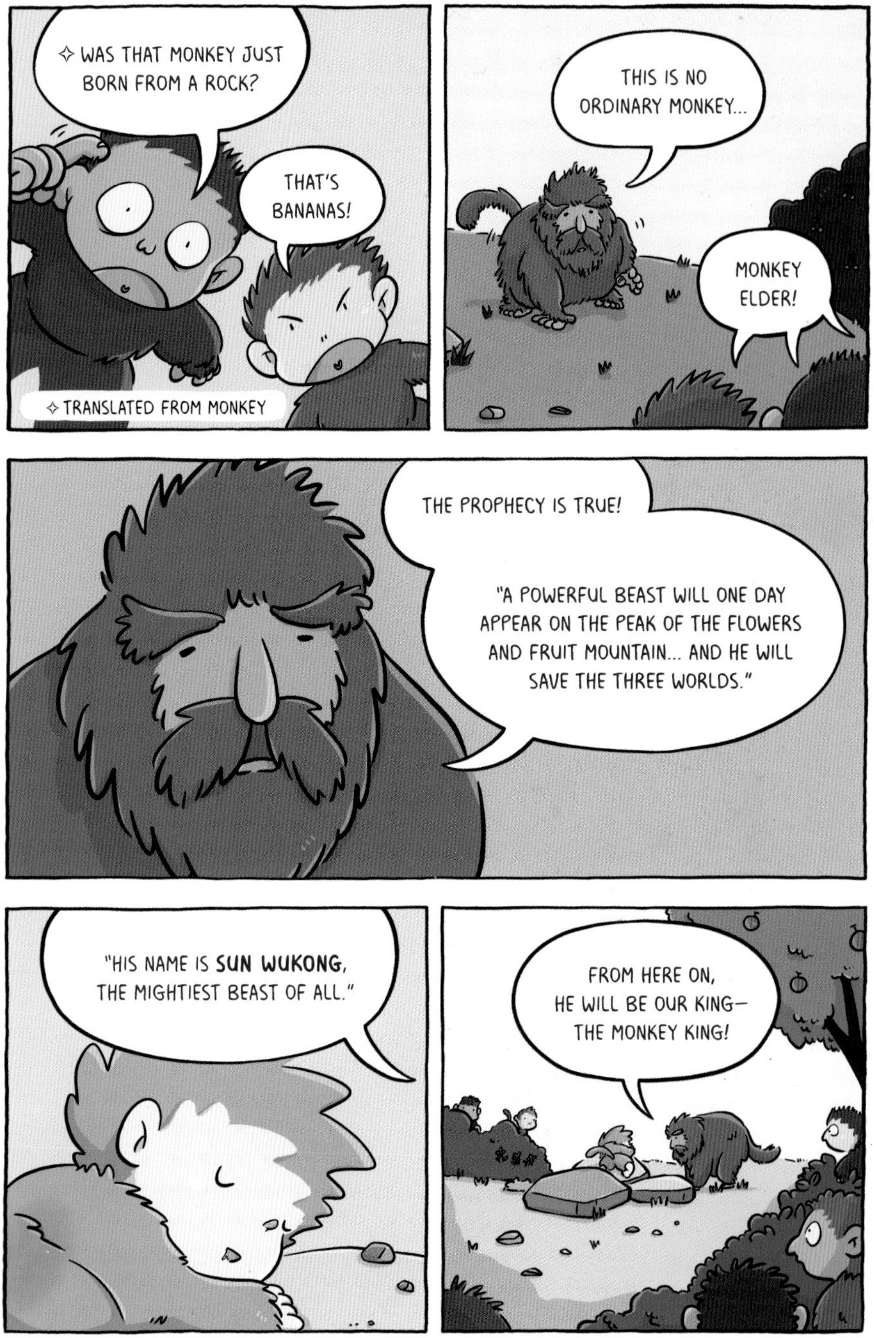
✧ WAS THAT MONKEY JUST BORN FROM A ROCK?
THAT'S BANANAS!
✧ TRANSLATED FROM MONKEY
THIS IS NO ORDINARY MONKEY...
MONKEY ELDER!
THE PROPHECY IS TRUE!
"A POWERFUL BEAST WILL ONE DAY APPEAR ON THE PEAK OF THE FLOWERS AND FRUIT MOUNTAIN... AND HE WILL SAVE THE THREE WORLDS."
"HIS NAME IS **SUN WUKONG**, THE MIGHTIEST BEAST OF ALL."
FROM HERE ON, HE WILL BE OUR KING— THE MONKEY KING!

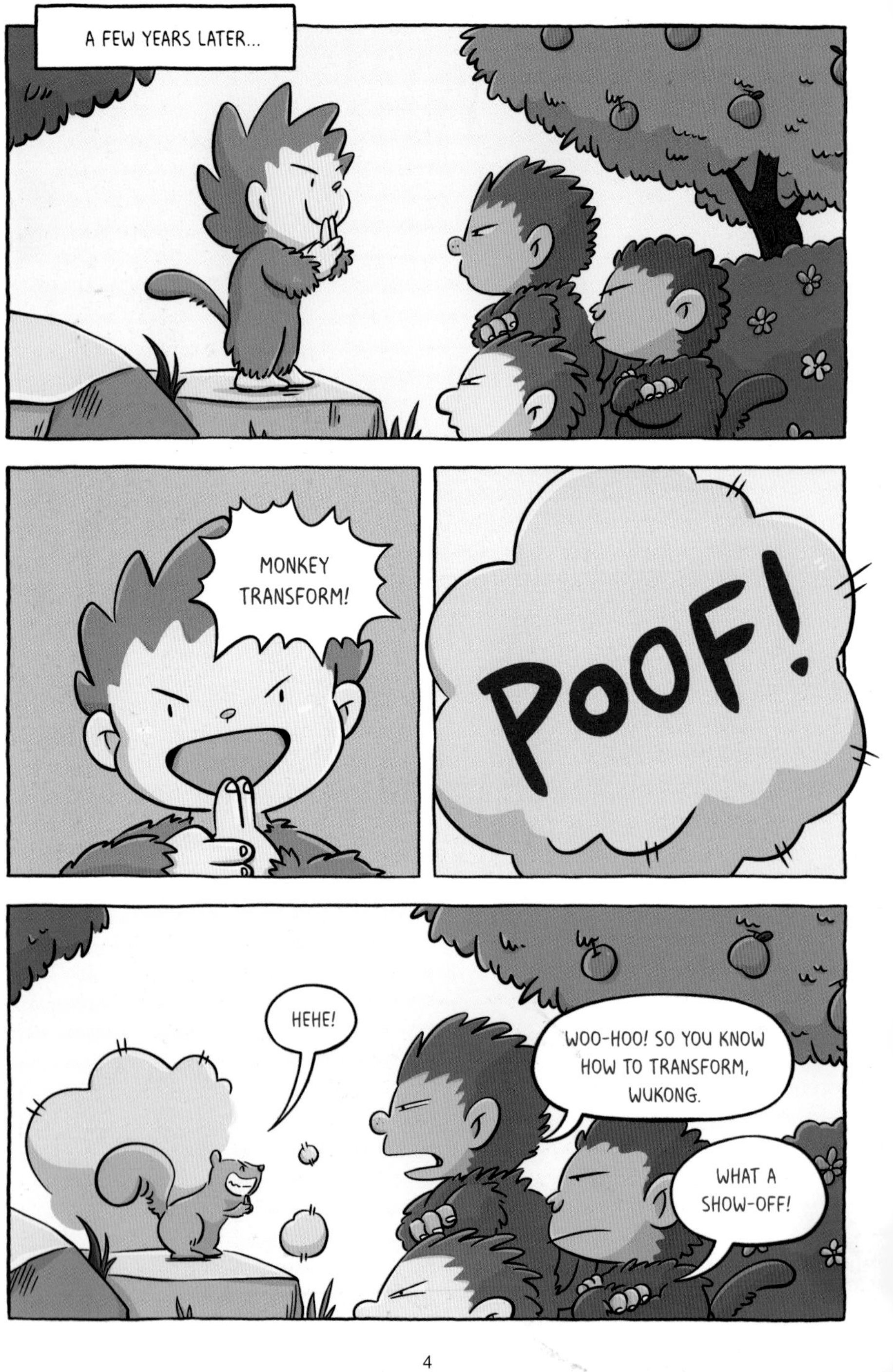
A FEW YEARS LATER...
MONKEY TRANSFORM!
POOF!
HEHE!
WOO-HOO! SO YOU KNOW HOW TO TRANSFORM, WUKONG.
WHAT A SHOW-OFF!

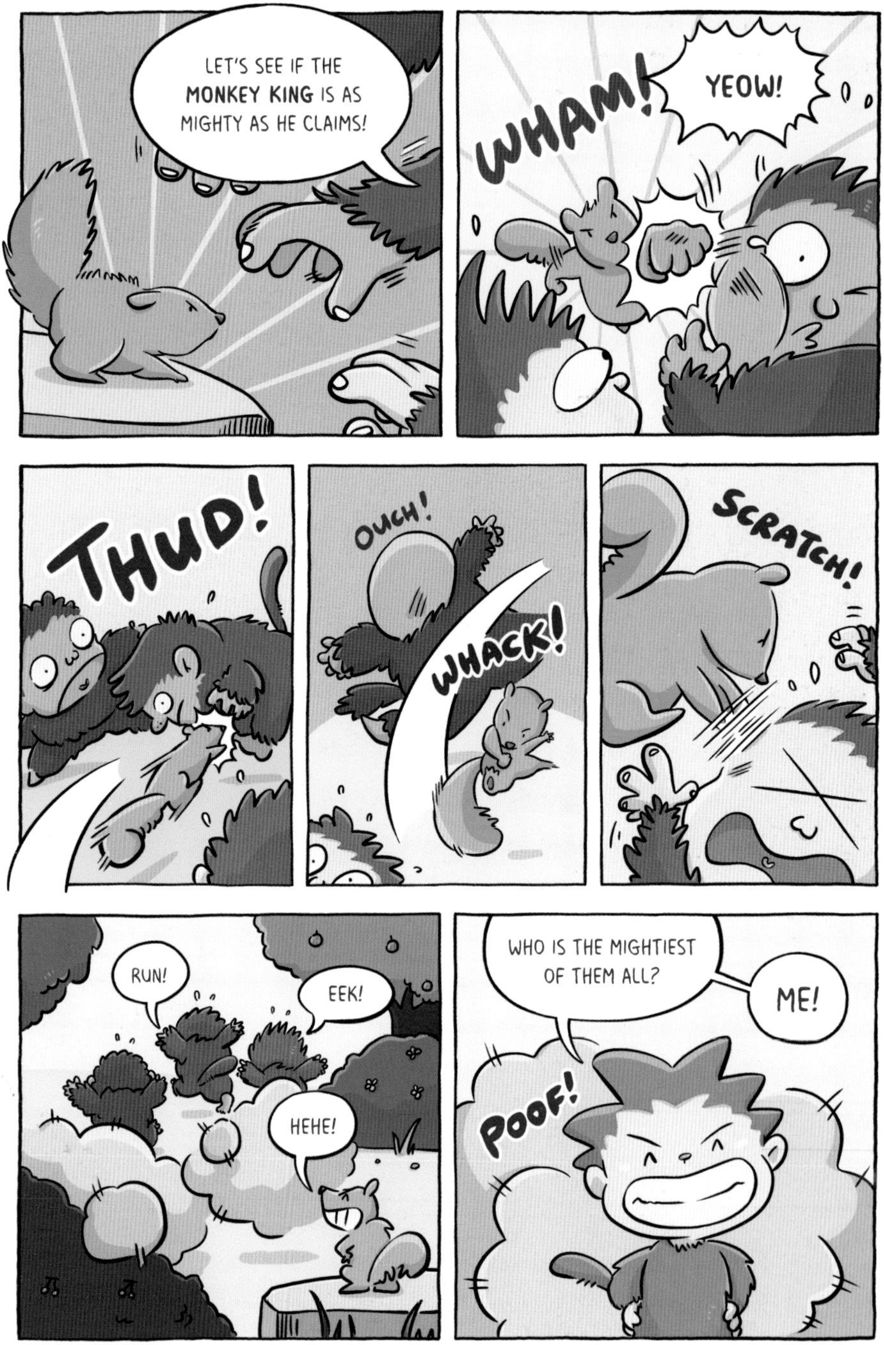

LET'S SEE IF THE MONKEY KING IS AS MIGHTY AS HE CLAIMS!
WHAM!
YEOW!
THUD!
OUCH!
WHACK!
SCRATCH!
RUN!
EEK!
HEHE!
WHO IS THE MIGHTIEST OF THEM ALL?
ME!
POOF!

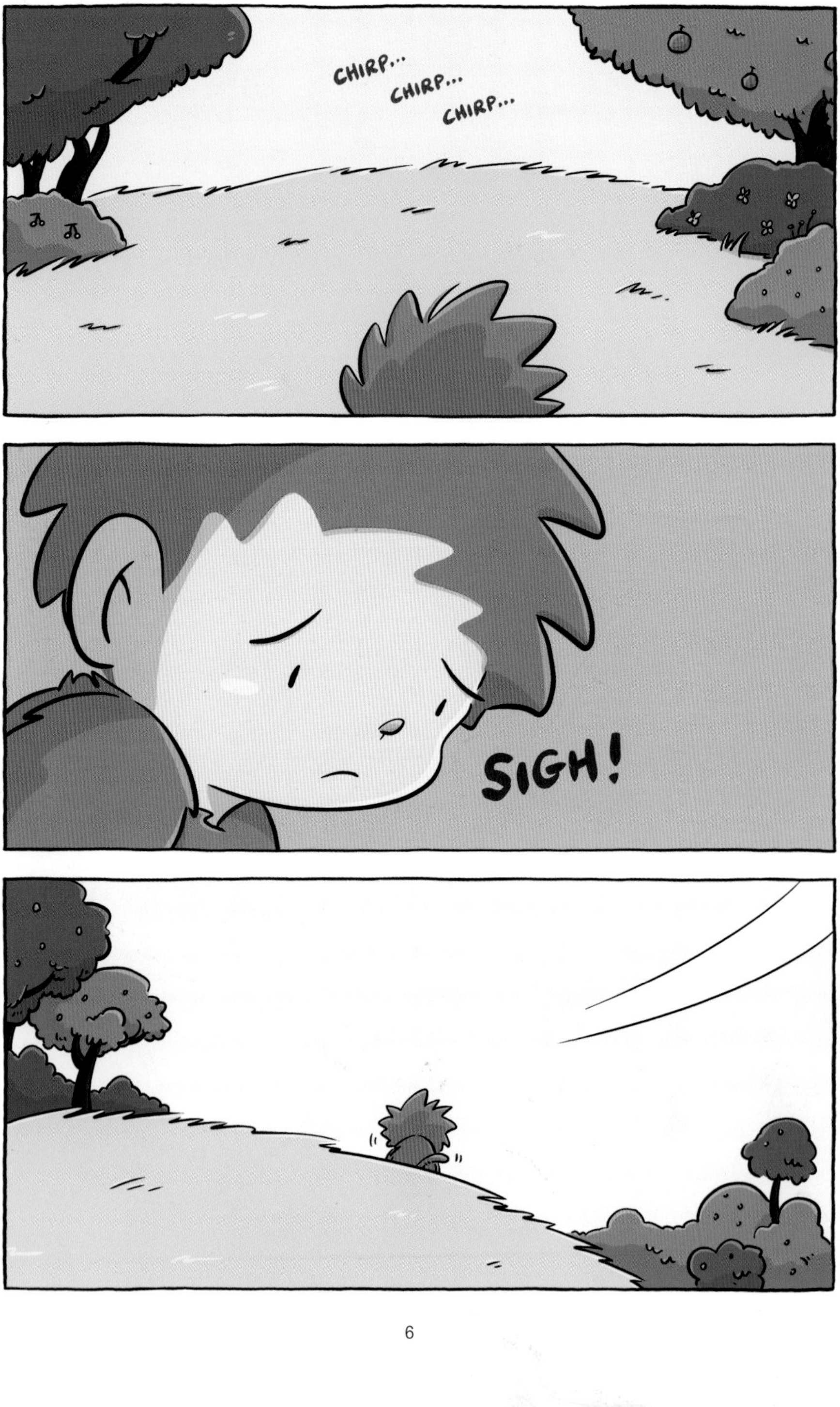
CHIRP...
CHIRP...
CHIRP...
SIGH!

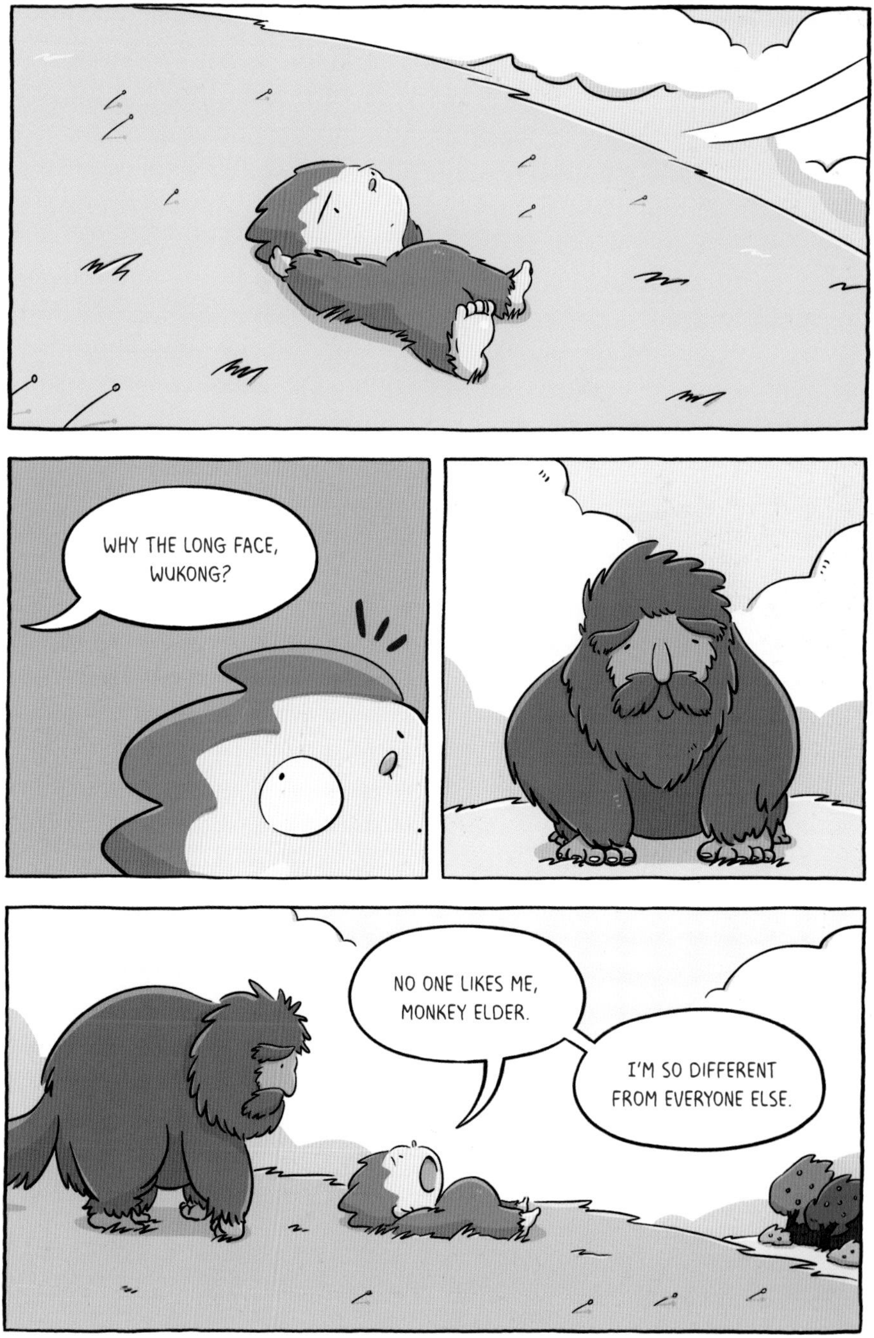
WHY THE LONG FACE, WUKONG?
NO ONE LIKES ME, MONKEY ELDER.
I'M SO DIFFERENT FROM EVERYONE ELSE.

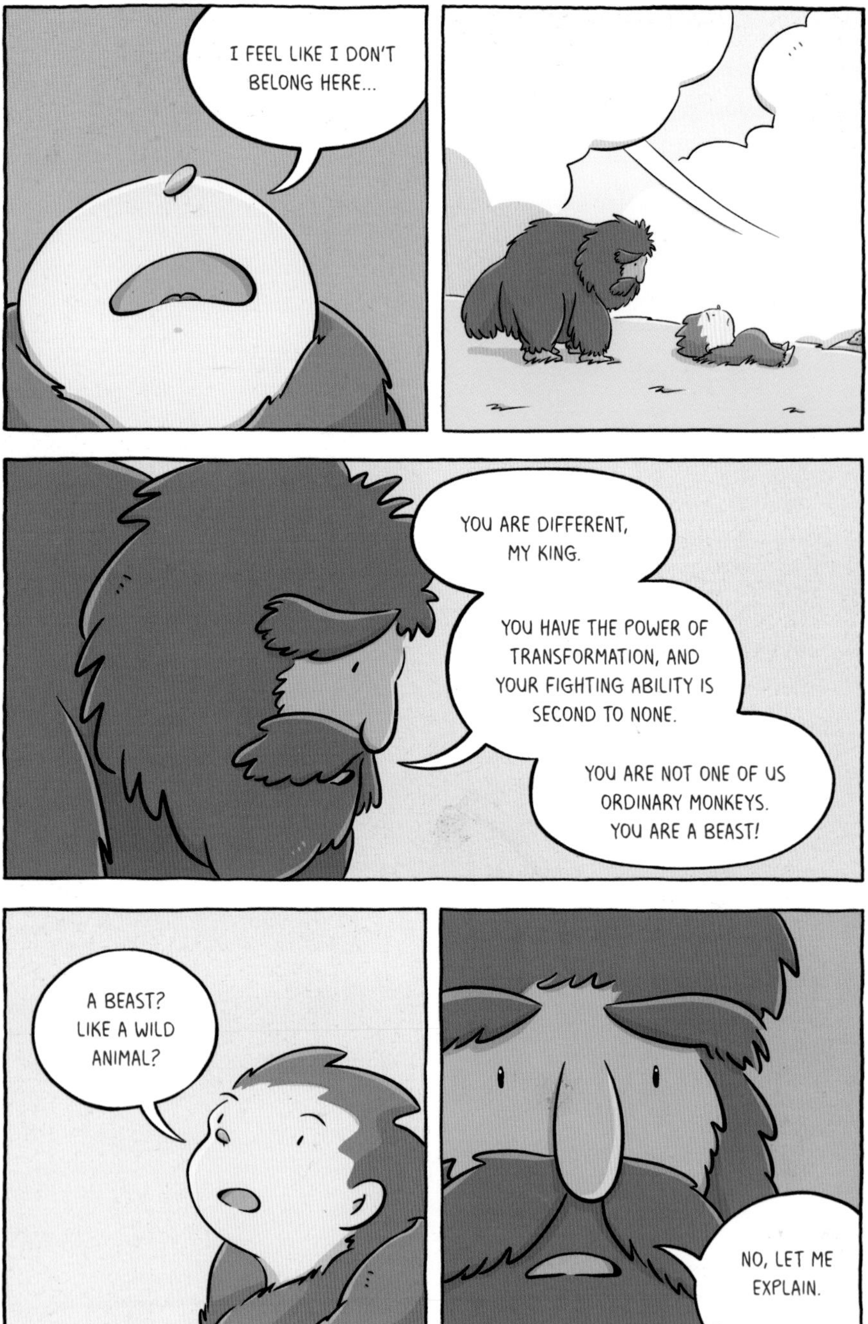
I FEEL LIKE I DON'T BELONG HERE...
...
YOU ARE DIFFERENT, MY KING.
YOU HAVE THE POWER OF TRANSFORMATION, AND YOUR FIGHTING ABILITY IS SECOND TO NONE.
YOU ARE NOT ONE OF US ORDINARY MONKEYS. YOU ARE A BEAST!
A BEAST? LIKE A WILD ANIMAL?
NO, LET ME EXPLAIN.

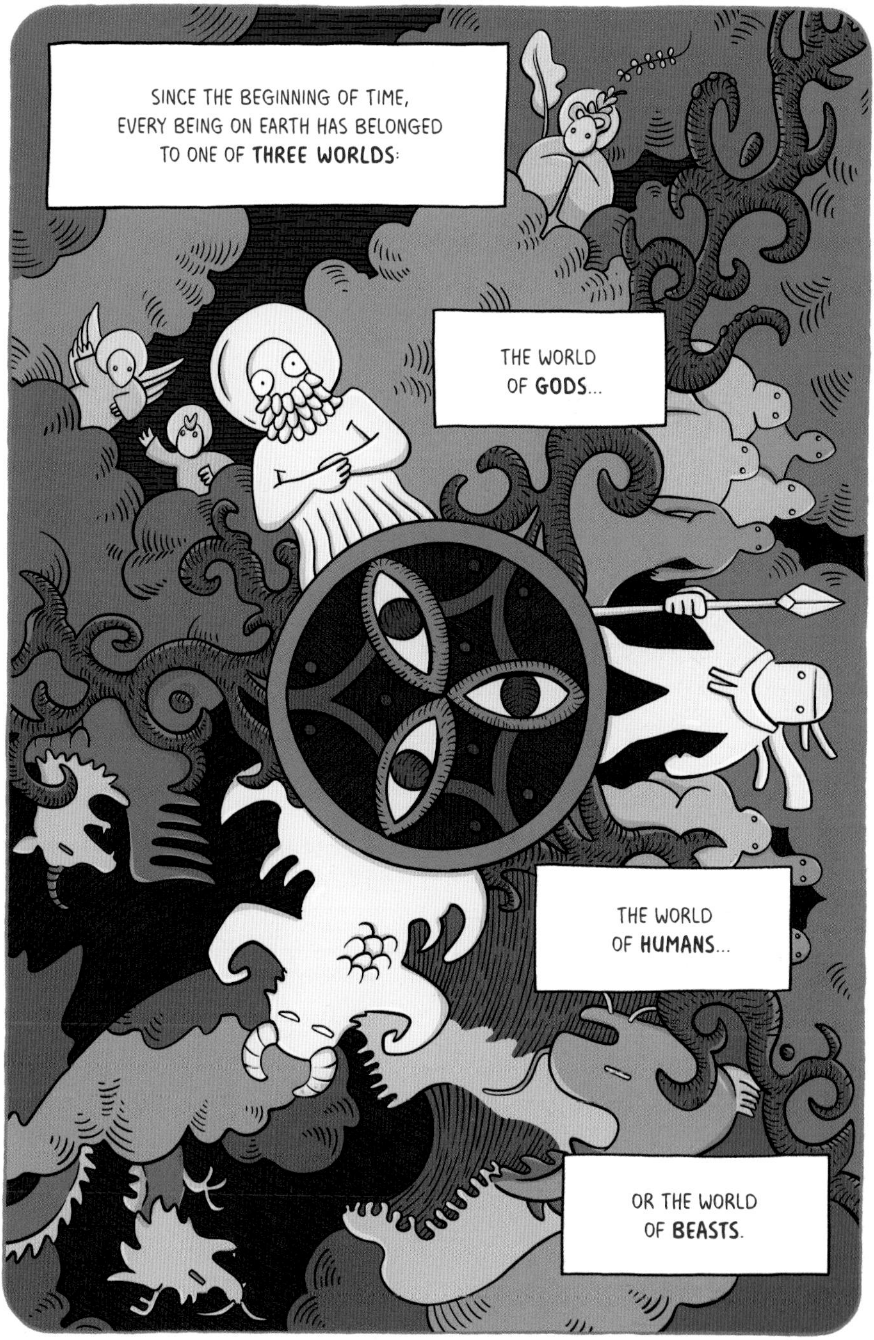
SINCE THE BEGINNING OF TIME, EVERY BEING ON EARTH HAS BELONGED TO ONE OF **THREE WORLDS**:
THE WORLD OF **GODS**...
THE WORLD OF **HUMANS**...
OR THE WORLD OF **BEASTS**.

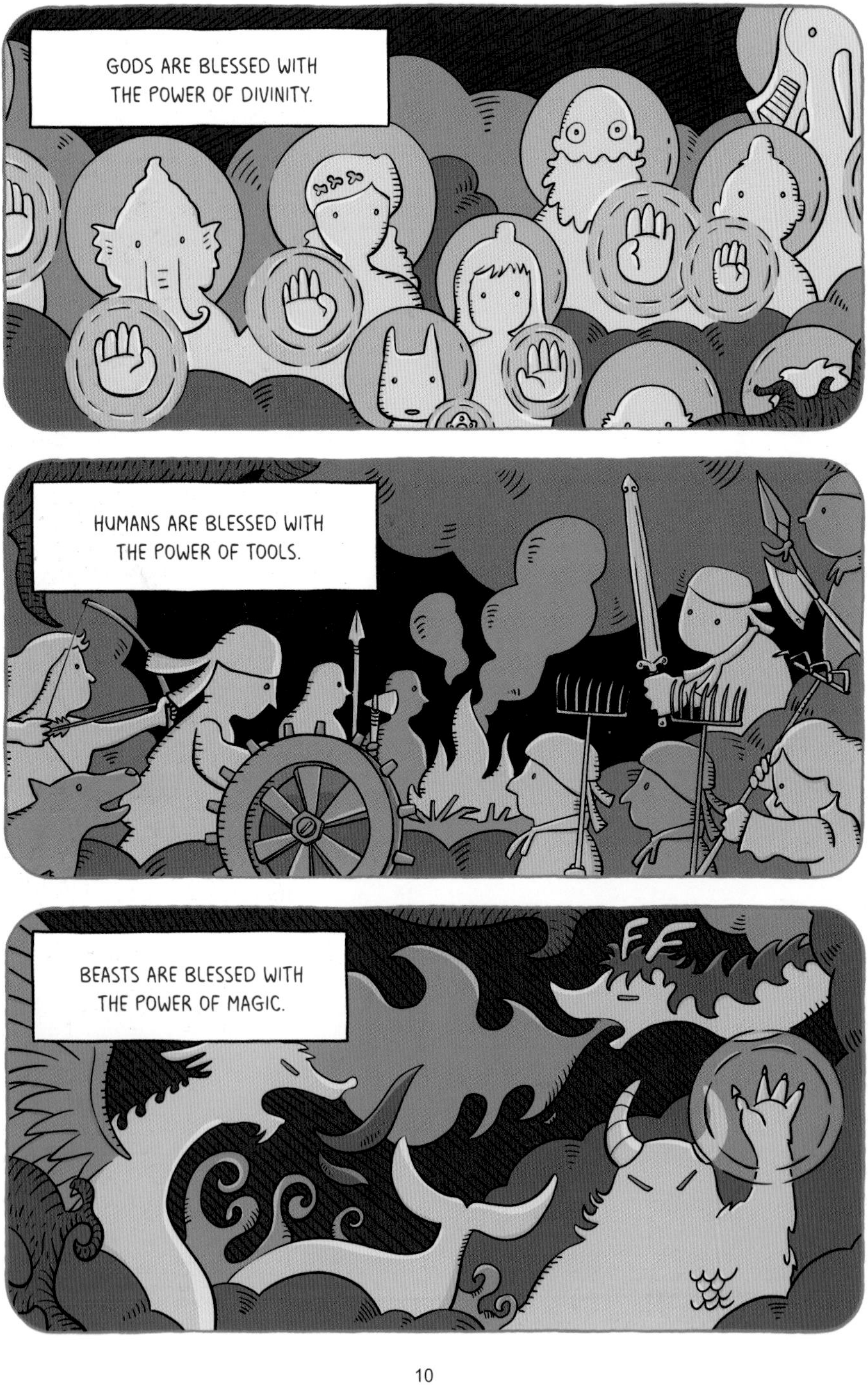
GODS ARE BLESSED WITH THE POWER OF DIVINITY.
HUMANS ARE BLESSED WITH THE POWER OF TOOLS.
BEASTS ARE BLESSED WITH THE POWER OF MAGIC.
FF

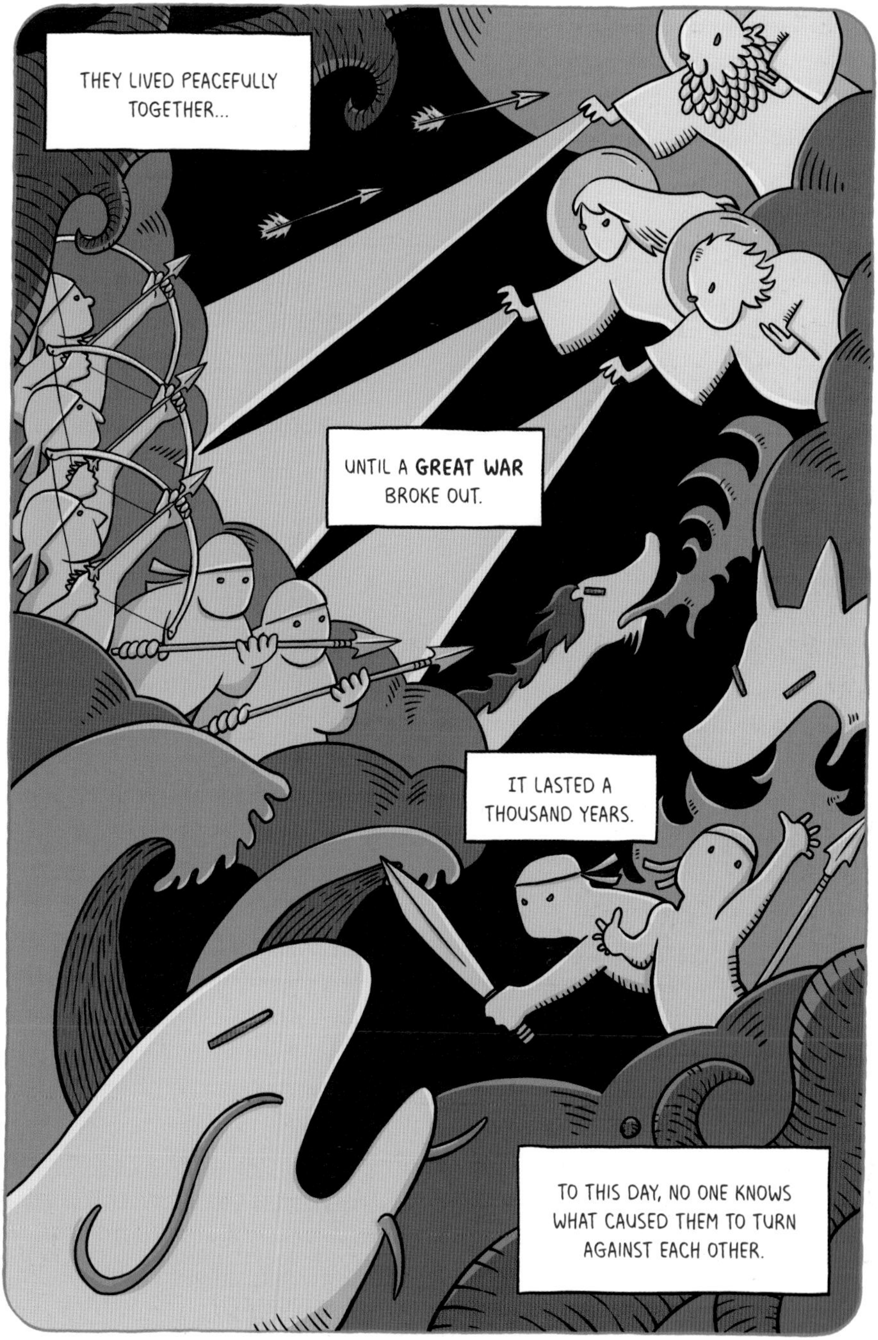
THEY LIVED PEACEFULLY TOGETHER...
UNTIL A **GREAT WAR** BROKE OUT.
IT LASTED A THOUSAND YEARS.
TO THIS DAY, NO ONE KNOWS WHAT CAUSED THEM TO TURN AGAINST EACH OTHER.

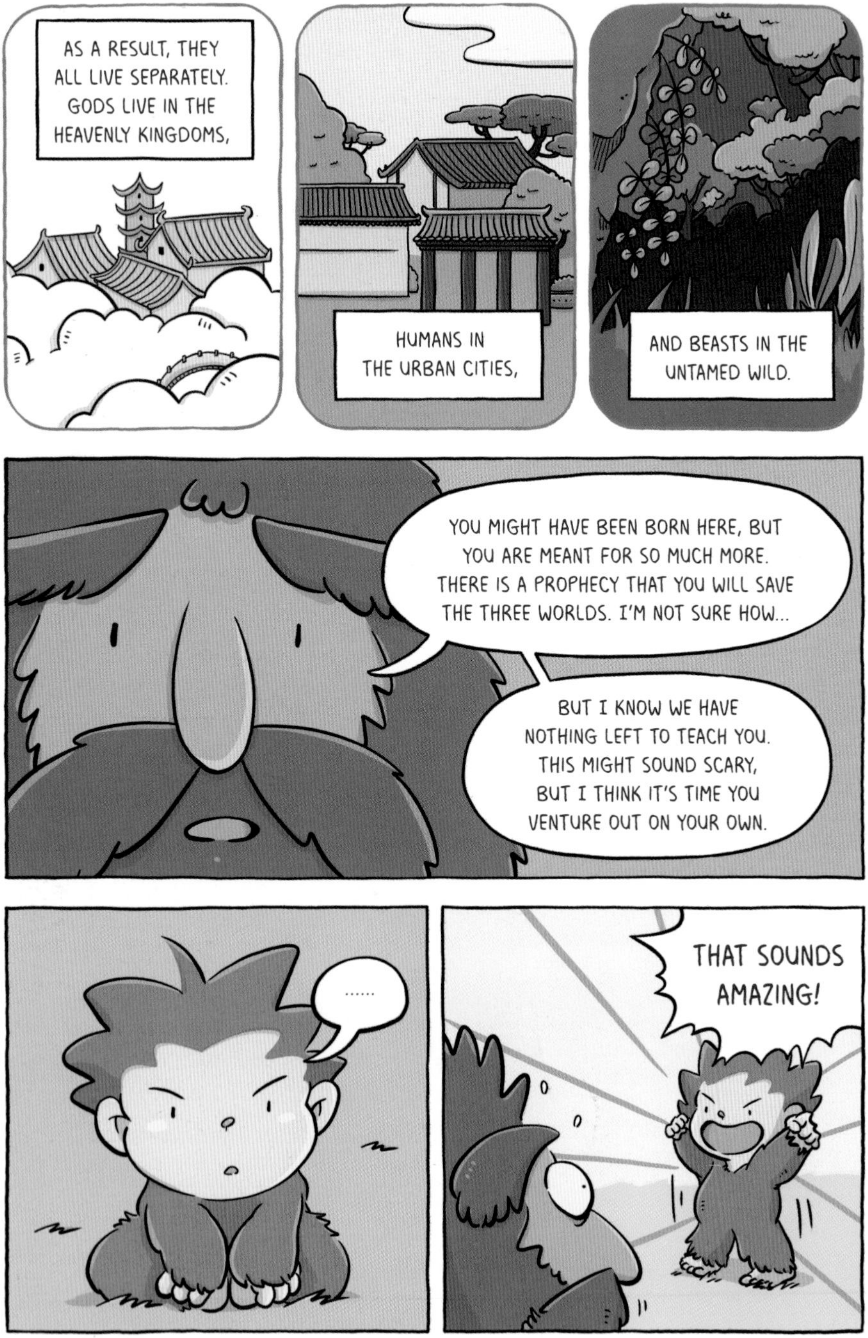
AS A RESULT, THEY ALL LIVE SEPARATELY. GODS LIVE IN THE HEAVENLY KINGDOMS,
HUMANS IN THE URBAN CITIES,
AND BEASTS IN THE UNTAMED WILD.
YOU MIGHT HAVE BEEN BORN HERE, BUT YOU ARE MEANT FOR SO MUCH MORE. THERE IS A PROPHECY THAT YOU WILL SAVE THE THREE WORLDS. I'M NOT SURE HOW...
BUT I KNOW WE HAVE NOTHING LEFT TO TEACH YOU. THIS MIGHT SOUND SCARY, BUT I THINK IT'S TIME YOU VENTURE OUT ON YOUR OWN.
......
THAT SOUNDS AMAZING!

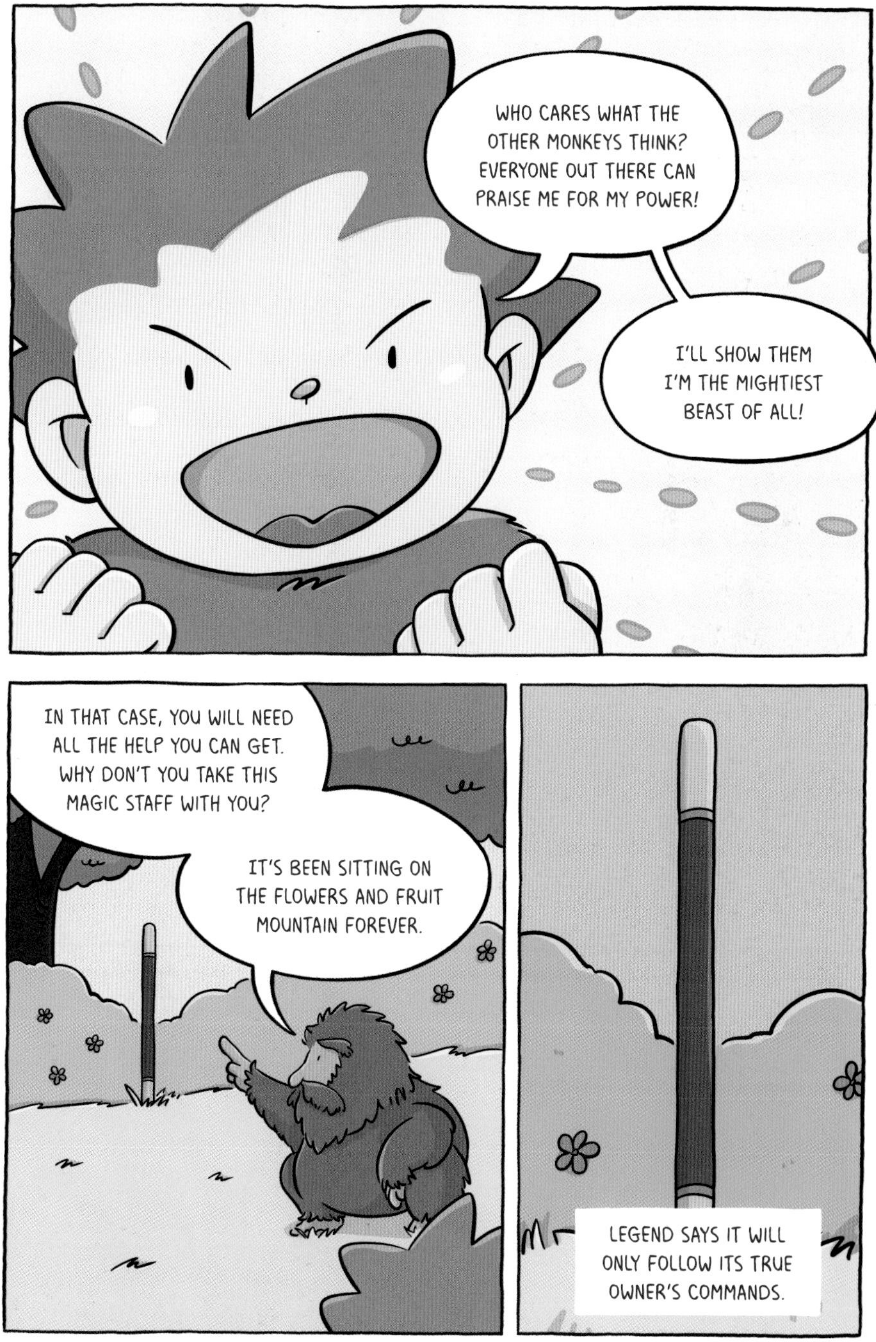
WHO CARES WHAT THE OTHER MONKEYS THINK? EVERYONE OUT THERE CAN PRAISE ME FOR MY POWER!
I'LL SHOW THEM I'M THE MIGHTIEST BEAST OF ALL!
IN THAT CASE, YOU WILL NEED ALL THE HELP YOU CAN GET. WHY DON'T YOU TAKE THIS MAGIC STAFF WITH YOU?
IT'S BEEN SITTING ON THE FLOWERS AND FRUIT MOUNTAIN FOREVER.
LEGEND SAYS IT WILL ONLY FOLLOW ITS TRUE OWNER'S COMMANDS.

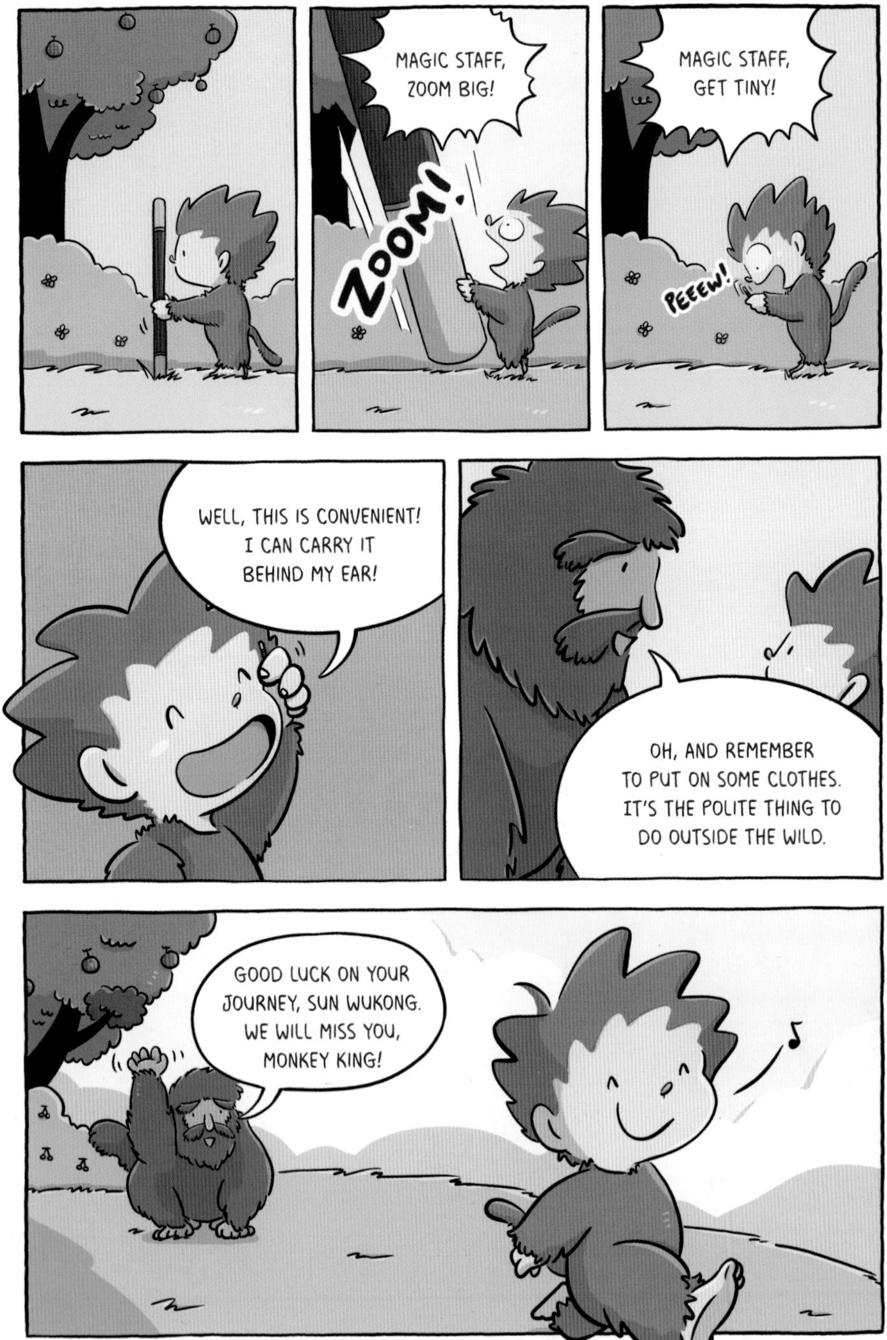
MAGIC STAFF, ZOOM BIG!
ZOOM!
MAGIC STAFF, GET TINY!
PEEEW!
WELL, THIS IS CONVENIENT! I CAN CARRY IT BEHIND MY EAR!
OH, AND REMEMBER TO PUT ON SOME CLOTHES. IT'S THE POLITE THING TO DO OUTSIDE THE WILD.
GOOD LUCK ON YOUR JOURNEY, SUN WUKONG. WE WILL MISS YOU, MONKEY KING!

CHAPTER 1

SUN WUKONG, THE MONKEY KING

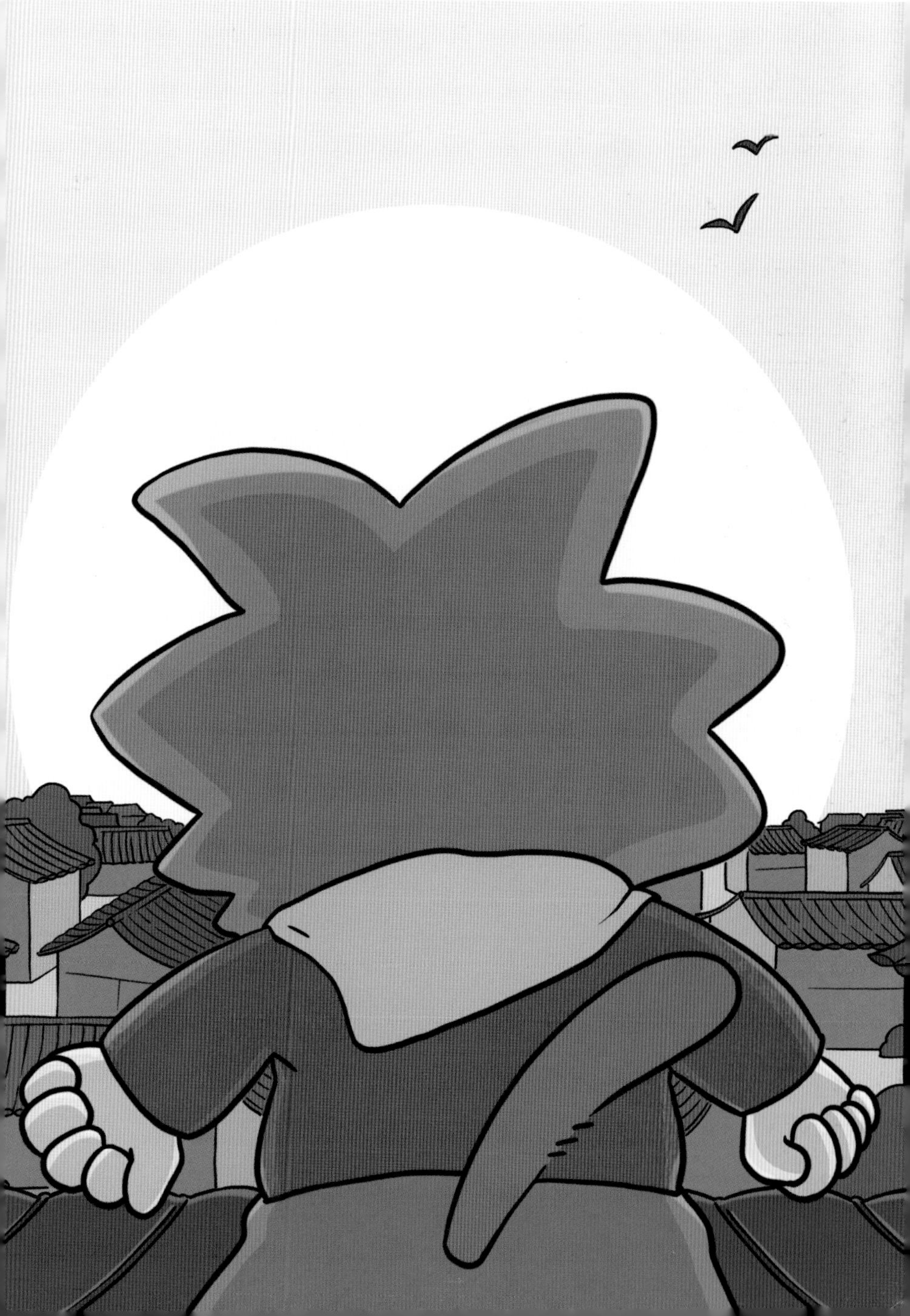

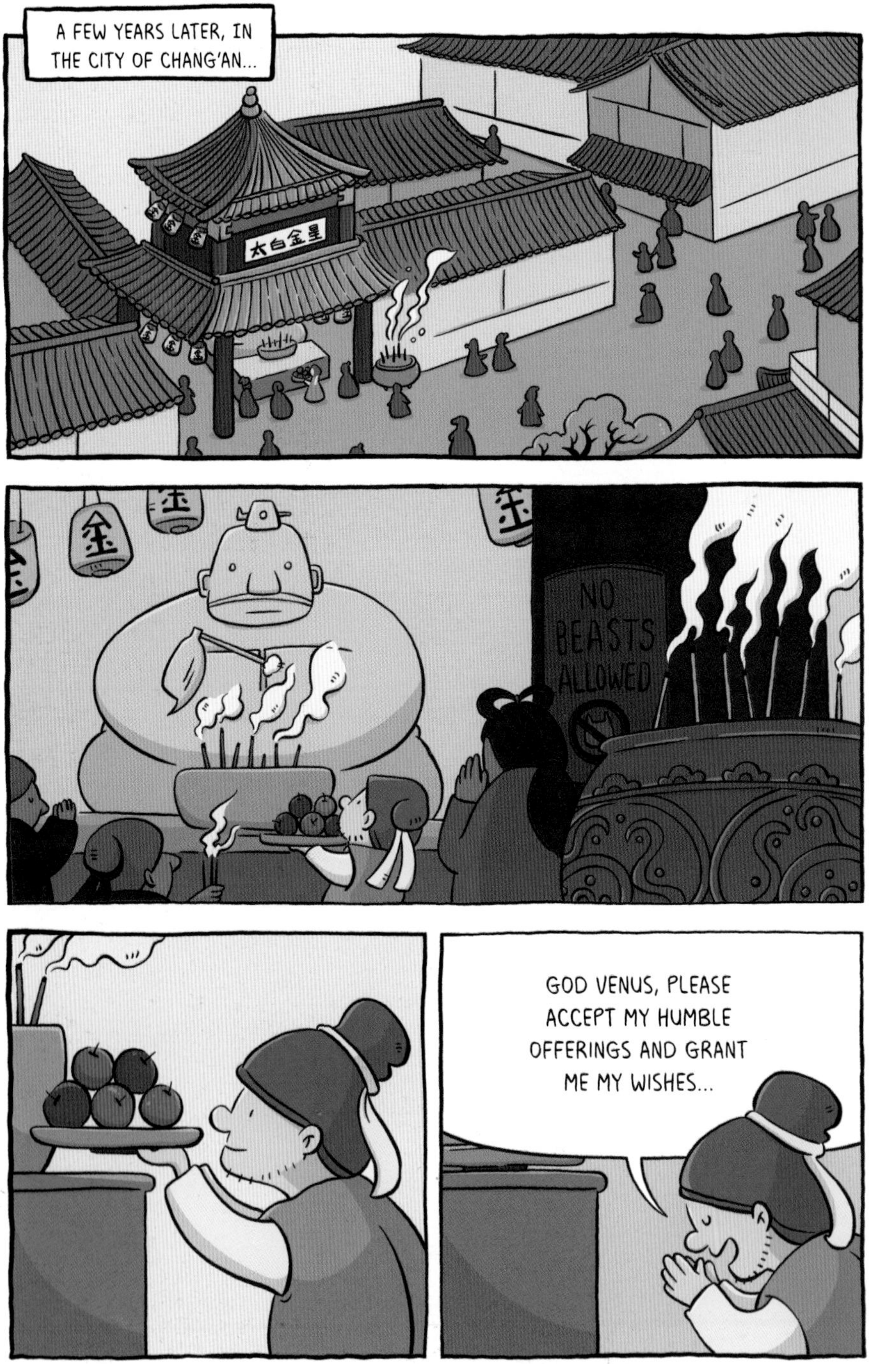
A FEW YEARS LATER, IN THE CITY OF CHANG'AN...
太白金星
NO BEASTS ALLOWED
GOD VENUS, PLEASE ACCEPT MY HUMBLE OFFERINGS AND GRANT ME MY WISHES...

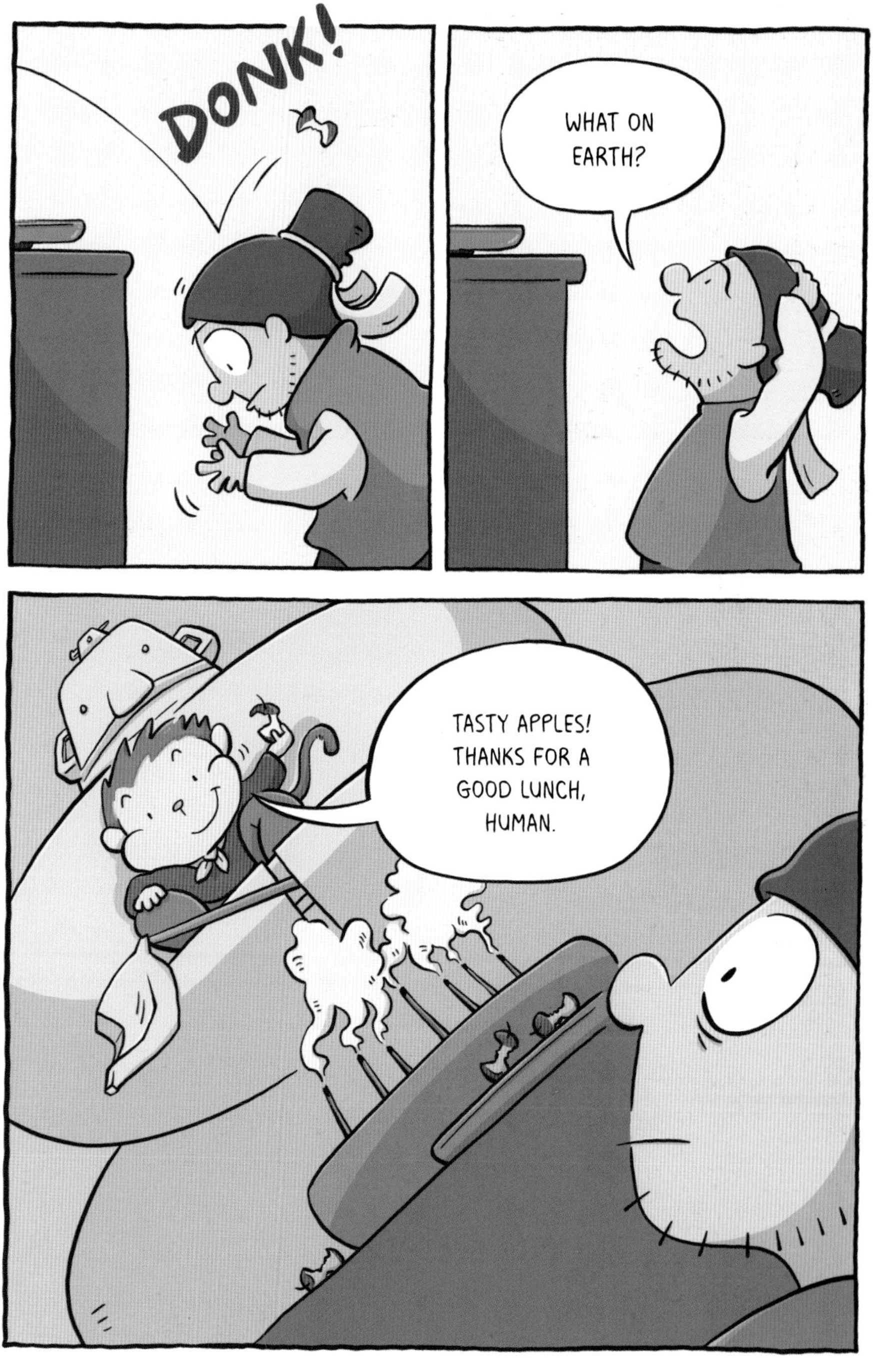
DONK!
WHAT ON EARTH?
TASTY APPLES! THANKS FOR A GOOD LUNCH, HUMAN.

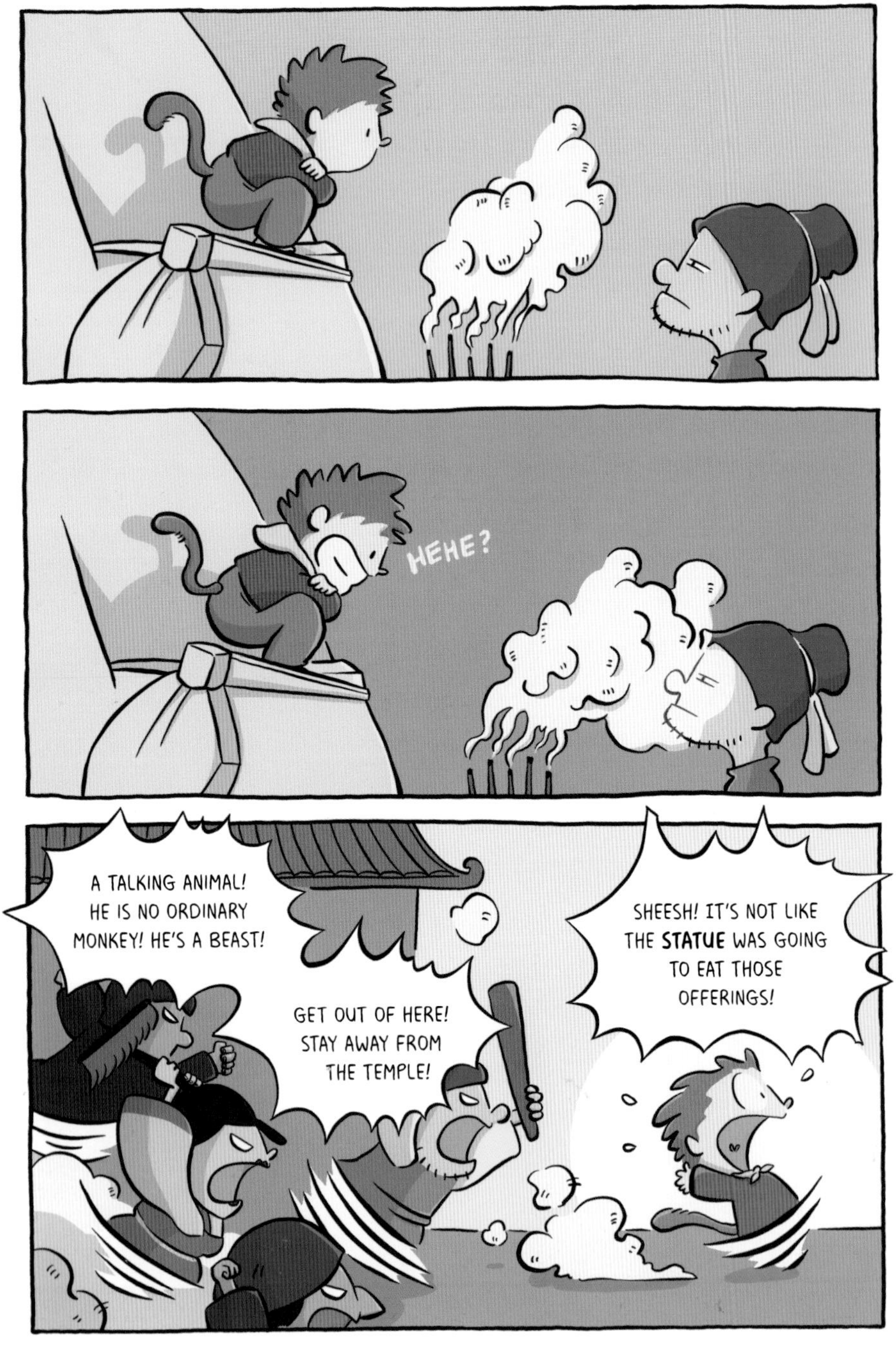
HEHE?
A TALKING ANIMAL! HE IS NO ORDINARY MONKEY! HE'S A BEAST!
GET OUT OF HERE! STAY AWAY FROM THE TEMPLE!
SHEESH! IT'S NOT LIKE THE **STATUE** WAS GOING TO EAT THOSE OFFERINGS!

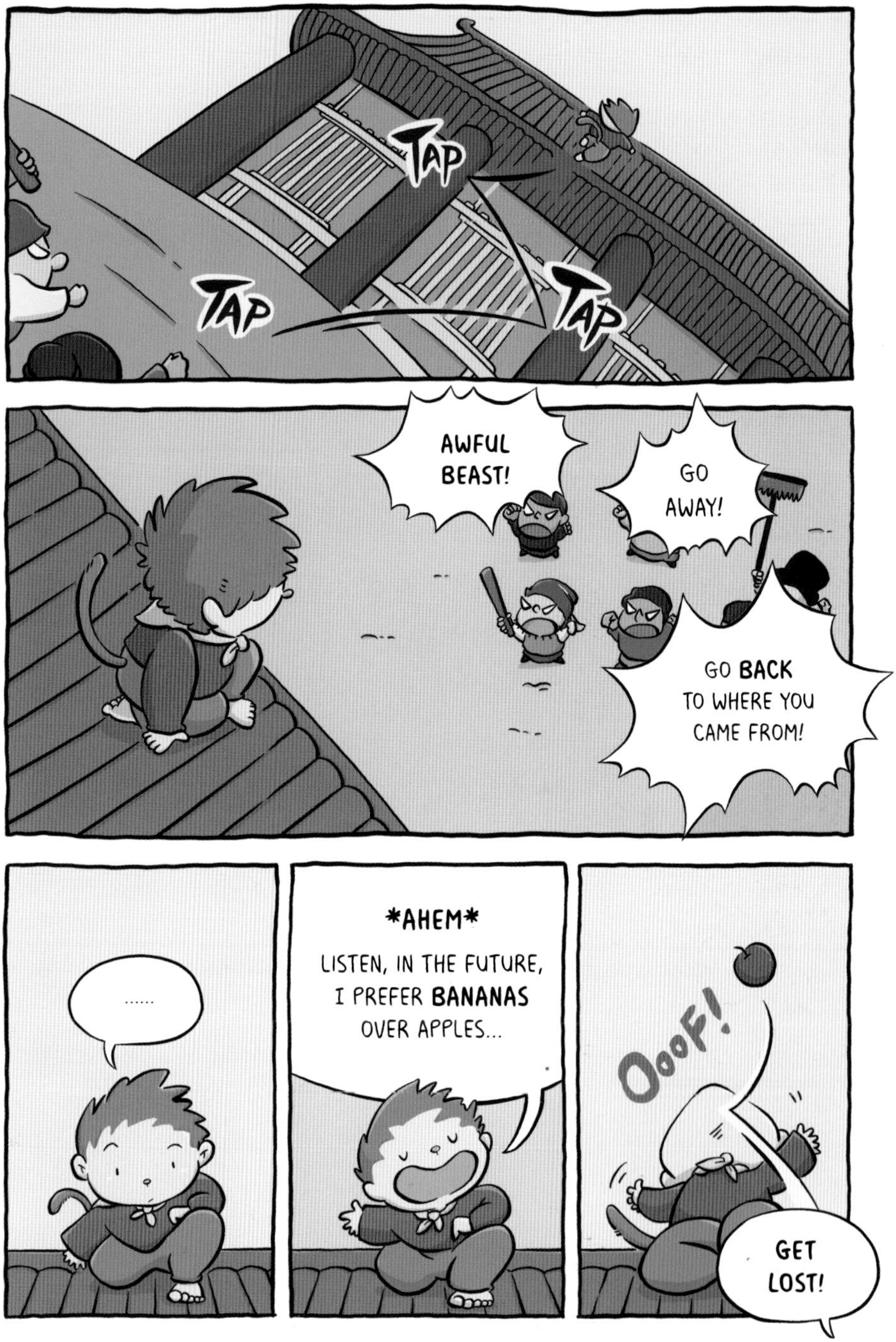
TAP
TAP
TAP
AWFUL BEAST!
GO AWAY!
GO BACK TO WHERE YOU CAME FROM!
......
AHEM
LISTEN, IN THE FUTURE, I PREFER BANANAS OVER APPLES...
OOOF!
GET LOST!

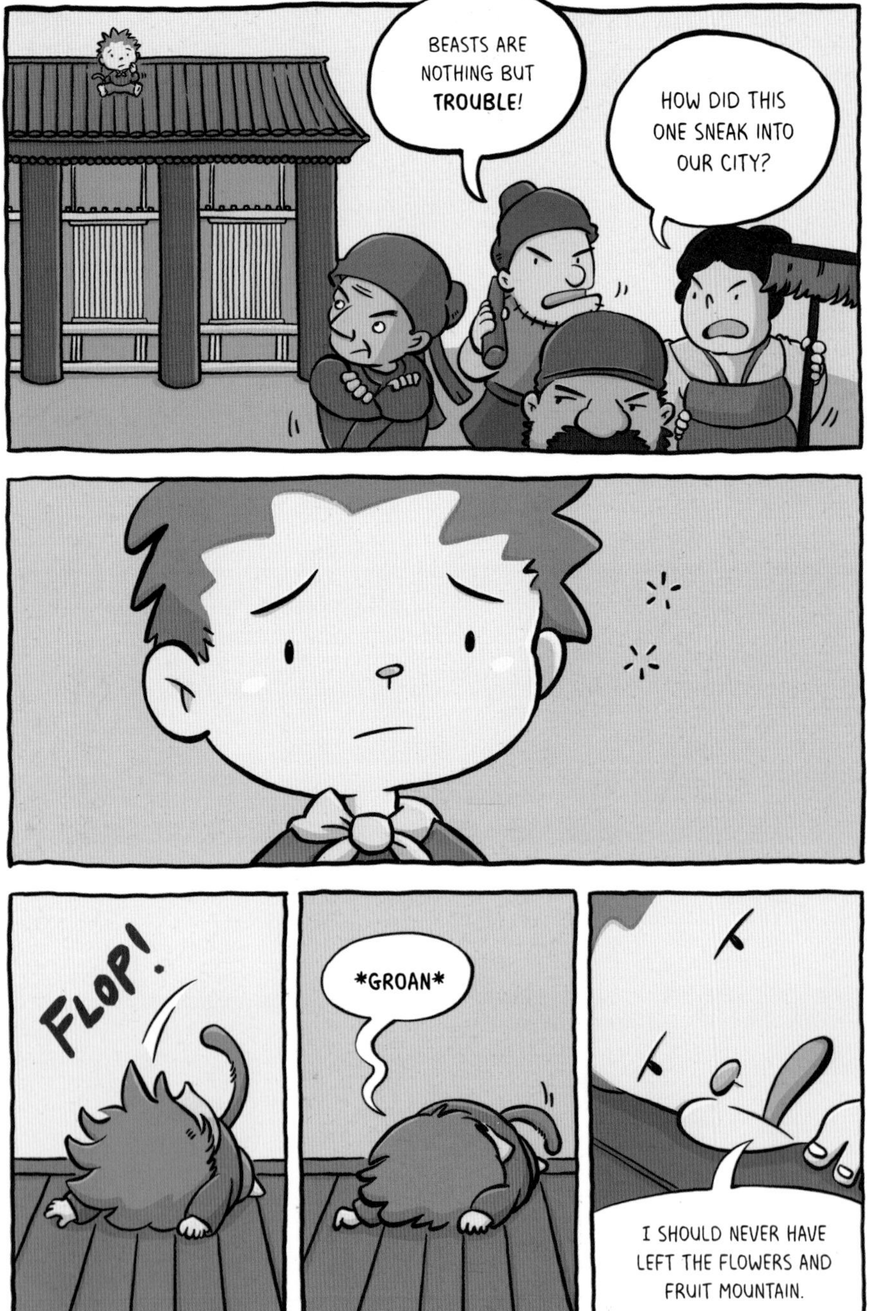
BEASTS ARE NOTHING BUT **TROUBLE**!
HOW DID THIS ONE SNEAK INTO OUR CITY?
FLOP!
GROAN
I SHOULD NEVER HAVE LEFT THE FLOWERS AND FRUIT MOUNTAIN.

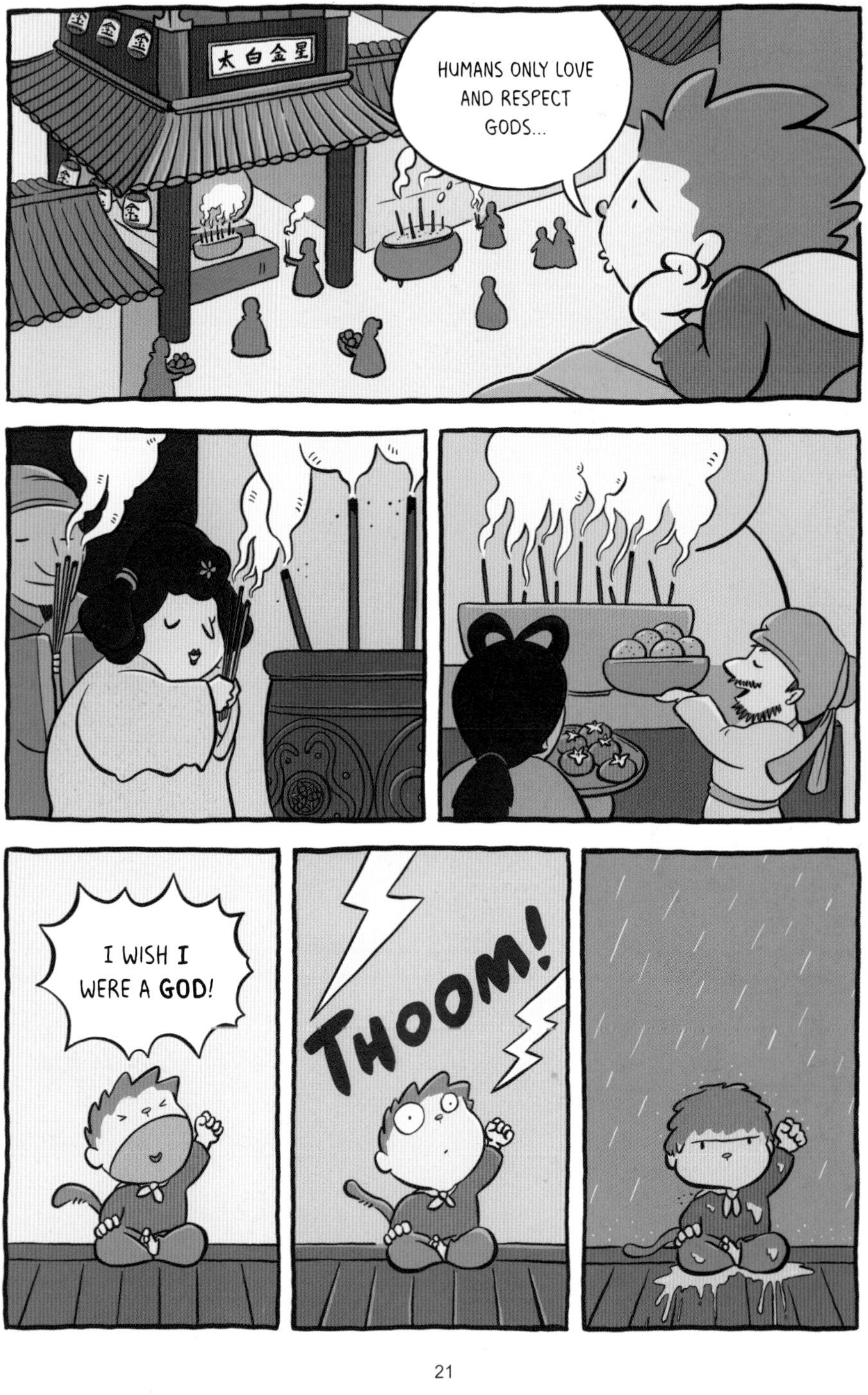
太白金星
HUMANS ONLY LOVE AND RESPECT GODS...
I WISH **I** WERE A **GOD**!
THOOM!

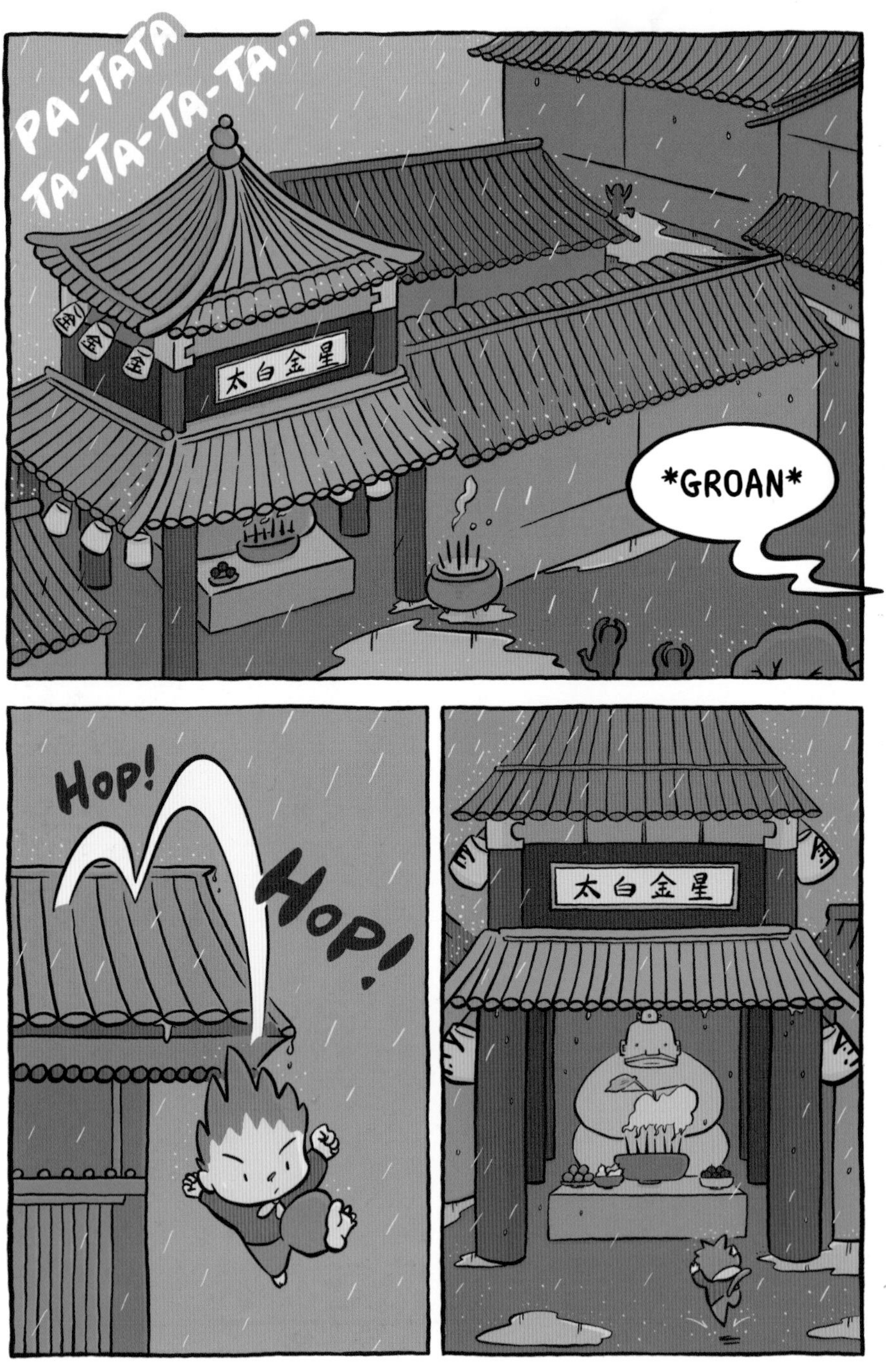
PA-TATA TA-TA-TA-TA...
太白金星
GROAN
HOP!
HOP!
太白金星

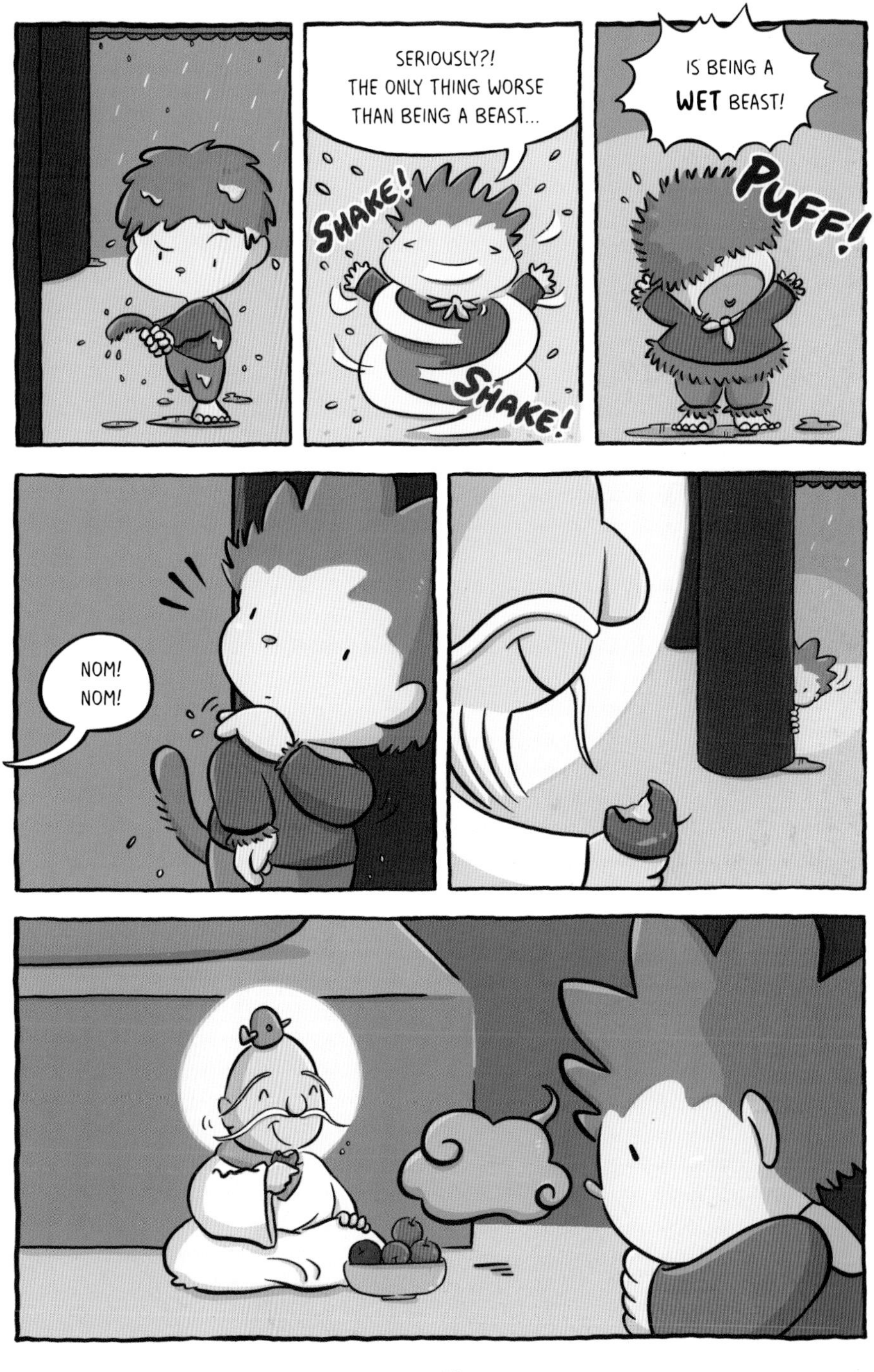
SERIOUSLY?! THE ONLY THING WORSE THAN BEING A BEAST...
SHAKE!
SHAKE!
IS BEING A WET BEAST!
PUFF!
NOM! NOM!

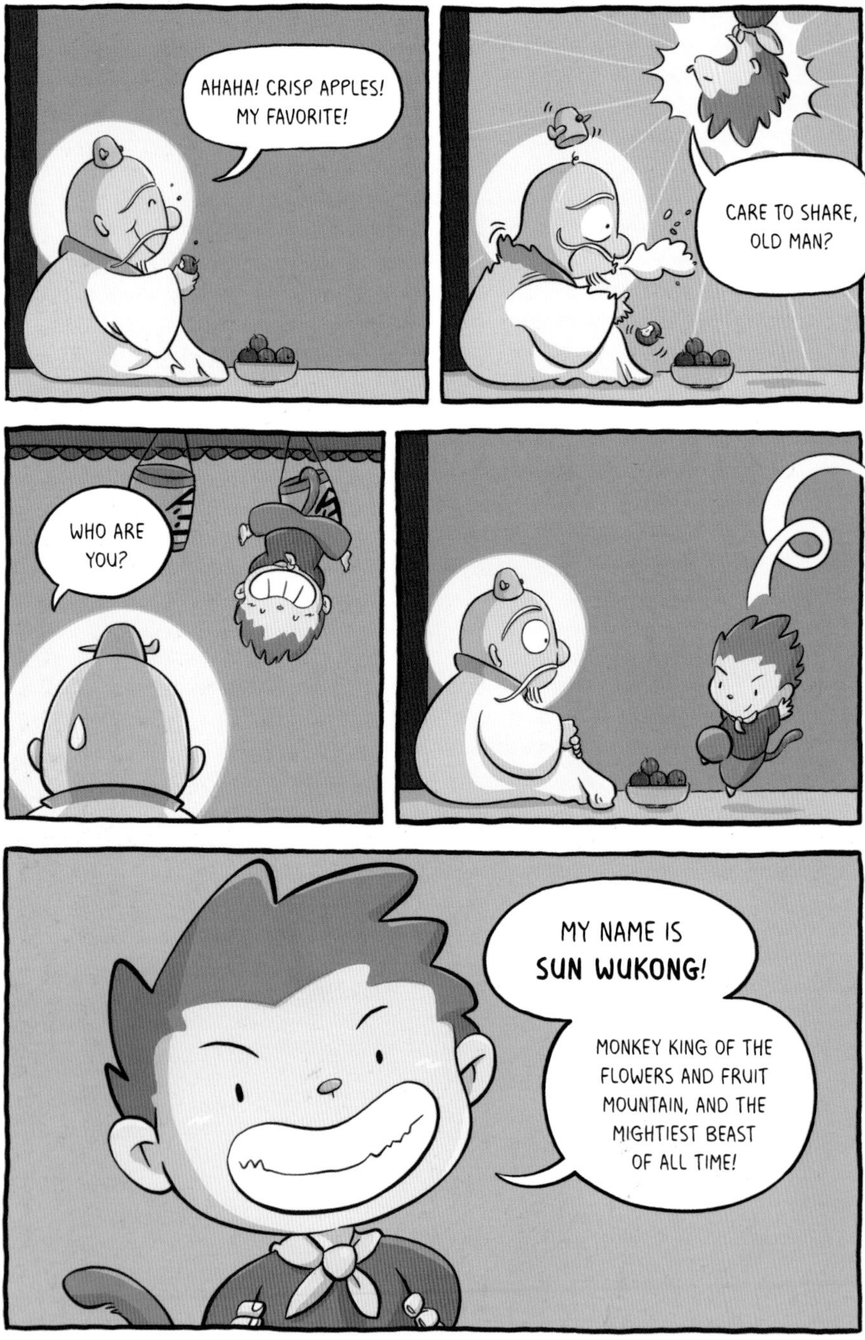

AHAHA! CRISP APPLES! MY FAVORITE!
CARE TO SHARE, OLD MAN?
WHO ARE YOU?
MY NAME IS **SUN WUKONG**!
MONKEY KING OF THE FLOWERS AND FRUIT MOUNTAIN, AND THE MIGHTIEST BEAST OF ALL TIME!

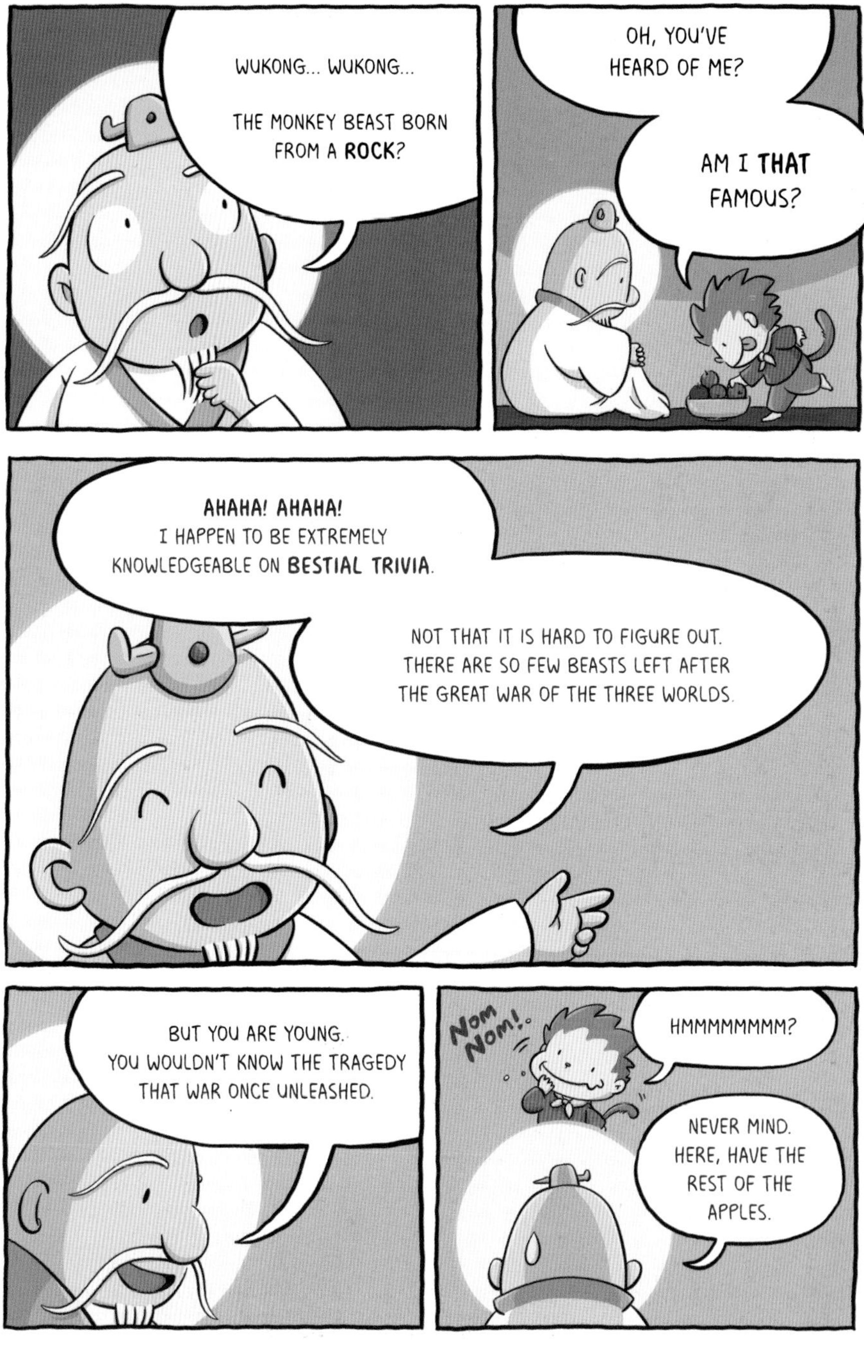
WUKONG... WUKONG...
THE MONKEY BEAST BORN FROM A ROCK?
OH, YOU'VE HEARD OF ME?
AM I THAT FAMOUS?
AHAHA! AHAHA! I HAPPEN TO BE EXTREMELY KNOWLEDGEABLE ON BESTIAL TRIVIA.
NOT THAT IT IS HARD TO FIGURE OUT. THERE ARE SO FEW BEASTS LEFT AFTER THE GREAT WAR OF THE THREE WORLDS.
BUT YOU ARE YOUNG. YOU WOULDN'T KNOW THE TRAGEDY THAT WAR ONCE UNLEASHED.
Nom Nom!
HMMMMMMMM?
NEVER MIND. HERE, HAVE THE REST OF THE APPLES.

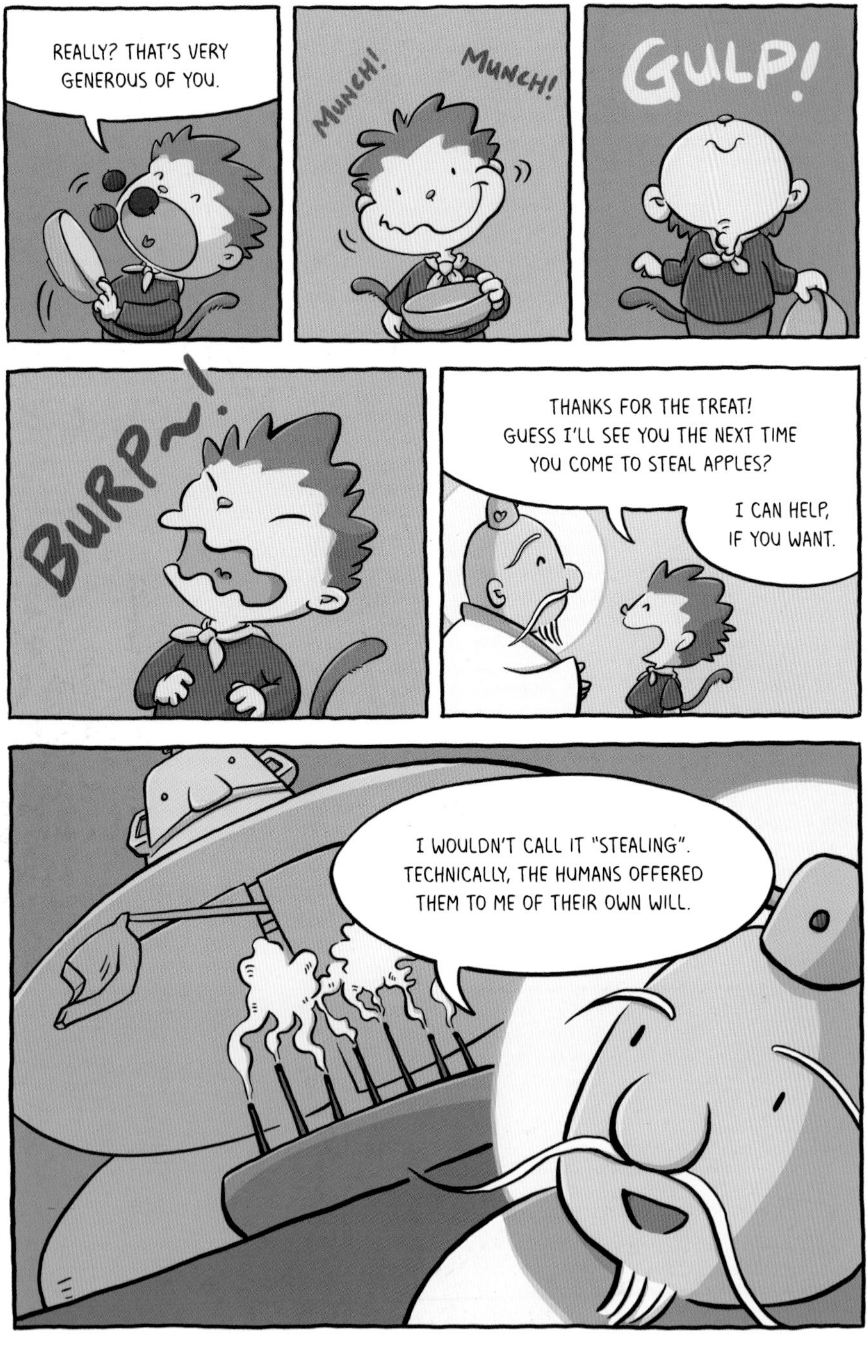
REALLY? THAT'S VERY GENEROUS OF YOU.
MUNCH!
MUNCH!
GULP!
BURP~!
THANKS FOR THE TREAT! GUESS I'LL SEE YOU THE NEXT TIME YOU COME TO STEAL APPLES?
I CAN HELP, IF YOU WANT.
I WOULDN'T CALL IT "STEALING". TECHNICALLY, THE HUMANS OFFERED THEM TO ME OF THEIR OWN WILL.

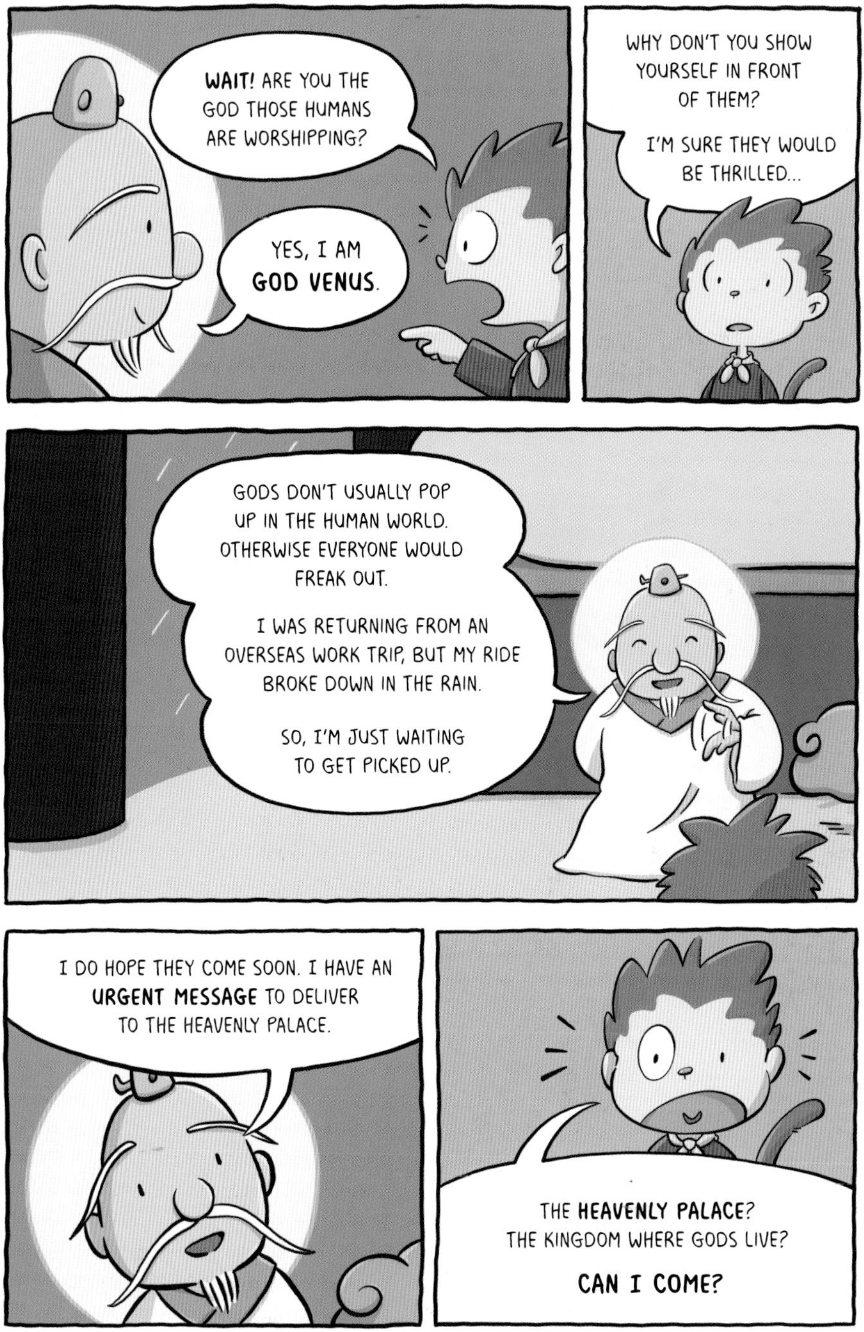
WAIT! ARE YOU THE GOD THOSE HUMANS ARE WORSHIPPING?
YES, I AM **GOD VENUS**.
WHY DON'T YOU SHOW YOURSELF IN FRONT OF THEM?
I'M SURE THEY WOULD BE THRILLED...
GODS DON'T USUALLY POP UP IN THE HUMAN WORLD. OTHERWISE EVERYONE WOULD FREAK OUT.
I WAS RETURNING FROM AN OVERSEAS WORK TRIP, BUT MY RIDE BROKE DOWN IN THE RAIN.
SO, I'M JUST WAITING TO GET PICKED UP.
I DO HOPE THEY COME SOON. I HAVE AN **URGENT MESSAGE** TO DELIVER TO THE HEAVENLY PALACE.
THE **HEAVENLY PALACE**? THE KINGDOM WHERE GODS LIVE?
CAN I COME?

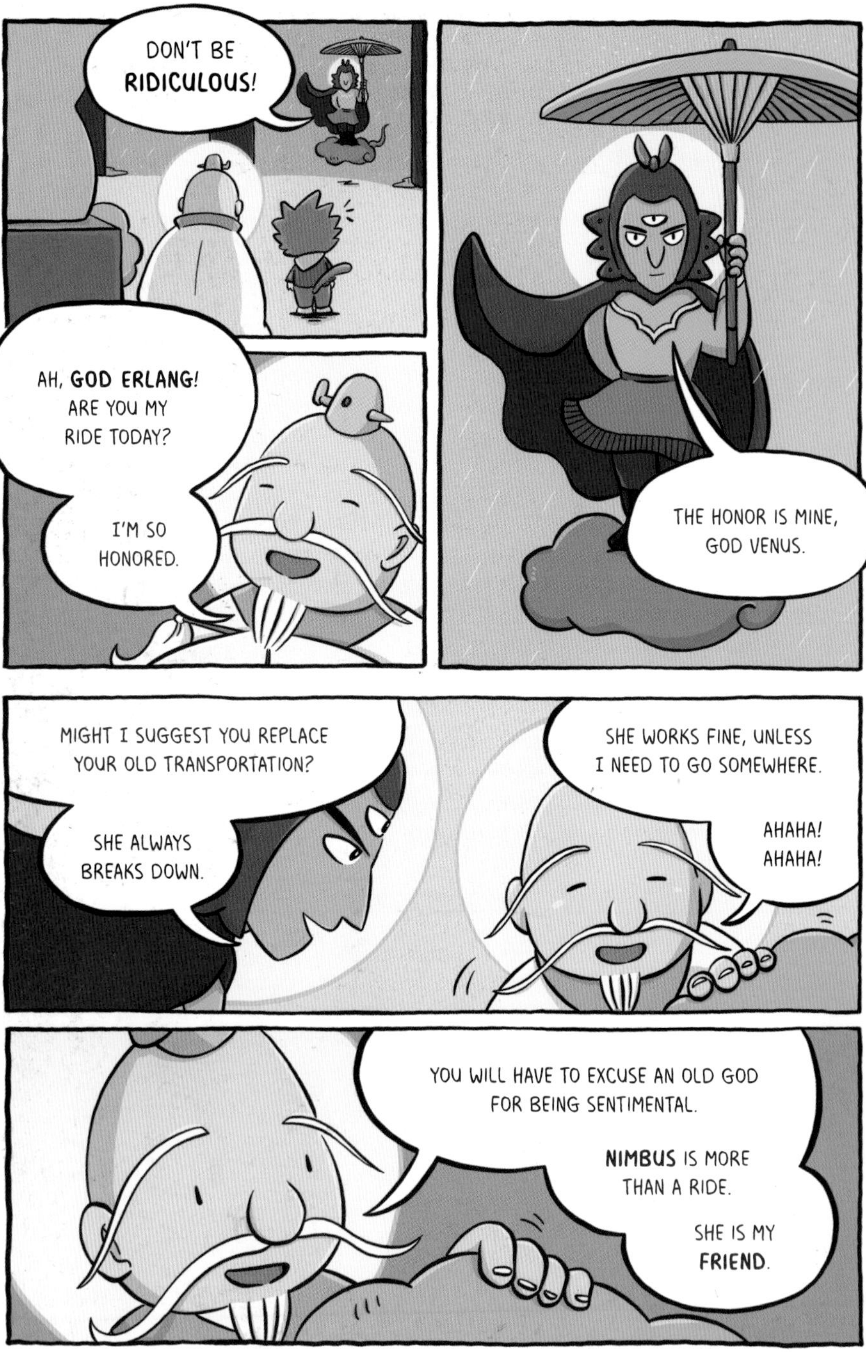
DON'T BE **RIDICULOUS**!
AH, **GOD ERLANG**! ARE YOU MY RIDE TODAY?
I'M SO HONORED.
THE HONOR IS MINE, GOD VENUS.
MIGHT I SUGGEST YOU REPLACE YOUR OLD TRANSPORTATION?
SHE ALWAYS BREAKS DOWN.
SHE WORKS FINE, UNLESS I NEED TO GO SOMEWHERE.
AHAHA! AHAHA!
YOU WILL HAVE TO EXCUSE AN OLD GOD FOR BEING SENTIMENTAL.
NIMBUS IS MORE THAN A RIDE.
SHE IS MY **FRIEND**.

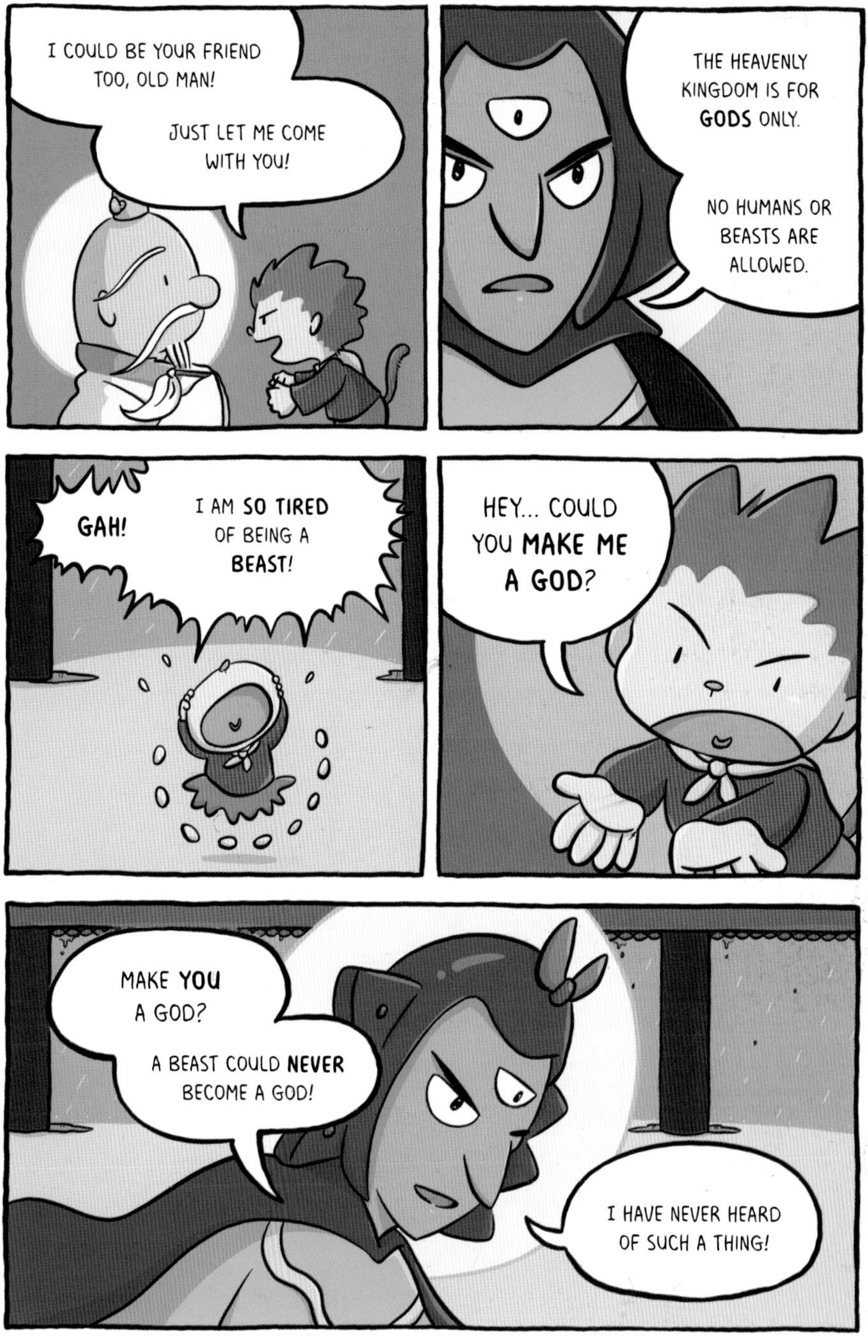
I COULD BE YOUR FRIEND TOO, OLD MAN!
JUST LET ME COME WITH YOU!
THE HEAVENLY KINGDOM IS FOR **GODS** ONLY.
NO HUMANS OR BEASTS ARE ALLOWED.
GAH!
I AM **SO TIRED** OF BEING A **BEAST!**
HEY... COULD YOU **MAKE ME A GOD?**
MAKE **YOU** A GOD?
A BEAST COULD **NEVER** BECOME A GOD!
I HAVE NEVER HEARD OF SUCH A THING!

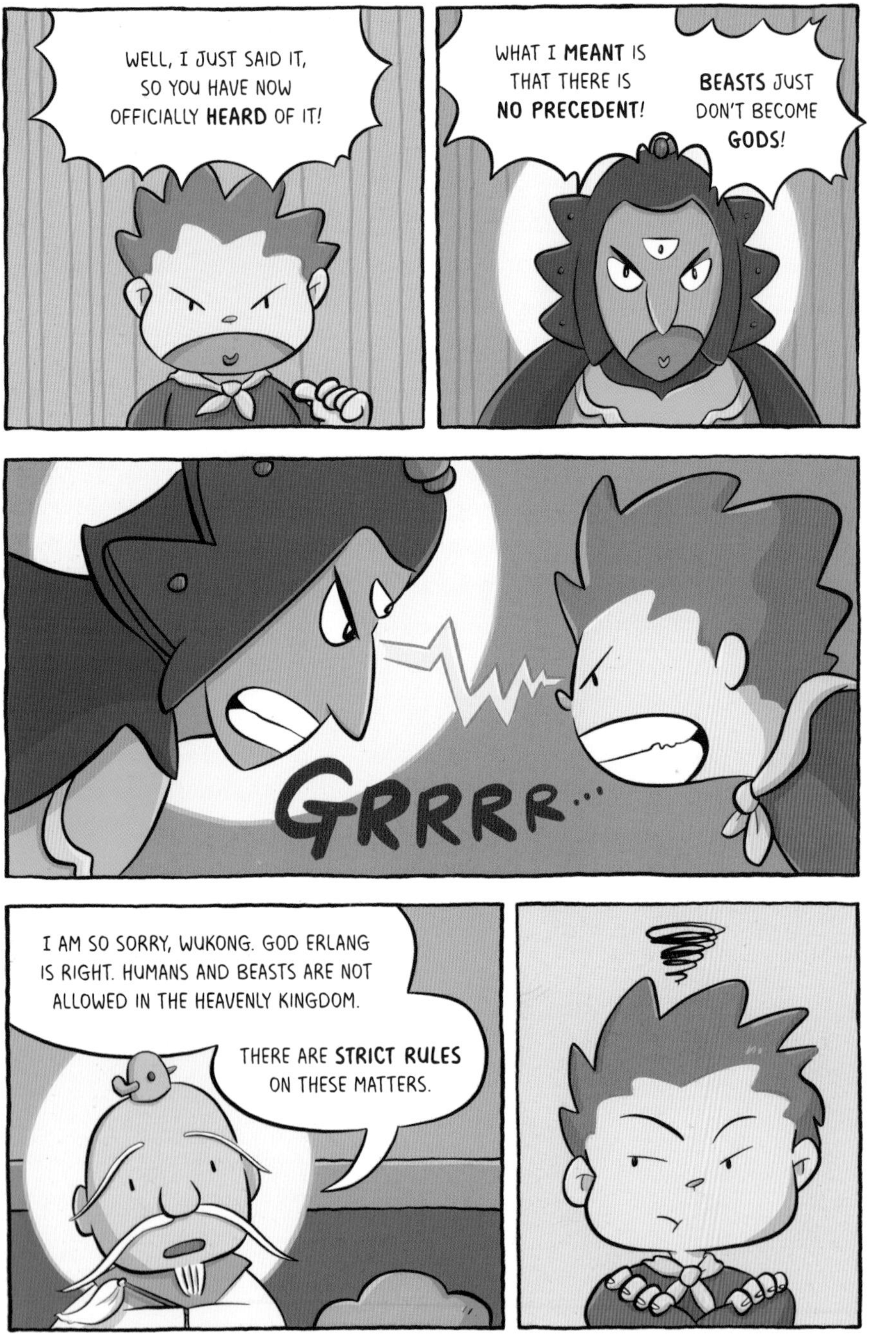
WELL, I JUST SAID IT, SO YOU HAVE NOW OFFICIALLY **HEARD** OF IT!
WHAT I **MEANT** IS THAT THERE IS **NO PRECEDENT**!
BEASTS JUST DON'T BECOME **GODS**!
GRRRR...
I AM SO SORRY, WUKONG. GOD ERLANG IS RIGHT. HUMANS AND BEASTS ARE NOT ALLOWED IN THE HEAVENLY KINGDOM.
THERE ARE **STRICT RULES** ON THESE MATTERS.

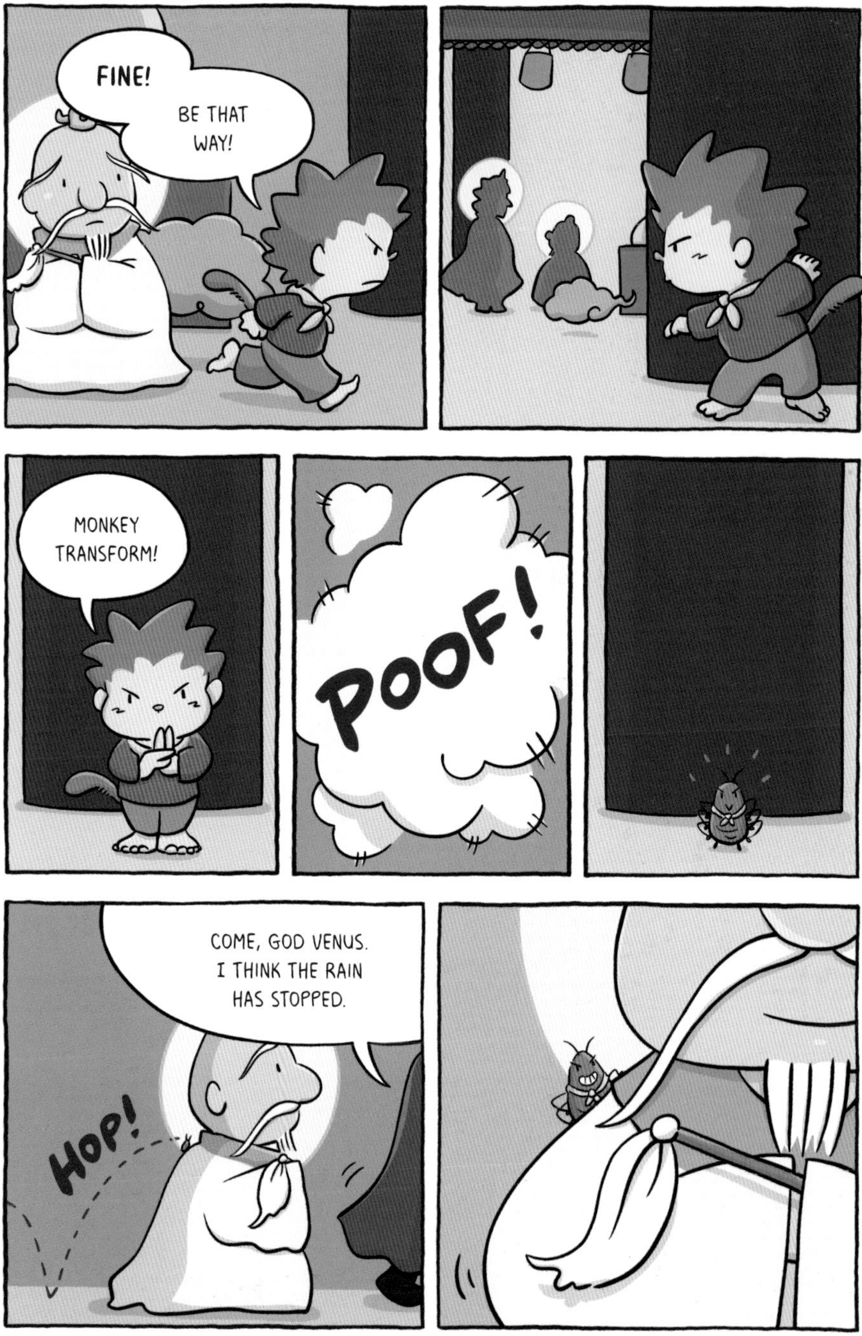
FINE!
BE THAT WAY!
MONKEY TRANSFORM!
POOF!
COME, GOD VENUS. I THINK THE RAIN HAS STOPPED.
HOP!

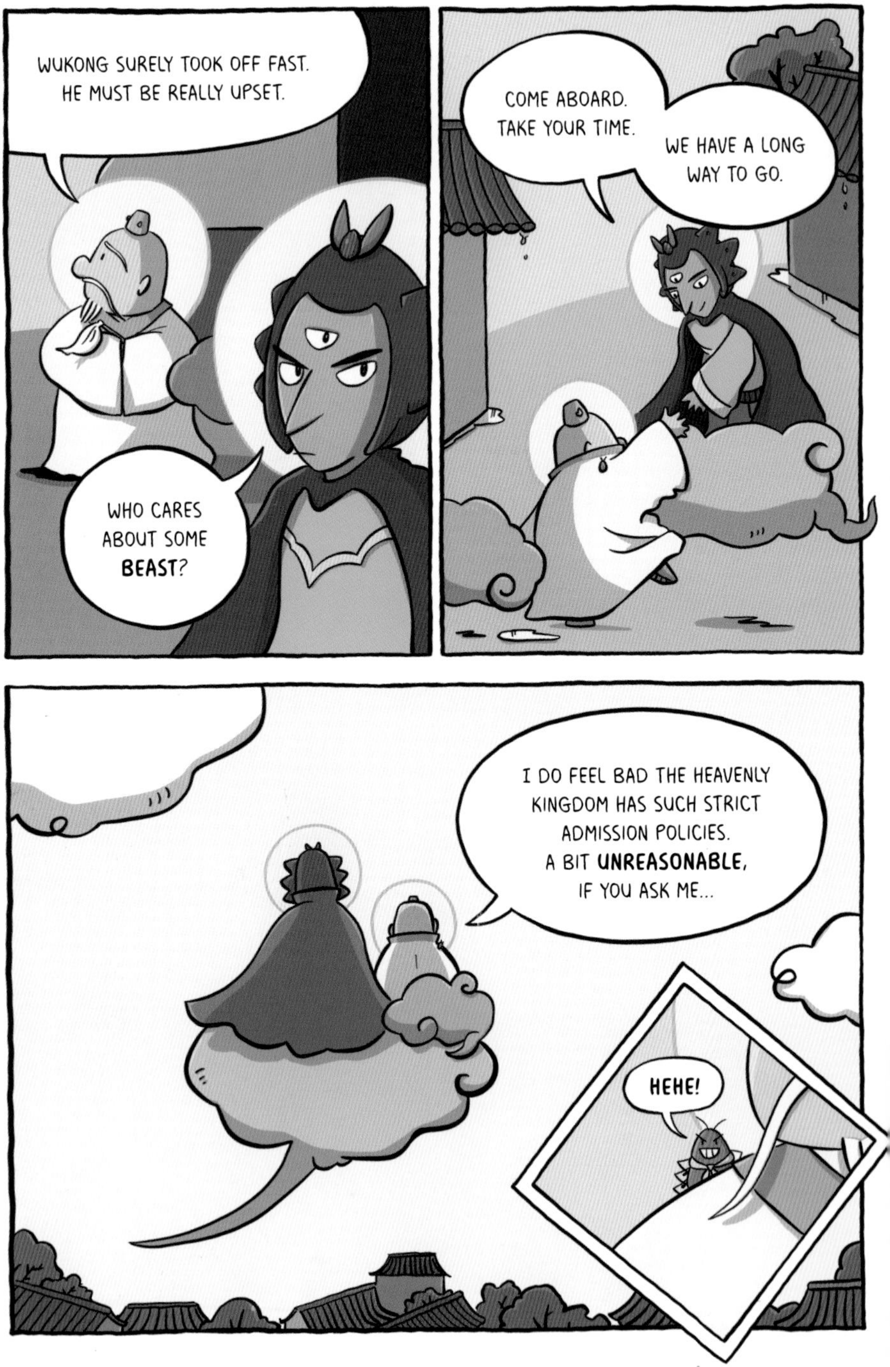
WUKONG SURELY TOOK OFF FAST. HE MUST BE REALLY UPSET.
WHO CARES ABOUT SOME **BEAST**?
COME ABOARD. TAKE YOUR TIME.
WE HAVE A LONG WAY TO GO.
I DO FEEL BAD THE HEAVENLY KINGDOM HAS SUCH STRICT ADMISSION POLICIES. A BIT **UNREASONABLE**, IF YOU ASK ME...
HEHE!

CHAPTER 2 THE HEAVENLY KINGDOM

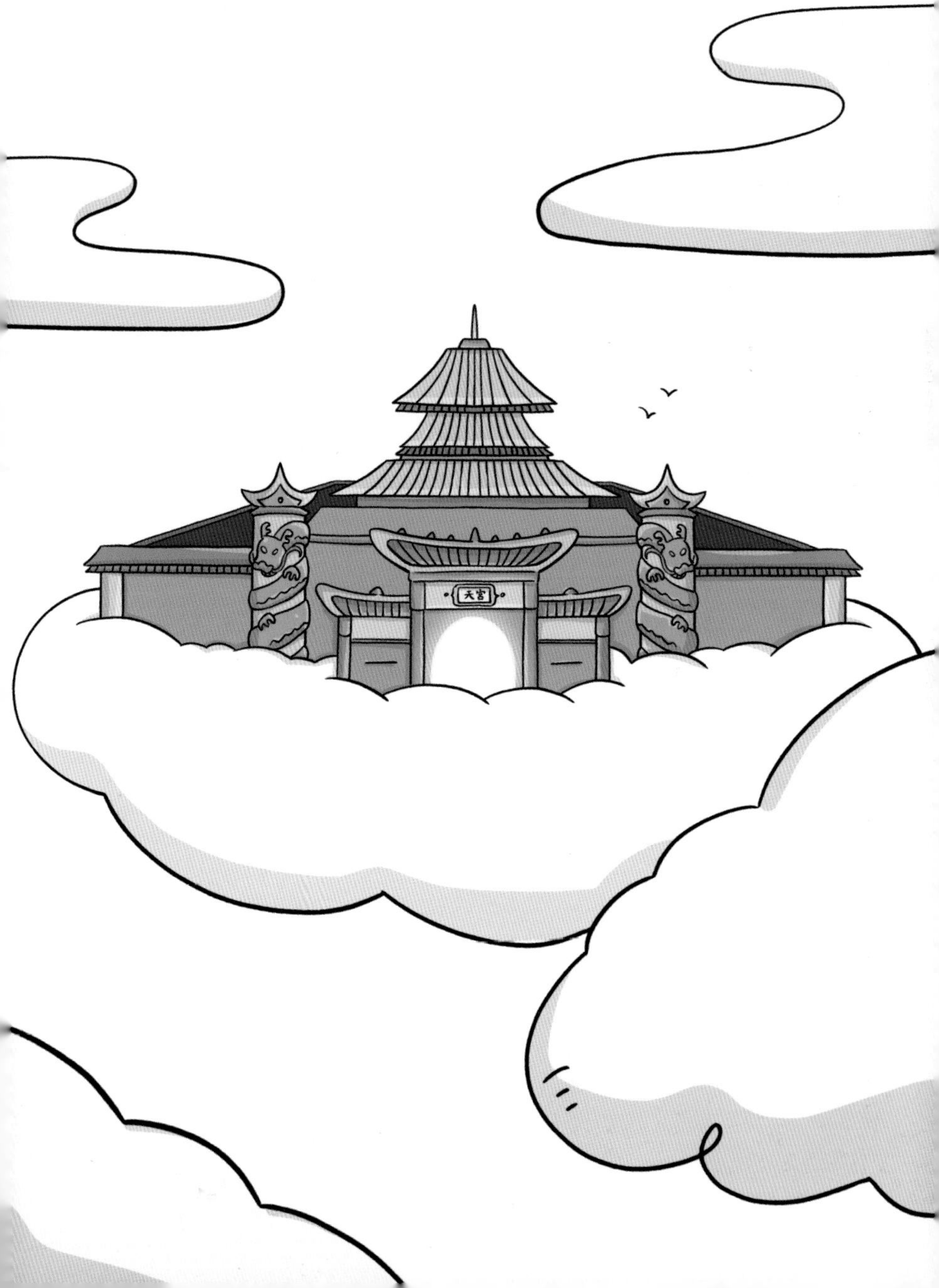

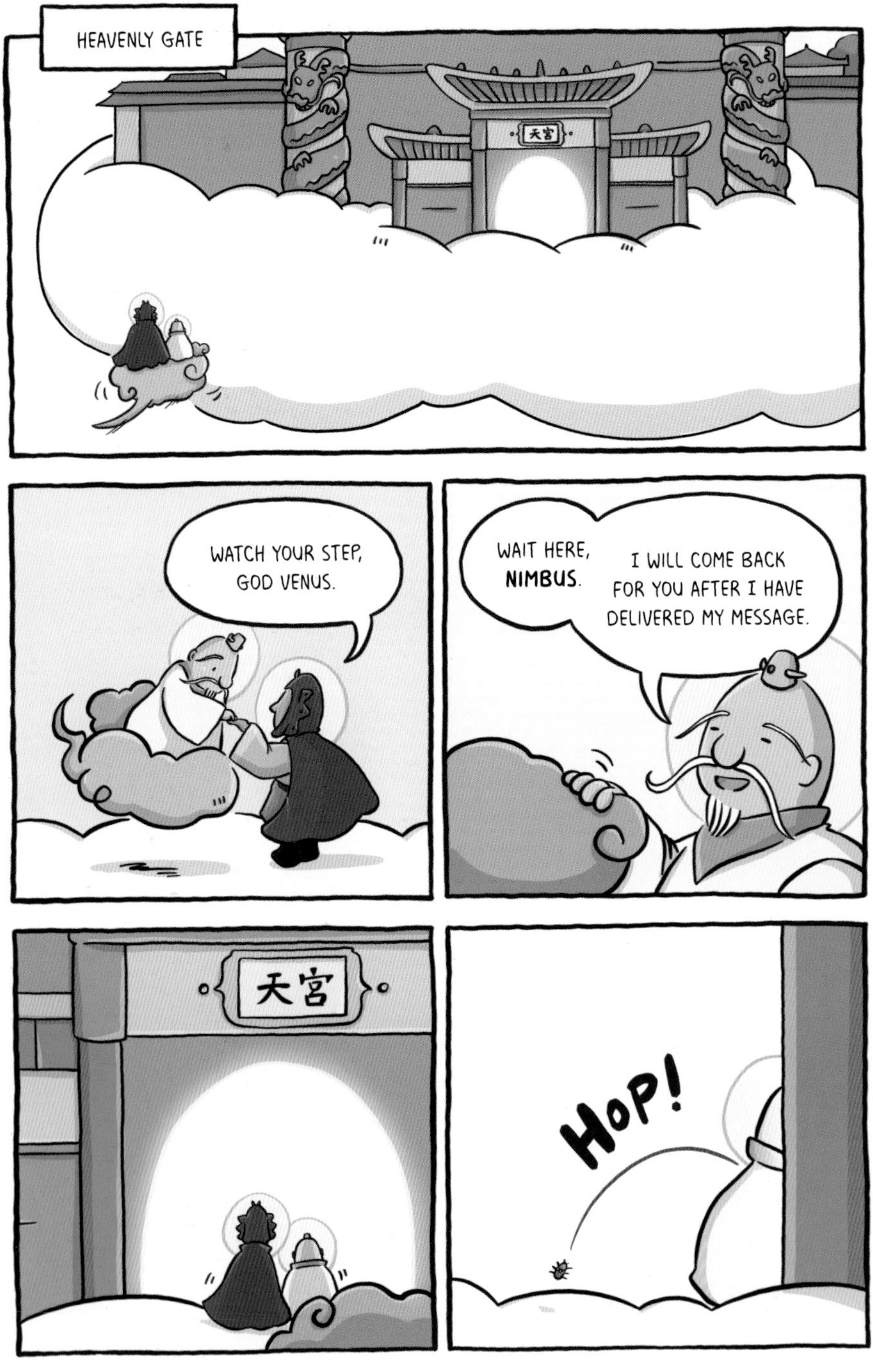
HEAVENLY GATE
天宫
WATCH YOUR STEP, GOD VENUS.
WAIT HERE, **NIMBUS**.
I WILL COME BACK FOR YOU AFTER I HAVE DELIVERED MY MESSAGE.
天宫
HOP!

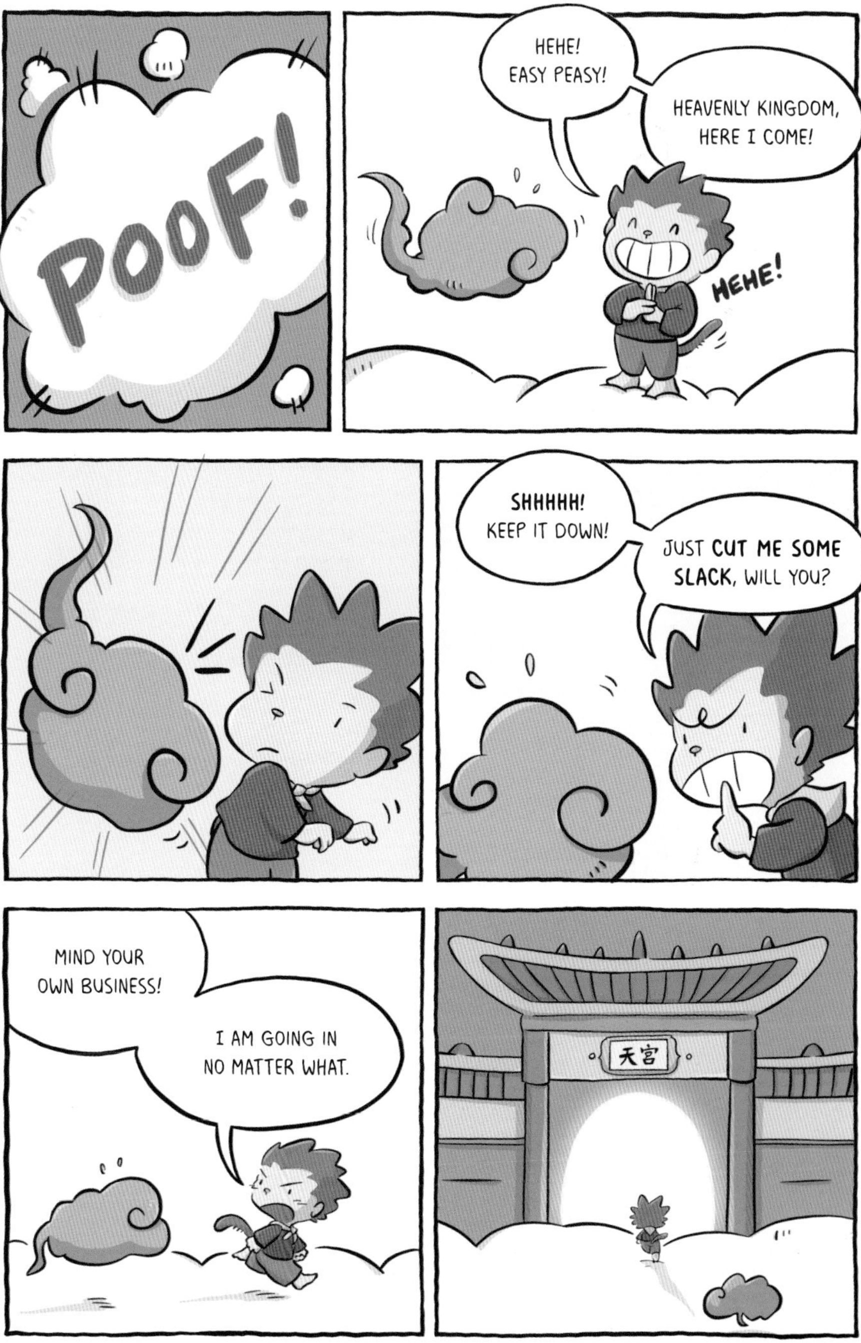
POOF!
HEHE!
EASY PEASY!
HEAVENLY KINGDOM,
HERE I COME!
HEHE!
SHHHHH!
KEEP IT DOWN!
JUST **CUT ME SOME SLACK**, WILL YOU?
MIND YOUR OWN BUSINESS!
I AM GOING IN NO MATTER WHAT.
天宫

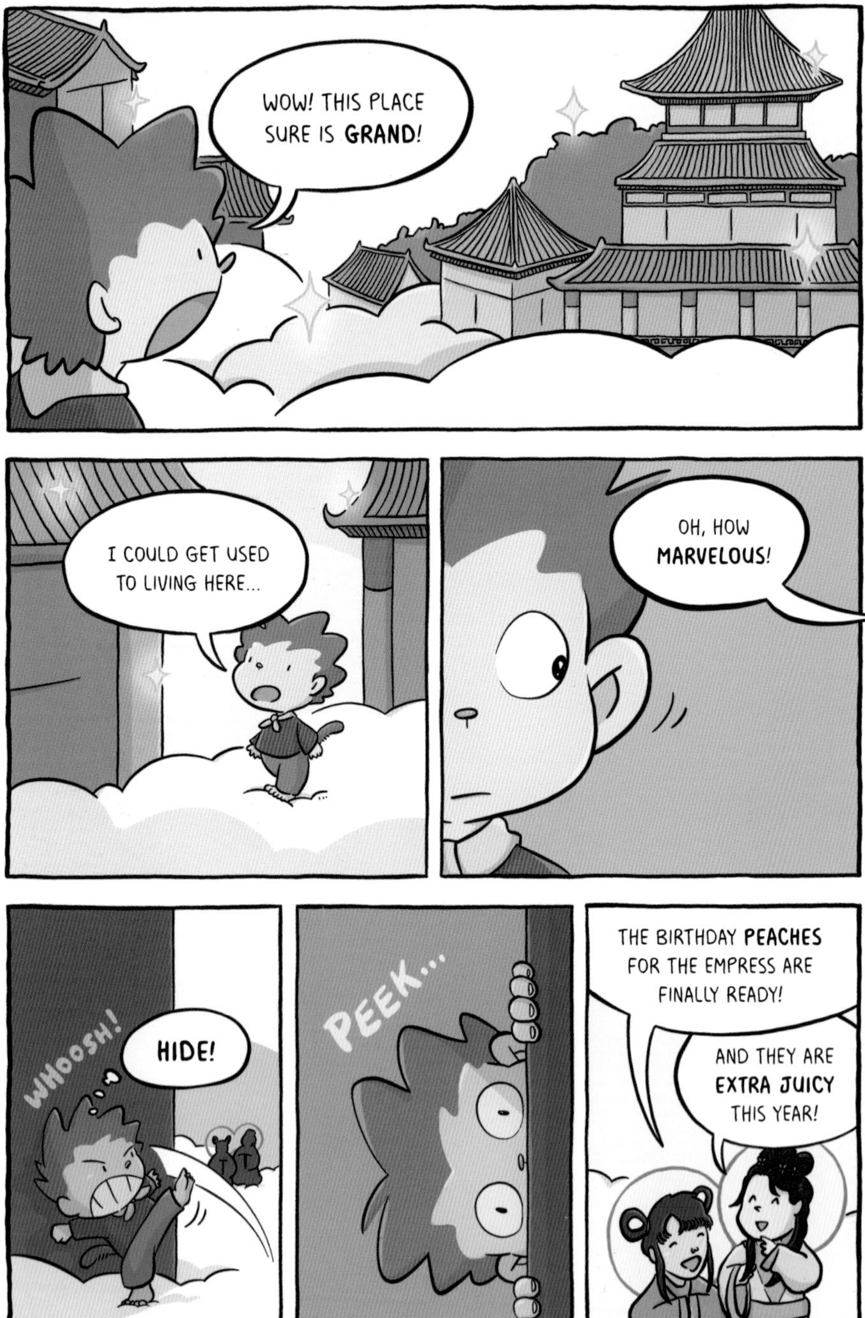
WOW! THIS PLACE SURE IS **GRAND**!
I COULD GET USED TO LIVING HERE...
OH, HOW **MARVELOUS**!
WHOOSH!
HIDE!
PEEK...
THE BIRTHDAY **PEACHES** FOR THE EMPRESS ARE FINALLY READY!
AND THEY ARE **EXTRA JUICY** THIS YEAR!

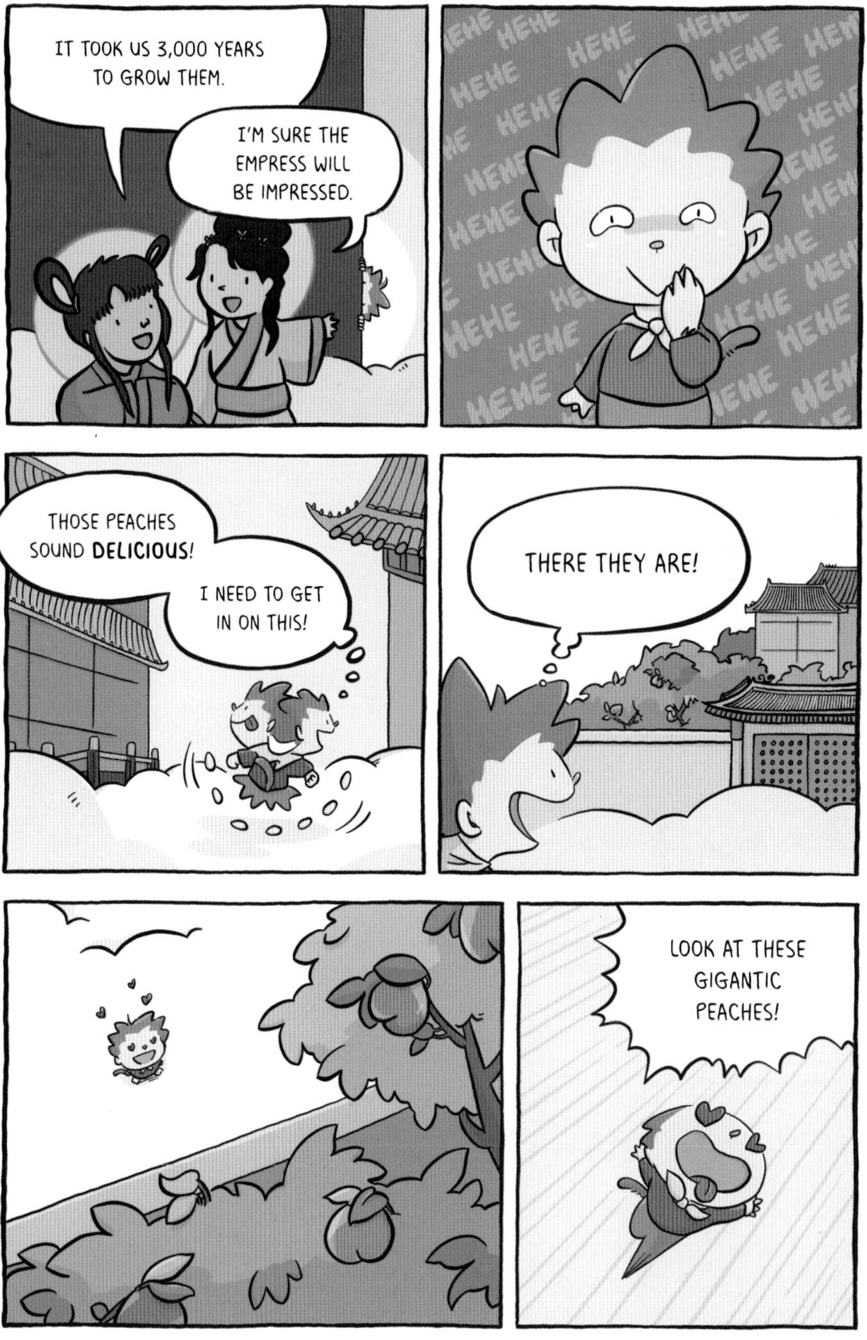
IT TOOK US 3,000 YEARS TO GROW THEM.
I'M SURE THE EMPRESS WILL BE IMPRESSED.
HEHE HEHE HEHE
THOSE PEACHES SOUND **DELICIOUS**!
I NEED TO GET IN ON THIS!
THERE THEY ARE!
LOOK AT THESE GIGANTIC PEACHES!

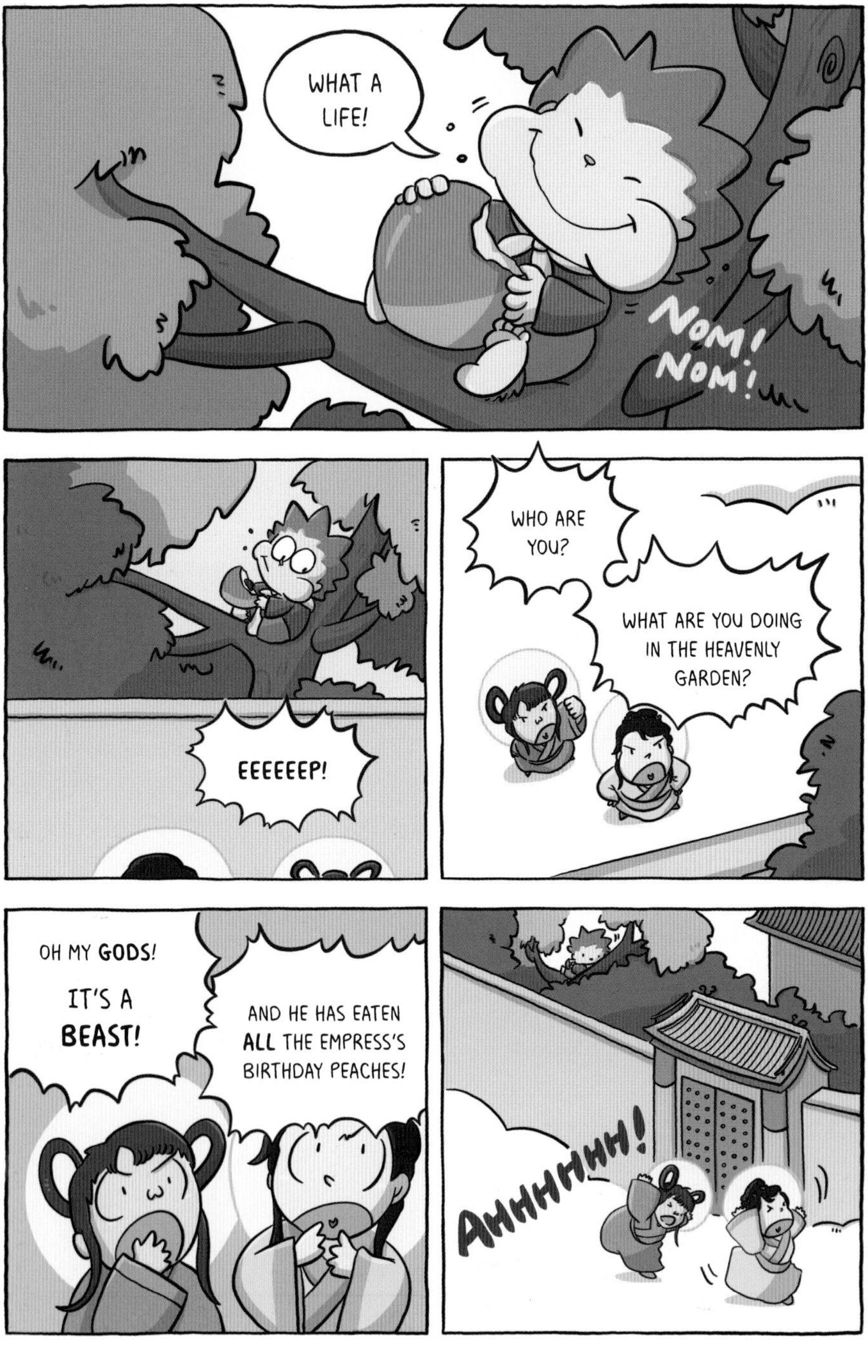
WHAT A LIFE!
NOM! NOM!
EEEEEEP!
WHO ARE YOU?
WHAT ARE YOU DOING IN THE HEAVENLY GARDEN?
OH MY **GODS**!
IT'S A **BEAST**!
AND HE HAS EATEN **ALL** THE EMPRESS'S BIRTHDAY PEACHES!
AHHHHHHH!

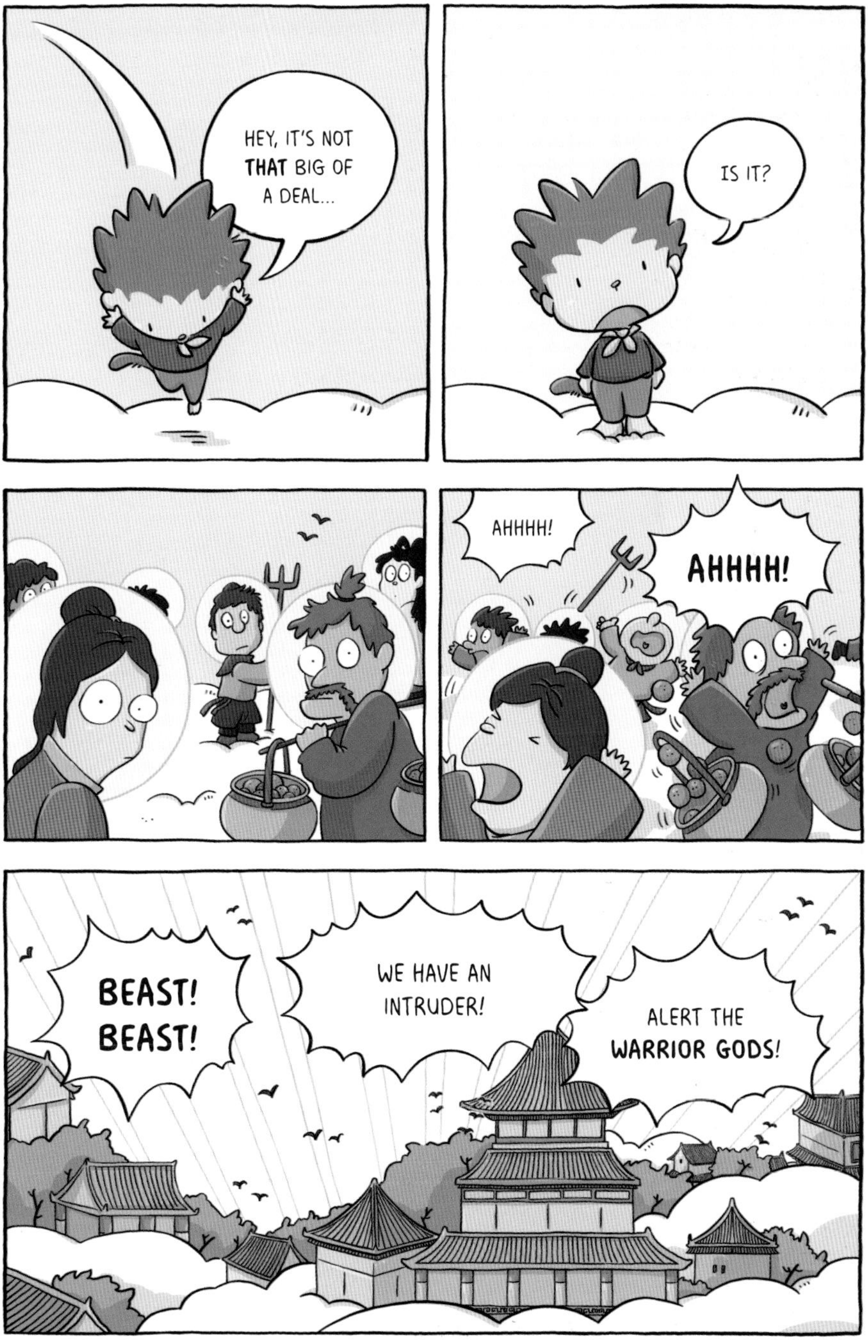
HEY, IT'S NOT **THAT** BIG OF A DEAL...
IS IT?
AHHHH!
AHHHH!
BEAST! BEAST!
WE HAVE AN INTRUDER!
ALERT THE WARRIOR GODS!

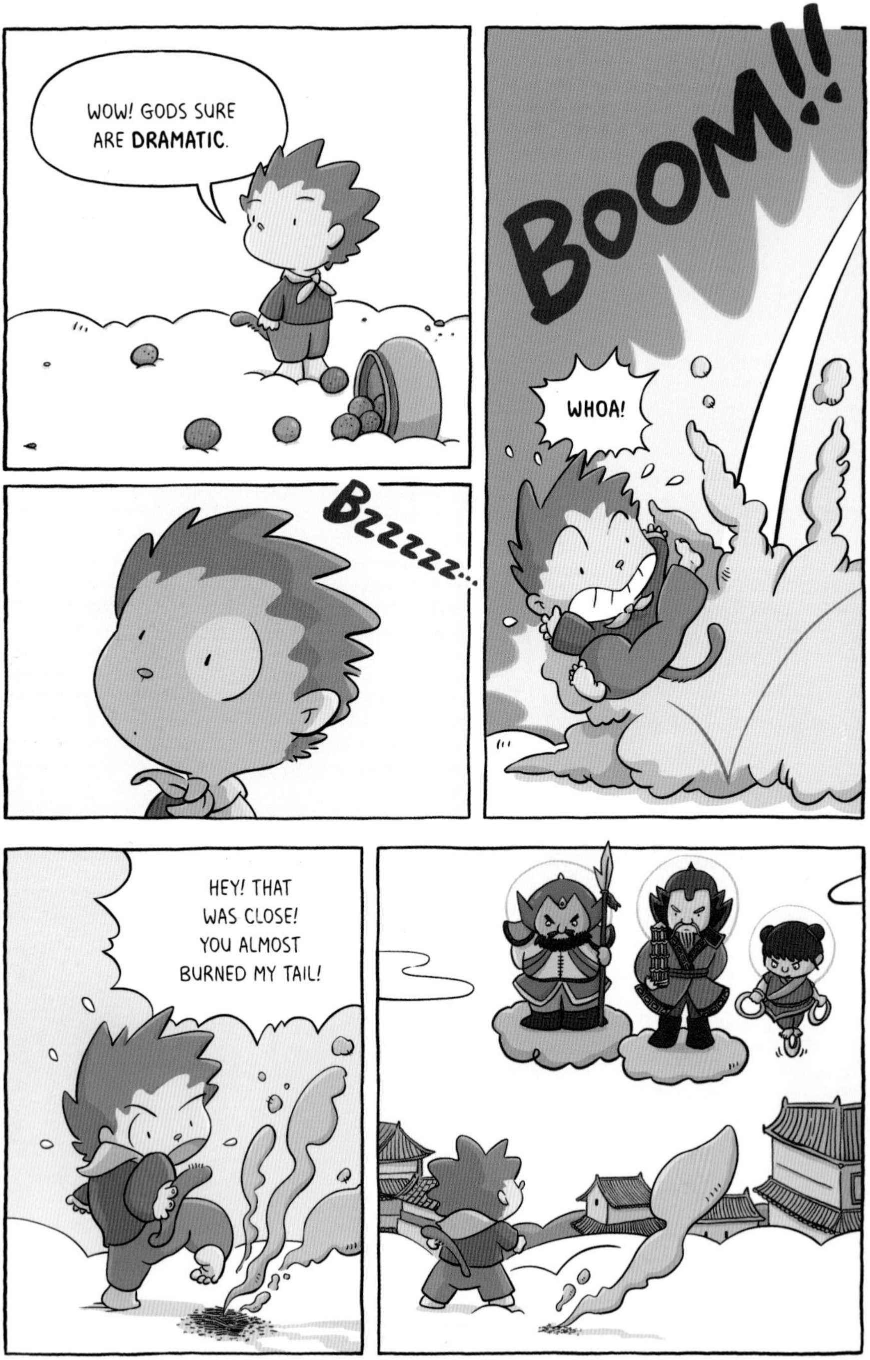
WOW! GODS SURE ARE **DRAMATIC**.
BOOM!!
WHOA!
Bzzzzzz...
HEY! THAT WAS CLOSE! YOU ALMOST BURNED MY TAIL!

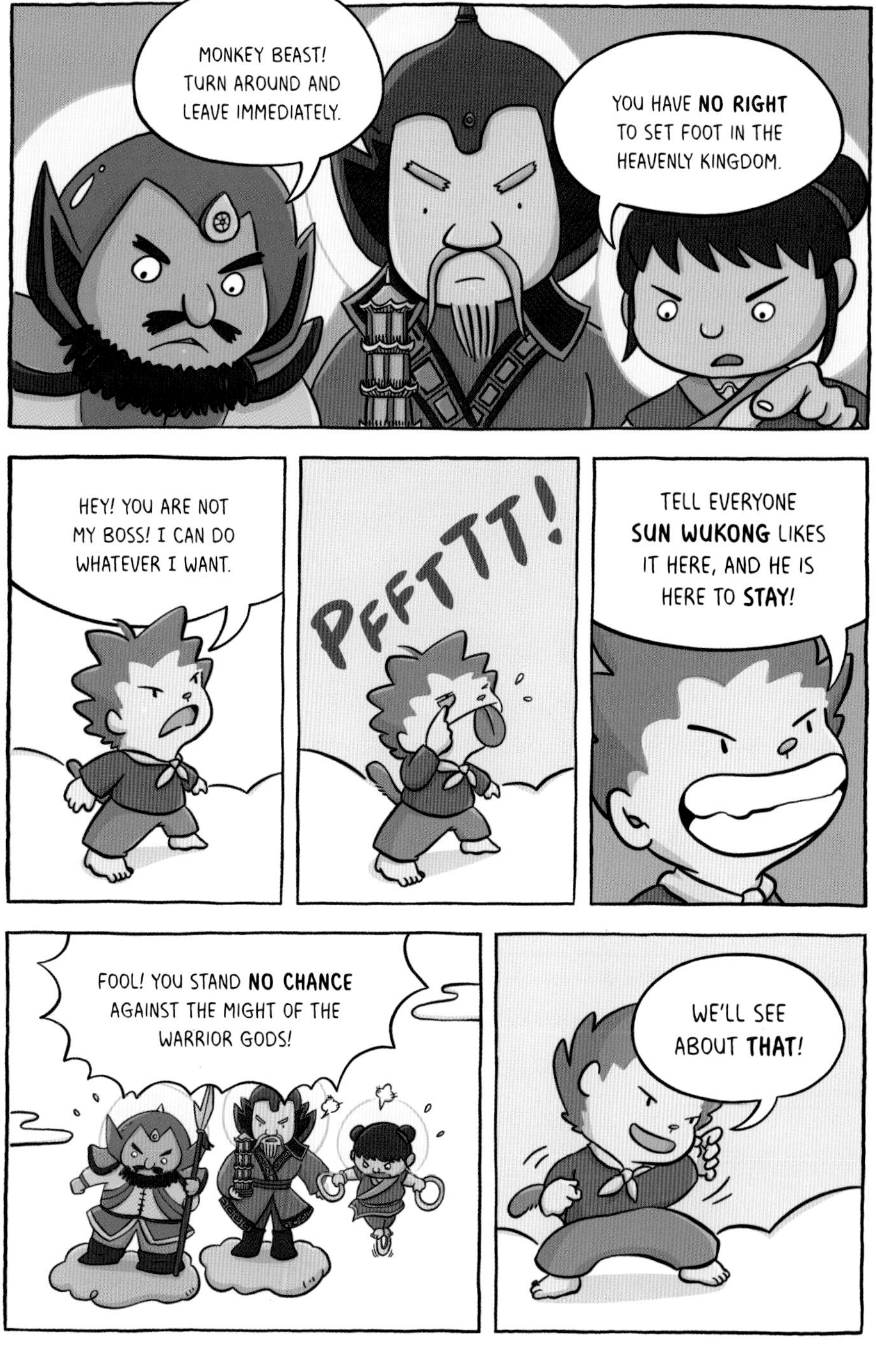
MONKEY BEAST! TURN AROUND AND LEAVE IMMEDIATELY.
YOU HAVE **NO RIGHT** TO SET FOOT IN THE HEAVENLY KINGDOM.
HEY! YOU ARE NOT MY BOSS! I CAN DO WHATEVER I WANT.
PFFTTT!
TELL EVERYONE **SUN WUKONG** LIKES IT HERE, AND HE IS HERE TO **STAY**!
FOOL! YOU STAND **NO CHANCE** AGAINST THE MIGHT OF THE WARRIOR GODS!
WE'LL SEE ABOUT **THAT**!

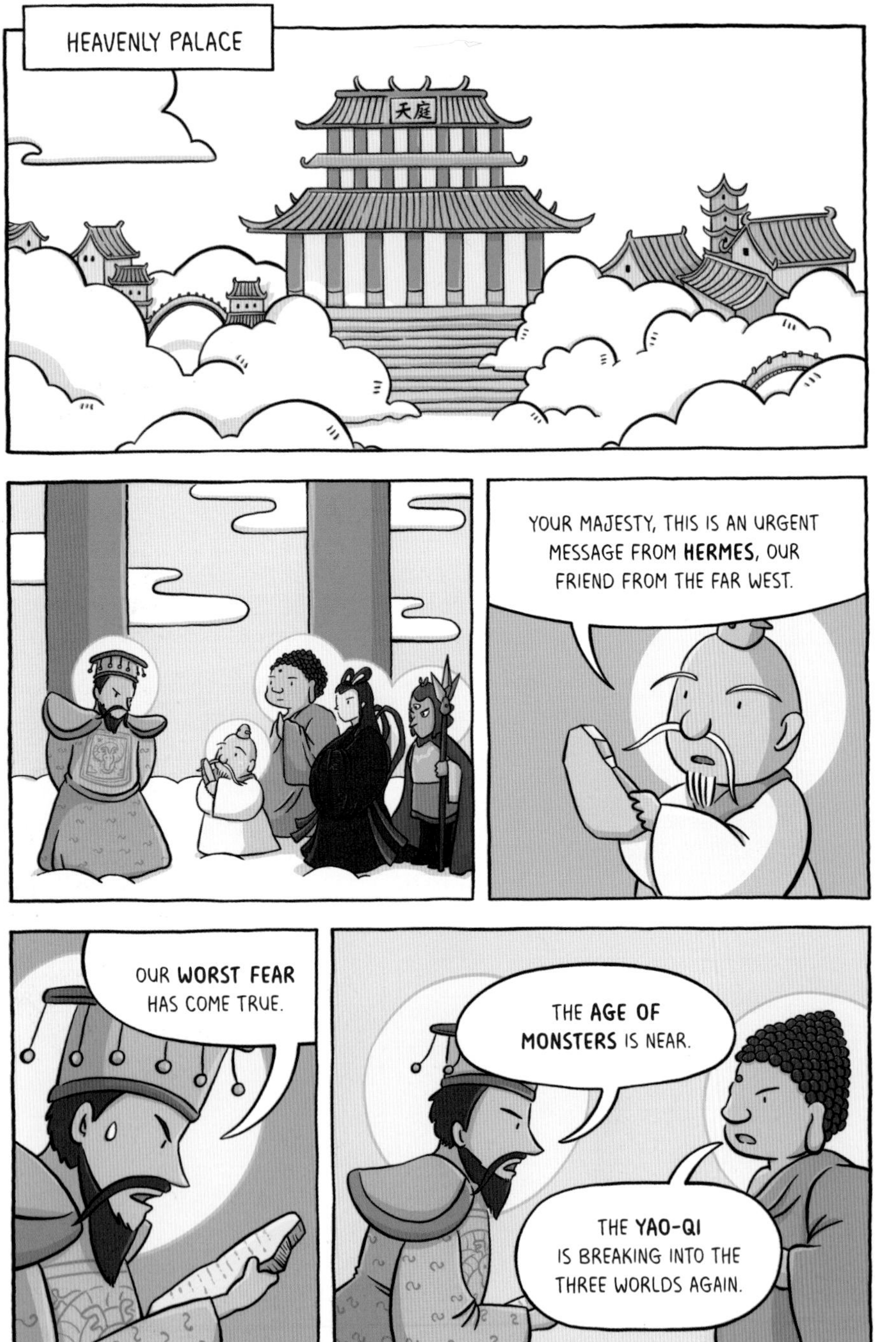
HEAVENLY PALACE
天庭
YOUR MAJESTY, THIS IS AN URGENT MESSAGE FROM **HERMES**, OUR FRIEND FROM THE FAR WEST.
OUR **WORST FEAR** HAS COME TRUE.
THE **AGE OF MONSTERS** IS NEAR.
THE **YAO-QI** IS BREAKING INTO THE THREE WORLDS AGAIN.

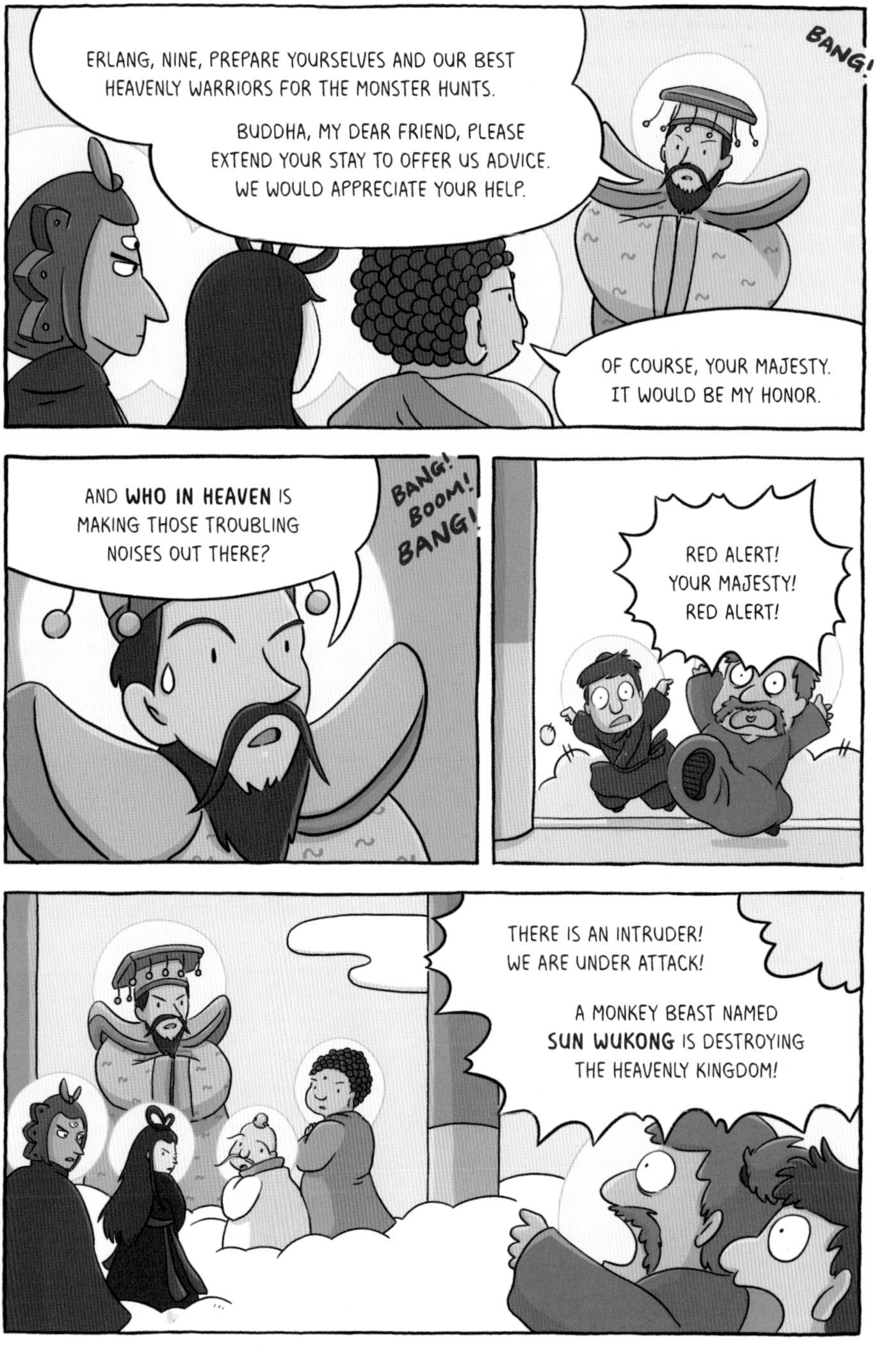
BANG!
ERLANG, NINE, PREPARE YOURSELVES AND OUR BEST HEAVENLY WARRIORS FOR THE MONSTER HUNTS.
BUDDHA, MY DEAR FRIEND, PLEASE EXTEND YOUR STAY TO OFFER US ADVICE. WE WOULD APPRECIATE YOUR HELP.
OF COURSE, YOUR MAJESTY. IT WOULD BE MY HONOR.
AND **WHO IN HEAVEN** IS MAKING THOSE TROUBLING NOISES OUT THERE?
BANG! BOOM! BANG!
RED ALERT! YOUR MAJESTY! RED ALERT!
THERE IS AN INTRUDER! WE ARE UNDER ATTACK!
A MONKEY BEAST NAMED **SUN WUKONG** IS DESTROYING THE HEAVENLY KINGDOM!

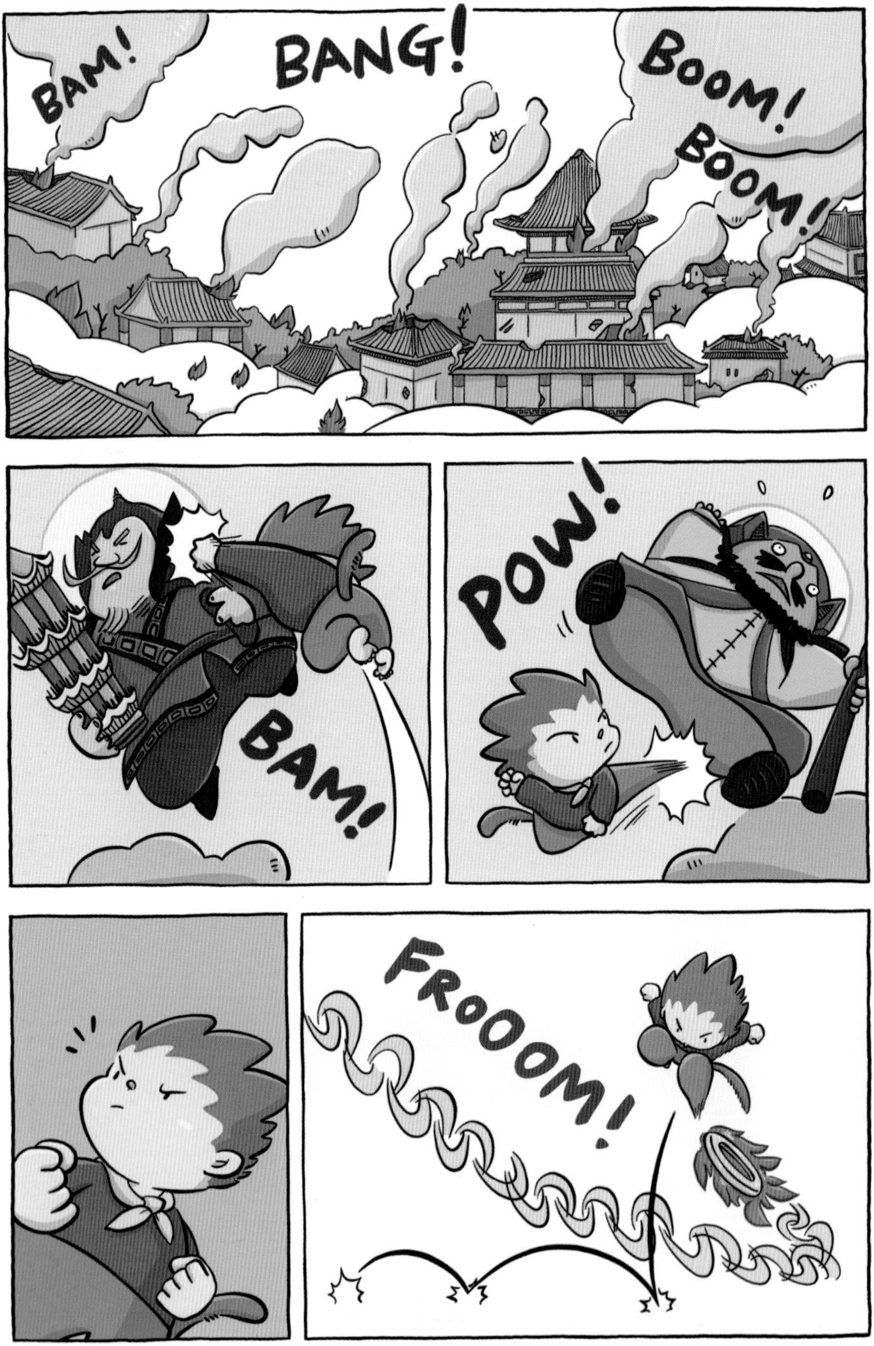
BAM!
BANG!
BOOM!
BOOM!
BAM!
POW!
FROOOOM!

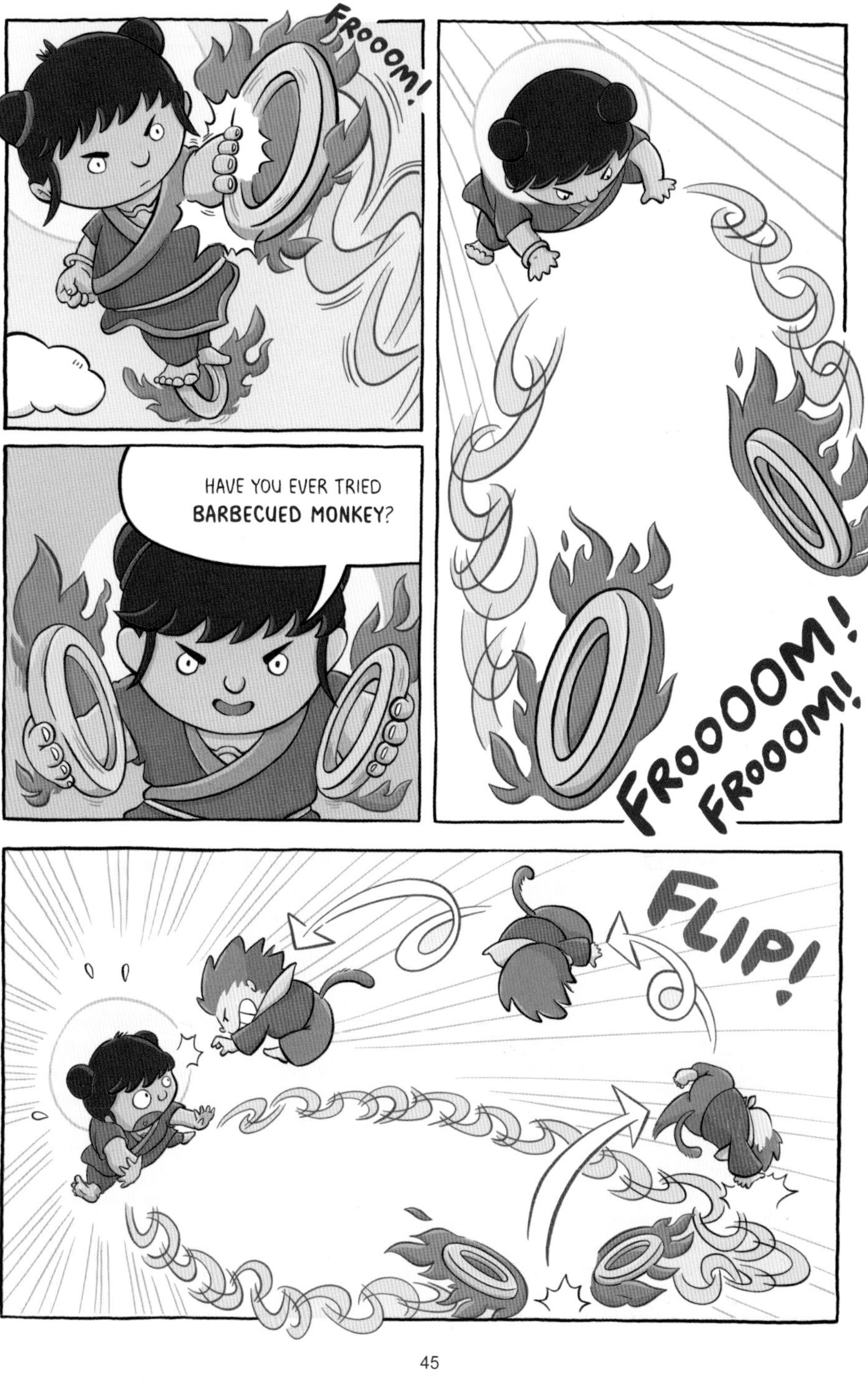
FROOOM!
HAVE YOU EVER TRIED
BARBECUED MONKEY?
FROOOOM!
FROOOM!
FLIP!

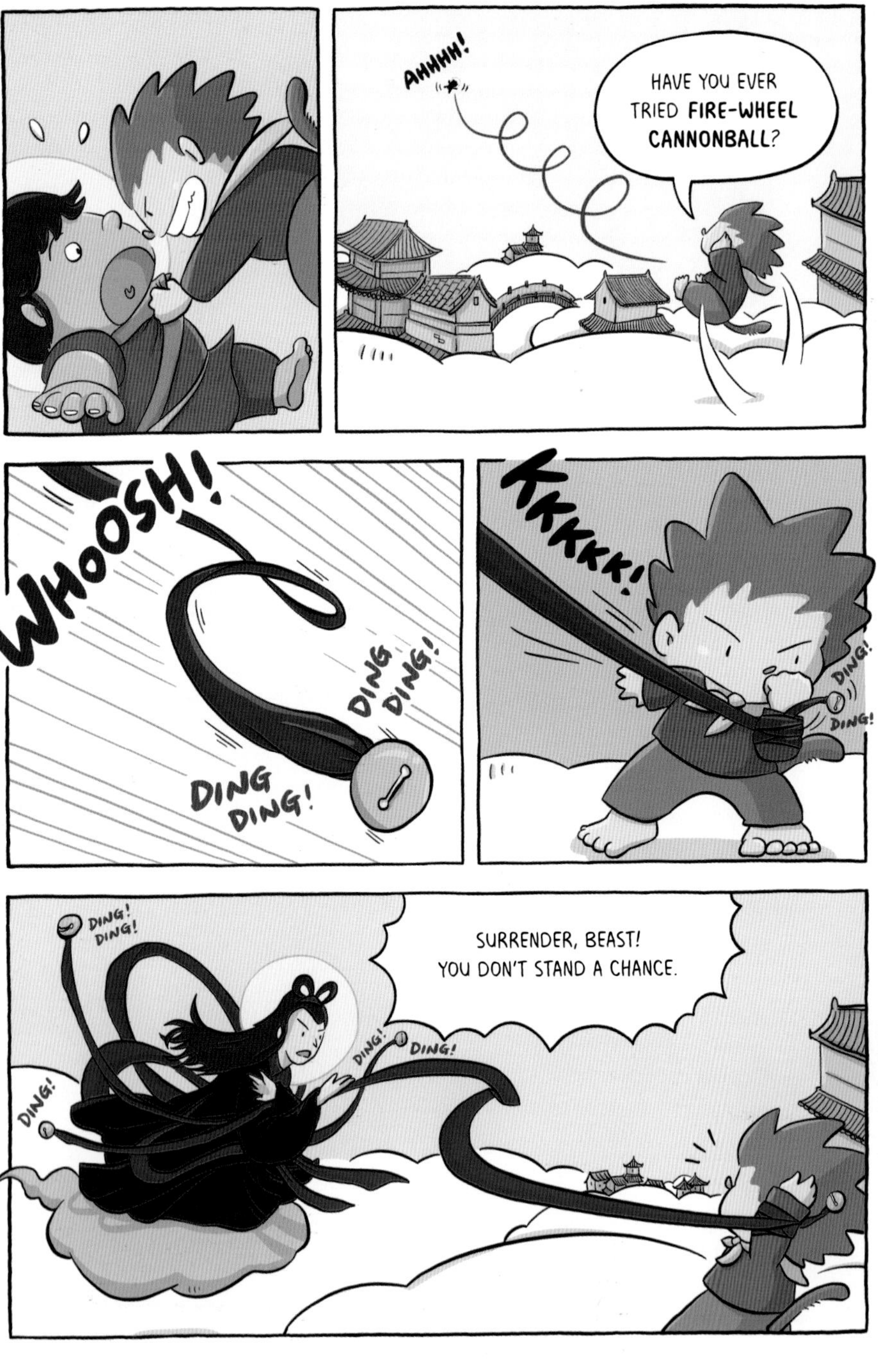
AHHHH!
HAVE YOU EVER TRIED **FIRE-WHEEL CANNONBALL**?
WHOOSH!
DING DING!
DING DING!
KKKKK!
DING!
DING!
DING! DING!
SURRENDER, BEAST! YOU DON'T STAND A CHANCE.
DING!
DING!
DING!

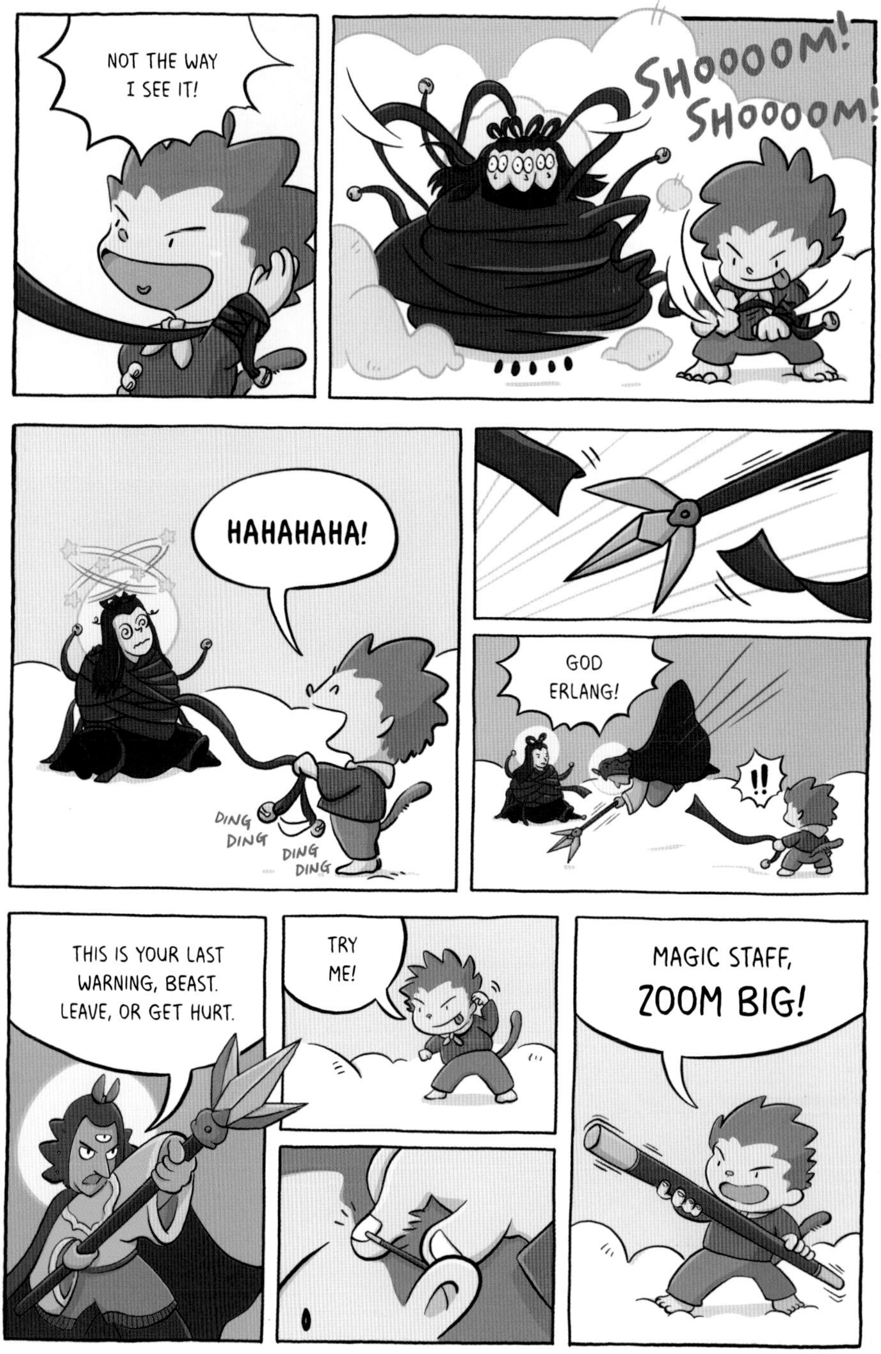
NOT THE WAY I SEE IT!
SHOOOOM! SHOOOOM!
HAHAHAHA!
DING DING
DING DING
GOD ERLANG!
!!
THIS IS YOUR LAST WARNING, BEAST. LEAVE, OR GET HURT.
TRY ME!
MAGIC STAFF, ZOOM BIG!

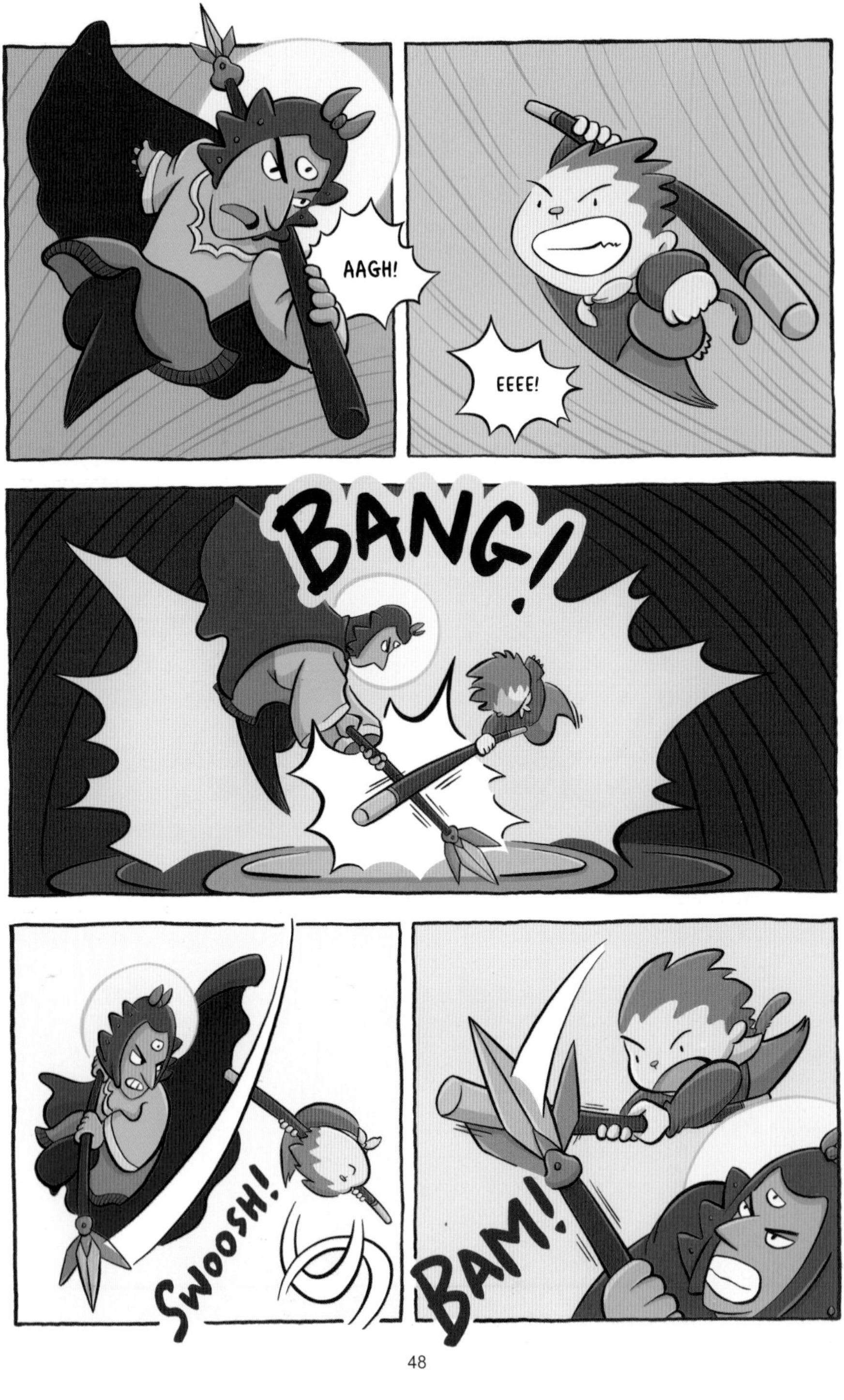
AAGH!
EEEE!
BANG!
SWOOSH!
BAM!

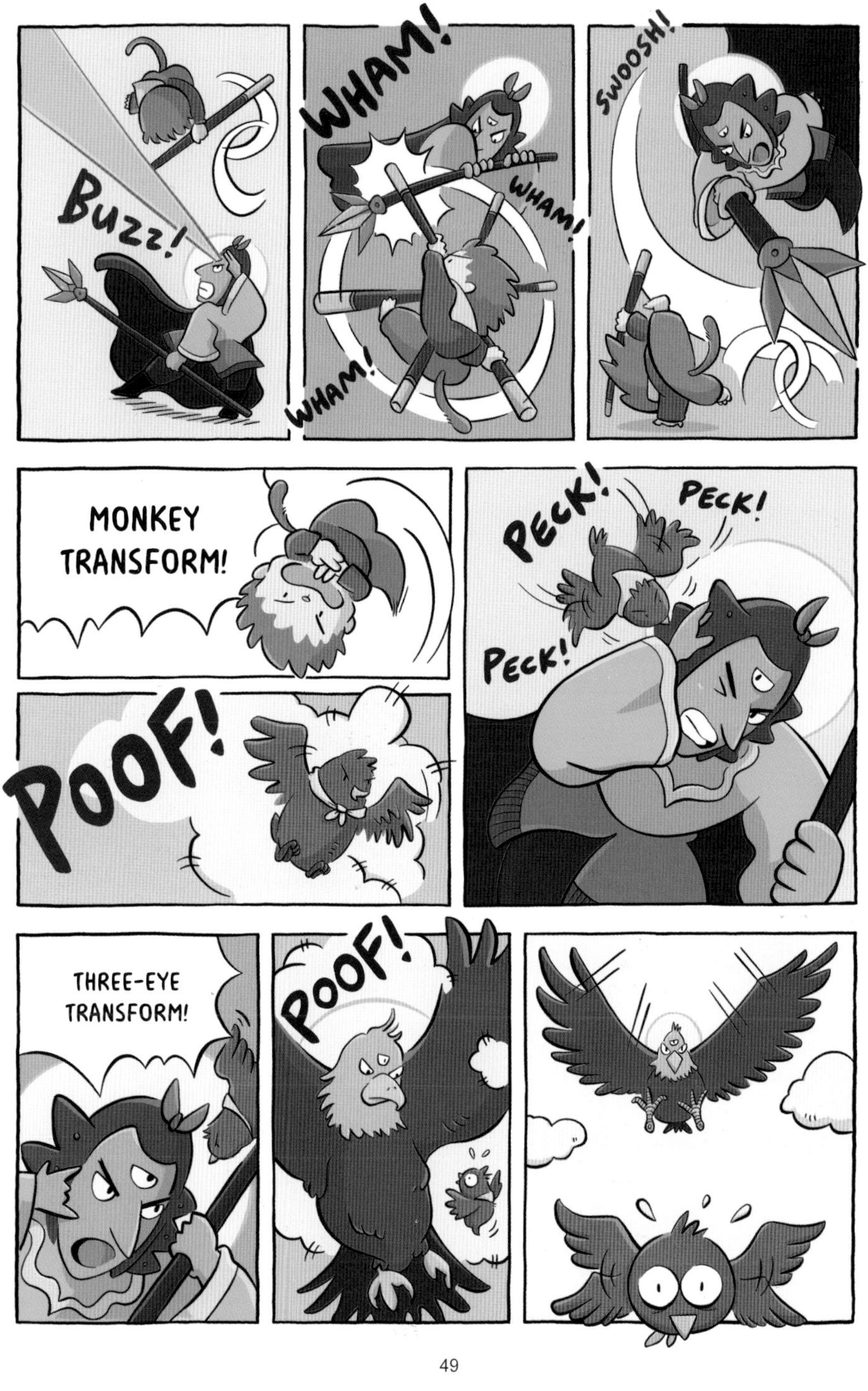
BUZZ!
WHAM!
WHAM!
WHAM!
SWOOSH!
MONKEY TRANSFORM!
POOF!
PECK!
PECK!
PECK!
THREE-EYE TRANSFORM!
POOF!

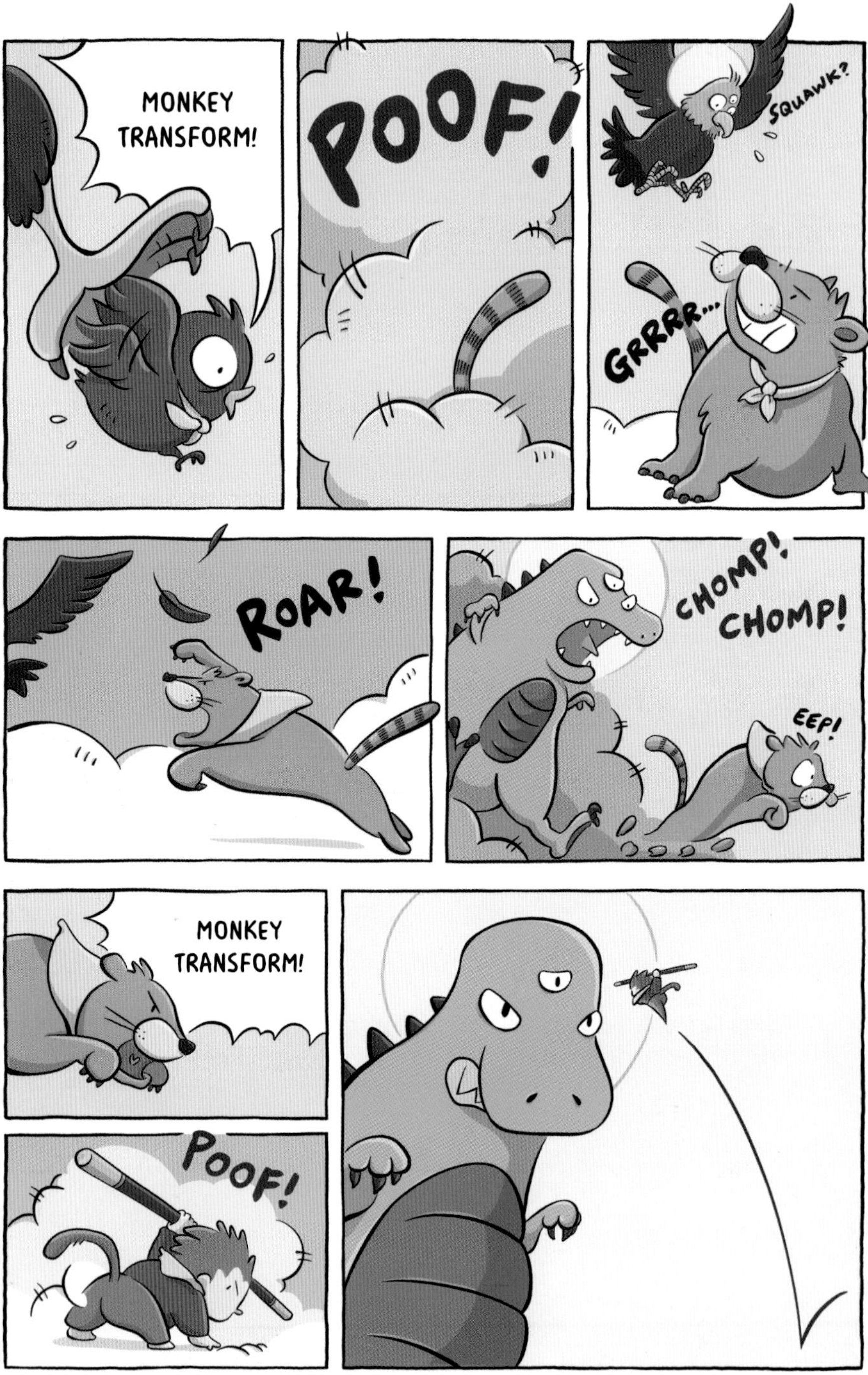
MONKEY TRANSFORM!
POOF!
SQUAWK?
GRRRR...
ROAR!
CHOMP! CHOMP!
EEP!
MONKEY TRANSFORM!
POOF!

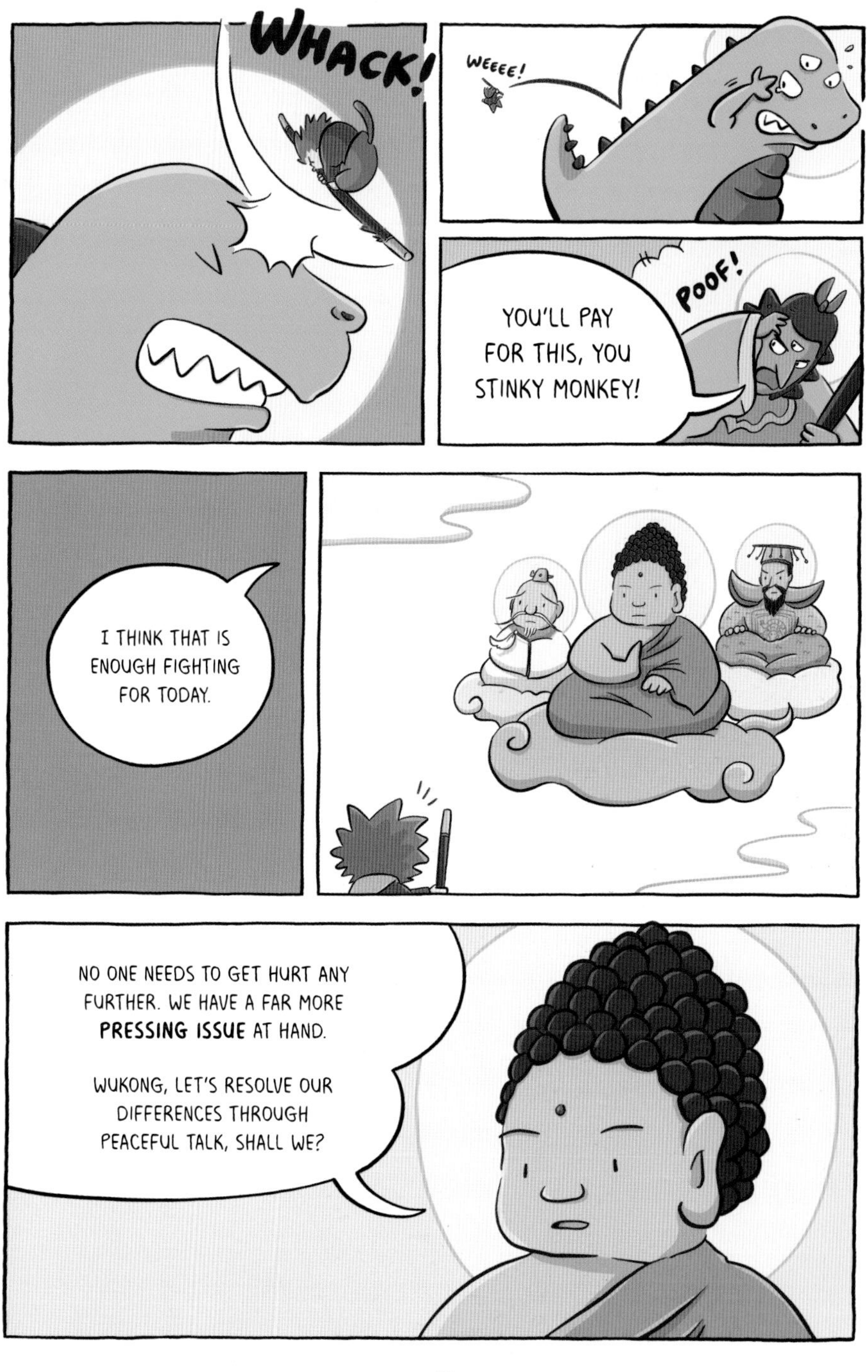
WHACK!
WEEEE!
POOF!
YOU'LL PAY FOR THIS, YOU STINKY MONKEY!
I THINK THAT IS ENOUGH FIGHTING FOR TODAY.
NO ONE NEEDS TO GET HURT ANY FURTHER. WE HAVE A FAR MORE **PRESSING ISSUE** AT HAND.
WUKONG, LET'S RESOLVE OUR DIFFERENCES THROUGH PEACEFUL TALK, SHALL WE?

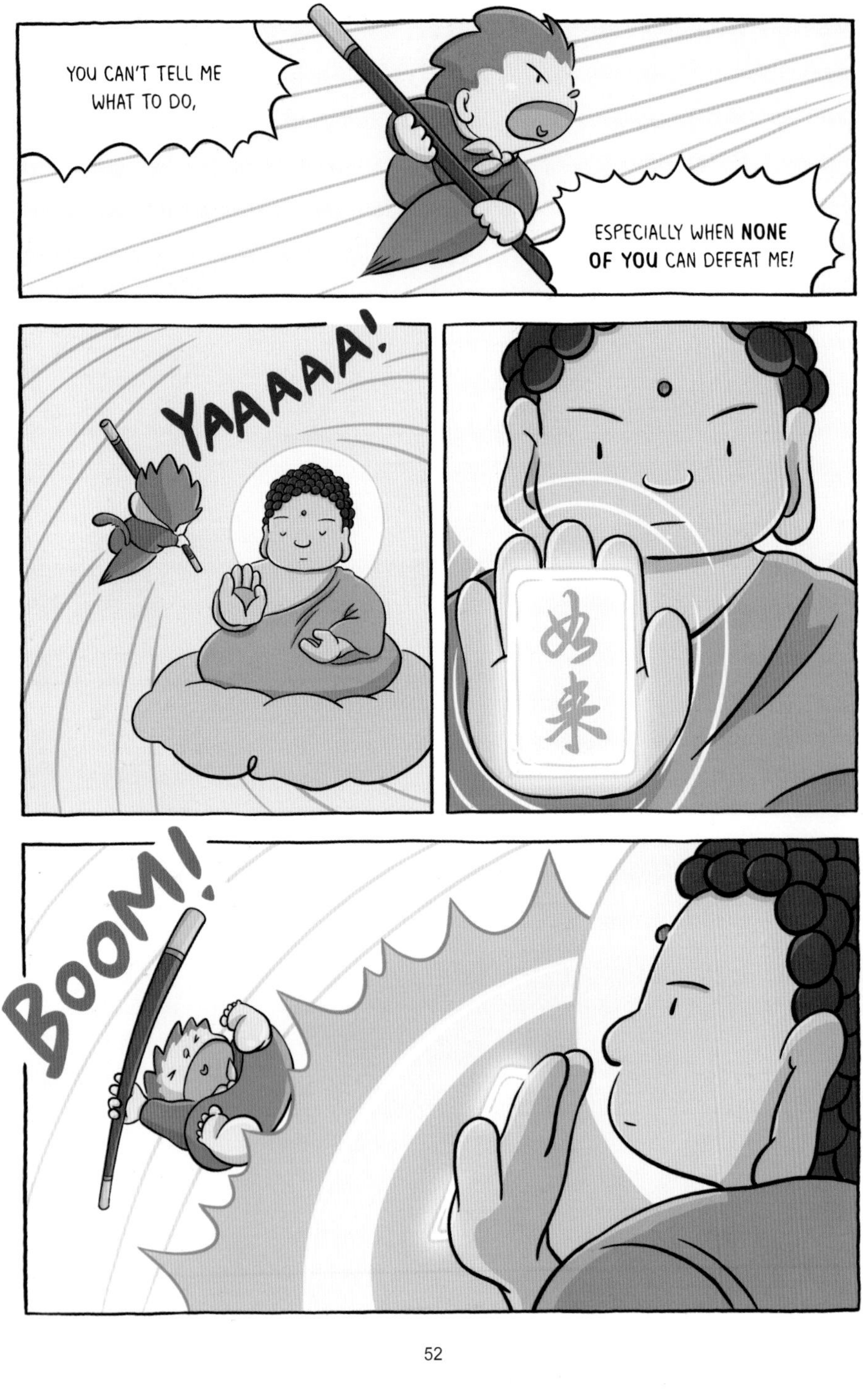

YOU CAN'T TELL ME WHAT TO DO,
ESPECIALLY WHEN **NONE OF YOU** CAN DEFEAT ME!
YAAAAA!
如来
BOOM!

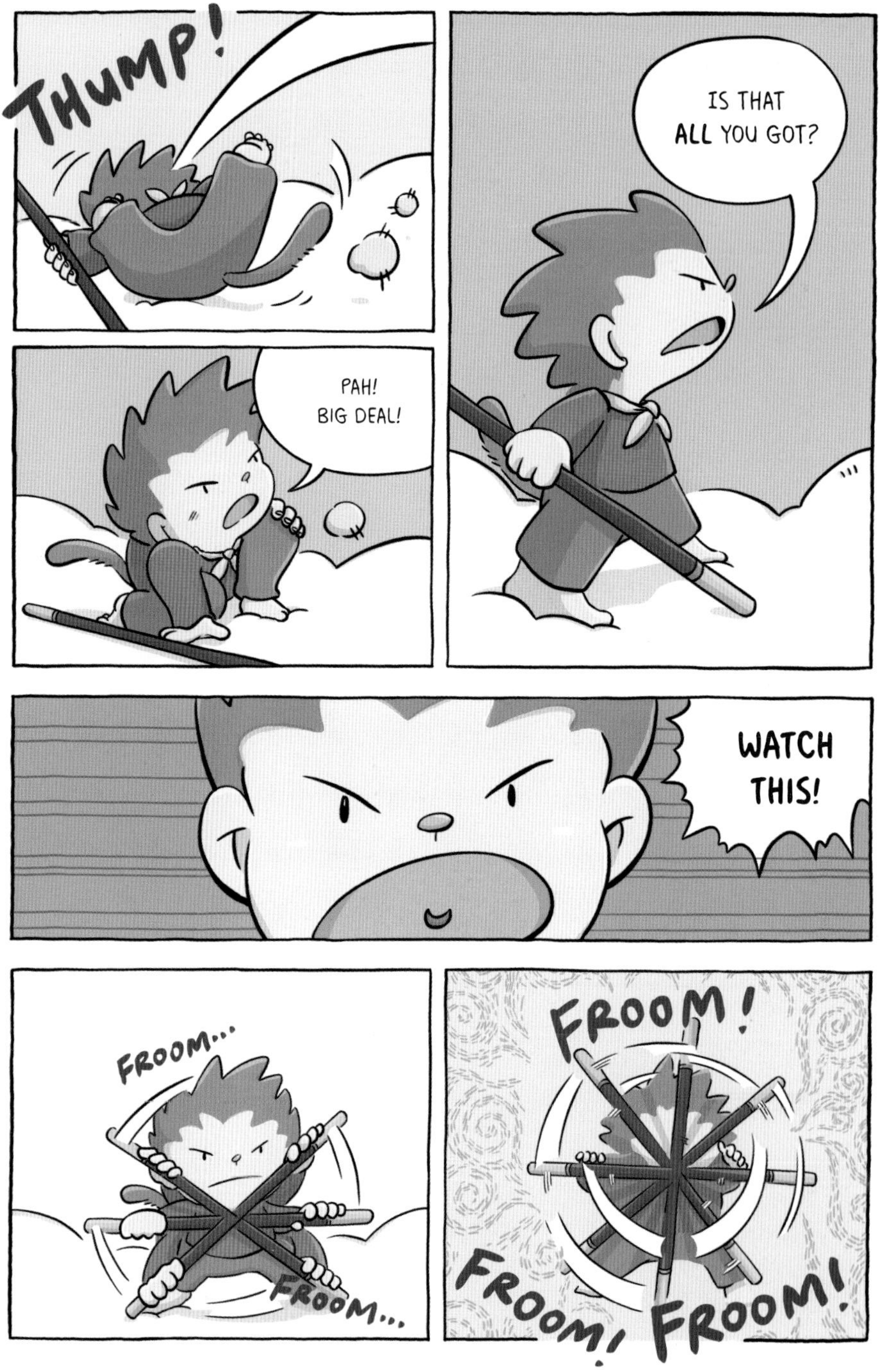
THUMP!
IS THAT ALL YOU GOT?
PAH! BIG DEAL!
WATCH THIS!
FROOM...
FROOM...
FROOM!
FROOM!
FROOM!

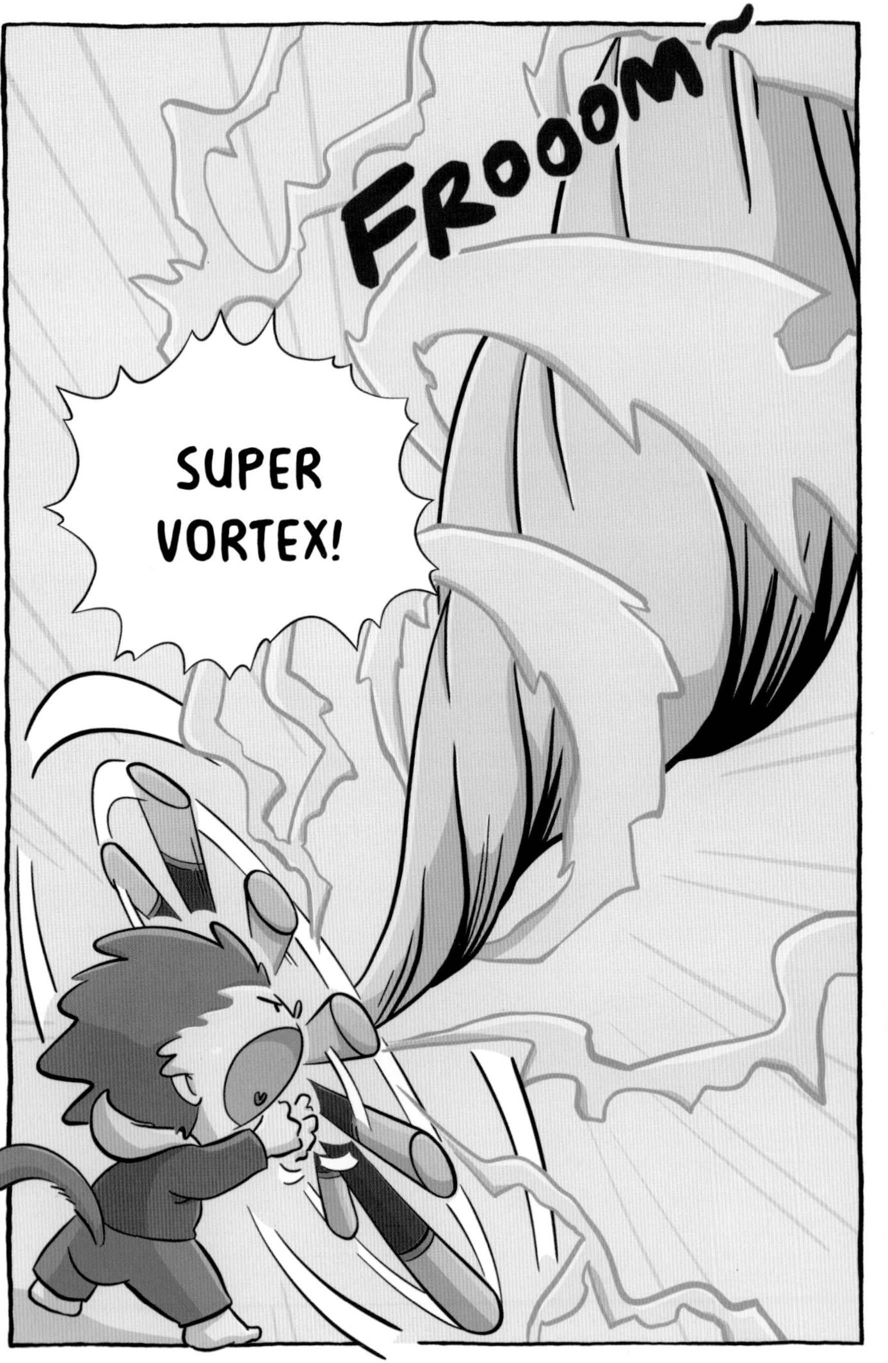
FROOOM~
SUPER VORTEX!

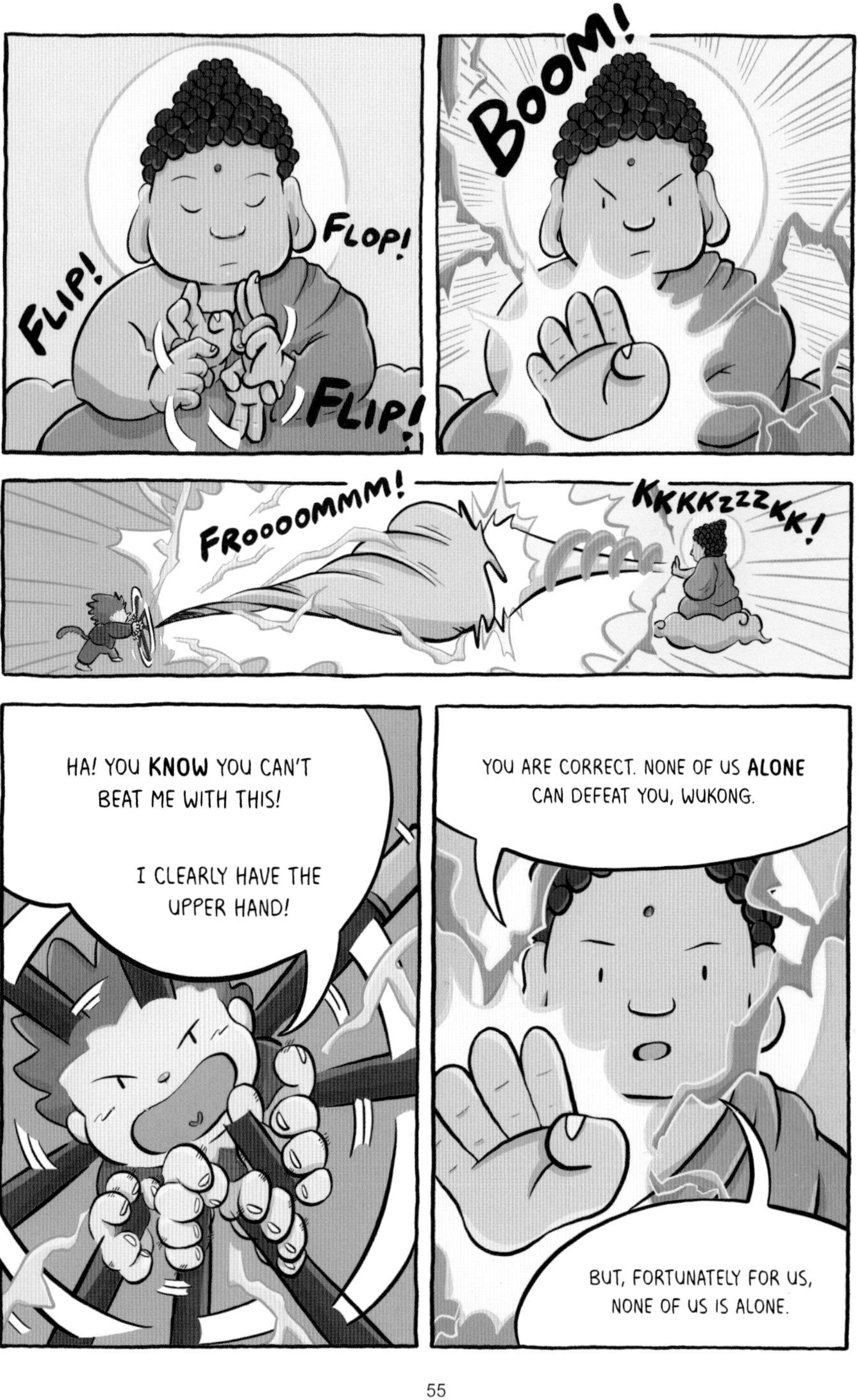
FLIP!
FLOP!
FLIP!
BOOM!
FROOOOMMM!
KKKKZZZKK!
HA! YOU **KNOW** YOU CAN'T BEAT ME WITH THIS!
I CLEARLY HAVE THE UPPER HAND!
YOU ARE CORRECT. NONE OF US **ALONE** CAN DEFEAT YOU, WUKONG.
BUT, FORTUNATELY FOR US, NONE OF US IS ALONE.

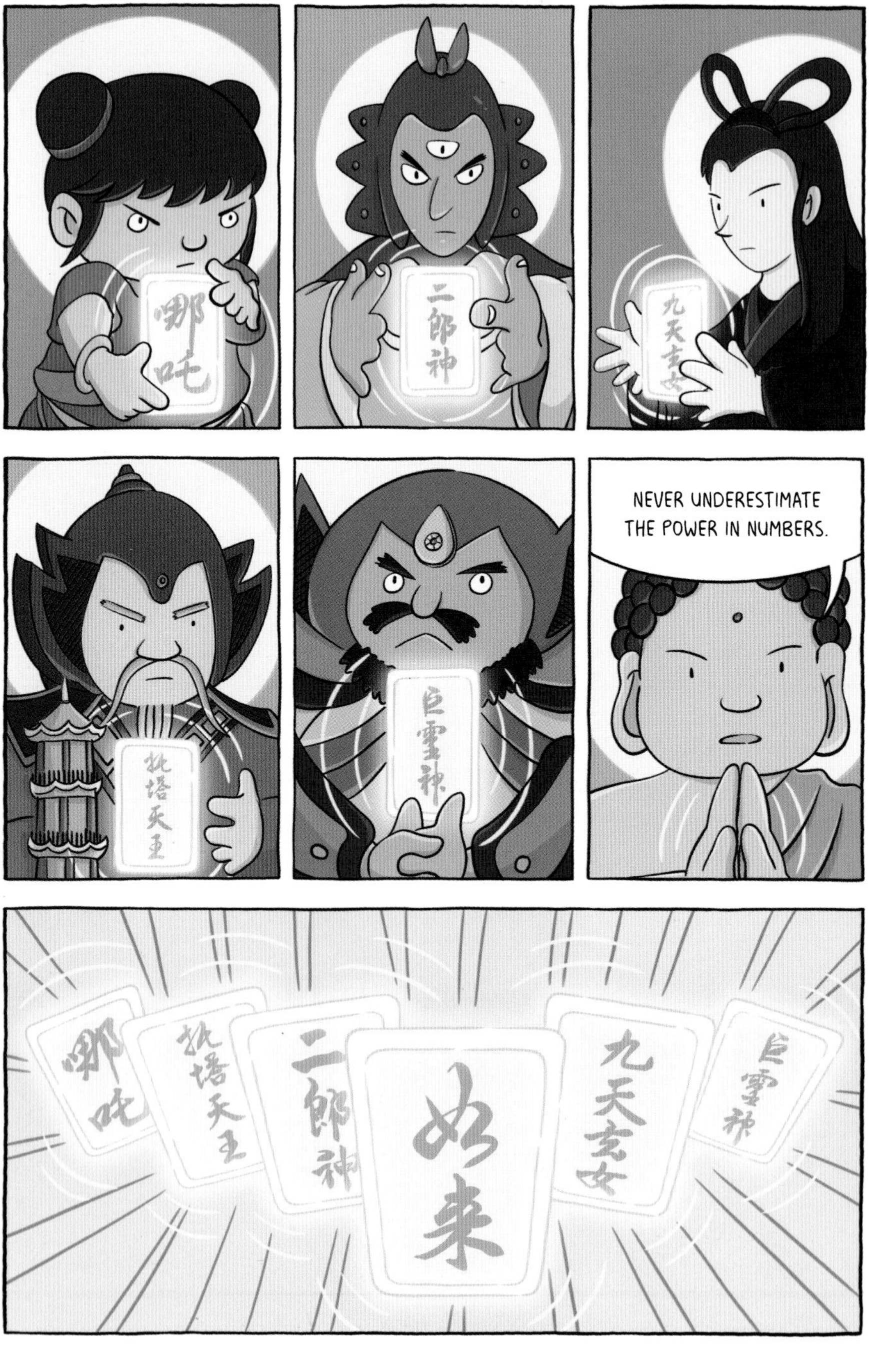
哪吒
二郎神
九天玄女
托塔天王
巨靈神
NEVER UNDERESTIMATE THE POWER IN NUMBERS.
哪吒
托塔天王
二郎神
如来
九天玄女
巨靈神

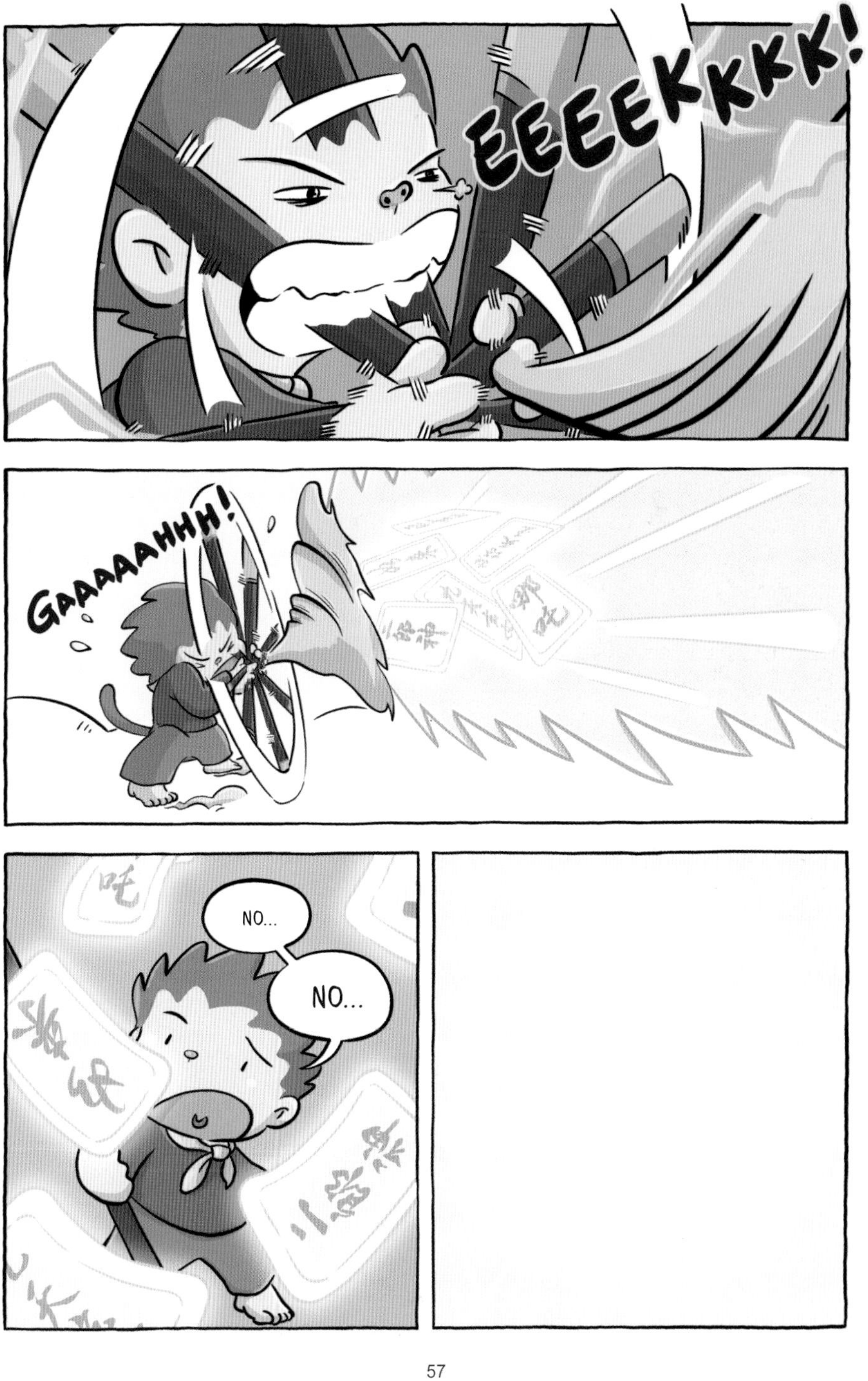
EEEEKKKK!
GAAAAAHHH!
NO...
NO...

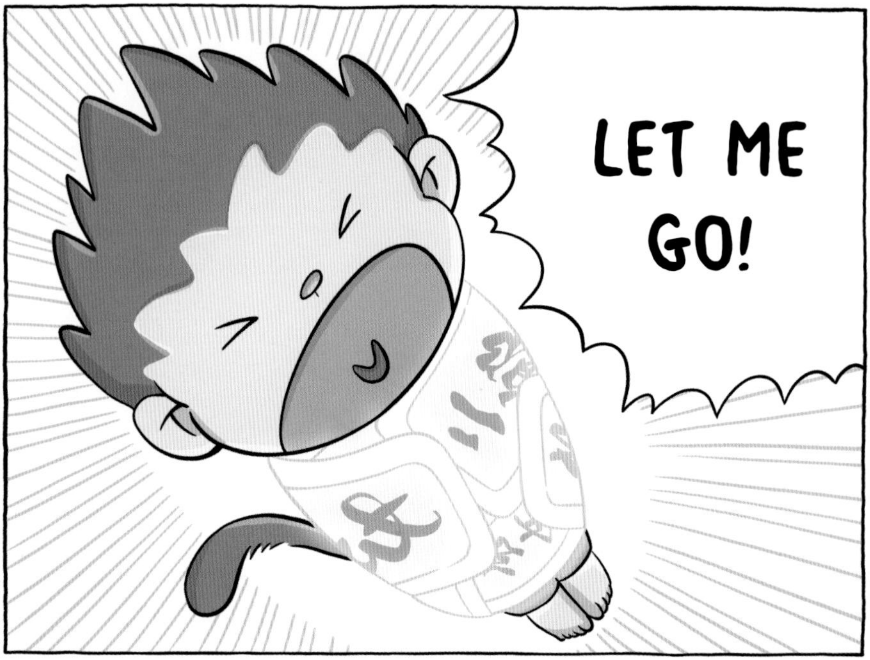
LET ME GO!

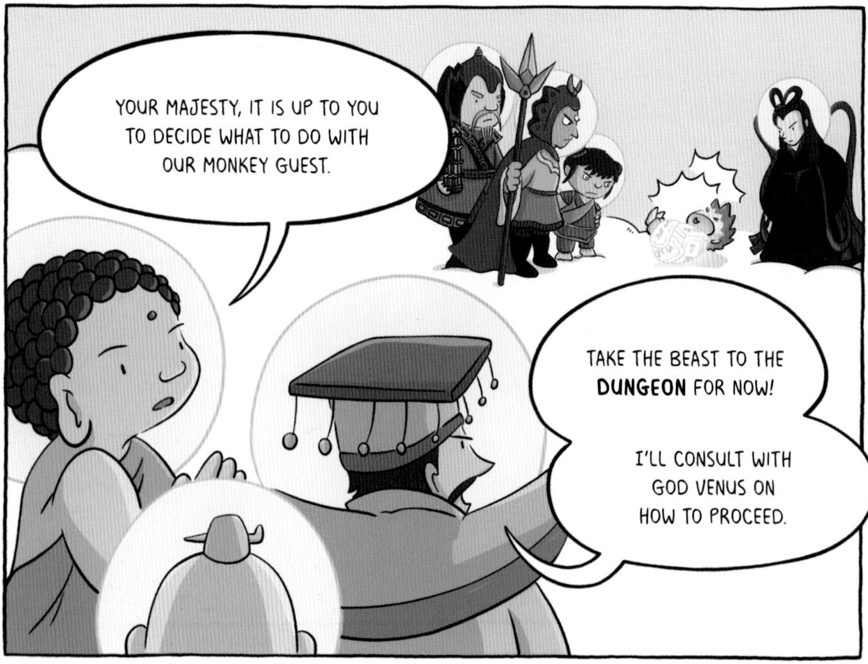
YOUR MAJESTY, IT IS UP TO YOU TO DECIDE WHAT TO DO WITH OUR MONKEY GUEST.
TAKE THE BEAST TO THE **DUNGEON** FOR NOW!
I'LL CONSULT WITH GOD VENUS ON HOW TO PROCEED.

CHAPTER 3 MONSTER HUNTER

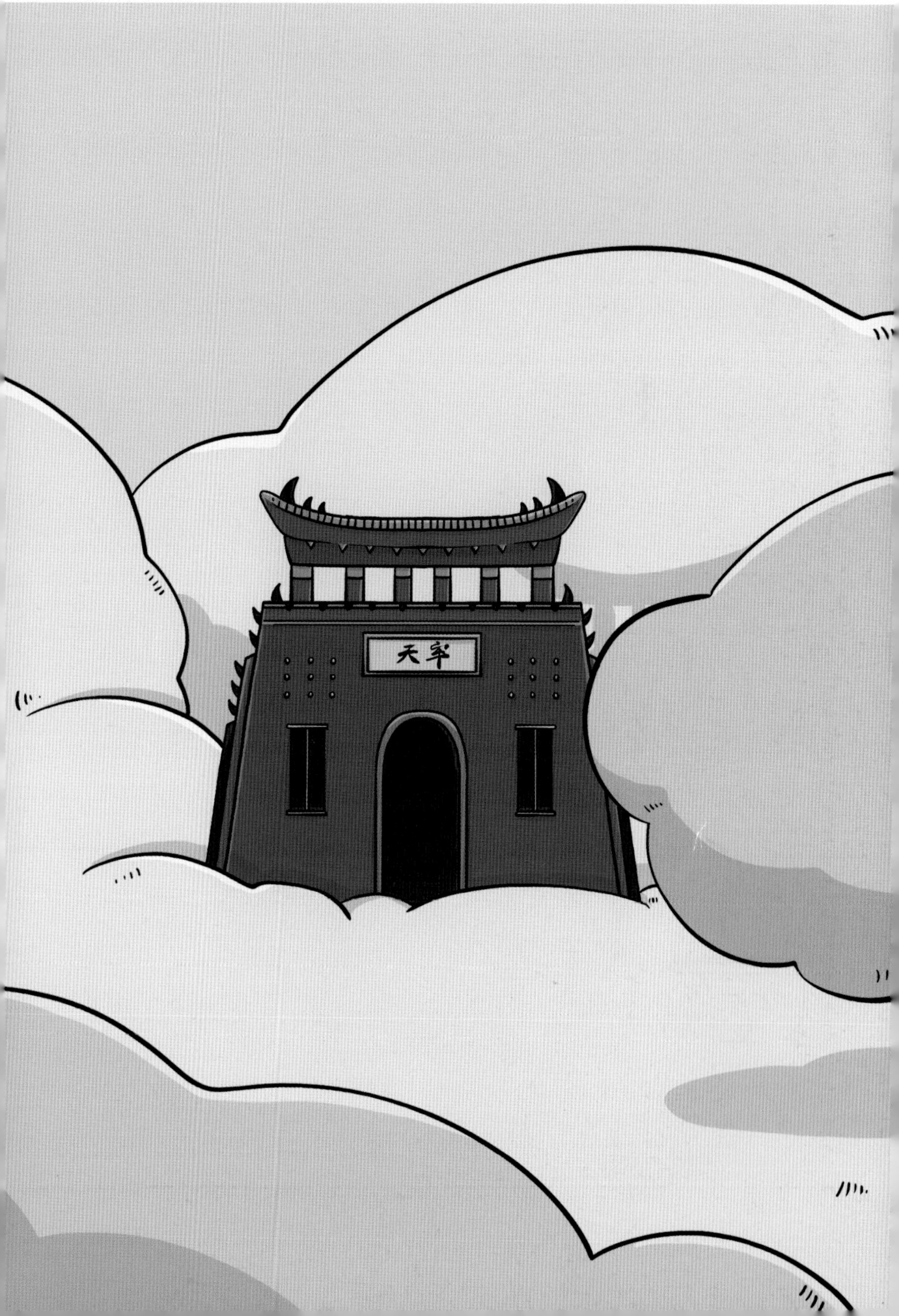
天牢

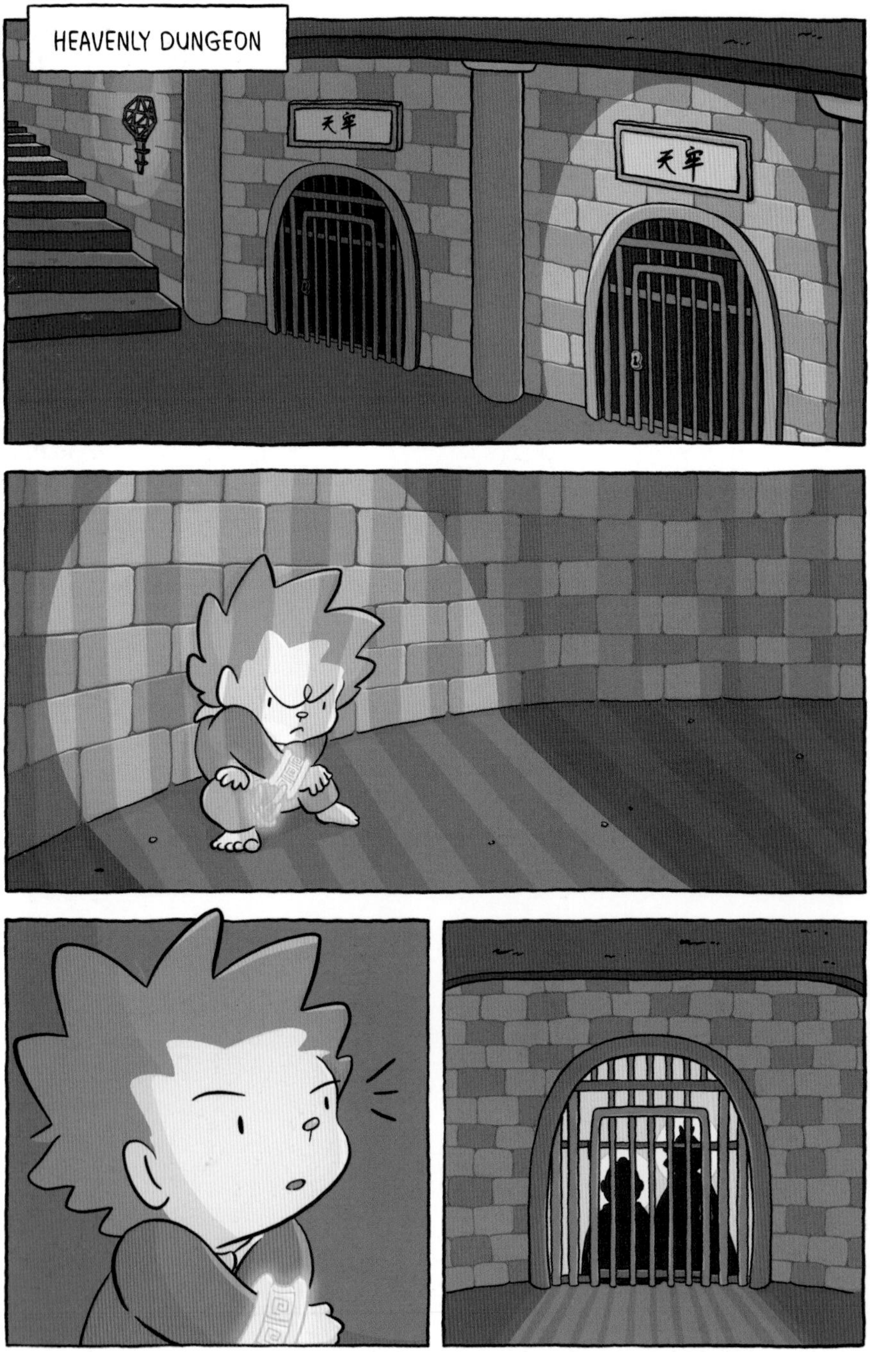
HEAVENLY DUNGEON
天牢
天牢

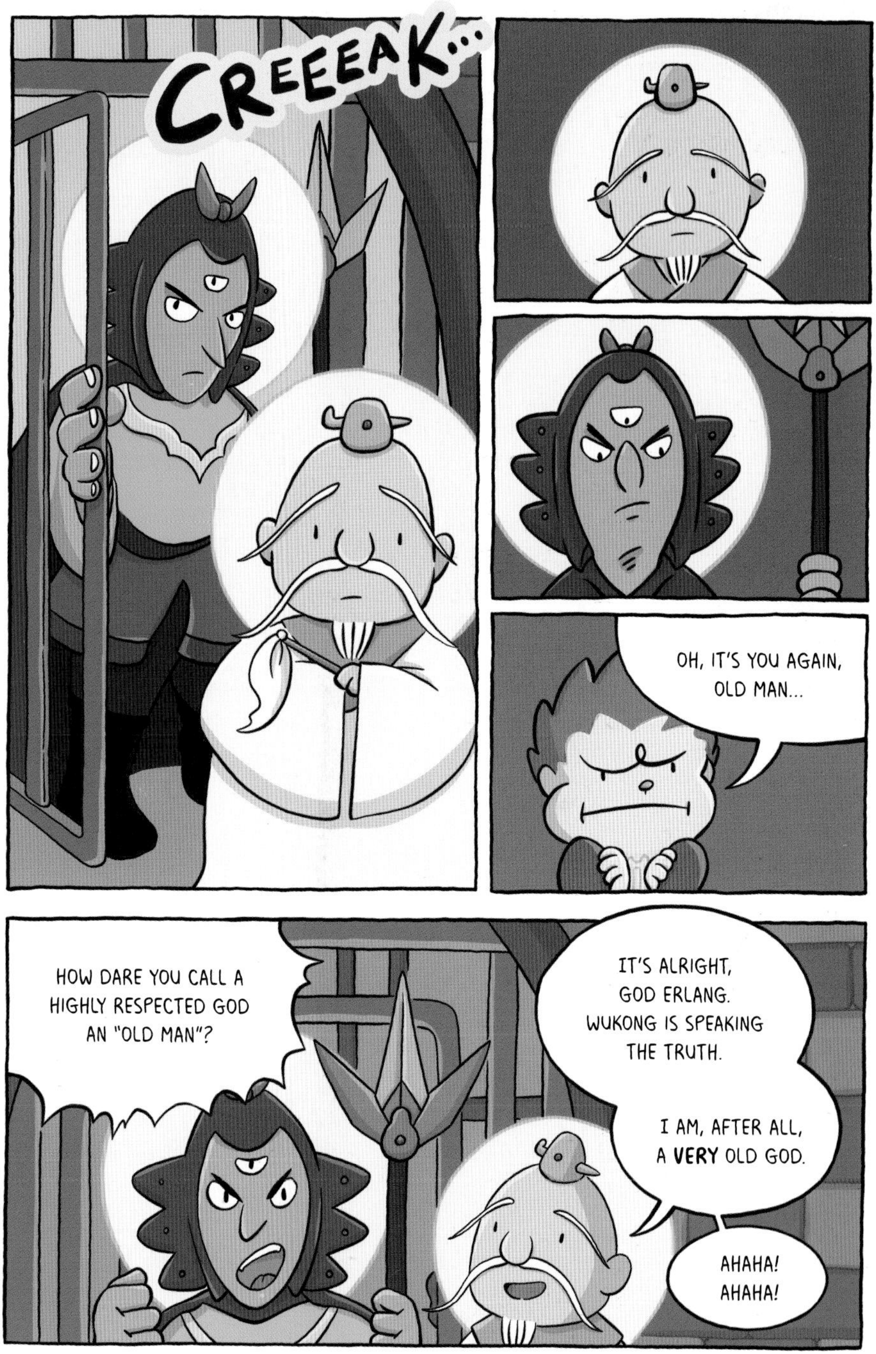
CREEEAK...
OH, IT'S YOU AGAIN, OLD MAN...
HOW DARE YOU CALL A HIGHLY RESPECTED GOD AN "OLD MAN"?
IT'S ALRIGHT, GOD ERLANG. WUKONG IS SPEAKING THE TRUTH.
I AM, AFTER ALL, A **VERY** OLD GOD.
AHAHA! AHAHA!

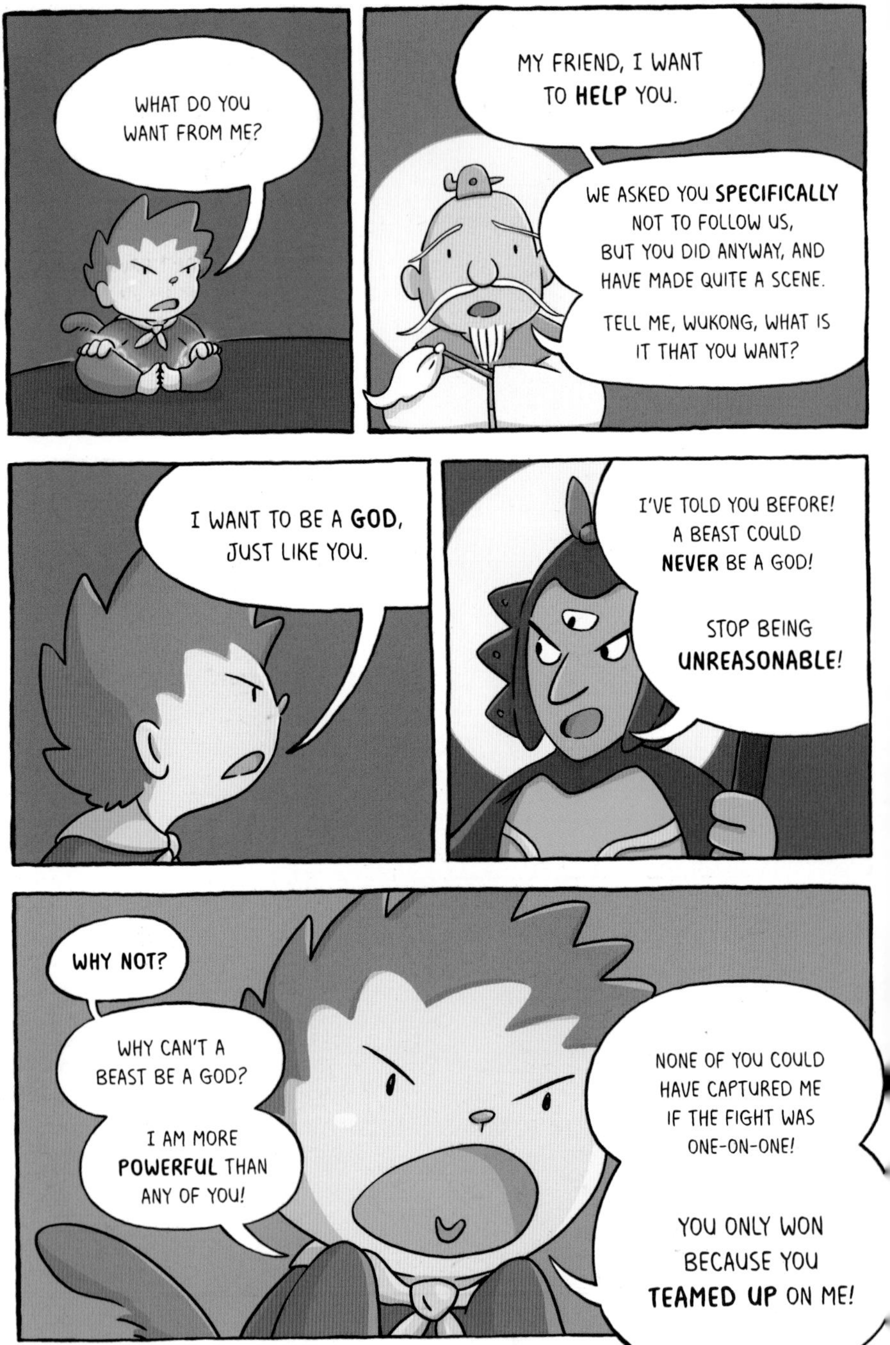
WHAT DO YOU WANT FROM ME?
MY FRIEND, I WANT TO **HELP** YOU.
WE ASKED YOU **SPECIFICALLY** NOT TO FOLLOW US, BUT YOU DID ANYWAY, AND HAVE MADE QUITE A SCENE.
TELL ME, WUKONG, WHAT IS IT THAT YOU WANT?
I WANT TO BE A **GOD**, JUST LIKE YOU.
I'VE TOLD YOU BEFORE! A BEAST COULD **NEVER** BE A GOD!
STOP BEING **UNREASONABLE**!
WHY NOT?
WHY CAN'T A BEAST BE A GOD?
I AM MORE **POWERFUL** THAN ANY OF YOU!
NONE OF YOU COULD HAVE CAPTURED ME IF THE FIGHT WAS ONE-ON-ONE!
YOU ONLY WON BECAUSE YOU **TEAMED UP** ON ME!

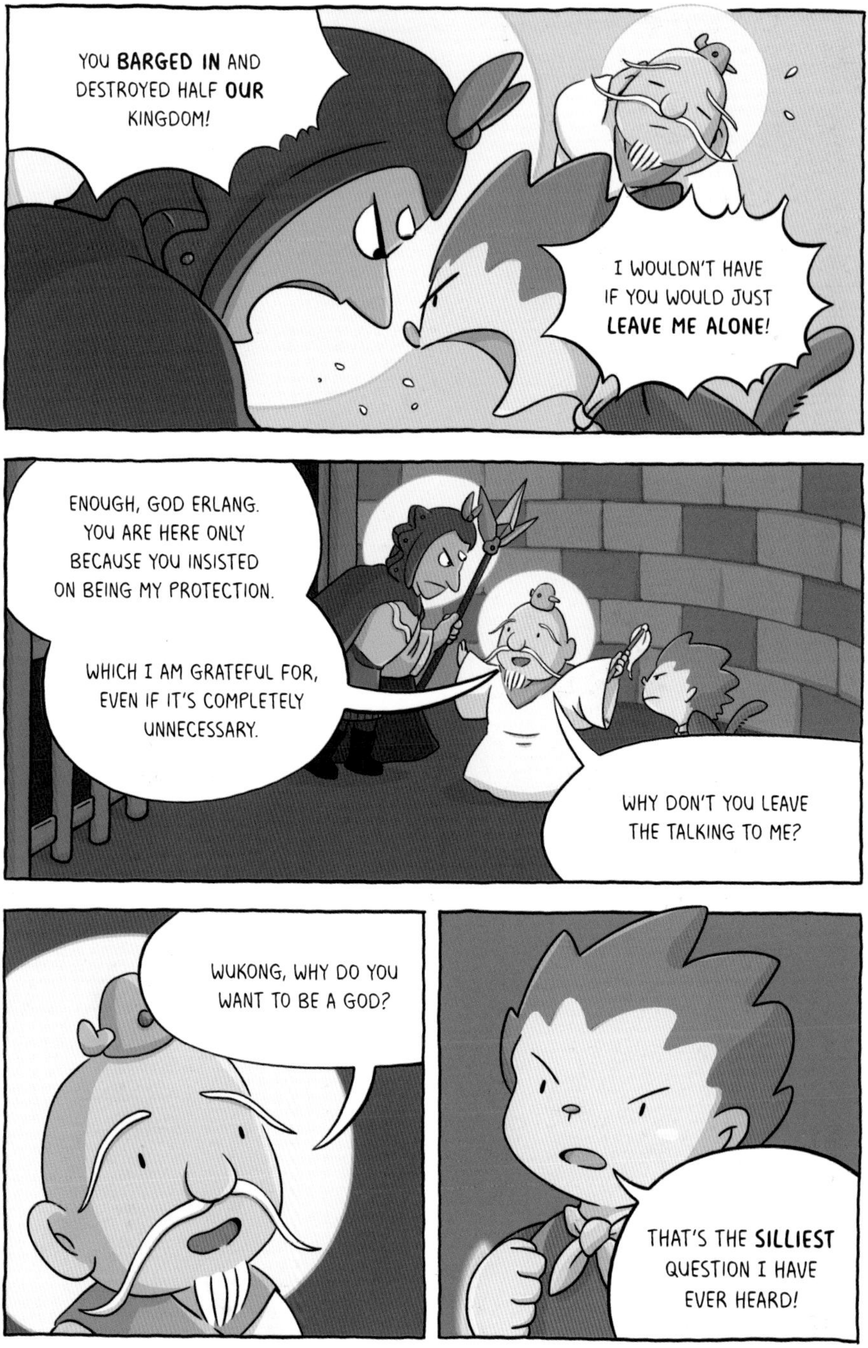
YOU **BARGED IN** AND DESTROYED HALF **OUR** KINGDOM!
I WOULDN'T HAVE IF YOU WOULD JUST **LEAVE ME ALONE**!
ENOUGH, GOD ERLANG. YOU ARE HERE ONLY BECAUSE YOU INSISTED ON BEING MY PROTECTION.
WHICH I AM GRATEFUL FOR, EVEN IF IT'S COMPLETELY UNNECESSARY.
WHY DON'T YOU LEAVE THE TALKING TO ME?
WUKONG, WHY DO YOU WANT TO BE A GOD?
THAT'S THE **SILLIEST** QUESTION I HAVE EVER HEARD!

EVERYONE **PRAISES, WORSHIPS, AND LOVES** THE GODS.

GODS GET TO DO **WHATEVER THEY WANT.**

WITH THAT KIND OF STATUS, I WOULD NEVER FEEL EMPTY OR BORED.

I WOULD BE **HAPPY FOREVER!**

OH, *WUKONG!*

YOU HAVE MISTAKEN THE MEANING OF **GODHOOD.**

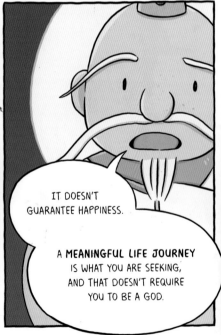

IT DOESN'T GUARANTEE HAPPINESS.

A **MEANINGFUL LIFE JOURNEY** IS WHAT YOU ARE SEEKING, AND THAT DOESN'T REQUIRE YOU TO BE A GOD.

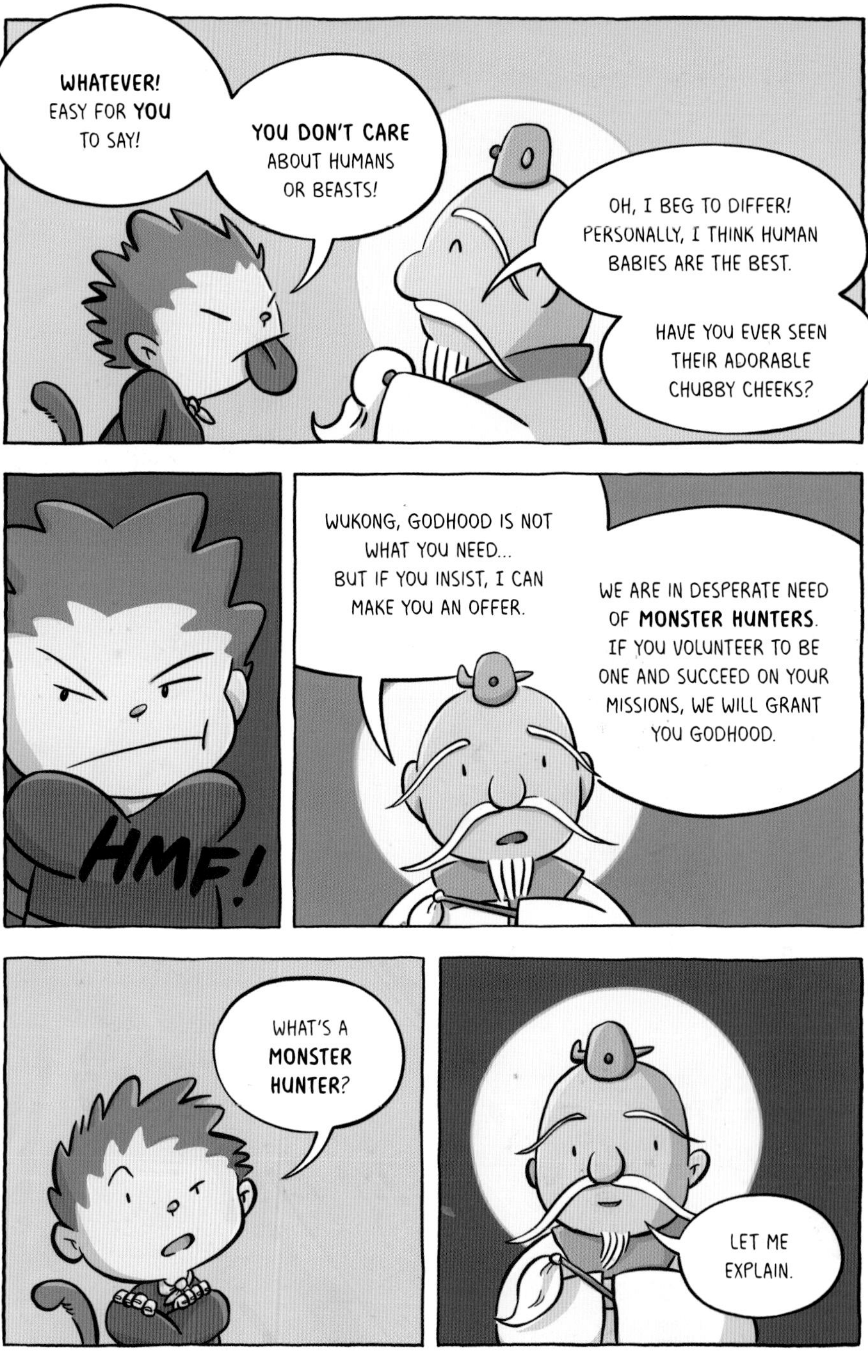
WHATEVER! EASY FOR YOU TO SAY!
YOU DON'T CARE ABOUT HUMANS OR BEASTS!
OH, I BEG TO DIFFER! PERSONALLY, I THINK HUMAN BABIES ARE THE BEST.
HAVE YOU EVER SEEN THEIR ADORABLE CHUBBY CHEEKS?
HMF!
WUKONG, GODHOOD IS NOT WHAT YOU NEED... BUT IF YOU INSIST, I CAN MAKE YOU AN OFFER.
WE ARE IN DESPERATE NEED OF MONSTER HUNTERS. IF YOU VOLUNTEER TO BE ONE AND SUCCEED ON YOUR MISSIONS, WE WILL GRANT YOU GODHOOD.
WHAT'S A MONSTER HUNTER?
LET ME EXPLAIN.

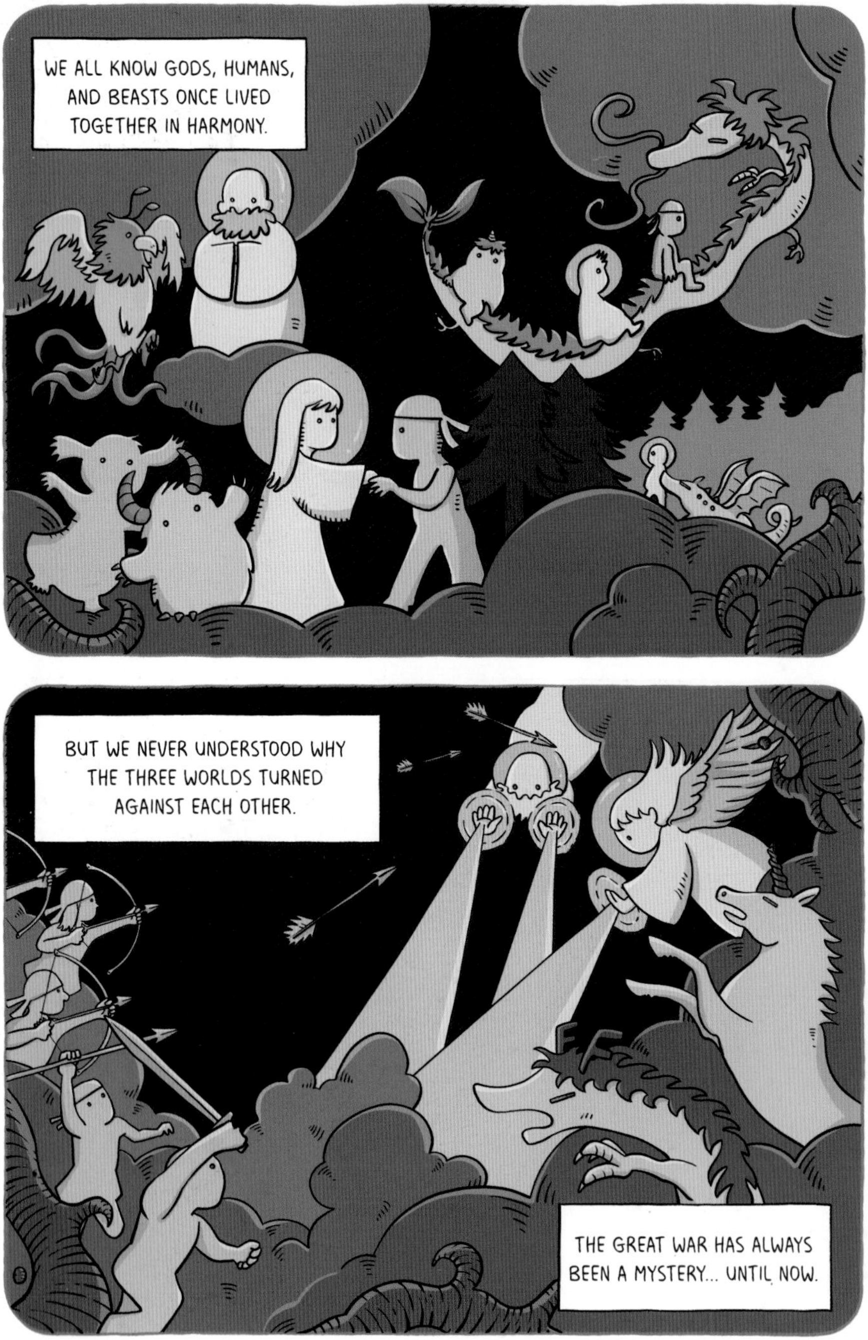
WE ALL KNOW GODS, HUMANS, AND BEASTS ONCE LIVED TOGETHER IN HARMONY.
BUT WE NEVER UNDERSTOOD WHY THE THREE WORLDS TURNED AGAINST EACH OTHER.
THE GREAT WAR HAS ALWAYS BEEN A MYSTERY... UNTIL NOW.

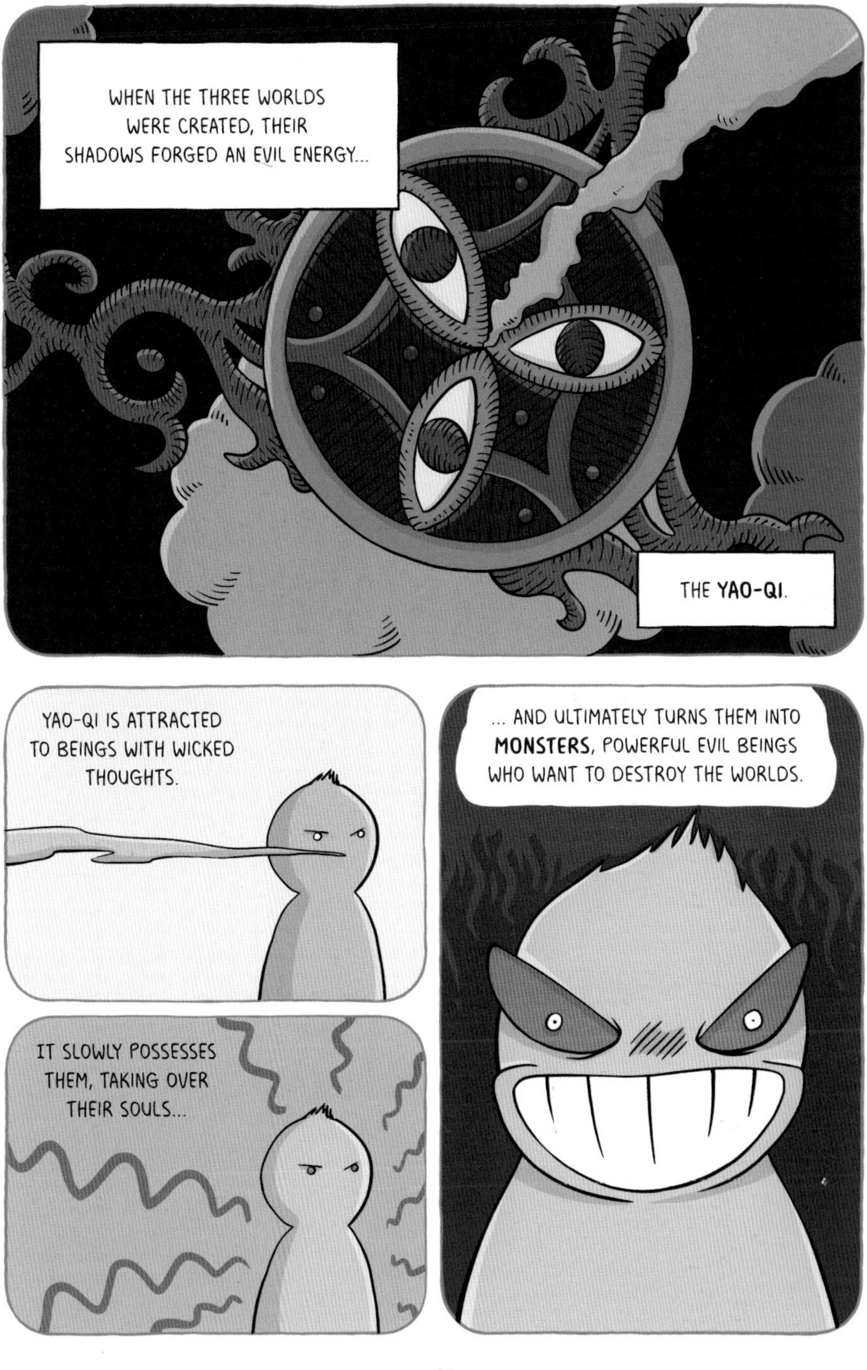
WHEN THE THREE WORLDS WERE CREATED, THEIR SHADOWS FORGED AN EVIL ENERGY...
THE **YAO-QI**.
YAO-QI IS ATTRACTED TO BEINGS WITH WICKED THOUGHTS.
IT SLOWLY POSSESSES THEM, TAKING OVER THEIR SOULS...
... AND ULTIMATELY TURNS THEM INTO **MONSTERS**, POWERFUL EVIL BEINGS WHO WANT TO DESTROY THE WORLDS.

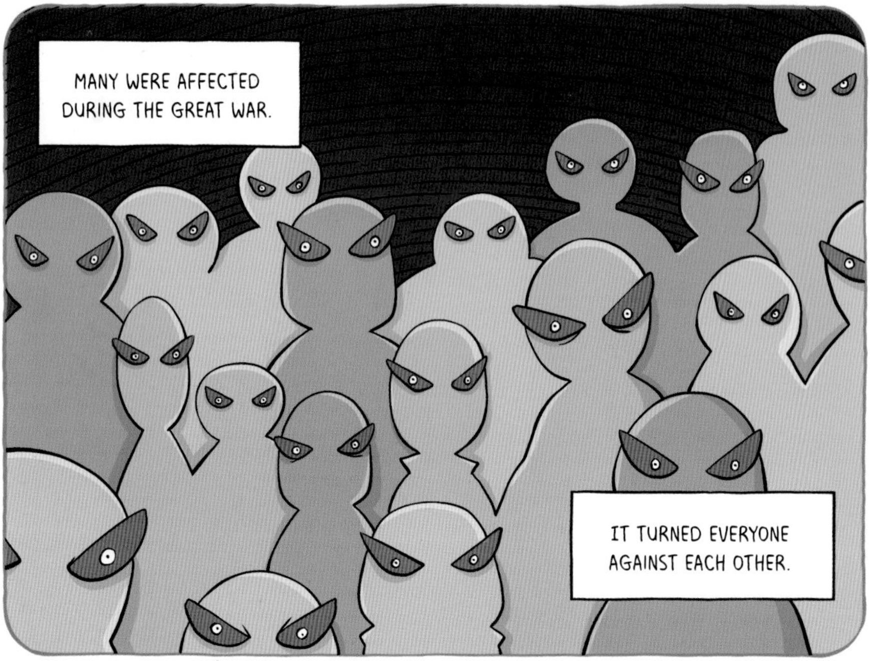
MANY WERE AFFECTED DURING THE GREAT WAR.
IT TURNED EVERYONE AGAINST EACH OTHER.

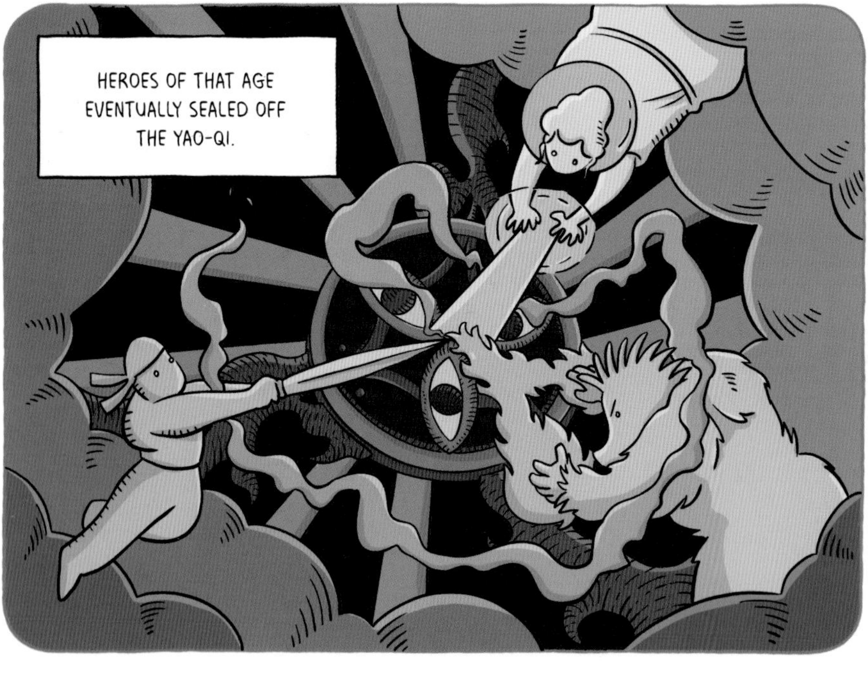
HEROES OF THAT AGE EVENTUALLY SEALED OFF THE YAO-QI.

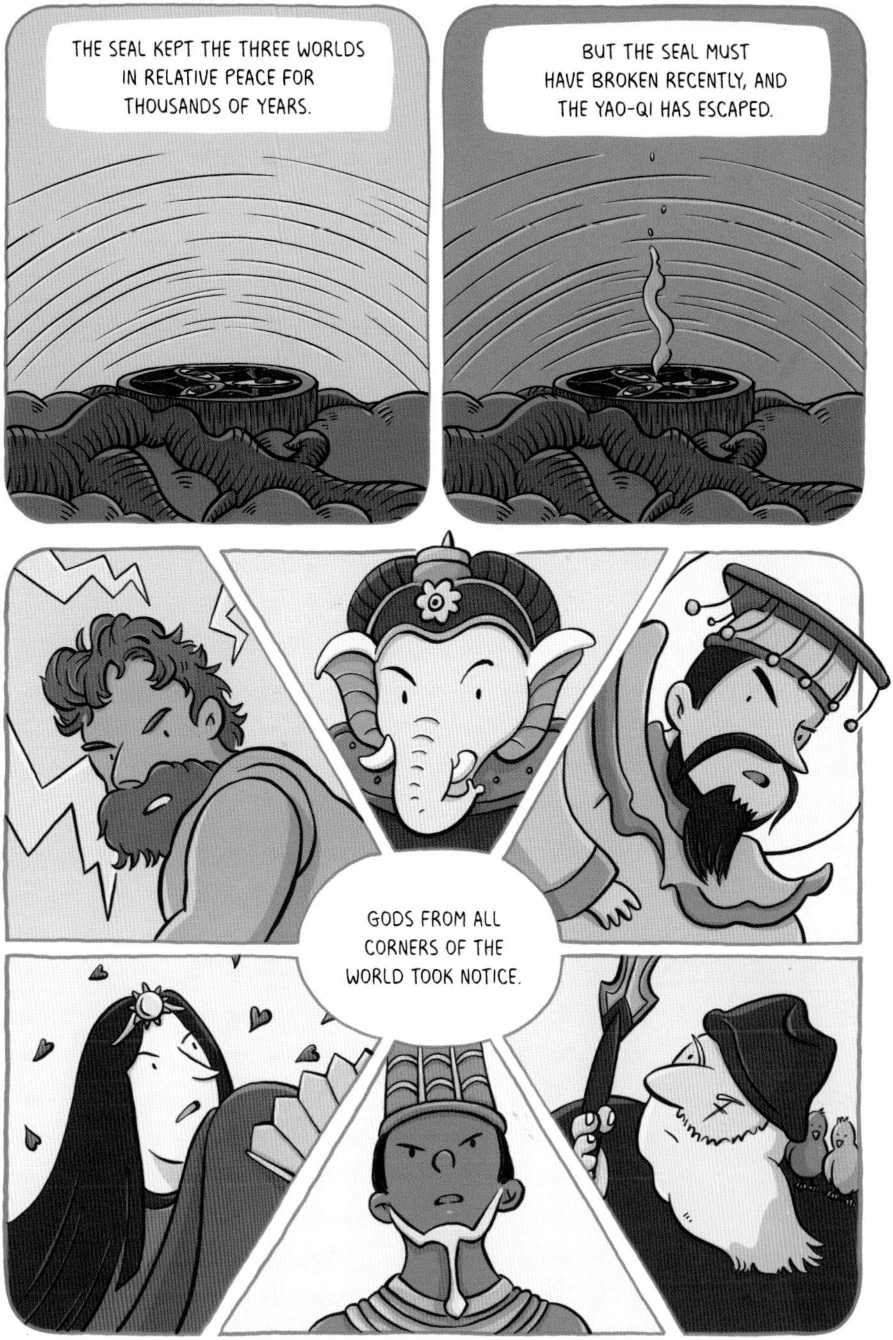
THE SEAL KEPT THE THREE WORLDS IN RELATIVE PEACE FOR THOUSANDS OF YEARS.
BUT THE SEAL MUST HAVE BROKEN RECENTLY, AND THE YAO-QI HAS ESCAPED.
GODS FROM ALL CORNERS OF THE WORLD TOOK NOTICE.

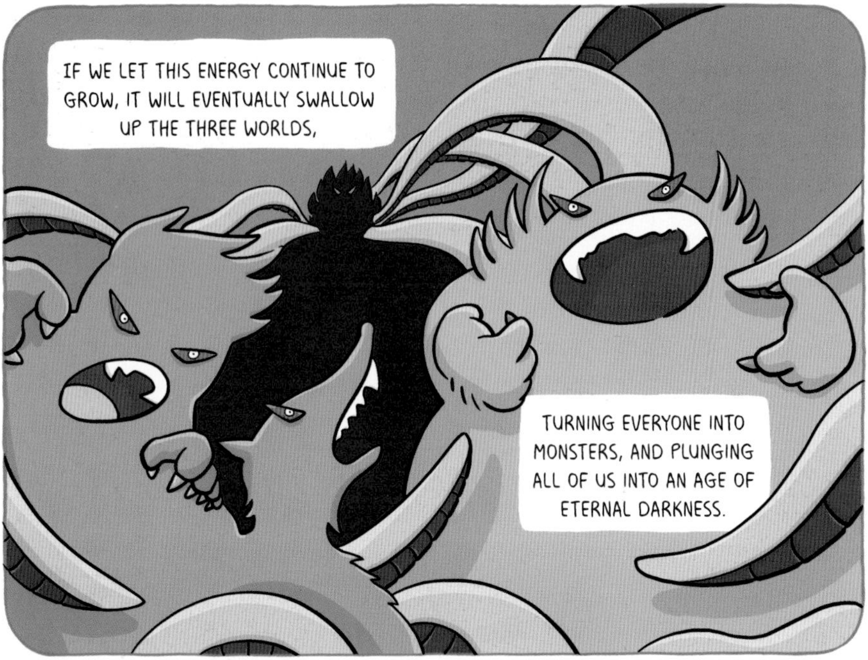
IF WE LET THIS ENERGY CONTINUE TO GROW, IT WILL EVENTUALLY SWALLOW UP THE THREE WORLDS,
TURNING EVERYONE INTO MONSTERS, AND PLUNGING ALL OF US INTO AN AGE OF ETERNAL DARKNESS.

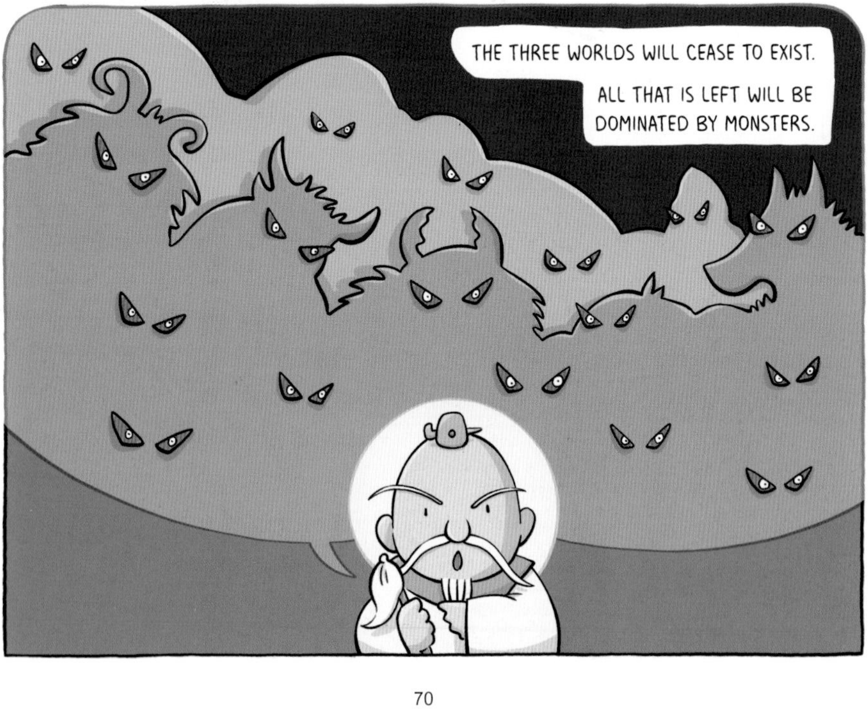
THE THREE WORLDS WILL CEASE TO EXIST.
ALL THAT IS LEFT WILL BE DOMINATED BY MONSTERS.

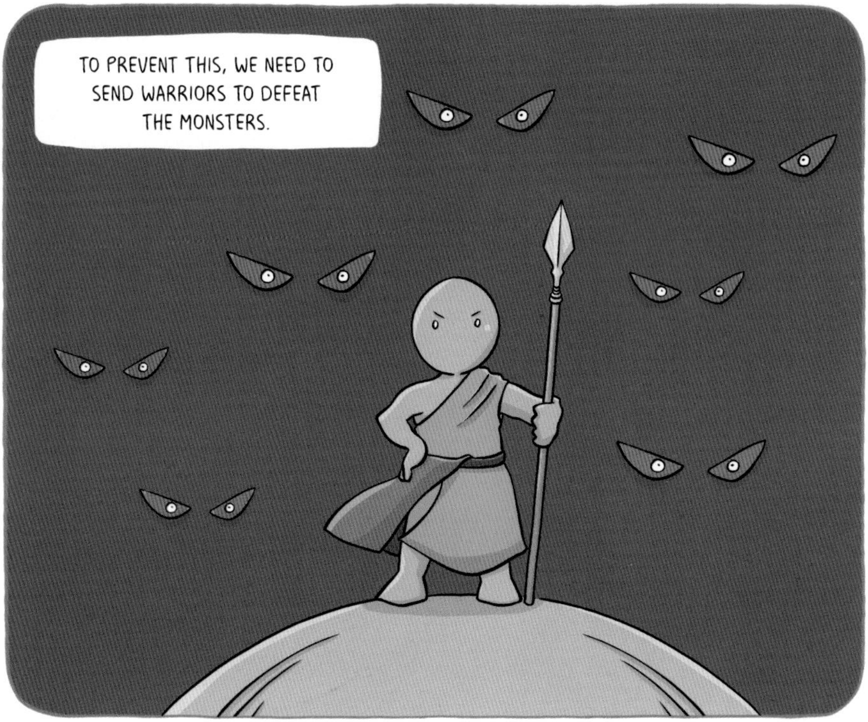
TO PREVENT THIS, WE NEED TO SEND WARRIORS TO DEFEAT THE MONSTERS.

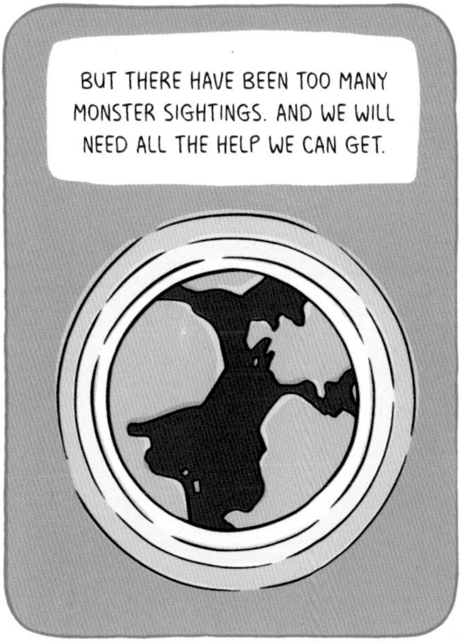
BUT THERE HAVE BEEN TOO MANY MONSTER SIGHTINGS. AND WE WILL NEED ALL THE HELP WE CAN GET.

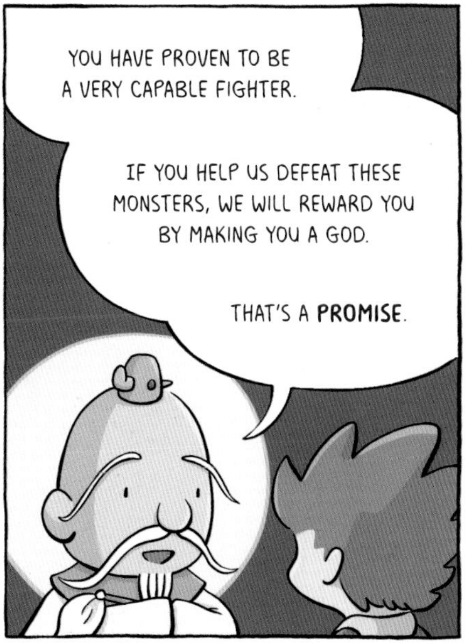
YOU HAVE PROVEN TO BE A VERY CAPABLE FIGHTER.
IF YOU HELP US DEFEAT THESE MONSTERS, WE WILL REWARD YOU BY MAKING YOU A GOD.
THAT'S A **PROMISE**.

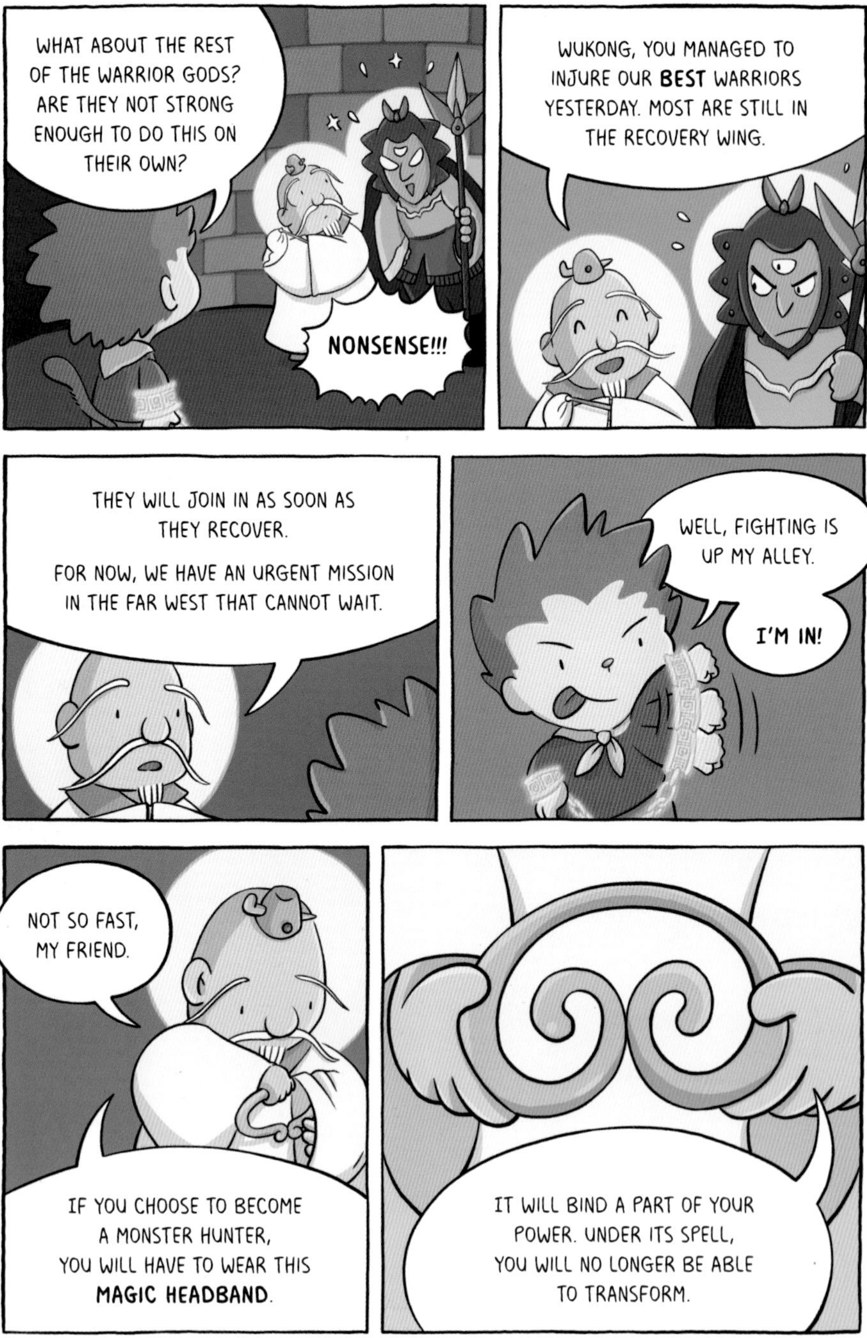
WHAT ABOUT THE REST OF THE WARRIOR GODS? ARE THEY NOT STRONG ENOUGH TO DO THIS ON THEIR OWN?
NONSENSE!!!
WUKONG, YOU MANAGED TO INJURE OUR **BEST** WARRIORS YESTERDAY. MOST ARE STILL IN THE RECOVERY WING.
THEY WILL JOIN IN AS SOON AS THEY RECOVER.
FOR NOW, WE HAVE AN URGENT MISSION IN THE FAR WEST THAT CANNOT WAIT.
WELL, FIGHTING IS UP MY ALLEY.
I'M IN!
NOT SO FAST, MY FRIEND.
IF YOU CHOOSE TO BECOME A MONSTER HUNTER, YOU WILL HAVE TO WEAR THIS **MAGIC HEADBAND**.
IT WILL BIND A PART OF YOUR POWER. UNDER ITS SPELL, YOU WILL NO LONGER BE ABLE TO TRANSFORM.

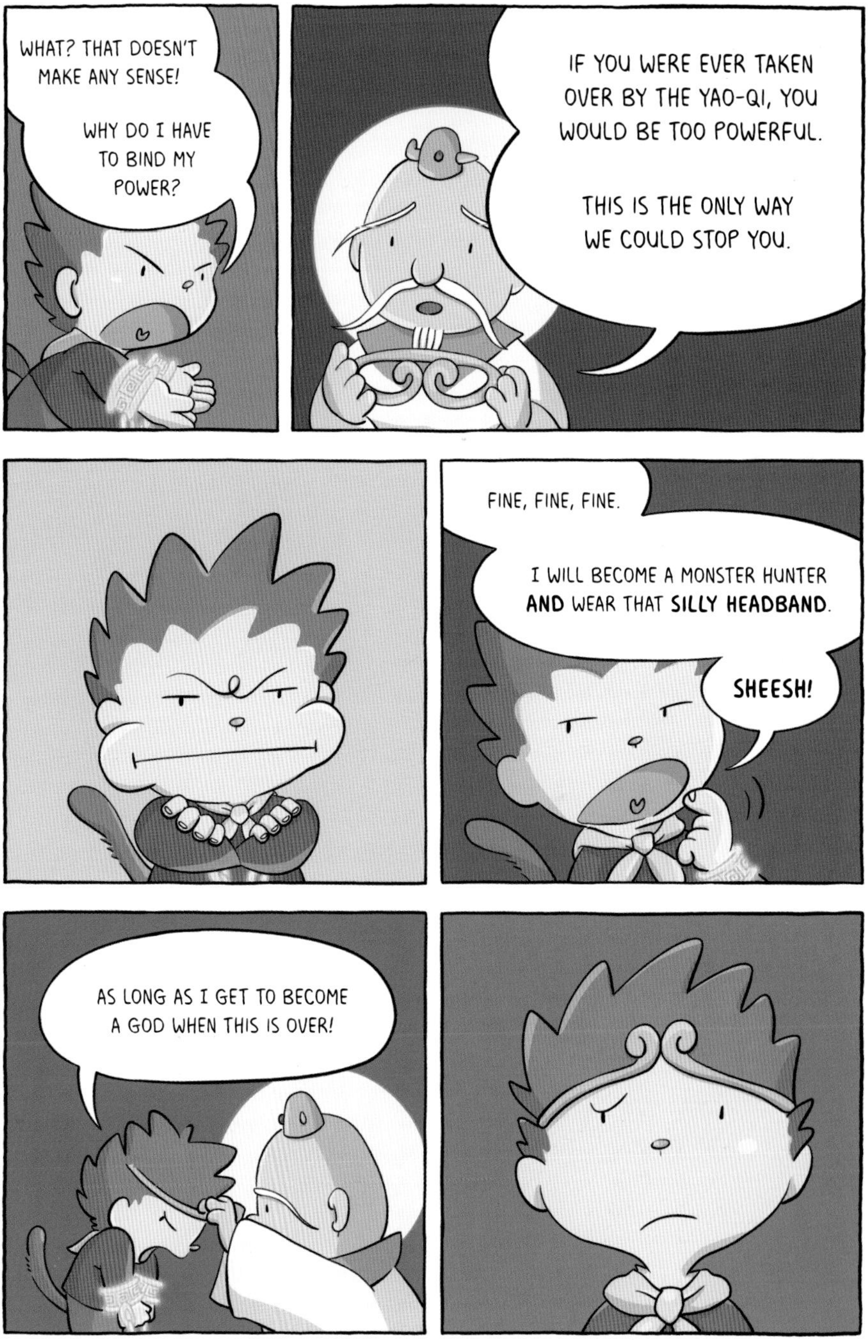
WHAT? THAT DOESN'T MAKE ANY SENSE!
WHY DO I HAVE TO BIND MY POWER?
IF YOU WERE EVER TAKEN OVER BY THE YAO-QI, YOU WOULD BE TOO POWERFUL.
THIS IS THE ONLY WAY WE COULD STOP YOU.
FINE, FINE, FINE.
I WILL BECOME A MONSTER HUNTER **AND** WEAR THAT **SILLY HEADBAND**.
SHEESH!
AS LONG AS I GET TO BECOME A GOD WHEN THIS IS OVER!

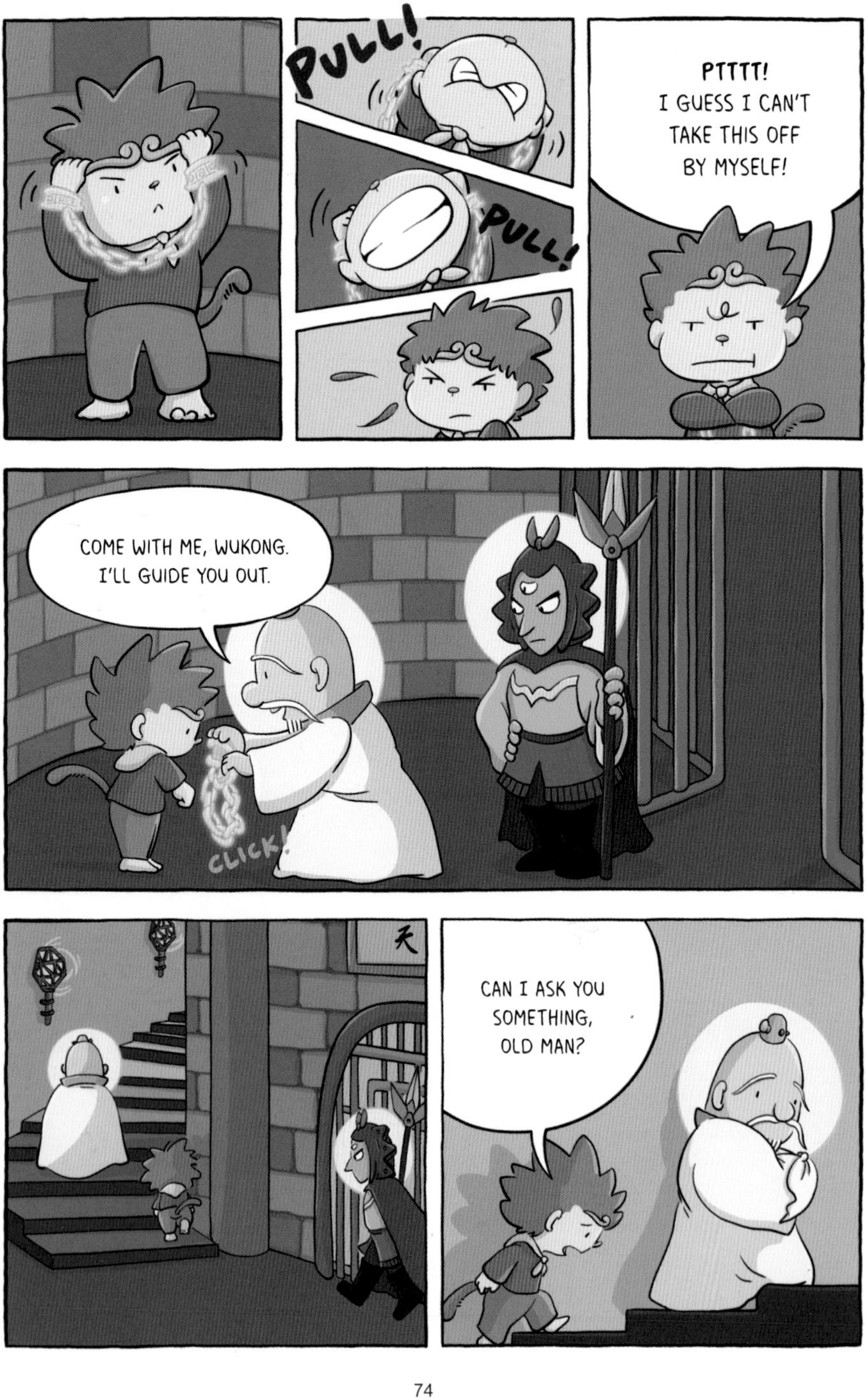
PULL!
PULL!
PTTTT!
I GUESS I CAN'T TAKE THIS OFF BY MYSELF!
COME WITH ME, WUKONG. I'LL GUIDE YOU OUT.
CLICK!
天
CAN I ASK YOU SOMETHING, OLD MAN?

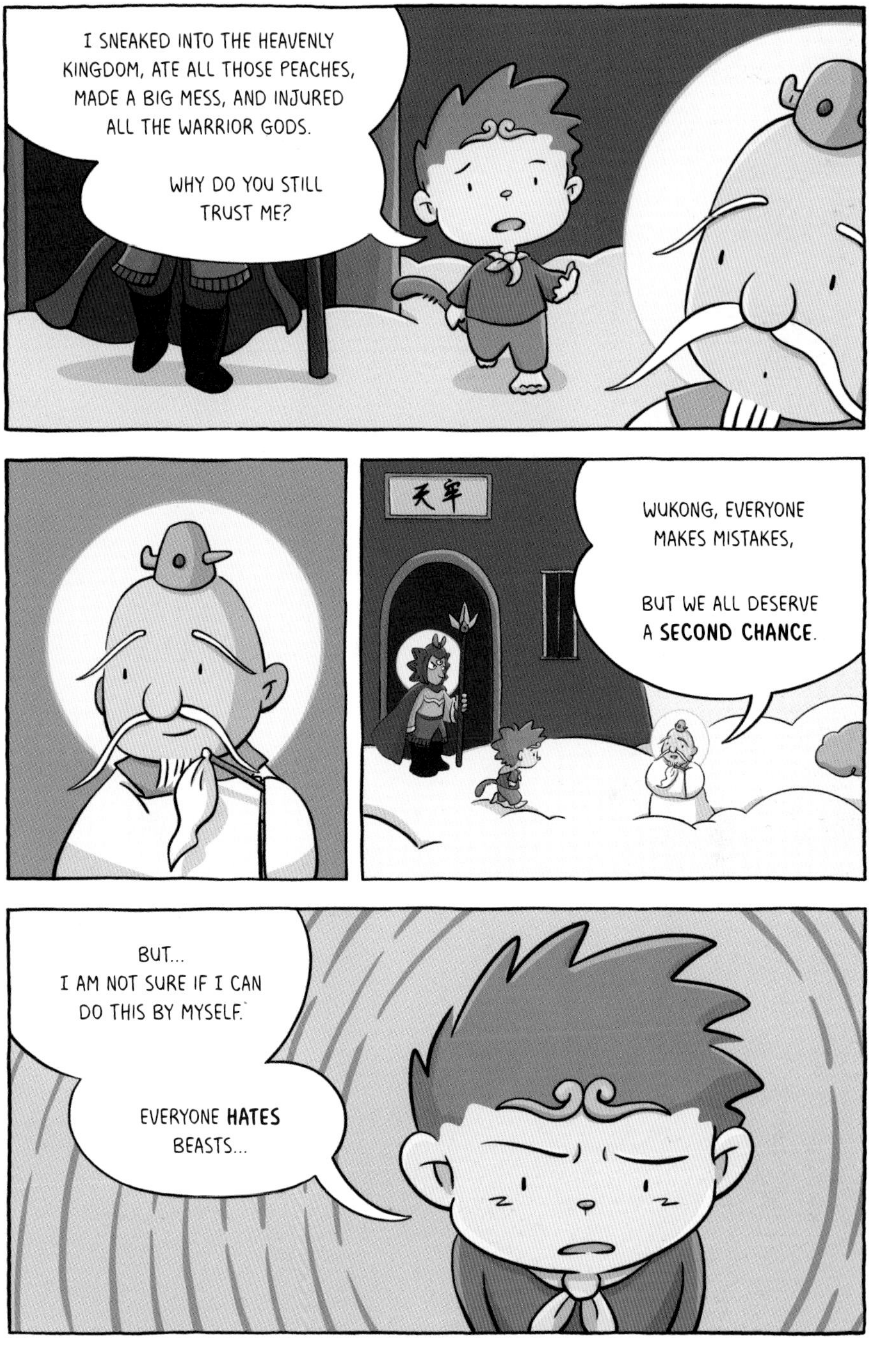
I SNEAKED INTO THE HEAVENLY KINGDOM, ATE ALL THOSE PEACHES, MADE A BIG MESS, AND INJURED ALL THE WARRIOR GODS.
WHY DO YOU STILL TRUST ME?
天牢
WUKONG, EVERYONE MAKES MISTAKES,
BUT WE ALL DESERVE A **SECOND CHANCE**.
BUT... I AM NOT SURE IF I CAN DO THIS BY MYSELF.
EVERYONE **HATES** BEASTS...

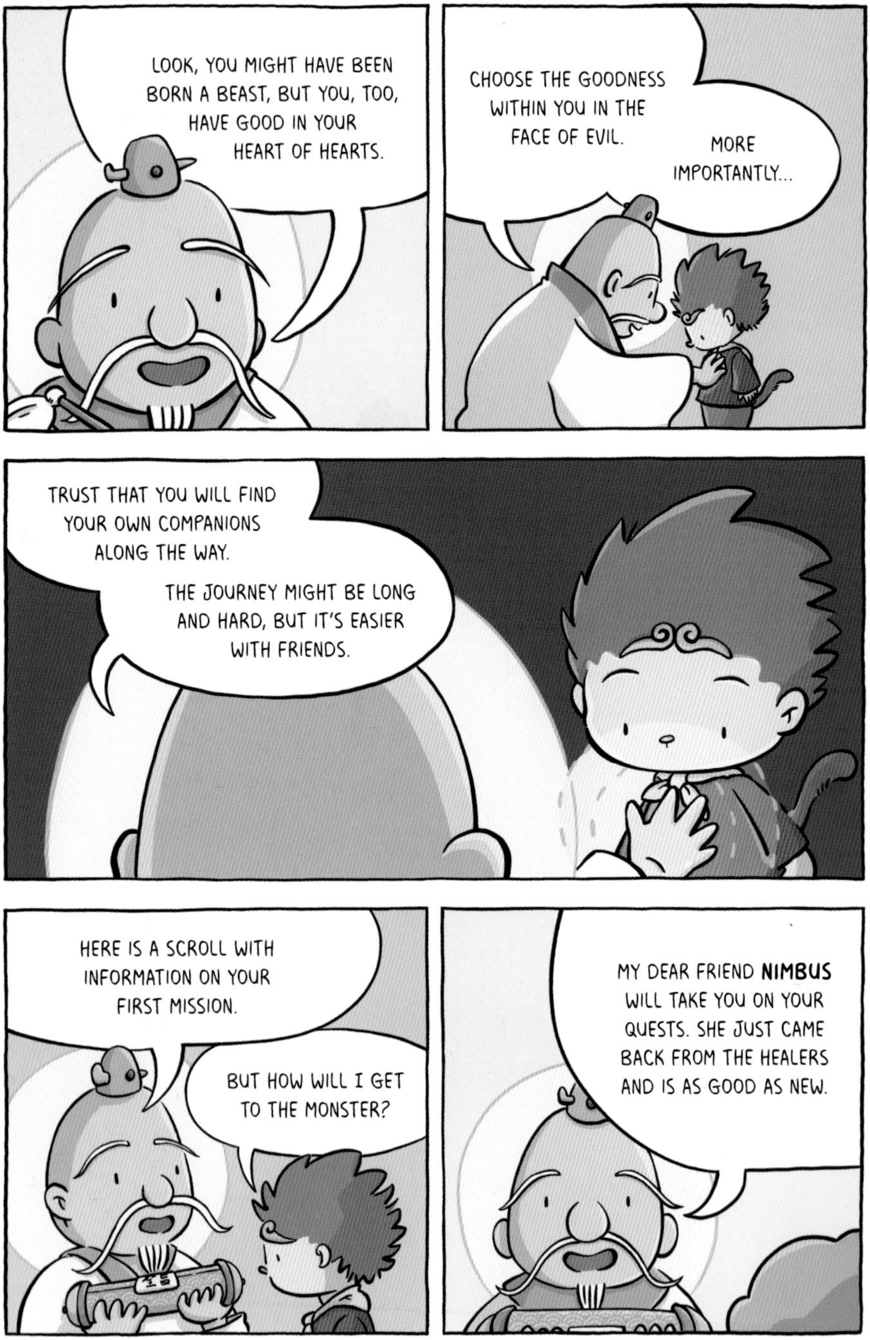
LOOK, YOU MIGHT HAVE BEEN BORN A BEAST, BUT YOU, TOO, HAVE GOOD IN YOUR HEART OF HEARTS.
CHOOSE THE GOODNESS WITHIN YOU IN THE FACE OF EVIL.
MORE IMPORTANTLY...
TRUST THAT YOU WILL FIND YOUR OWN COMPANIONS ALONG THE WAY.
THE JOURNEY MIGHT BE LONG AND HARD, BUT IT'S EASIER WITH FRIENDS.
HERE IS A SCROLL WITH INFORMATION ON YOUR FIRST MISSION.
BUT HOW WILL I GET TO THE MONSTER?
MY DEAR FRIEND **NIMBUS** WILL TAKE YOU ON YOUR QUESTS. SHE JUST CAME BACK FROM THE HEALERS AND IS AS GOOD AS NEW.

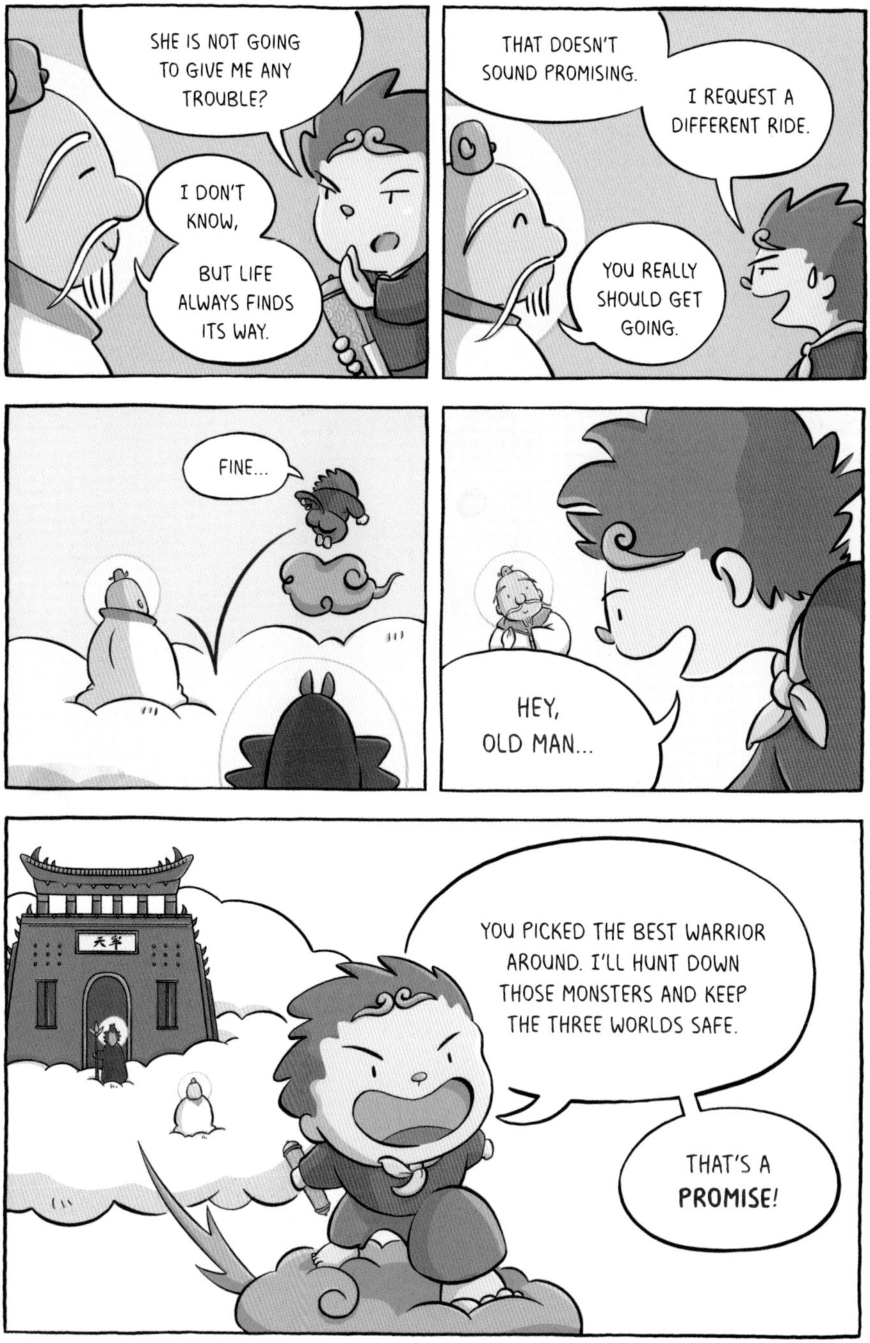
SHE IS NOT GOING TO GIVE ME ANY TROUBLE?
I DON'T KNOW,
BUT LIFE ALWAYS FINDS ITS WAY.
THAT DOESN'T SOUND PROMISING.
I REQUEST A DIFFERENT RIDE.
YOU REALLY SHOULD GET GOING.
FINE...
HEY, OLD MAN...
天牢
YOU PICKED THE BEST WARRIOR AROUND. I'LL HUNT DOWN THOSE MONSTERS AND KEEP THE THREE WORLDS SAFE.
THAT'S A **PROMISE**!

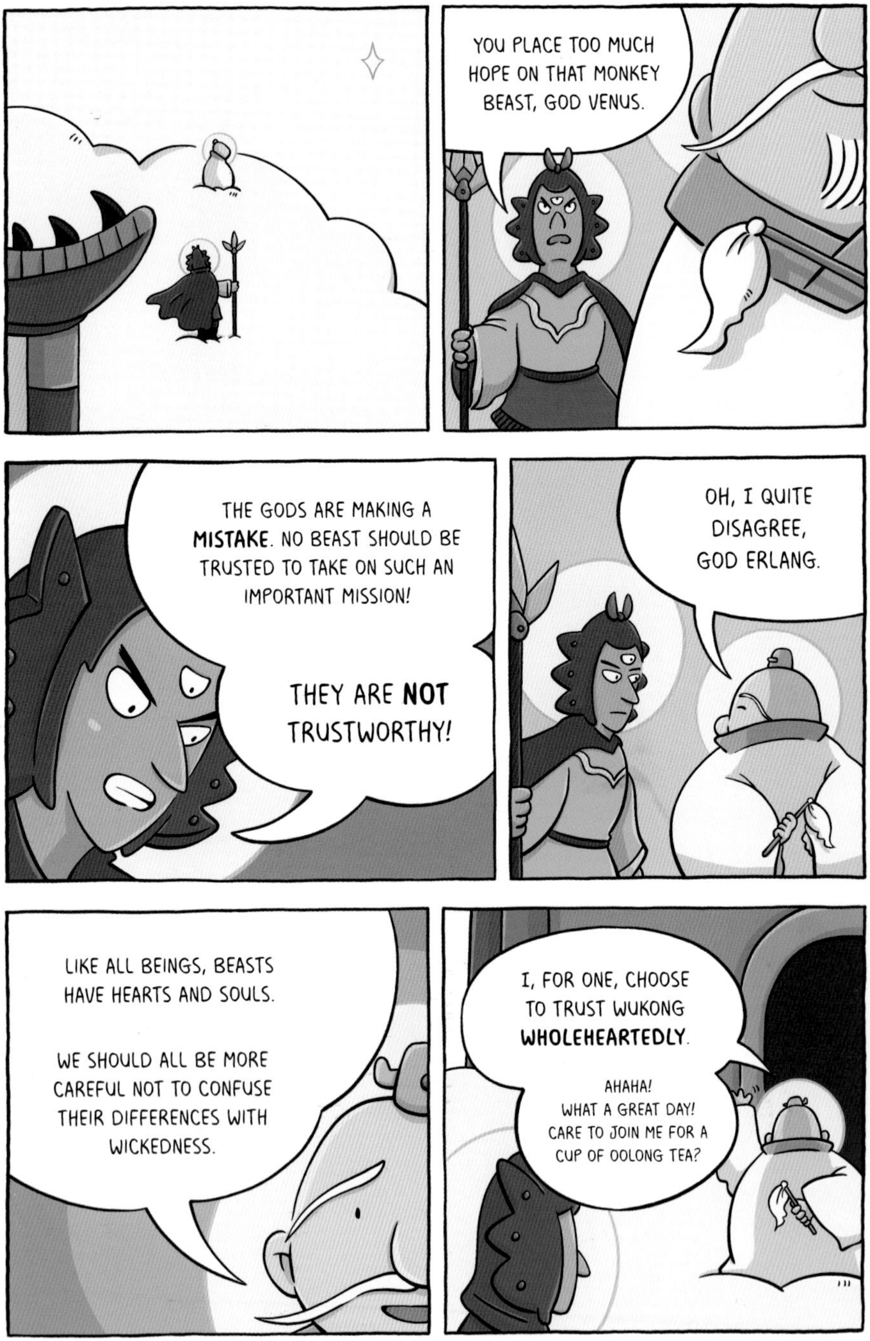
YOU PLACE TOO MUCH HOPE ON THAT MONKEY BEAST, GOD VENUS.
THE GODS ARE MAKING A MISTAKE. NO BEAST SHOULD BE TRUSTED TO TAKE ON SUCH AN IMPORTANT MISSION!
THEY ARE NOT TRUSTWORTHY!
OH, I QUITE DISAGREE, GOD ERLANG.
LIKE ALL BEINGS, BEASTS HAVE HEARTS AND SOULS.
WE SHOULD ALL BE MORE CAREFUL NOT TO CONFUSE THEIR DIFFERENCES WITH WICKEDNESS.
I, FOR ONE, CHOOSE TO TRUST WUKONG WHOLEHEARTEDLY.
AHAHA! WHAT A GREAT DAY! CARE TO JOIN ME FOR A CUP OF OOLONG TEA?

CHAPTER 4 THE UNDERWORLD

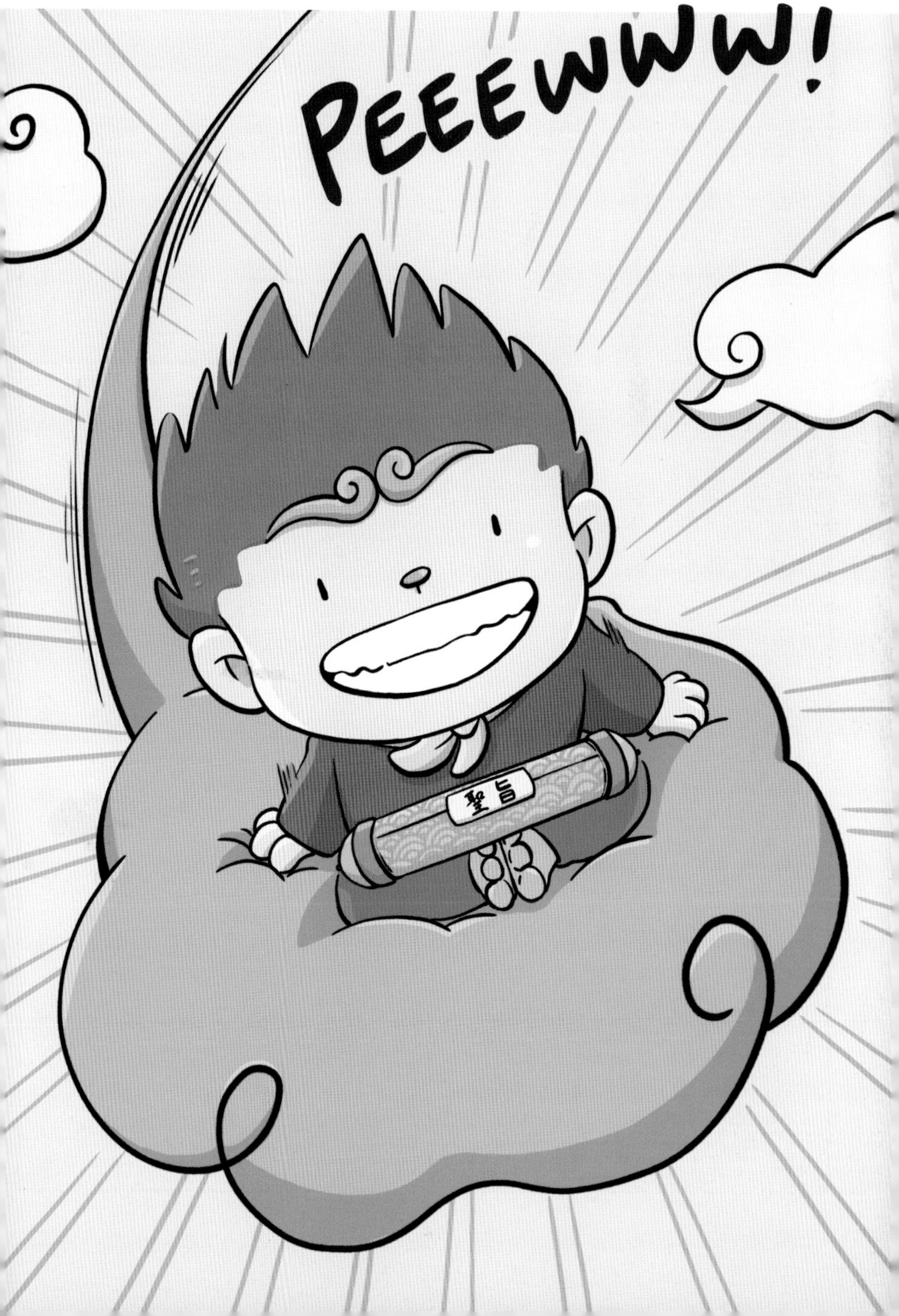
PEEEWWW!
聖旨

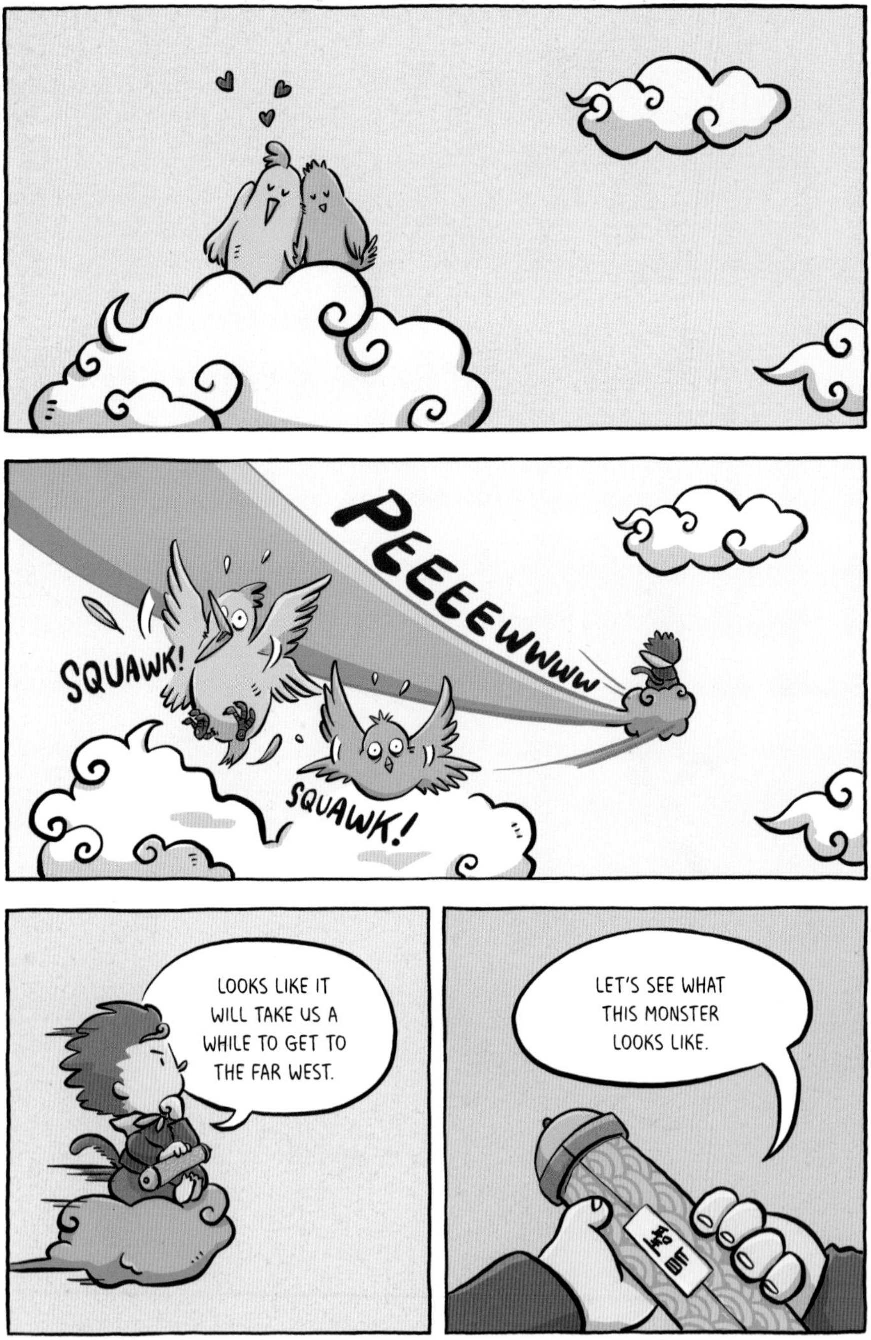
PEEEEWWWWW
SQUAWK!
SQUAWK!
LOOKS LIKE IT WILL TAKE US A WHILE TO GET TO THE FAR WEST.
LET'S SEE WHAT THIS MONSTER LOOKS LIKE.

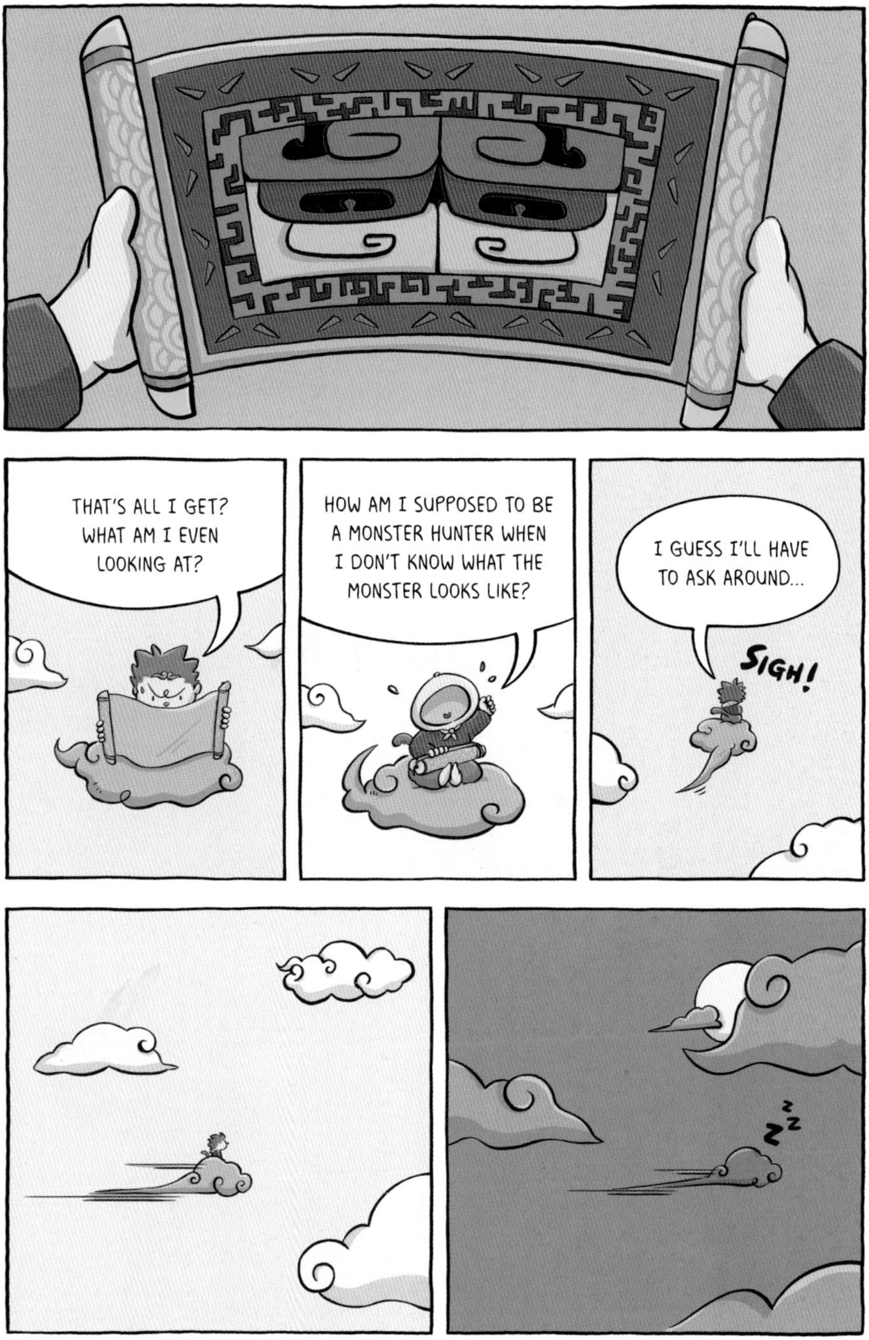
THAT'S ALL I GET? WHAT AM I EVEN LOOKING AT?
HOW AM I SUPPOSED TO BE A MONSTER HUNTER WHEN I DON'T KNOW WHAT THE MONSTER LOOKS LIKE?
I GUESS I'LL HAVE TO ASK AROUND...
SIGH!
Z Z Z

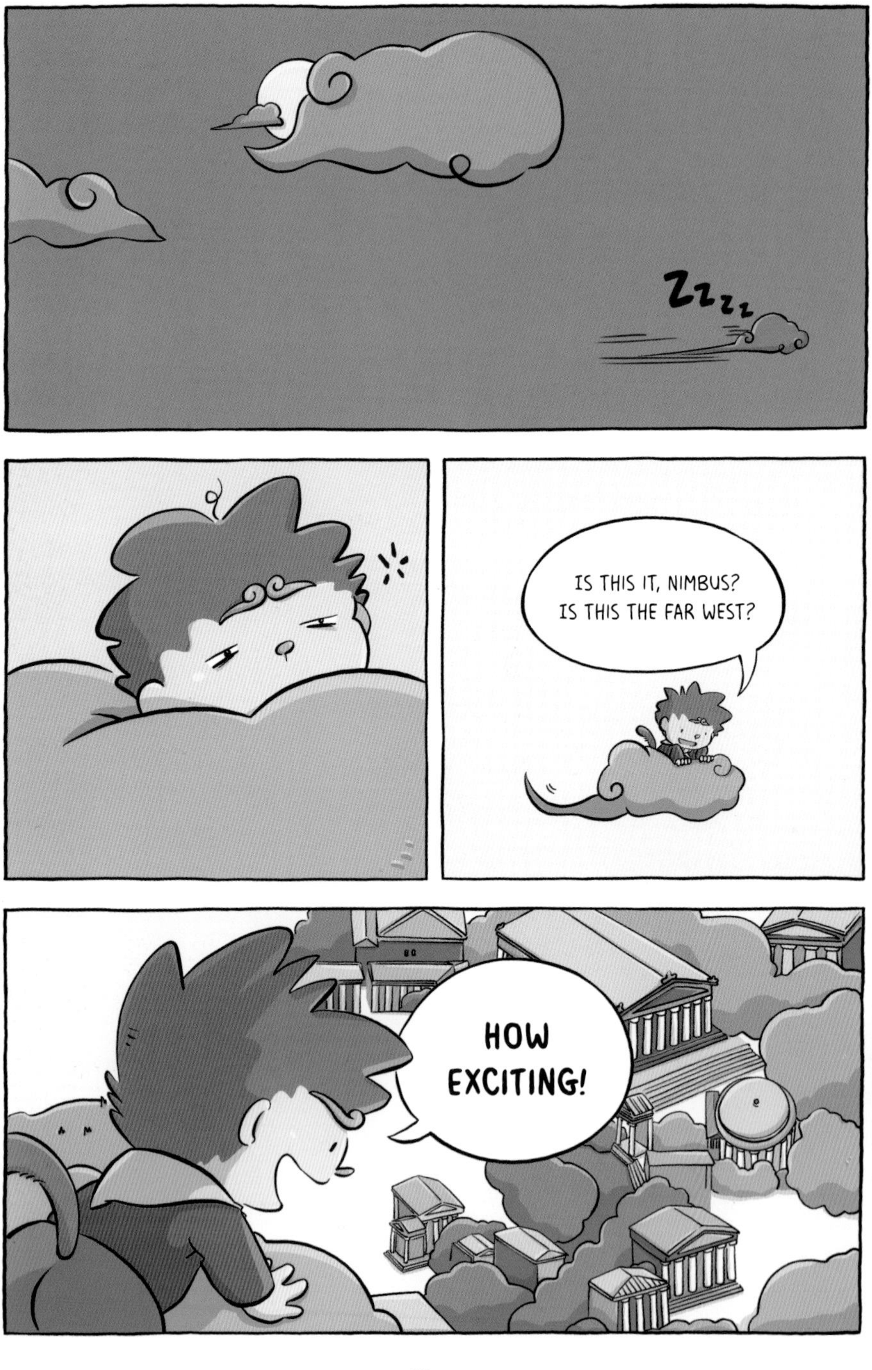
ZZZZ
IS THIS IT, NIMBUS?
IS THIS THE FAR WEST?
HOW
EXCITING!

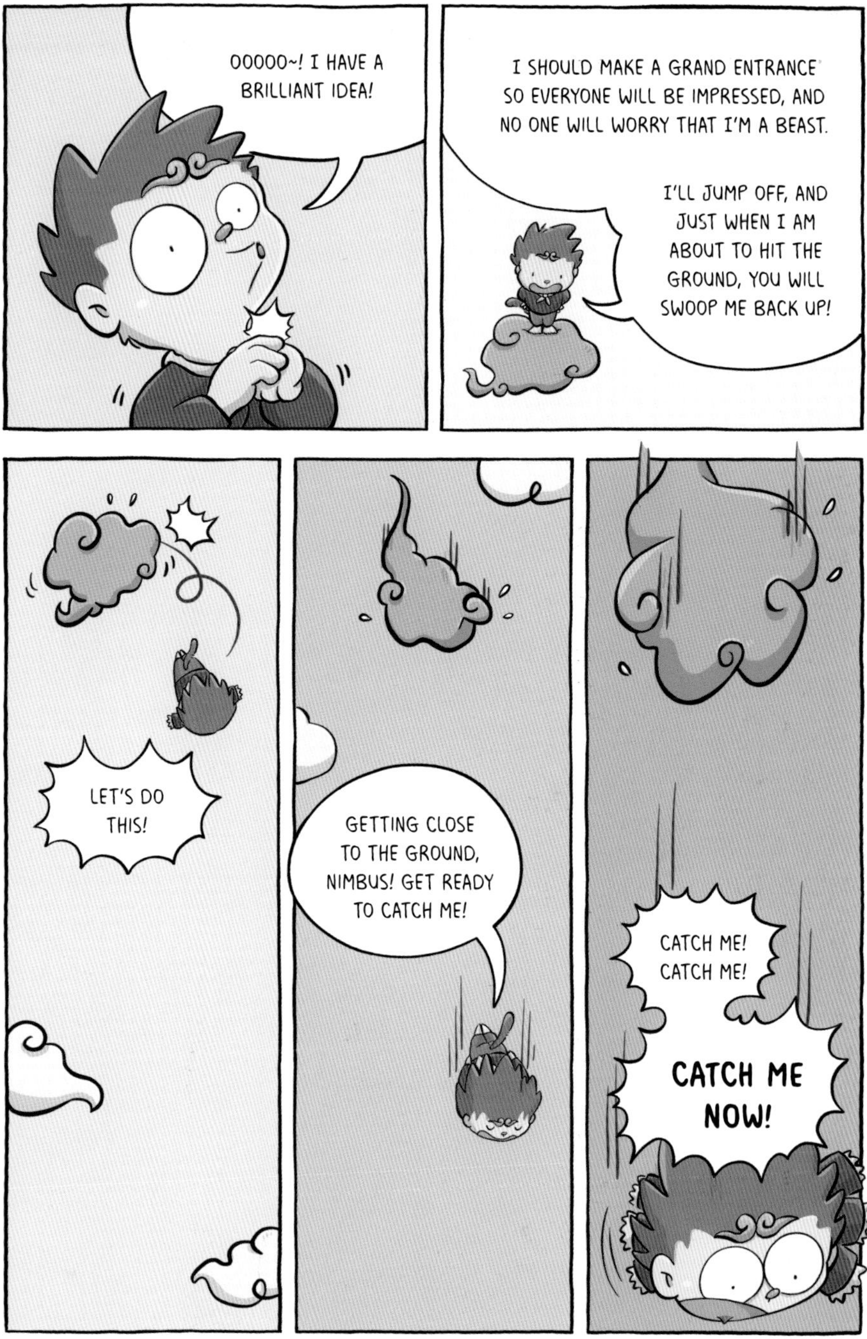
OOOOO~! I HAVE A BRILLIANT IDEA!
I SHOULD MAKE A GRAND ENTRANCE SO EVERYONE WILL BE IMPRESSED, AND NO ONE WILL WORRY THAT I'M A BEAST.
I'LL JUMP OFF, AND JUST WHEN I AM ABOUT TO HIT THE GROUND, YOU WILL SWOOP ME BACK UP!
LET'S DO THIS!
GETTING CLOSE TO THE GROUND, NIMBUS! GET READY TO CATCH ME!
CATCH ME! CATCH ME!
CATCH ME NOW!

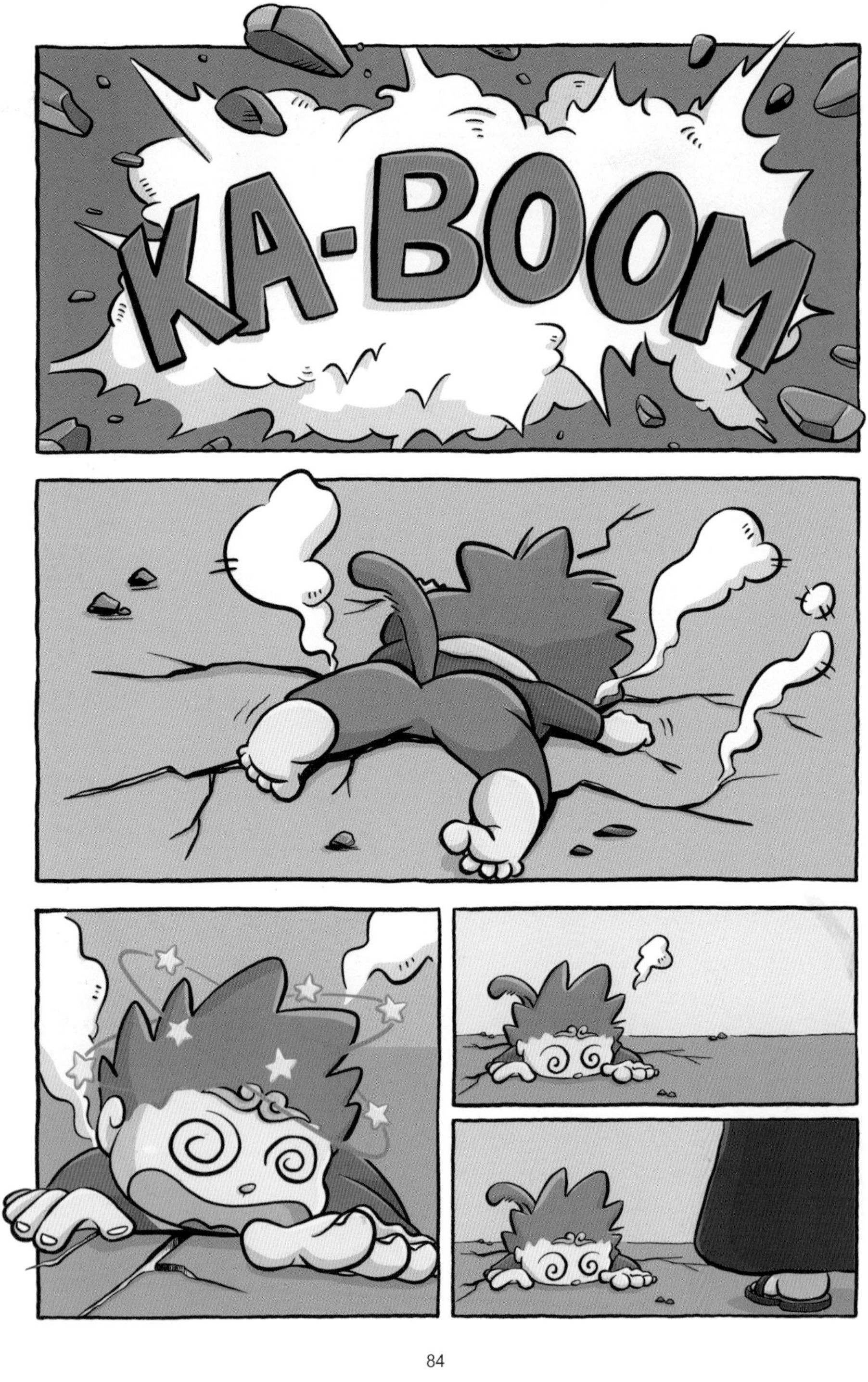
KA-BOOM

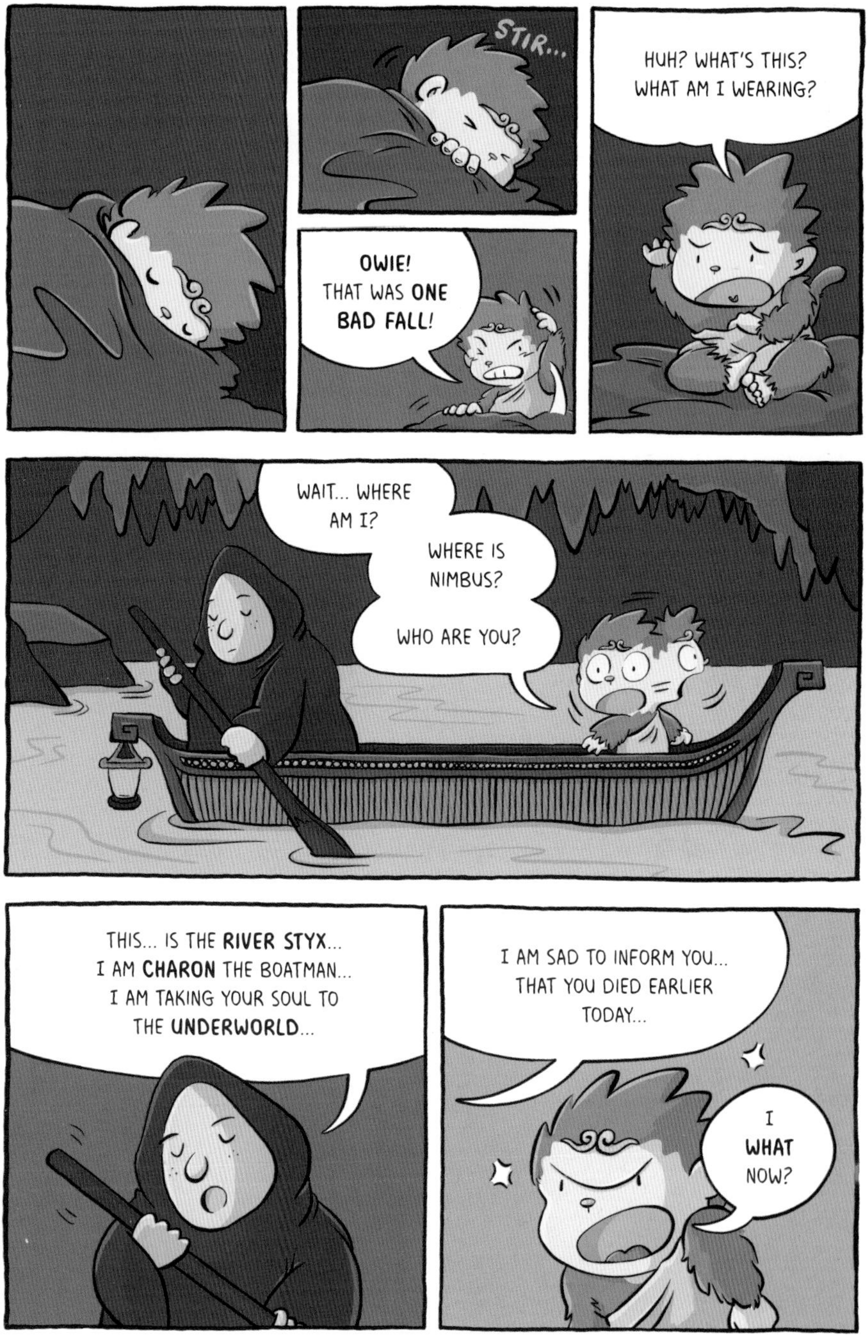
STIR...
HUH? WHAT'S THIS? WHAT AM I WEARING?
OWIE! THAT WAS ONE BAD FALL!
WAIT... WHERE AM I?
WHERE IS NIMBUS?
WHO ARE YOU?
THIS... IS THE RIVER STYX... I AM CHARON THE BOATMAN... I AM TAKING YOUR SOUL TO THE UNDERWORLD...
I AM SAD TO INFORM YOU... THAT YOU DIED EARLIER TODAY...
I WHAT NOW?

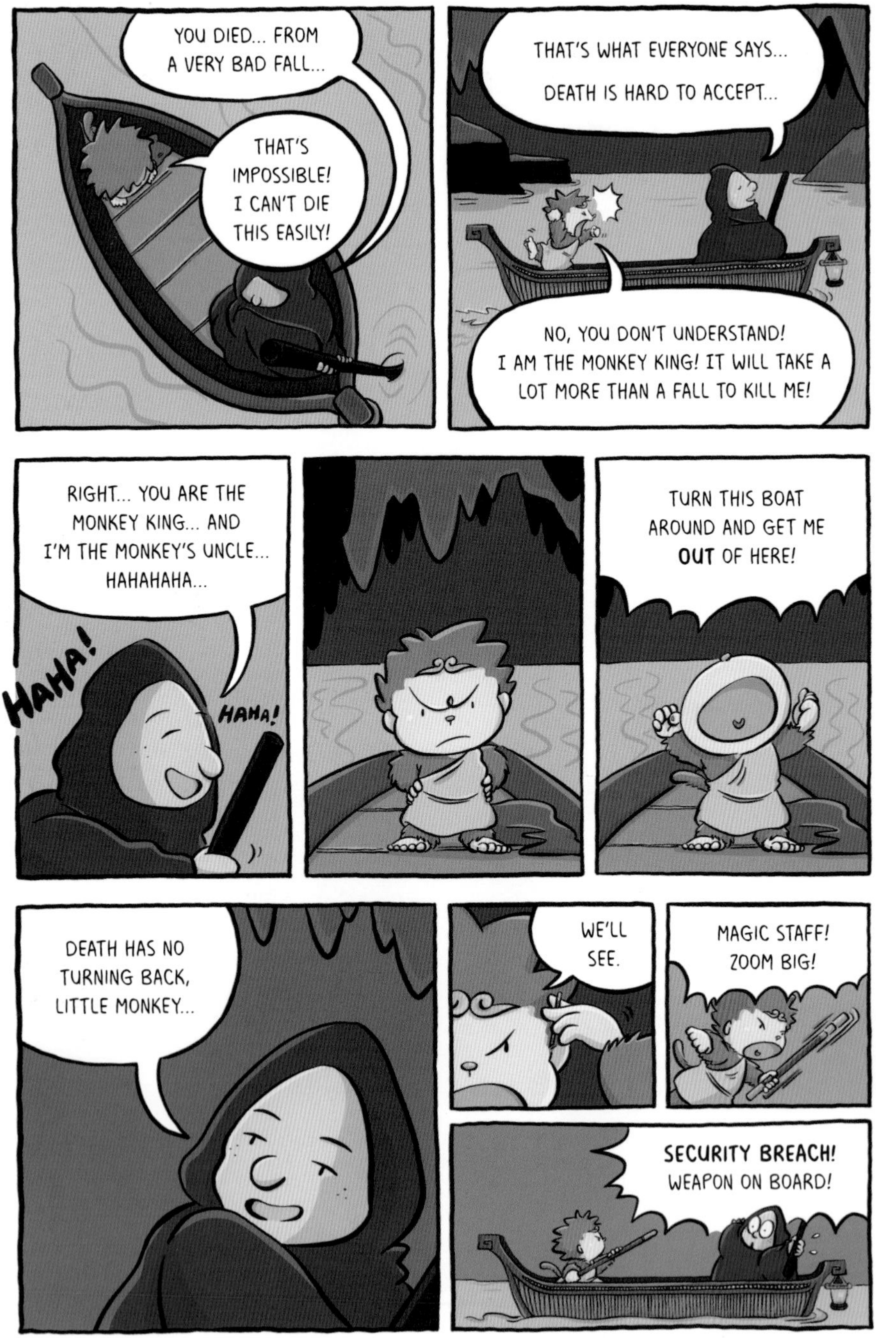
YOU DIED... FROM A VERY BAD FALL...
THAT'S IMPOSSIBLE! I CAN'T DIE THIS EASILY!
THAT'S WHAT EVERYONE SAYS...
DEATH IS HARD TO ACCEPT...
NO, YOU DON'T UNDERSTAND! I AM THE MONKEY KING! IT WILL TAKE A LOT MORE THAN A FALL TO KILL ME!
RIGHT... YOU ARE THE MONKEY KING... AND I'M THE MONKEY'S UNCLE... HAHAHAHA...
HAHA!
HAHA!
TURN THIS BOAT AROUND AND GET ME **OUT** OF HERE!
DEATH HAS NO TURNING BACK, LITTLE MONKEY...
WE'LL SEE.
MAGIC STAFF! ZOOM BIG!
SECURITY BREACH! WEAPON ON BOARD!

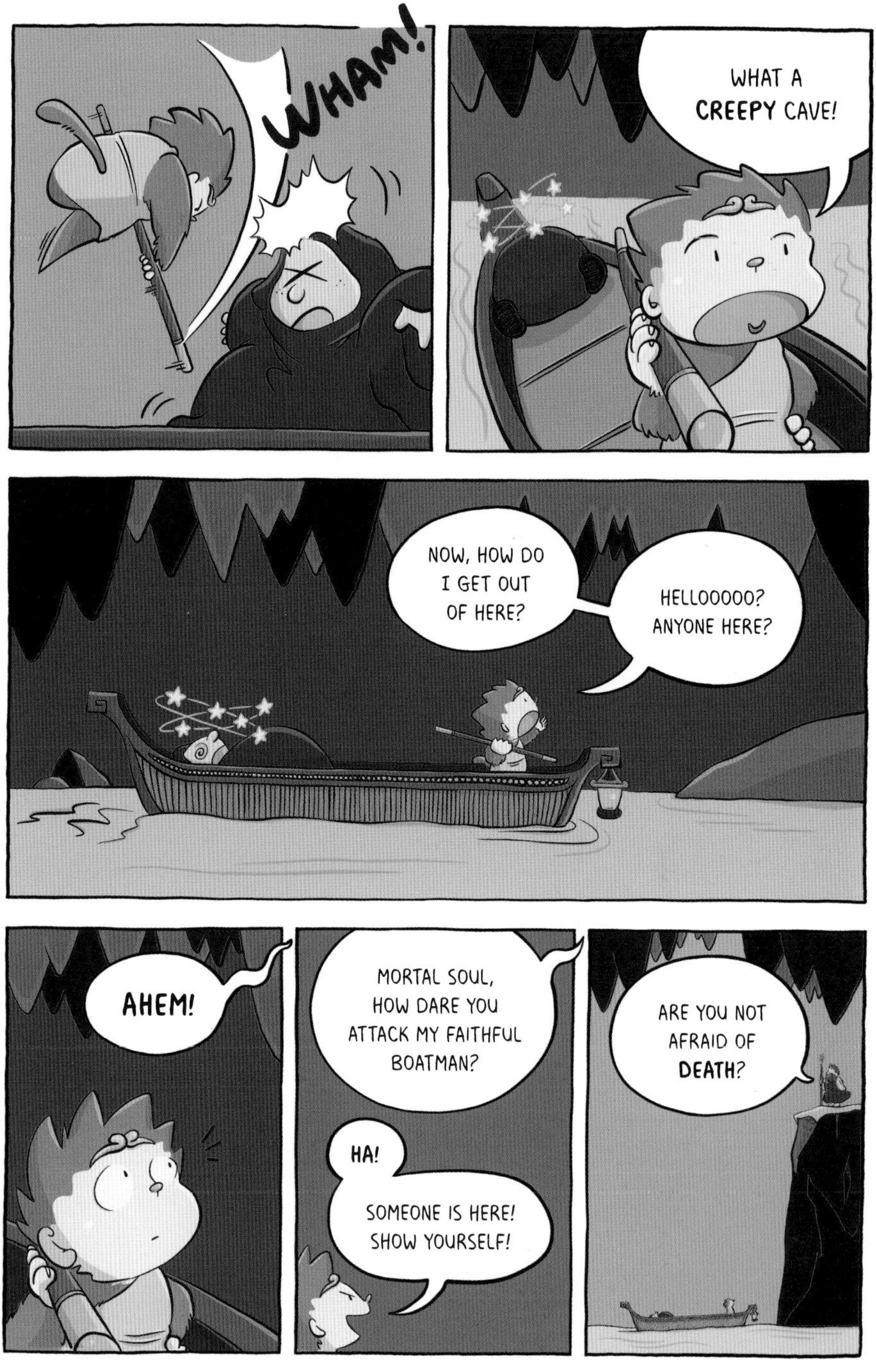
WHAM!
WHAT A CREEPY CAVE!
NOW, HOW DO I GET OUT OF HERE?
HELLOOOOO? ANYONE HERE?
AHEM!
MORTAL SOUL, HOW DARE YOU ATTACK MY FAITHFUL BOATMAN?
HA!
SOMEONE IS HERE! SHOW YOURSELF!
ARE YOU NOT AFRAID OF DEATH?

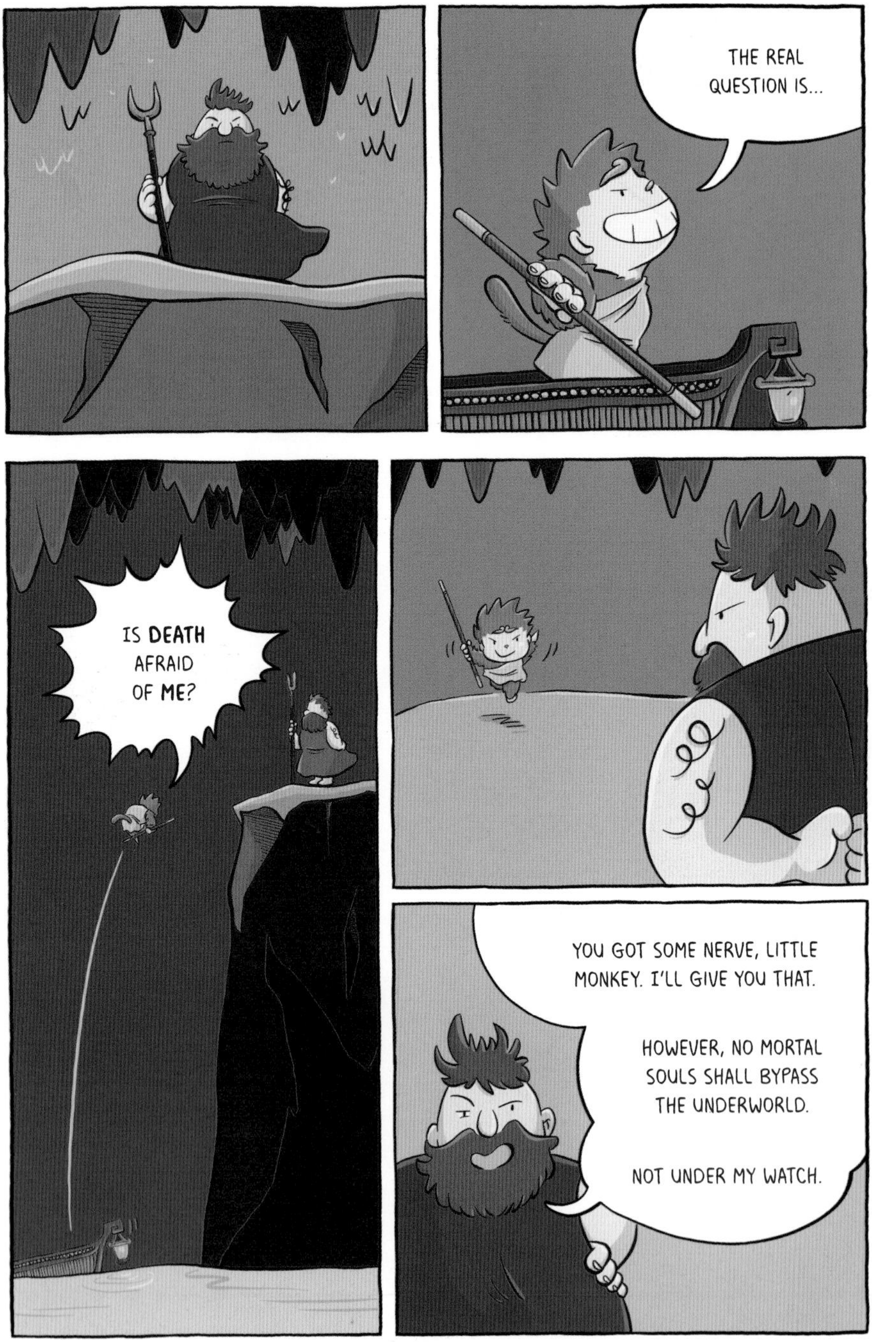
THE REAL QUESTION IS...
IS DEATH AFRAID OF ME?
YOU GOT SOME NERVE, LITTLE MONKEY. I'LL GIVE YOU THAT.
HOWEVER, NO MORTAL SOULS SHALL BYPASS THE UNDERWORLD.
NOT UNDER MY WATCH.

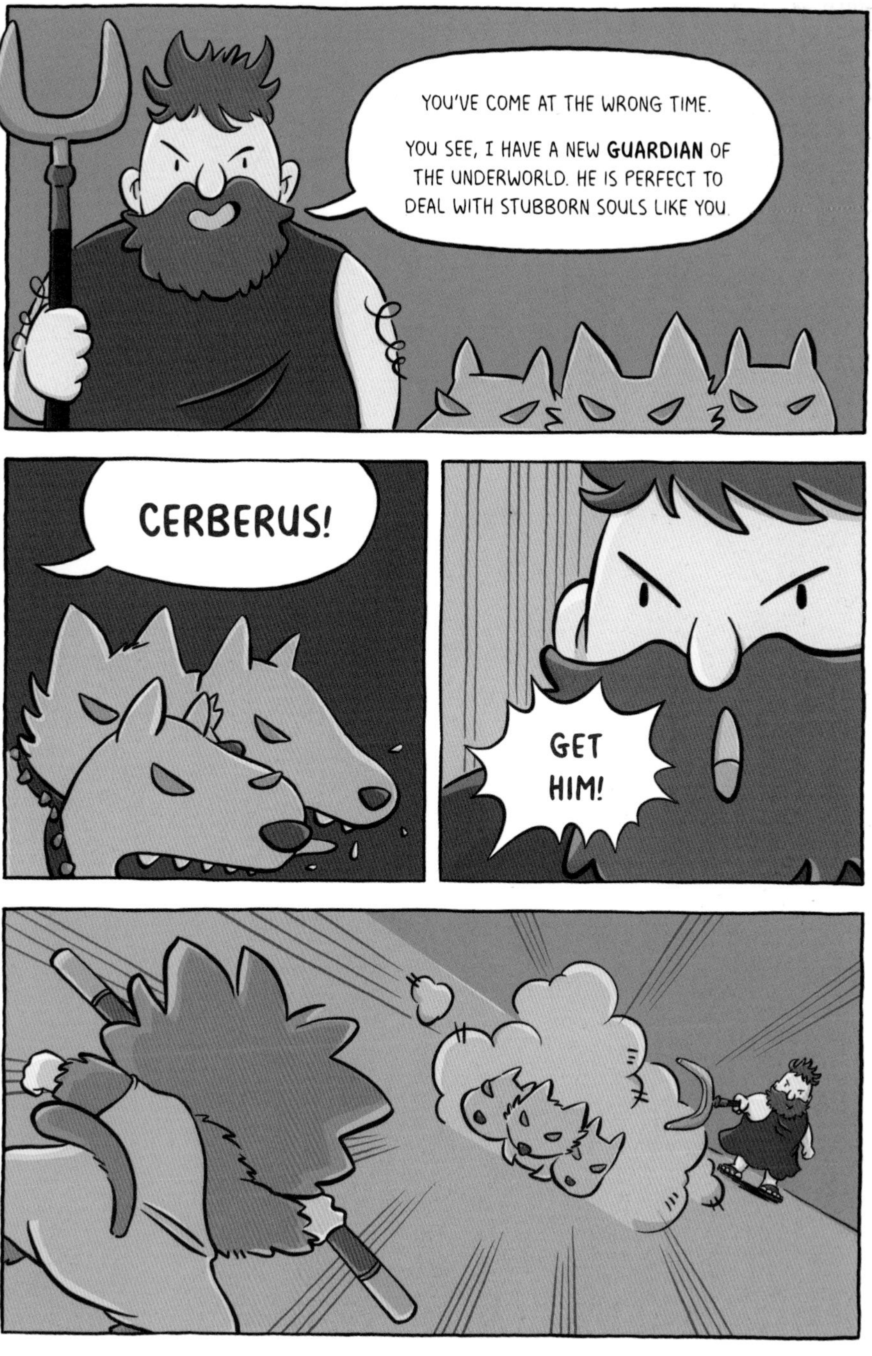
YOU'VE COME AT THE WRONG TIME.
YOU SEE, I HAVE A NEW **GUARDIAN** OF THE UNDERWORLD. HE IS PERFECT TO DEAL WITH STUBBORN SOULS LIKE YOU.
CERBERUS!
GET HIM!

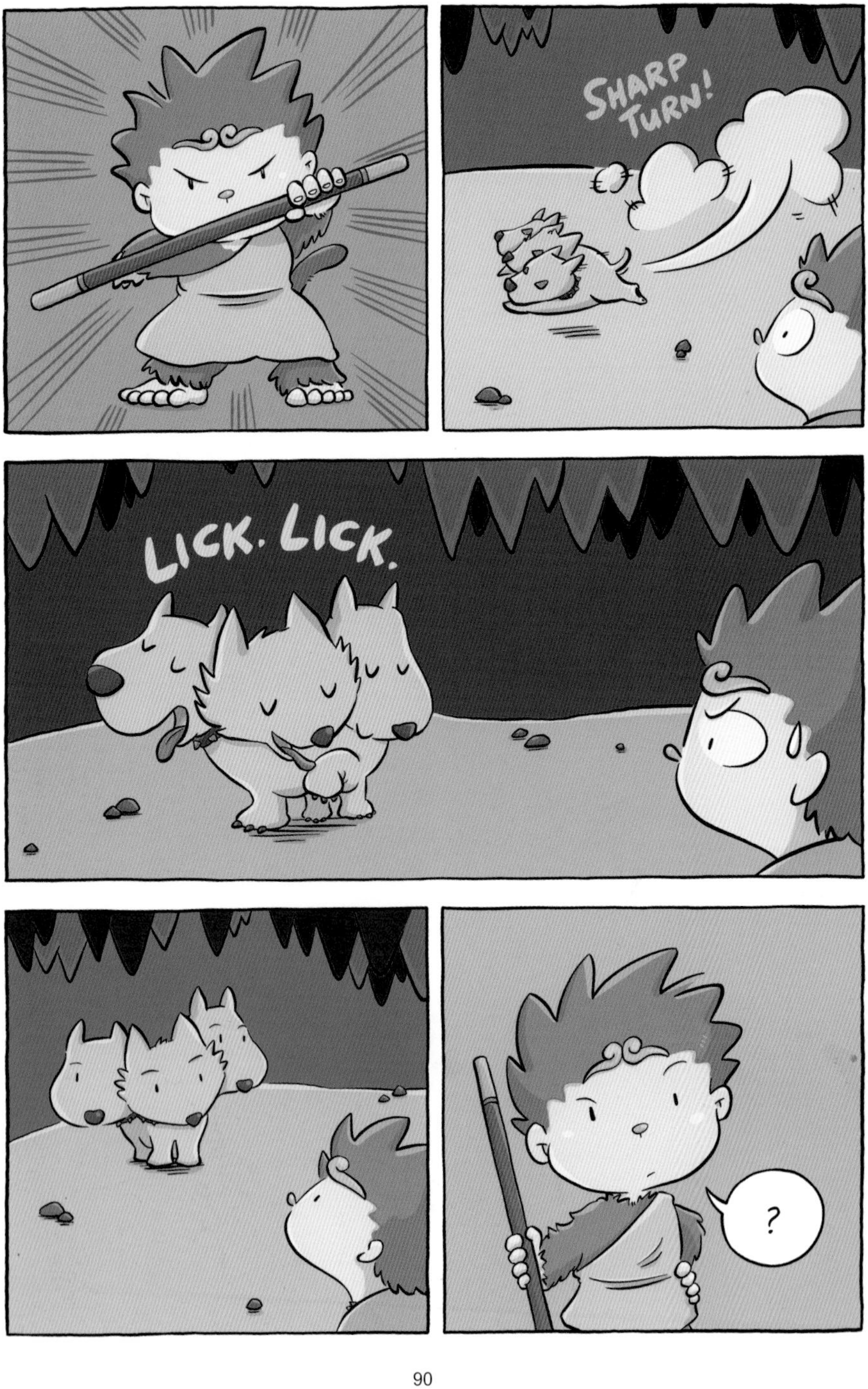
SHARP TURN!
LICK. LICK.
?

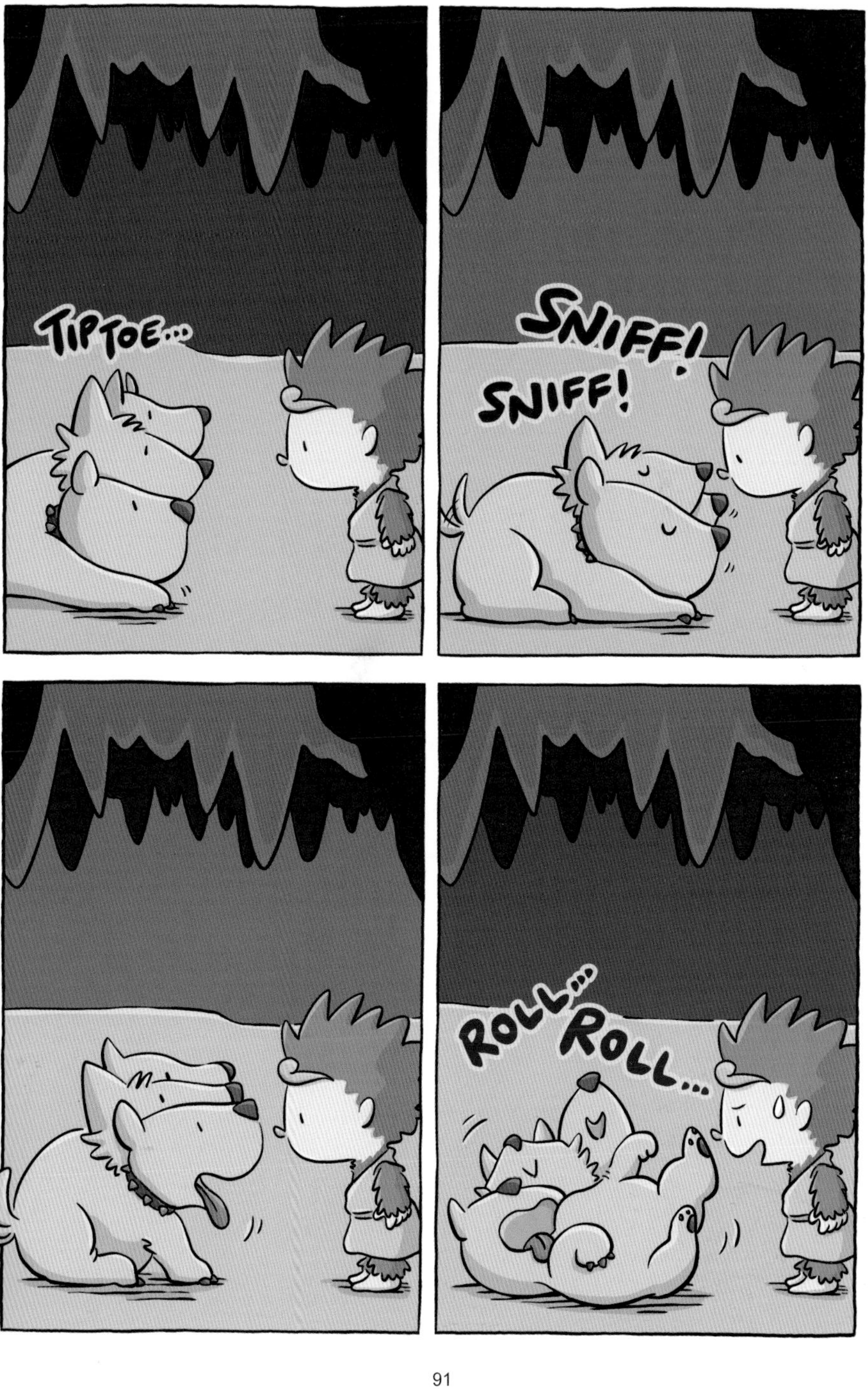
TIPTOE...
SNIFF!
SNIFF!
ROLL...
ROLL...

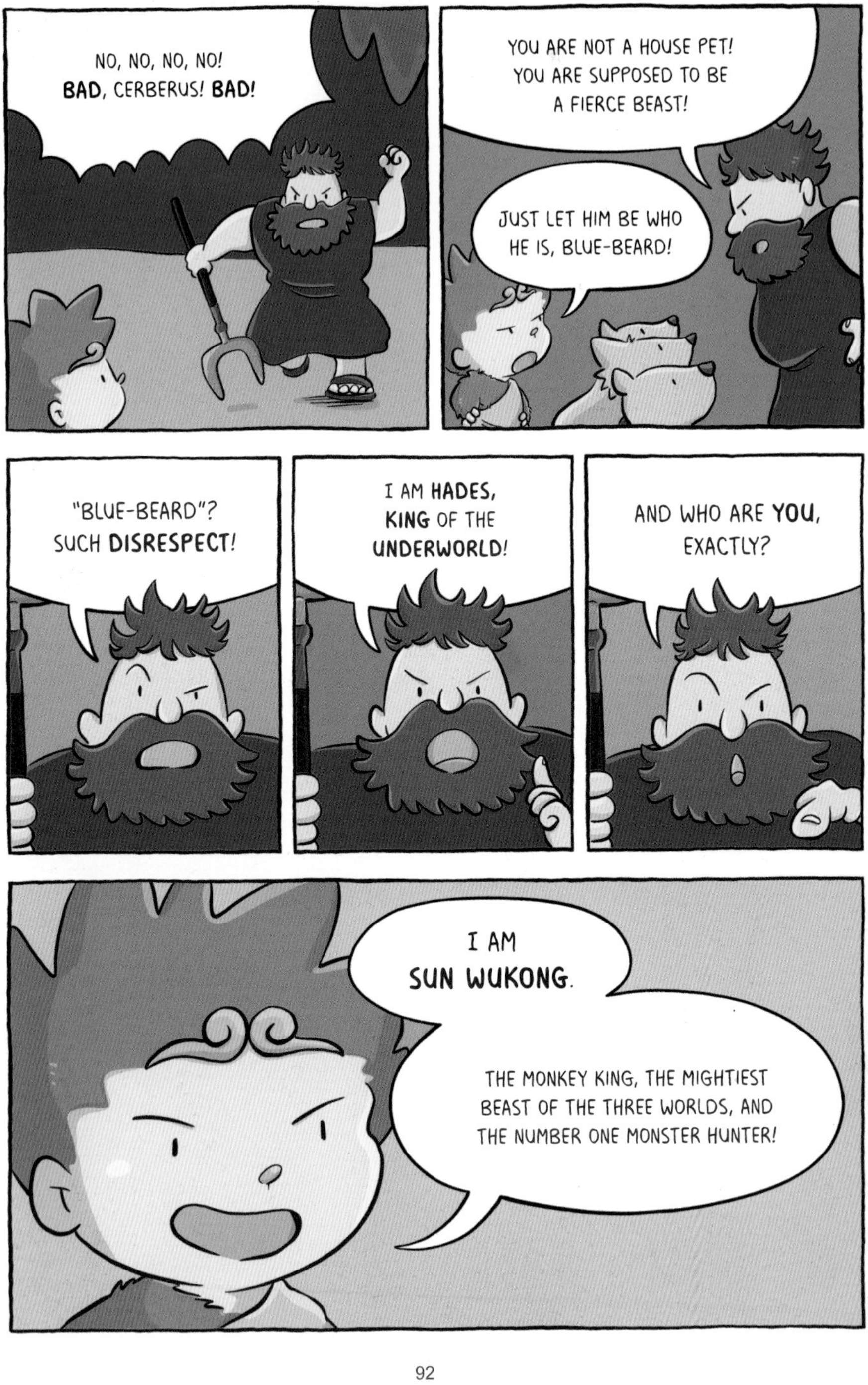
NO, NO, NO, NO! **BAD**, CERBERUS! **BAD**!
YOU ARE NOT A HOUSE PET! YOU ARE SUPPOSED TO BE A FIERCE BEAST!
JUST LET HIM BE WHO HE IS, BLUE-BEARD!
"BLUE-BEARD"? SUCH **DISRESPECT**!
I AM **HADES, KING** OF THE **UNDERWORLD**!
AND WHO ARE **YOU**, EXACTLY?
I AM **SUN WUKONG**.
THE MONKEY KING, THE MIGHTIEST BEAST OF THE THREE WORLDS, AND THE NUMBER ONE MONSTER HUNTER!

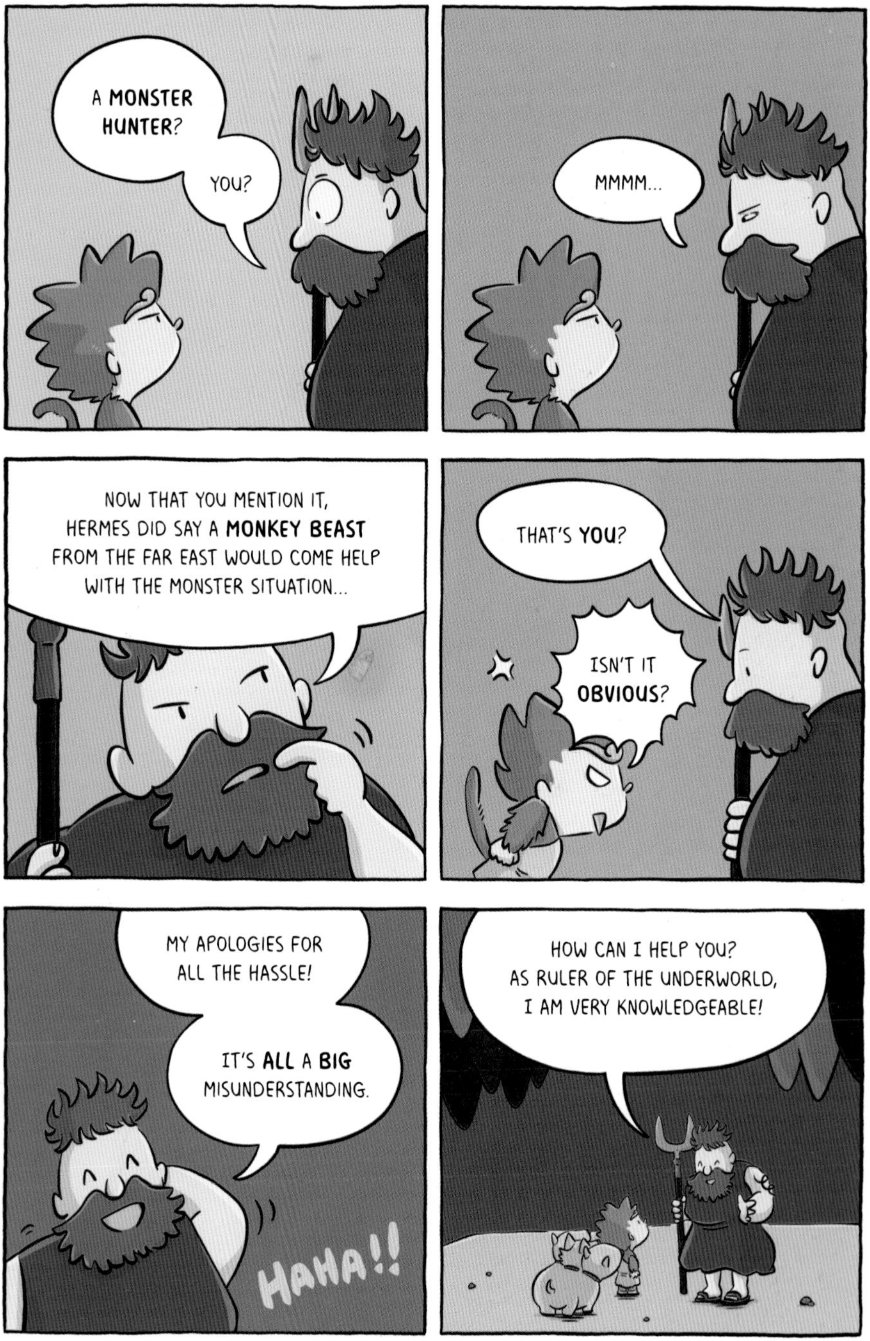
A **MONSTER HUNTER**?
YOU?
MMMM...
NOW THAT YOU MENTION IT, HERMES DID SAY A **MONKEY BEAST** FROM THE FAR EAST WOULD COME HELP WITH THE MONSTER SITUATION...
THAT'S **YOU**?
ISN'T IT **OBVIOUS**?
MY APOLOGIES FOR ALL THE HASSLE!
IT'S **ALL** A **BIG** MISUNDERSTANDING.
HAHA!!
HOW CAN I HELP YOU? AS RULER OF THE UNDERWORLD, I AM VERY KNOWLEDGEABLE!

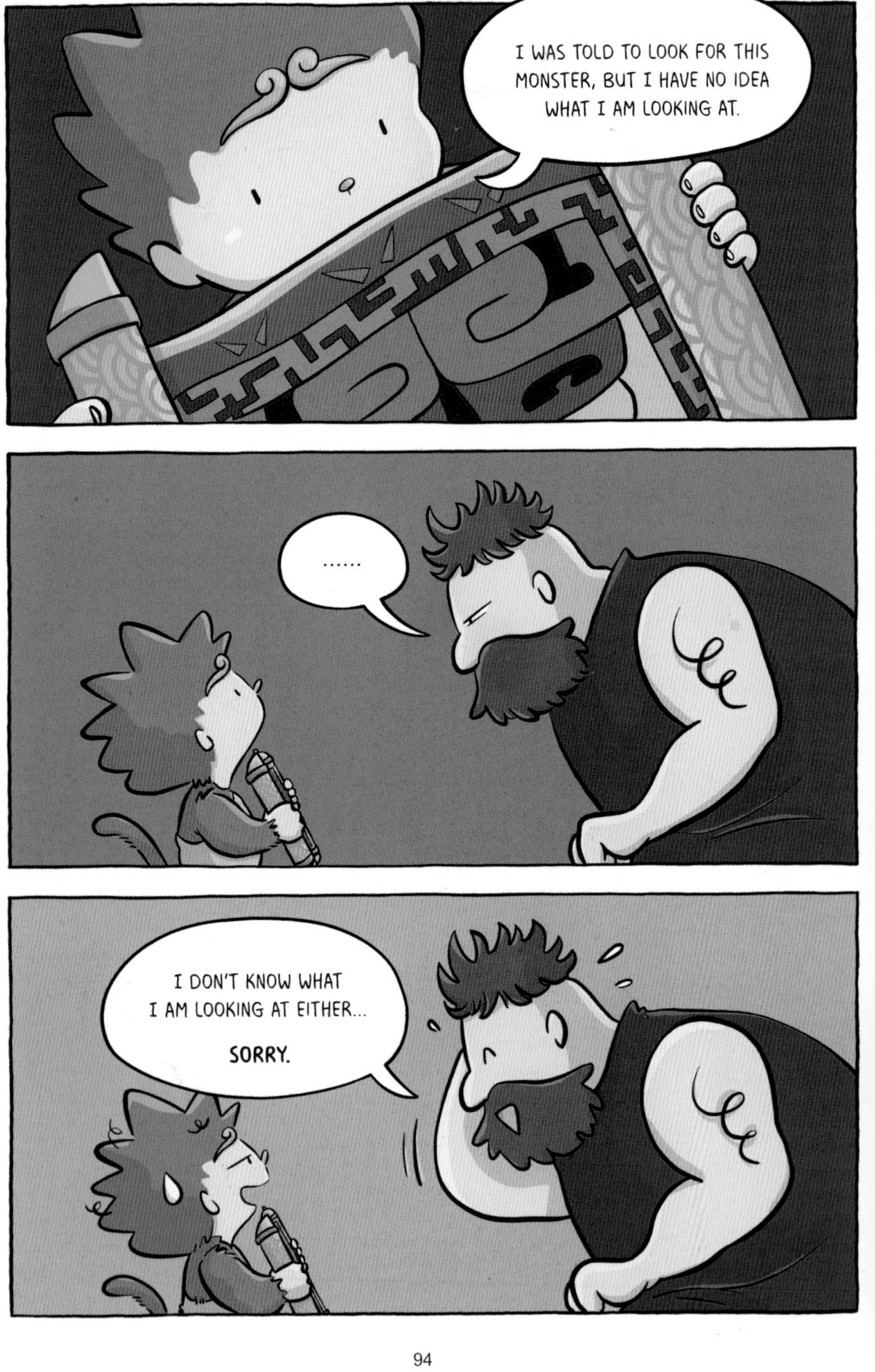
I WAS TOLD TO LOOK FOR THIS MONSTER, BUT I HAVE NO IDEA WHAT I AM LOOKING AT.
......
I DON'T KNOW WHAT I AM LOOKING AT EITHER...
SORRY.

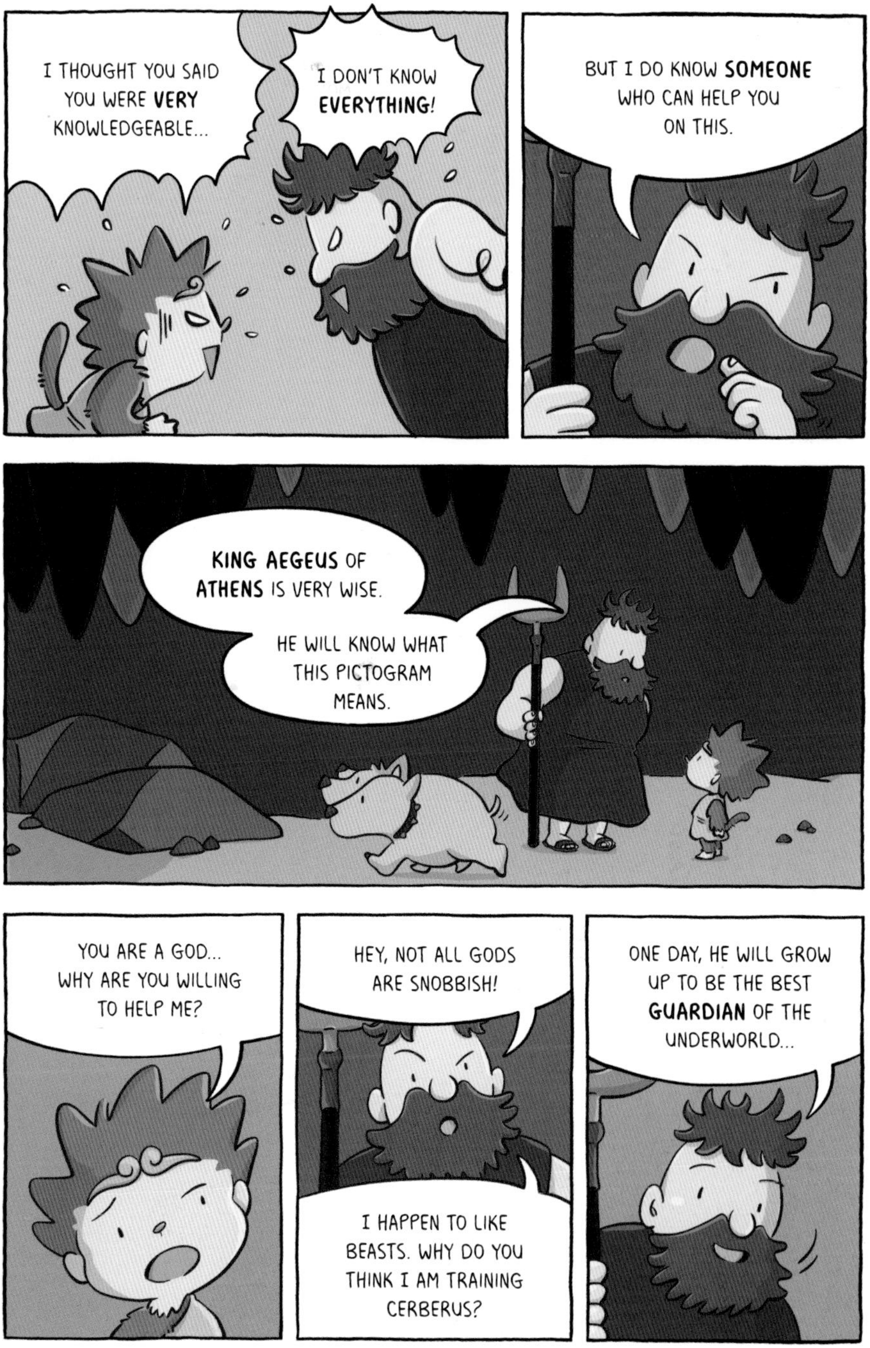
I THOUGHT YOU SAID YOU WERE **VERY** KNOWLEDGEABLE...
I DON'T KNOW **EVERYTHING**!
BUT I DO KNOW **SOMEONE** WHO CAN HELP YOU ON THIS.
KING AEGEUS OF **ATHENS** IS VERY WISE.
HE WILL KNOW WHAT THIS PICTOGRAM MEANS.
YOU ARE A GOD... WHY ARE YOU WILLING TO HELP ME?
HEY, NOT ALL GODS ARE SNOBBISH!
I HAPPEN TO LIKE BEASTS. WHY DO YOU THINK I AM TRAINING CERBERUS?
ONE DAY, HE WILL GROW UP TO BE THE BEST **GUARDIAN** OF THE UNDERWORLD...

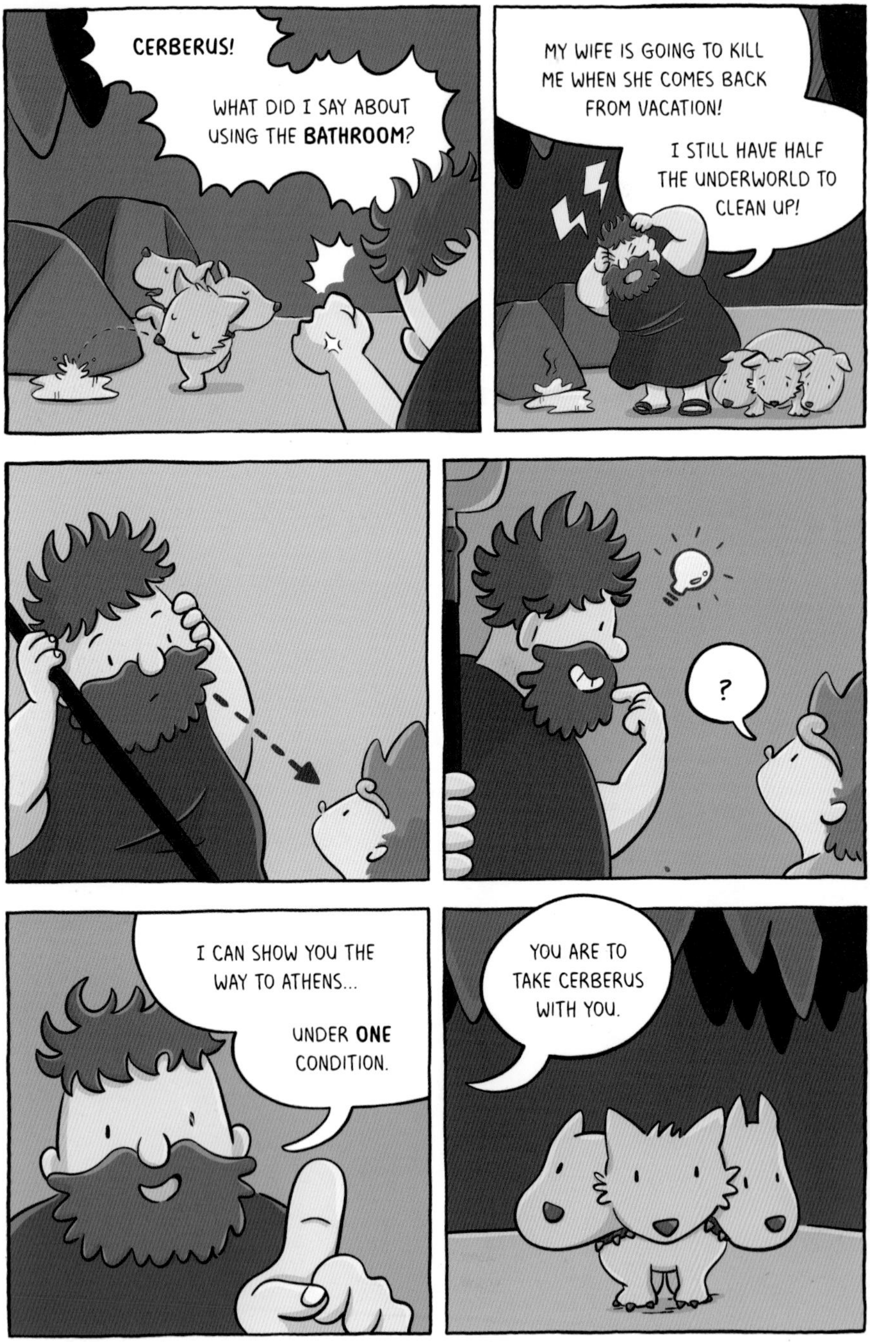
CERBERUS!
WHAT DID I SAY ABOUT USING THE **BATHROOM**?
MY WIFE IS GOING TO KILL ME WHEN SHE COMES BACK FROM VACATION!
I STILL HAVE HALF THE UNDERWORLD TO CLEAN UP!
?
I CAN SHOW YOU THE WAY TO ATHENS...
UNDER **ONE** CONDITION.
YOU ARE TO TAKE CERBERUS WITH YOU.

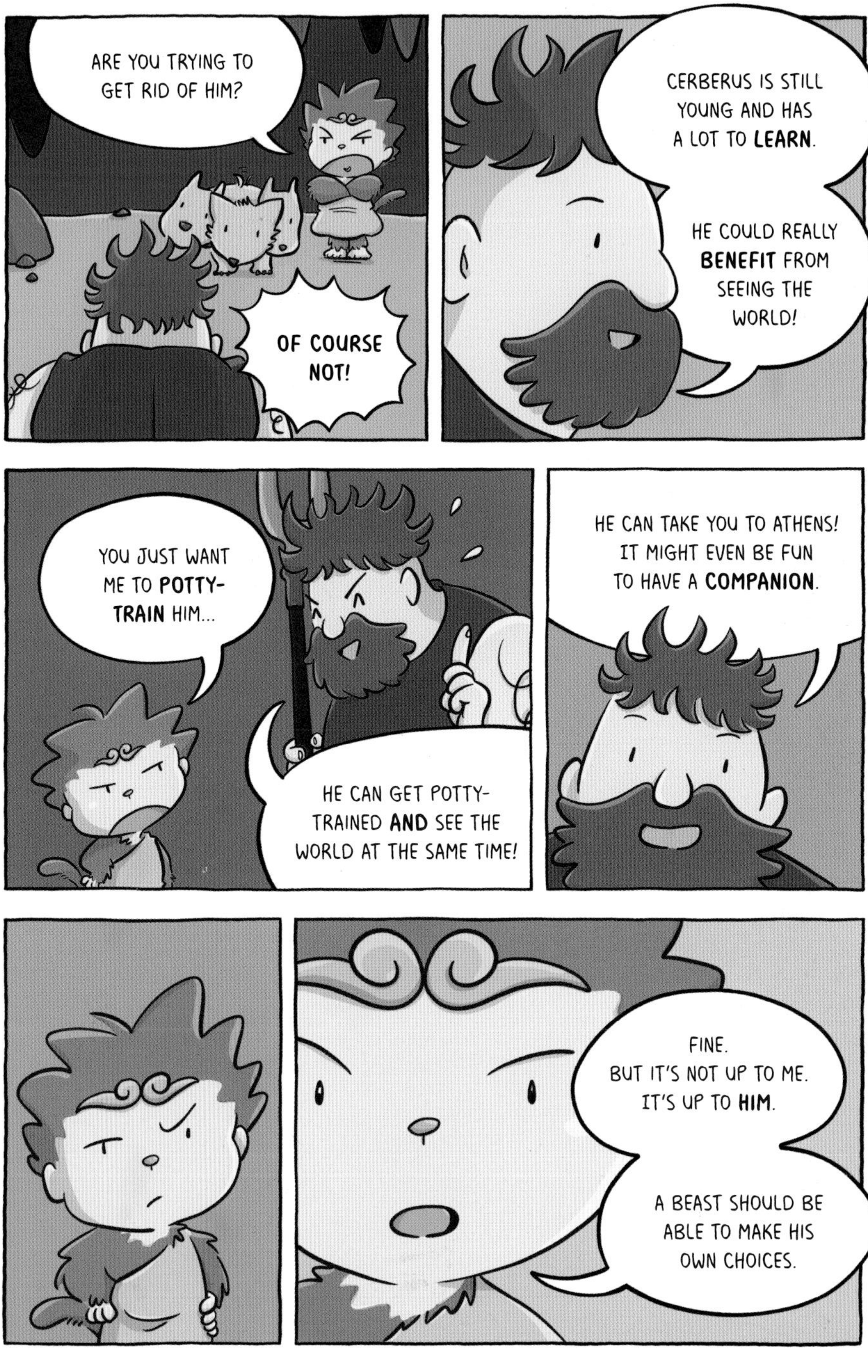
ARE YOU TRYING TO GET RID OF HIM?
OF COURSE NOT!
CERBERUS IS STILL YOUNG AND HAS A LOT TO LEARN.
HE COULD REALLY BENEFIT FROM SEEING THE WORLD!
YOU JUST WANT ME TO POTTY-TRAIN HIM...
HE CAN GET POTTY-TRAINED AND SEE THE WORLD AT THE SAME TIME!
HE CAN TAKE YOU TO ATHENS! IT MIGHT EVEN BE FUN TO HAVE A COMPANION.
FINE. BUT IT'S NOT UP TO ME. IT'S UP TO HIM.
A BEAST SHOULD BE ABLE TO MAKE HIS OWN CHOICES.

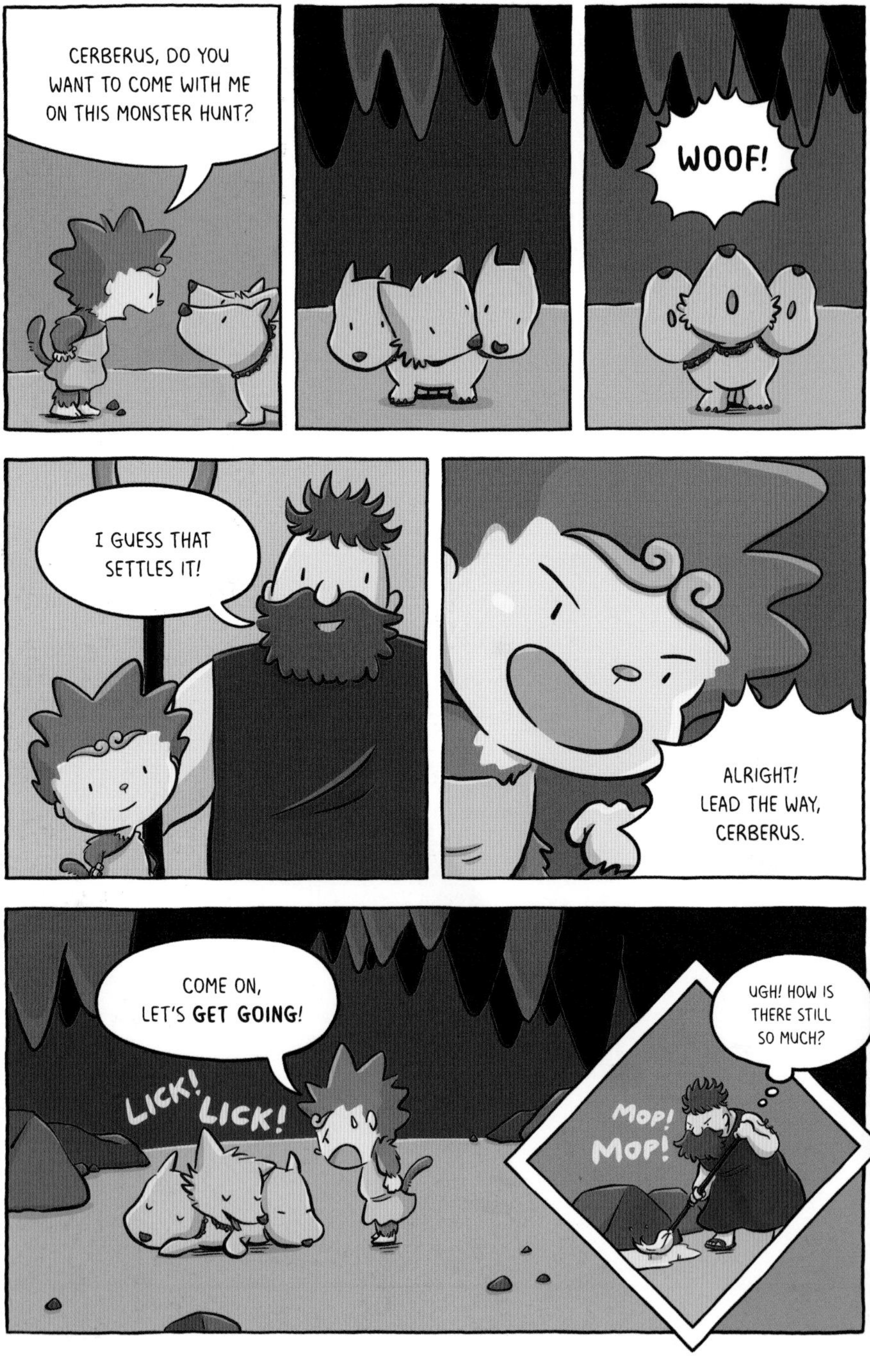

CERBERUS, DO YOU WANT TO COME WITH ME ON THIS MONSTER HUNT?
WOOF!
I GUESS THAT SETTLES IT!
ALRIGHT! LEAD THE WAY, CERBERUS.
COME ON, LET'S **GET GOING**!
LICK! LICK!
UGH! HOW IS THERE STILL SO MUCH?
MOP! MOP!

CHAPTER 5 THE BUZZING CITY OF ATHENS

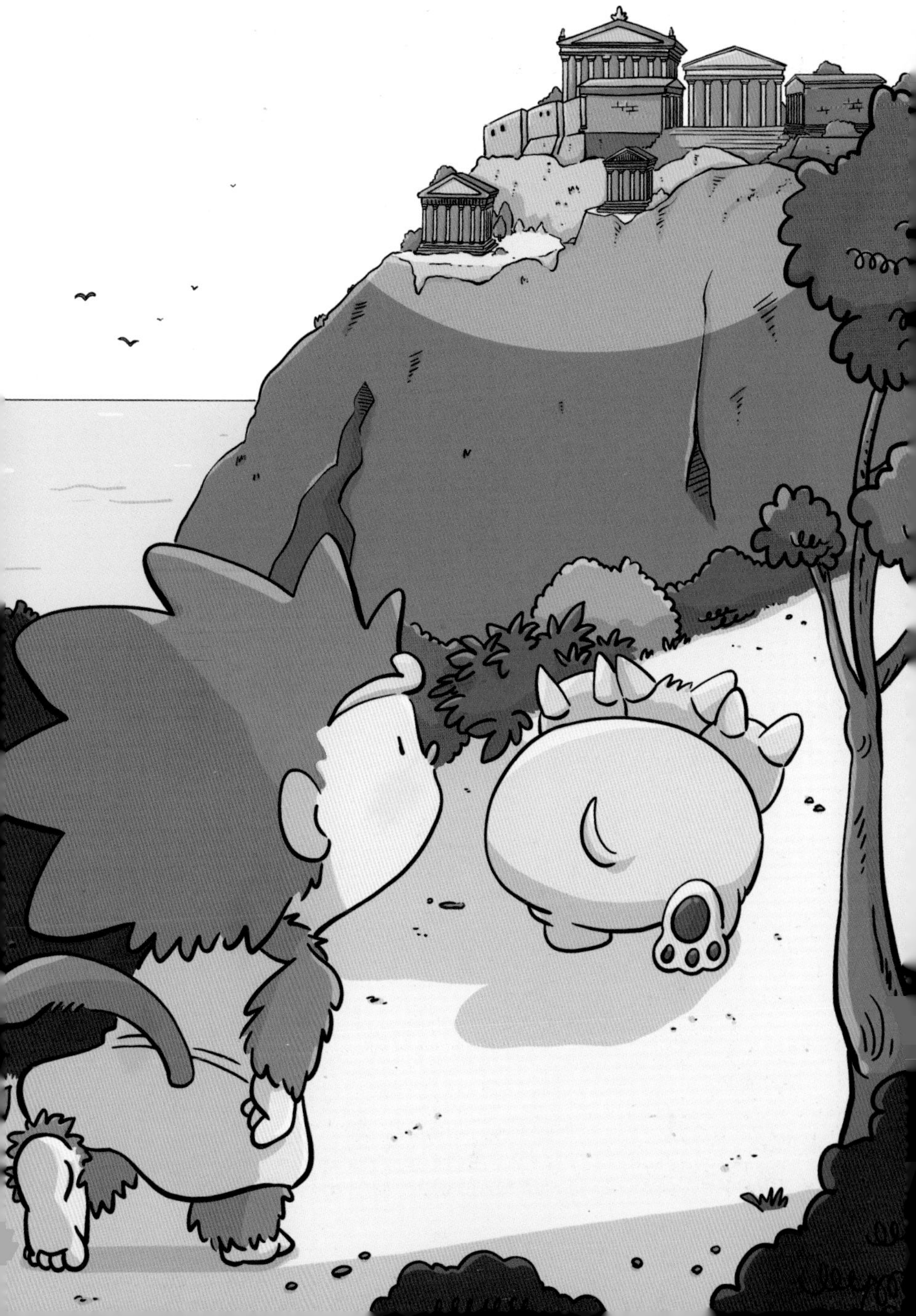

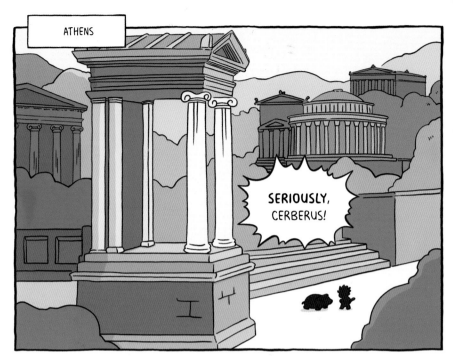

ATHENS

SERIOUSLY, CERBERUS!

IF YOU ARE COMING WITH ME, THERE ARE **A FEW RULES!**

NAMELY, YOU CANNOT **POOP** EVERYWHERE!

I AM A **MONSTER HUNTER!** I CAN'T FOCUS WHEN I AM BUSY CLEANING UP AFTER YOU!

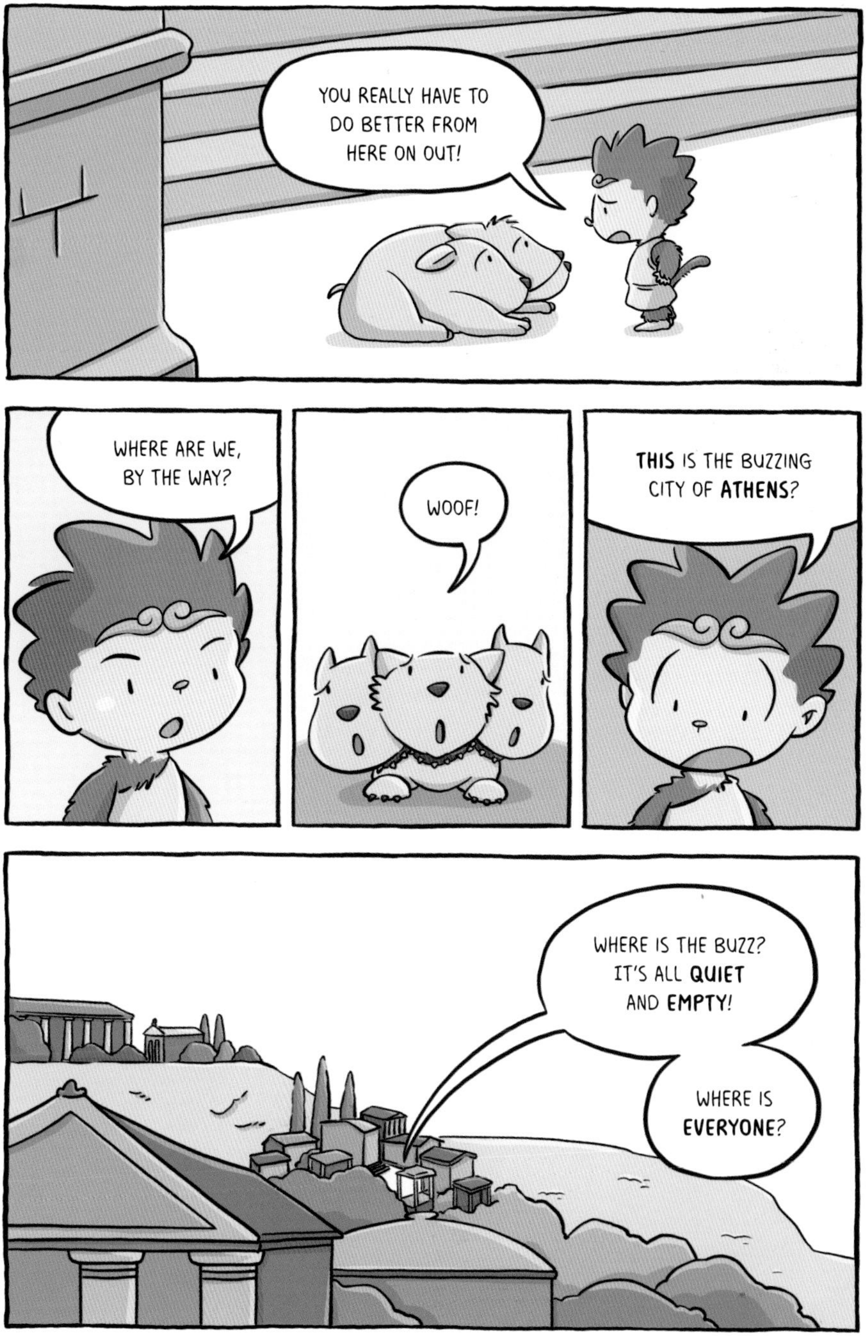
YOU REALLY HAVE TO DO BETTER FROM HERE ON OUT!
WHERE ARE WE, BY THE WAY?
WOOF!
THIS IS THE BUZZING CITY OF **ATHENS**?
WHERE IS THE BUZZ? IT'S ALL **QUIET** AND **EMPTY**!
WHERE IS **EVERYONE**?

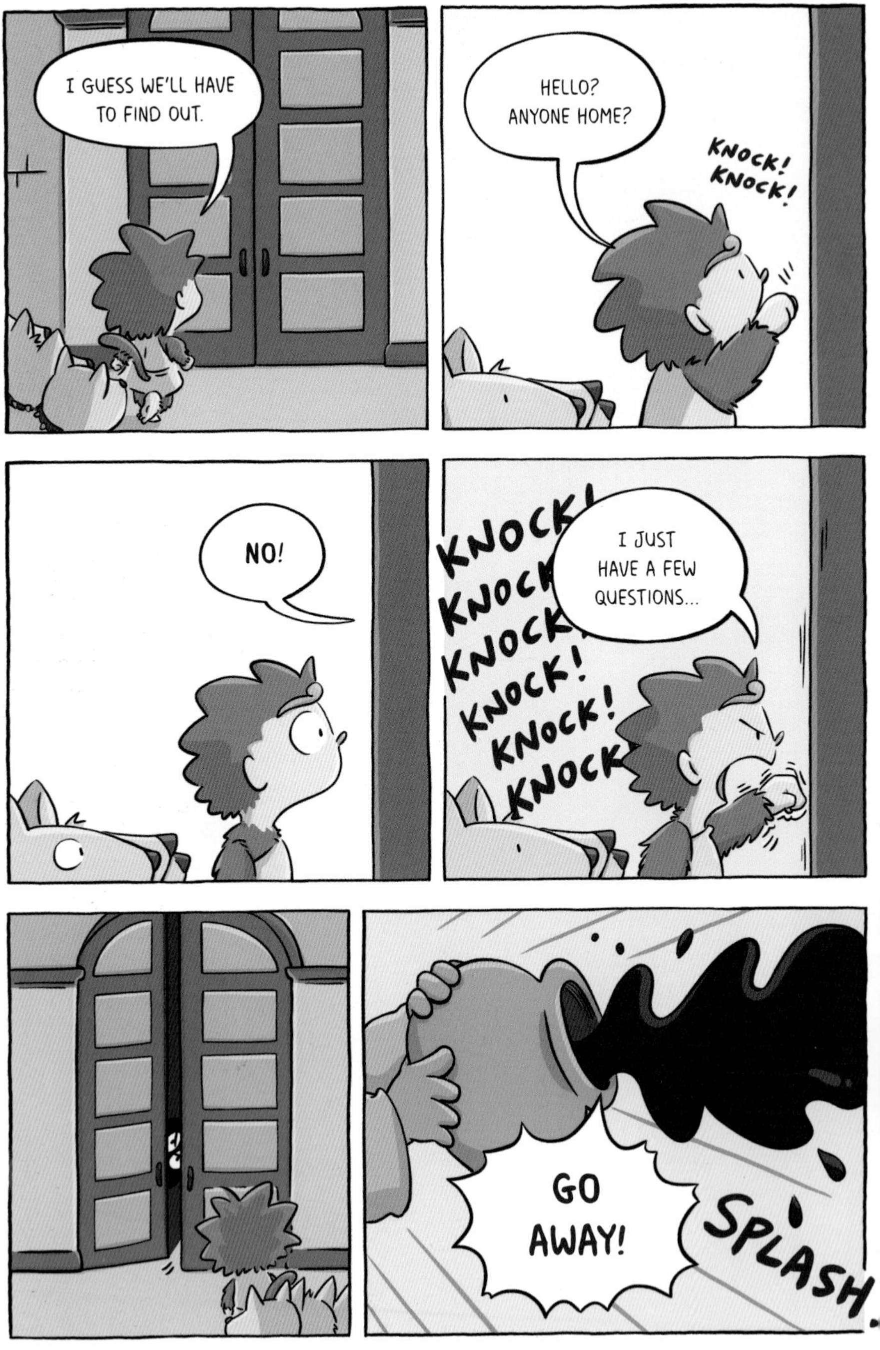
I GUESS WE'LL HAVE TO FIND OUT.
HELLO? ANYONE HOME?
KNOCK! KNOCK!
NO!
KNOCK! KNOCK! KNOCK! KNOCK! KNOCK! KNOCK
I JUST HAVE A FEW QUESTIONS...
GO AWAY!
SPLASH.

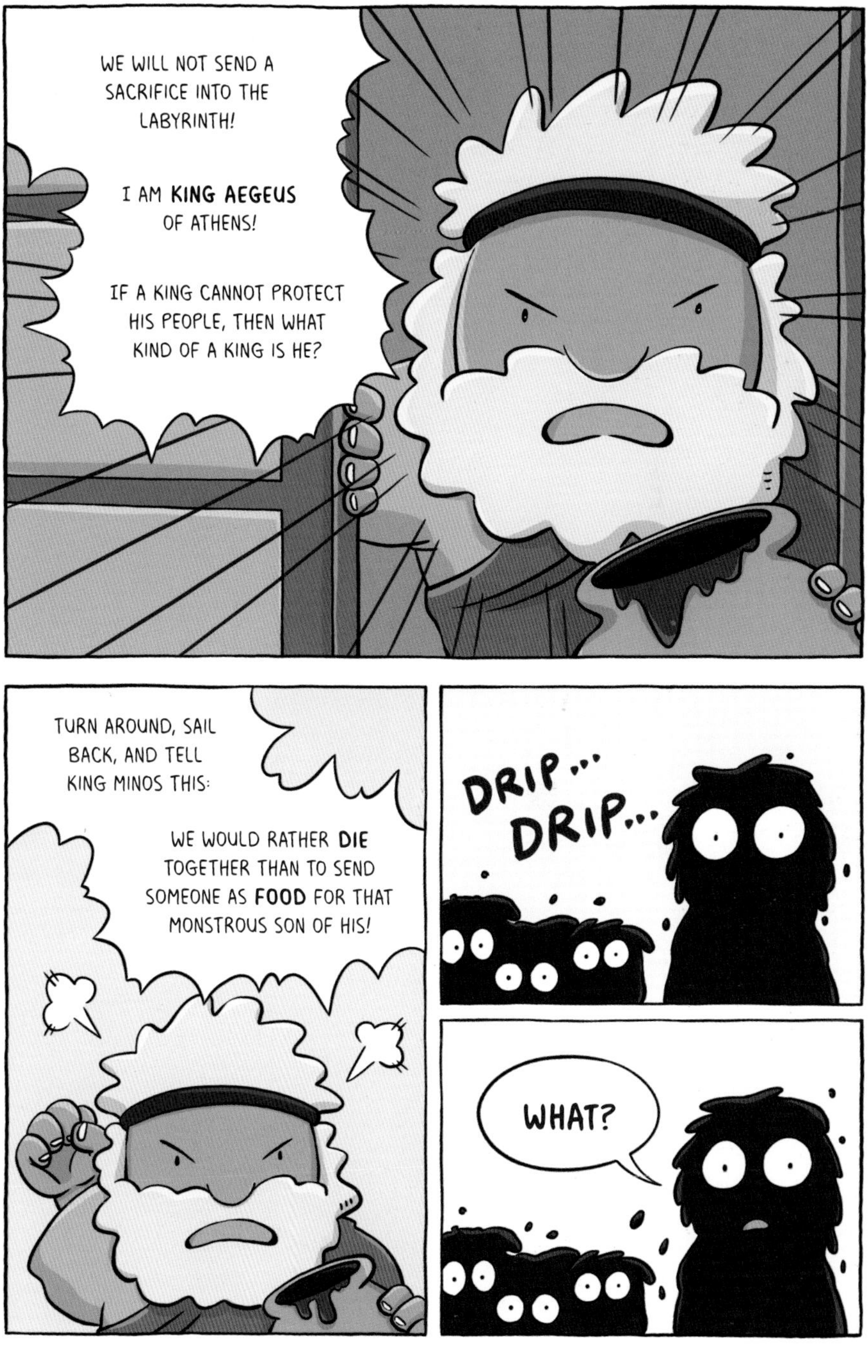
WE WILL NOT SEND A SACRIFICE INTO THE LABYRINTH!
I AM **KING AEGEUS** OF ATHENS!
IF A KING CANNOT PROTECT HIS PEOPLE, THEN WHAT KIND OF A KING IS HE?
TURN AROUND, SAIL BACK, AND TELL KING MINOS THIS:
WE WOULD RATHER **DIE** TOGETHER THAN TO SEND SOMEONE AS **FOOD** FOR THAT MONSTROUS SON OF HIS!
DRIP...
DRIP...
WHAT?

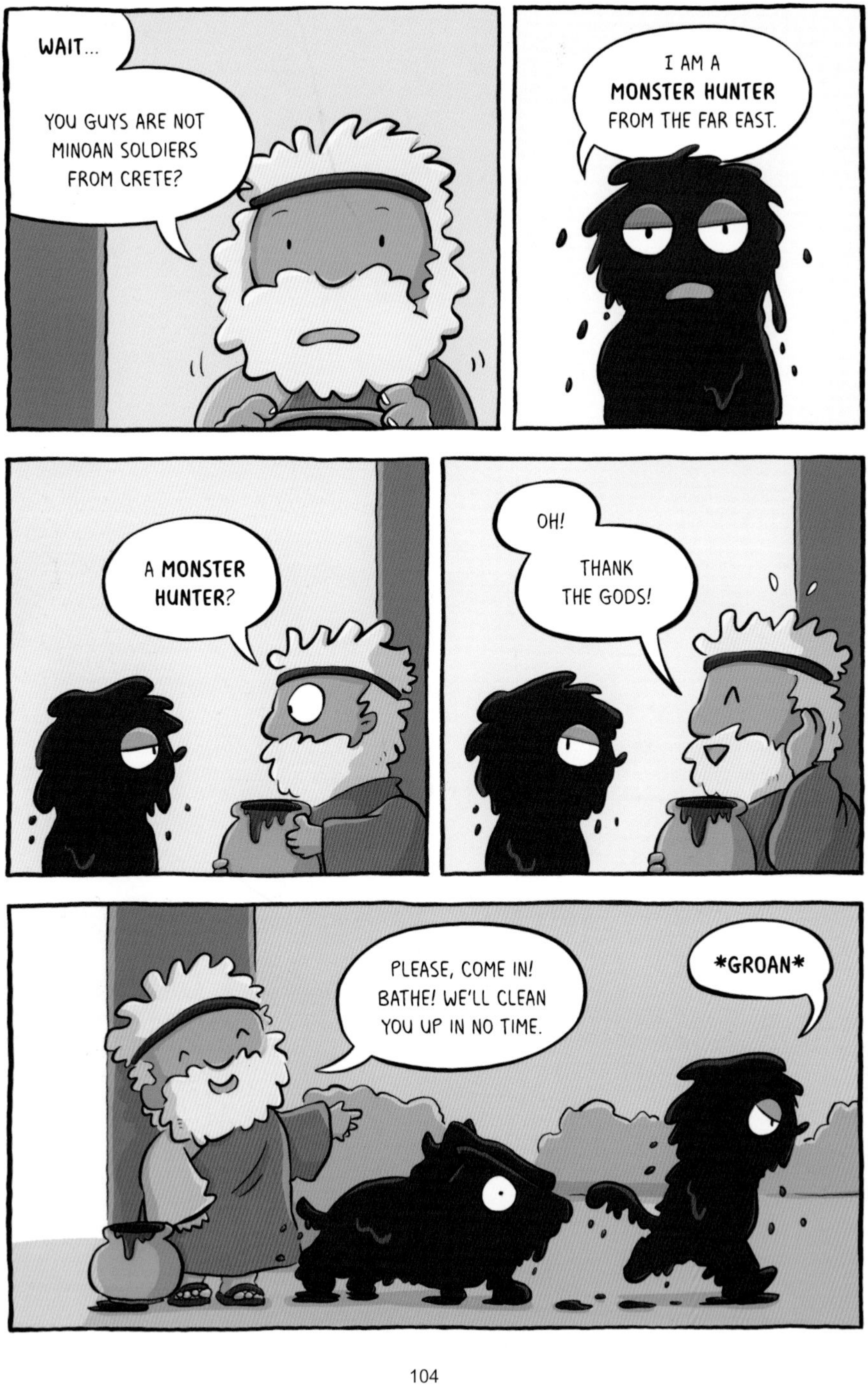
WAIT...
YOU GUYS ARE NOT MINOAN SOLDIERS FROM CRETE?
I AM A MONSTER HUNTER FROM THE FAR EAST.
A MONSTER HUNTER?
OH!
THANK THE GODS!
PLEASE, COME IN! BATHE! WE'LL CLEAN YOU UP IN NO TIME.
GROAN

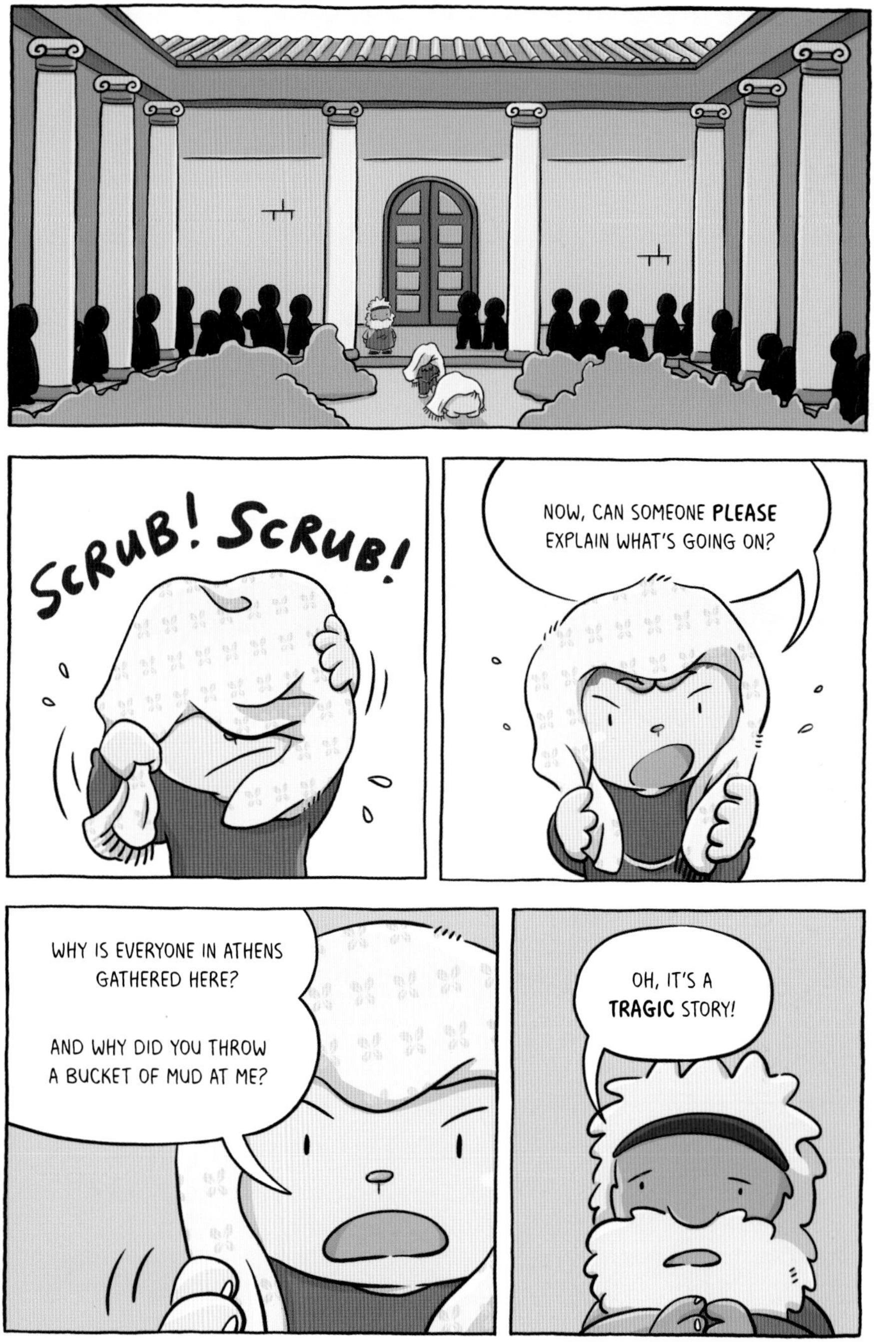
SCRUB! SCRUB!
NOW, CAN SOMEONE **PLEASE** EXPLAIN WHAT'S GOING ON?
WHY IS EVERYONE IN ATHENS GATHERED HERE?
AND WHY DID YOU THROW A BUCKET OF MUD AT ME?
OH, IT'S A **TRAGIC** STORY!

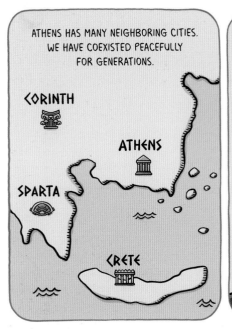

ATHENS HAS MANY NEIGHBORING CITIES. WE HAVE COEXISTED PEACEFULLY FOR GENERATIONS.

CORINTH

ATHENS

SPARTA

CRETE

BUT THERE IS ONE MAN WHO ISN'T SATISFIED. HE WANTS MORE— MORE MONEY, MORE LAND, MORE POWER.

HE IS **KING MINOS**, RULER OF THE **MINOANS**.

THE MINOANS LIVE ON THE SMALL ISLAND OF **CRETE**, BUT THEY HAVE THE MIGHTIEST NAVY IN THE THREE WORLDS.

WHAT WE FEAR THE MOST, HOWEVER, IS NOT KING MINOS'S NAVY...

IT'S SOMETHING MUCH, MUCH **WORSE**.

KING MINOS HAD A MONSTROUS CHILD— HALF HUMAN, HALF BULL.

HE IS THE **MINOTAUR**. RUMOR HAS IT, HE EATS HUMANS!

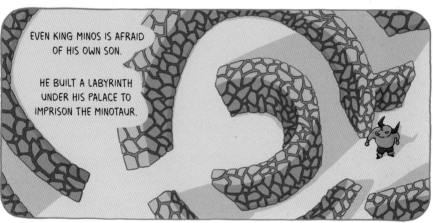

EVEN KING MINOS IS AFRAID OF HIS OWN SON.

HE BUILT A LABYRINTH UNDER HIS PALACE TO IMPRISON THE MINOTAUR.

HE DEMANDED ATHENS PROVIDE A SACRIFICE TO GO INTO THE LABYRINTH TO SATISFY THE MONSTER'S HUNGER.

IF WE DISOBEY, WE WILL HAVE TO FACE THE DESTRUCTIVE WRATH OF HIS NAVY.

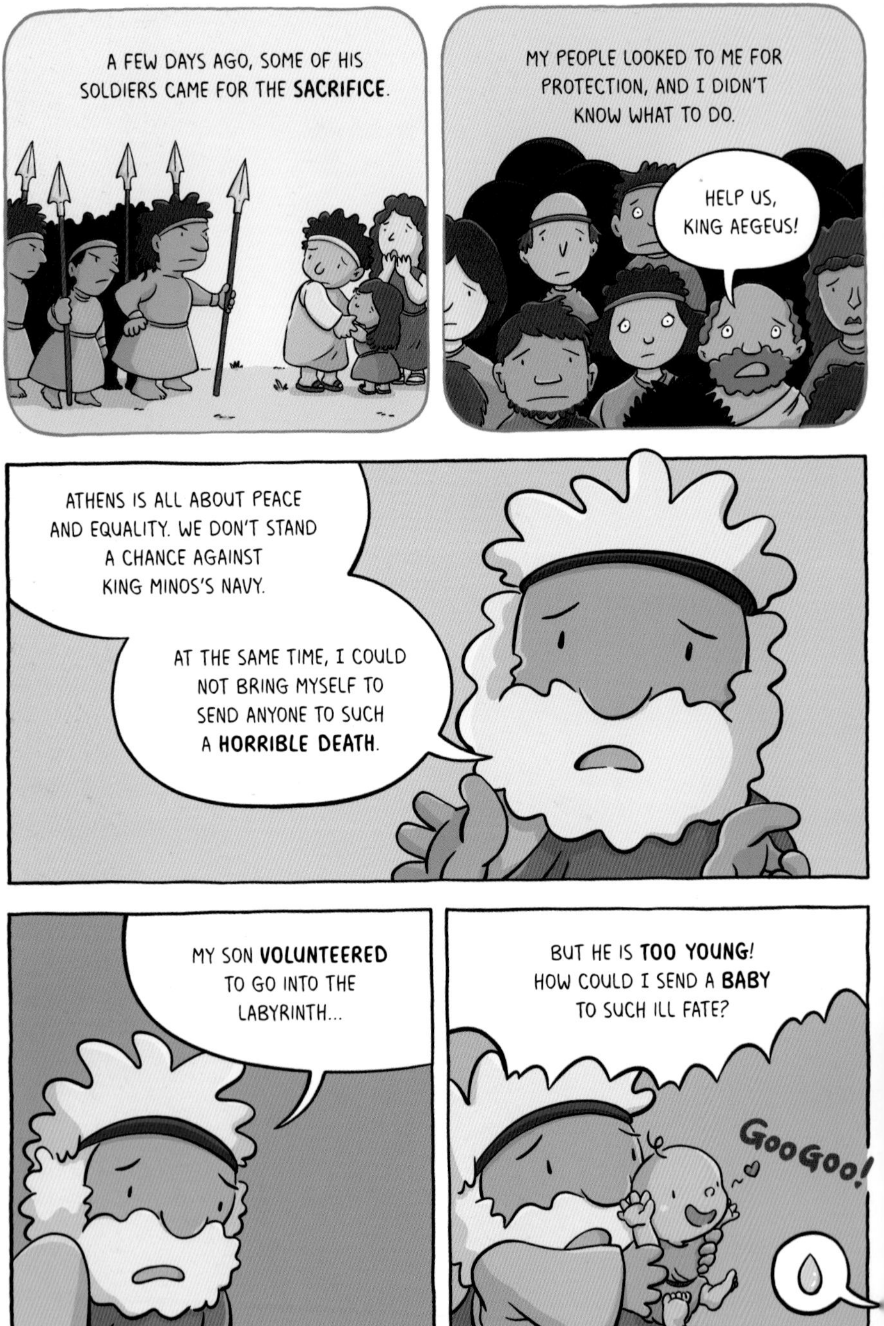
A FEW DAYS AGO, SOME OF HIS SOLDIERS CAME FOR THE **SACRIFICE**.
MY PEOPLE LOOKED TO ME FOR PROTECTION, AND I DIDN'T KNOW WHAT TO DO.
HELP US, KING AEGEUS!
ATHENS IS ALL ABOUT PEACE AND EQUALITY. WE DON'T STAND A CHANCE AGAINST KING MINOS'S NAVY.
AT THE SAME TIME, I COULD NOT BRING MYSELF TO SEND ANYONE TO SUCH A **HORRIBLE DEATH**.
MY SON **VOLUNTEERED** TO GO INTO THE LABYRINTH...
BUT HE IS **TOO YOUNG**! HOW COULD I SEND A **BABY** TO SUCH ILL FATE?
GOOGOO!

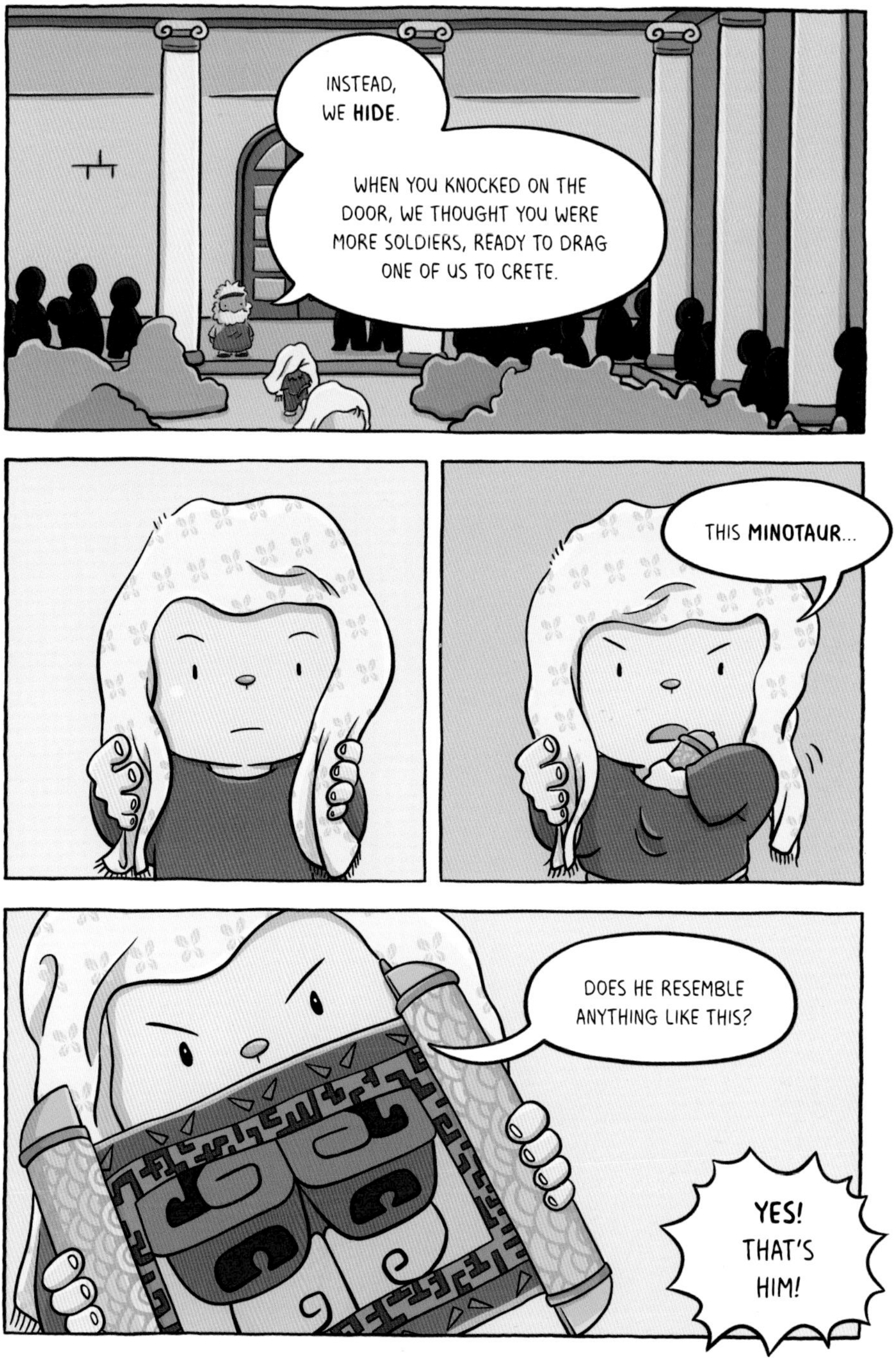
INSTEAD, WE HIDE.
WHEN YOU KNOCKED ON THE DOOR, WE THOUGHT YOU WERE MORE SOLDIERS, READY TO DRAG ONE OF US TO CRETE.
THIS MINOTAUR...
DOES HE RESEMBLE ANYTHING LIKE THIS?
YES! THAT'S HIM!

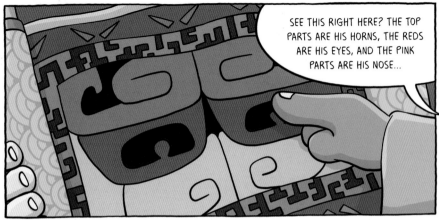

SEE THIS RIGHT HERE? THE TOP PARTS ARE HIS HORNS, THE REDS ARE HIS EYES, AND THE PINK PARTS ARE HIS NOSE...

HEHE!

WHY ARE YOU SMILING?

WHAT'S FUNNY?

TELL YOU WHAT, KING AEGEUS...

SHOW ME THE WAY TO CRETE,

AND I WILL GET RID OF THE MONSTER FOR YOU.

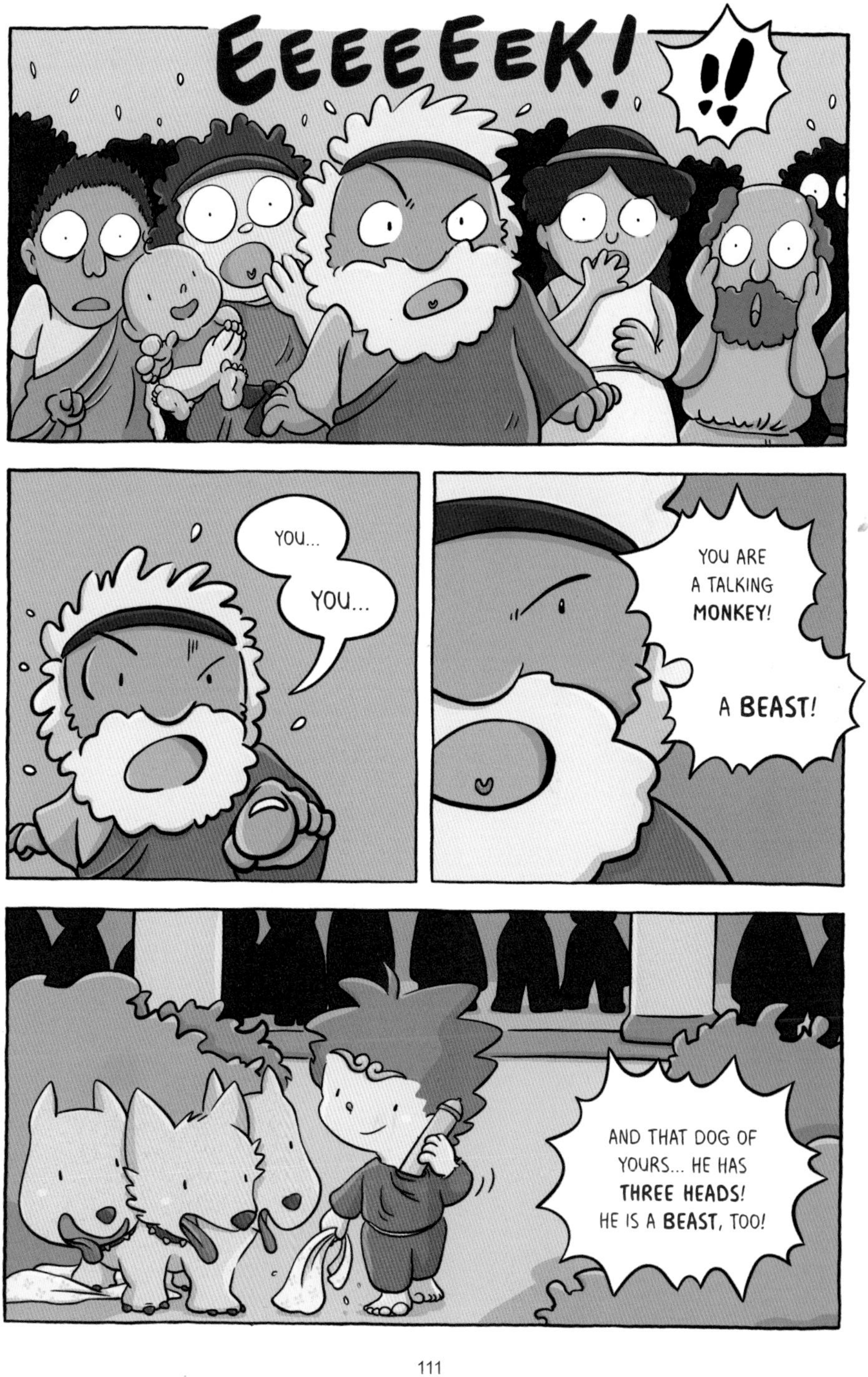
EEEEEEK!
!!
YOU...
YOU...
YOU ARE A TALKING MONKEY!
A BEAST!
AND THAT DOG OF YOURS... HE HAS THREE HEADS! HE IS A BEAST, TOO!

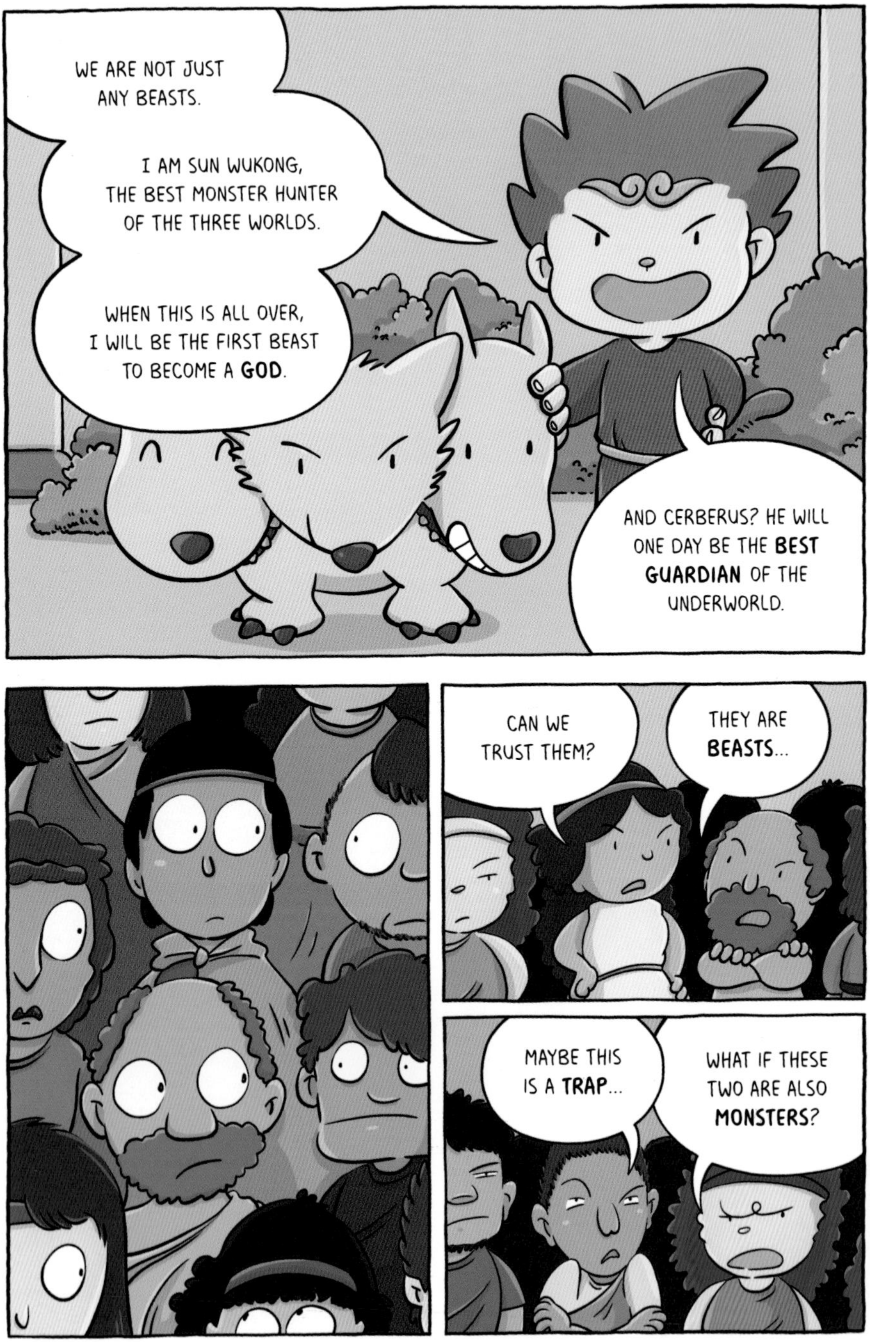
WE ARE NOT JUST ANY BEASTS.
I AM SUN WUKONG, THE BEST MONSTER HUNTER OF THE THREE WORLDS.
WHEN THIS IS ALL OVER, I WILL BE THE FIRST BEAST TO BECOME A **GOD**.
AND CERBERUS? HE WILL ONE DAY BE THE **BEST GUARDIAN** OF THE UNDERWORLD.
CAN WE TRUST THEM?
THEY ARE **BEASTS**...
MAYBE THIS IS A **TRAP**...
WHAT IF THESE TWO ARE ALSO **MONSTERS**?

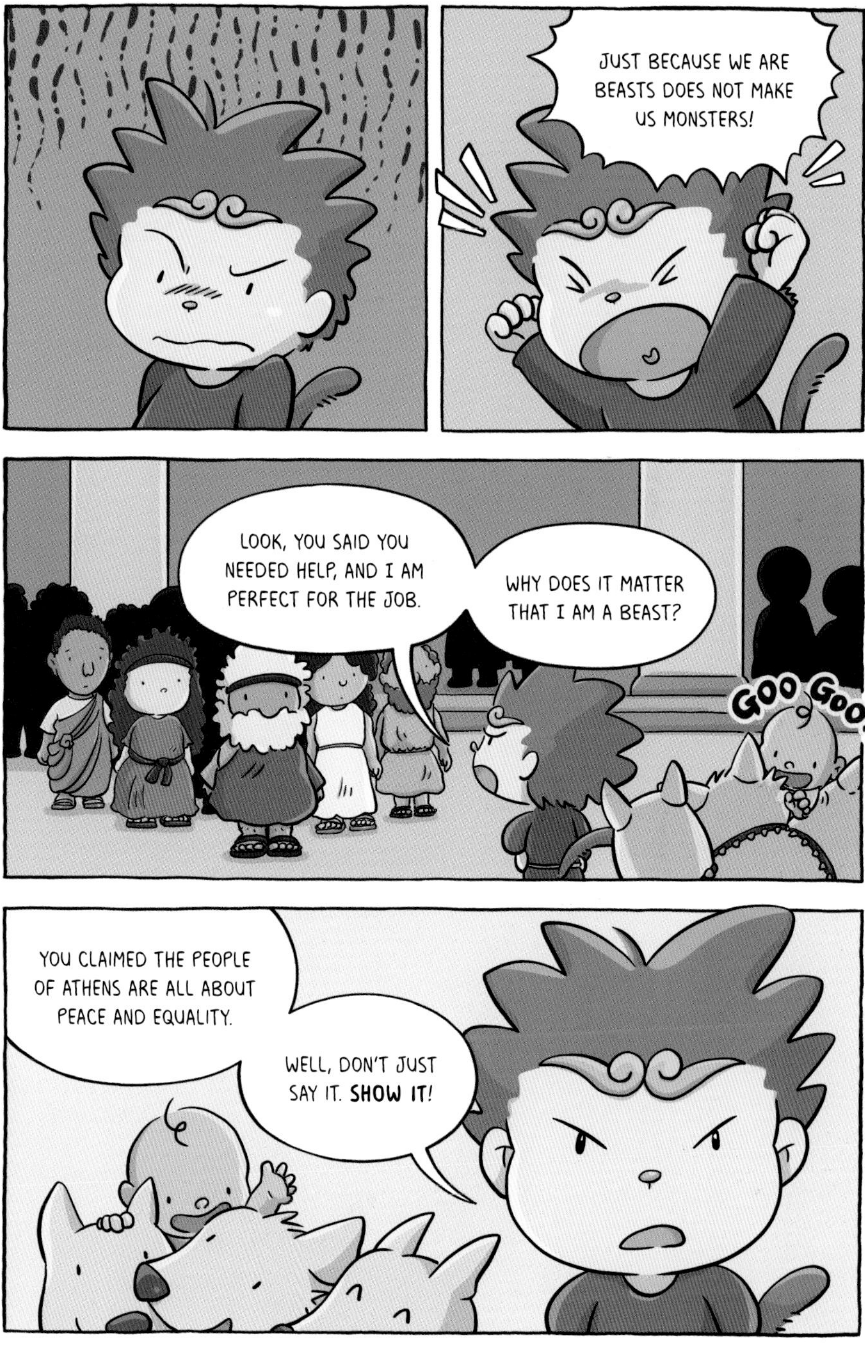
JUST BECAUSE WE ARE BEASTS DOES NOT MAKE US MONSTERS!
LOOK, YOU SAID YOU NEEDED HELP, AND I AM PERFECT FOR THE JOB.
WHY DOES IT MATTER THAT I AM A BEAST?
GOO GOO!
YOU CLAIMED THE PEOPLE OF ATHENS ARE ALL ABOUT PEACE AND EQUALITY.
WELL, DON'T JUST SAY IT. **SHOW IT**!

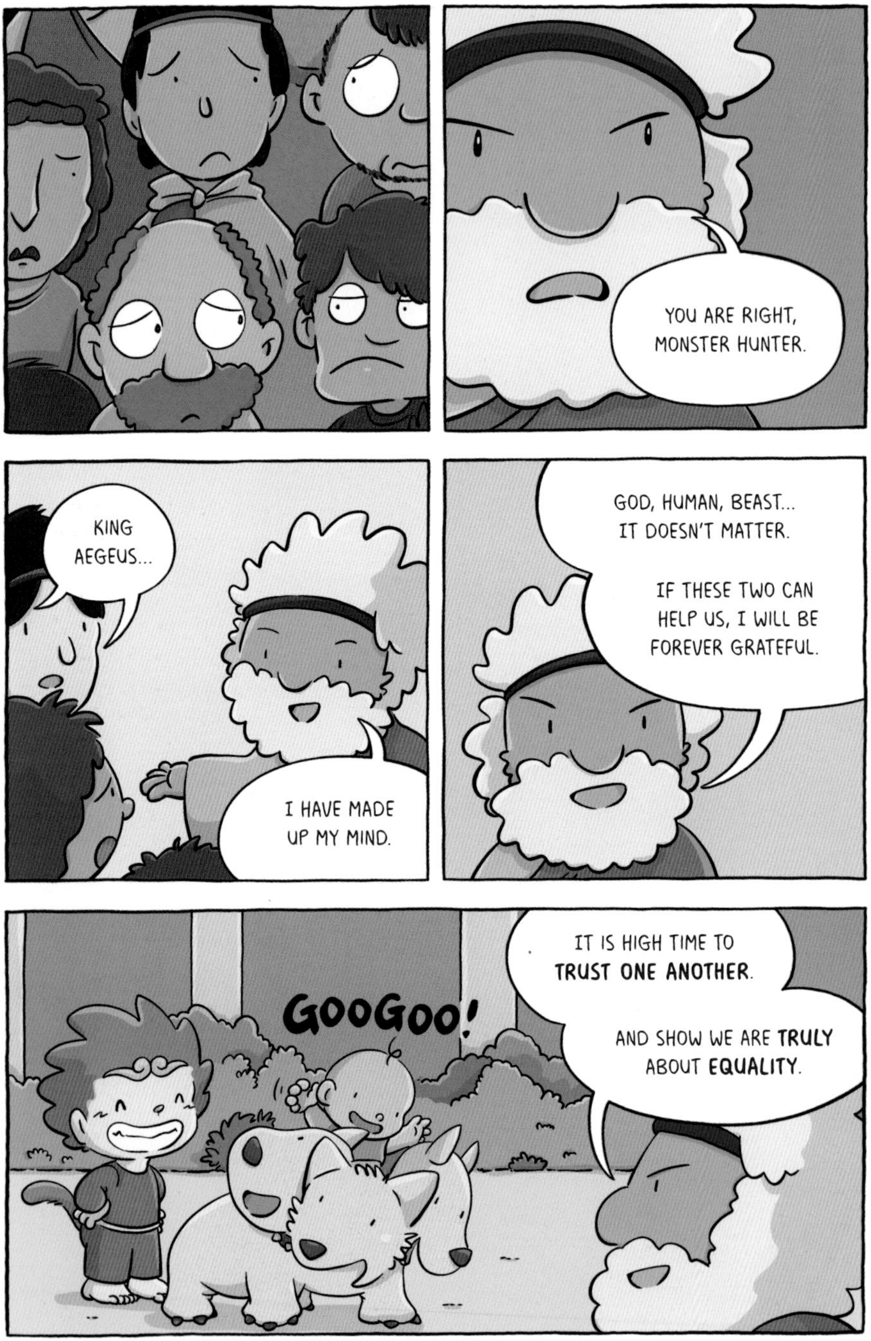
YOU ARE RIGHT, MONSTER HUNTER.
KING AEGEUS...
I HAVE MADE UP MY MIND.
GOD, HUMAN, BEAST... IT DOESN'T MATTER.
IF THESE TWO CAN HELP US, I WILL BE FOREVER GRATEFUL.
GOOGOO!
IT IS HIGH TIME TO **TRUST ONE ANOTHER**.
AND SHOW WE ARE **TRULY** ABOUT **EQUALITY**.

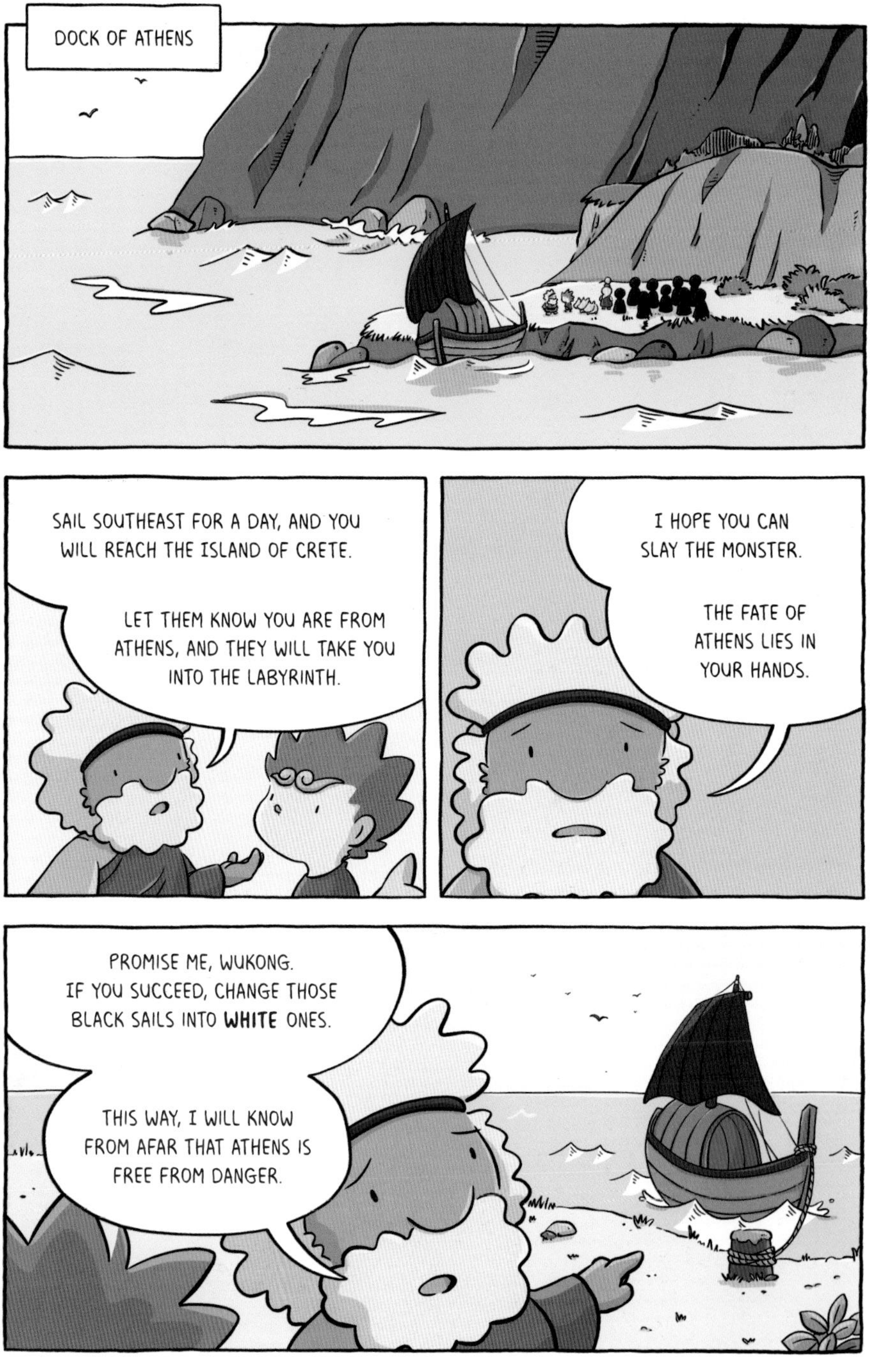
DOCK OF ATHENS
SAIL SOUTHEAST FOR A DAY, AND YOU WILL REACH THE ISLAND OF CRETE.
LET THEM KNOW YOU ARE FROM ATHENS, AND THEY WILL TAKE YOU INTO THE LABYRINTH.
I HOPE YOU CAN SLAY THE MONSTER.
THE FATE OF ATHENS LIES IN YOUR HANDS.
PROMISE ME, WUKONG. IF YOU SUCCEED, CHANGE THOSE BLACK SAILS INTO **WHITE** ONES.
THIS WAY, I WILL KNOW FROM AFAR THAT ATHENS IS FREE FROM DANGER.

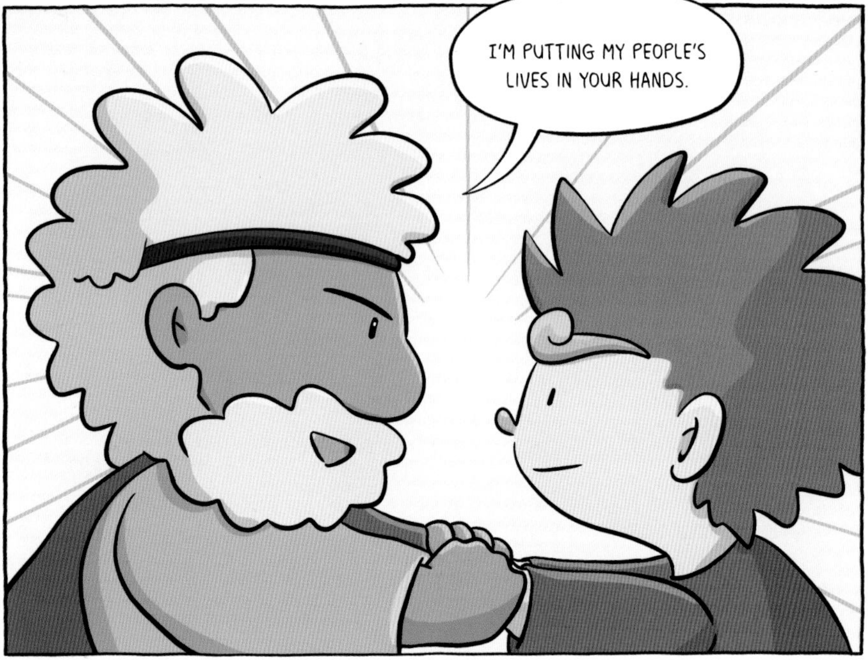
I'M PUTTING MY PEOPLE'S LIVES IN YOUR HANDS.

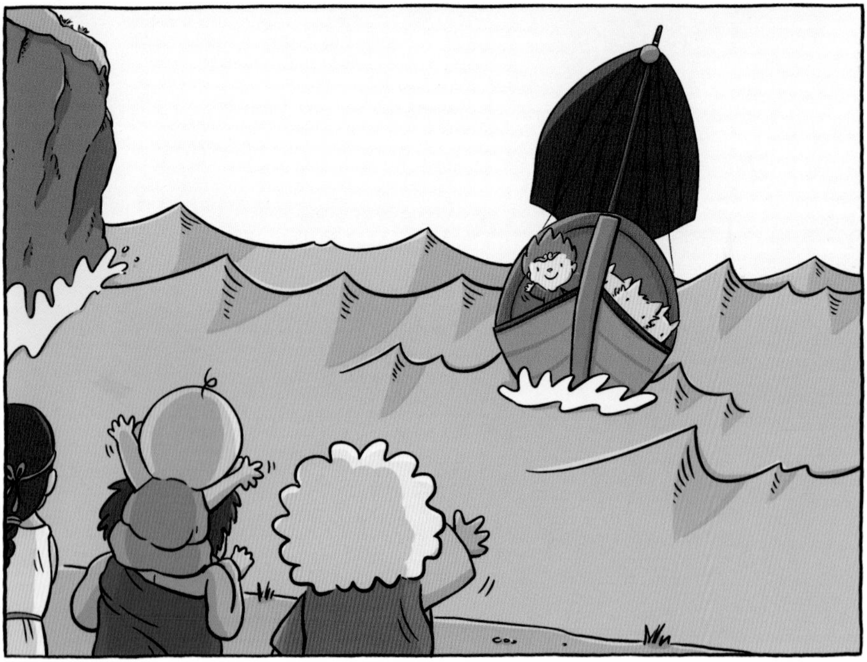

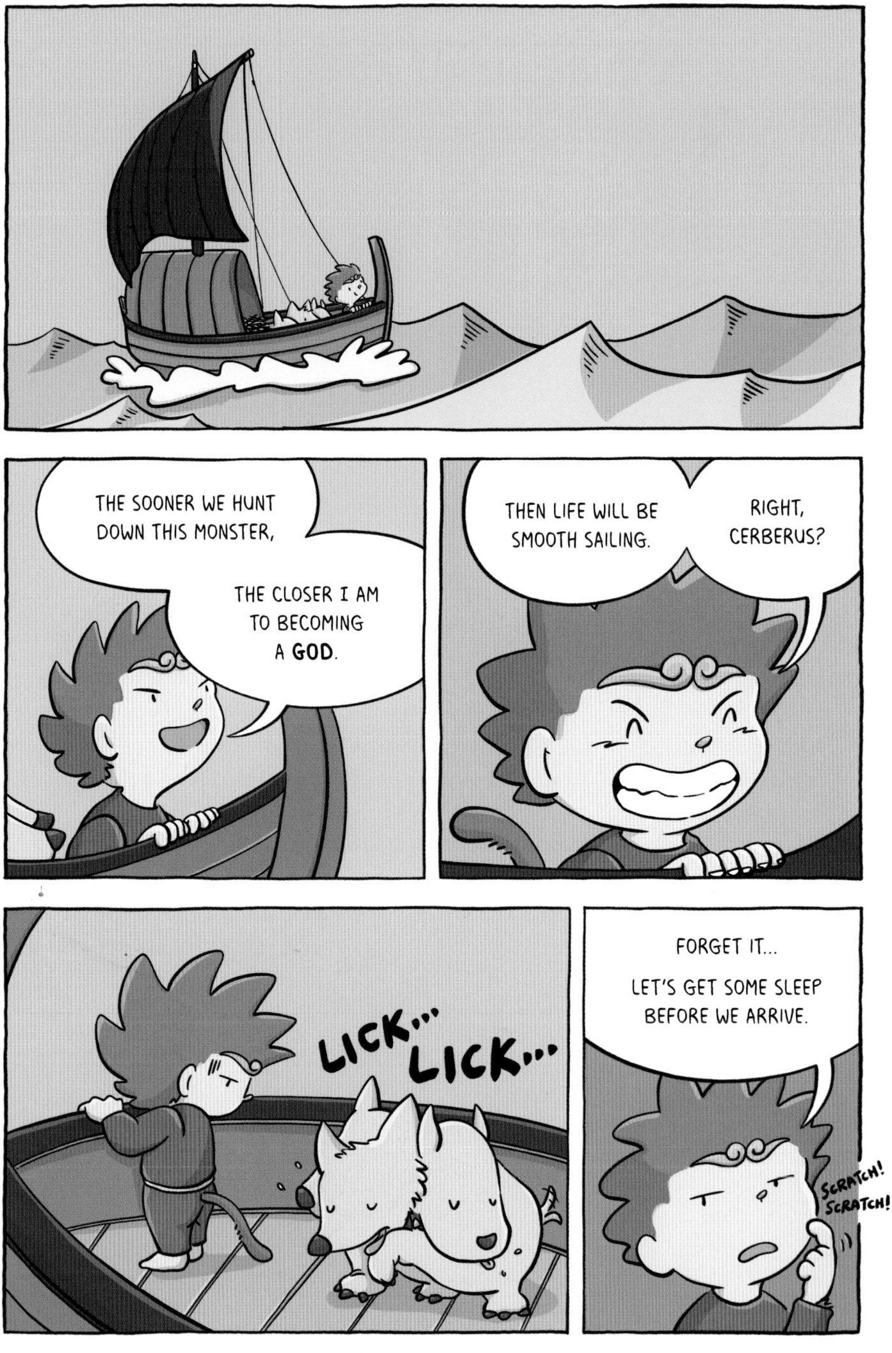
THE SOONER WE HUNT DOWN THIS MONSTER,
THE CLOSER I AM TO BECOMING A **GOD**.
THEN LIFE WILL BE SMOOTH SAILING.
RIGHT, CERBERUS?
LICK... LICK...
FORGET IT...
LET'S GET SOME SLEEP BEFORE WE ARRIVE.
SCRATCH! SCRATCH!

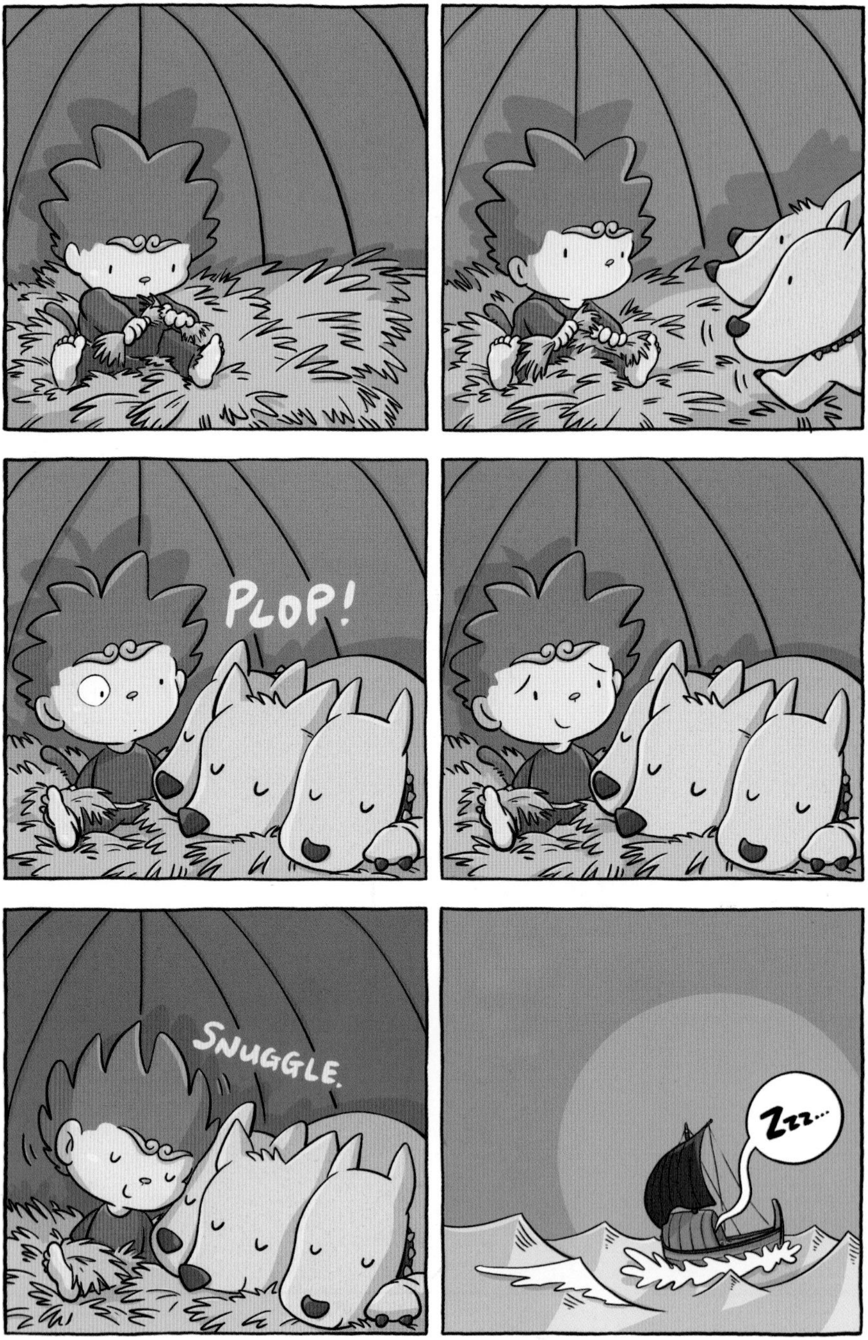
PLOP!
SNUGGLE.
Zzz...

CHAPTER 6 THE ISLAND OF CRETE

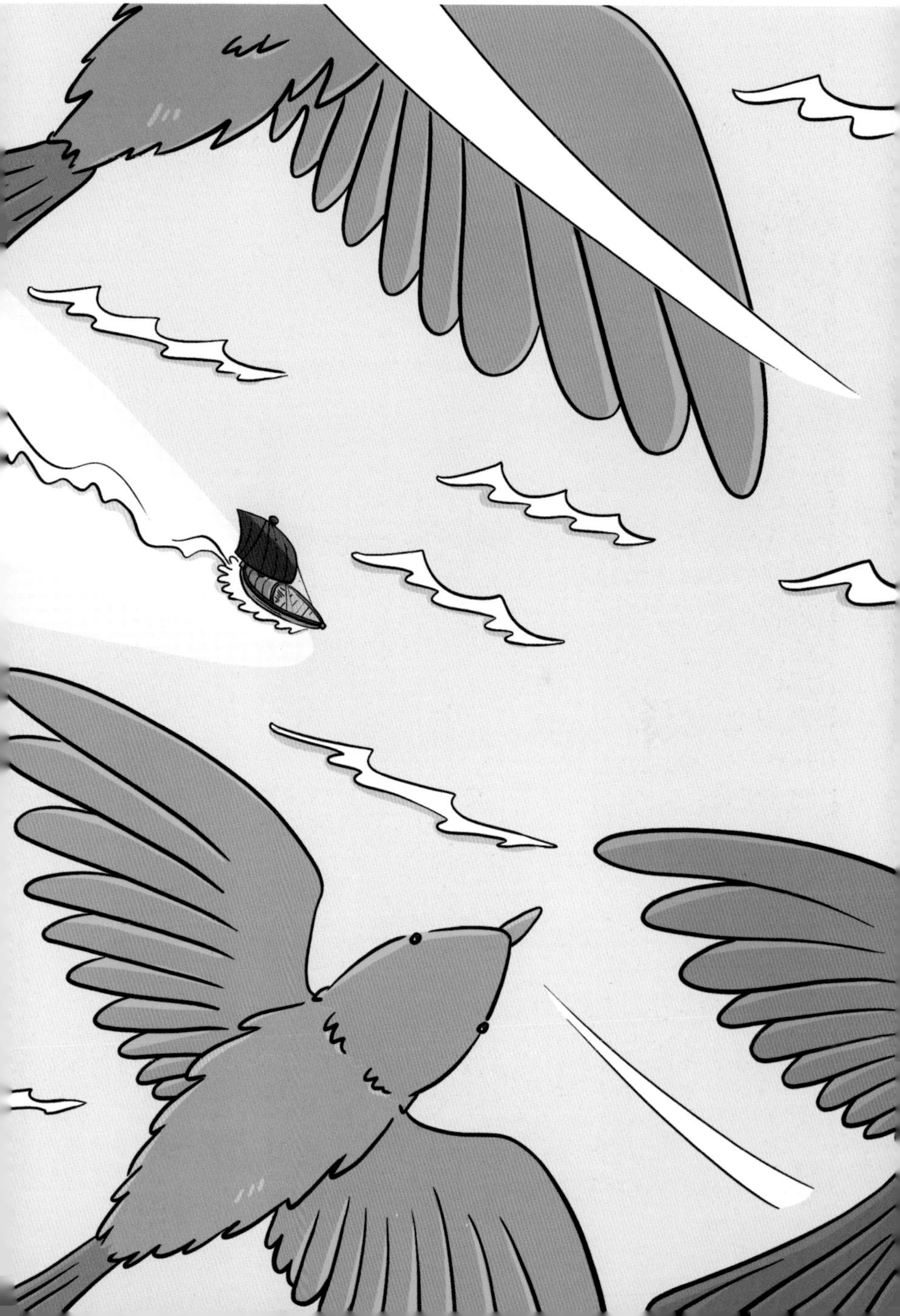

ISLAND OF CRETE

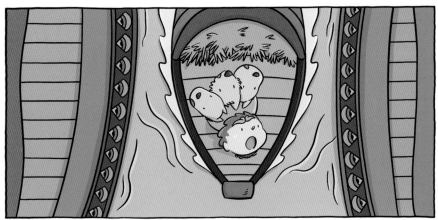

WOW! THE MINOAN NAVAL FLEETS **ARE** IMPRESSIVE.

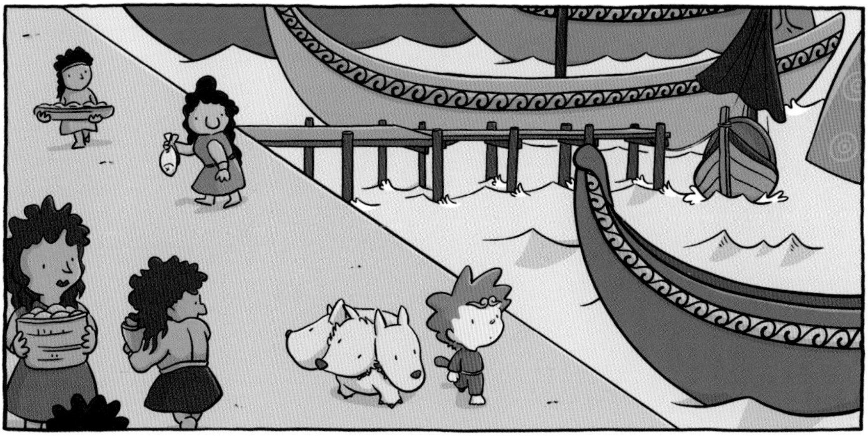

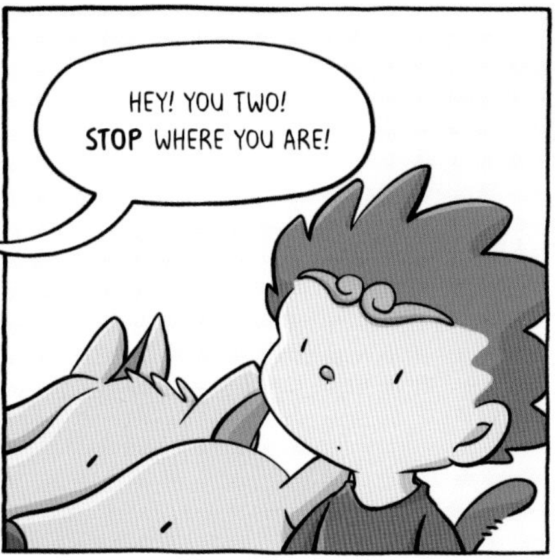
HEY! YOU TWO!
STOP WHERE YOU ARE!

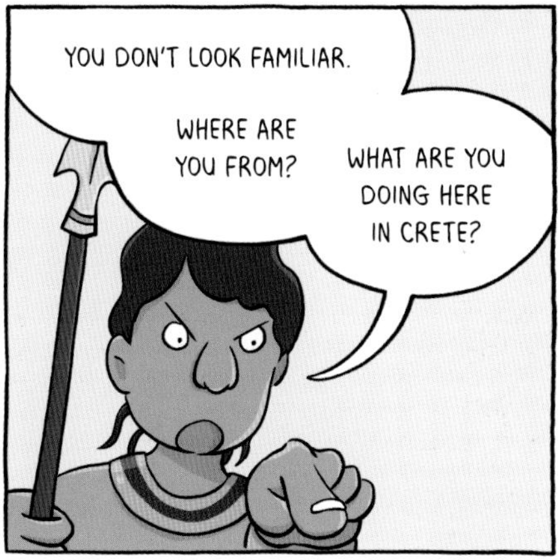
YOU DON'T LOOK FAMILIAR.
WHERE ARE YOU FROM?
WHAT ARE YOU DOING HERE IN CRETE?

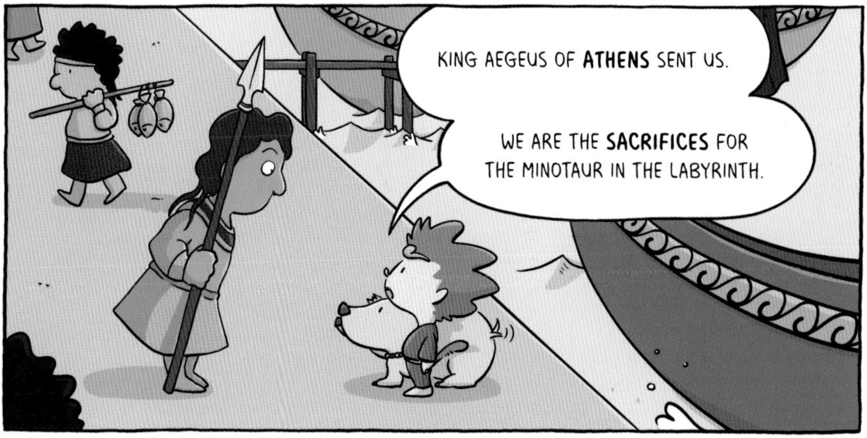
KING AEGEUS OF **ATHENS** SENT US.
WE ARE THE **SACRIFICES** FOR THE MINOTAUR IN THE LABYRINTH.

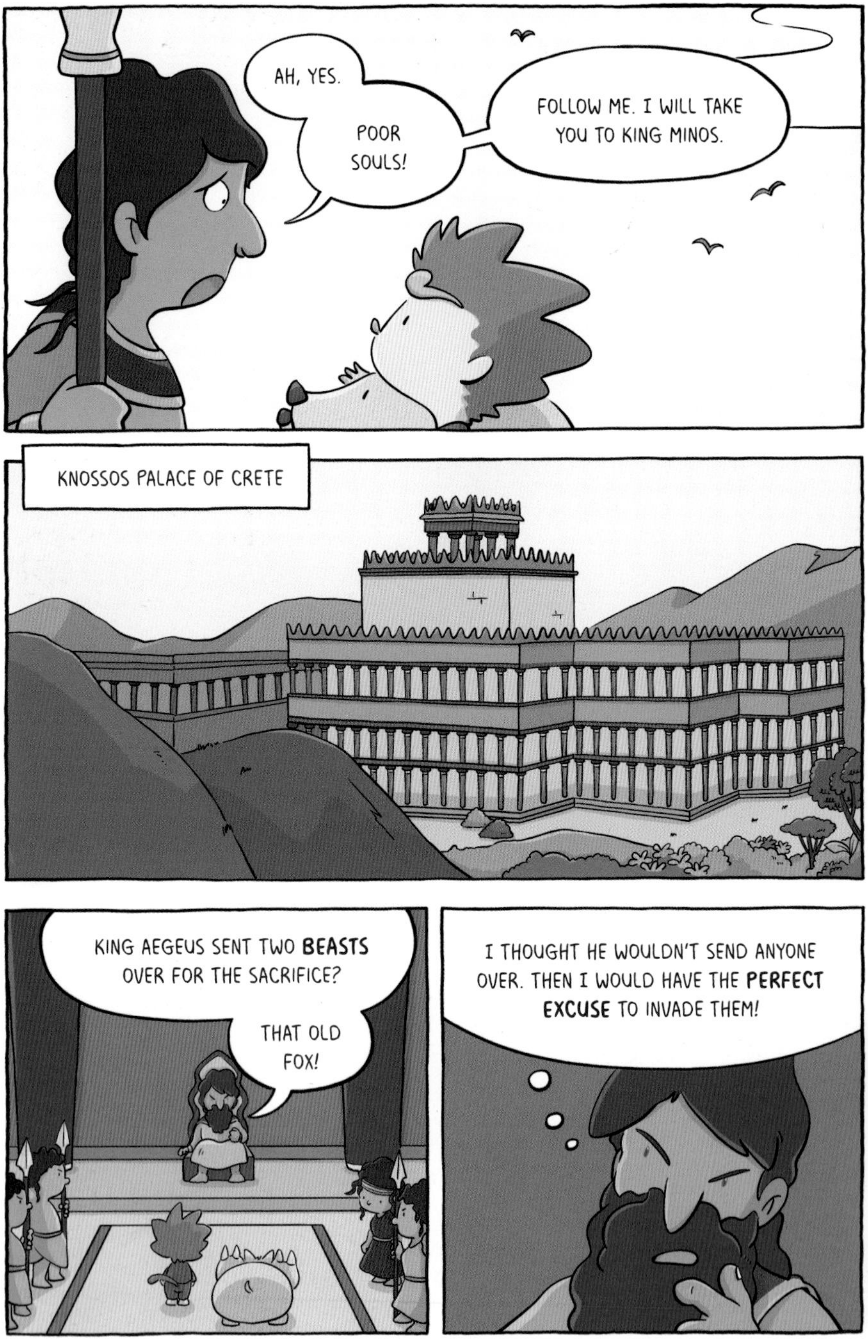
AH, YES.
POOR SOULS!
FOLLOW ME. I WILL TAKE YOU TO KING MINOS.
KNOSSOS PALACE OF CRETE
KING AEGEUS SENT TWO **BEASTS** OVER FOR THE SACRIFICE?
THAT OLD FOX!
I THOUGHT HE WOULDN'T SEND ANYONE OVER. THEN I WOULD HAVE THE **PERFECT EXCUSE** TO INVADE THEM!

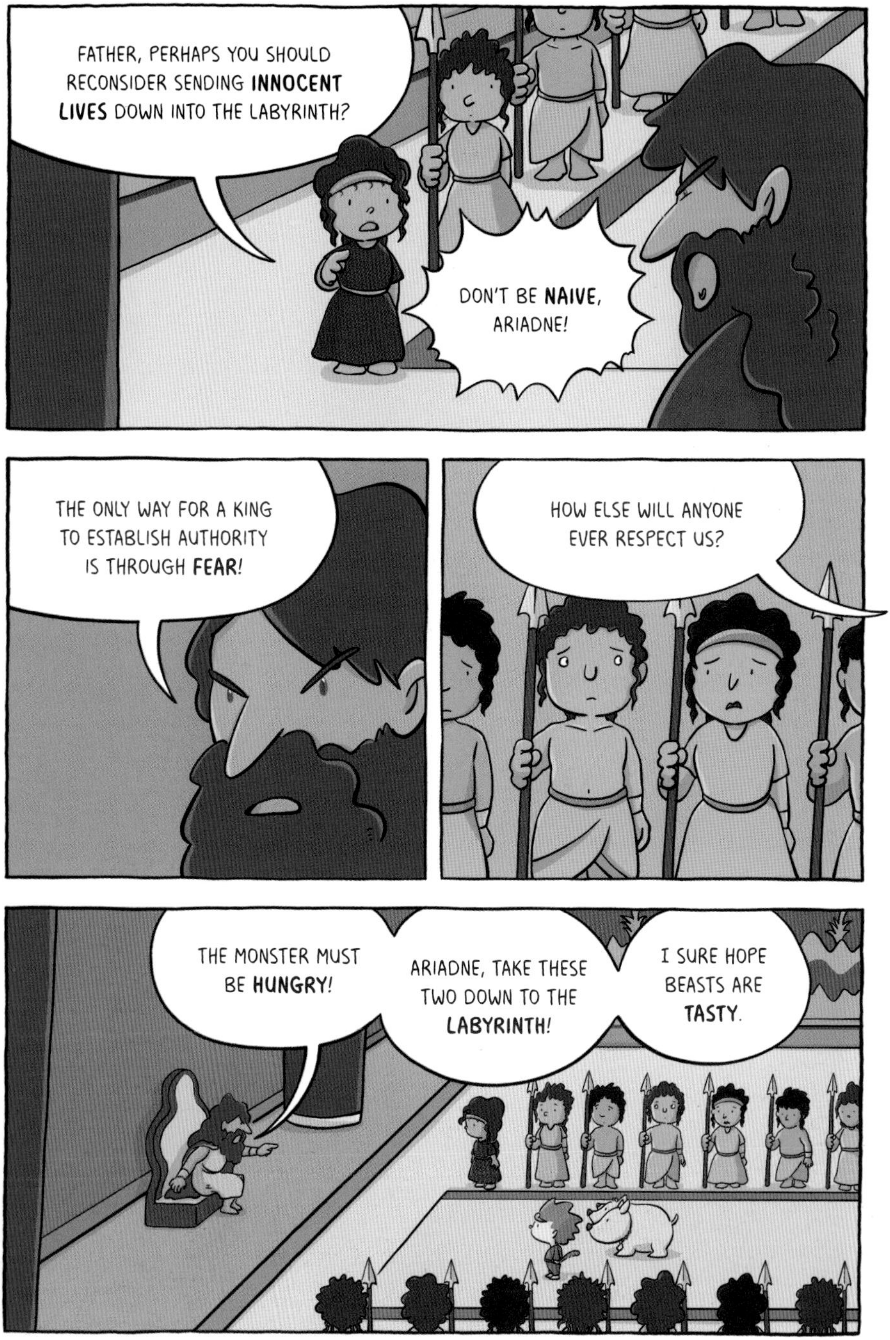
FATHER, PERHAPS YOU SHOULD RECONSIDER SENDING **INNOCENT LIVES** DOWN INTO THE LABYRINTH?
DON'T BE **NAIVE**, ARIADNE!
THE ONLY WAY FOR A KING TO ESTABLISH AUTHORITY IS THROUGH **FEAR**!
HOW ELSE WILL ANYONE EVER RESPECT US?
THE MONSTER MUST BE **HUNGRY**!
ARIADNE, TAKE THESE TWO DOWN TO THE **LABYRINTH**!
I SURE HOPE BEASTS ARE **TASTY**.

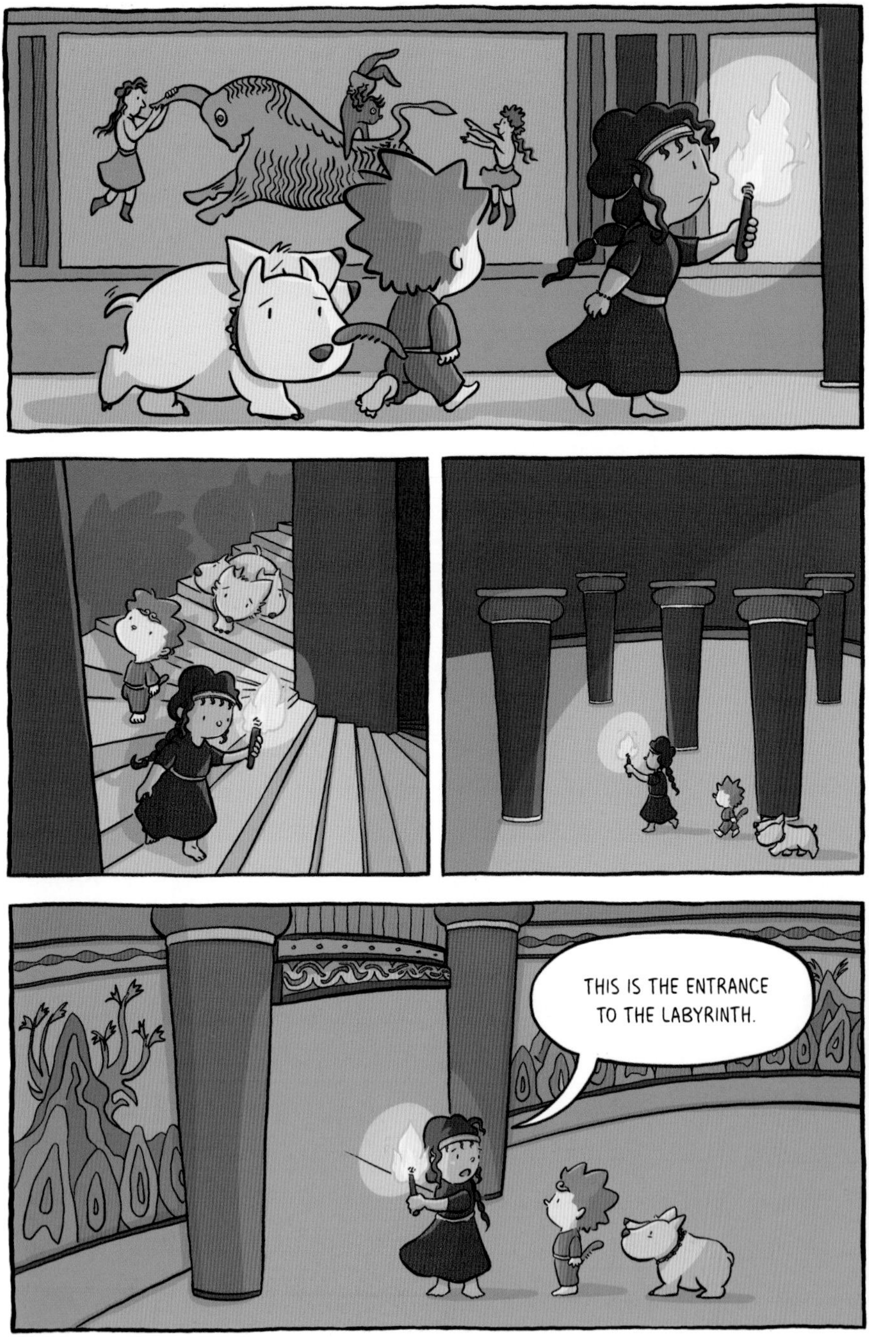
THIS IS THE ENTRANCE TO THE LABYRINTH.

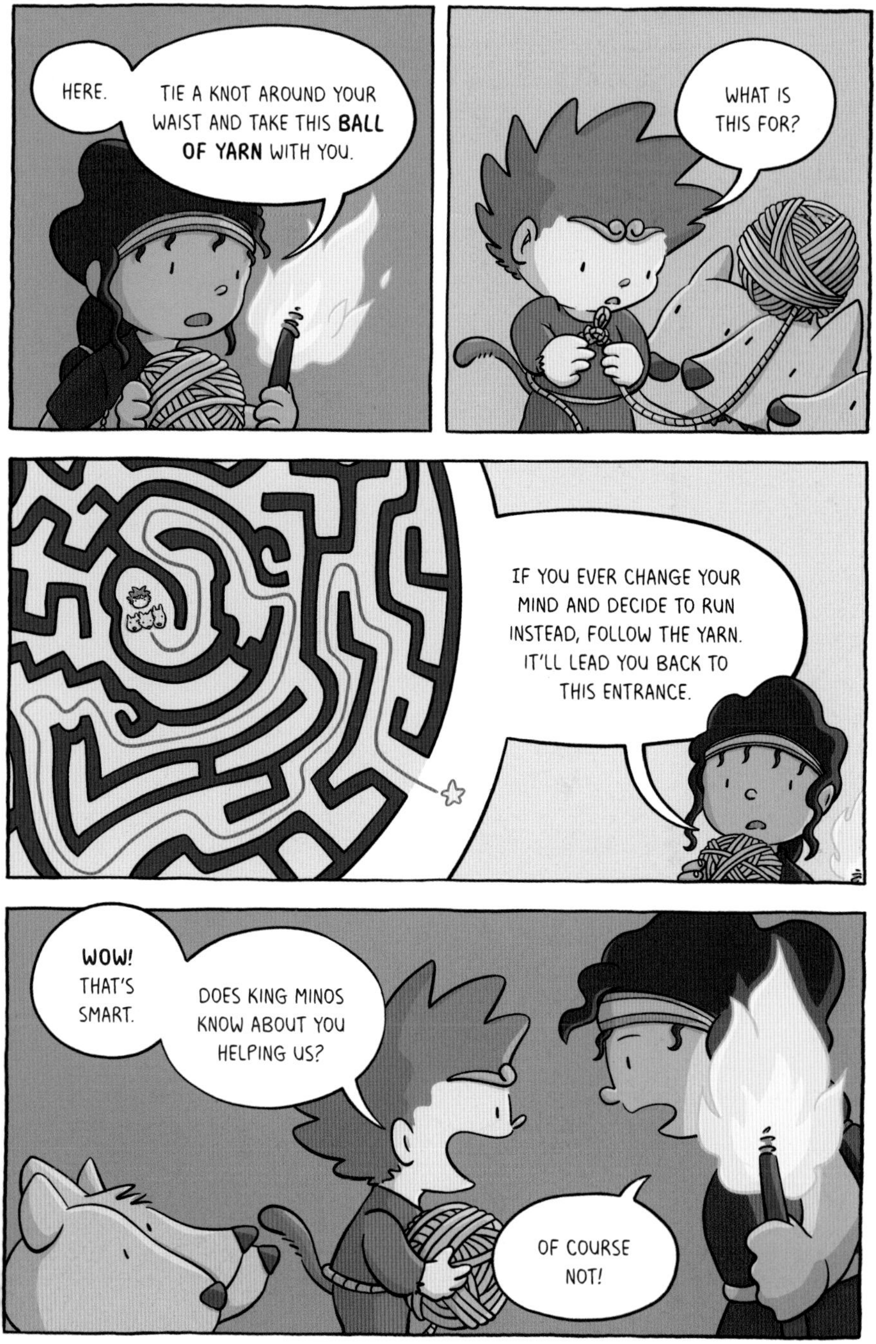
HERE.
TIE A KNOT AROUND YOUR WAIST AND TAKE THIS **BALL OF YARN** WITH YOU.
WHAT IS THIS FOR?
IF YOU EVER CHANGE YOUR MIND AND DECIDE TO RUN INSTEAD, FOLLOW THE YARN. IT'LL LEAD YOU BACK TO THIS ENTRANCE.
WOW! THAT'S SMART.
DOES KING MINOS KNOW ABOUT YOU HELPING US?
OF COURSE NOT!

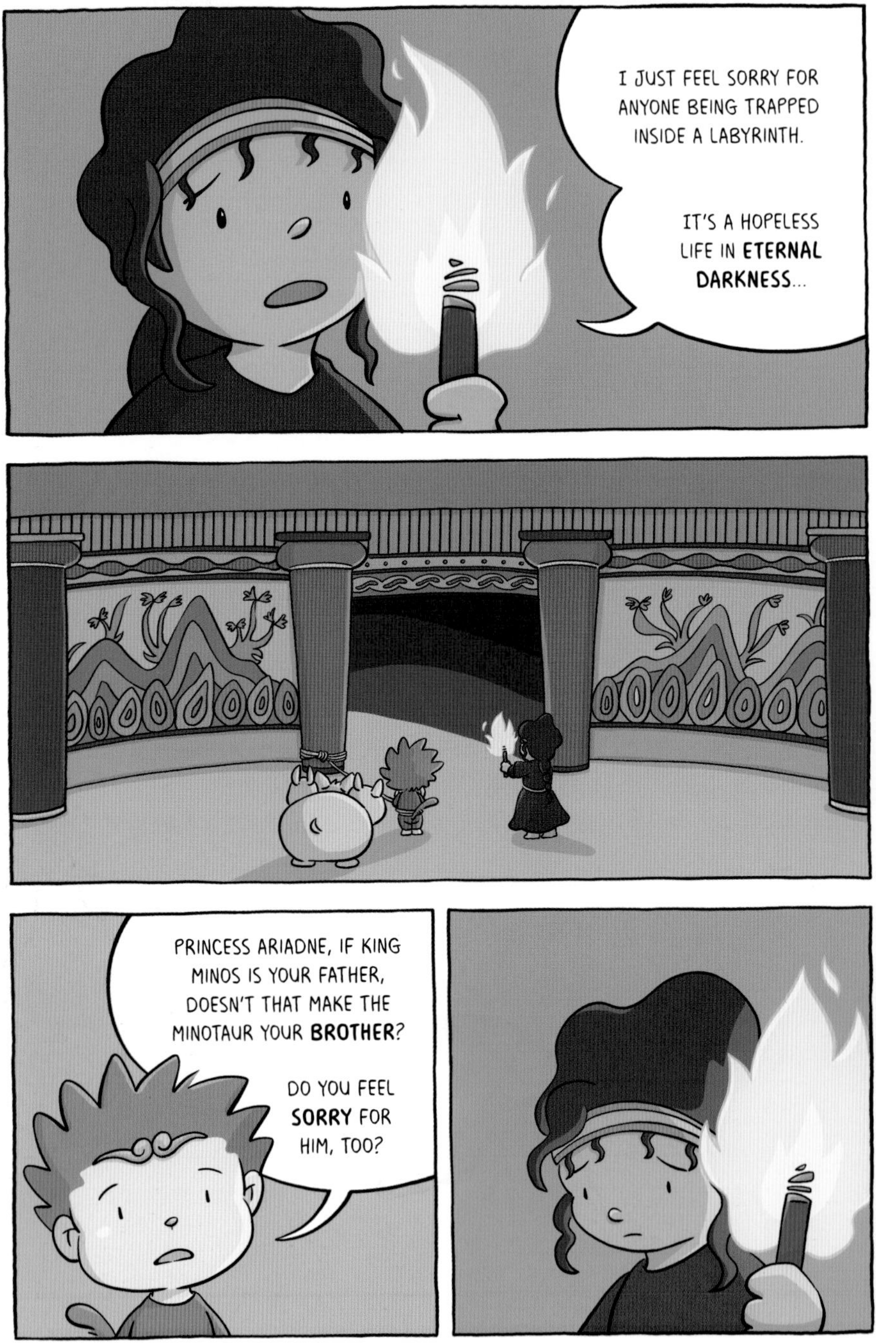
I JUST FEEL SORRY FOR ANYONE BEING TRAPPED INSIDE A LABYRINTH.
IT'S A HOPELESS LIFE IN **ETERNAL DARKNESS**...
PRINCESS ARIADNE, IF KING MINOS IS YOUR FATHER, DOESN'T THAT MAKE THE MINOTAUR YOUR **BROTHER**?
DO YOU FEEL **SORRY** FOR HIM, TOO?

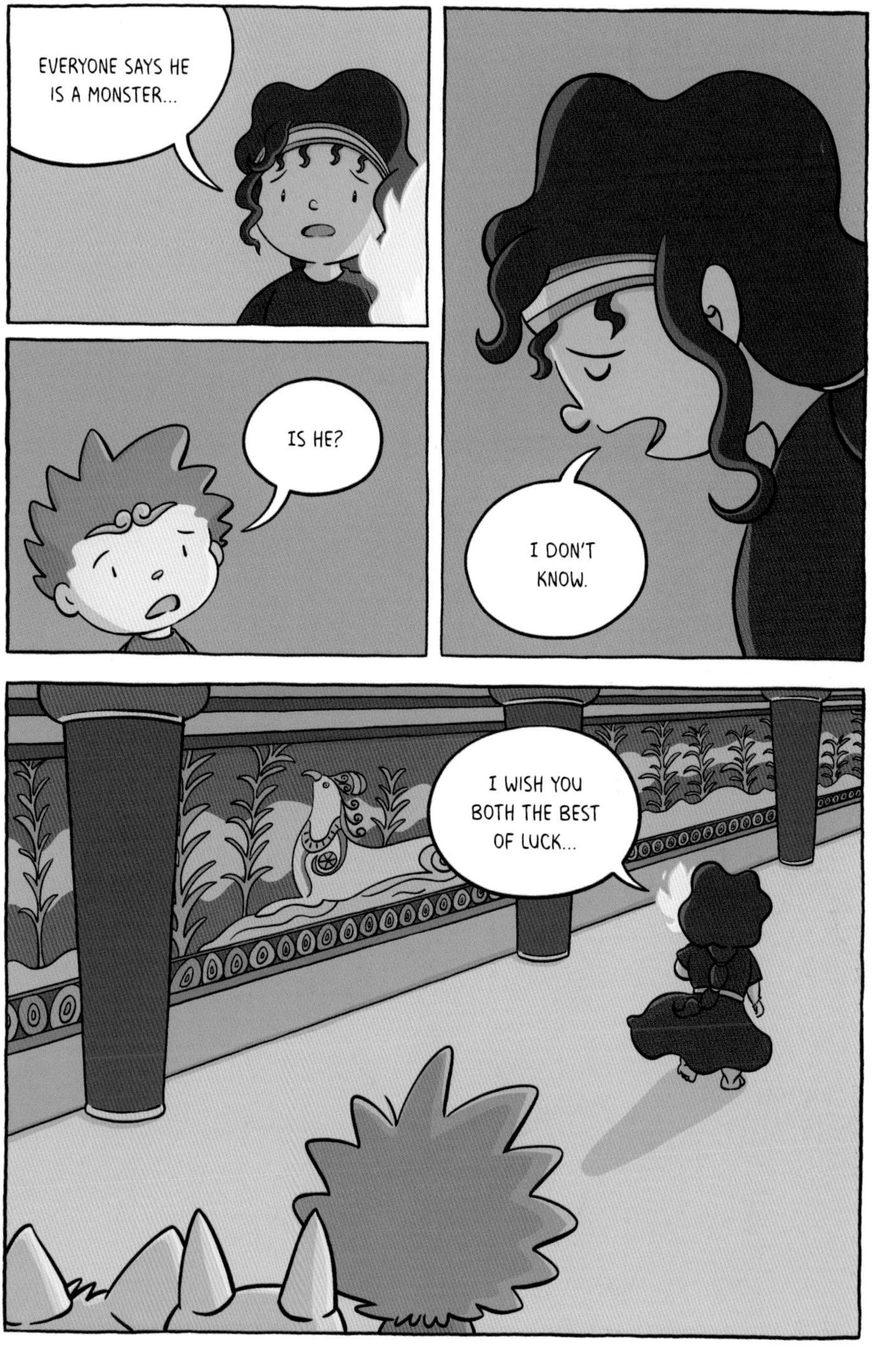
EVERYONE SAYS HE IS A MONSTER...
IS HE?
I DON'T KNOW.
I WISH YOU BOTH THE BEST OF LUCK...

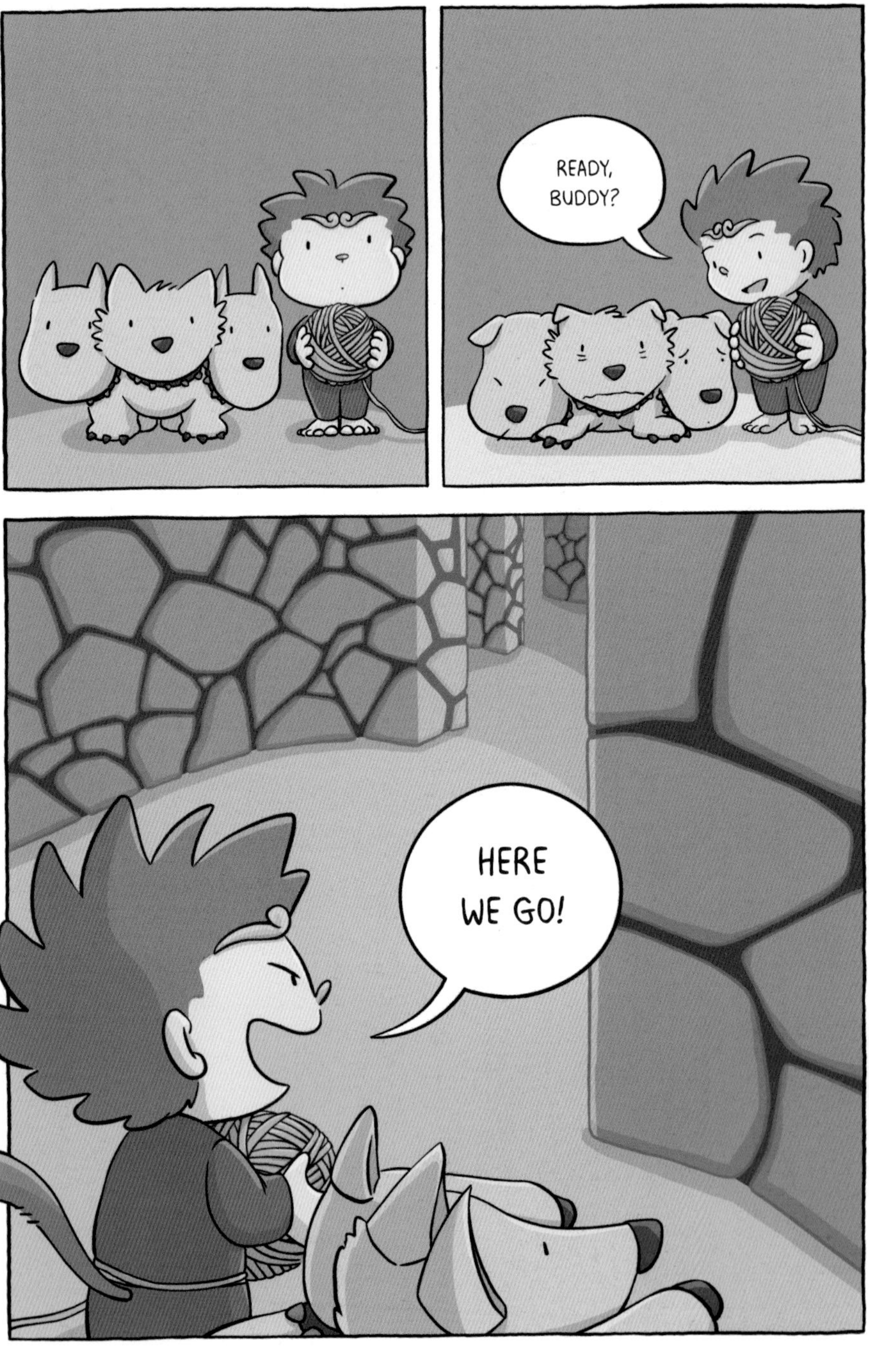
READY, BUDDY?
HERE WE GO!

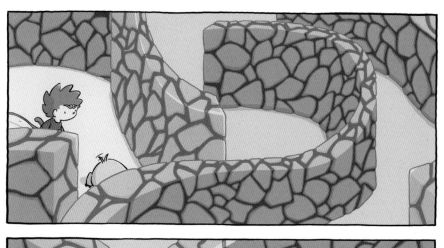

SERIOUSLY, CERBERUS!

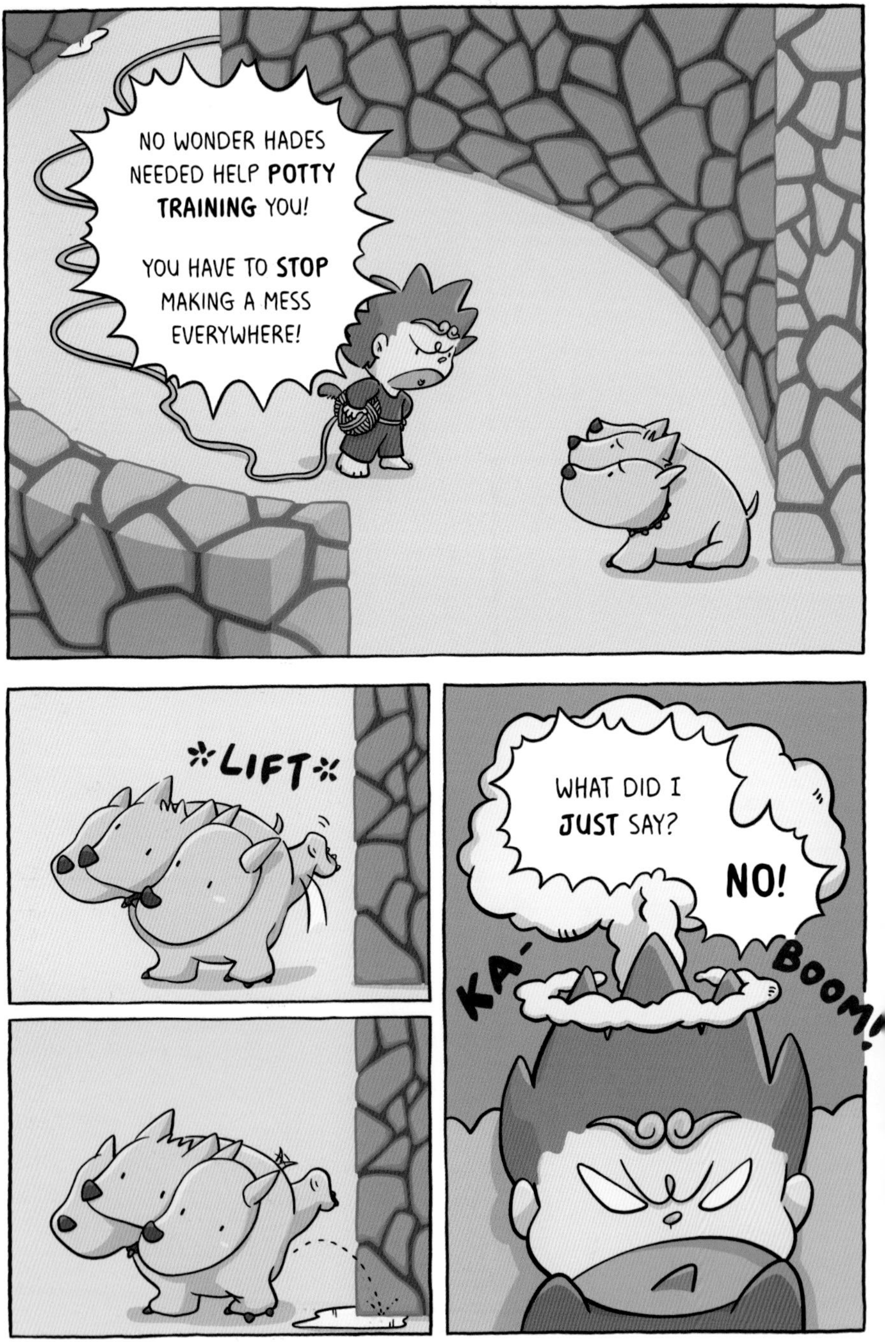
NO WONDER HADES NEEDED HELP POTTY TRAINING YOU!
YOU HAVE TO STOP MAKING A MESS EVERYWHERE!
LIFT
WHAT DID I JUST SAY?
NO!
KA-BOOM!

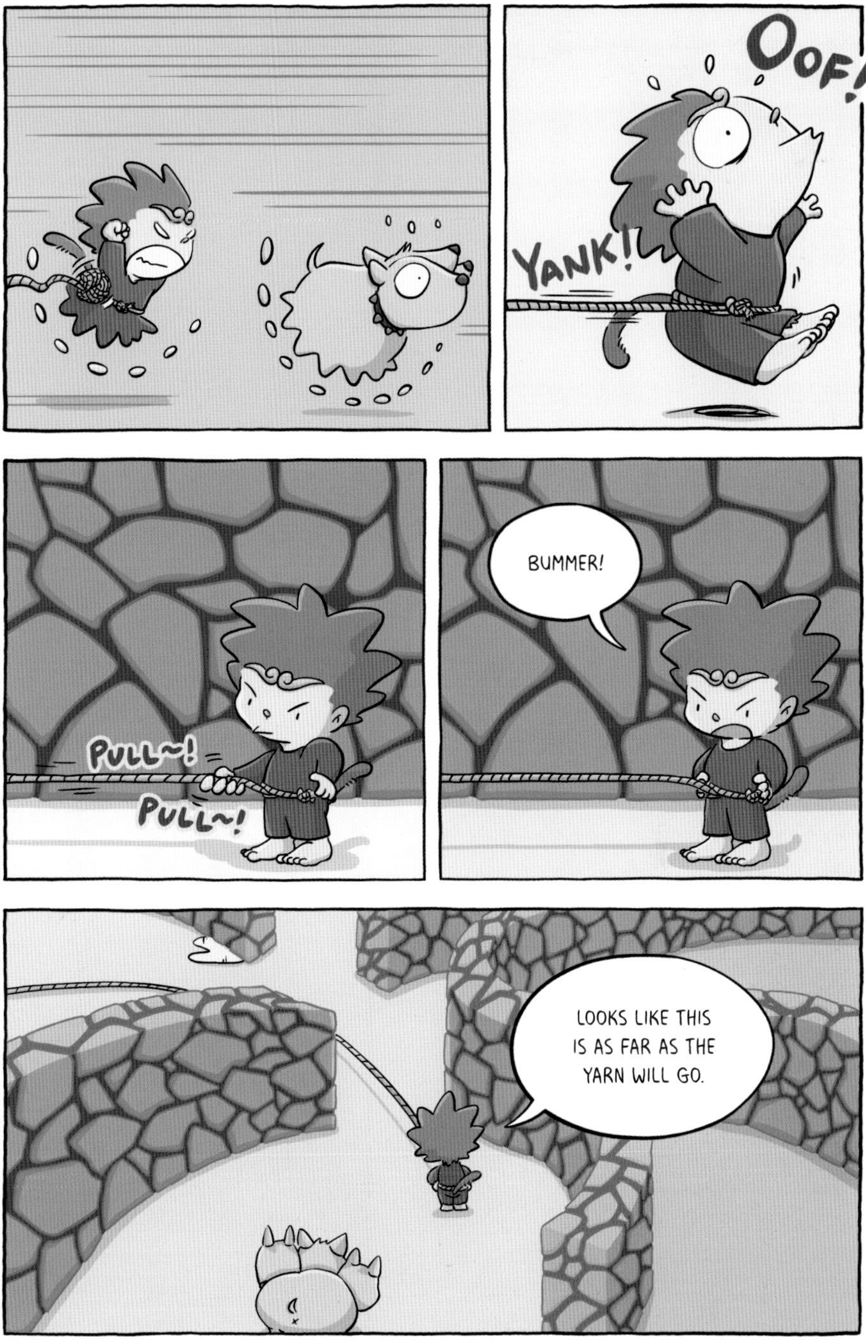
OOF!
YANK!
PULL~!
PULL~!
BUMMER!
LOOKS LIKE THIS IS AS FAR AS THE YARN WILL GO.

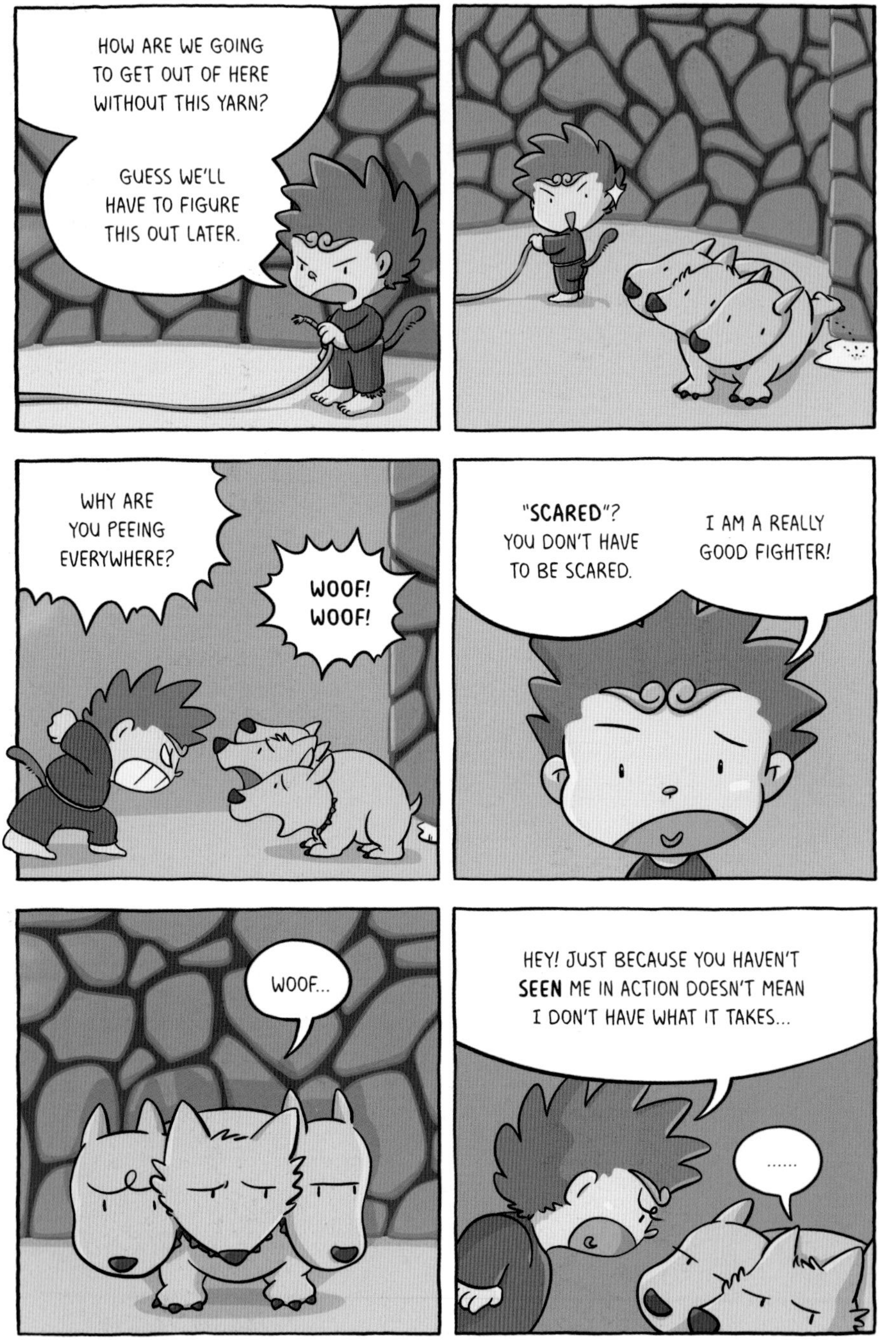
HOW ARE WE GOING TO GET OUT OF HERE WITHOUT THIS YARN?
GUESS WE'LL HAVE TO FIGURE THIS OUT LATER.
WHY ARE YOU PEEING EVERYWHERE?
WOOF! WOOF!
"SCARED"? YOU DON'T HAVE TO BE SCARED.
I AM A REALLY GOOD FIGHTER!
WOOF...
HEY! JUST BECAUSE YOU HAVEN'T SEEN ME IN ACTION DOESN'T MEAN I DON'T HAVE WHAT IT TAKES...
......

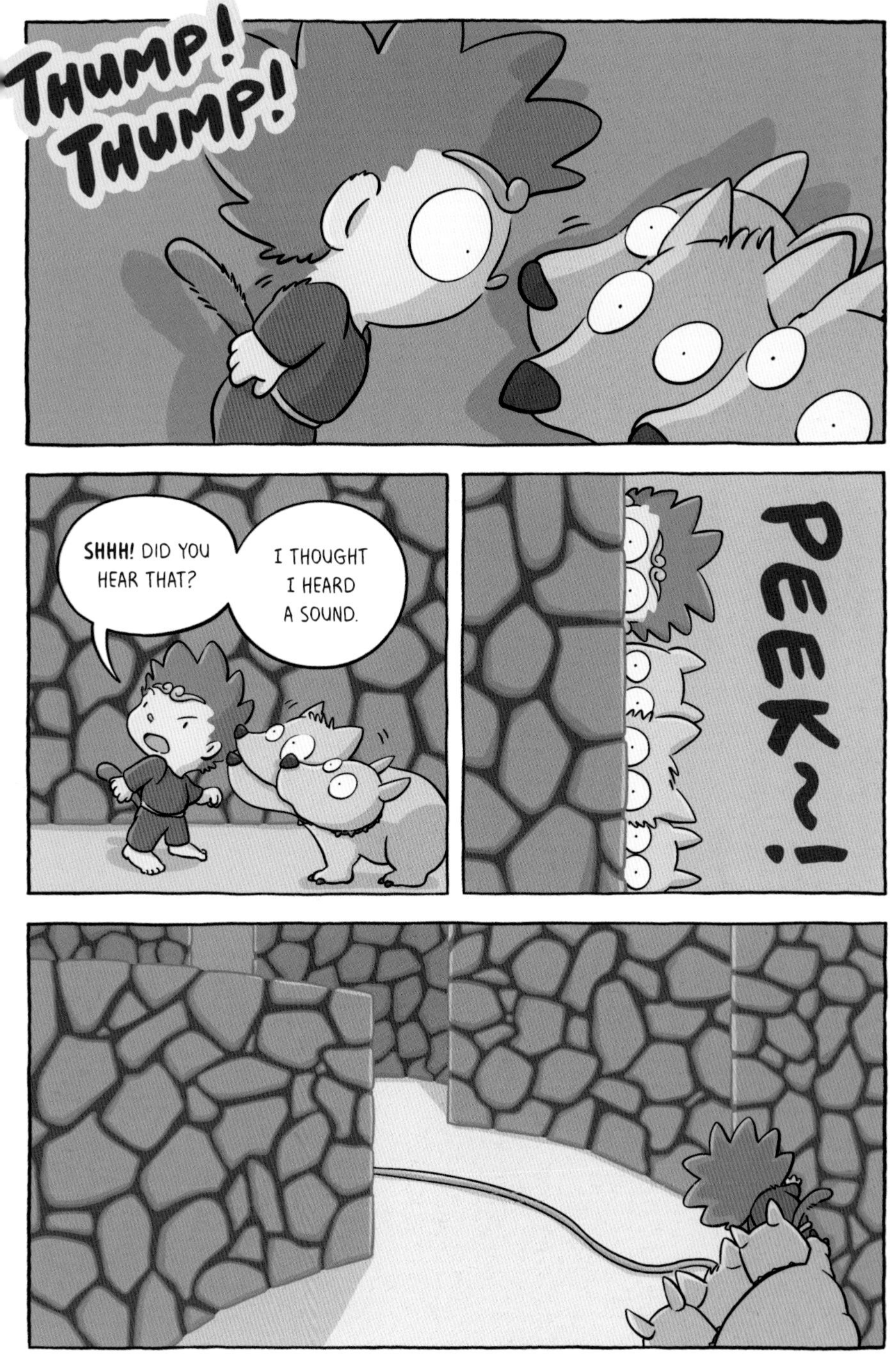
THUMP! THUMP!
SHHH! DID YOU HEAR THAT?
I THOUGHT I HEARD A SOUND.
PEEK~!

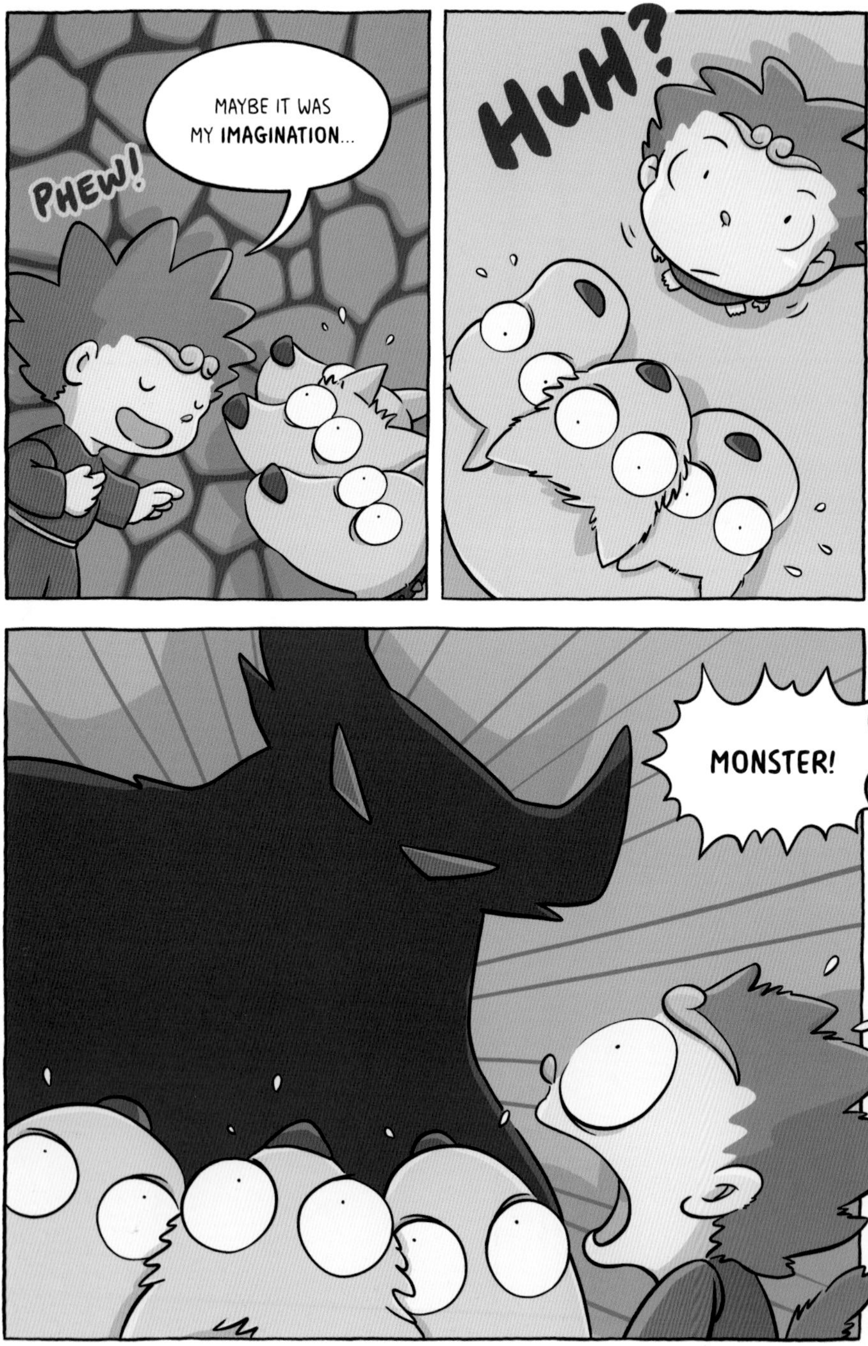
PHEW!
MAYBE IT WAS MY **IMAGINATION**...
HUH?
MONSTER!

CHAPTER 7

THE MINOTAUR OF THE LABYRINTH

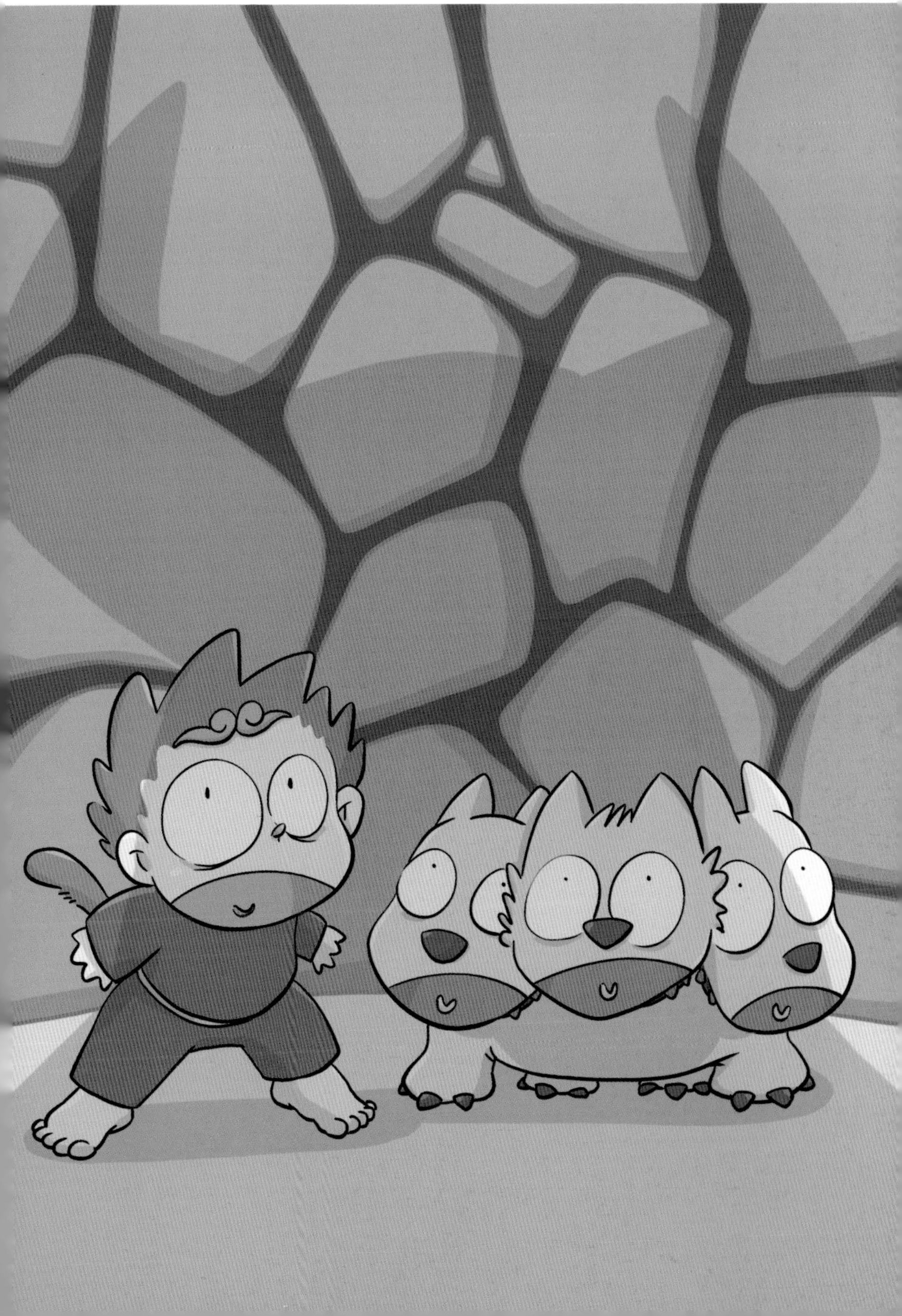

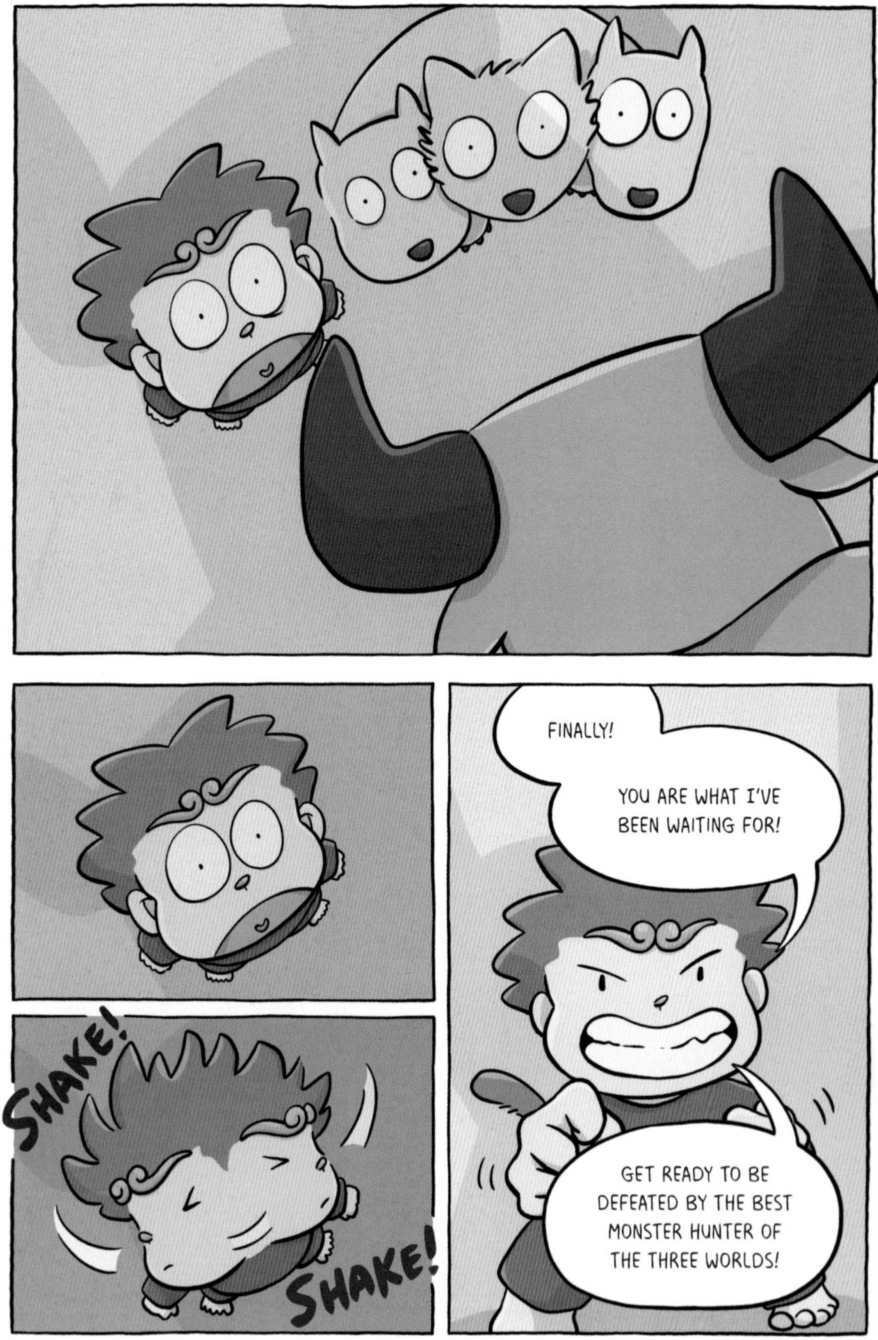
SHAKE!
SHAKE!
FINALLY!
YOU ARE WHAT I'VE BEEN WAITING FOR!
GET READY TO BE DEFEATED BY THE BEST MONSTER HUNTER OF THE THREE WORLDS!

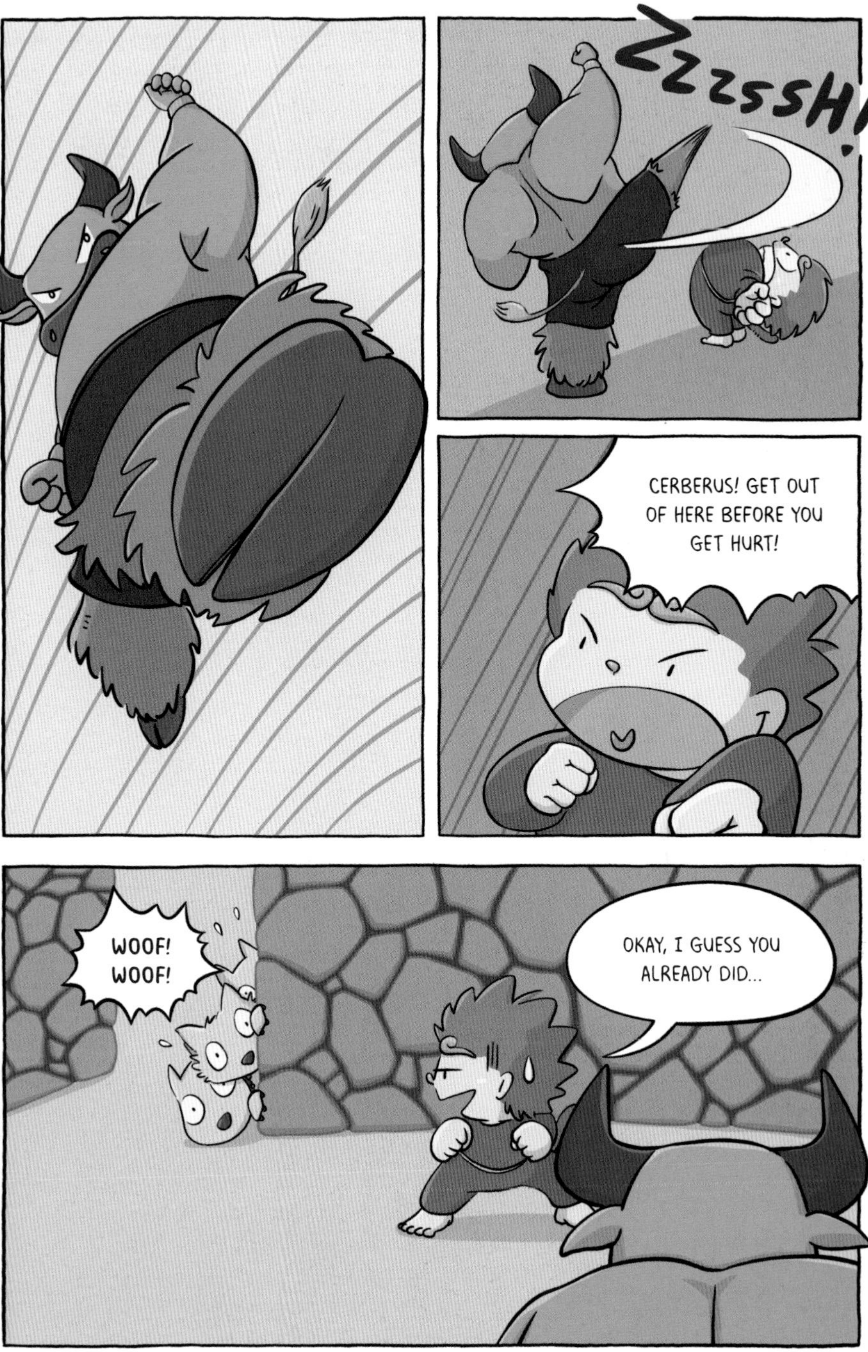
ZZZSSH!
CERBERUS! GET OUT OF HERE BEFORE YOU GET HURT!
WOOF! WOOF!
OKAY, I GUESS YOU ALREADY DID...

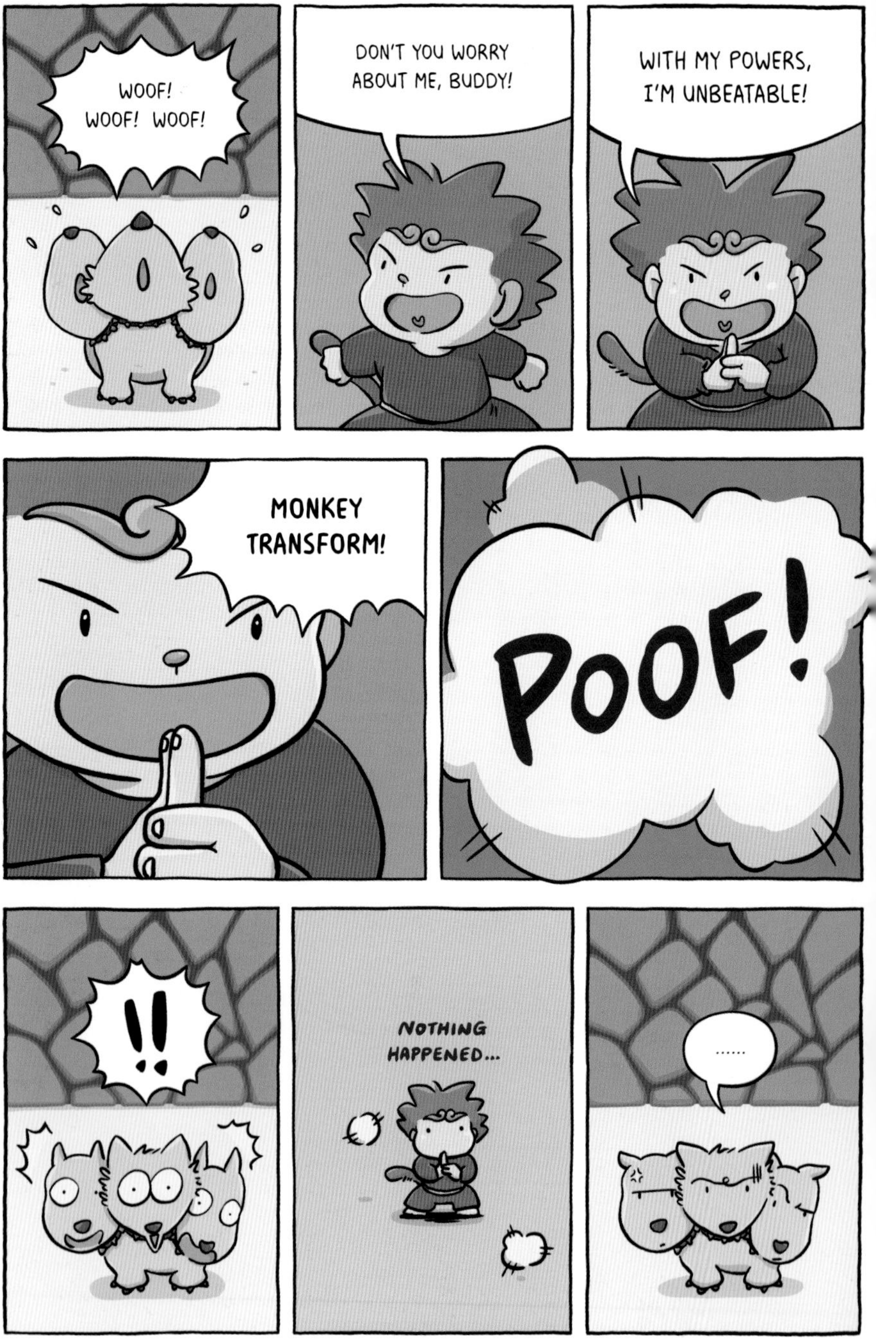
WOOF!
WOOF! WOOF!
DON'T YOU WORRY ABOUT ME, BUDDY!
WITH MY POWERS, I'M UNBEATABLE!
MONKEY TRANSFORM!
POOF!
!!
NOTHING HAPPENED...
......

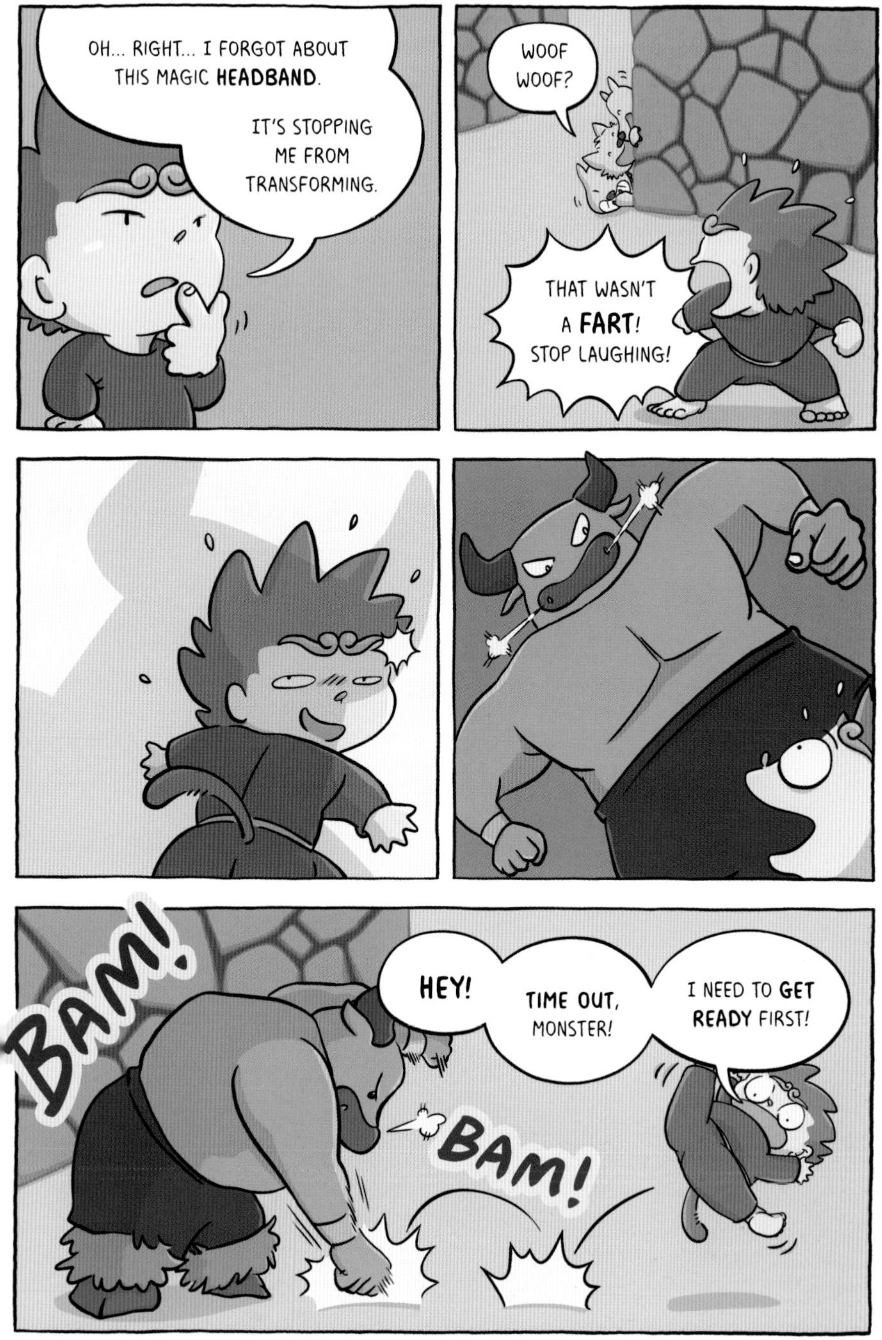
OH... RIGHT... I FORGOT ABOUT THIS MAGIC **HEADBAND**.
IT'S STOPPING ME FROM TRANSFORMING.
WOOF WOOF?
THAT WASN'T A **FART**! STOP LAUGHING!
BAM!
HEY!
TIME OUT, MONSTER!
I NEED TO **GET READY** FIRST!
BAM!

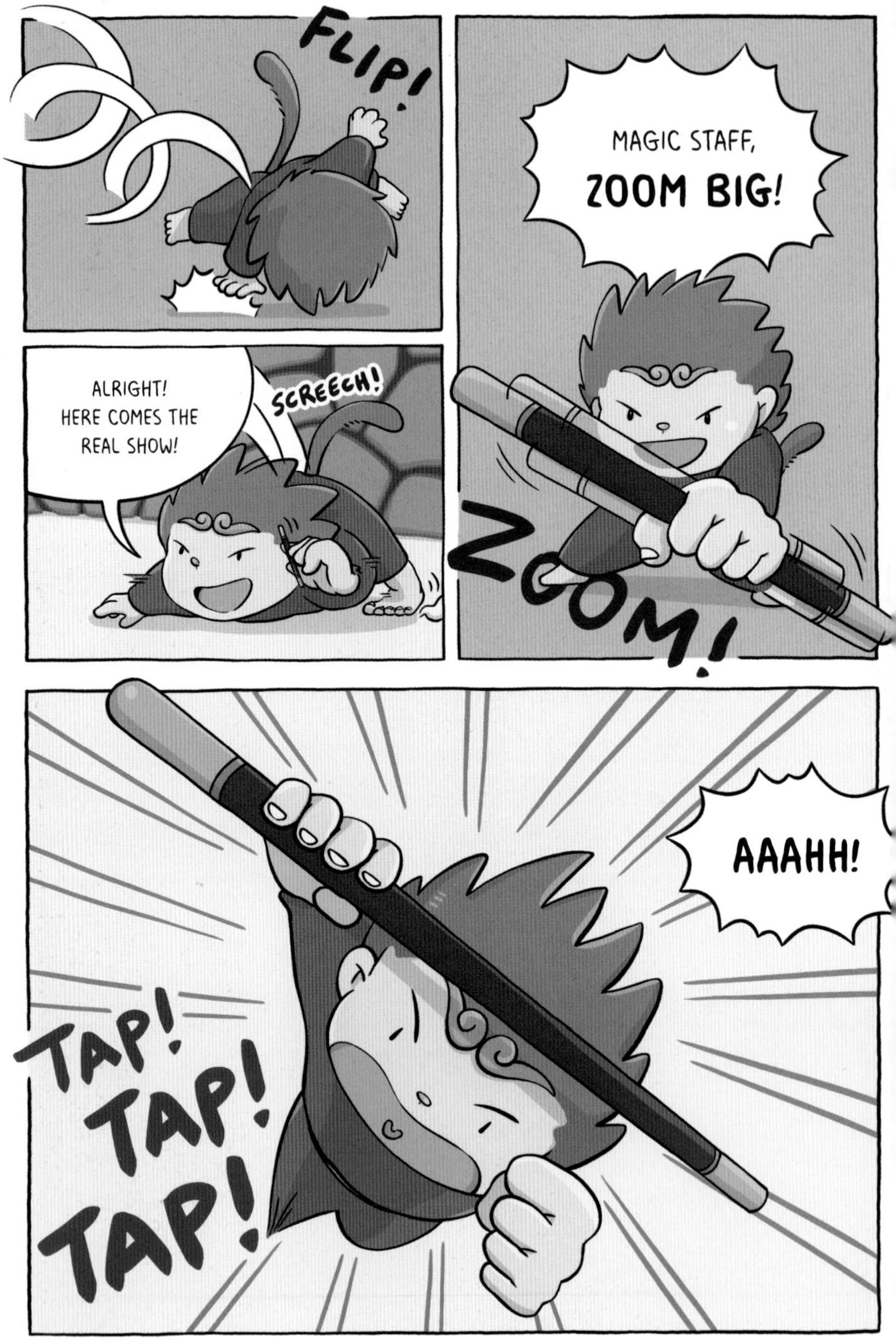
FLIP!
MAGIC STAFF, ZOOM BIG!
ALRIGHT! HERE COMES THE REAL SHOW!
SCREECH!
ZOOM!
AAAHH!
TAP! TAP! TAP!

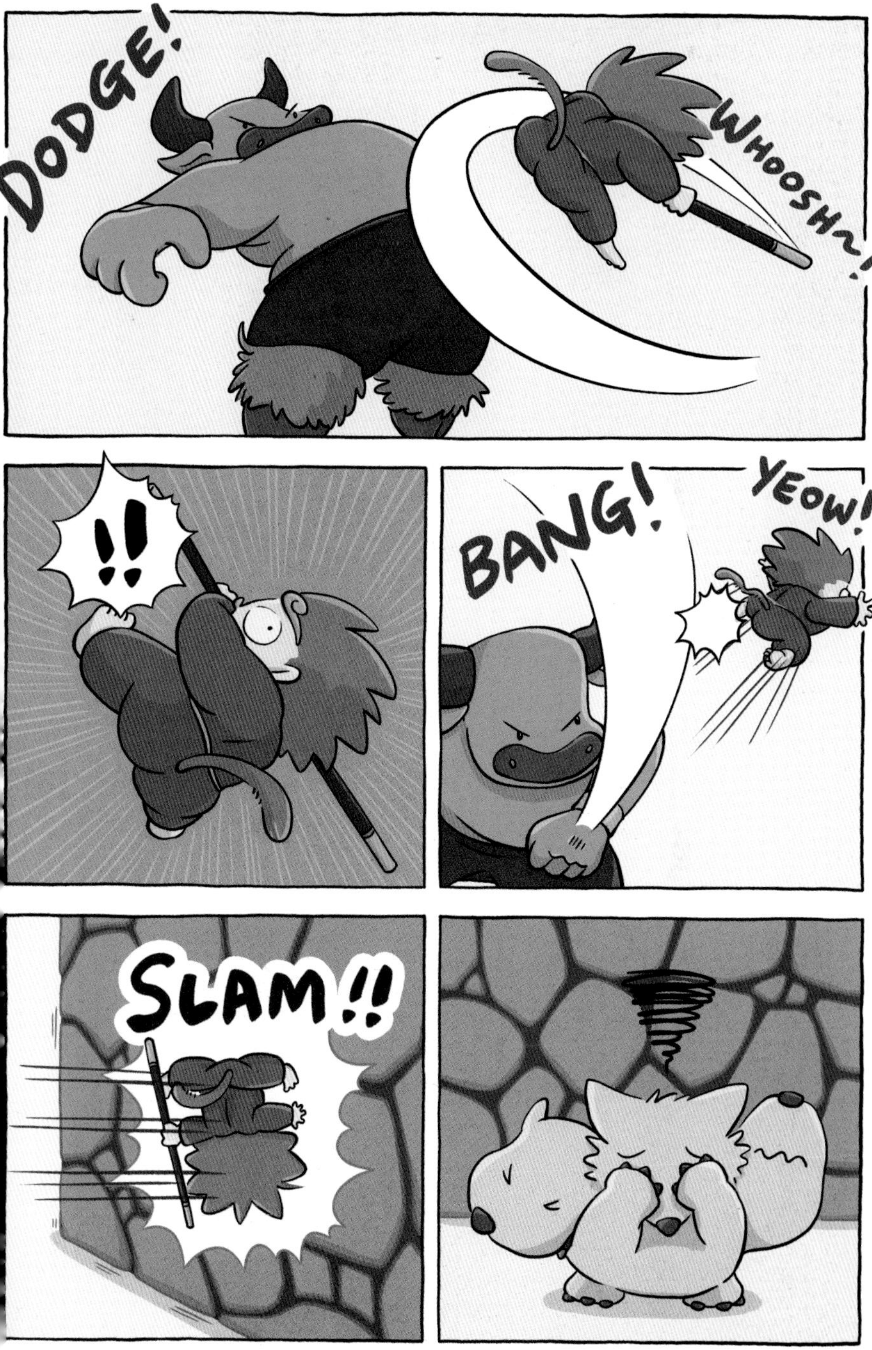
DODGE!
WHOOSH~!
!!
BANG!
YEOW!
SLAM!!

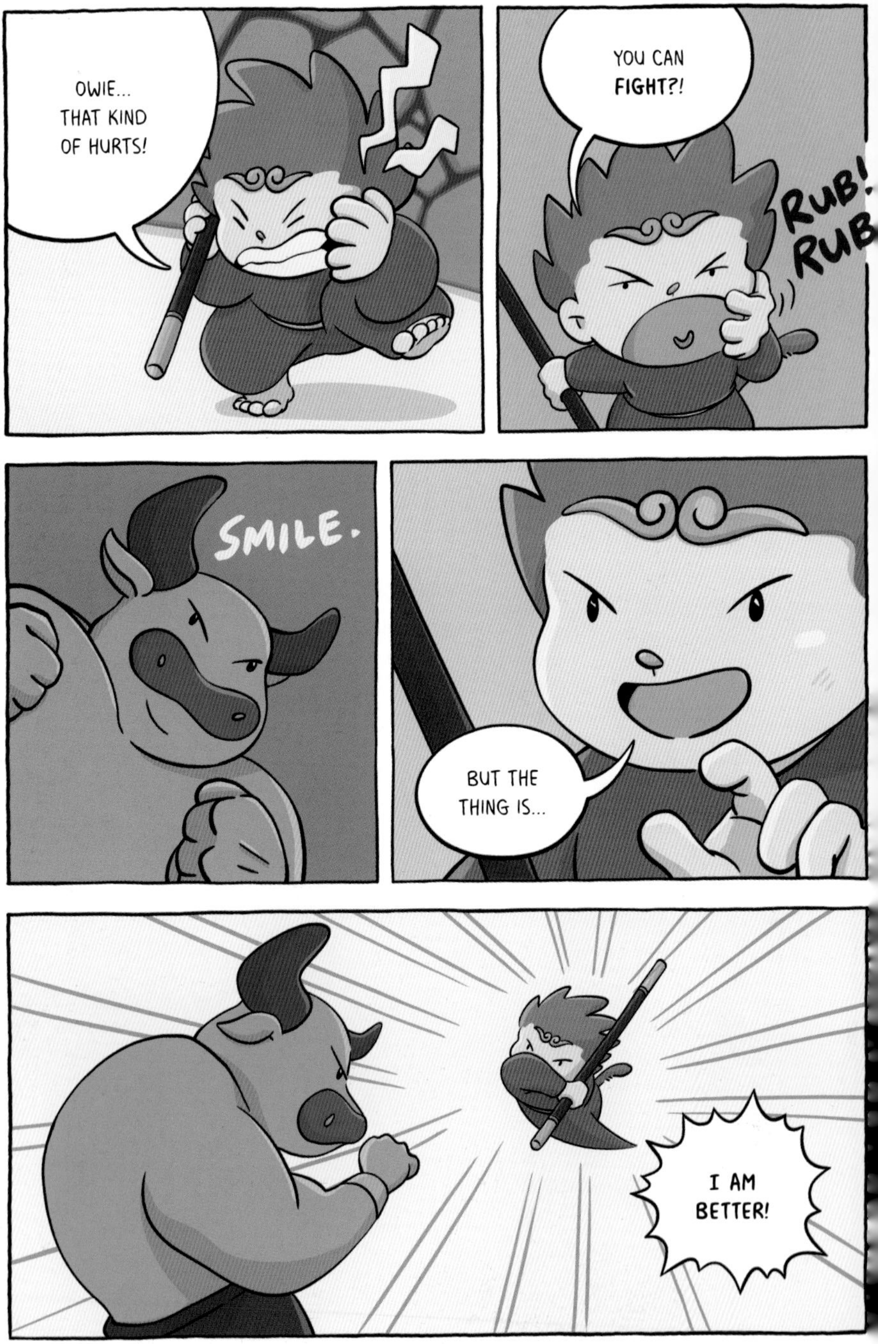
OWIE... THAT KIND OF HURTS!
YOU CAN FIGHT?!
RUB! RUB
SMILE.
BUT THE THING IS...
I AM BETTER!

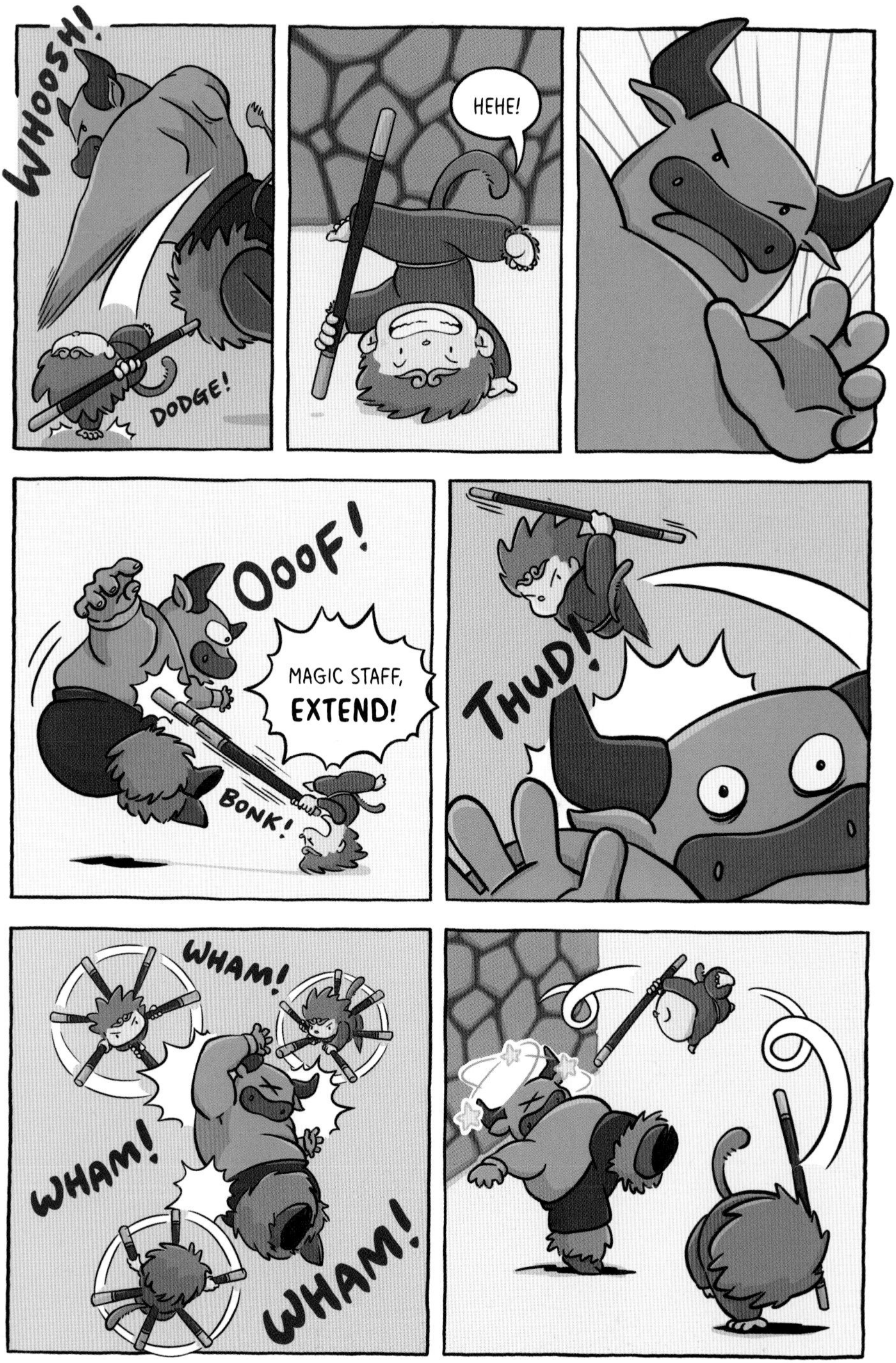
WHOOSH!
DODGE!
HEHE!
OOOF!
MAGIC STAFF,
EXTEND!
BONK!
THUD!
WHAM!
WHAM!
WHAM!

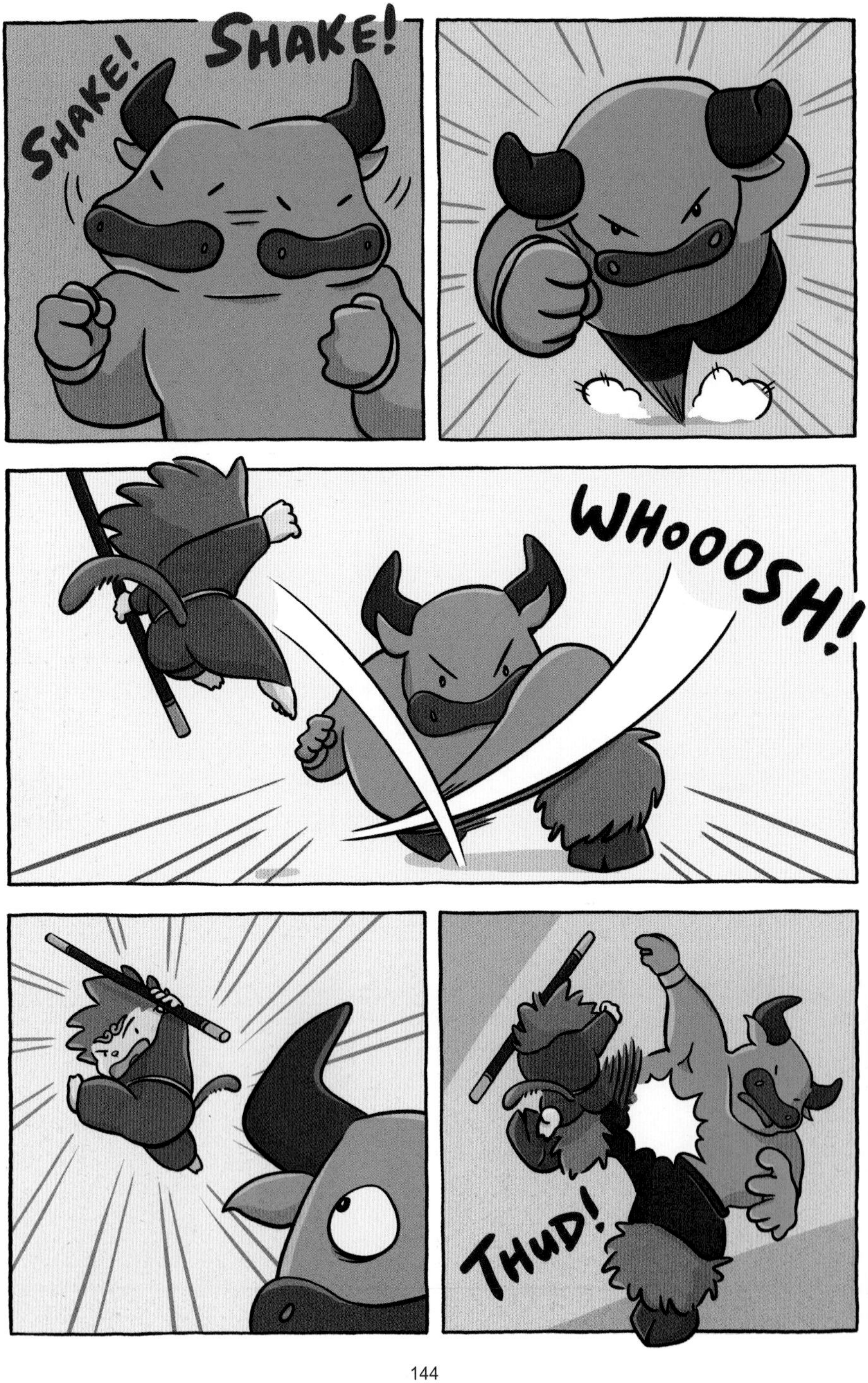
SHAKE!
SHAKE!
WHOOOOSH!
THUD!

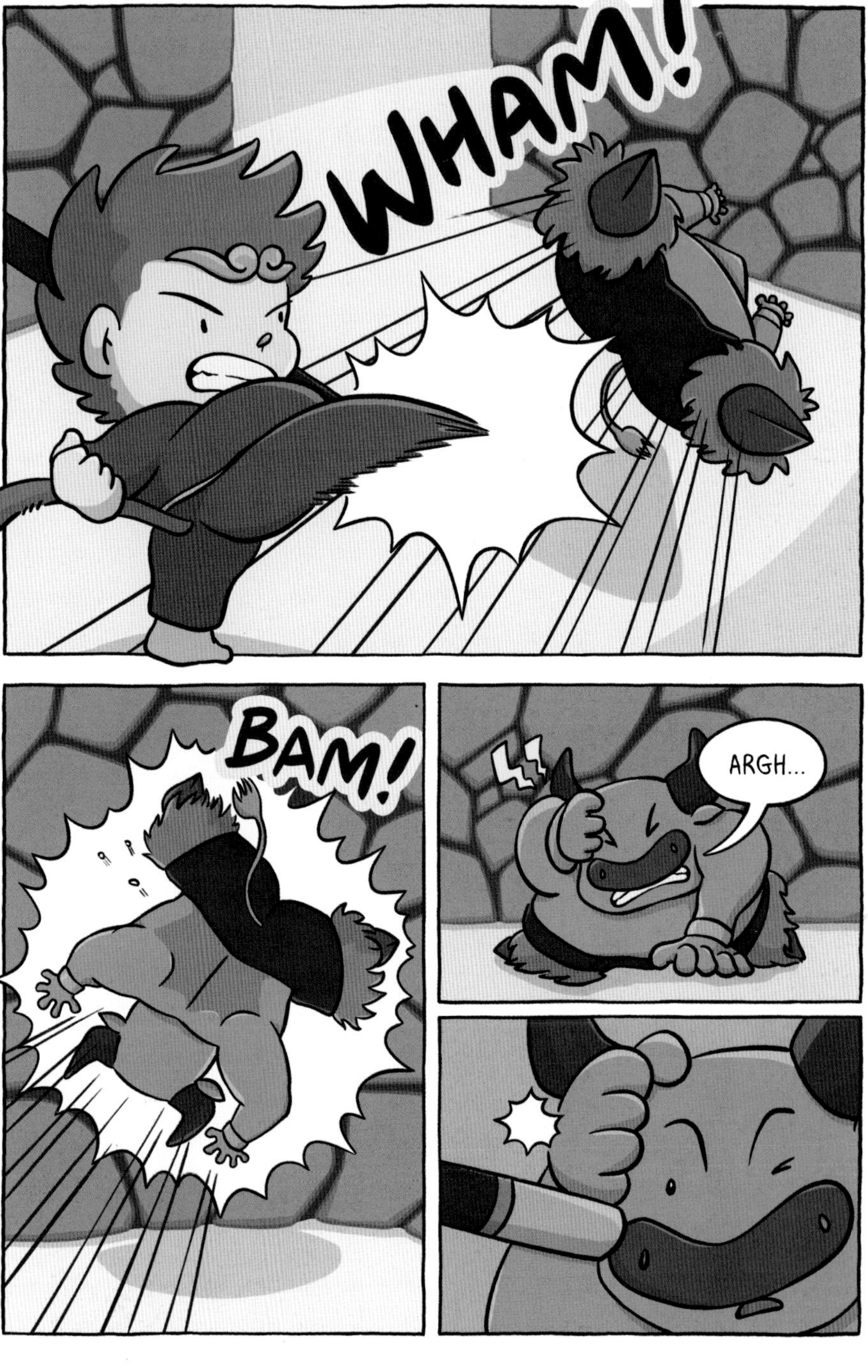
WHAM!
BAM!
ARGH...

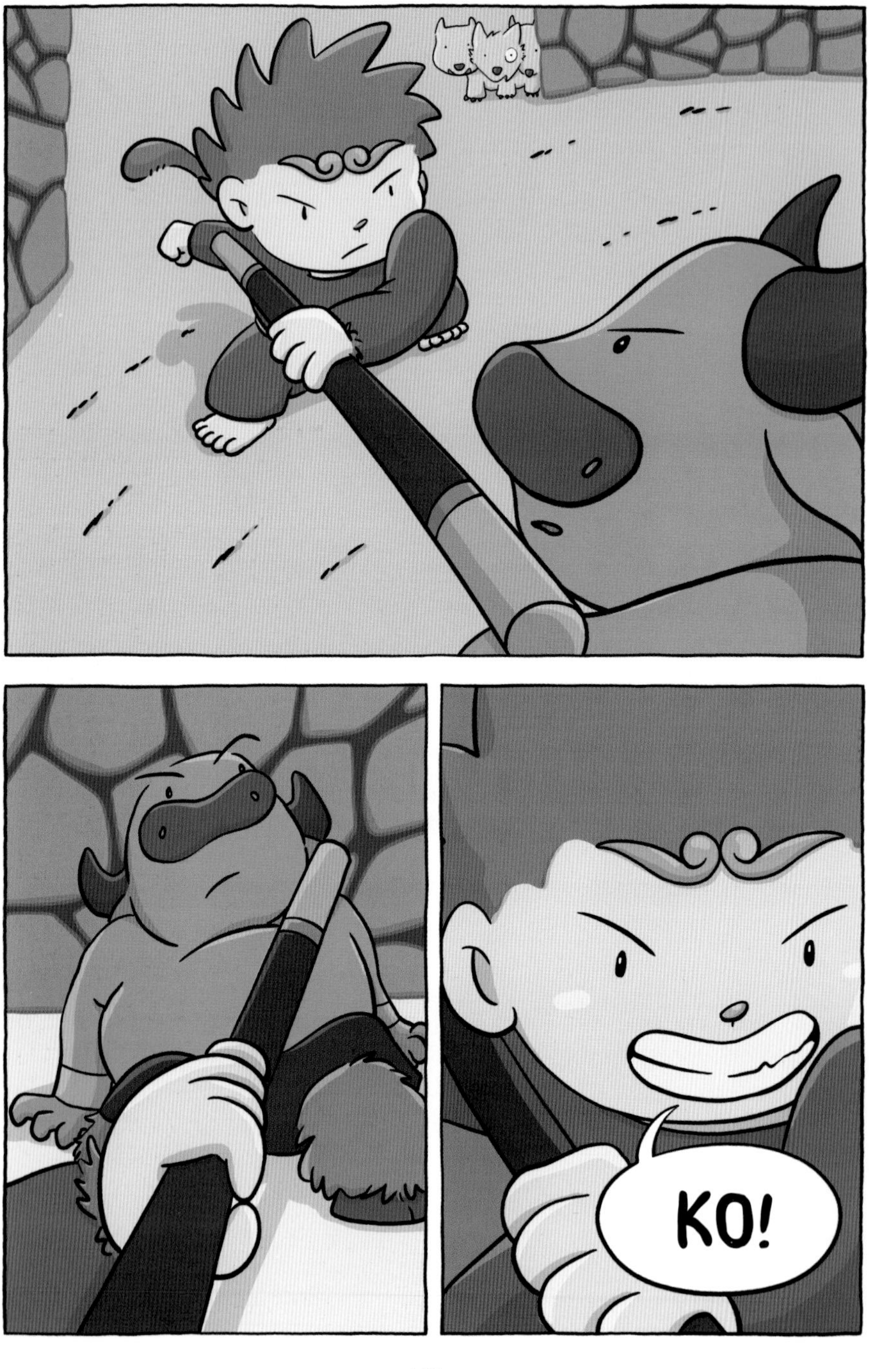
KO!

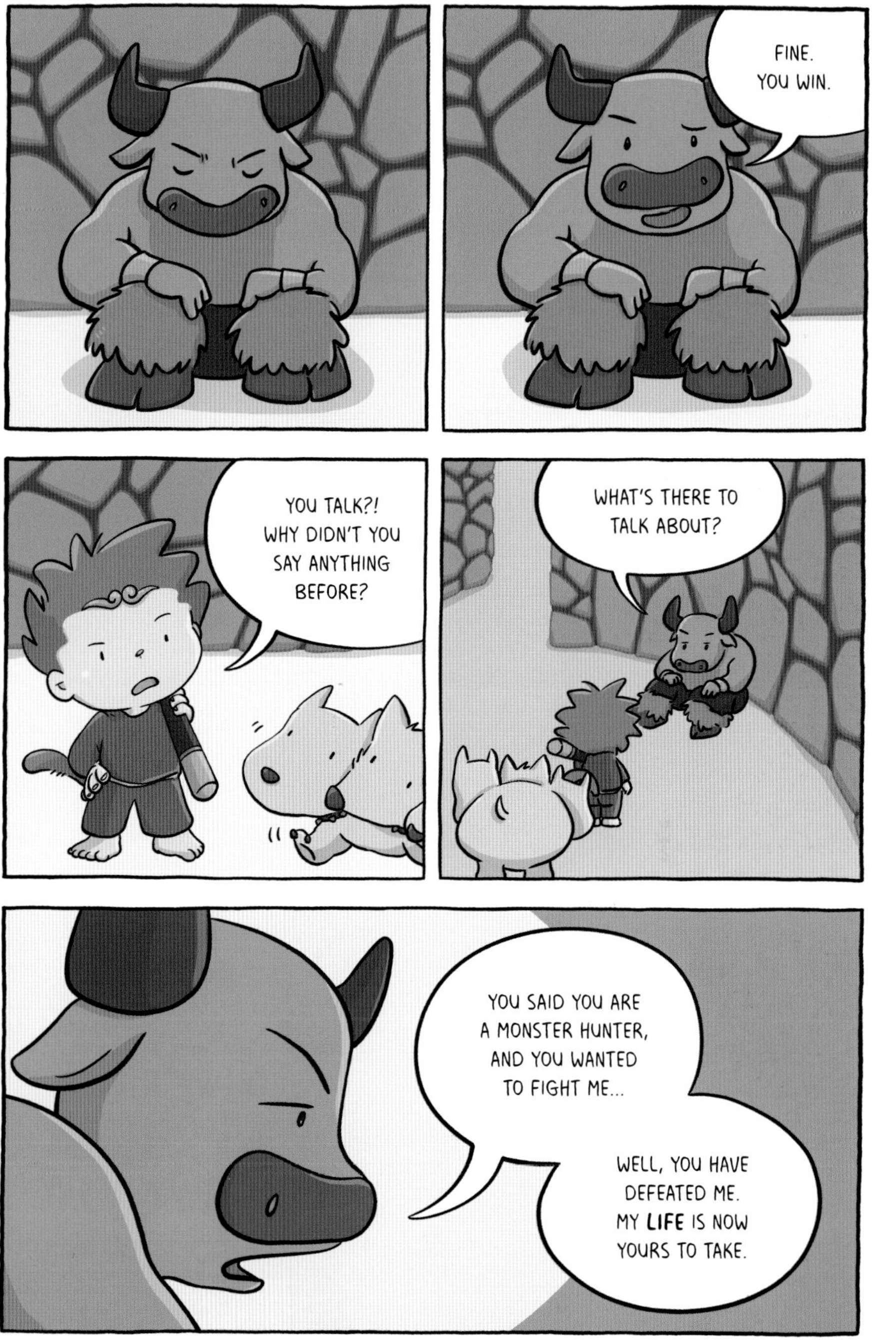
FINE. YOU WIN.
YOU TALK?! WHY DIDN'T YOU SAY ANYTHING BEFORE?
WHAT'S THERE TO TALK ABOUT?
YOU SAID YOU ARE A MONSTER HUNTER, AND YOU WANTED TO FIGHT ME...
WELL, YOU HAVE DEFEATED ME. MY **LIFE** IS NOW YOURS TO TAKE.

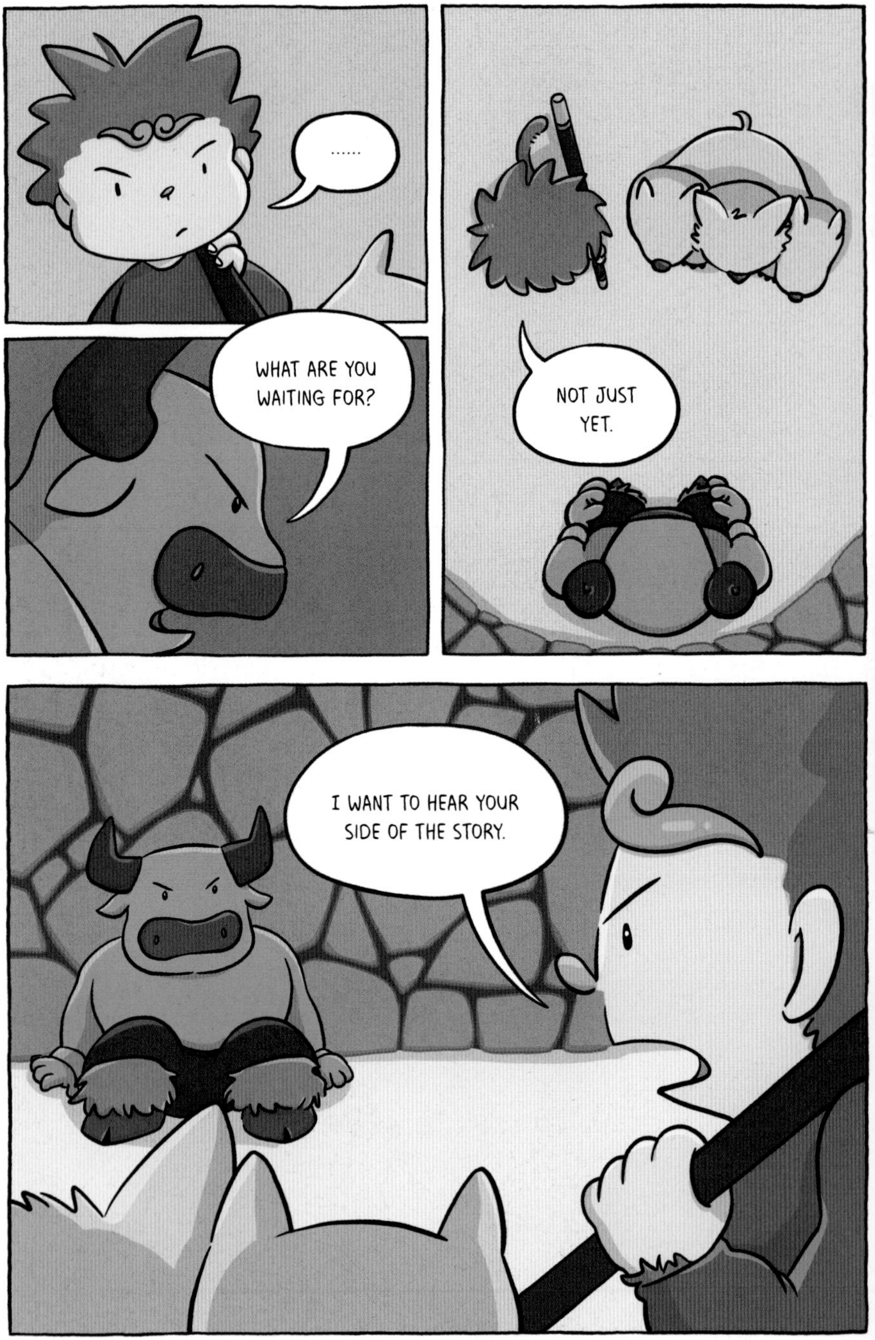
......
WHAT ARE YOU WAITING FOR?
NOT JUST YET.
I WANT TO HEAR YOUR SIDE OF THE STORY.

CHAPTER 8

THE MINOTAUR'S STORY

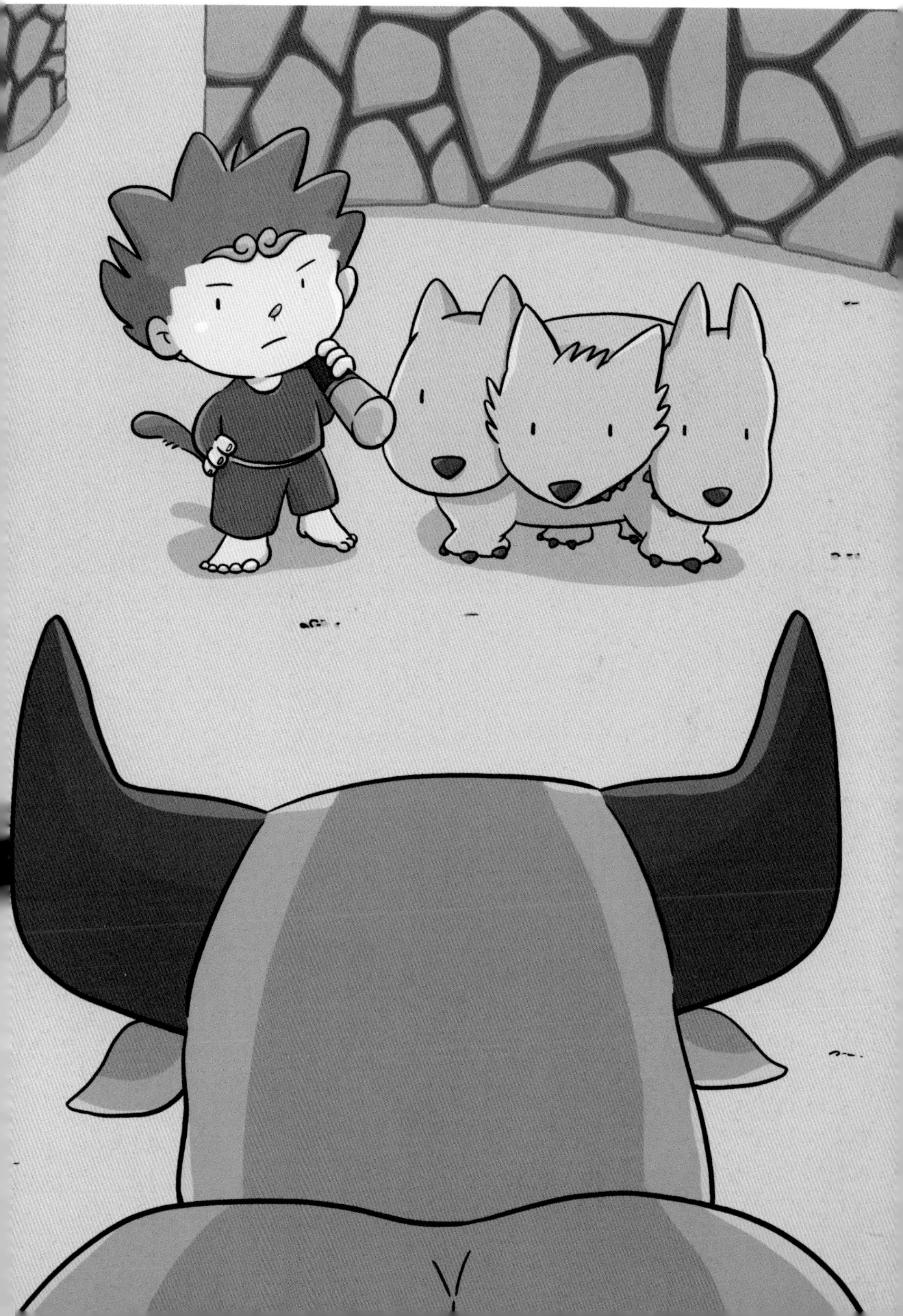

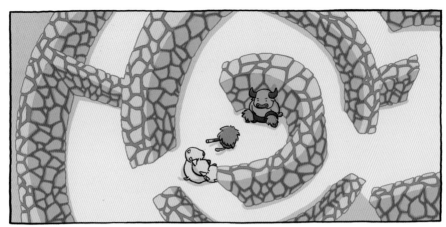

"MY SIDE OF THE STORY"? WHAT DOES THAT EVEN **MEAN**?

I AM A **MONSTER**. IT IS YOUR JOB TO HUNT ME DOWN AND **DESTROY** ME, RIGHT?

WHAT MAKES YOU A MONSTER?

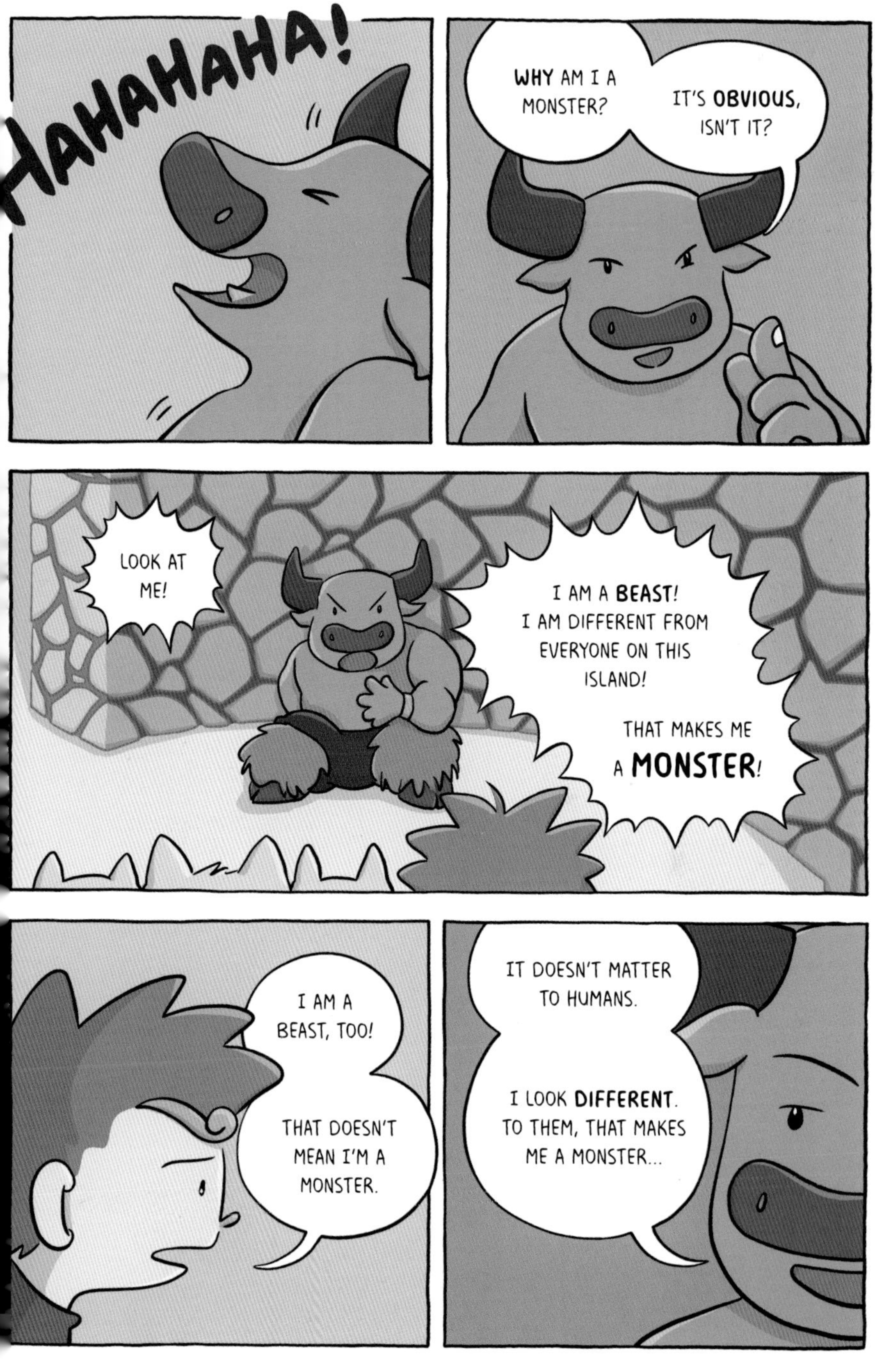
HAHAHAHA!
WHY AM I A MONSTER?
IT'S OBVIOUS, ISN'T IT?
LOOK AT ME!
I AM A BEAST! I AM DIFFERENT FROM EVERYONE ON THIS ISLAND!
THAT MAKES ME A MONSTER!
I AM A BEAST, TOO!
THAT DOESN'T MEAN I'M A MONSTER.
IT DOESN'T MATTER TO HUMANS.
I LOOK DIFFERENT. TO THEM, THAT MAKES ME A MONSTER...

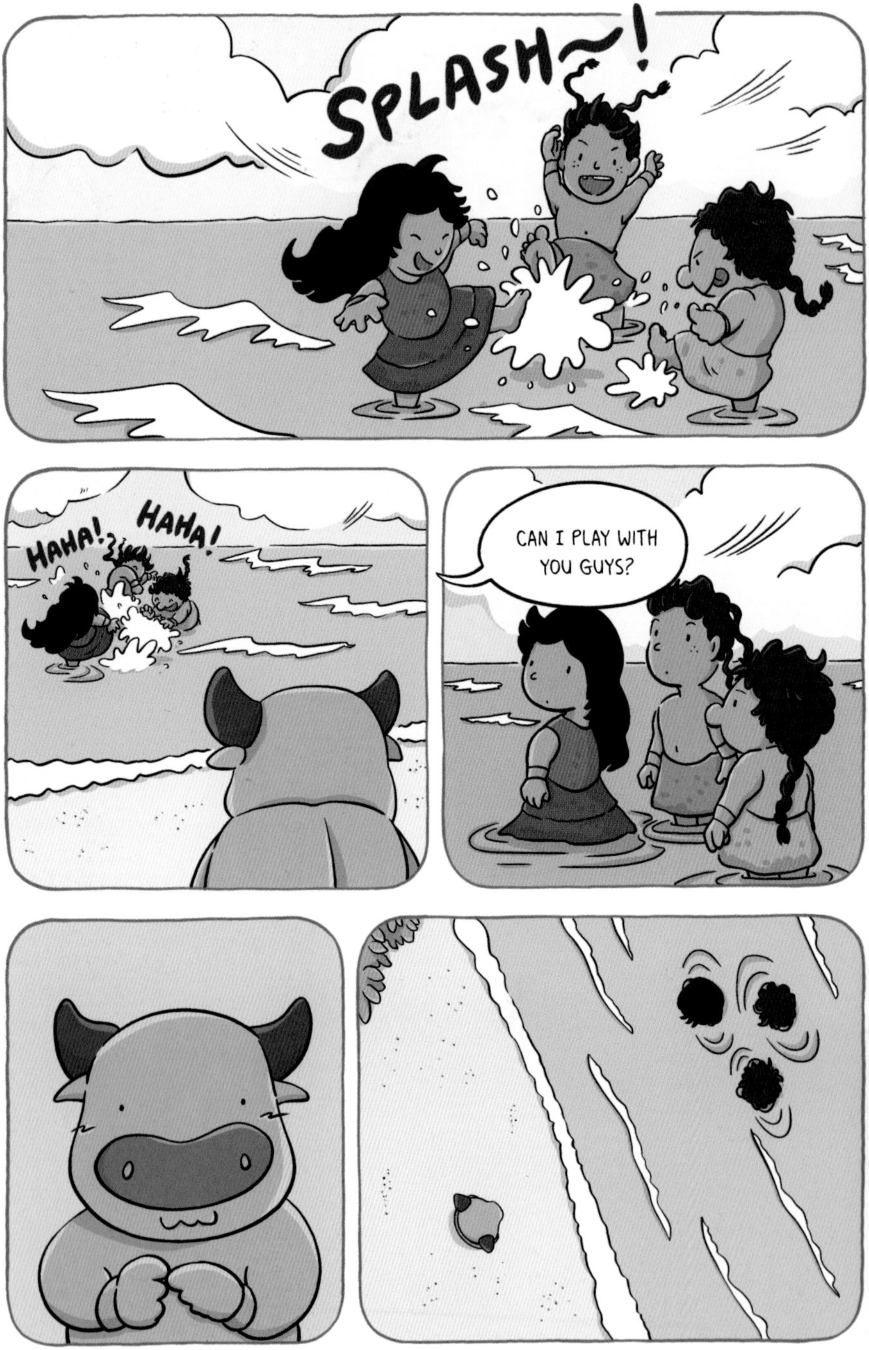
SPLASH~!
HAHA!
HAHA!
CAN I PLAY WITH YOU GUYS?

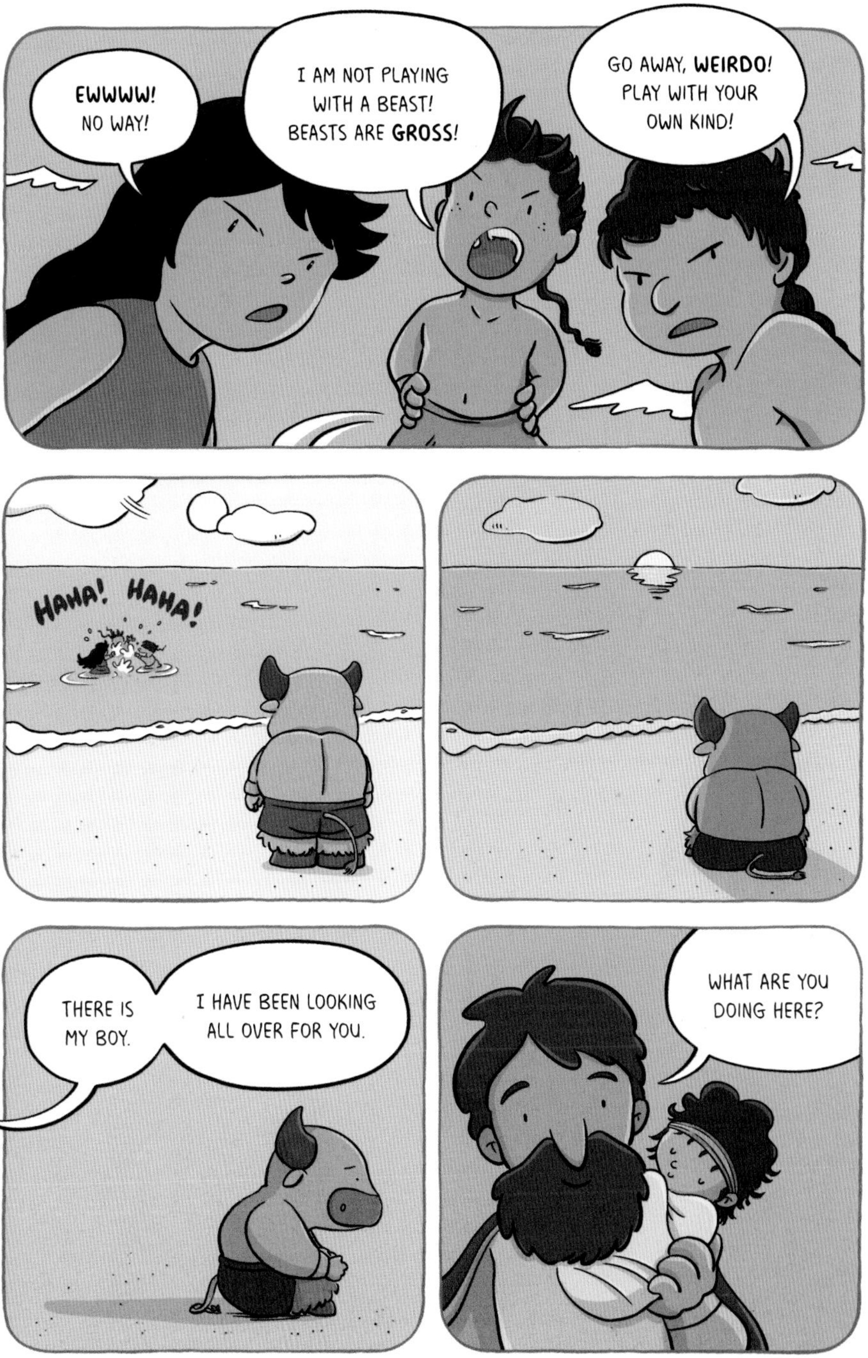
EWWWW! NO WAY!
I AM NOT PLAYING WITH A BEAST! BEASTS ARE GROSS!
GO AWAY, WEIRDO! PLAY WITH YOUR OWN KIND!
HAHA! HAHA!
THERE IS MY BOY.
I HAVE BEEN LOOKING ALL OVER FOR YOU.
WHAT ARE YOU DOING HERE?

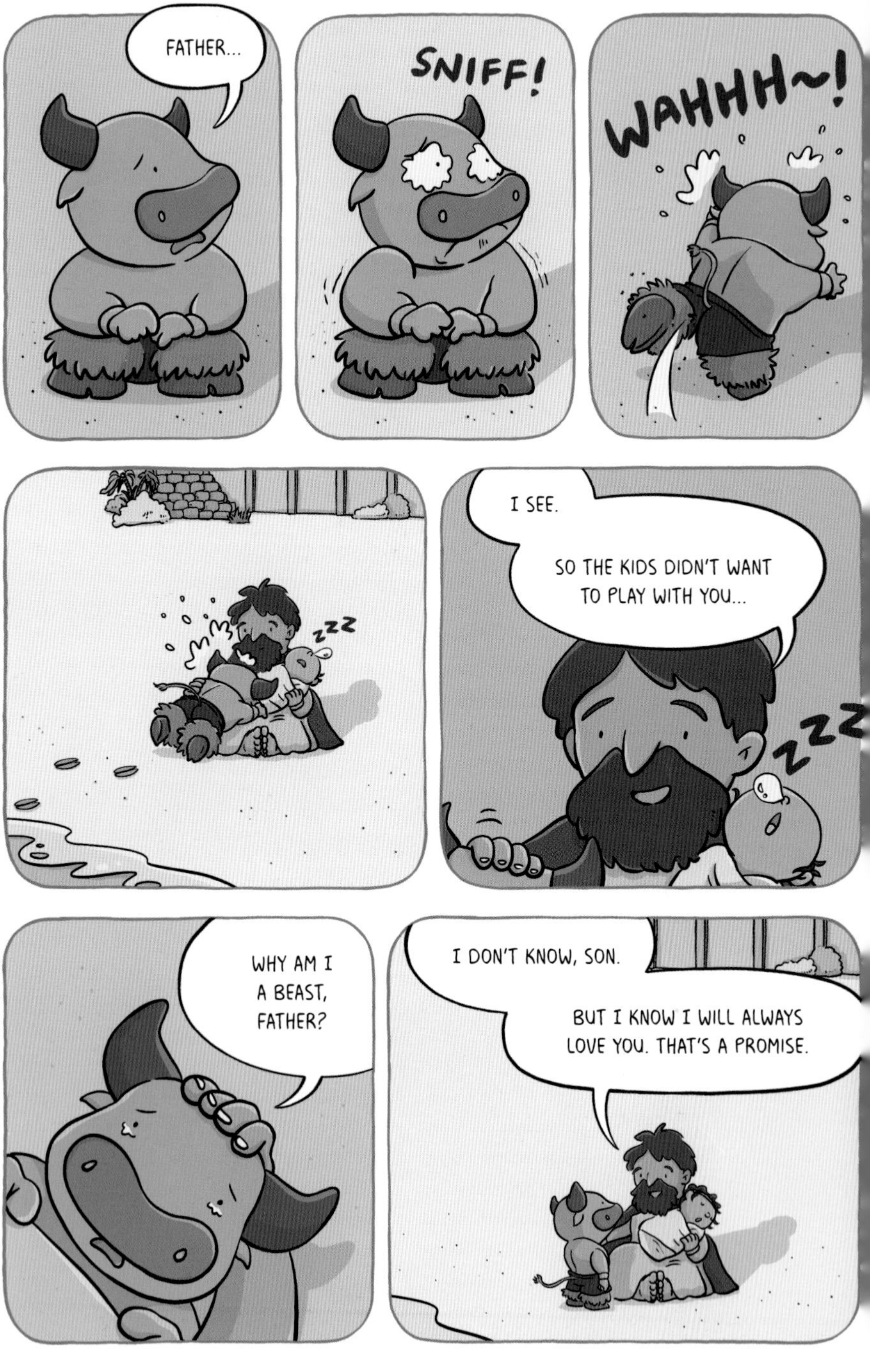
FATHER...
SNIFF!
WAHHH~!
ZZZ
I SEE.
SO THE KIDS DIDN'T WANT TO PLAY WITH YOU...
ZZZ
WHY AM I A BEAST, FATHER?
I DON'T KNOW, SON.
BUT I KNOW I WILL ALWAYS LOVE YOU. THAT'S A PROMISE.

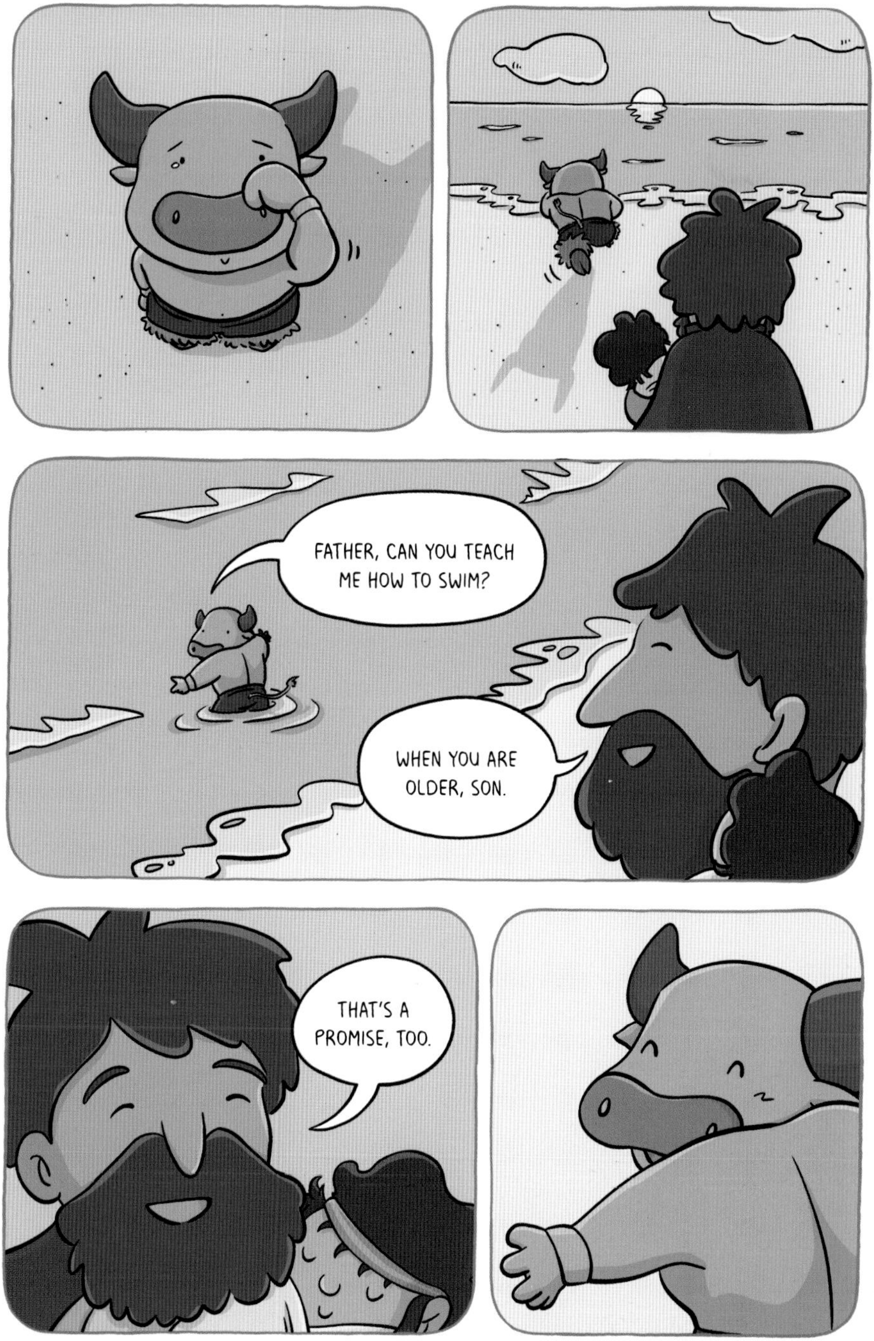
FATHER, CAN YOU TEACH ME HOW TO SWIM?
WHEN YOU ARE OLDER, SON.
THAT'S A PROMISE, TOO.

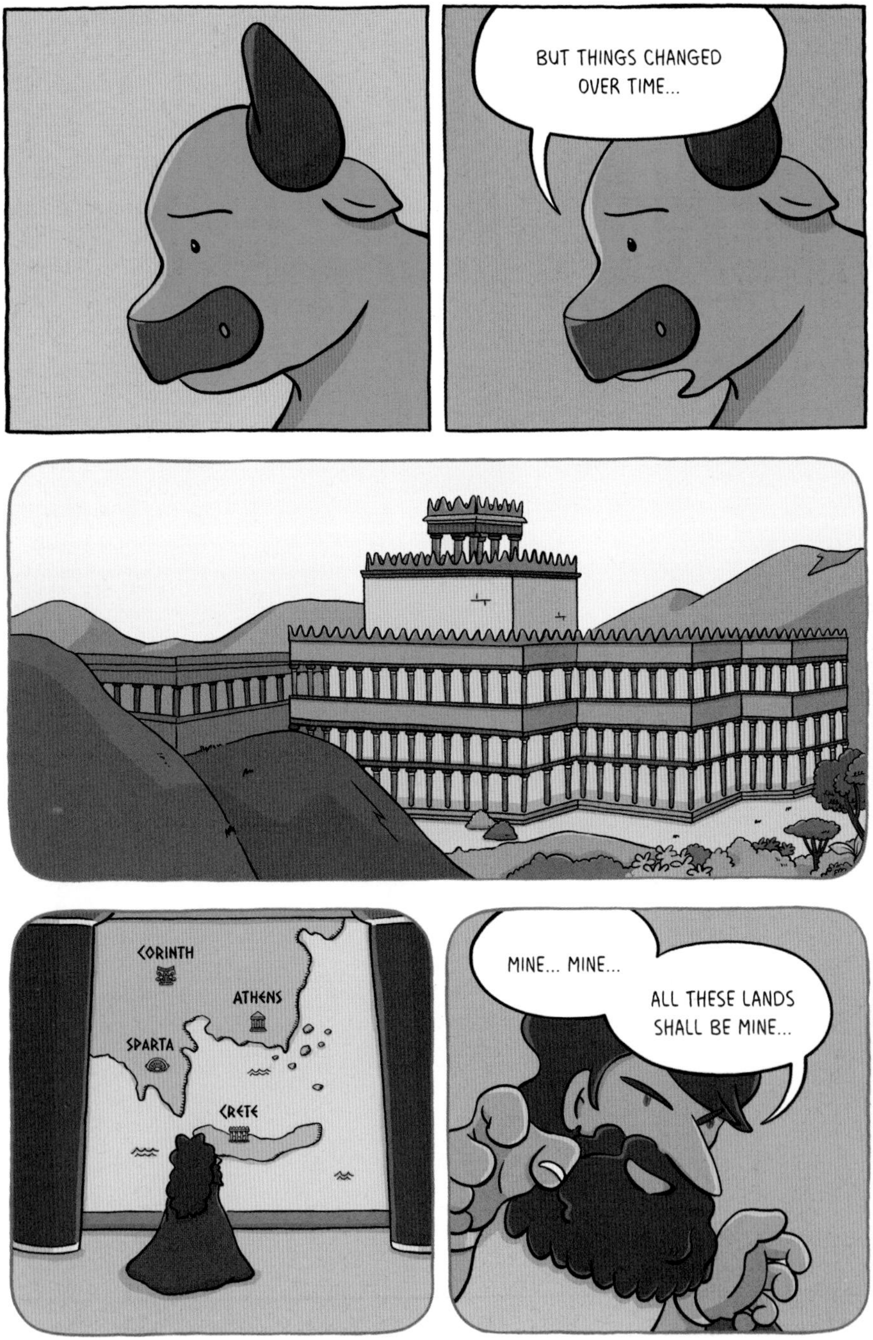
BUT THINGS CHANGED OVER TIME...
CORINTH
ATHENS
SPARTA
CRETE
MINE... MINE...
ALL THESE LANDS SHALL BE MINE...

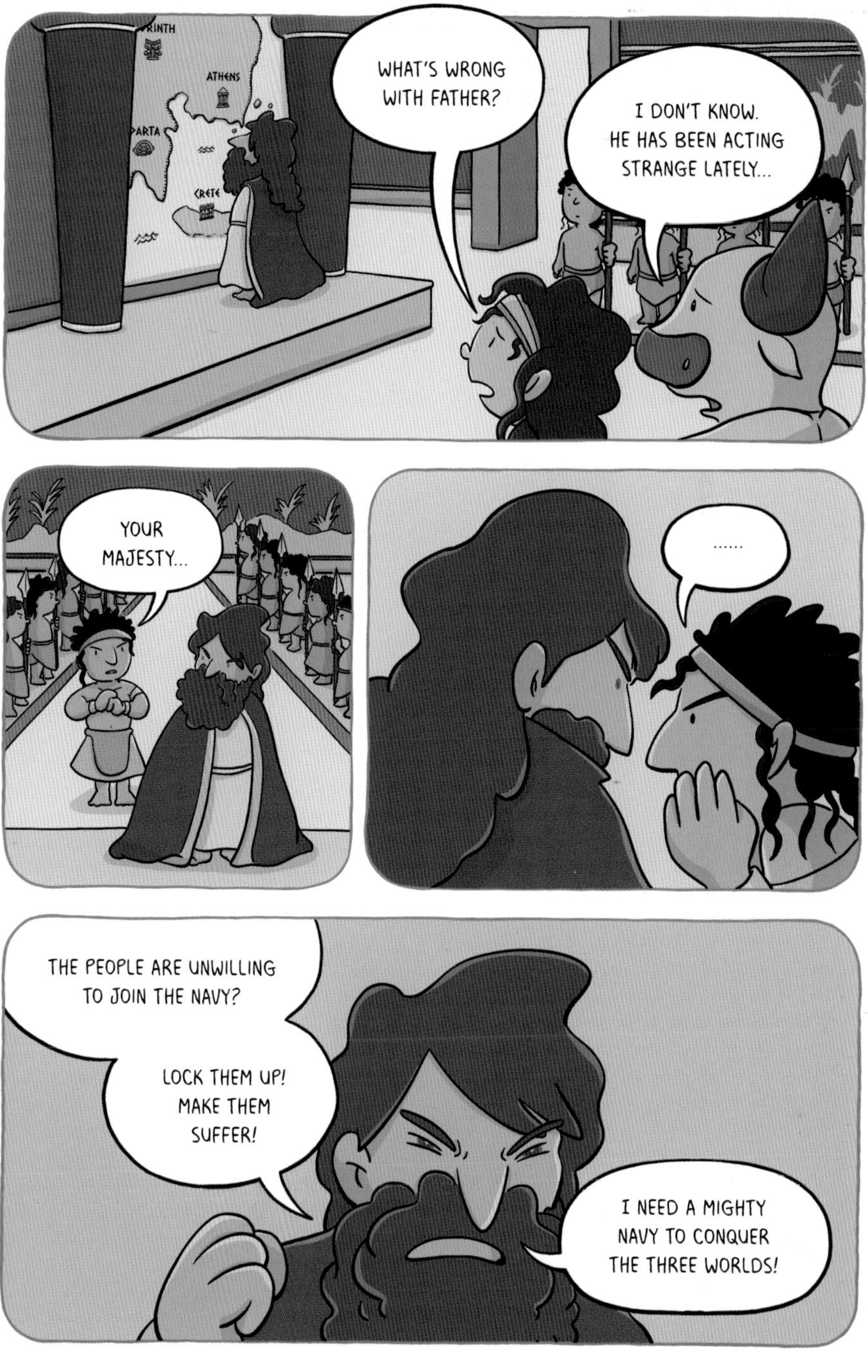
ATHENS
CRETE
WHAT'S WRONG WITH FATHER?
I DON'T KNOW. HE HAS BEEN ACTING STRANGE LATELY...
YOUR MAJESTY...
......
THE PEOPLE ARE UNWILLING TO JOIN THE NAVY?
LOCK THEM UP! MAKE THEM SUFFER!
I NEED A MIGHTY NAVY TO CONQUER THE THREE WORLDS!

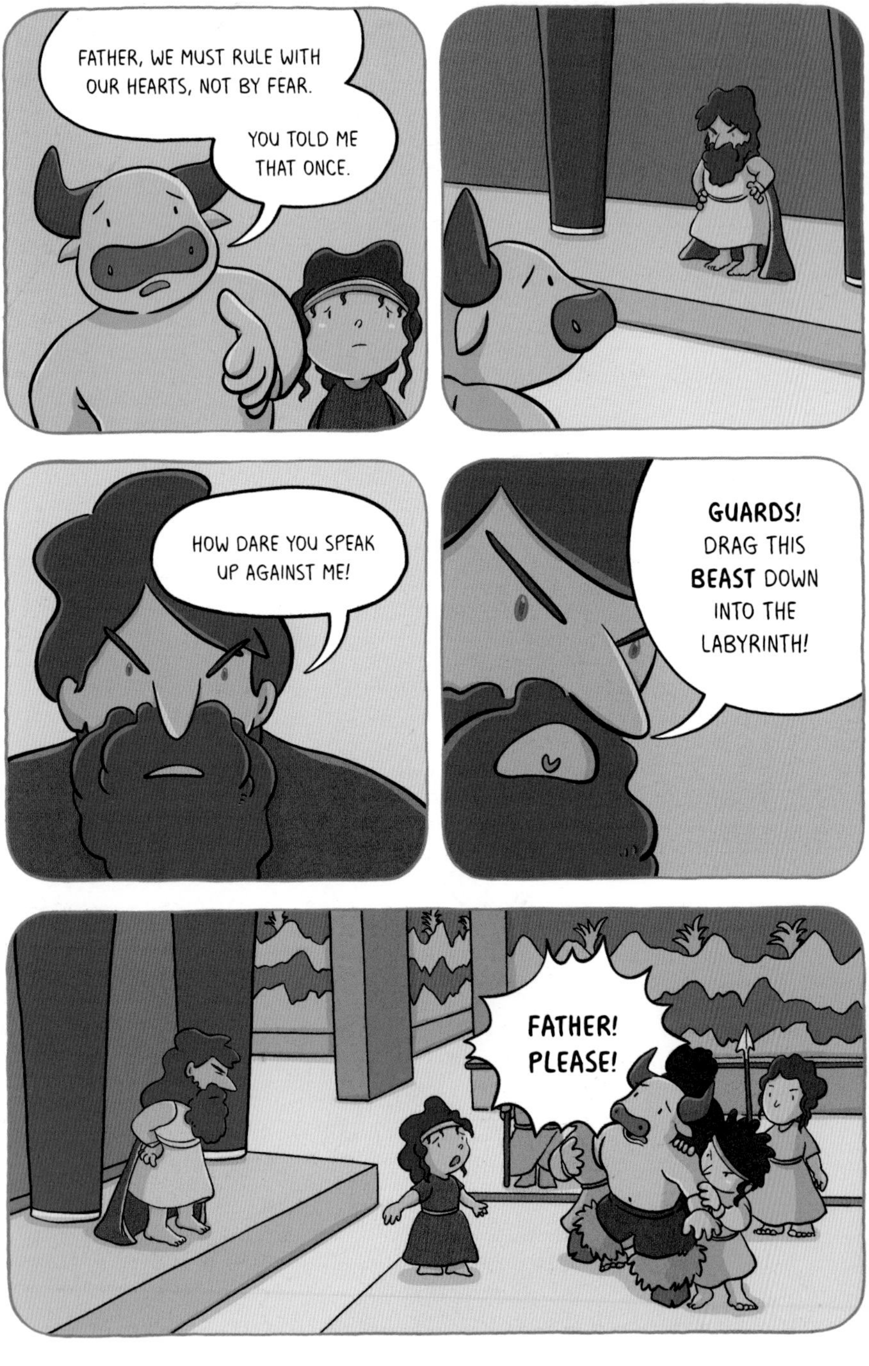
FATHER, WE MUST RULE WITH OUR HEARTS, NOT BY FEAR.
YOU TOLD ME THAT ONCE.
HOW DARE YOU SPEAK UP AGAINST ME!
GUARDS! DRAG THIS **BEAST** DOWN INTO THE LABYRINTH!
FATHER! PLEASE!

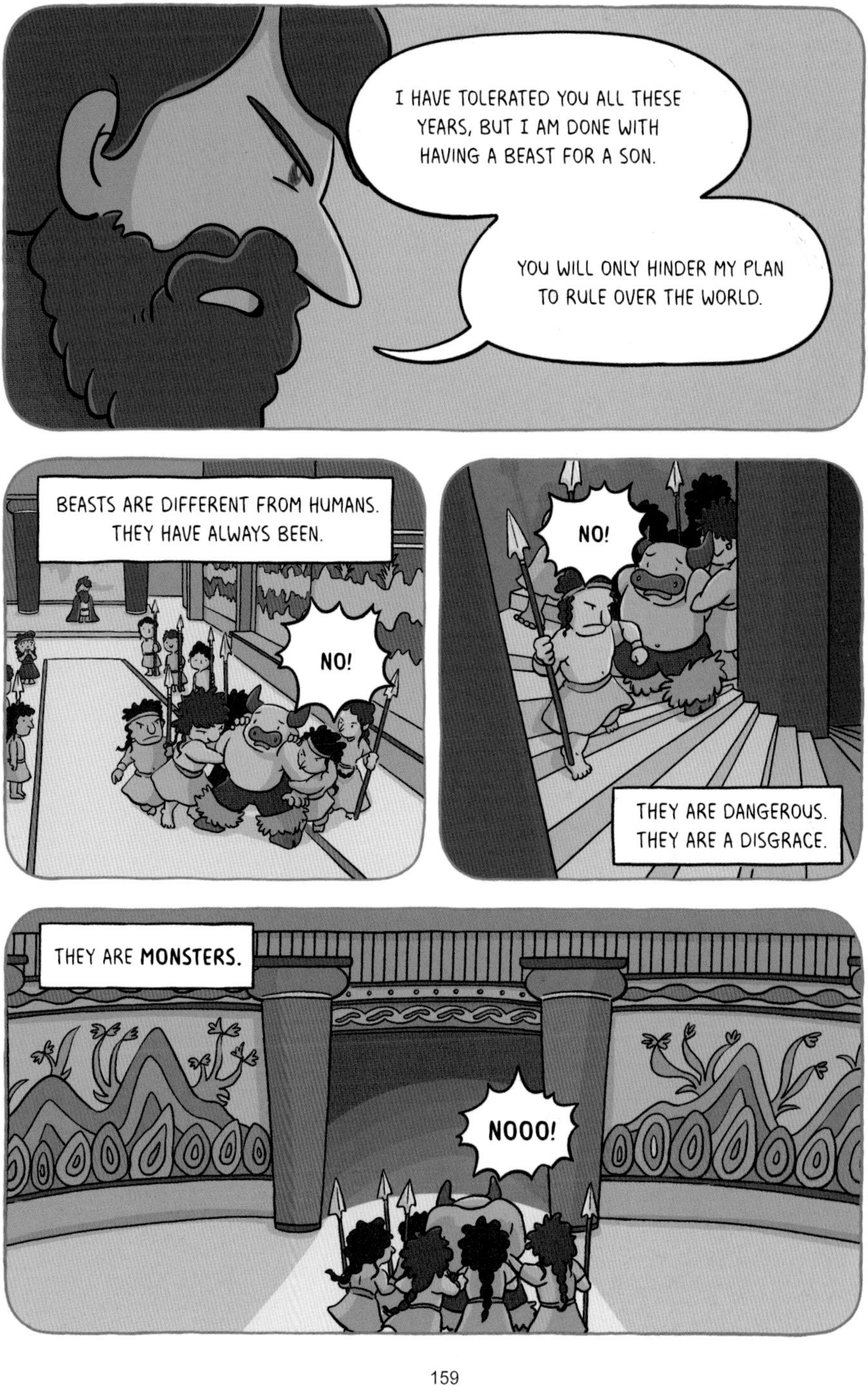
I HAVE TOLERATED YOU ALL THESE YEARS, BUT I AM DONE WITH HAVING A BEAST FOR A SON.
YOU WILL ONLY HINDER MY PLAN TO RULE OVER THE WORLD.
BEASTS ARE DIFFERENT FROM HUMANS. THEY HAVE ALWAYS BEEN.
NO!
NO!
THEY ARE DANGEROUS. THEY ARE A DISGRACE.
THEY ARE **MONSTERS.**
NOOO!

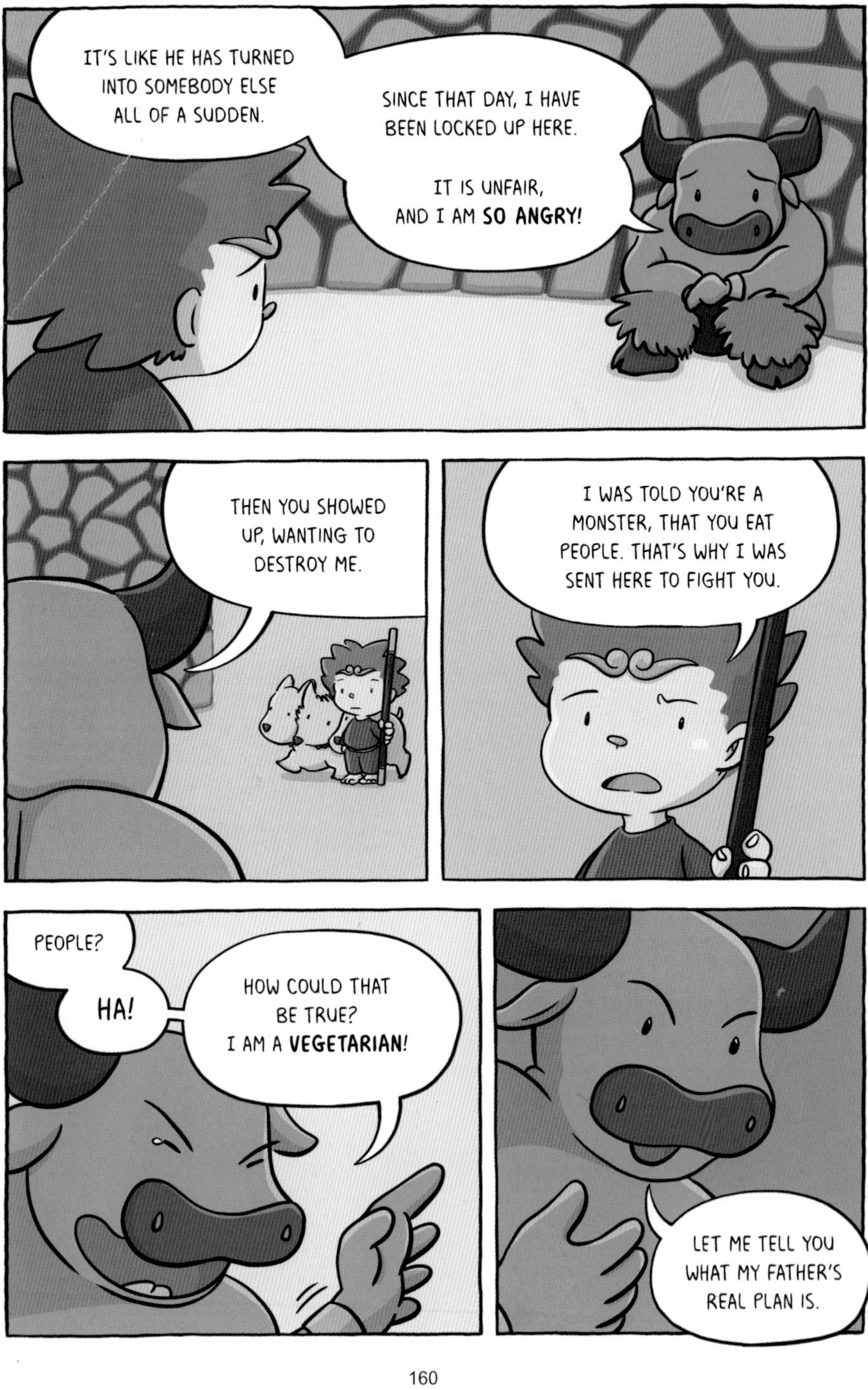
IT'S LIKE HE HAS TURNED INTO SOMEBODY ELSE ALL OF A SUDDEN.
SINCE THAT DAY, I HAVE BEEN LOCKED UP HERE.
IT IS UNFAIR, AND I AM **SO ANGRY!**
THEN YOU SHOWED UP, WANTING TO DESTROY ME.
I WAS TOLD YOU'RE A MONSTER, THAT YOU EAT PEOPLE. THAT'S WHY I WAS SENT HERE TO FIGHT YOU.
PEOPLE?
HA!
HOW COULD THAT BE TRUE? I AM A **VEGETARIAN!**
LET ME TELL YOU WHAT MY FATHER'S REAL PLAN IS.

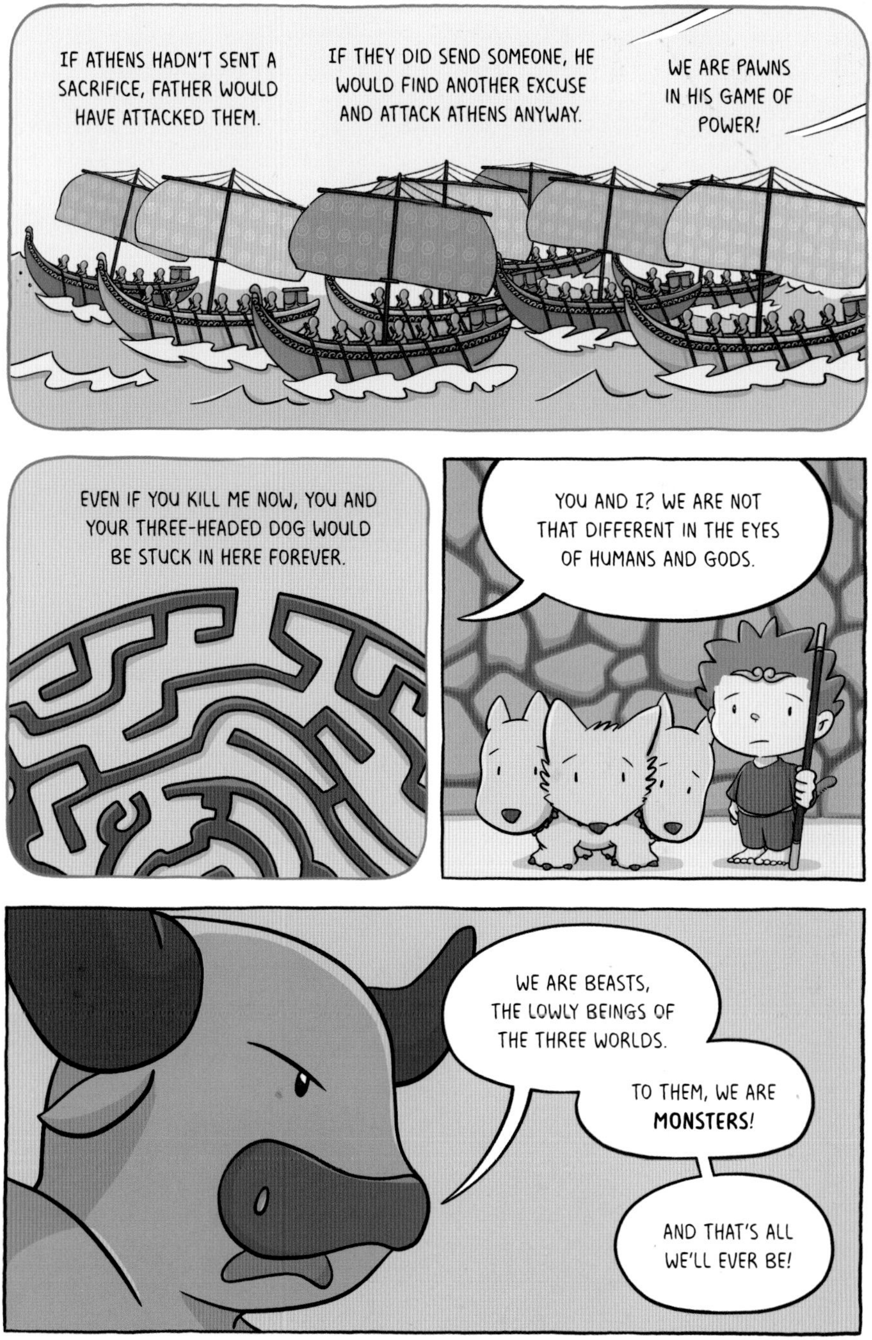
IF ATHENS HADN'T SENT A SACRIFICE, FATHER WOULD HAVE ATTACKED THEM.
IF THEY DID SEND SOMEONE, HE WOULD FIND ANOTHER EXCUSE AND ATTACK ATHENS ANYWAY.
WE ARE PAWNS IN HIS GAME OF POWER!
EVEN IF YOU KILL ME NOW, YOU AND YOUR THREE-HEADED DOG WOULD BE STUCK IN HERE FOREVER.
YOU AND I? WE ARE NOT THAT DIFFERENT IN THE EYES OF HUMANS AND GODS.
WE ARE BEASTS, THE LOWLY BEINGS OF THE THREE WORLDS.
TO THEM, WE ARE **MONSTERS**!
AND THAT'S ALL WE'LL EVER BE!

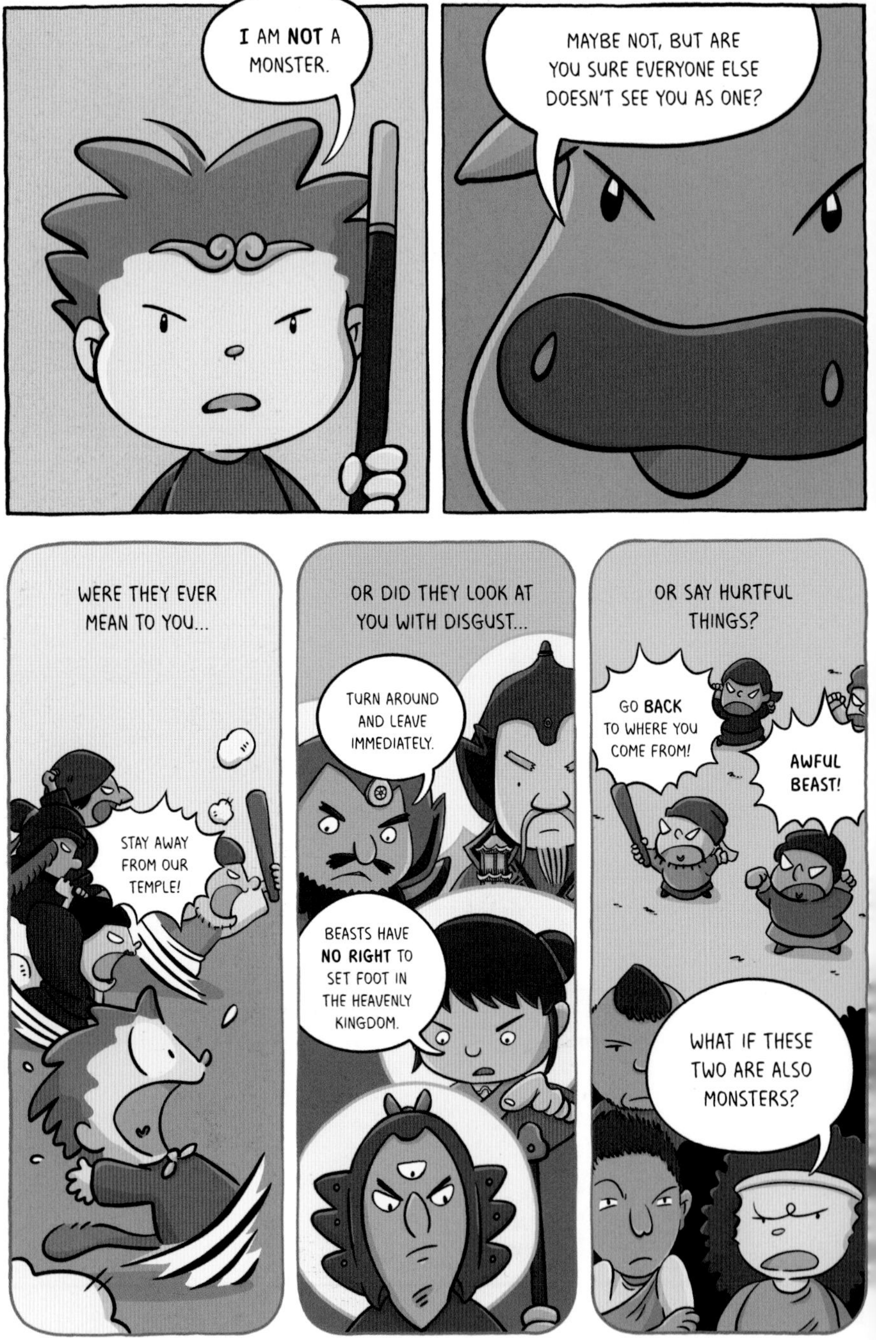
I AM **NOT** A MONSTER.
MAYBE NOT, BUT ARE YOU SURE EVERYONE ELSE DOESN'T SEE YOU AS ONE?
WERE THEY EVER MEAN TO YOU...
STAY AWAY FROM OUR TEMPLE!
OR DID THEY LOOK AT YOU WITH DISGUST...
TURN AROUND AND LEAVE IMMEDIATELY.
BEASTS HAVE **NO RIGHT** TO SET FOOT IN THE HEAVENLY KINGDOM.
OR SAY HURTFUL THINGS?
GO **BACK** TO WHERE YOU COME FROM!
AWFUL BEAST!
WHAT IF THESE TWO ARE ALSO MONSTERS?

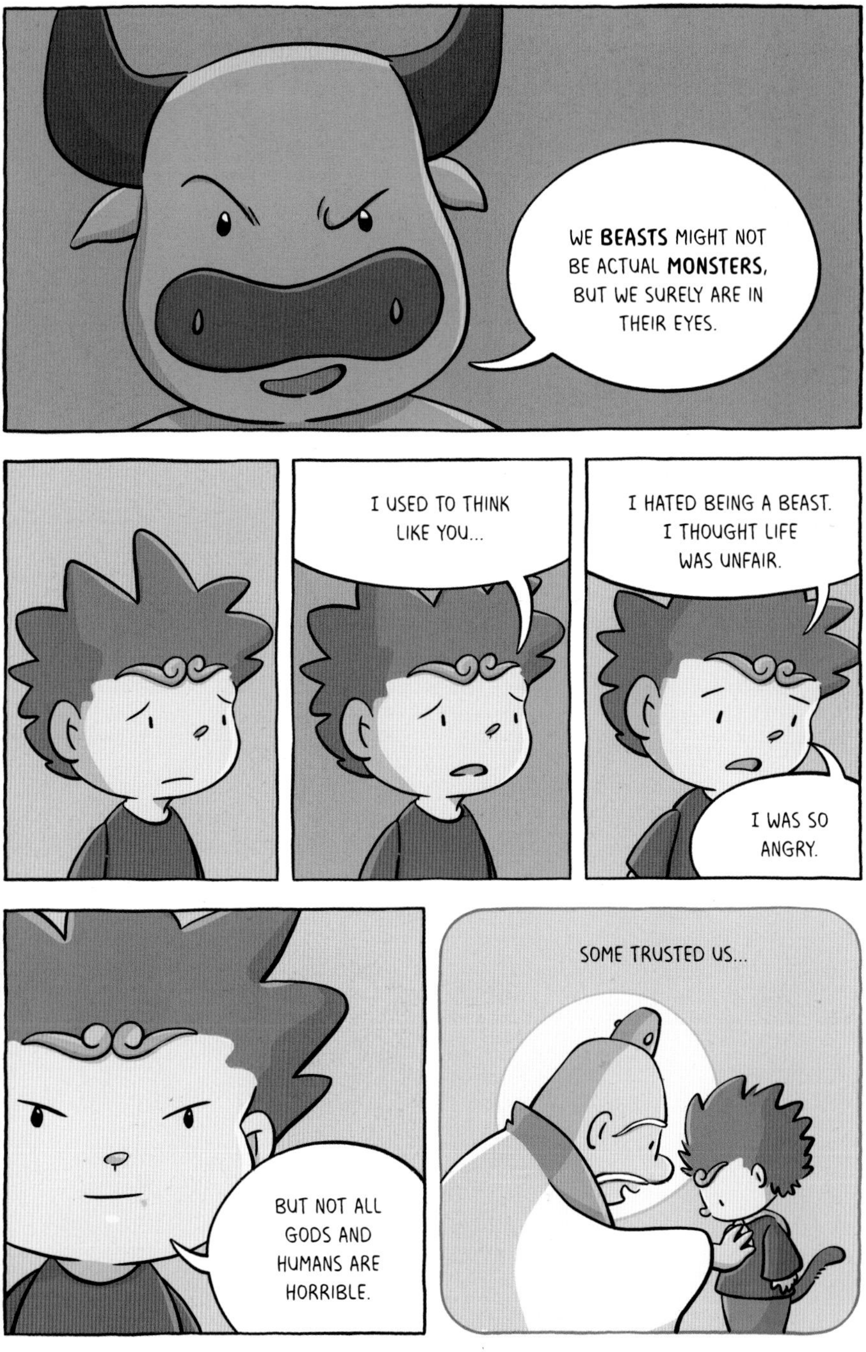
WE **BEASTS** MIGHT NOT BE ACTUAL **MONSTERS,** BUT WE SURELY ARE IN THEIR EYES.
I USED TO THINK LIKE YOU...
I HATED BEING A BEAST. I THOUGHT LIFE WAS UNFAIR.
I WAS SO ANGRY.
BUT NOT ALL GODS AND HUMANS ARE HORRIBLE.
SOME TRUSTED US...

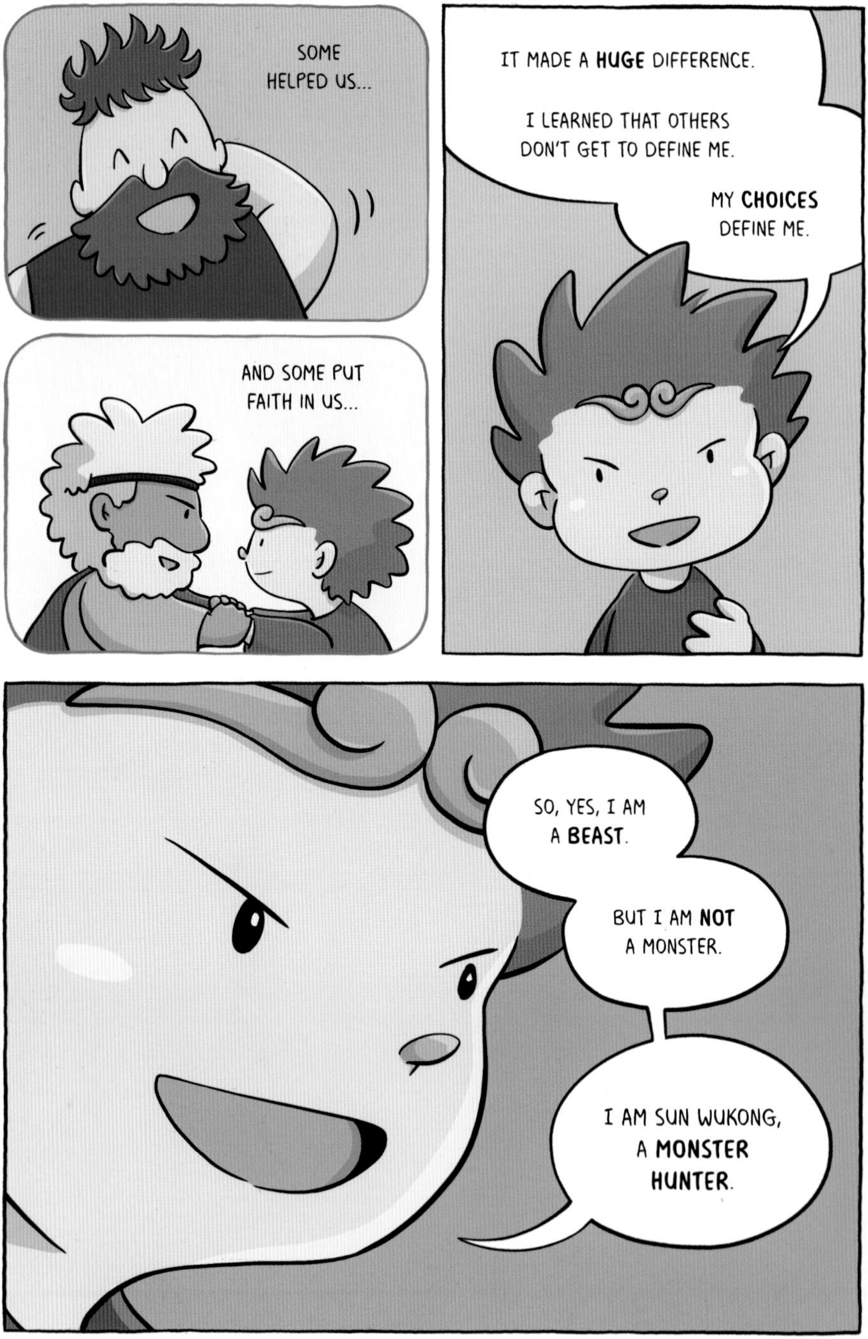
SOME HELPED US...
AND SOME PUT FAITH IN US...
IT MADE A **HUGE** DIFFERENCE.
I LEARNED THAT OTHERS DON'T GET TO DEFINE ME.
MY **CHOICES** DEFINE ME.
SO, YES, I AM A **BEAST**.
BUT I AM **NOT** A MONSTER.
I AM SUN WUKONG, A **MONSTER HUNTER**.

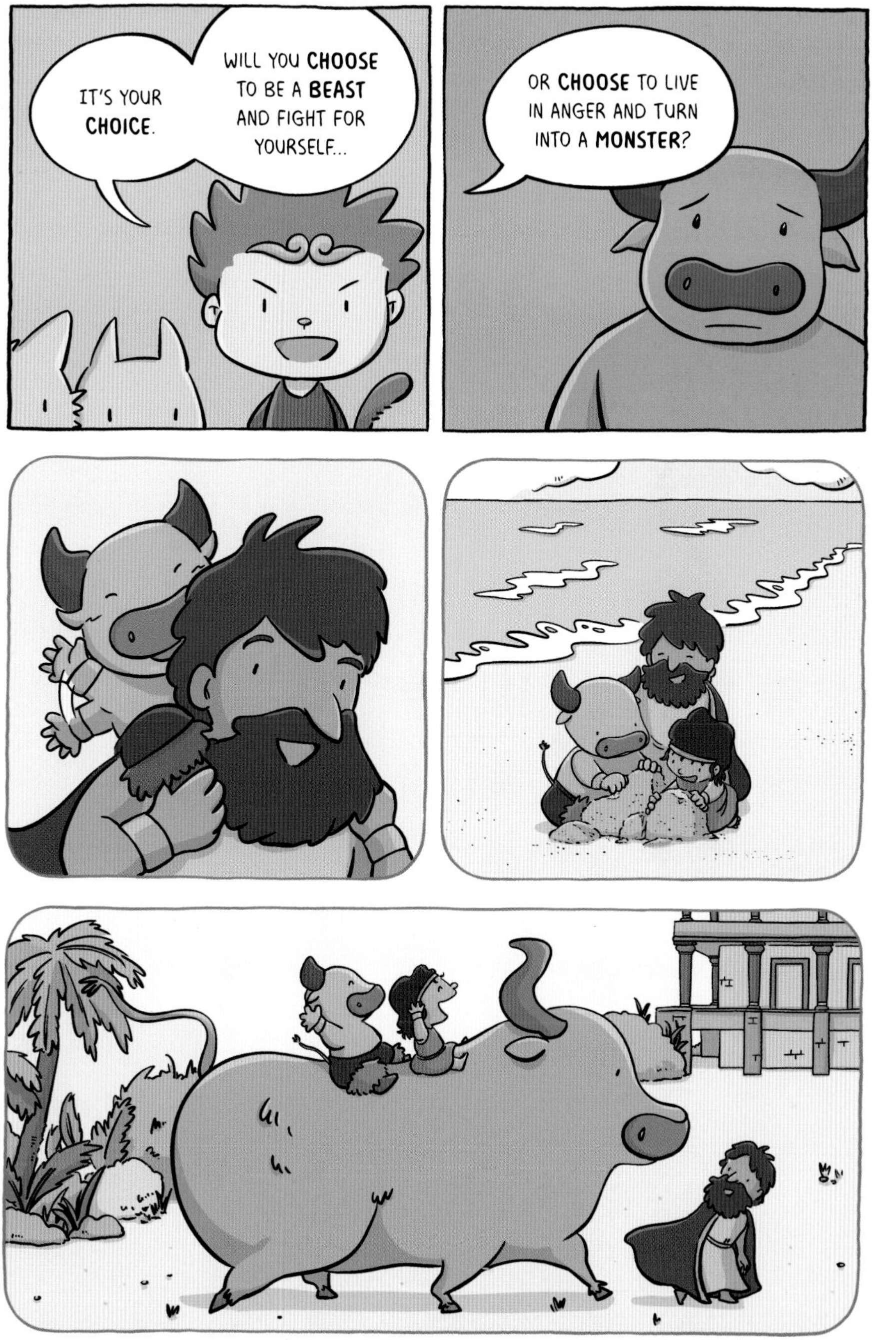
IT'S YOUR CHOICE.
WILL YOU CHOOSE TO BE A BEAST AND FIGHT FOR YOURSELF...
OR CHOOSE TO LIVE IN ANGER AND TURN INTO A MONSTER?

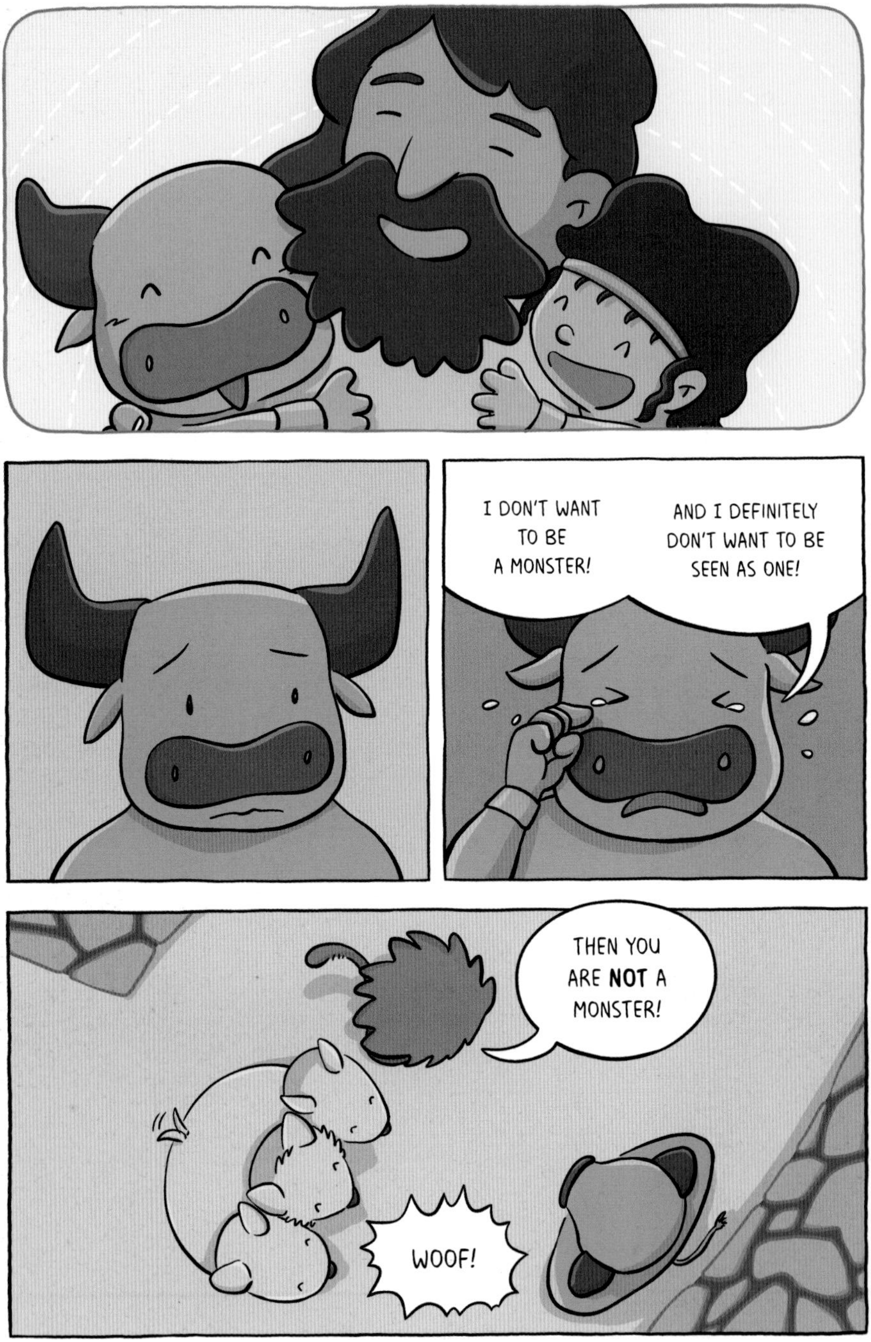
I DON'T WANT TO BE A MONSTER!
AND I DEFINITELY DON'T WANT TO BE SEEN AS ONE!
THEN YOU ARE **NOT** A MONSTER!
WOOF!

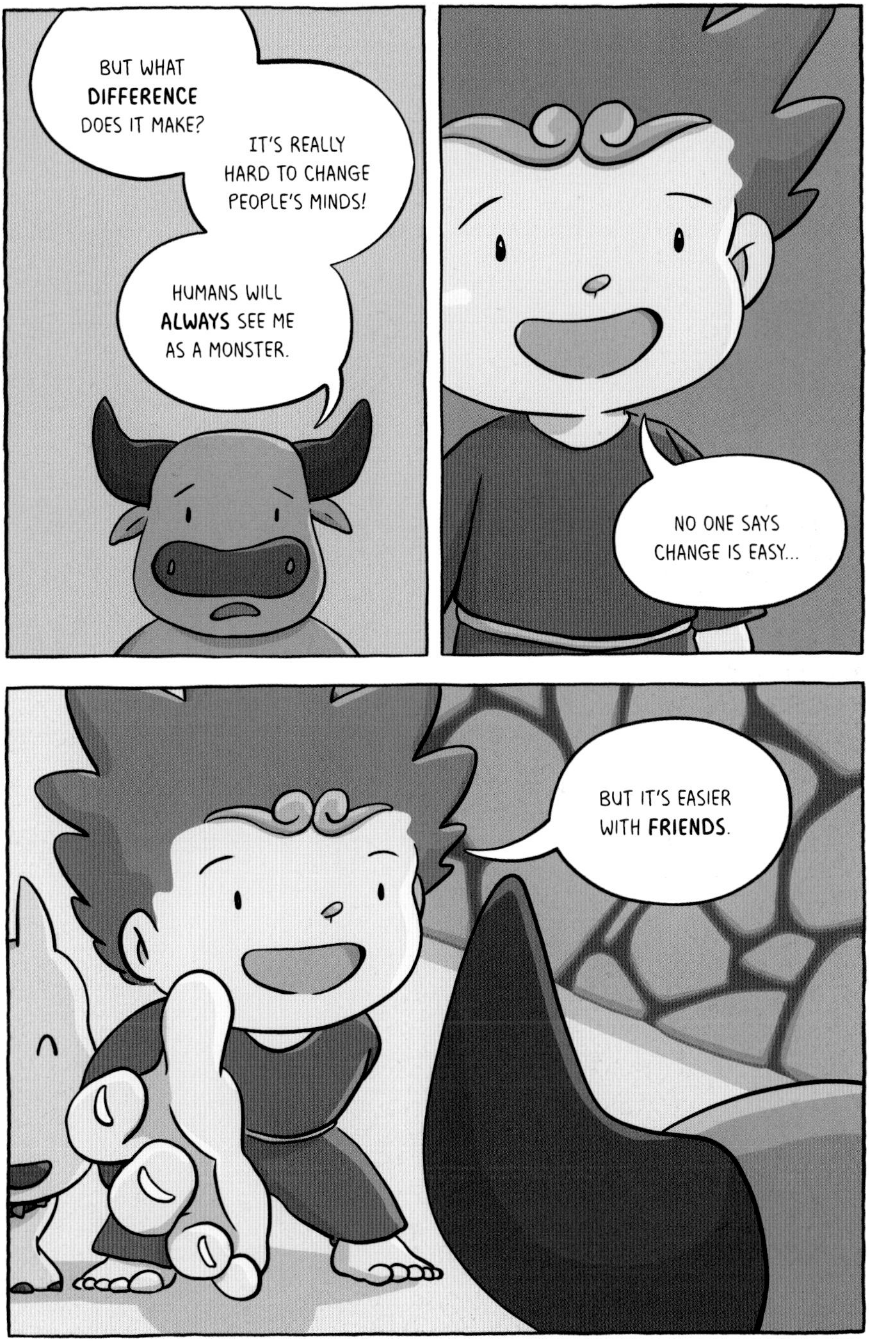

BUT WHAT **DIFFERENCE** DOES IT MAKE?
IT'S REALLY HARD TO CHANGE PEOPLE'S MINDS!
HUMANS WILL **ALWAYS** SEE ME AS A MONSTER.
NO ONE SAYS CHANGE IS EASY...
BUT IT'S EASIER WITH **FRIENDS**.

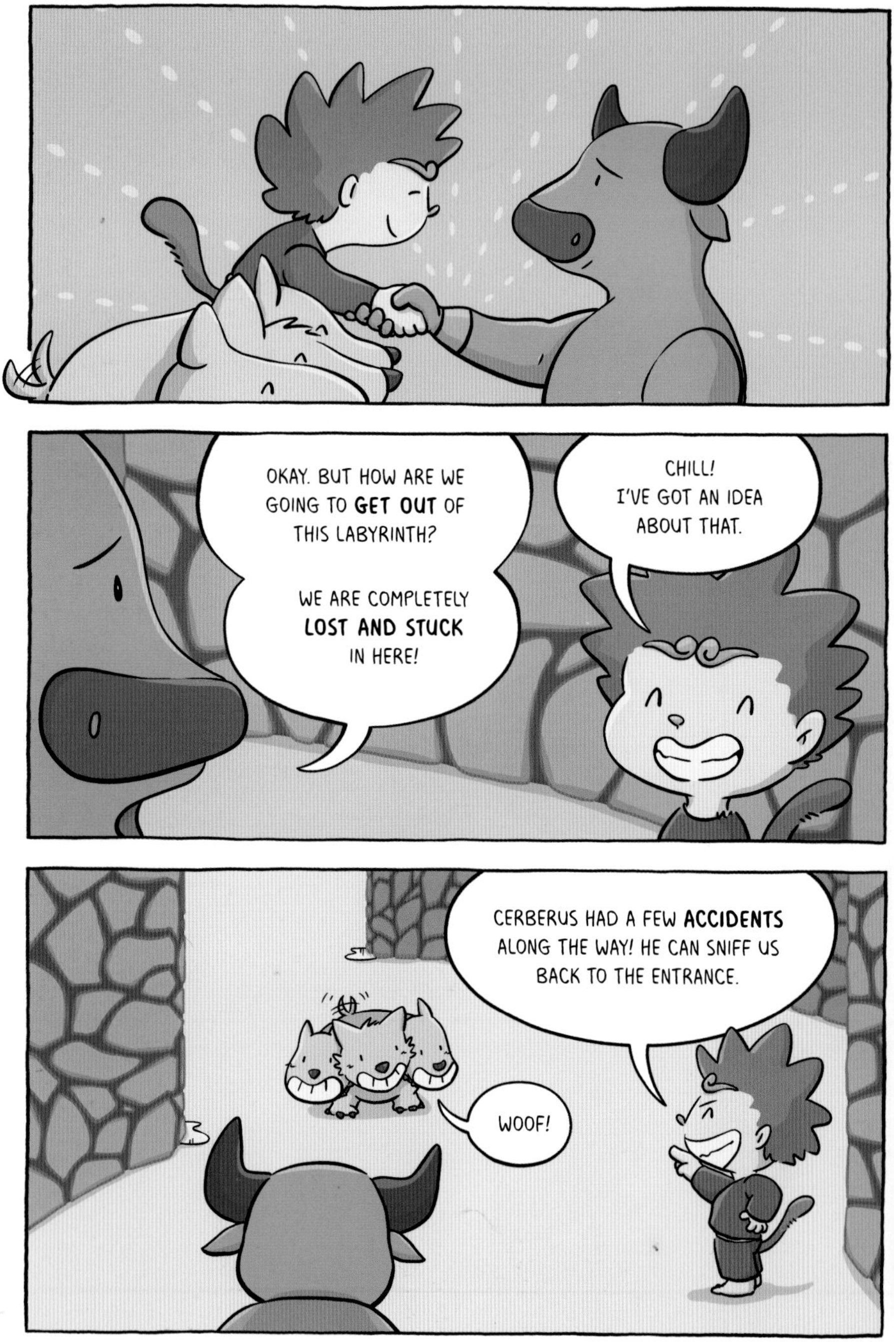
OKAY. BUT HOW ARE WE GOING TO GET OUT OF THIS LABYRINTH?
WE ARE COMPLETELY LOST AND STUCK IN HERE!
CHILL! I'VE GOT AN IDEA ABOUT THAT.
CERBERUS HAD A FEW ACCIDENTS ALONG THE WAY! HE CAN SNIFF US BACK TO THE ENTRANCE.
WOOF!

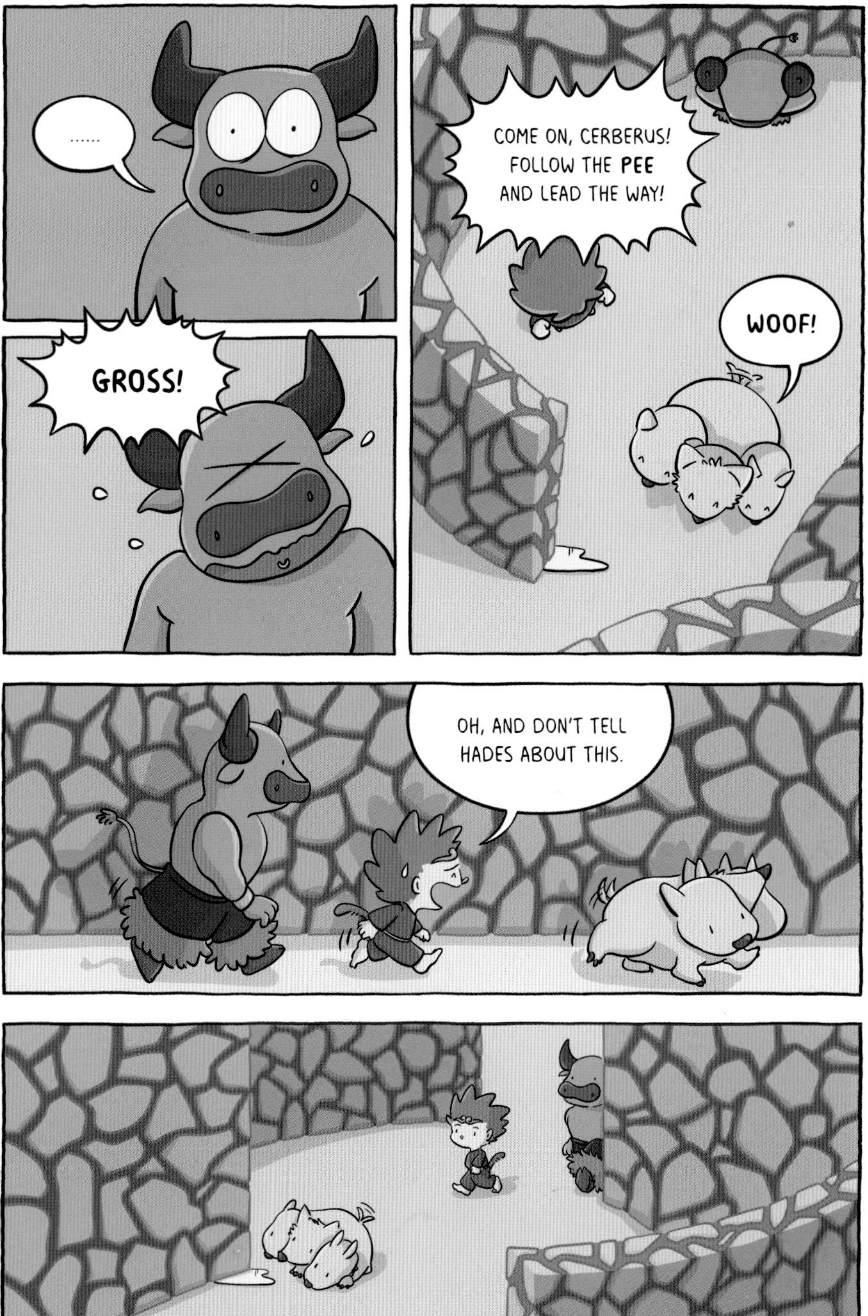
......
GROSS!
COME ON, CERBERUS! FOLLOW THE **PEE** AND LEAD THE WAY!
WOOF!
OH, AND DON'T TELL HADES ABOUT THIS.

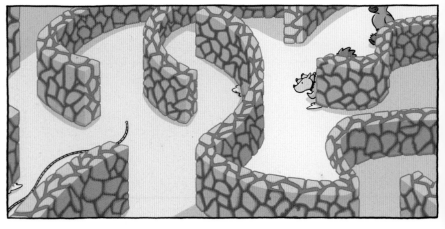

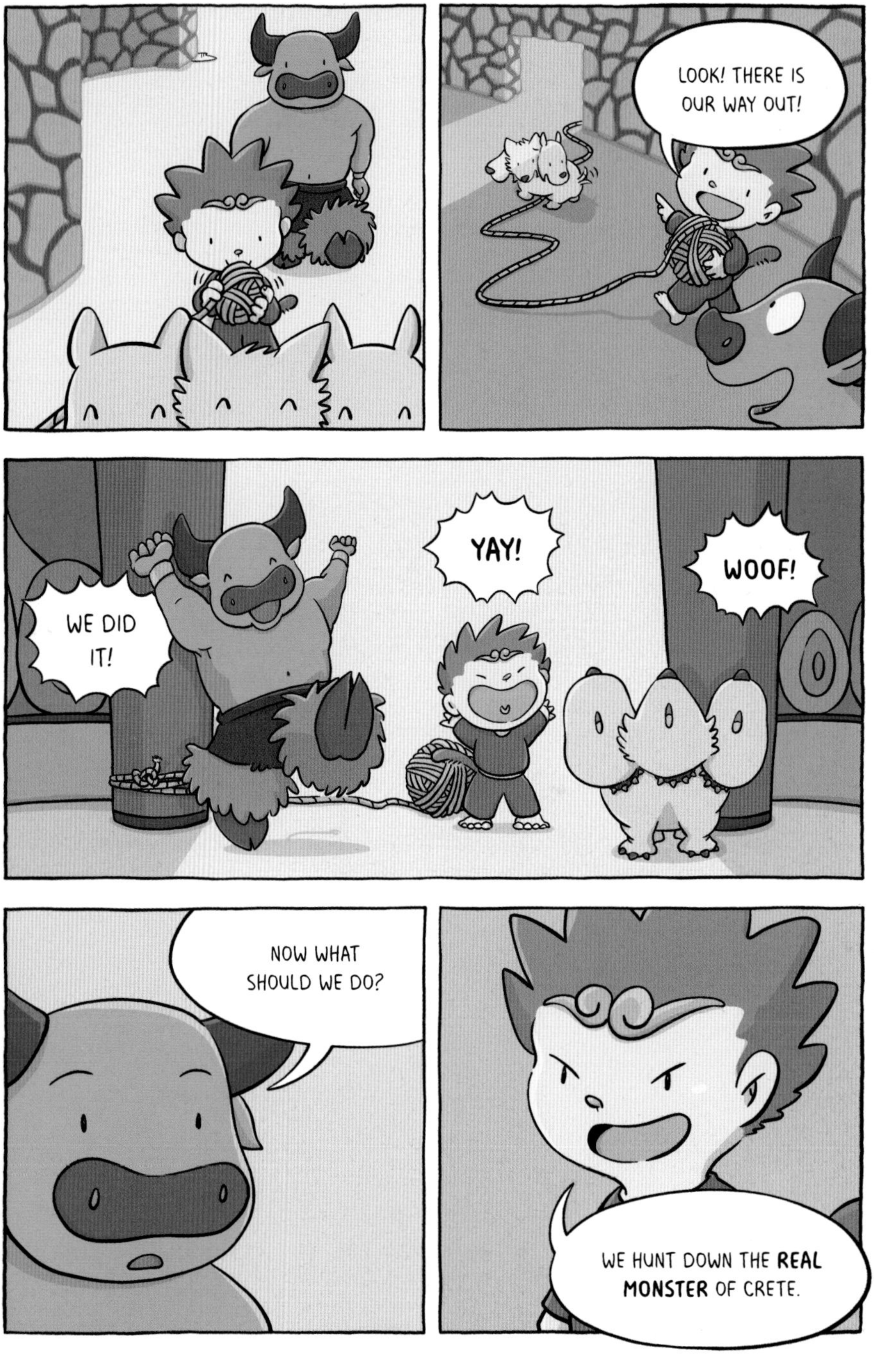
LOOK! THERE IS OUR WAY OUT!
WE DID IT!
YAY!
WOOF!
NOW WHAT SHOULD WE DO?
WE HUNT DOWN THE **REAL MONSTER** OF CRETE.

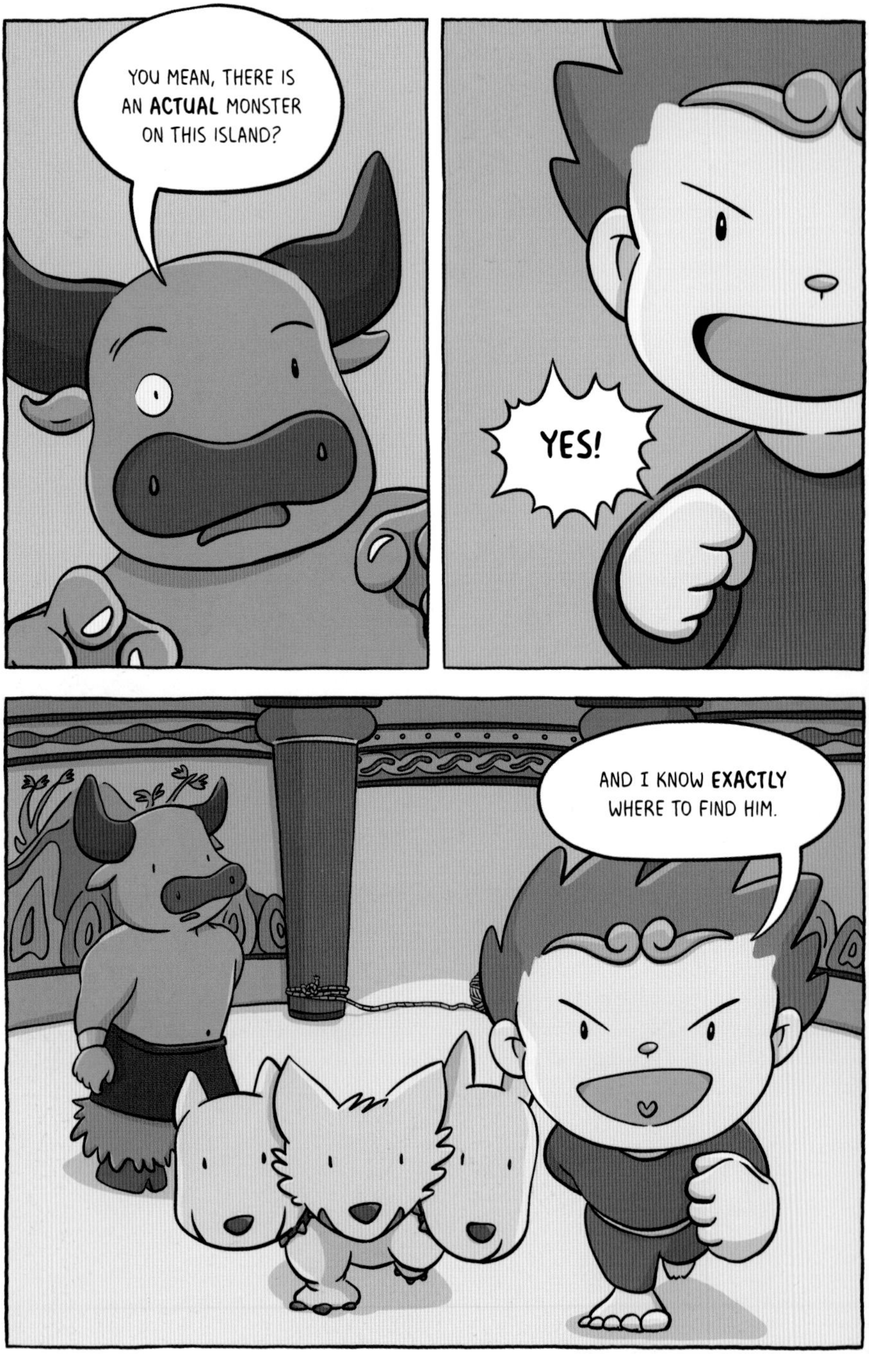
YOU MEAN, THERE IS AN ACTUAL MONSTER ON THIS ISLAND?
YES!
AND I KNOW EXACTLY WHERE TO FIND HIM.

CHAPTER 9

THE MONSTER

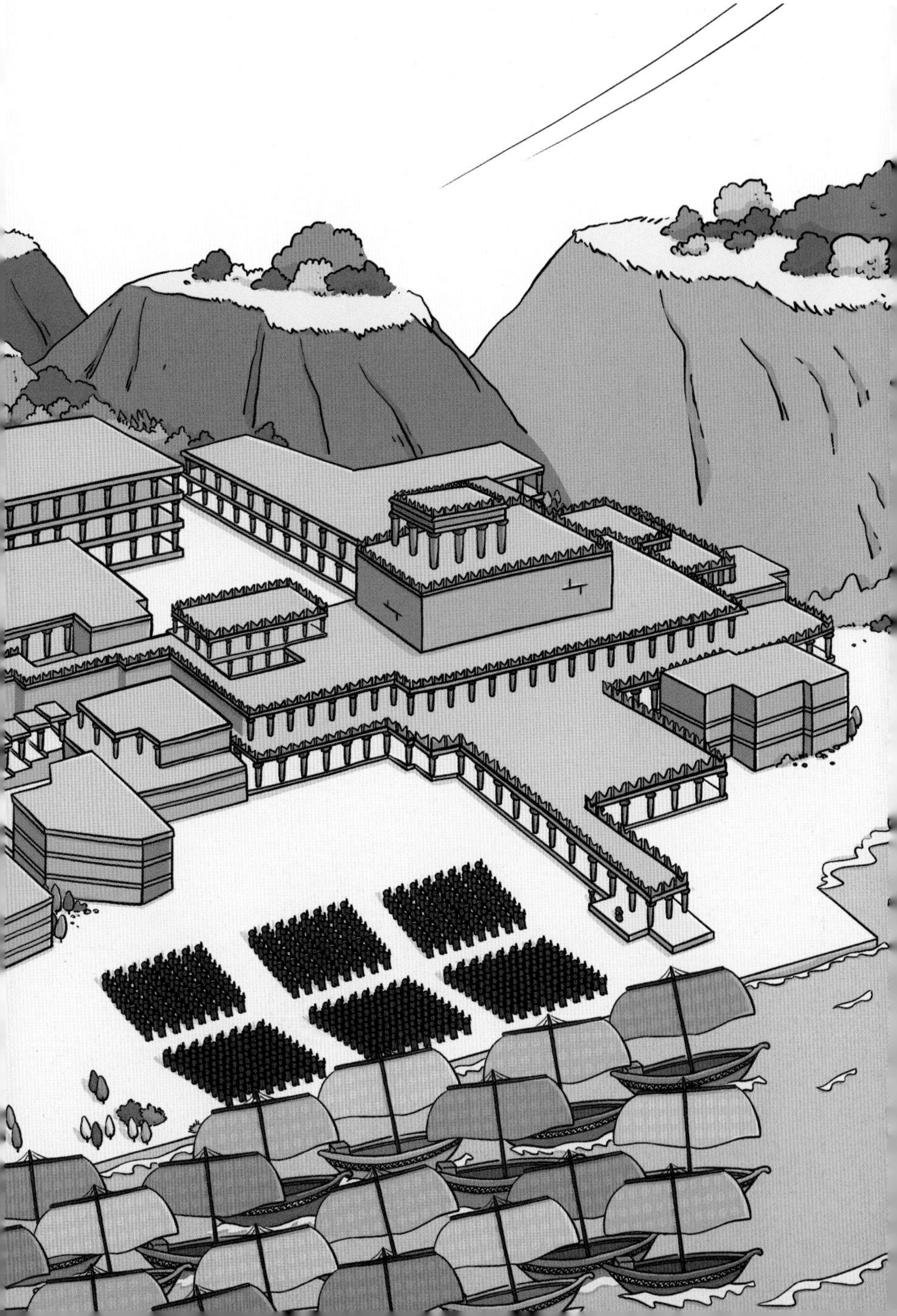

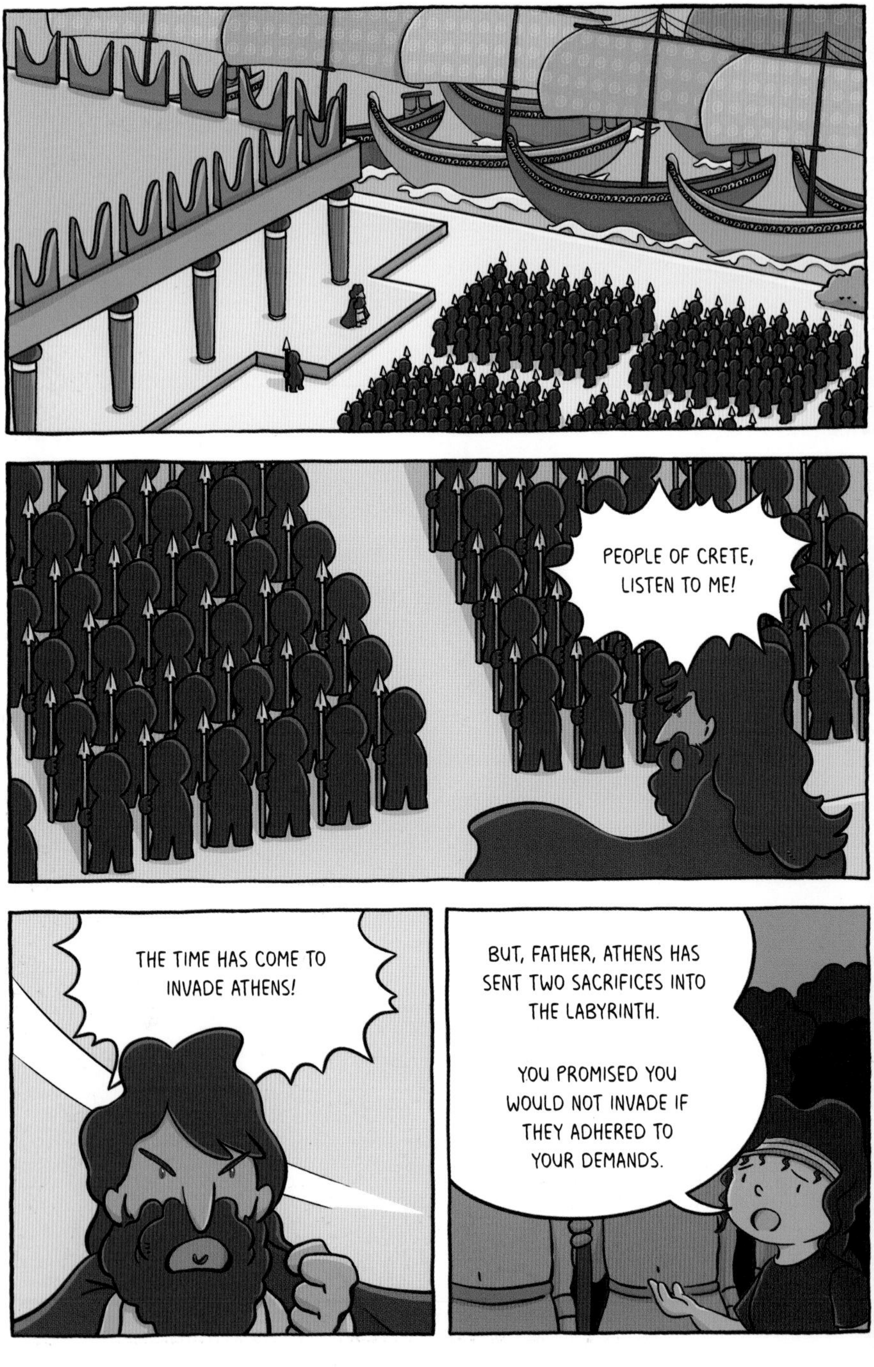
PEOPLE OF CRETE, LISTEN TO ME!
THE TIME HAS COME TO INVADE ATHENS!
BUT, FATHER, ATHENS HAS SENT TWO SACRIFICES INTO THE LABYRINTH.
YOU PROMISED YOU WOULD NOT INVADE IF THEY ADHERED TO YOUR DEMANDS.

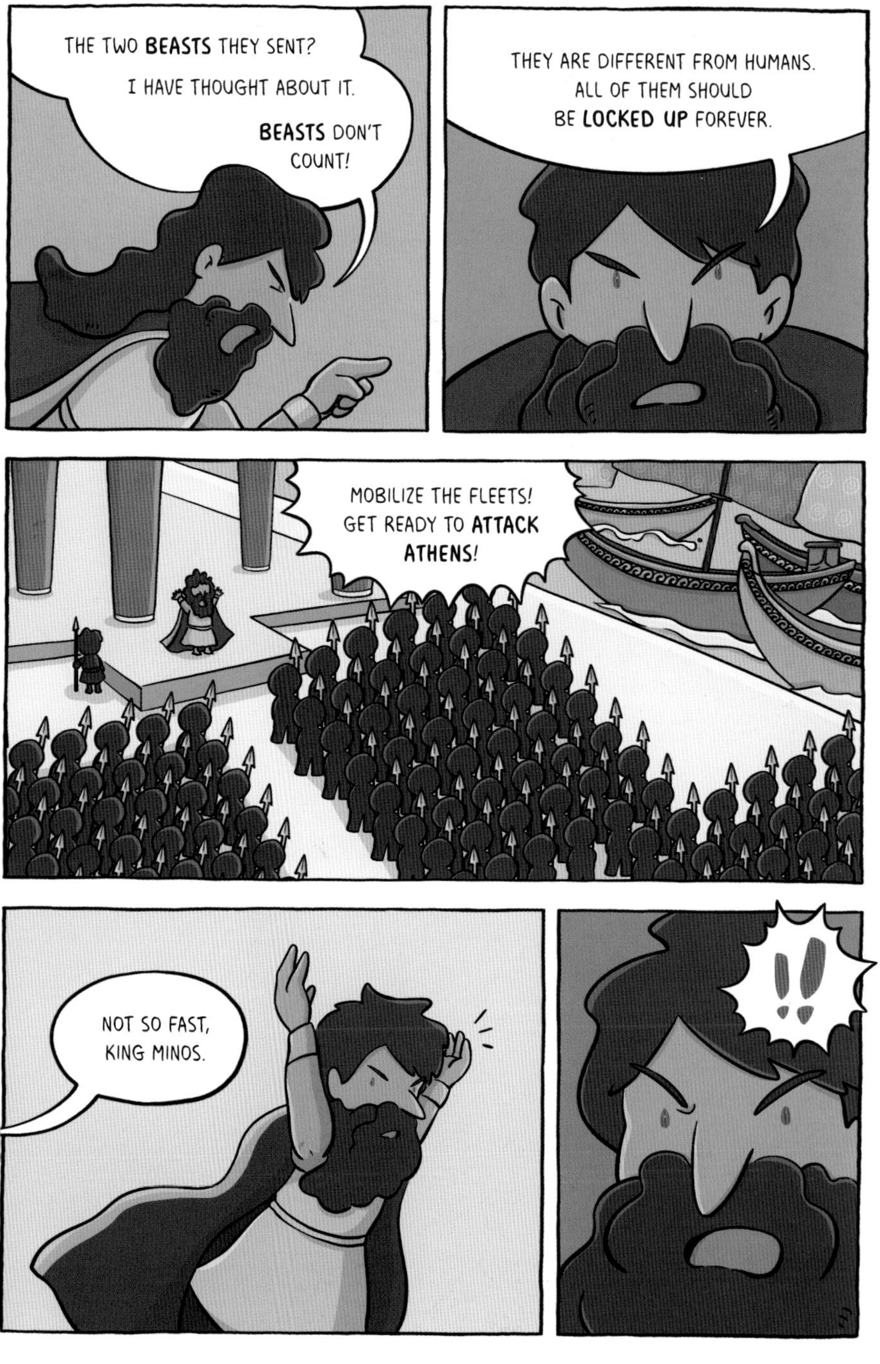
THE TWO BEASTS THEY SENT? I HAVE THOUGHT ABOUT IT. BEASTS DON'T COUNT!
THEY ARE DIFFERENT FROM HUMANS. ALL OF THEM SHOULD BE LOCKED UP FOREVER.
MOBILIZE THE FLEETS! GET READY TO ATTACK ATHENS!
NOT SO FAST, KING MINOS.
!!

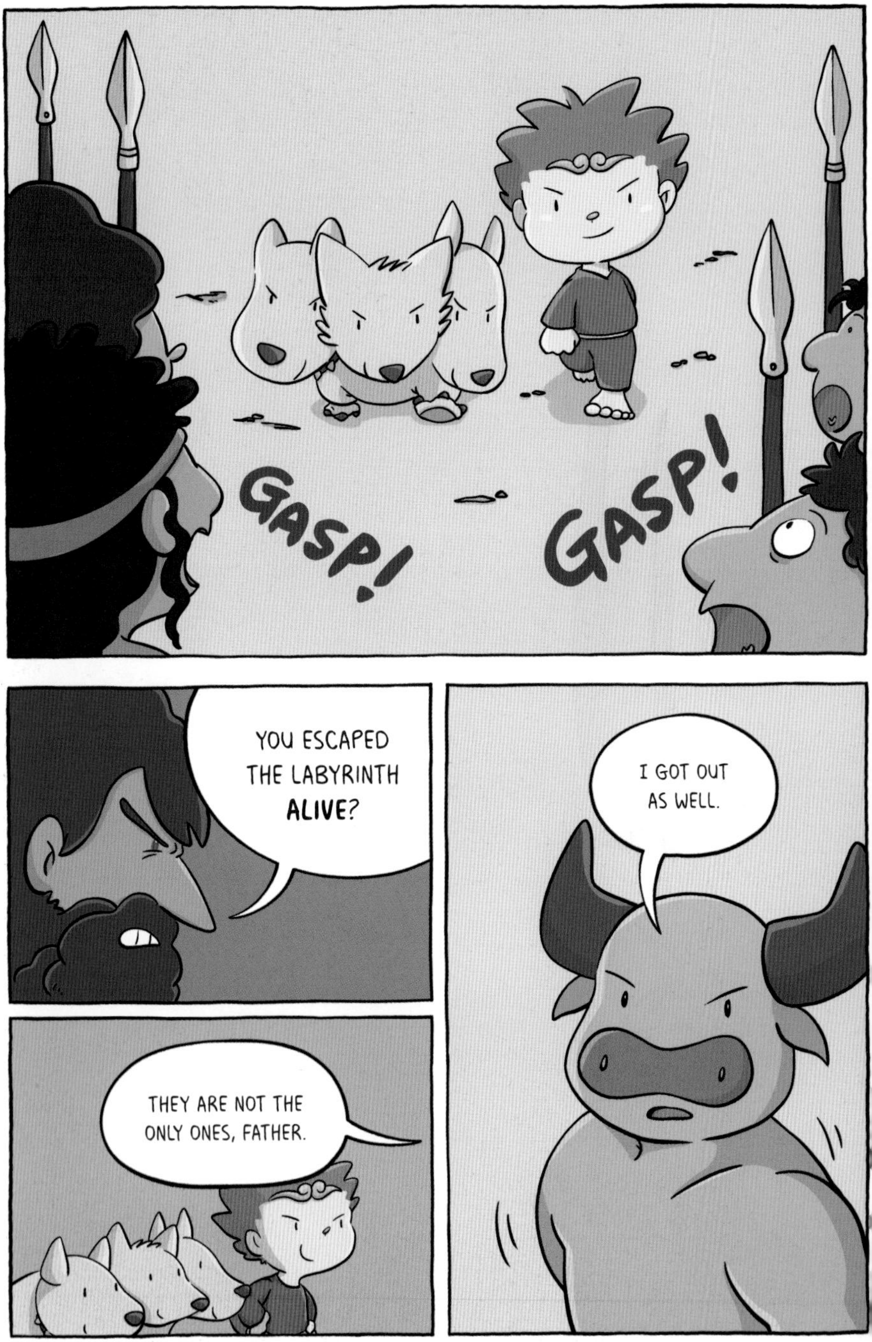
GASP!
GASP!
YOU ESCAPED THE LABYRINTH **ALIVE**?
THEY ARE NOT THE ONLY ONES, FATHER.
I GOT OUT AS WELL.

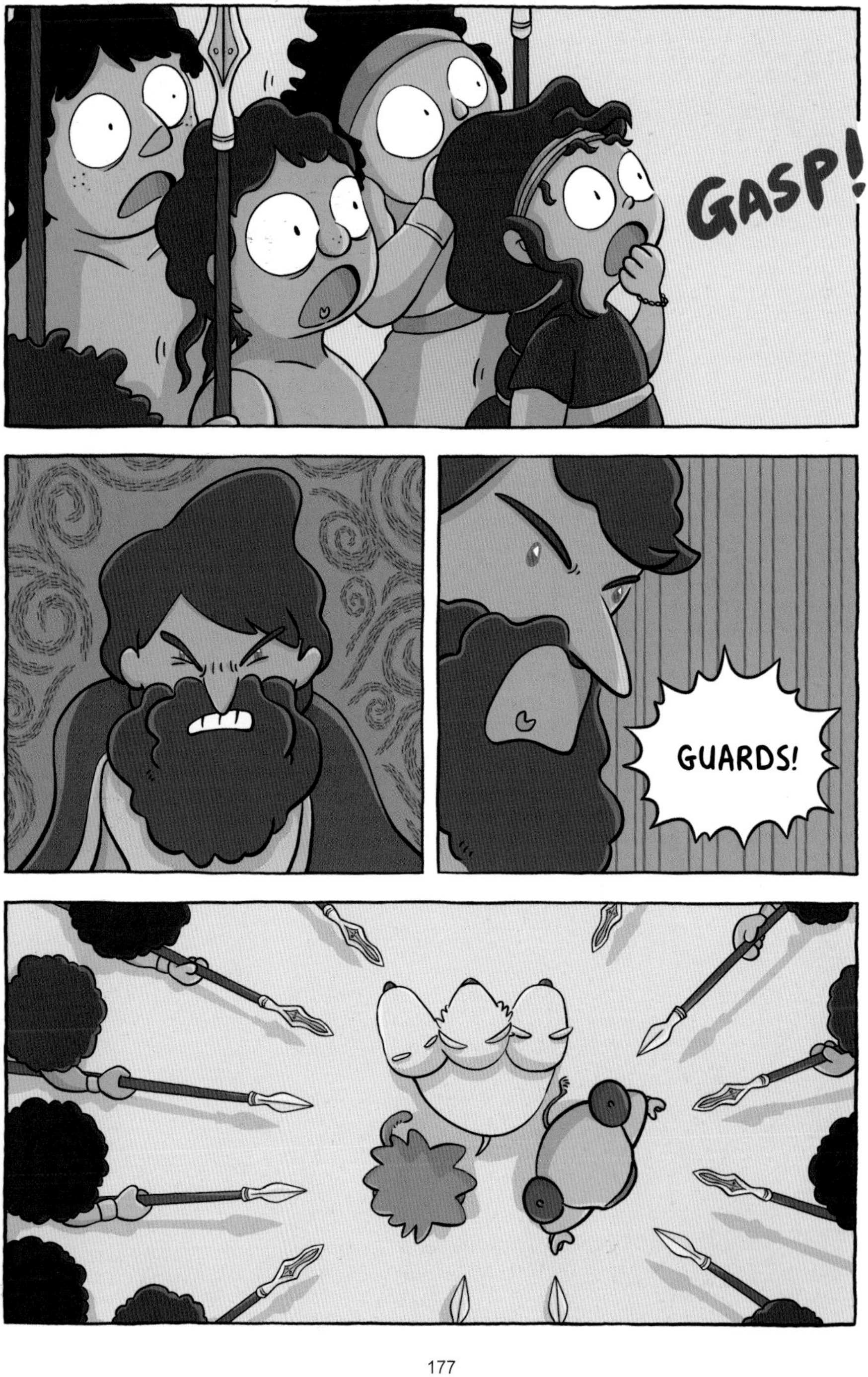
GASP!
GUARDS!

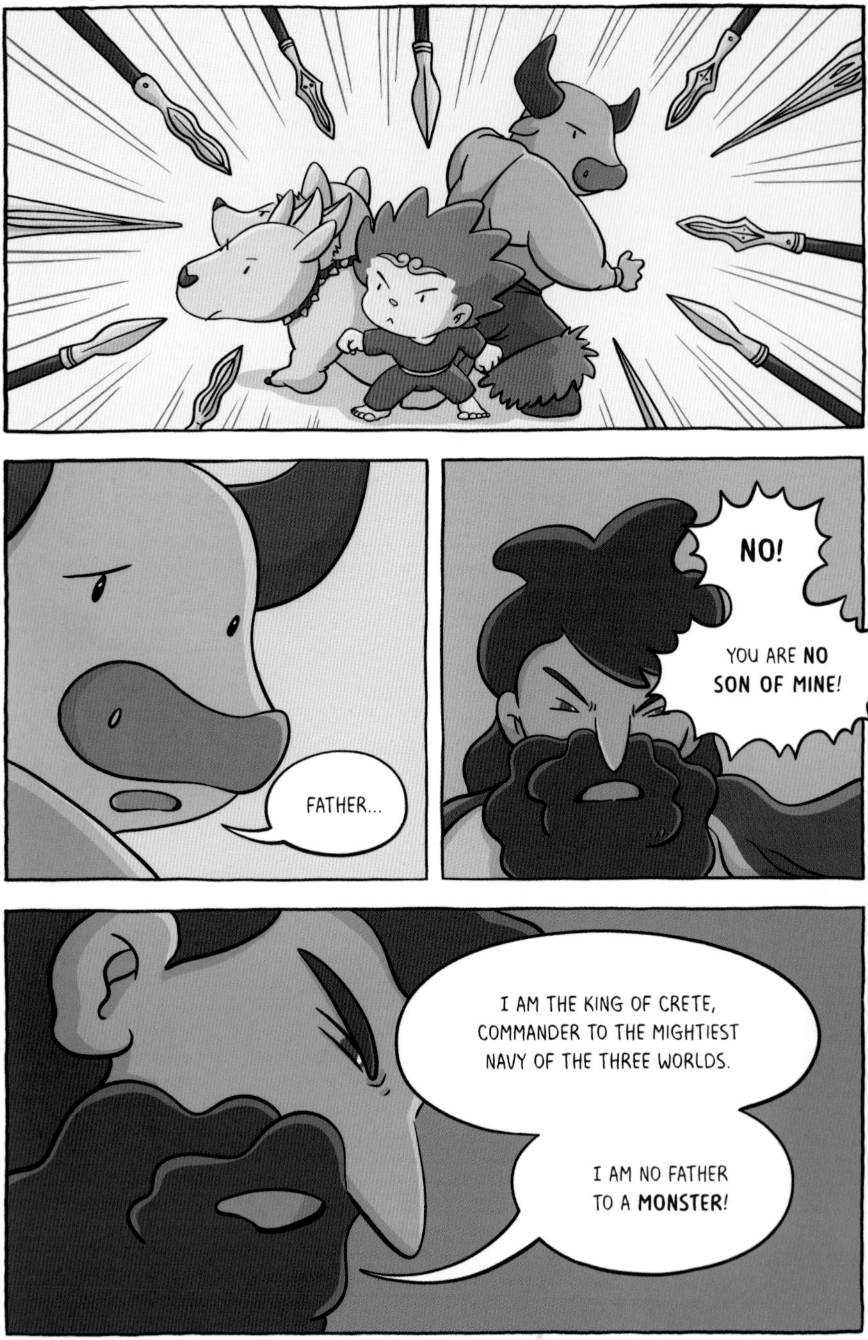
FATHER...
NO!
YOU ARE NO SON OF MINE!
I AM THE KING OF CRETE, COMMANDER TO THE MIGHTIEST NAVY OF THE THREE WORLDS.
I AM NO FATHER TO A MONSTER!

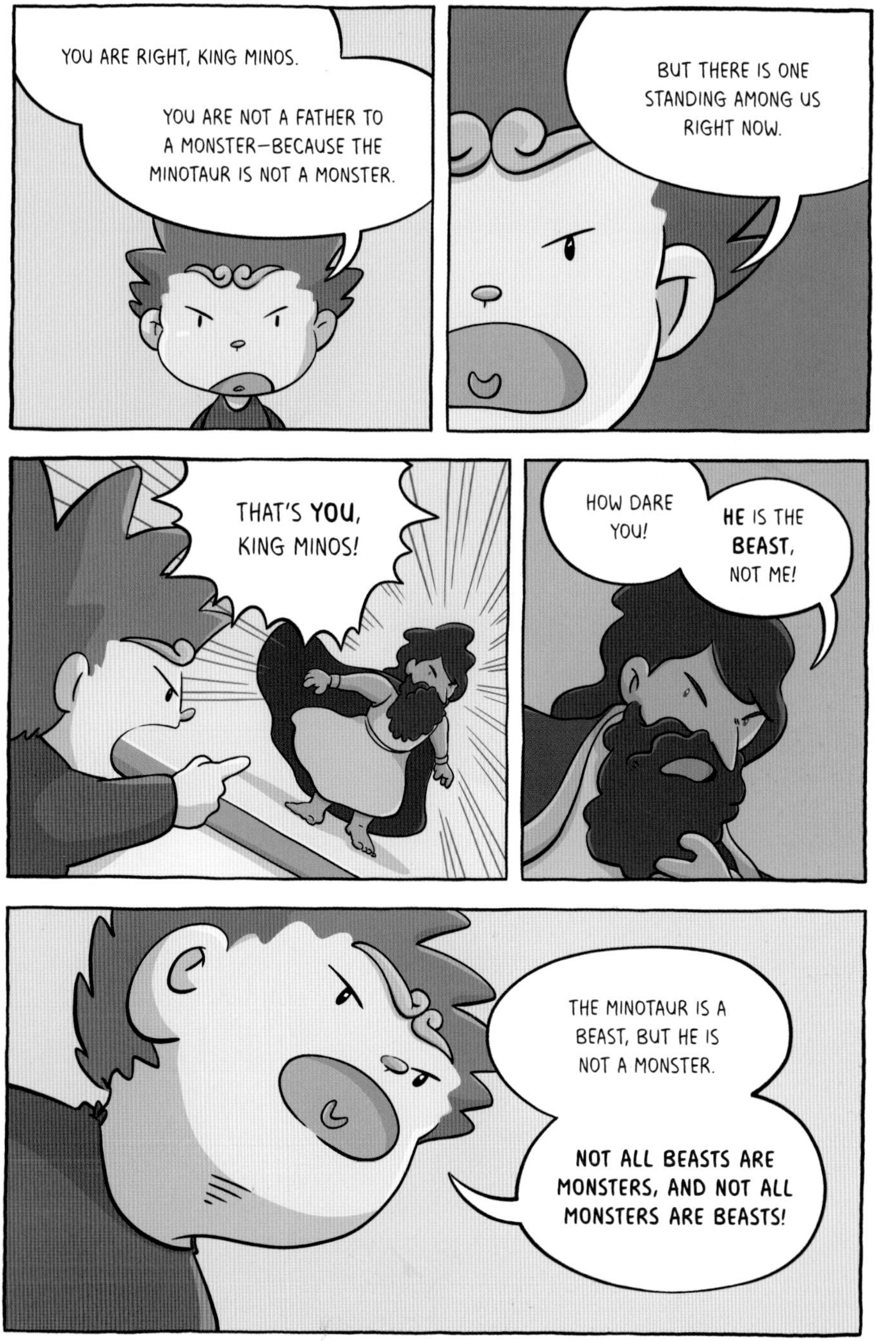
YOU ARE RIGHT, KING MINOS.
YOU ARE NOT A FATHER TO A MONSTER—BECAUSE THE MINOTAUR IS NOT A MONSTER.
BUT THERE IS ONE STANDING AMONG US RIGHT NOW.
THAT'S **YOU**, KING MINOS!
HOW DARE YOU!
HE IS THE **BEAST**, NOT ME!
THE MINOTAUR IS A BEAST, BUT HE IS NOT A MONSTER.
NOT ALL BEASTS ARE MONSTERS, AND NOT ALL MONSTERS ARE BEASTS!

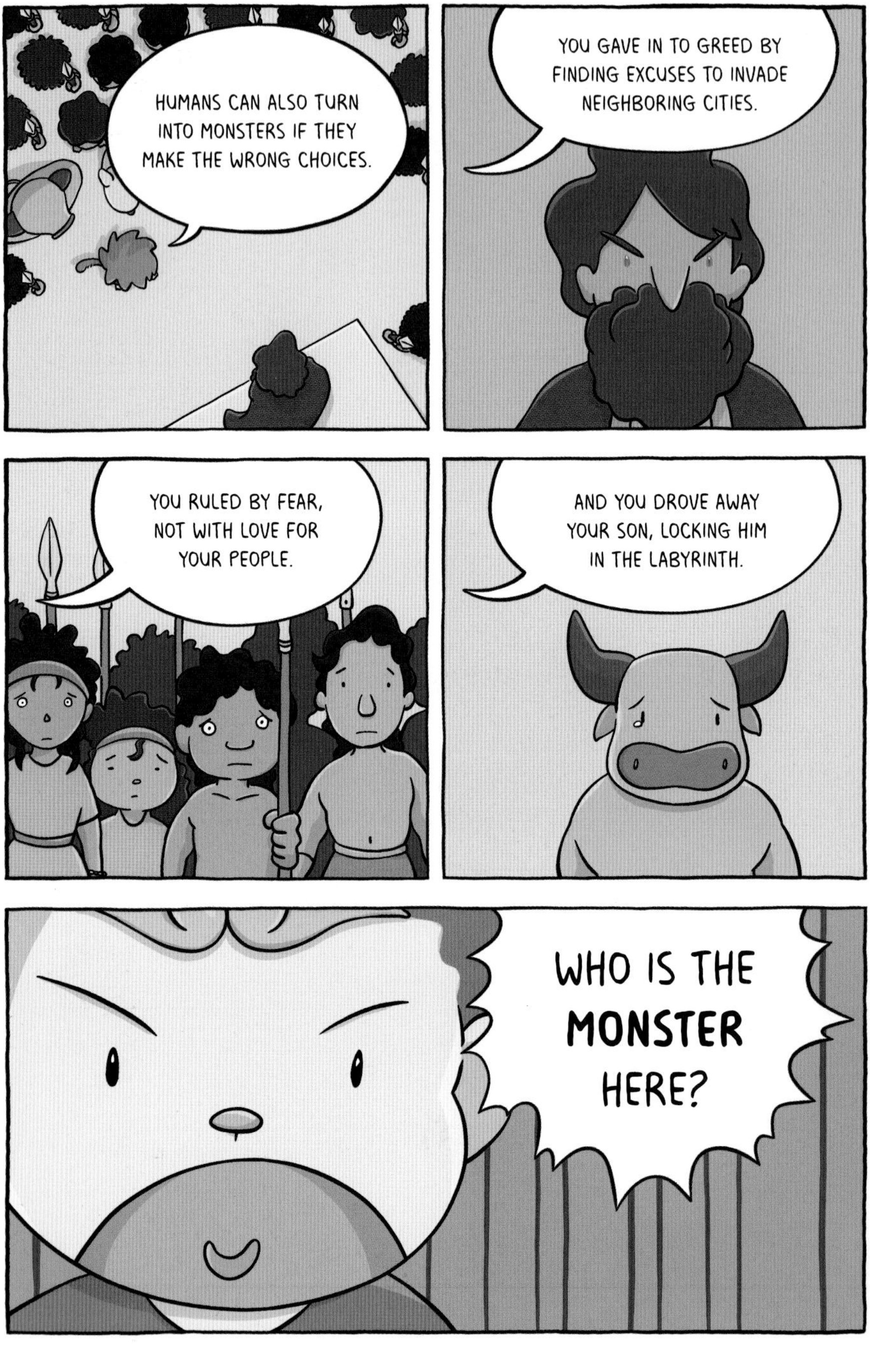
HUMANS CAN ALSO TURN INTO MONSTERS IF THEY MAKE THE WRONG CHOICES.
YOU GAVE IN TO GREED BY FINDING EXCUSES TO INVADE NEIGHBORING CITIES.
YOU RULED BY FEAR, NOT WITH LOVE FOR YOUR PEOPLE.
AND YOU DROVE AWAY YOUR SON, LOCKING HIM IN THE LABYRINTH.
WHO IS THE **MONSTER** HERE?

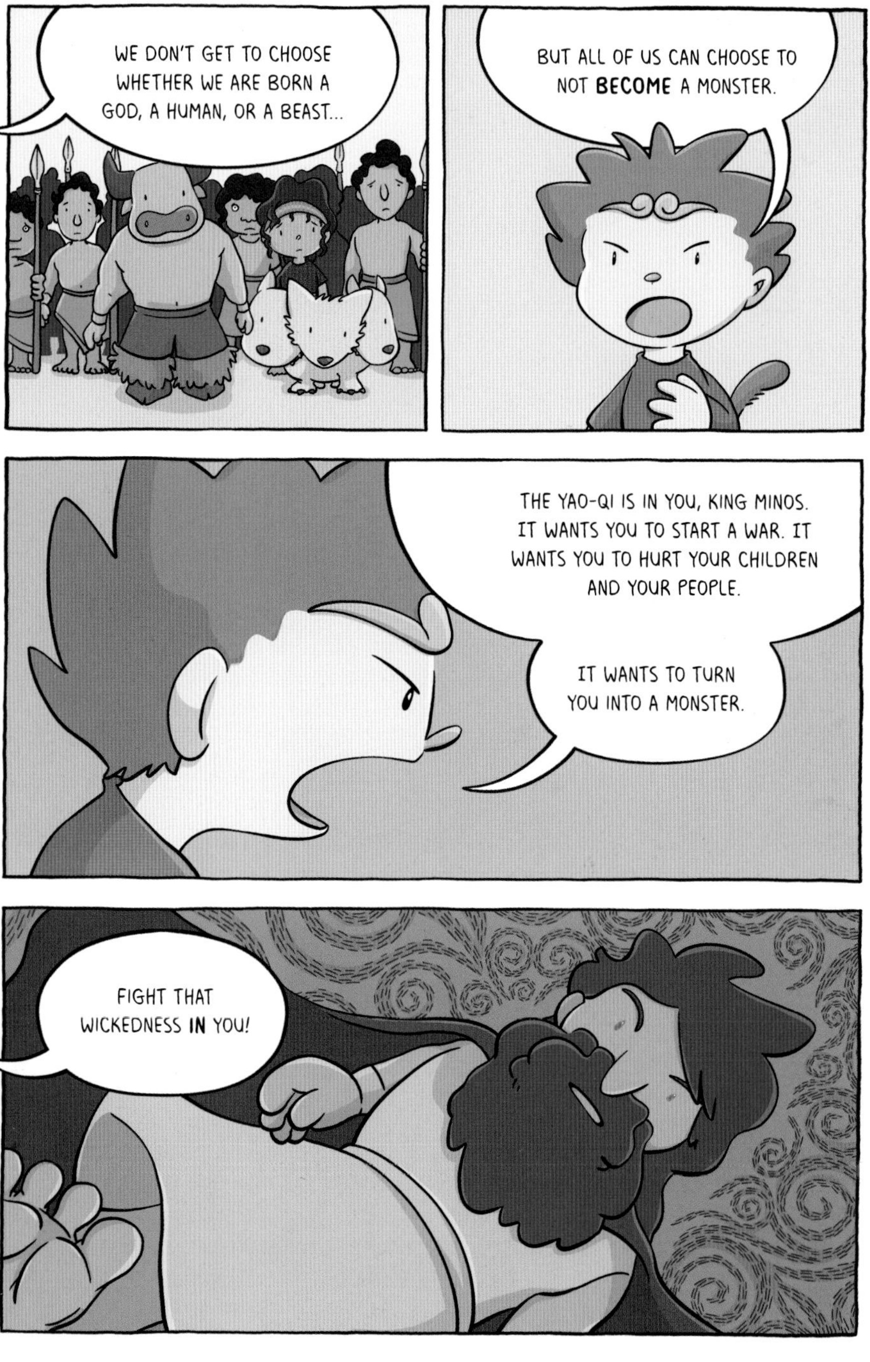
WE DON'T GET TO CHOOSE WHETHER WE ARE BORN A GOD, A HUMAN, OR A BEAST...
BUT ALL OF US CAN CHOOSE TO NOT **BECOME** A MONSTER.
THE YAO-QI IS IN YOU, KING MINOS. IT WANTS YOU TO START A WAR. IT WANTS YOU TO HURT YOUR CHILDREN AND YOUR PEOPLE.
IT WANTS TO TURN YOU INTO A MONSTER.
FIGHT THAT WICKEDNESS **IN** YOU!

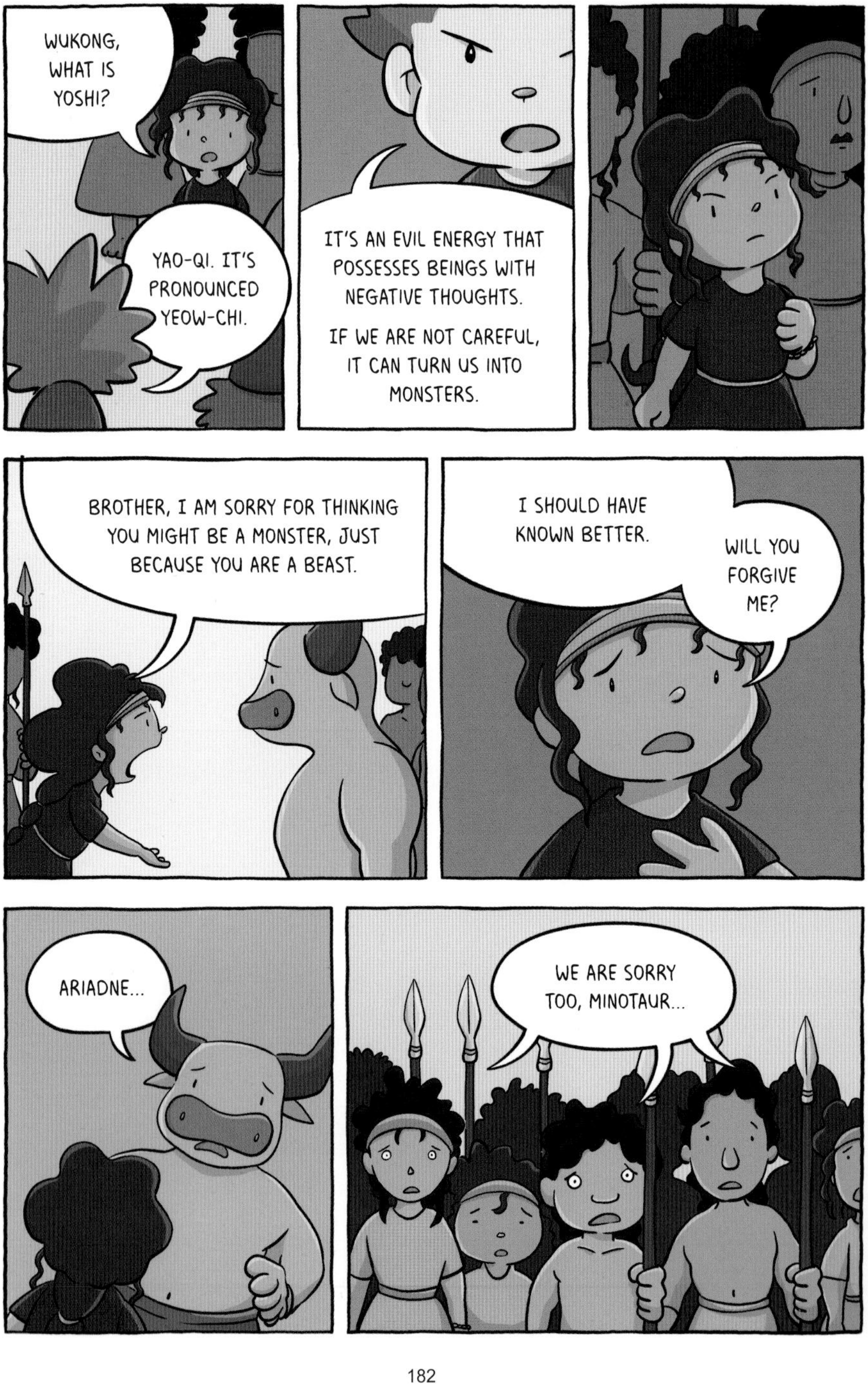
WUKONG, WHAT IS YOSHI?
YAO-QI. IT'S PRONOUNCED YEOW-CHI.
IT'S AN EVIL ENERGY THAT POSSESSES BEINGS WITH NEGATIVE THOUGHTS.
IF WE ARE NOT CAREFUL, IT CAN TURN US INTO MONSTERS.
BROTHER, I AM SORRY FOR THINKING YOU MIGHT BE A MONSTER, JUST BECAUSE YOU ARE A BEAST.
I SHOULD HAVE KNOWN BETTER.
WILL YOU FORGIVE ME?
ARIADNE...
WE ARE SORRY TOO, MINOTAUR...

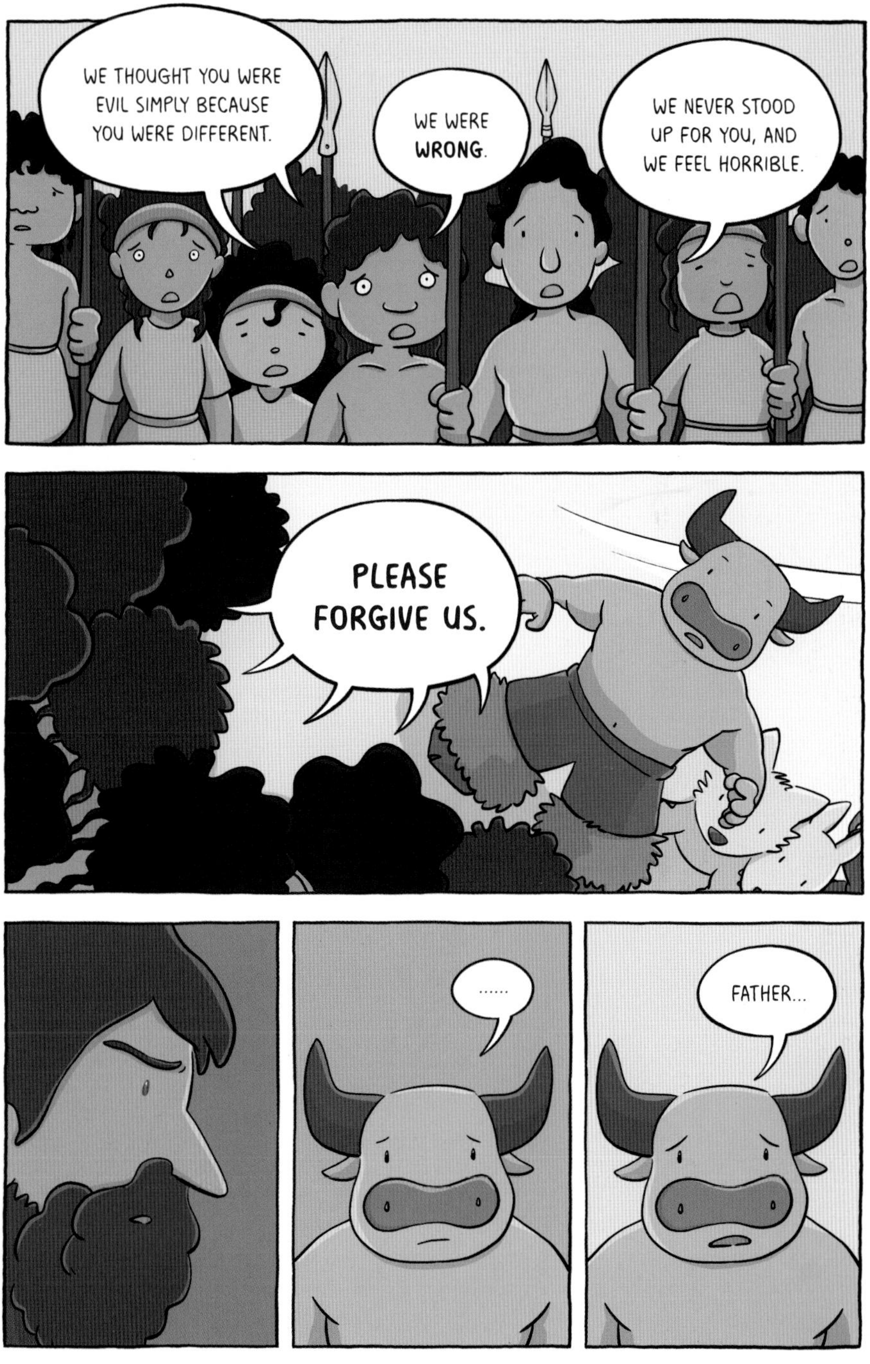
WE THOUGHT YOU WERE EVIL SIMPLY BECAUSE YOU WERE DIFFERENT.
WE WERE **WRONG**.
WE NEVER STOOD UP FOR YOU, AND WE FEEL HORRIBLE.
PLEASE FORGIVE US.
......
FATHER...

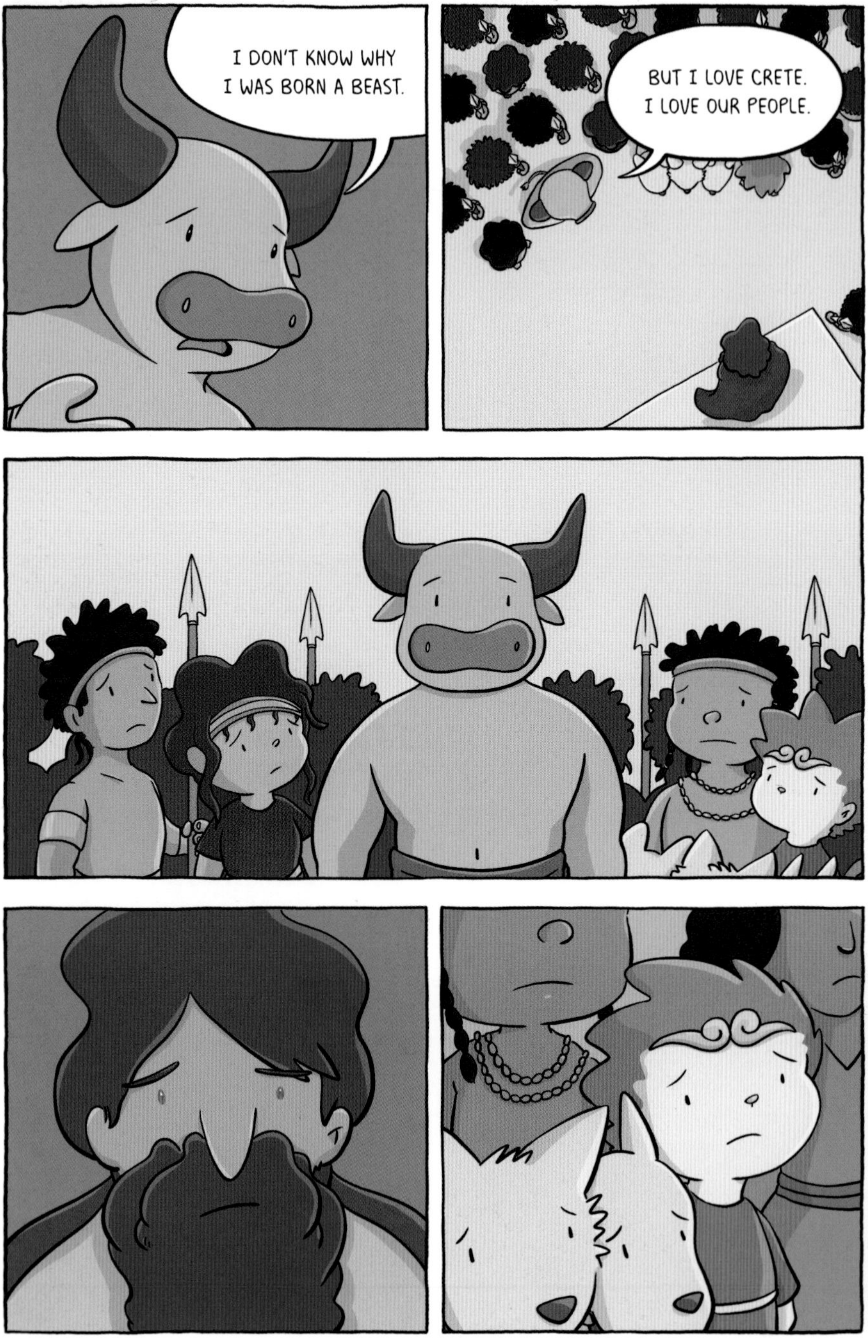
I DON'T KNOW WHY
I WAS BORN A BEAST.
BUT I LOVE CRETE.
I LOVE OUR PEOPLE.

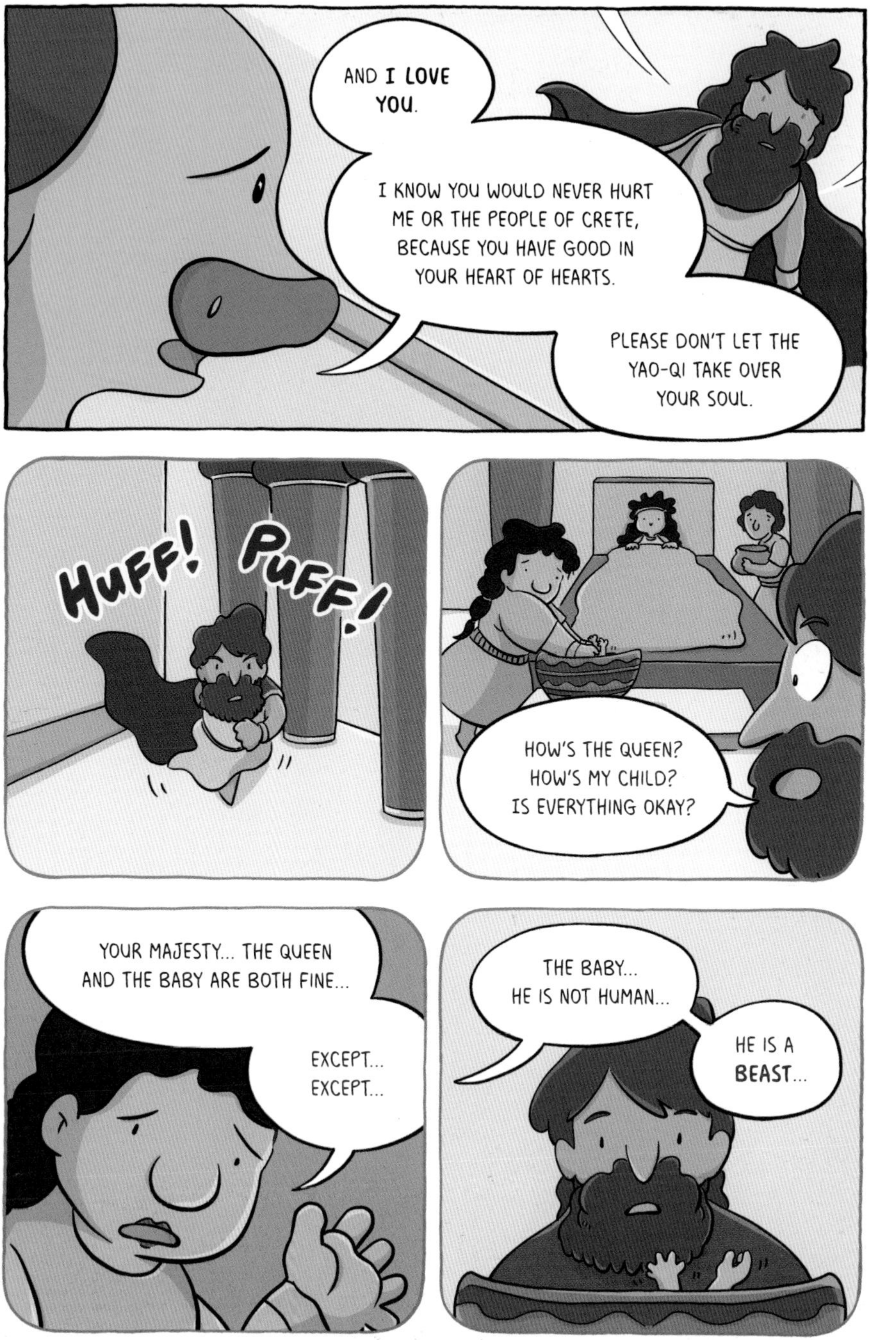
AND I LOVE YOU.
I KNOW YOU WOULD NEVER HURT ME OR THE PEOPLE OF CRETE, BECAUSE YOU HAVE GOOD IN YOUR HEART OF HEARTS.
PLEASE DON'T LET THE YAO-QI TAKE OVER YOUR SOUL.
HUFF! PUFF!
HOW'S THE QUEEN? HOW'S MY CHILD? IS EVERYTHING OKAY?
YOUR MAJESTY... THE QUEEN AND THE BABY ARE BOTH FINE...
EXCEPT... EXCEPT...
THE BABY... HE IS NOT HUMAN...
HE IS A BEAST...

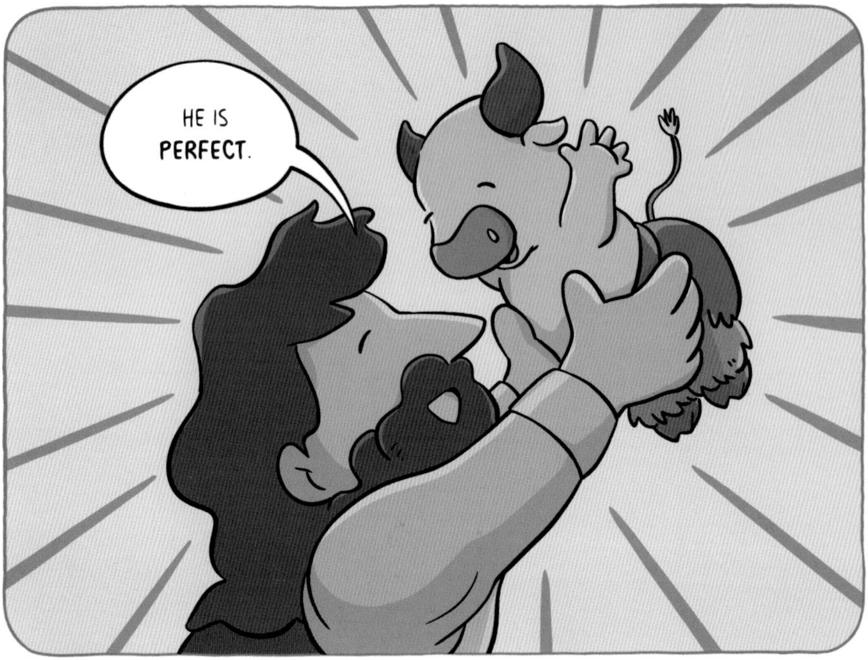
HE IS
PERFECT.

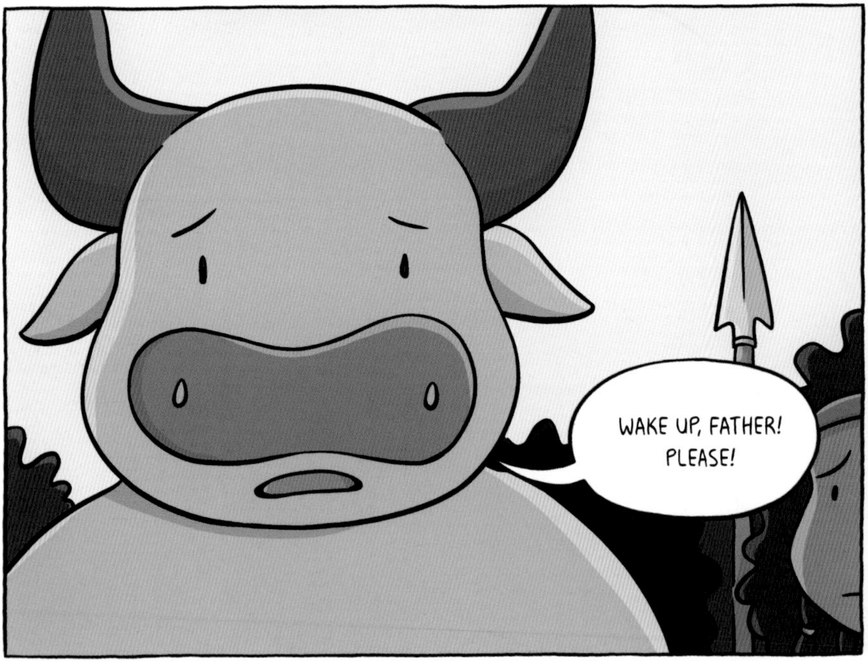
WAKE UP, FATHER!
PLEASE!

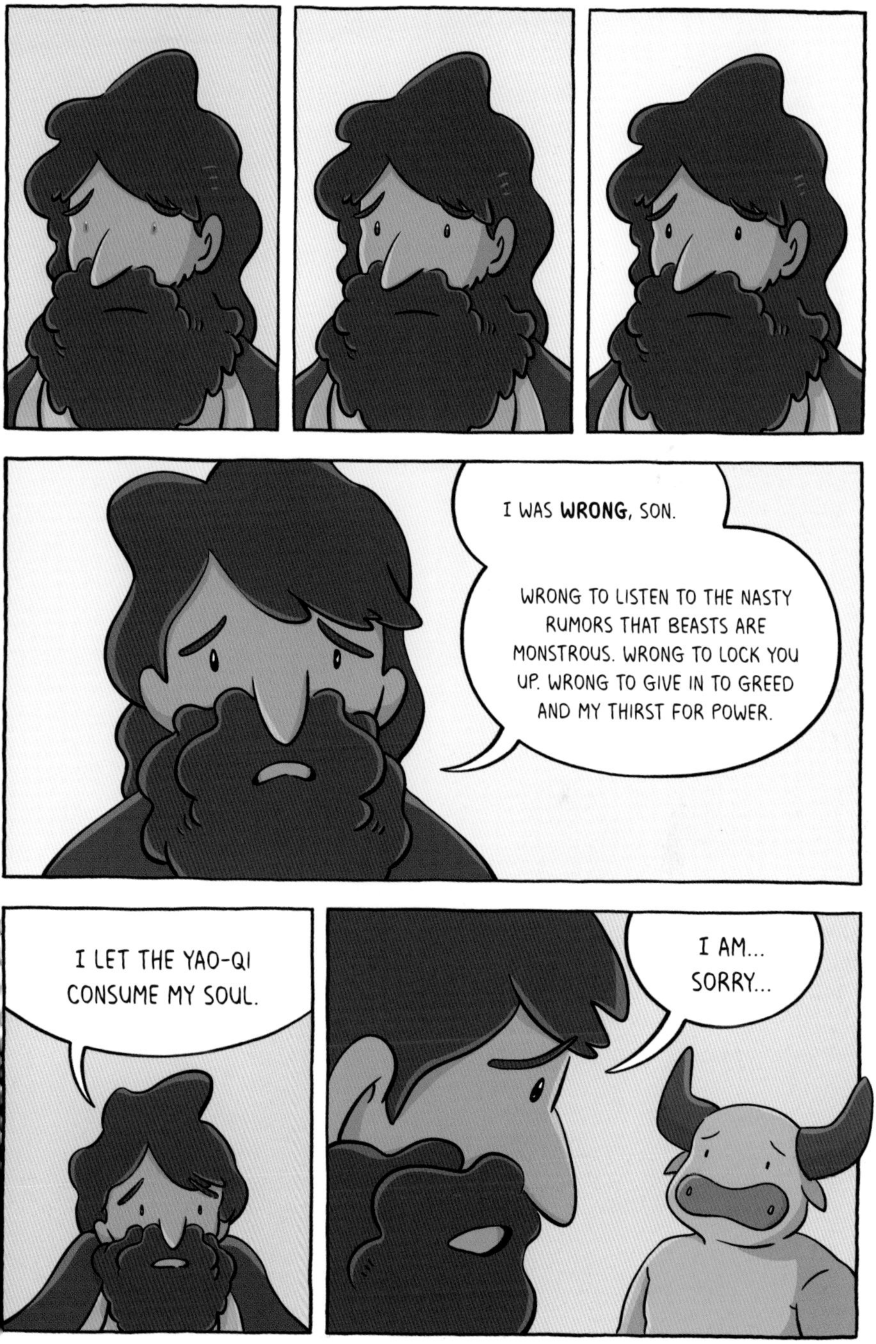
I WAS **WRONG**, SON.
WRONG TO LISTEN TO THE NASTY RUMORS THAT BEASTS ARE MONSTROUS. WRONG TO LOCK YOU UP. WRONG TO GIVE IN TO GREED AND MY THIRST FOR POWER.
I LET THE YAO-QI CONSUME MY SOUL.
I AM... SORRY...

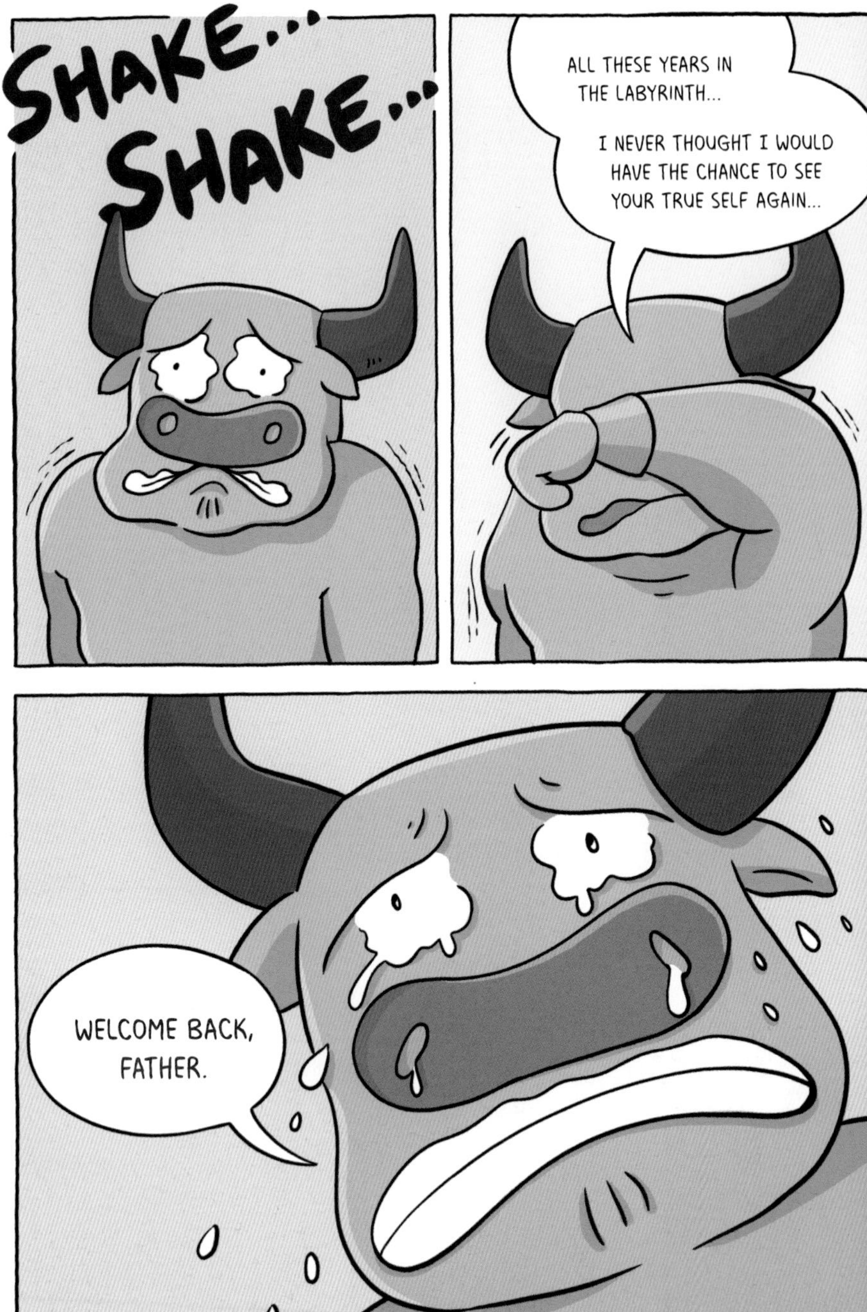
SHAKE...
SHAKE...
ALL THESE YEARS IN THE LABYRINTH...
I NEVER THOUGHT I WOULD HAVE THE CHANCE TO SEE YOUR TRUE SELF AGAIN...
WELCOME BACK, FATHER.

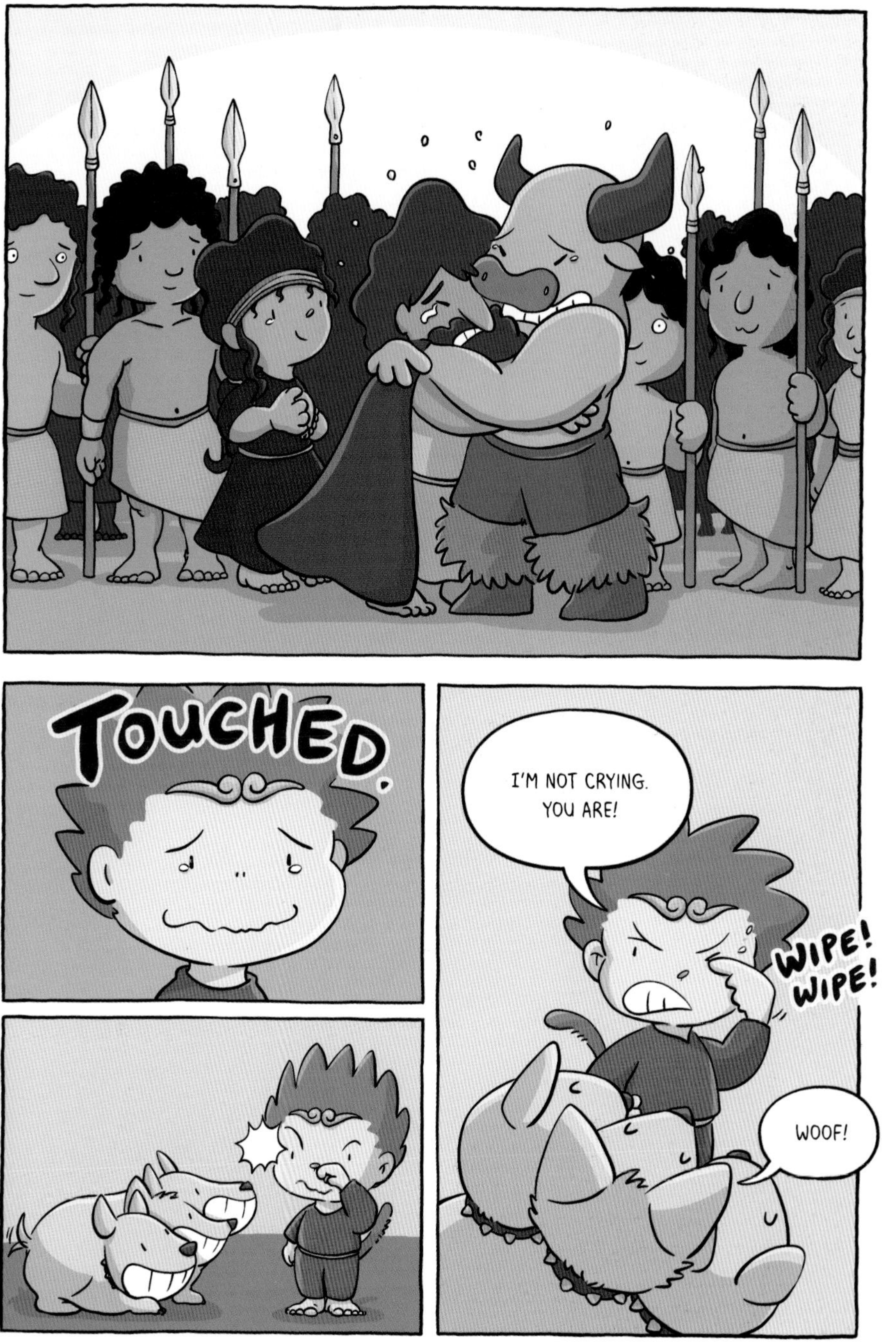
TOUCHED.
I'M NOT CRYING. YOU ARE!
WIPE! WIPE!
WOOF!

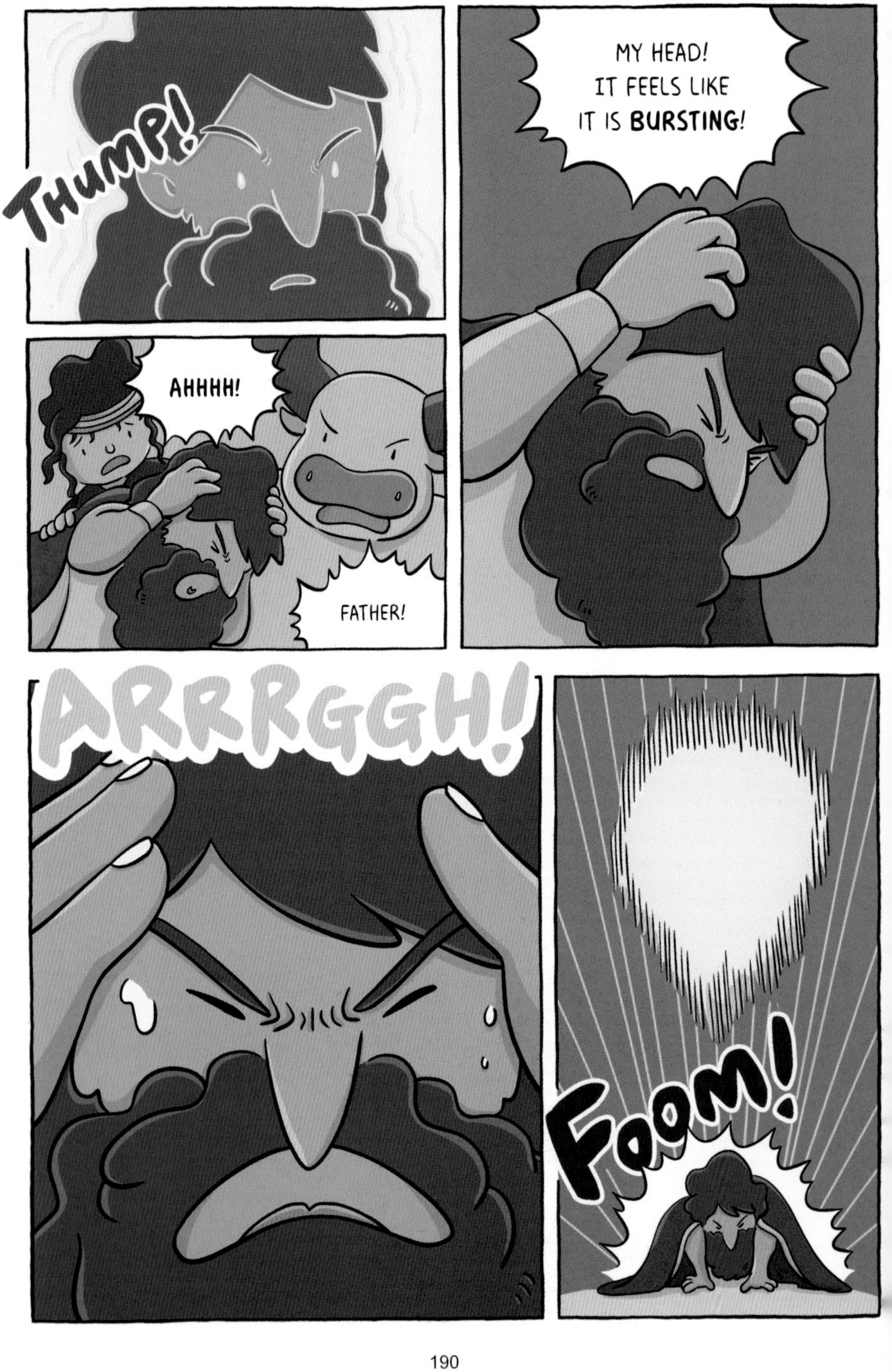
THUMP!
MY HEAD!
IT FEELS LIKE
IT IS **BURSTING**!
AHHHH!
FATHER!
ARRRGGH!
FOOM!

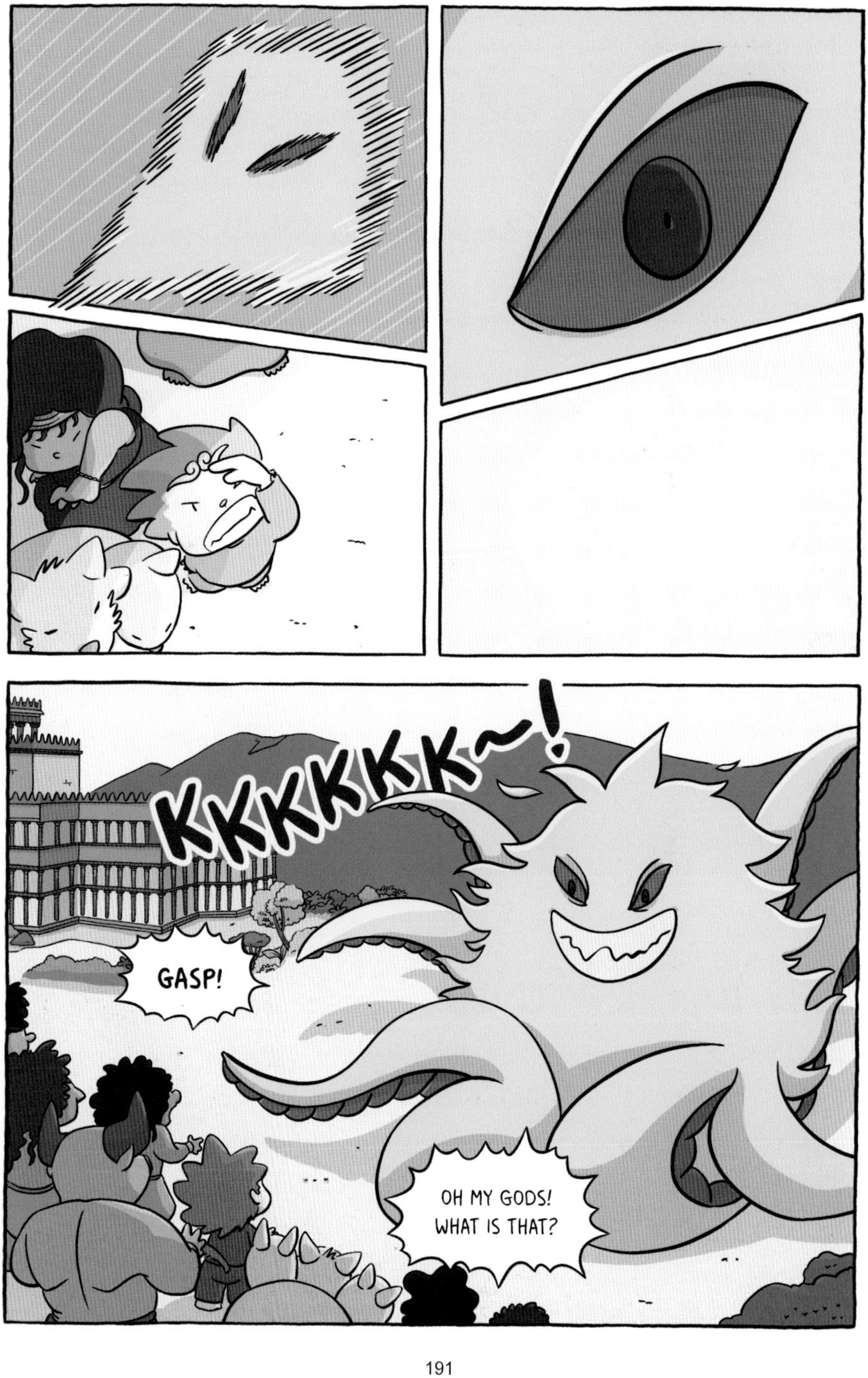
KKKKKK~!
GASP!
OH MY GODS!
WHAT IS THAT?

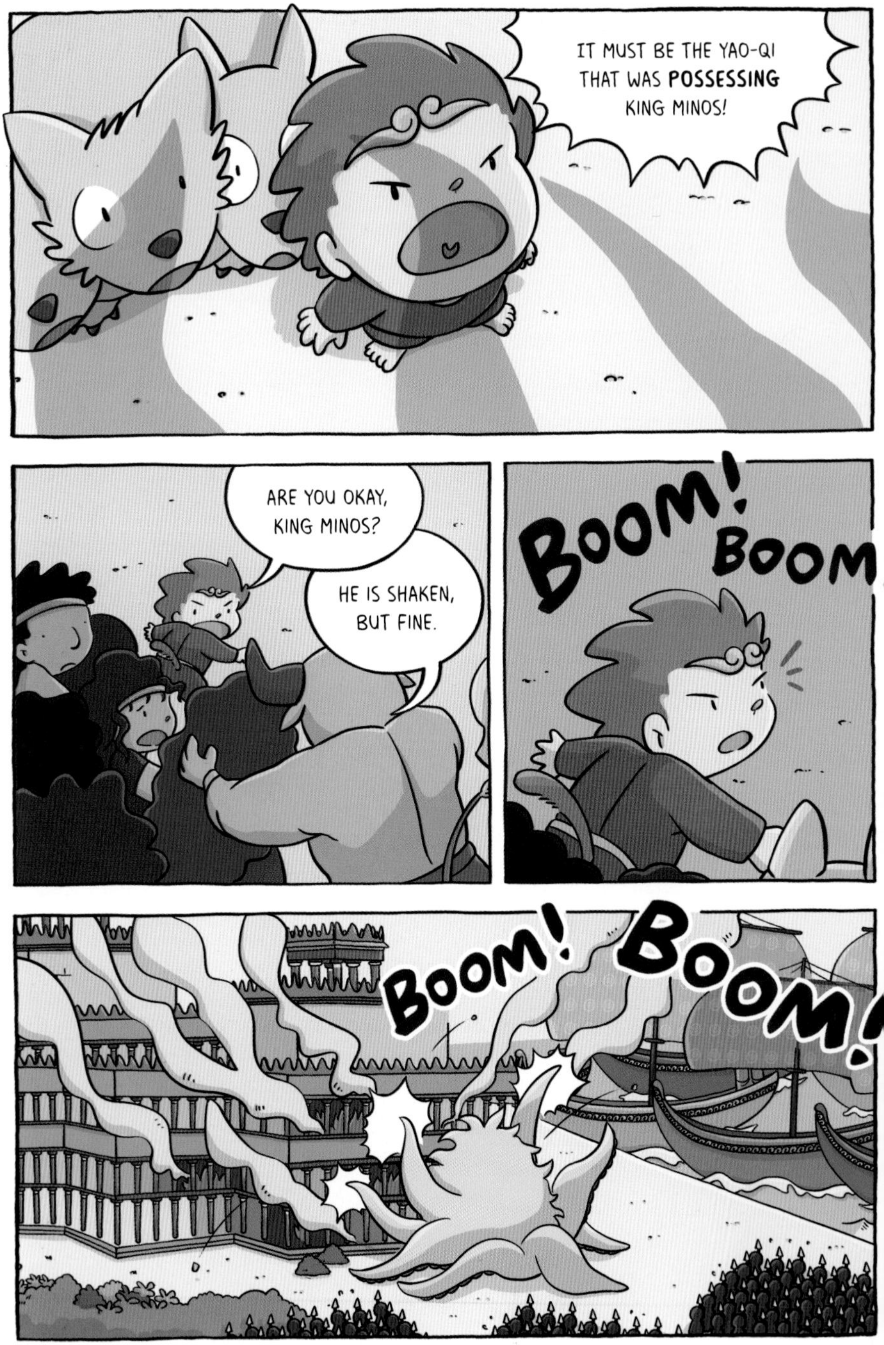
IT MUST BE THE YAO-QI THAT WAS **POSSESSING** KING MINOS!
ARE YOU OKAY, KING MINOS?
HE IS SHAKEN, BUT FINE.
BOOM! BOOM
BOOM! BOOM!

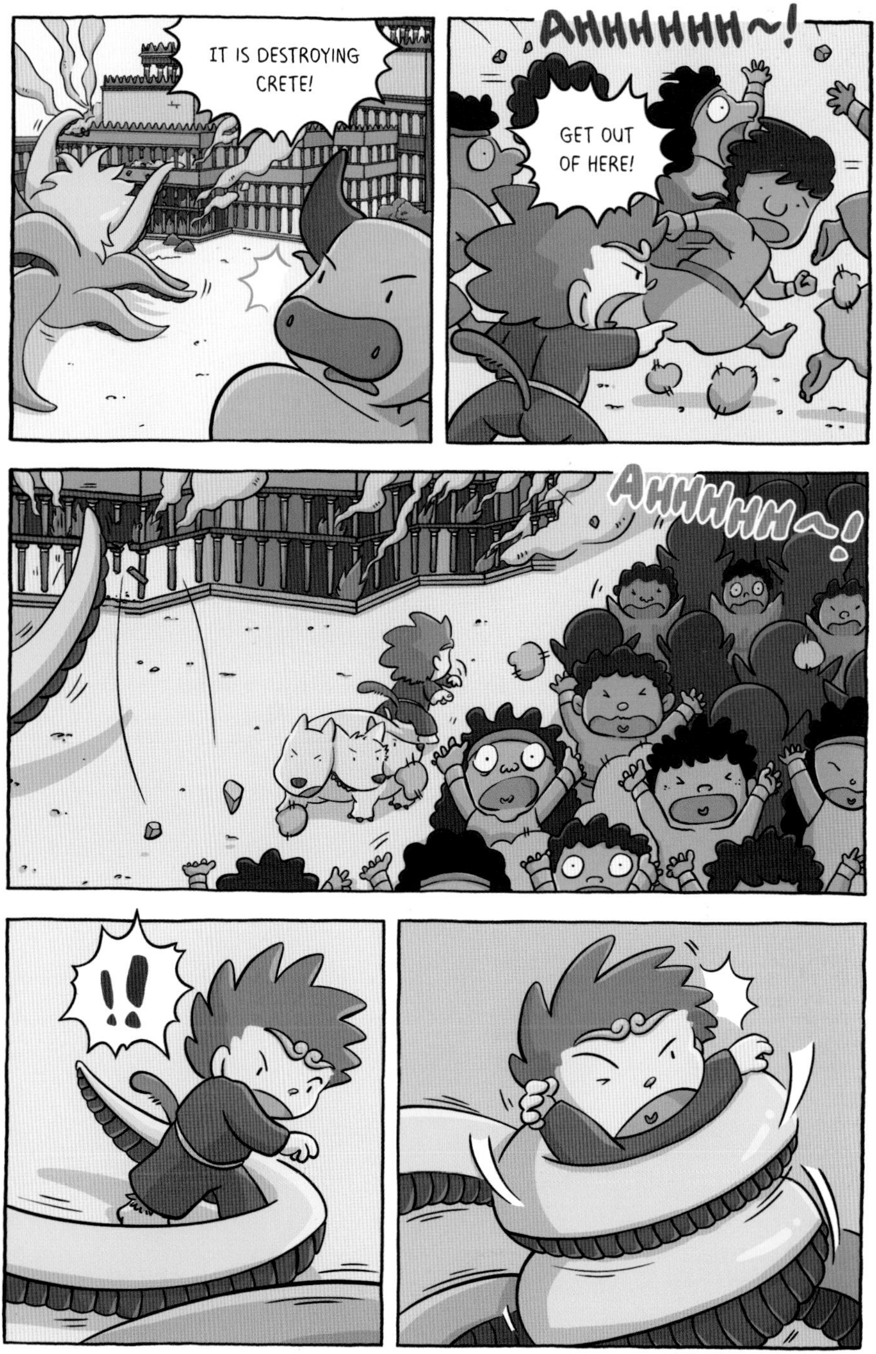
IT IS DESTROYING CRETE!
AHHHHHH~!
GET OUT OF HERE!
AHHHHHH~!
!!

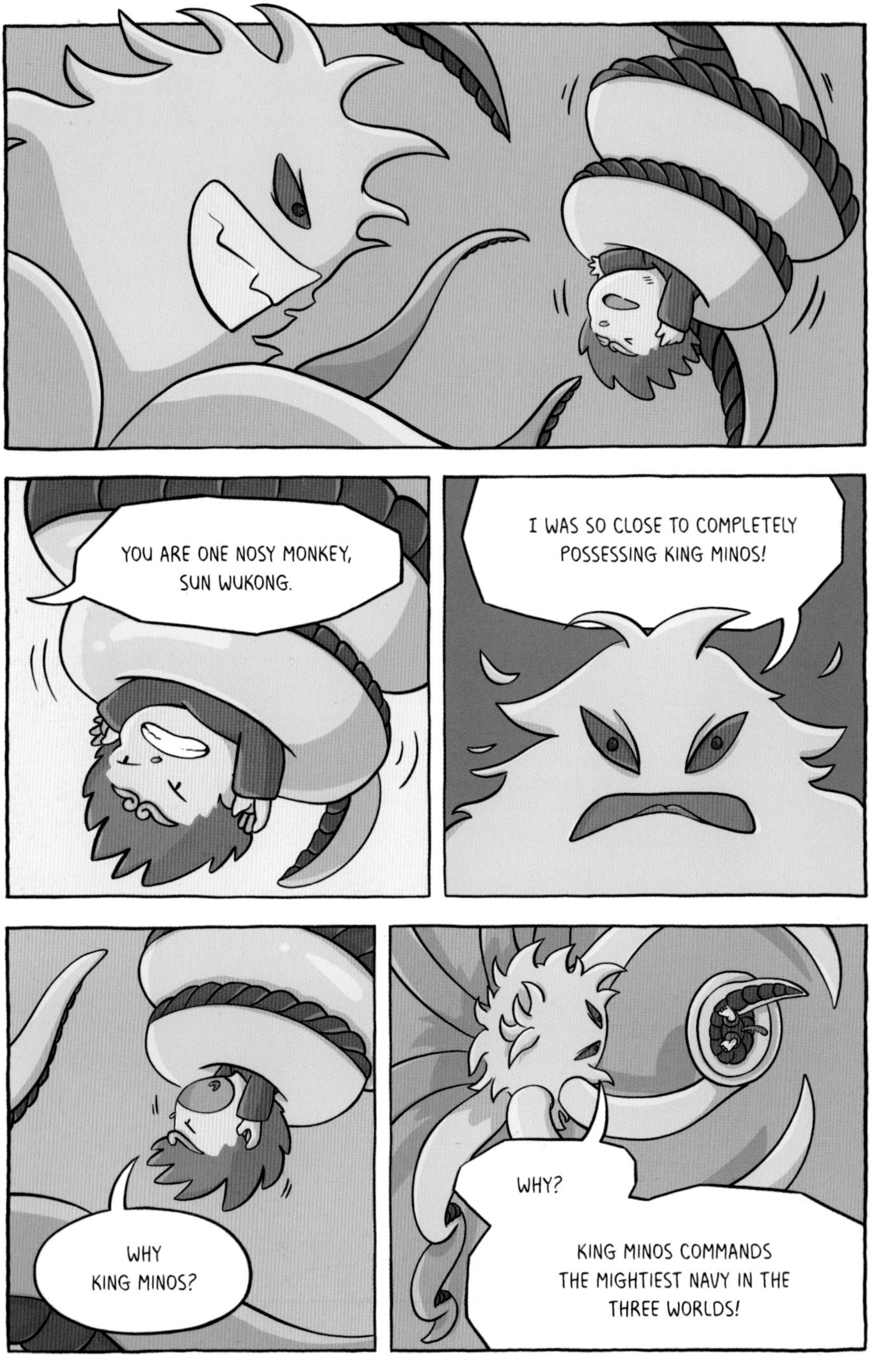
YOU ARE ONE NOSY MONKEY, SUN WUKONG.
I WAS SO CLOSE TO COMPLETELY POSSESSING KING MINOS!
WHY KING MINOS?
WHY?
KING MINOS COMMANDS THE MIGHTIEST NAVY IN THE THREE WORLDS!

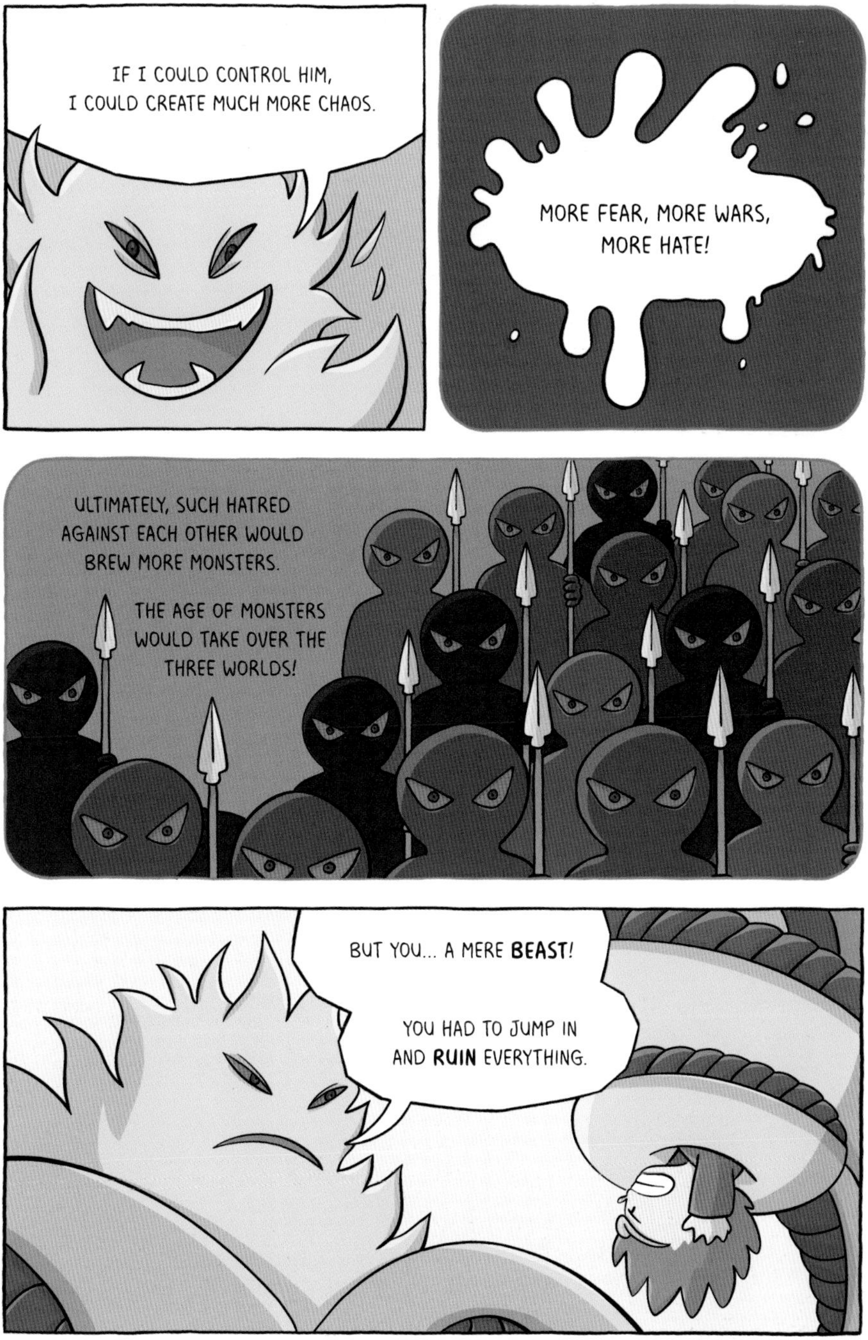
IF I COULD CONTROL HIM,
I COULD CREATE MUCH MORE CHAOS.
MORE FEAR, MORE WARS,
MORE HATE!
ULTIMATELY, SUCH HATRED AGAINST EACH OTHER WOULD BREW MORE MONSTERS.
THE AGE OF MONSTERS WOULD TAKE OVER THE THREE WORLDS!
BUT YOU... A MERE **BEAST**!
YOU HAD TO JUMP IN AND **RUIN** EVERYTHING.

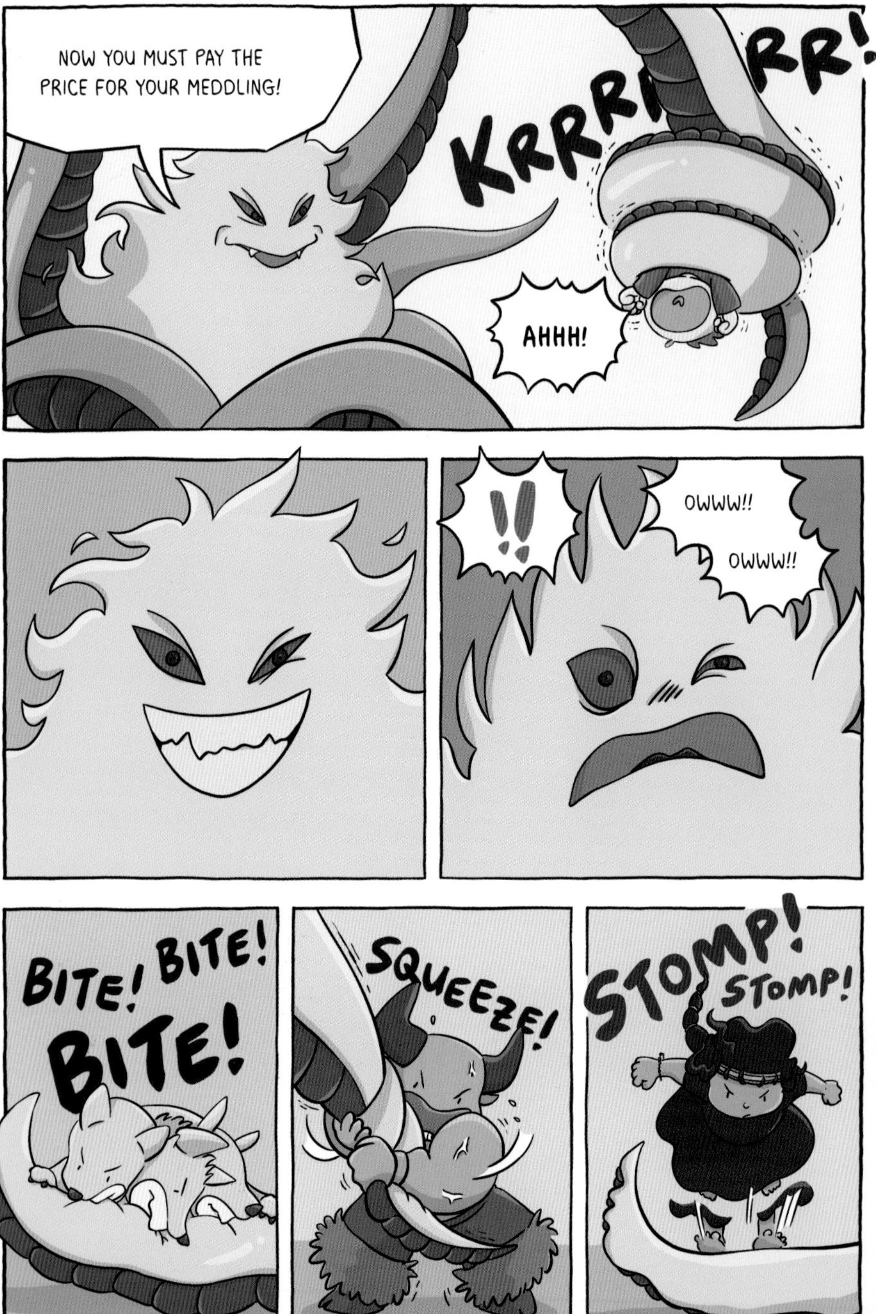
NOW YOU MUST PAY THE PRICE FOR YOUR MEDDLING!
KRRRRRRR!
AHHH!
!!
OWWW!!
OWWW!!
BITE! BITE!
BITE!
SQUEEZE!
STOMP!
STOMP!

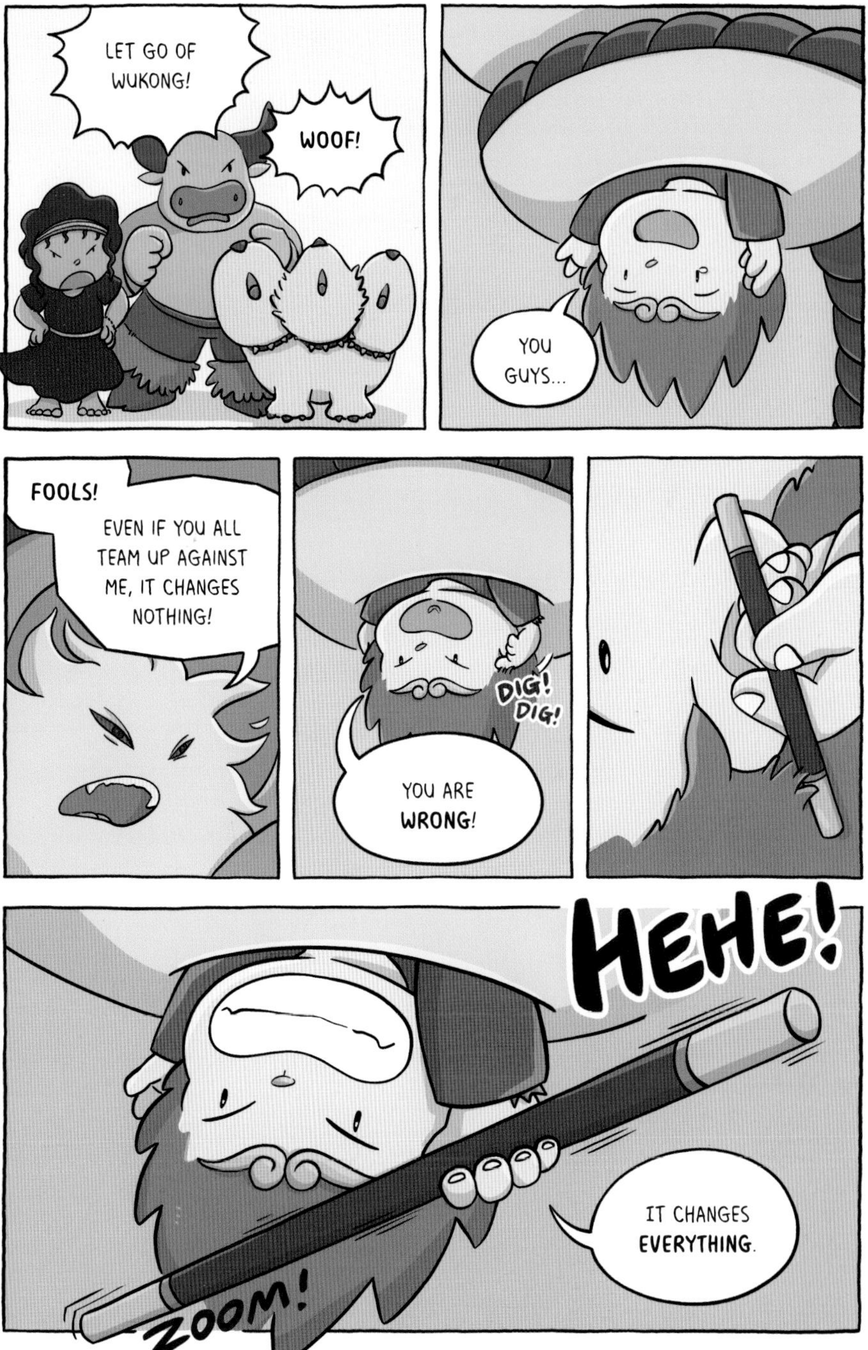
LET GO OF WUKONG!
WOOF!
YOU GUYS...
FOOLS!
EVEN IF YOU ALL TEAM UP AGAINST ME, IT CHANGES NOTHING!
DIG! DIG!
YOU ARE WRONG!
HEHE!
IT CHANGES EVERYTHING.
ZOOM!

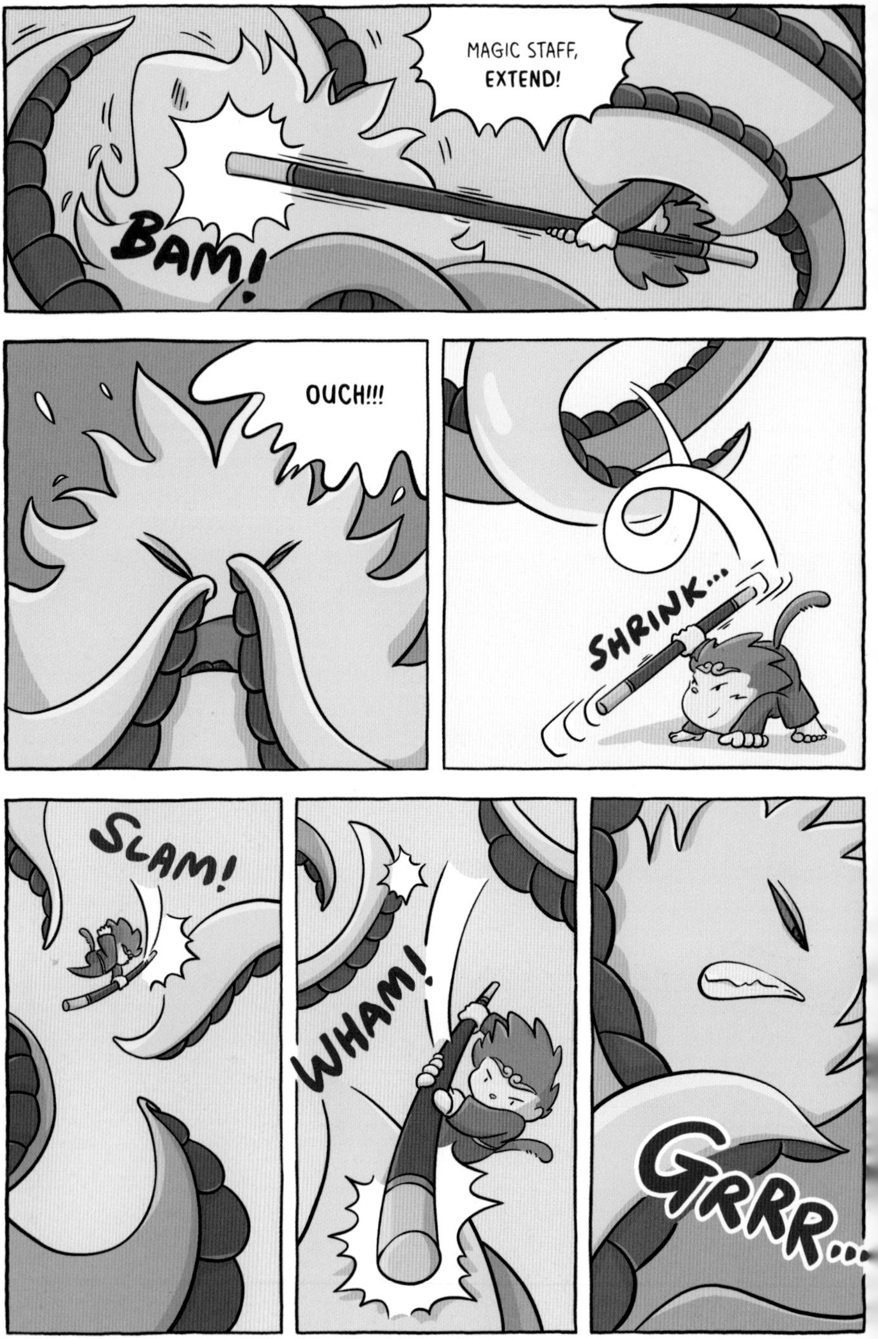
MAGIC STAFF,
EXTEND!
BAM!
OUCH!!!
SHRINK...
SLAM!
WHAM!
GRRR...

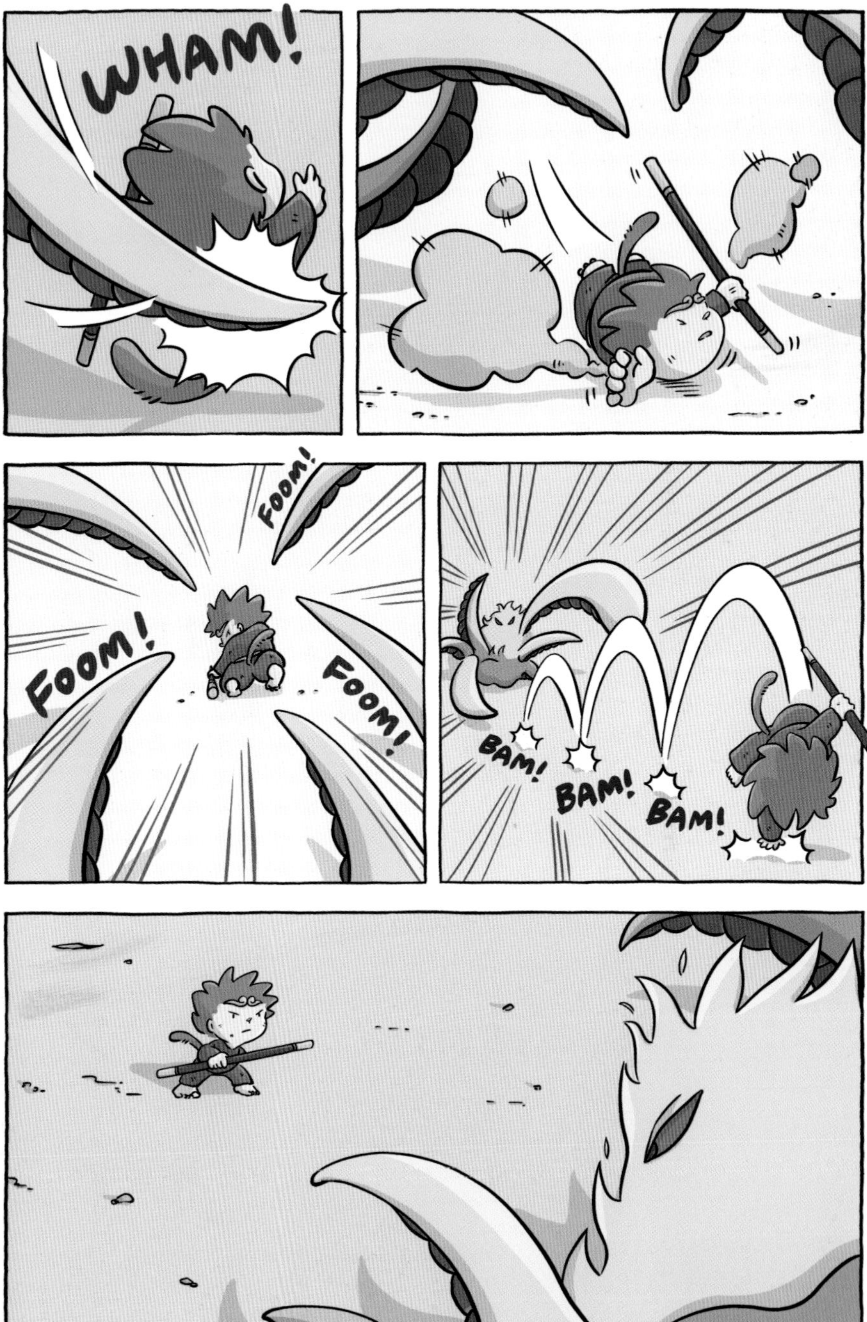
WHAM!
FOOM!
FOOM!
FOOM!
BAM!
BAM!
BAM!

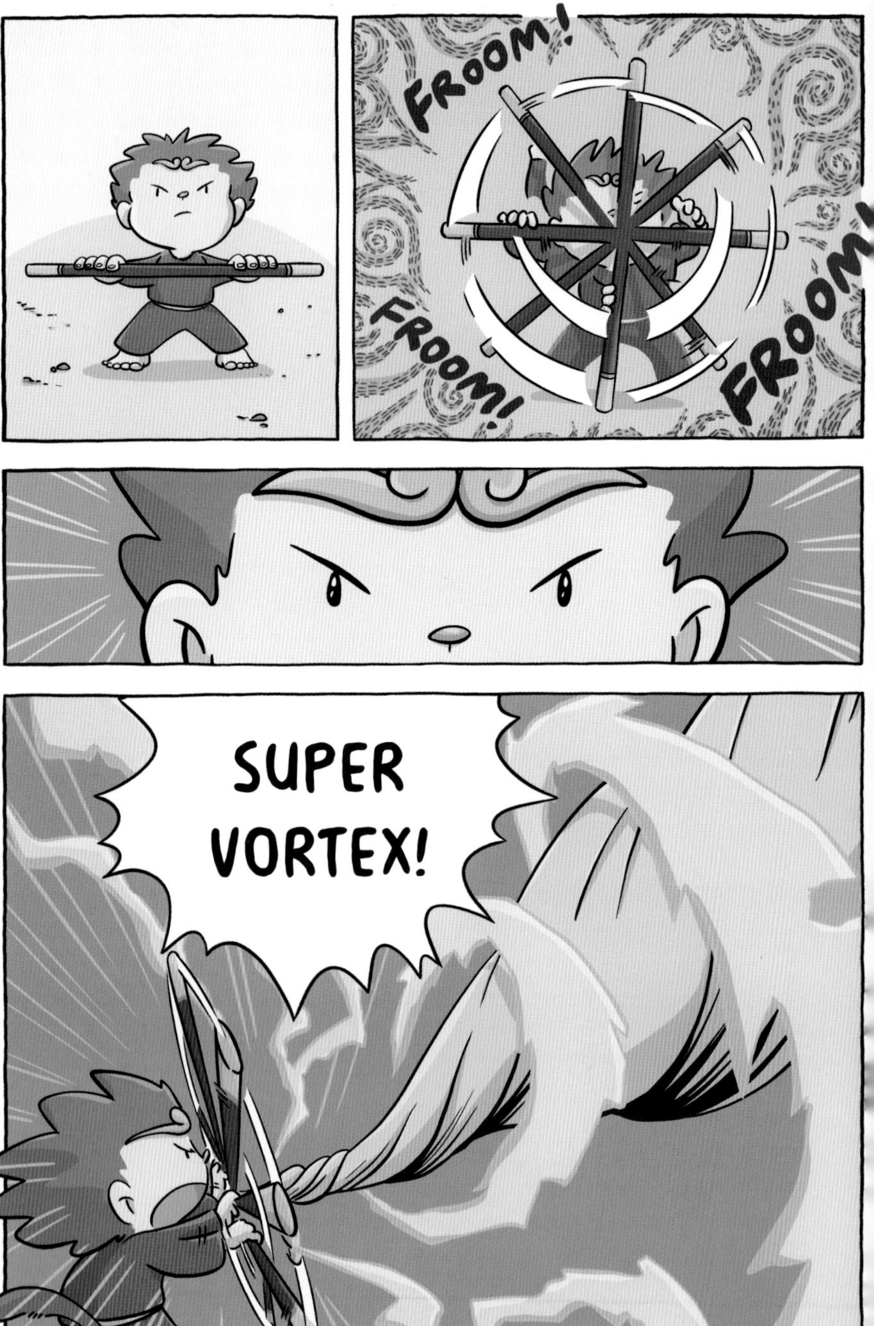
FROOM!
FROOM!
FROOM!
SUPER VORTEX!

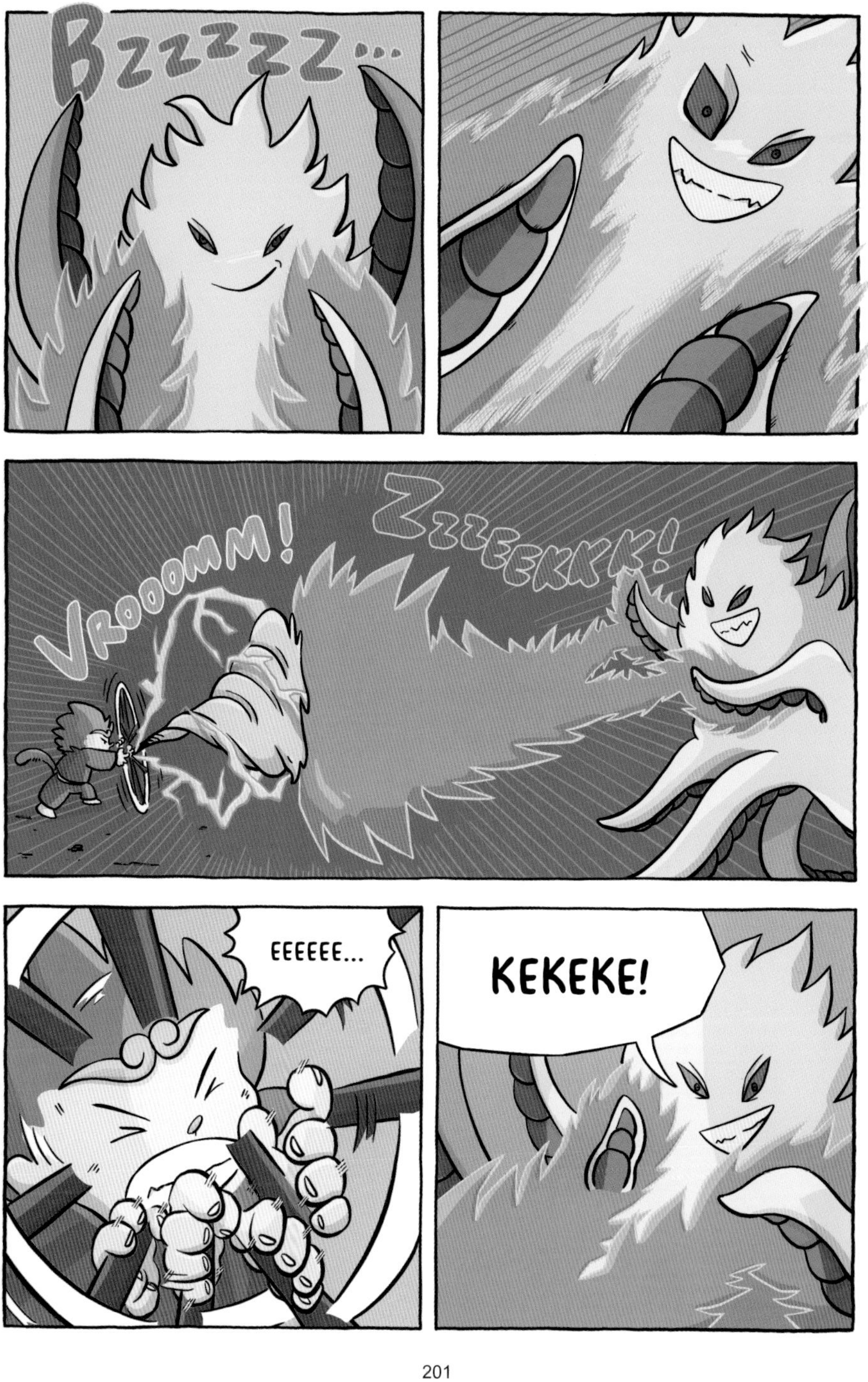
Bzzzzz...
VROOOMM!
ZZZEEKKK!
EEEEEE...
KEKEKE!

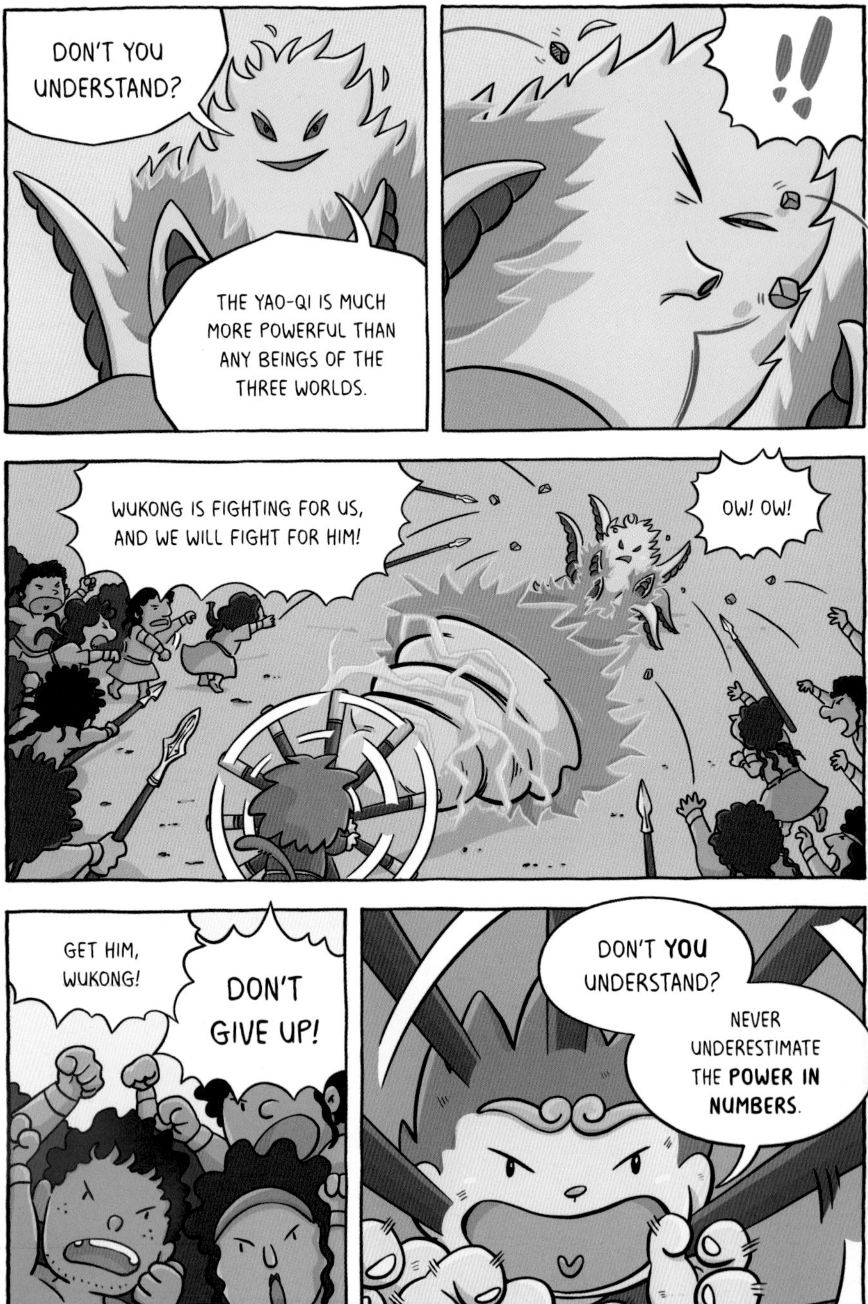
DON'T YOU UNDERSTAND?
THE YAO-QI IS MUCH MORE POWERFUL THAN ANY BEINGS OF THE THREE WORLDS.
!!
WUKONG IS FIGHTING FOR US, AND WE WILL FIGHT FOR HIM!
OW! OW!
GET HIM, WUKONG!
DON'T GIVE UP!
DON'T **YOU** UNDERSTAND?
NEVER UNDERESTIMATE THE **POWER IN NUMBERS**.

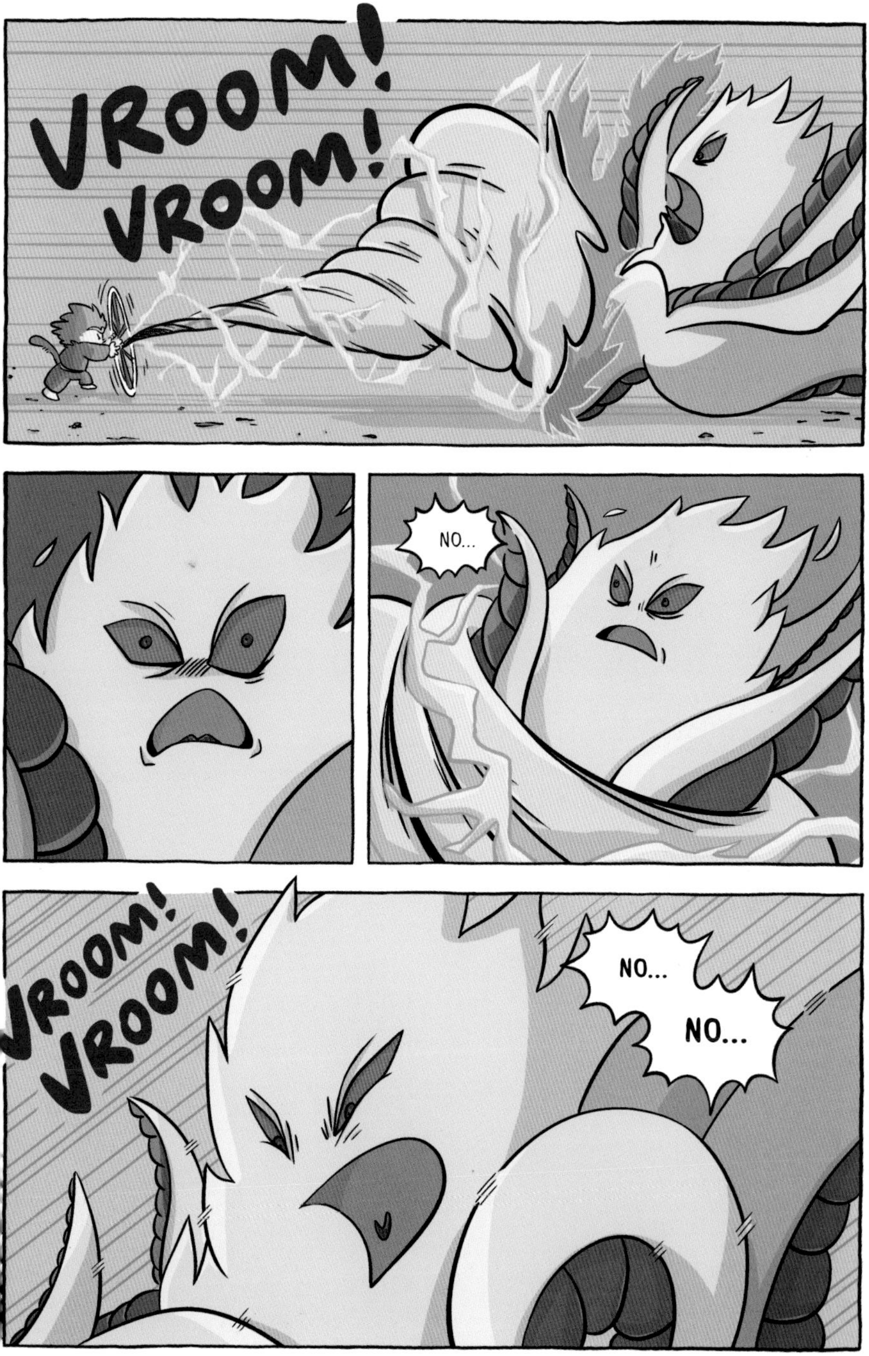
VROOM!
VROOM!
NO...
VROOM!
VROOM!
NO...
NO...

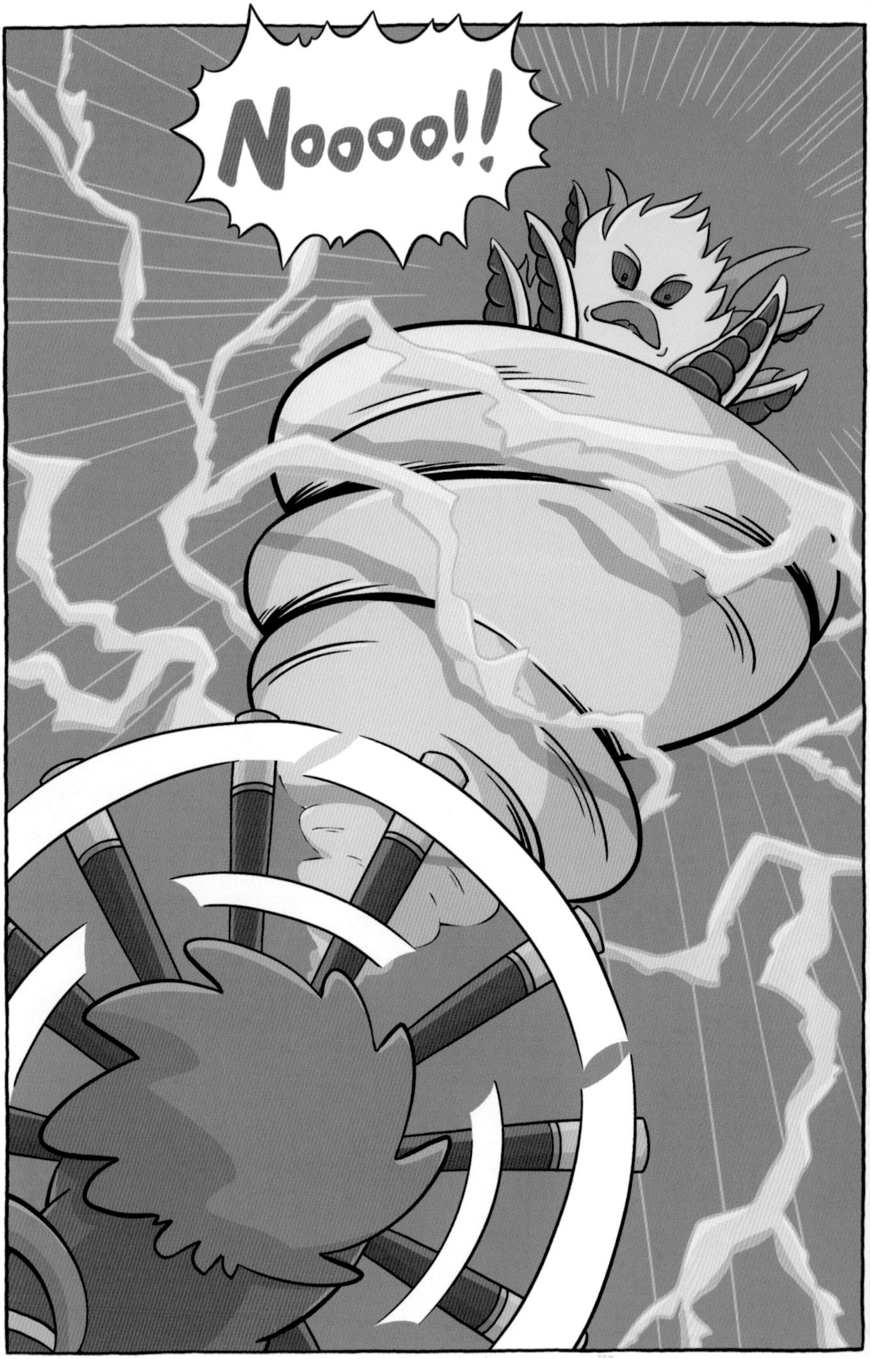
Noooo!!

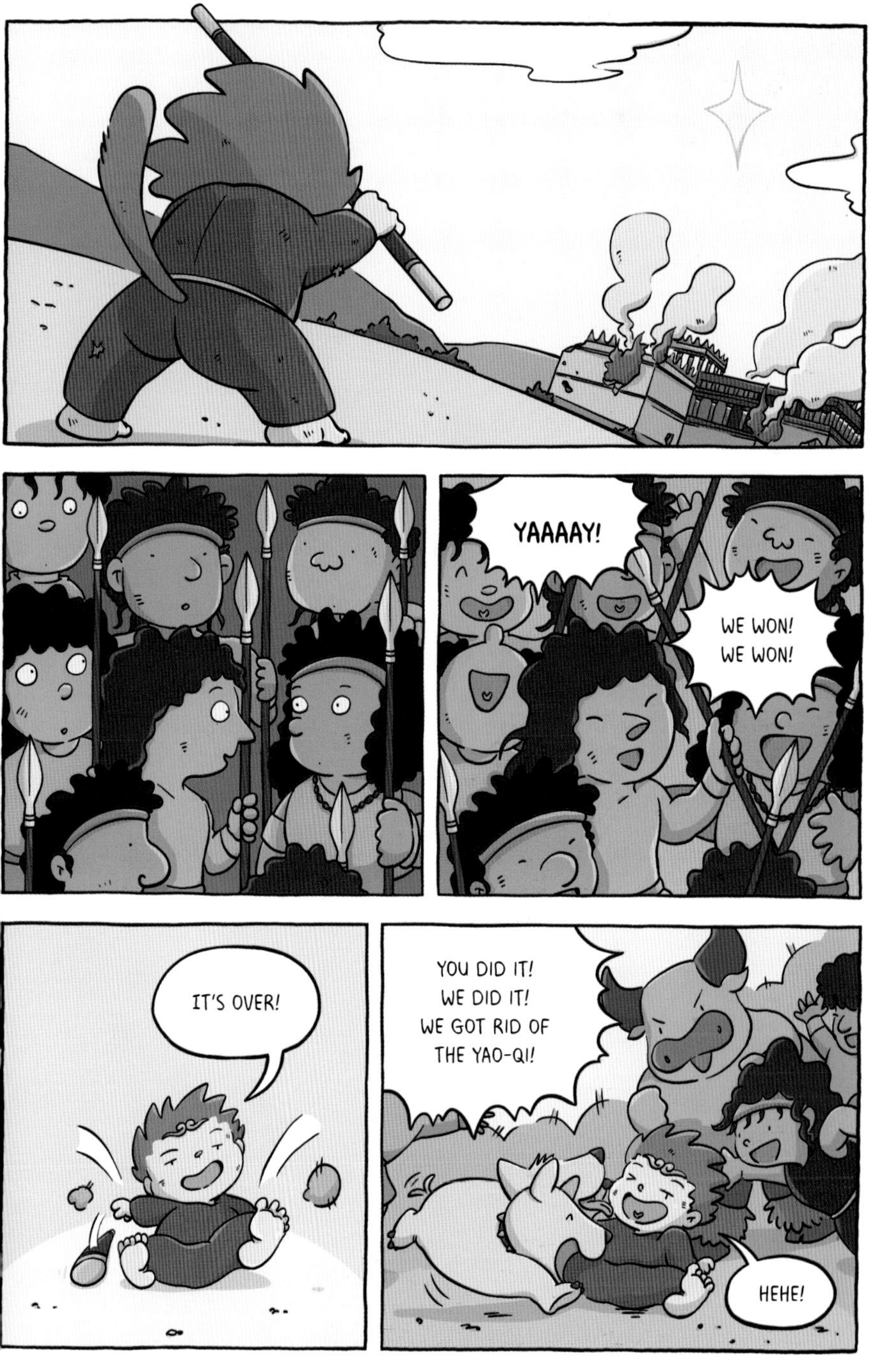
YAAAAY!
WE WON!
WE WON!
IT'S OVER!
YOU DID IT!
WE DID IT!
WE GOT RID OF
THE YAO-QI!
HEHE!

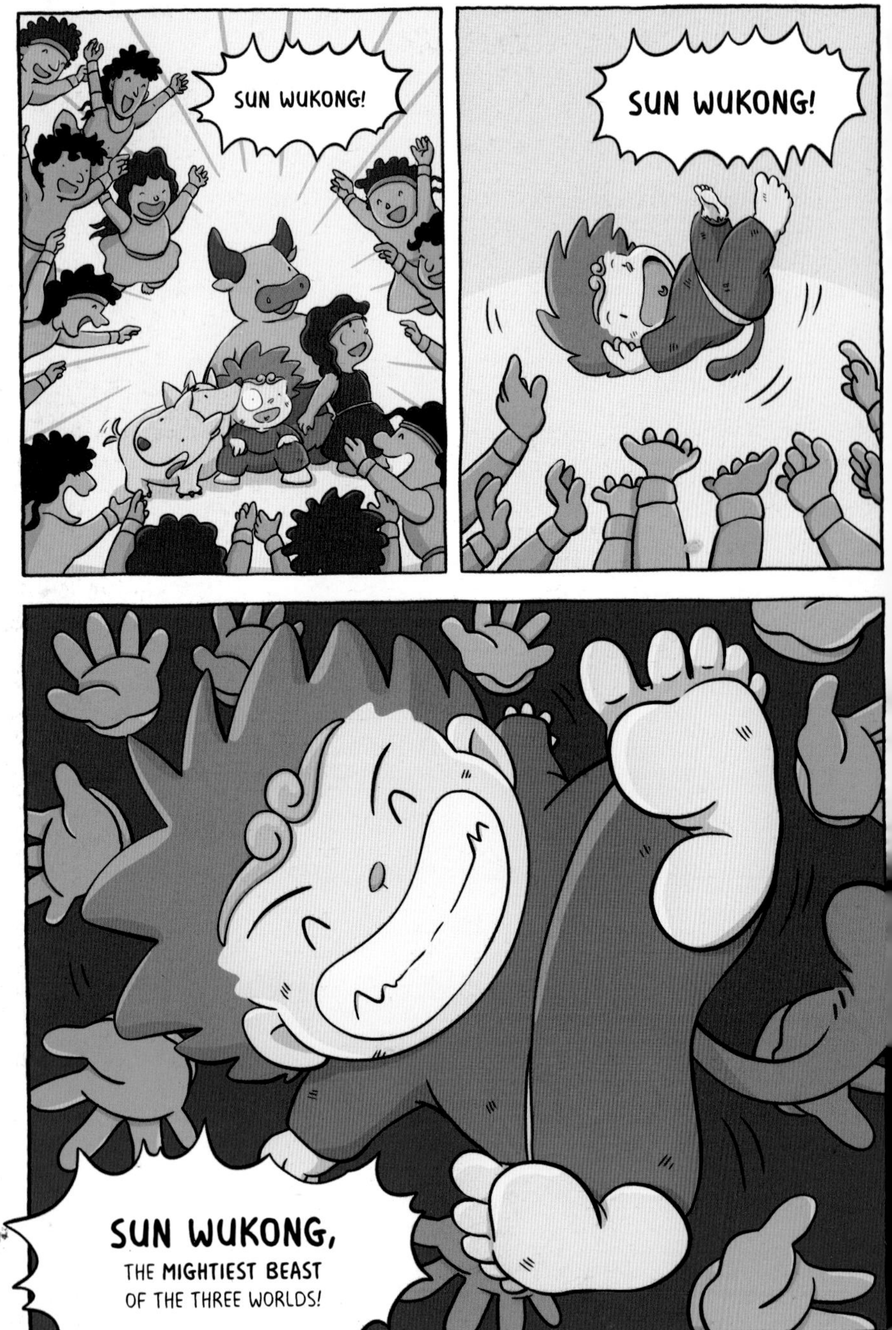
SUN WUKONG!
SUN WUKONG!
SUN WUKONG,
THE MIGHTIEST BEAST
OF THE THREE WORLDS!

CHAPTER 10 THE JOURNEY CONTINUES

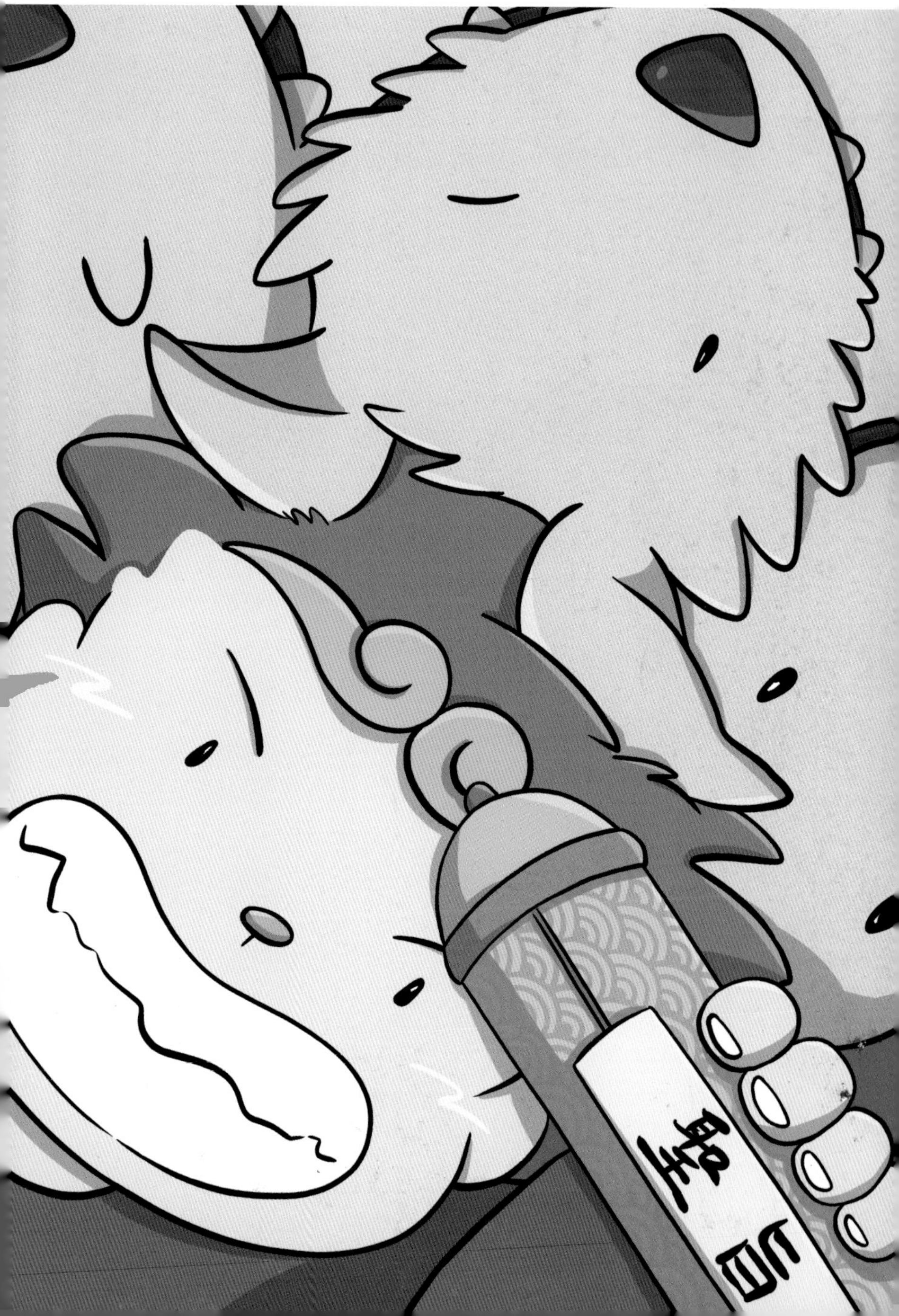
聖旨

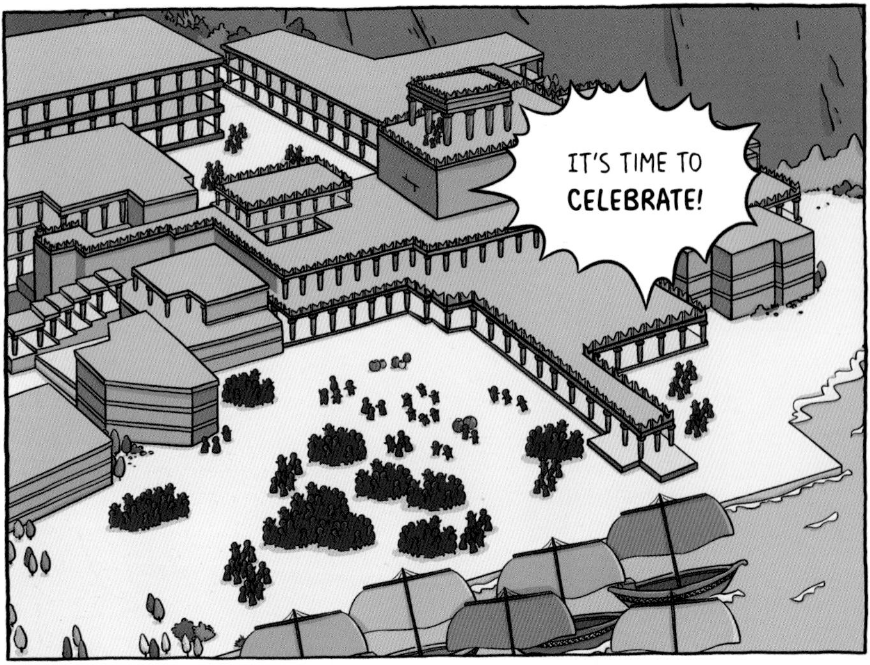
IT'S TIME TO
CELEBRATE!

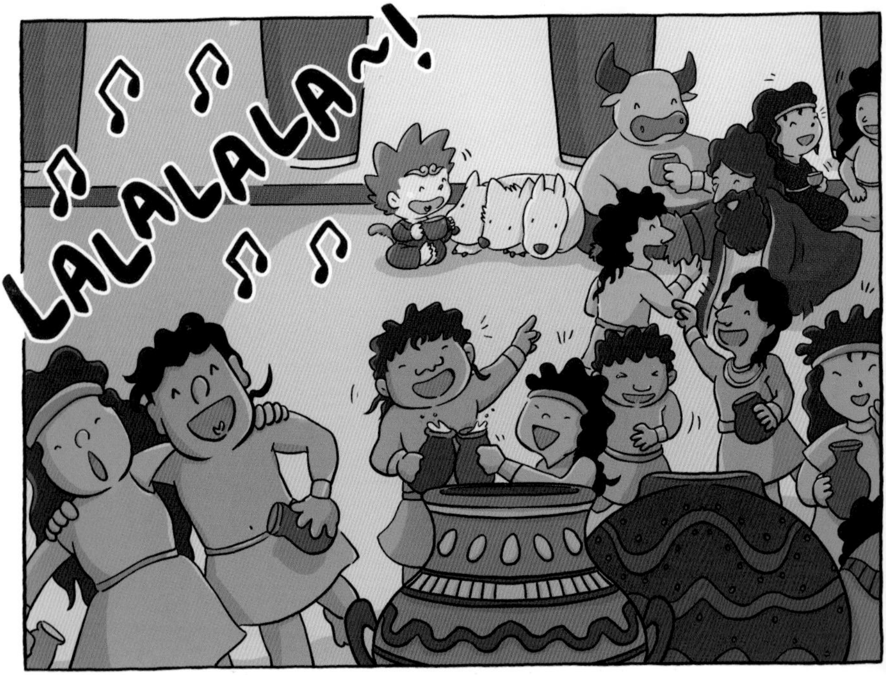
LALALALA~!

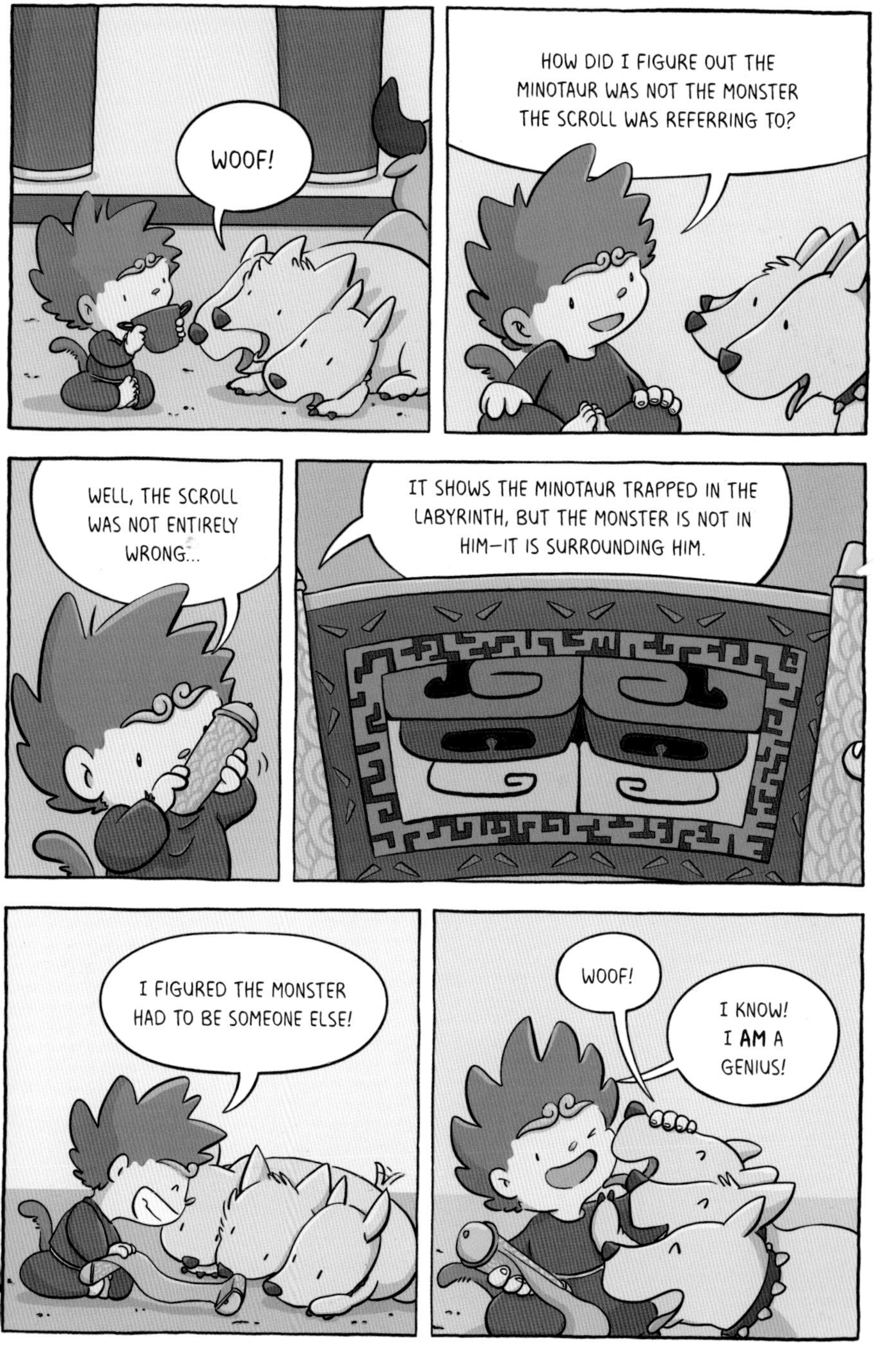
WOOF!
HOW DID I FIGURE OUT THE MINOTAUR WAS NOT THE MONSTER THE SCROLL WAS REFERRING TO?
WELL, THE SCROLL WAS NOT ENTIRELY WRONG...
IT SHOWS THE MINOTAUR TRAPPED IN THE LABYRINTH, BUT THE MONSTER IS NOT IN HIM—IT IS SURROUNDING HIM.
I FIGURED THE MONSTER HAD TO BE SOMEONE ELSE!
WOOF!
I KNOW! I **AM** A GENIUS!

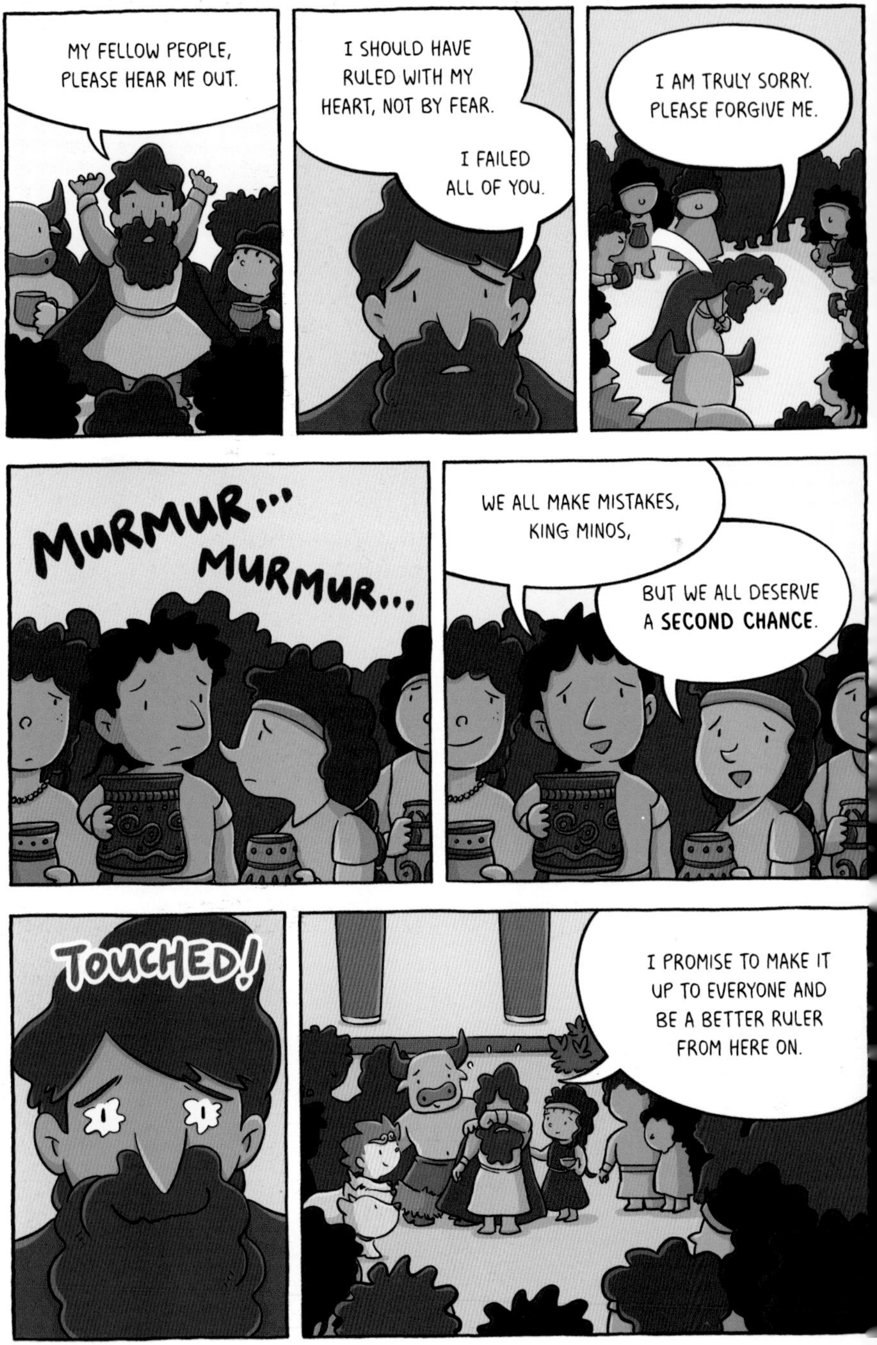
MY FELLOW PEOPLE, PLEASE HEAR ME OUT.
I SHOULD HAVE RULED WITH MY HEART, NOT BY FEAR.
I FAILED ALL OF YOU.
I AM TRULY SORRY. PLEASE FORGIVE ME.
MURMUR...
MURMUR...
WE ALL MAKE MISTAKES, KING MINOS,
BUT WE ALL DESERVE A **SECOND CHANCE**.
TOUCHED!
I PROMISE TO MAKE IT UP TO EVERYONE AND BE A BETTER RULER FROM HERE ON.

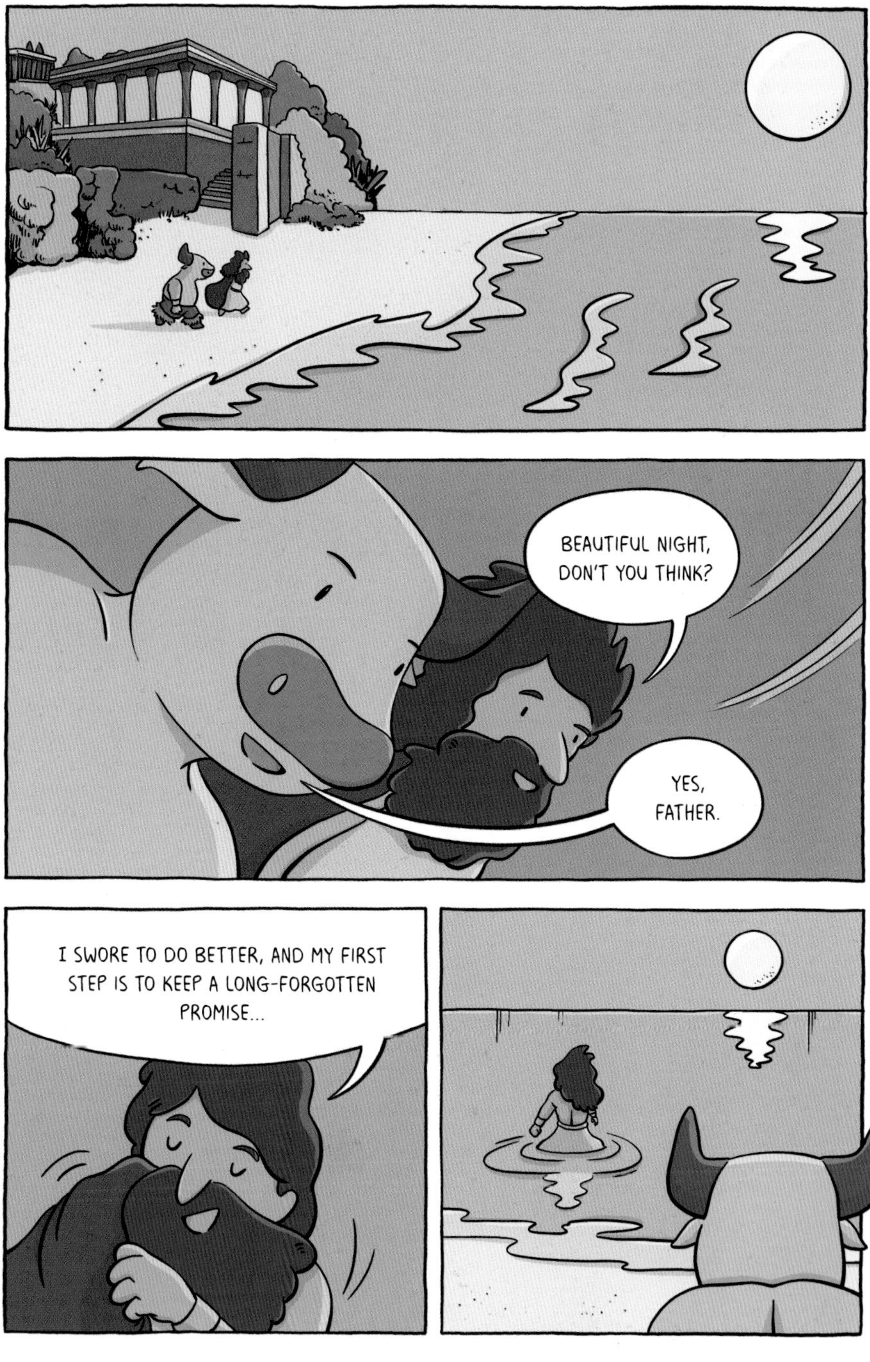
BEAUTIFUL NIGHT, DON'T YOU THINK?
YES, FATHER.
I SWORE TO DO BETTER, AND MY FIRST STEP IS TO KEEP A LONG-FORGOTTEN PROMISE...

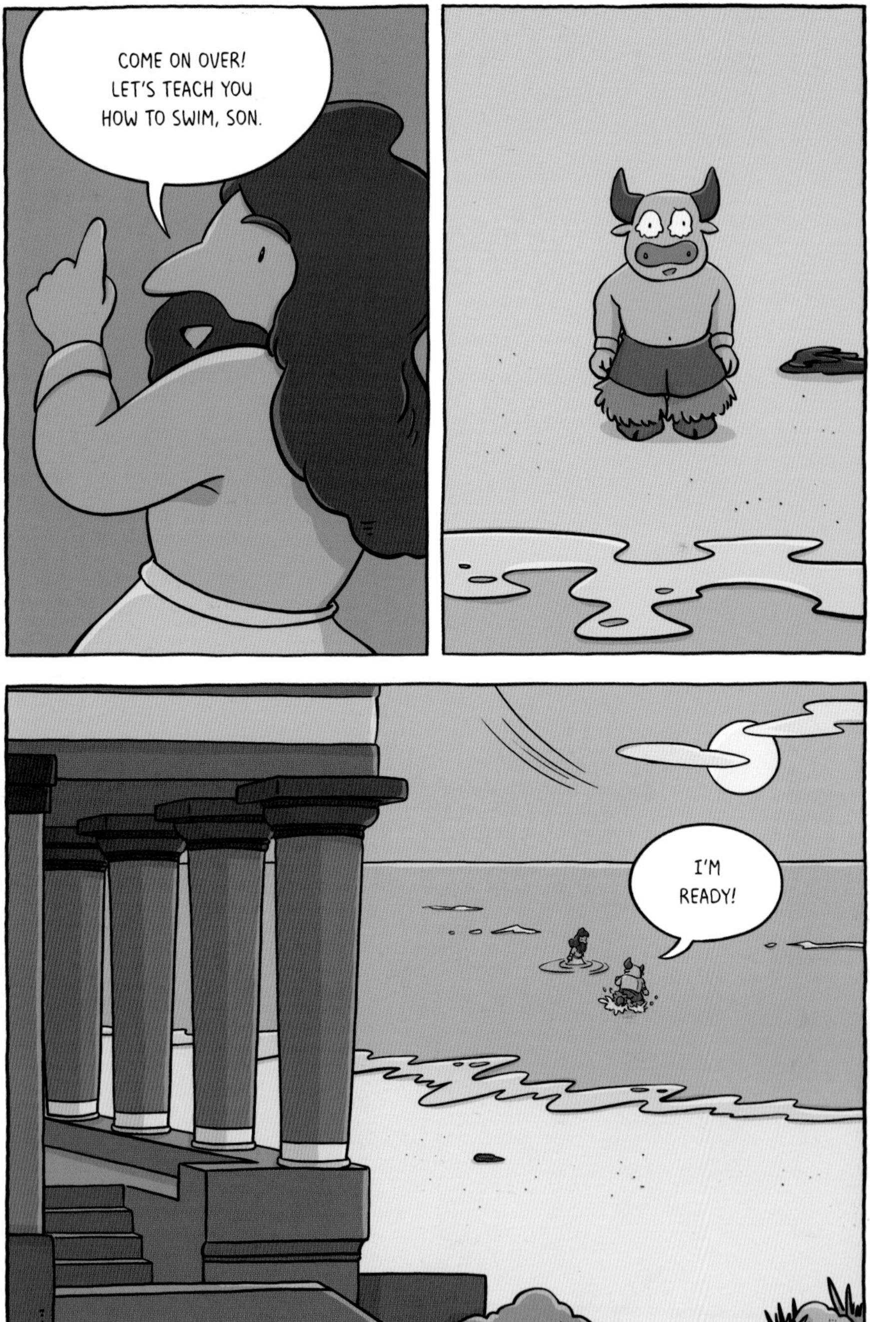
COME ON OVER! LET'S TEACH YOU HOW TO SWIM, SON.
I'M READY!

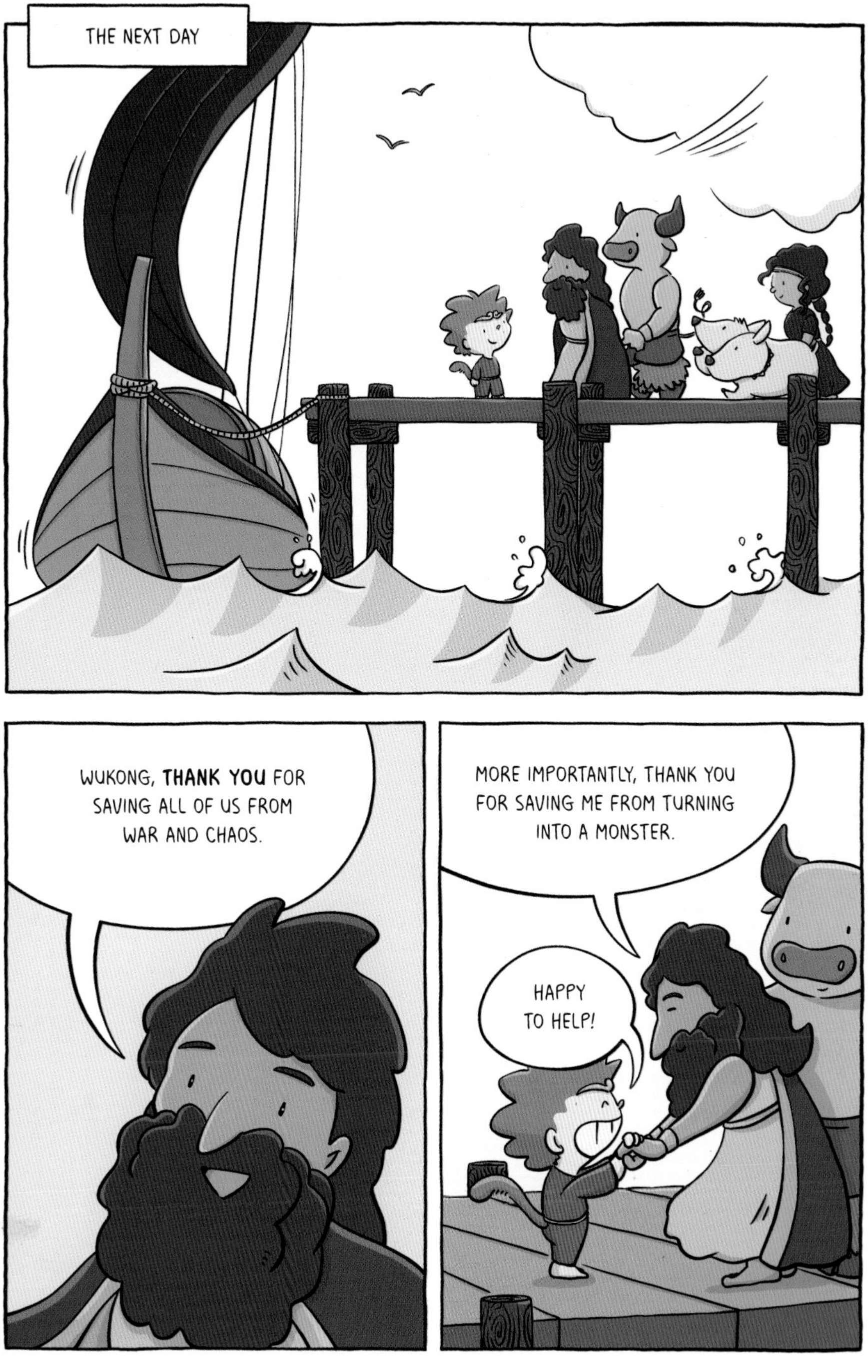
THE NEXT DAY
WUKONG, **THANK YOU** FOR SAVING ALL OF US FROM WAR AND CHAOS.
MORE IMPORTANTLY, THANK YOU FOR SAVING ME FROM TURNING INTO A MONSTER.
HAPPY TO HELP!

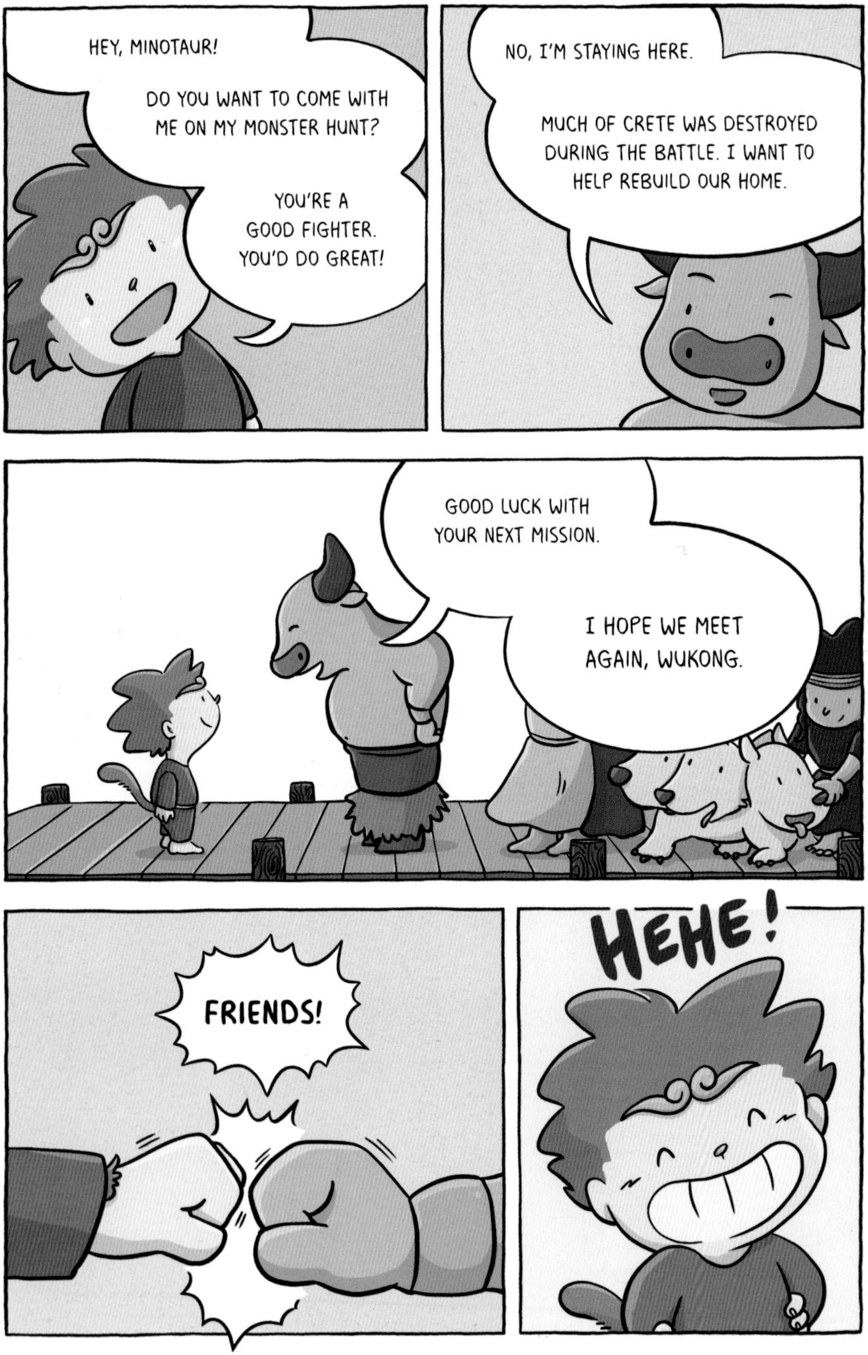
HEY, MINOTAUR!
DO YOU WANT TO COME WITH ME ON MY MONSTER HUNT?
YOU'RE A GOOD FIGHTER. YOU'D DO GREAT!
NO, I'M STAYING HERE.
MUCH OF CRETE WAS DESTROYED DURING THE BATTLE. I WANT TO HELP REBUILD OUR HOME.
GOOD LUCK WITH YOUR NEXT MISSION.
I HOPE WE MEET AGAIN, WUKONG.
FRIENDS!
HEHE!

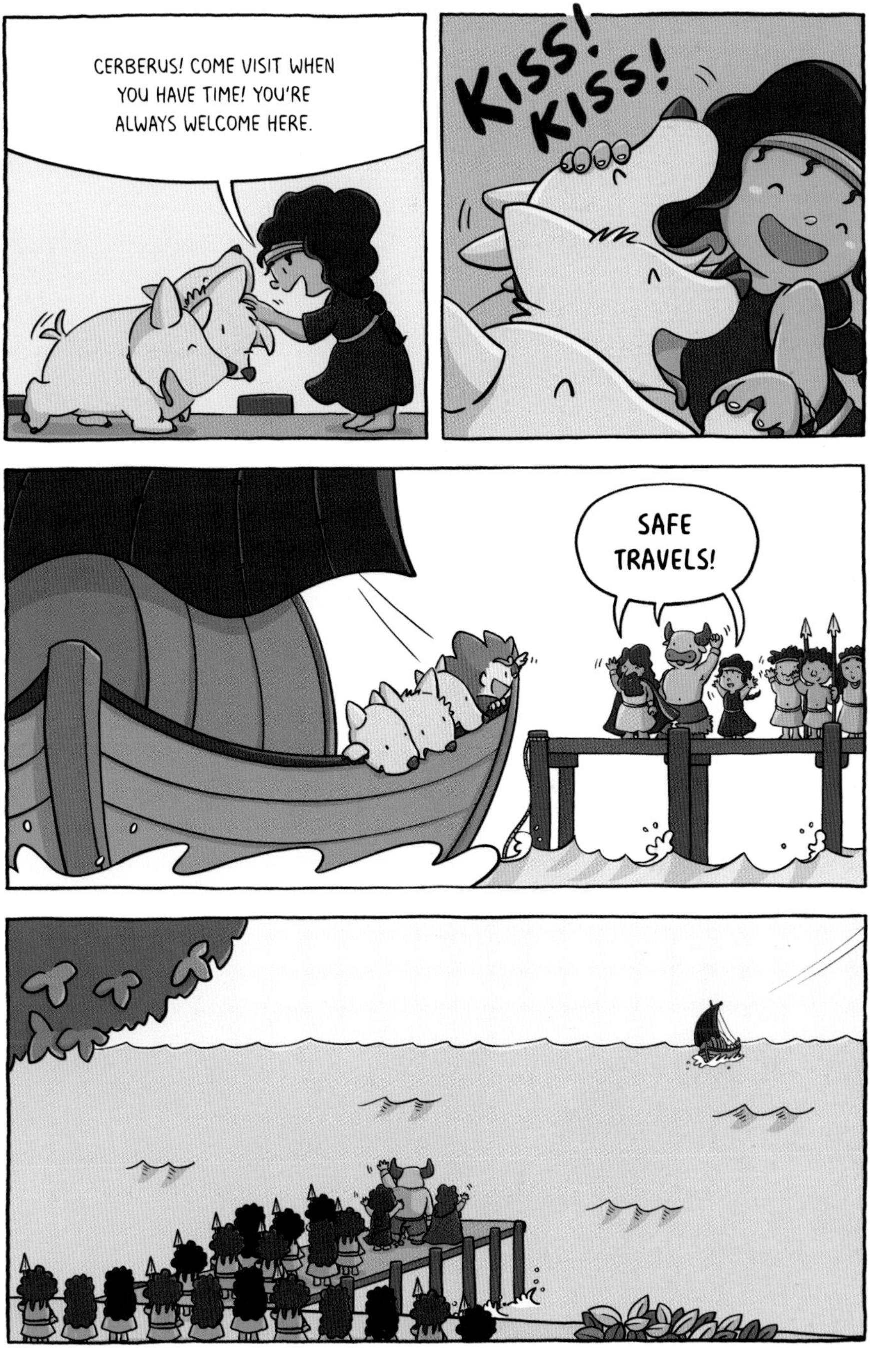
CERBERUS! COME VISIT WHEN YOU HAVE TIME! YOU'RE ALWAYS WELCOME HERE.
KISS! KISS!
SAFE TRAVELS!

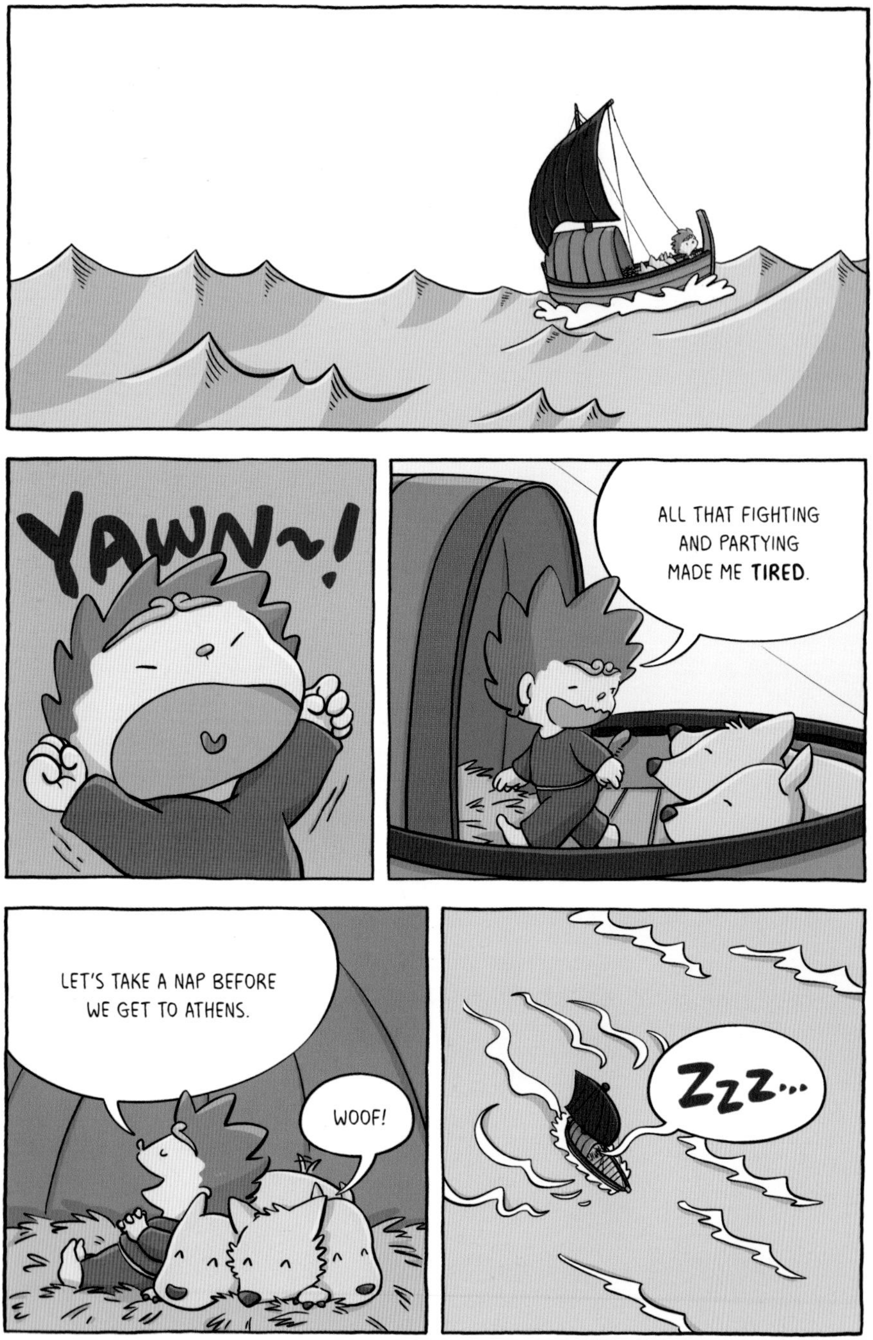
YAWN~!
ALL THAT FIGHTING AND PARTYING MADE ME **TIRED**.
LET'S TAKE A NAP BEFORE WE GET TO ATHENS.
WOOF!
ZZZ...

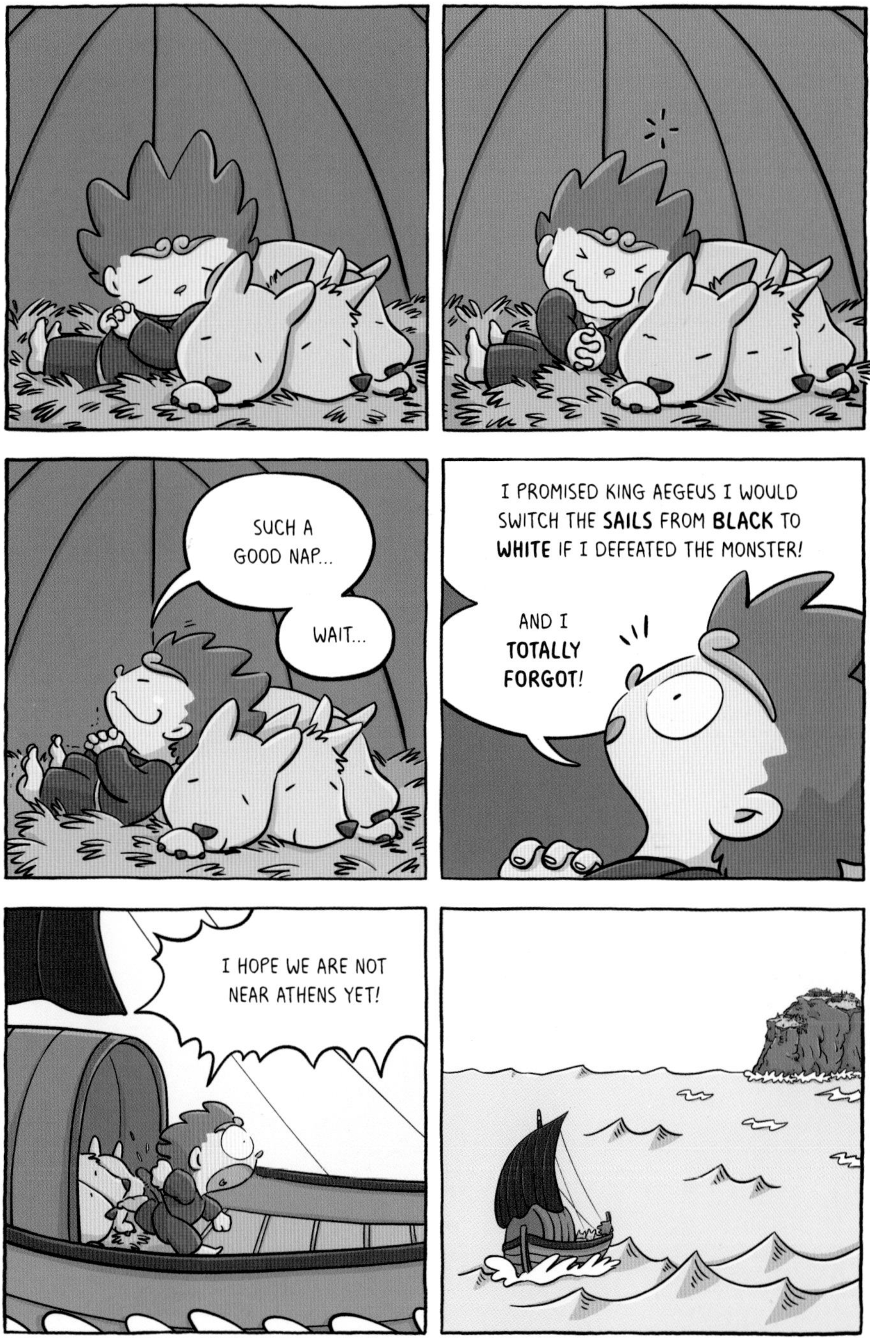
SUCH A GOOD NAP...
WAIT...
I PROMISED KING AEGEUS I WOULD SWITCH THE **SAILS** FROM **BLACK** TO **WHITE** IF I DEFEATED THE MONSTER!
AND I **TOTALLY FORGOT**!
I HOPE WE ARE NOT NEAR ATHENS YET!

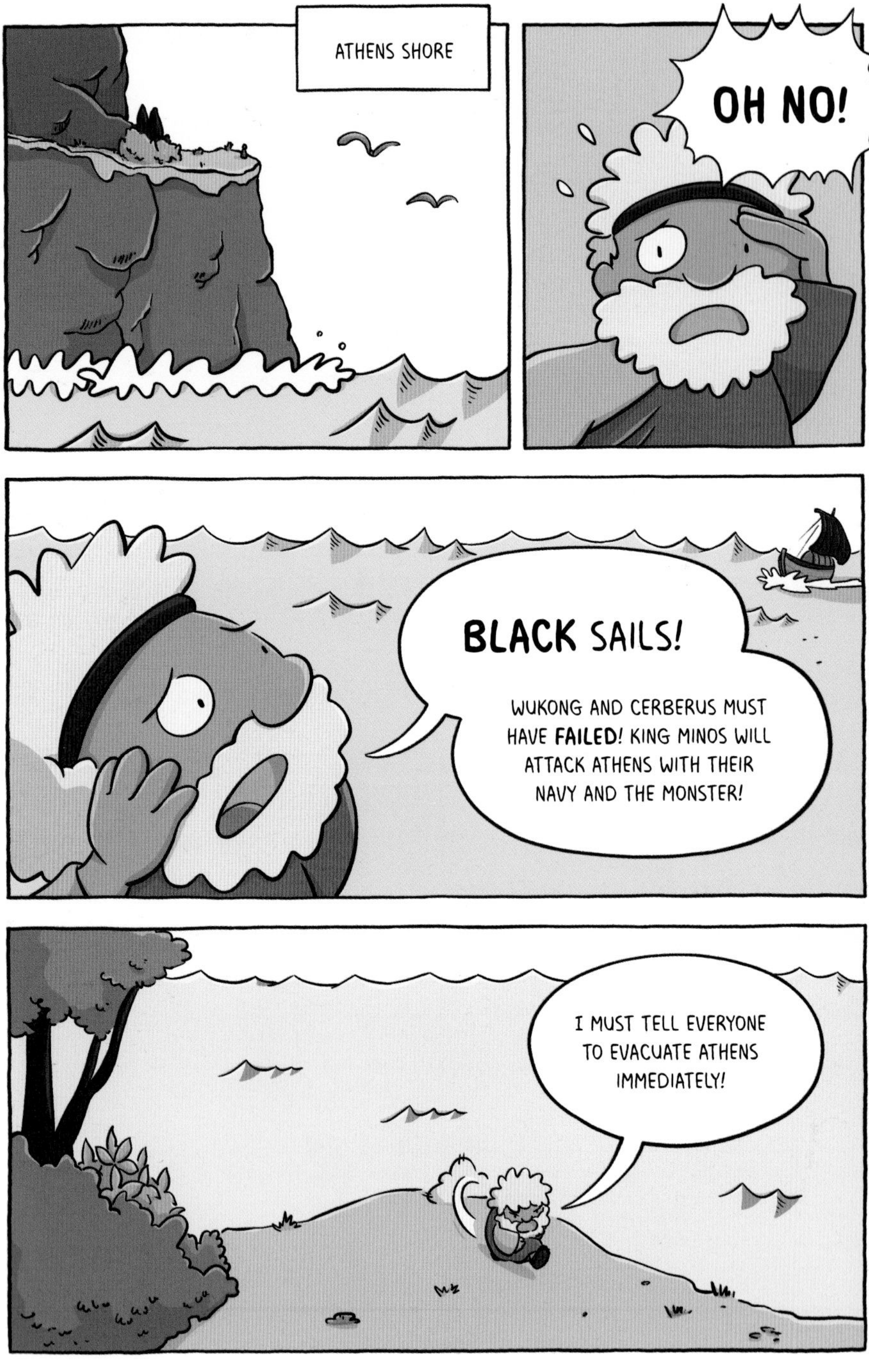
ATHENS SHORE
OH NO!
BLACK SAILS!
WUKONG AND CERBERUS MUST HAVE **FAILED**! KING MINOS WILL ATTACK ATHENS WITH THEIR NAVY AND THE MONSTER!
I MUST TELL EVERYONE TO EVACUATE ATHENS IMMEDIATELY!

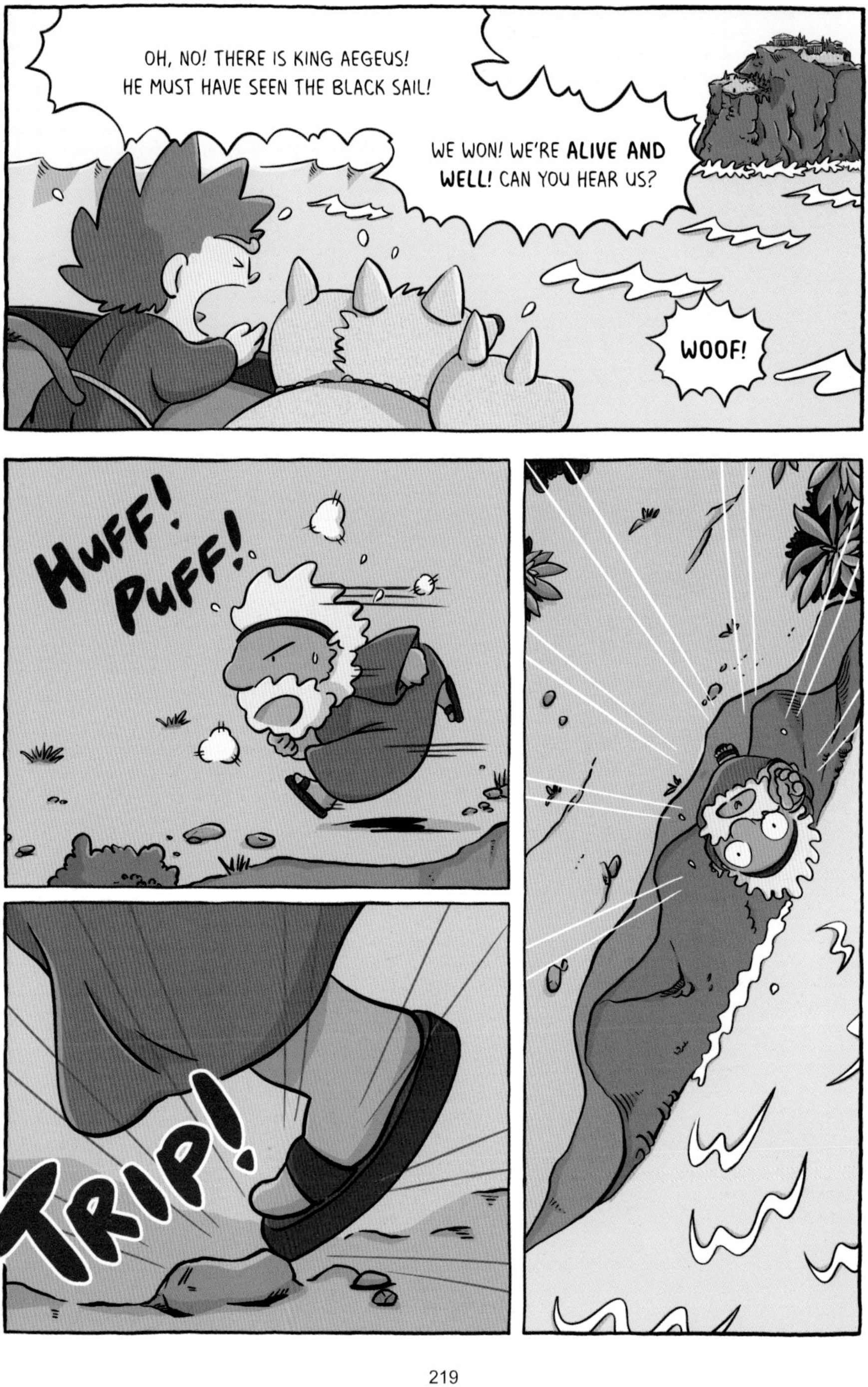
OH, NO! THERE IS KING AEGEUS! HE MUST HAVE SEEN THE BLACK SAIL!
WE WON! WE'RE **ALIVE AND WELL!** CAN YOU HEAR US?
WOOF!
HUFF! PUFF!
TRIP!

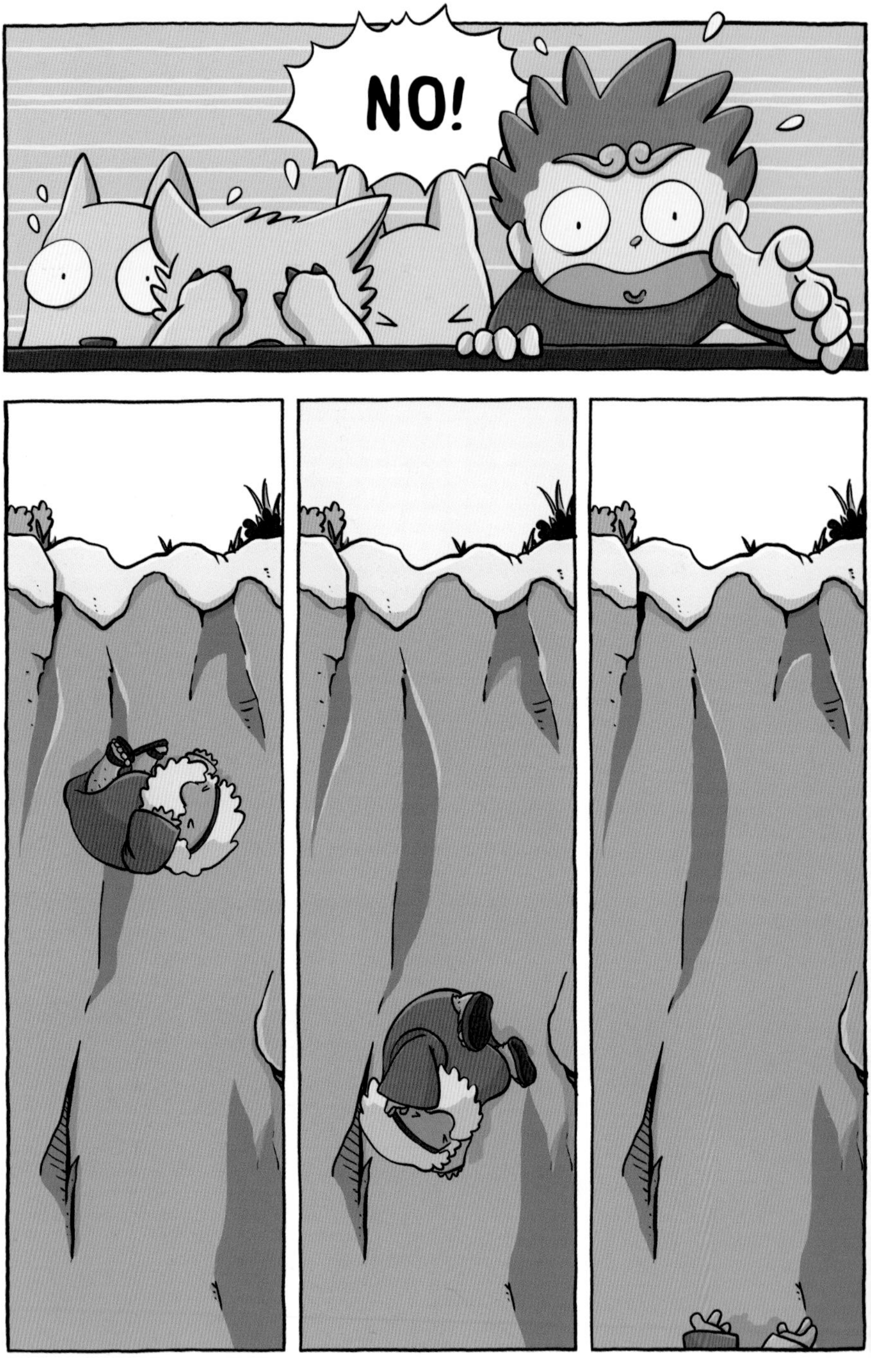
NO!

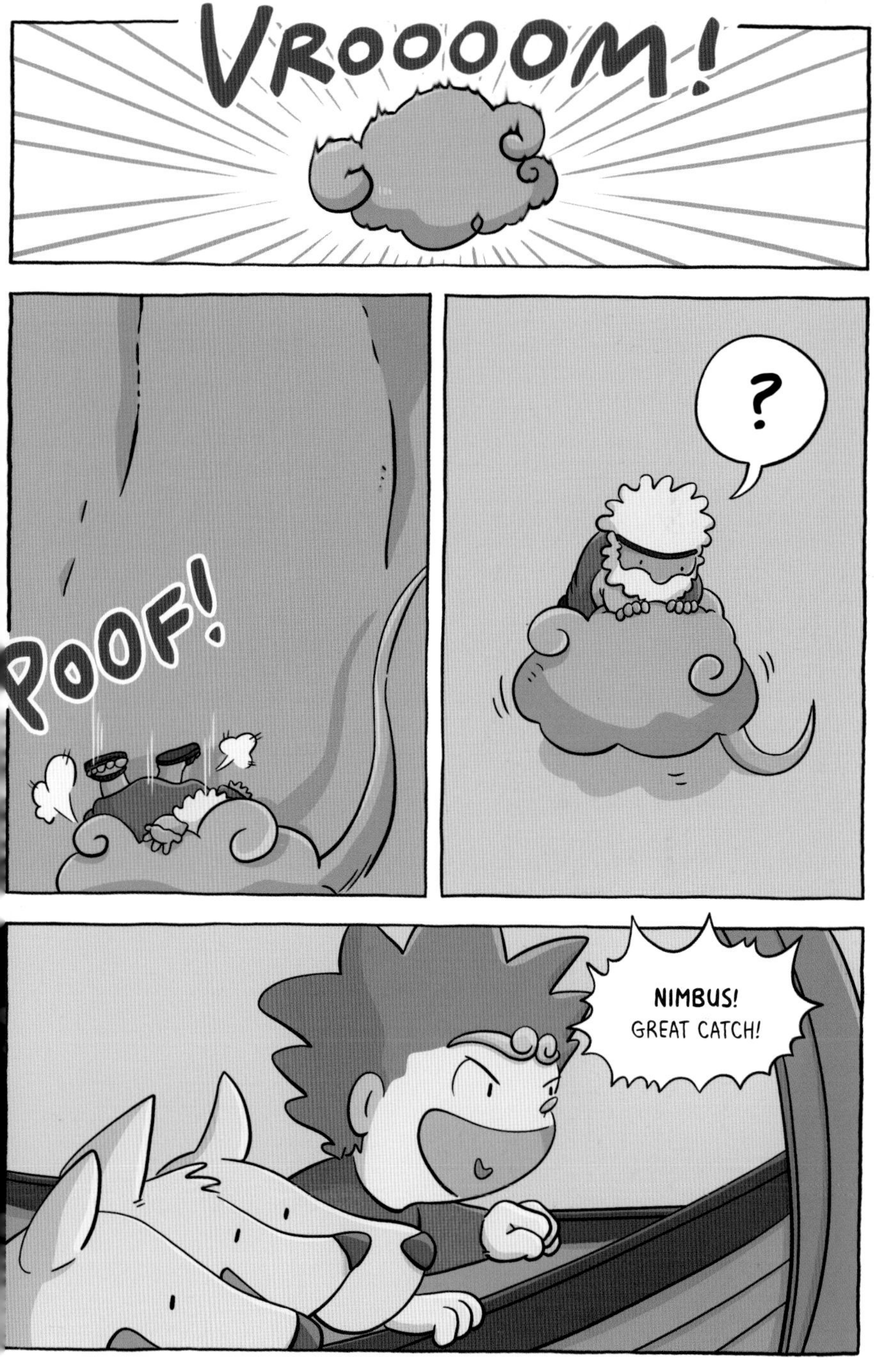
VROOOOM!
POOF!
?
NIMBUS!
GREAT CATCH!

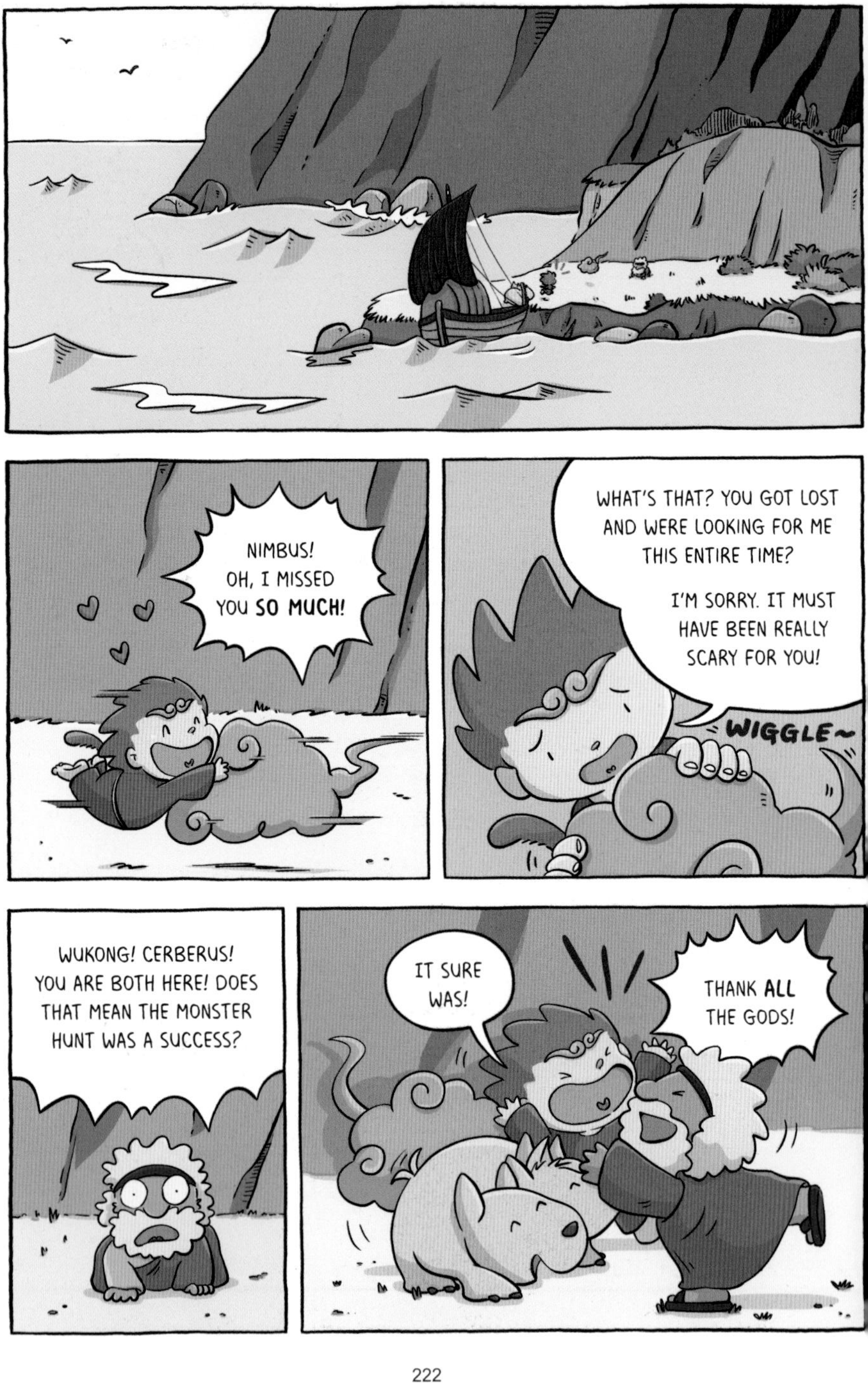
NIMBUS!
OH, I MISSED YOU **SO MUCH**!
WHAT'S THAT? YOU GOT LOST AND WERE LOOKING FOR ME THIS ENTIRE TIME?
I'M SORRY. IT MUST HAVE BEEN REALLY SCARY FOR YOU!
WIGGLE~
WUKONG! CERBERUS! YOU ARE BOTH HERE! DOES THAT MEAN THE MONSTER HUNT WAS A SUCCESS?
IT SURE WAS!
THANK **ALL** THE GODS!

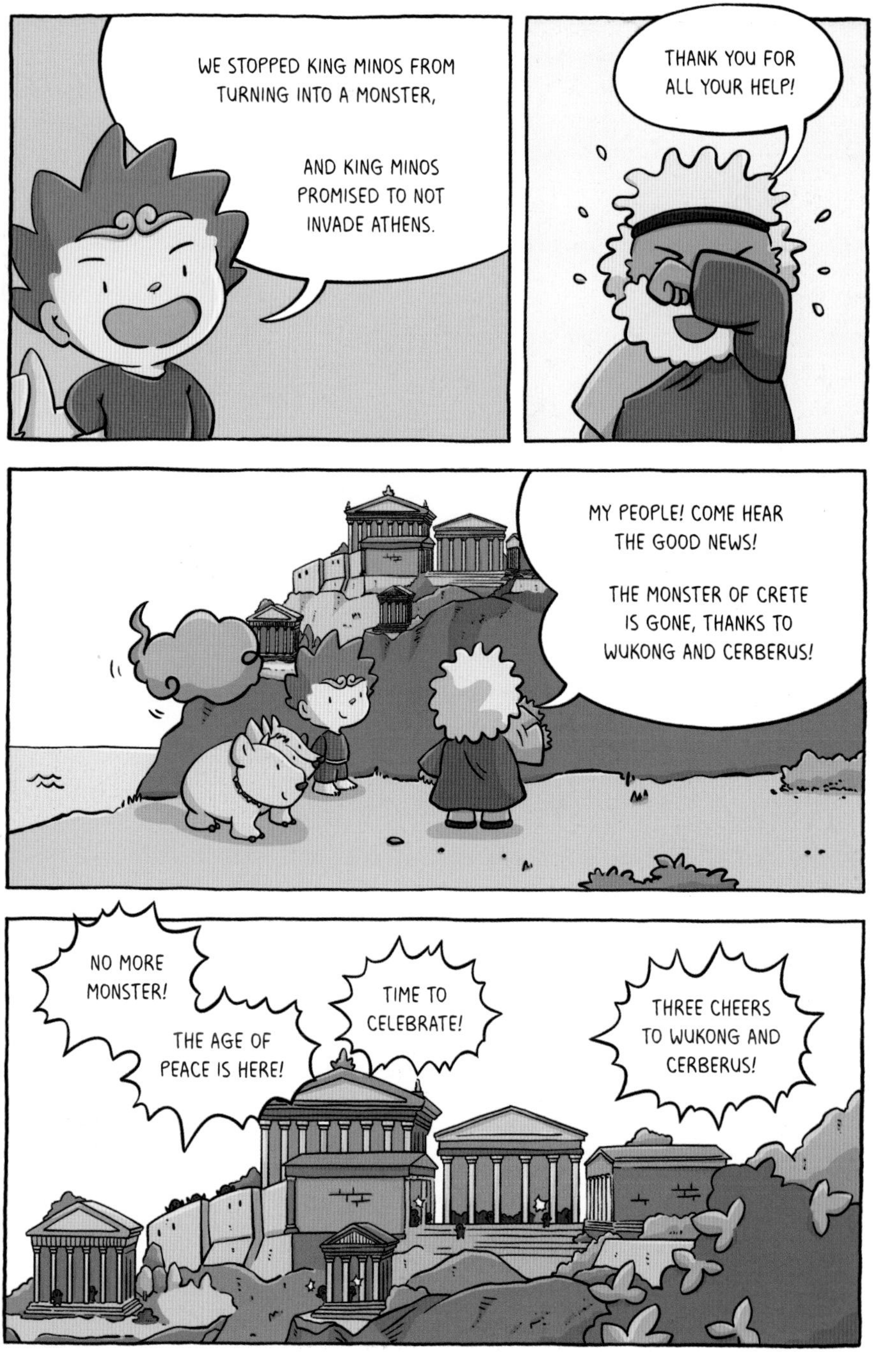
WE STOPPED KING MINOS FROM TURNING INTO A MONSTER,
AND KING MINOS PROMISED TO NOT INVADE ATHENS.
THANK YOU FOR ALL YOUR HELP!
MY PEOPLE! COME HEAR THE GOOD NEWS!
THE MONSTER OF CRETE IS GONE, THANKS TO WUKONG AND CERBERUS!
NO MORE MONSTER!
THE AGE OF PEACE IS HERE!
TIME TO CELEBRATE!
THREE CHEERS TO WUKONG AND CERBERUS!

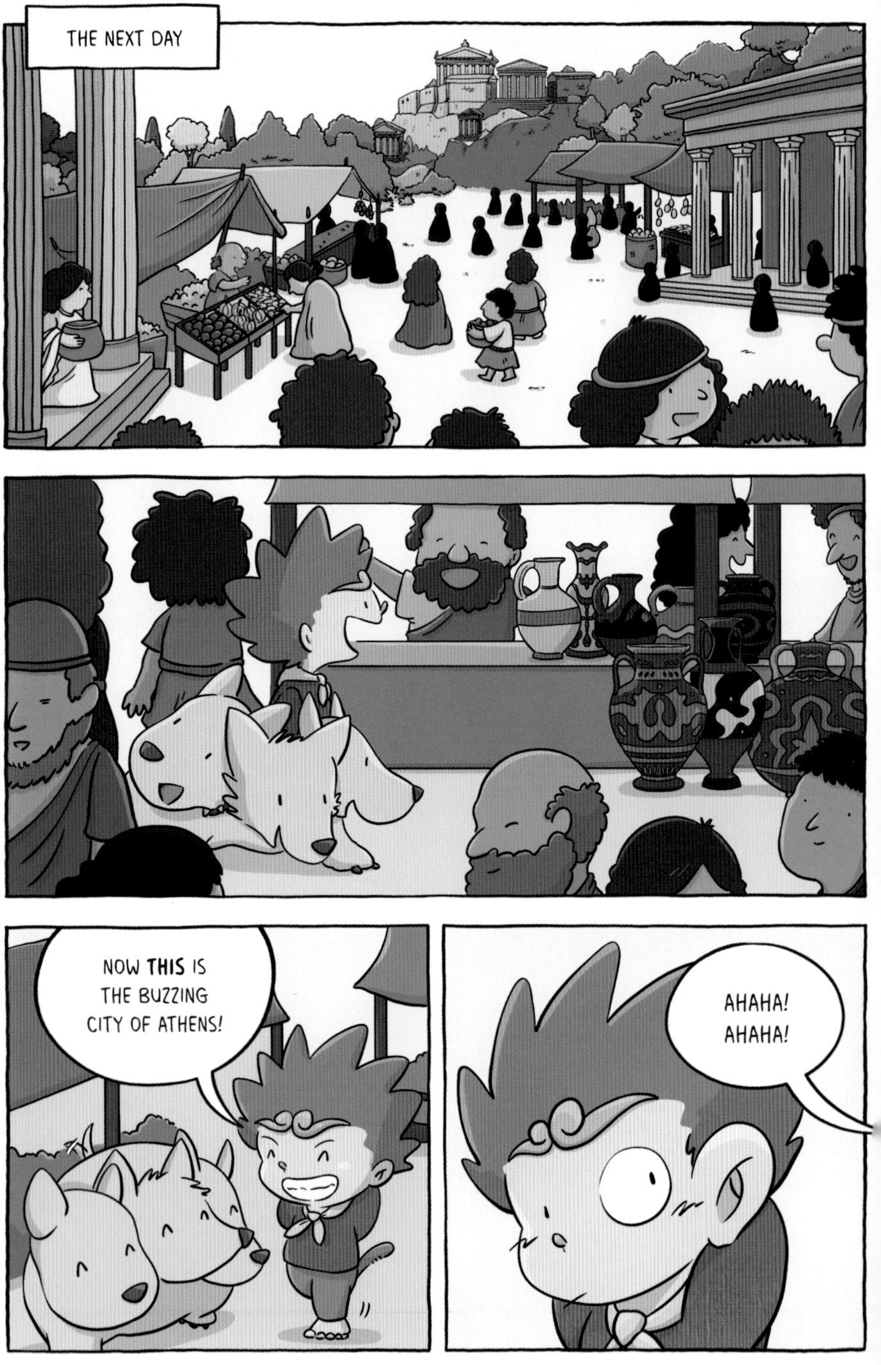
THE NEXT DAY
NOW **THIS** IS THE BUZZING CITY OF ATHENS!
AHAHA! AHAHA!

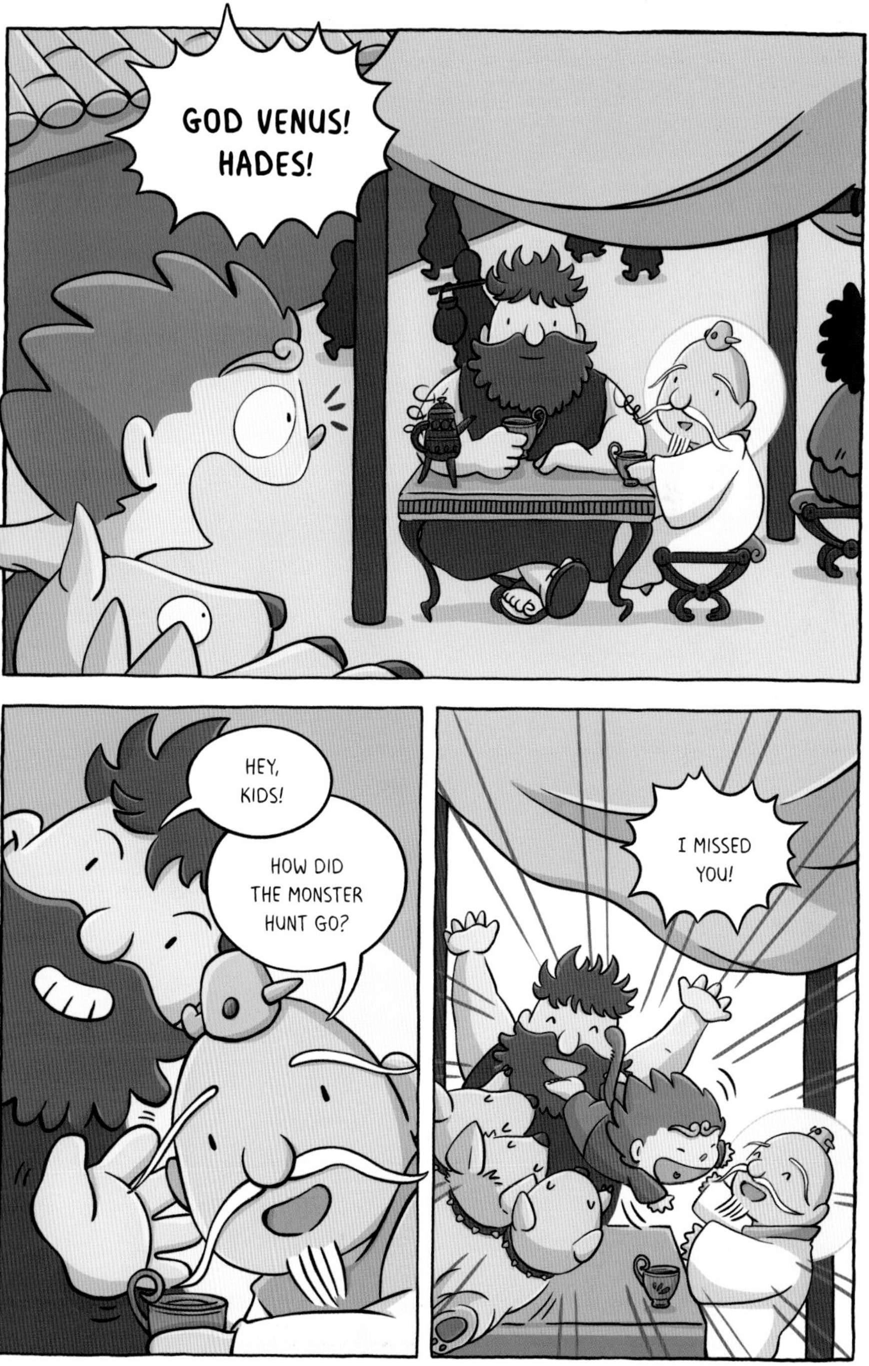
GOD VENUS!
HADES!
HEY, KIDS!
HOW DID THE MONSTER HUNT GO?
I MISSED YOU!

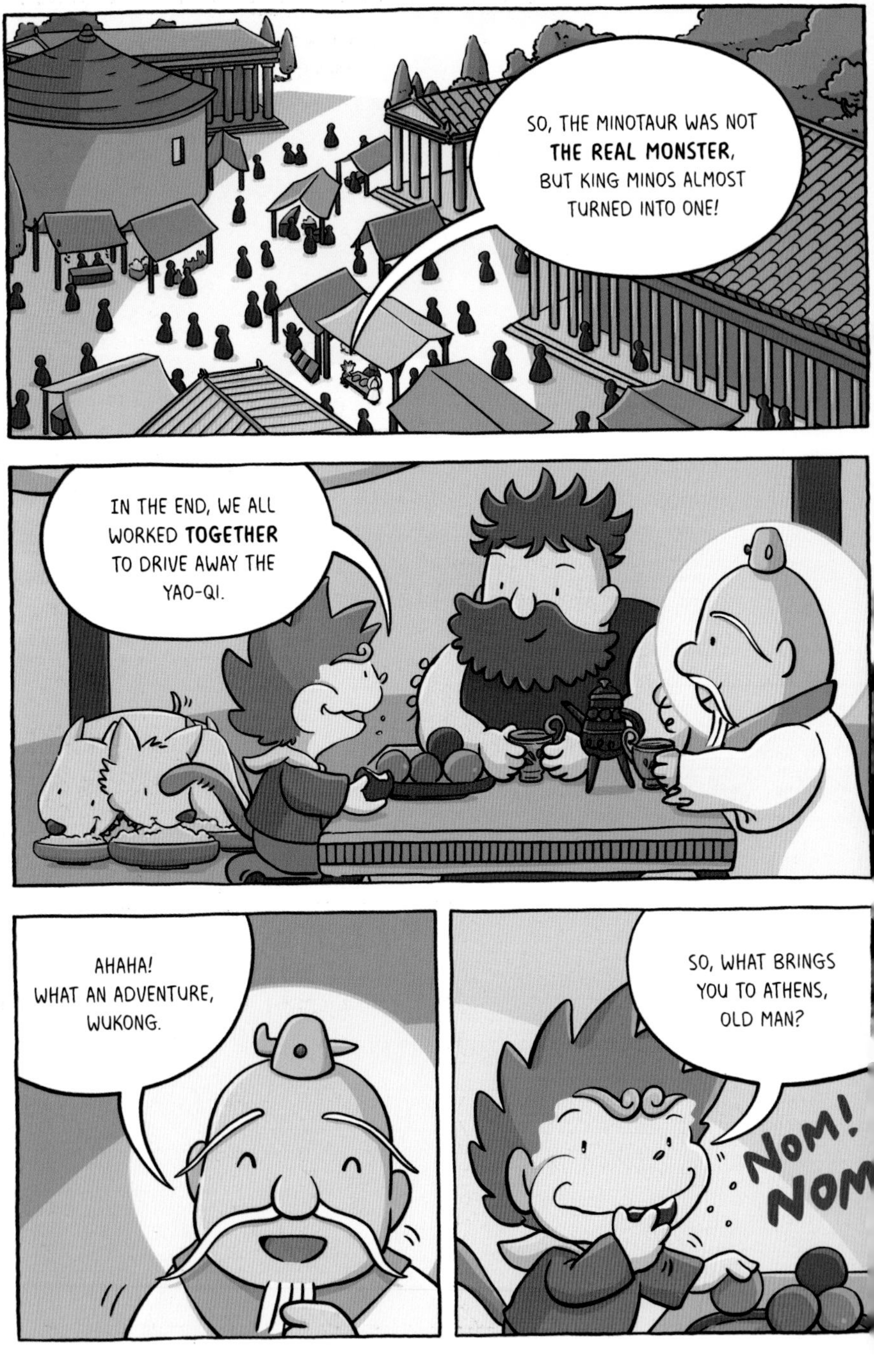
SO, THE MINOTAUR WAS NOT **THE REAL MONSTER**, BUT KING MINOS ALMOST TURNED INTO ONE!
IN THE END, WE ALL WORKED **TOGETHER** TO DRIVE AWAY THE YAO-QI.
AHAHA! WHAT AN ADVENTURE, WUKONG.
SO, WHAT BRINGS YOU TO ATHENS, OLD MAN?
NOM! NOM

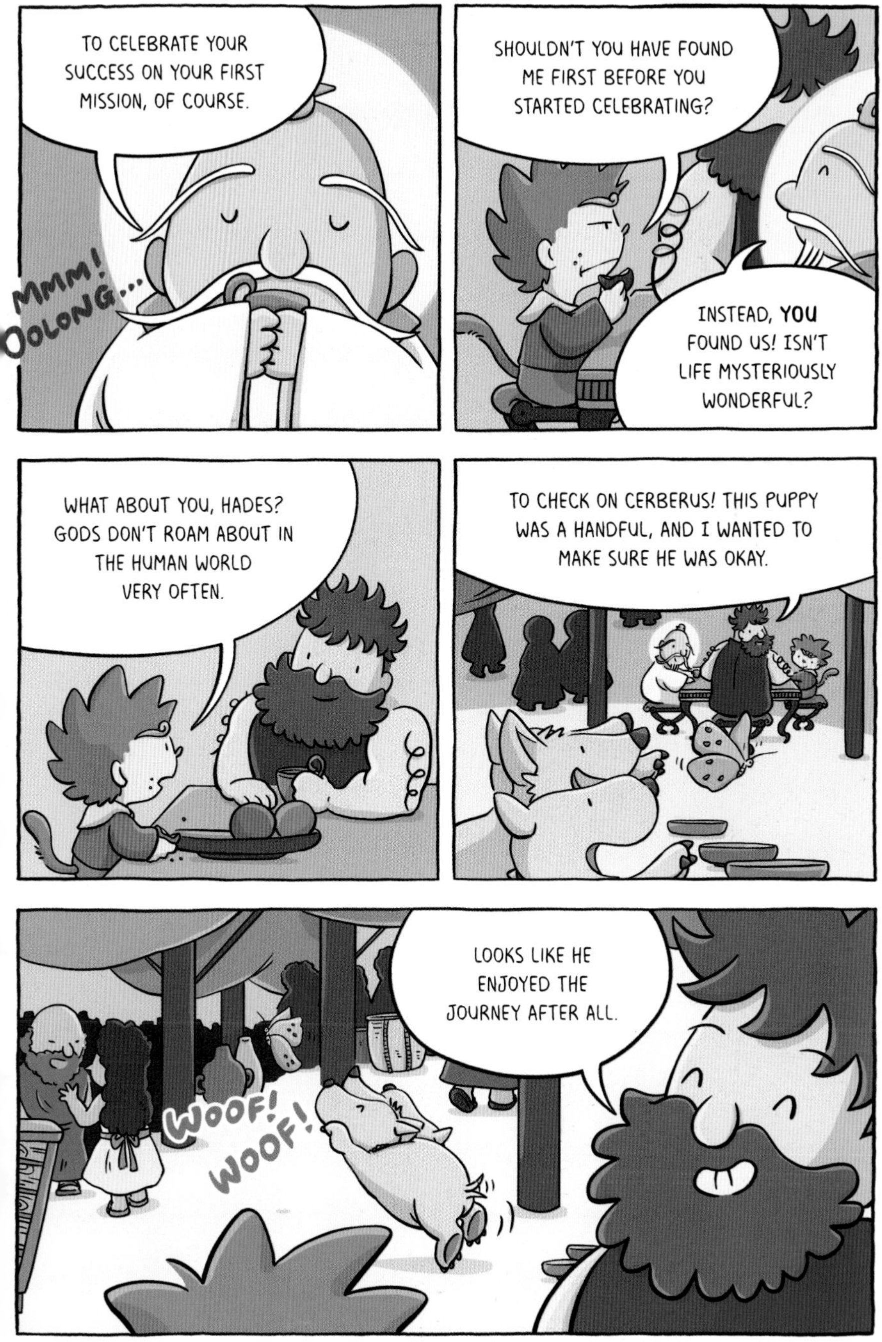
TO CELEBRATE YOUR SUCCESS ON YOUR FIRST MISSION, OF COURSE.
MMM! OOLONG...
SHOULDN'T YOU HAVE FOUND ME FIRST BEFORE YOU STARTED CELEBRATING?
INSTEAD, **YOU** FOUND US! ISN'T LIFE MYSTERIOUSLY WONDERFUL?
WHAT ABOUT YOU, HADES? GODS DON'T ROAM ABOUT IN THE HUMAN WORLD VERY OFTEN.
TO CHECK ON CERBERUS! THIS PUPPY WAS A HANDFUL, AND I WANTED TO MAKE SURE HE WAS OKAY.
LOOKS LIKE HE ENJOYED THE JOURNEY AFTER ALL.
WOOF! WOOF!

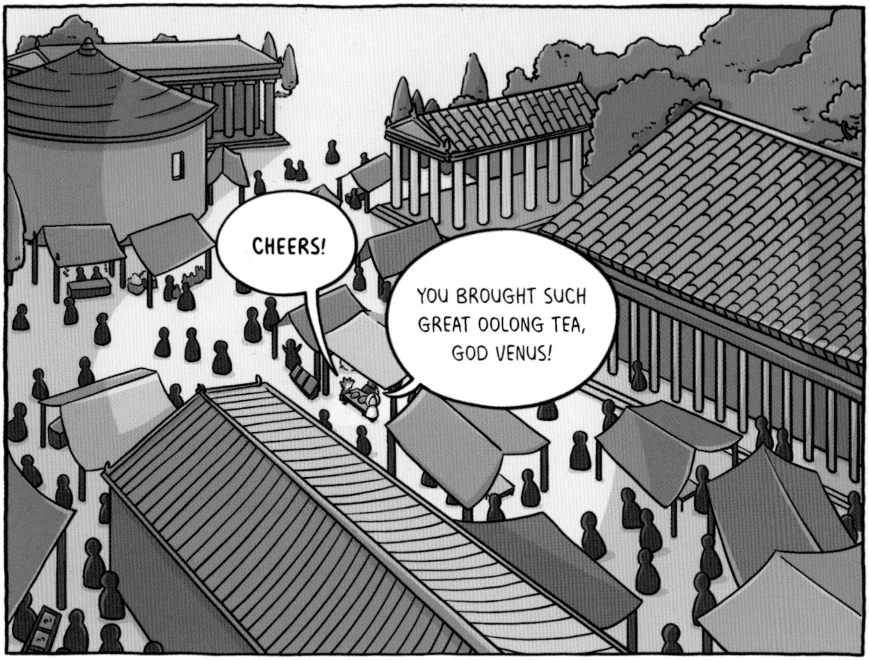
CHEERS!
YOU BROUGHT SUCH GREAT OOLONG TEA, GOD VENUS!

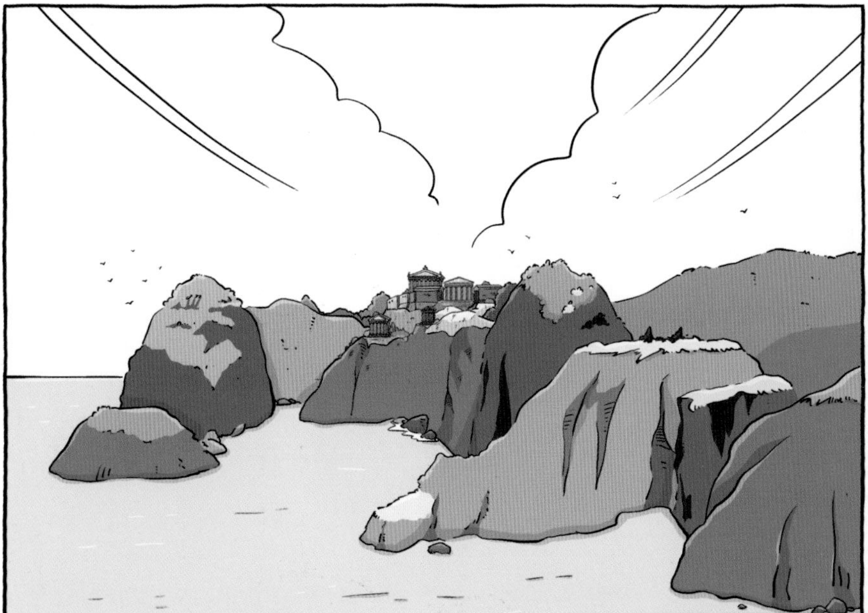

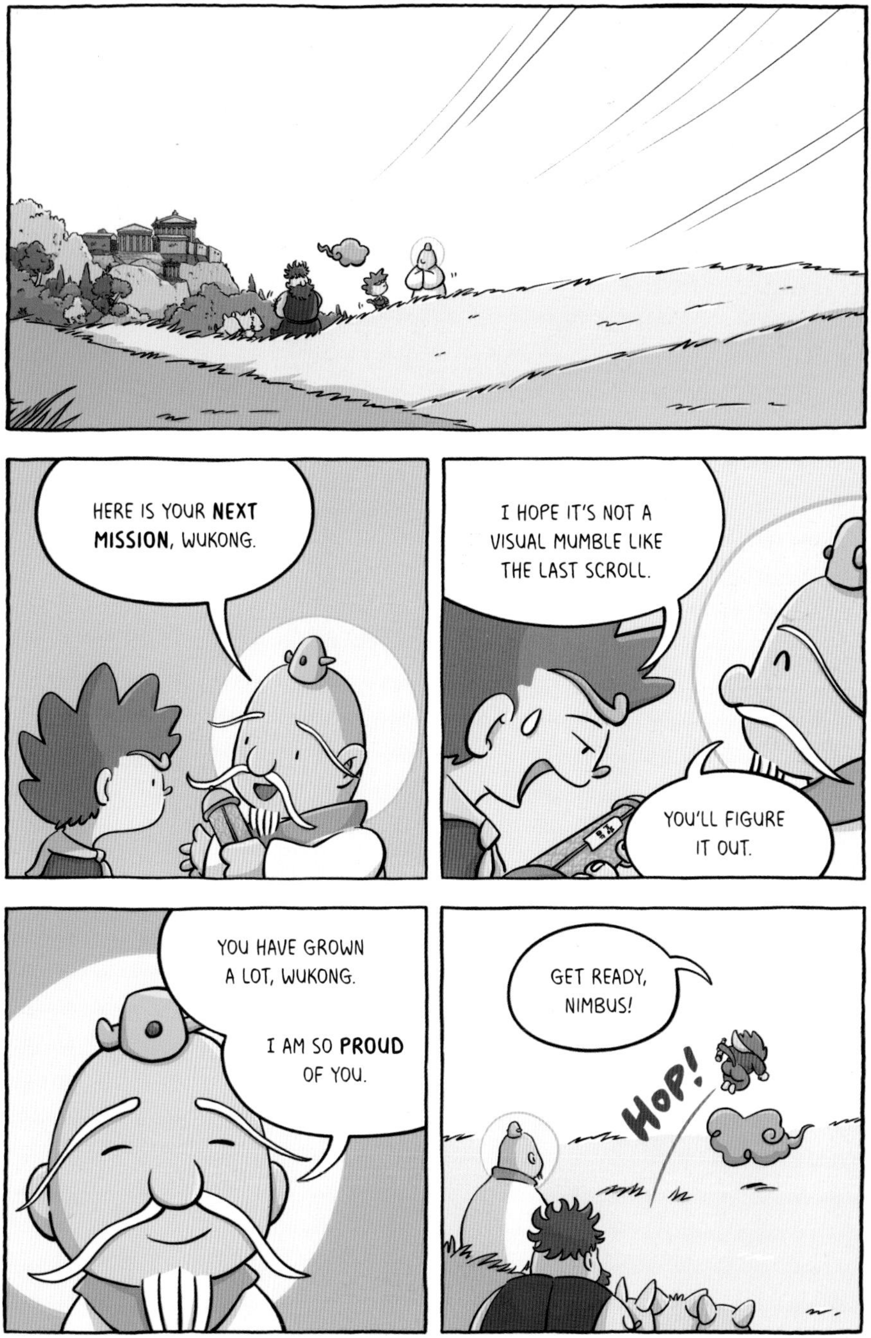
HERE IS YOUR **NEXT MISSION**, WUKONG.
I HOPE IT'S NOT A VISUAL MUMBLE LIKE THE LAST SCROLL.
YOU'LL FIGURE IT OUT.
YOU HAVE GROWN A LOT, WUKONG.
I AM SO **PROUD** OF YOU.
GET READY, NIMBUS!
HOP!

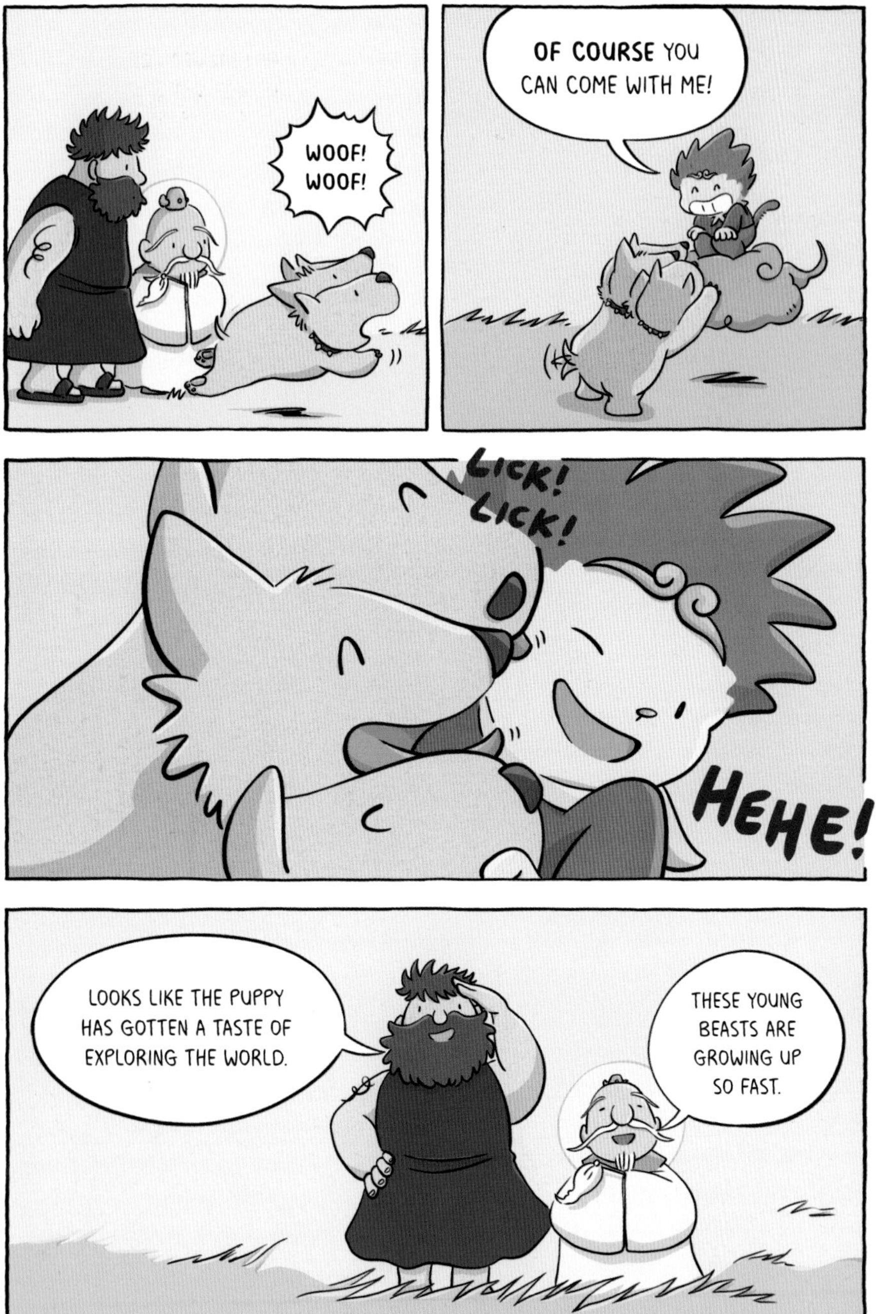
WOOF!
WOOF!
OF COURSE YOU CAN COME WITH ME!
LICK!
LICK!
HEHE!
LOOKS LIKE THE PUPPY HAS GOTTEN A TASTE OF EXPLORING THE WORLD.
THESE YOUNG BEASTS ARE GROWING UP SO FAST.

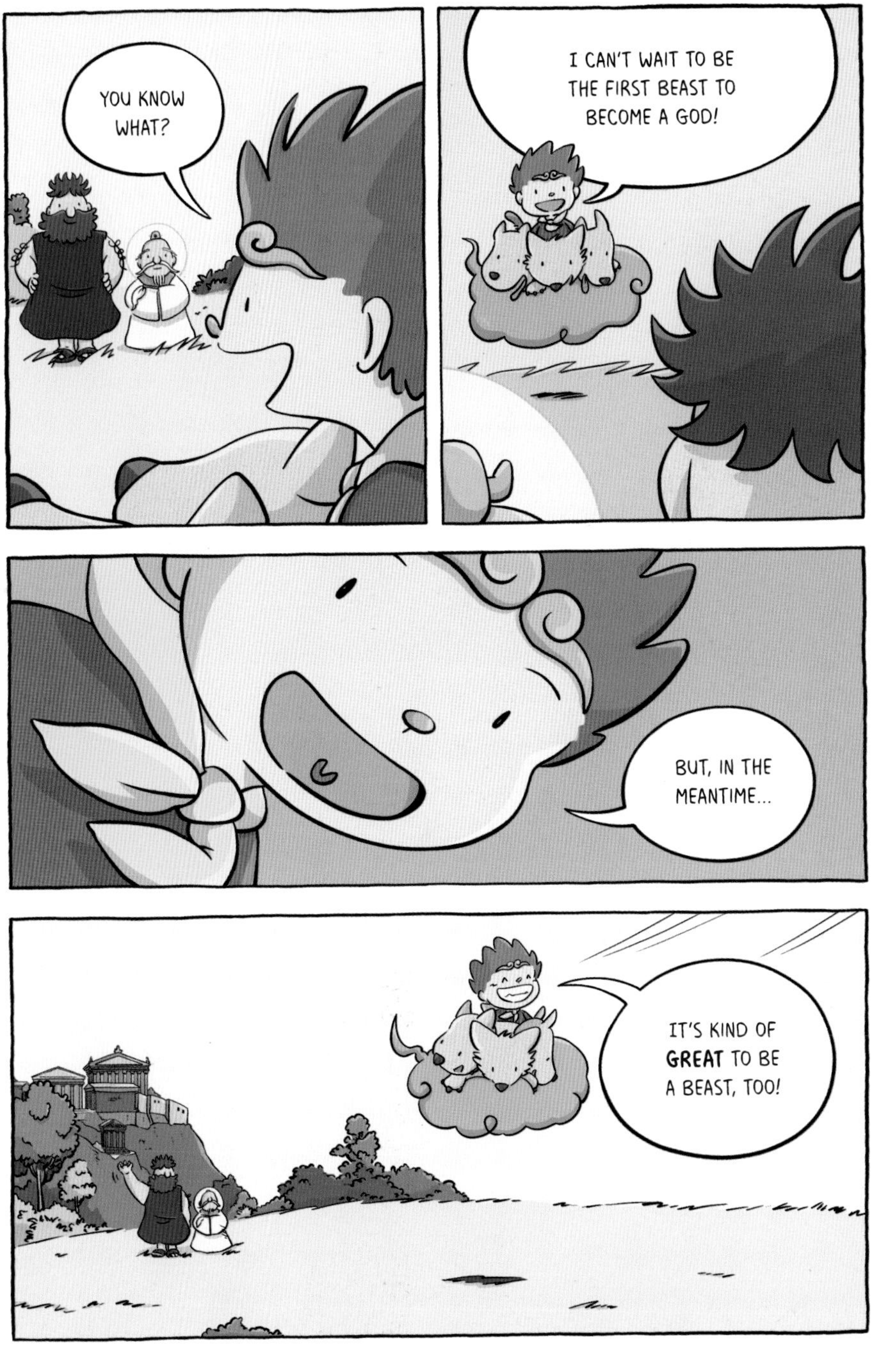
YOU KNOW WHAT?
I CAN'T WAIT TO BE THE FIRST BEAST TO BECOME A GOD!
BUT, IN THE MEANTIME...
IT'S KIND OF **GREAT** TO BE A BEAST, TOO!

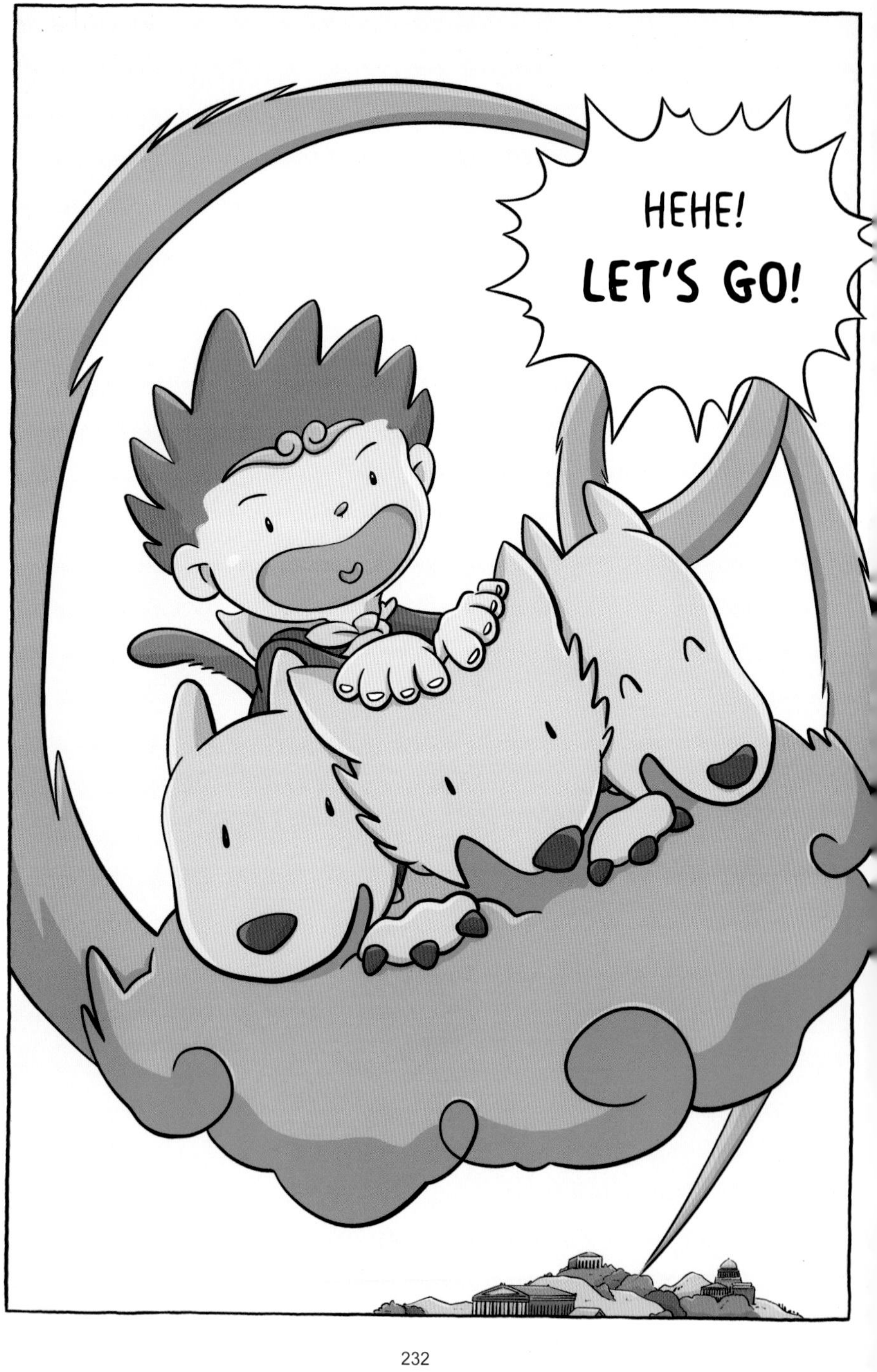
HEHE!
LET'S GO!

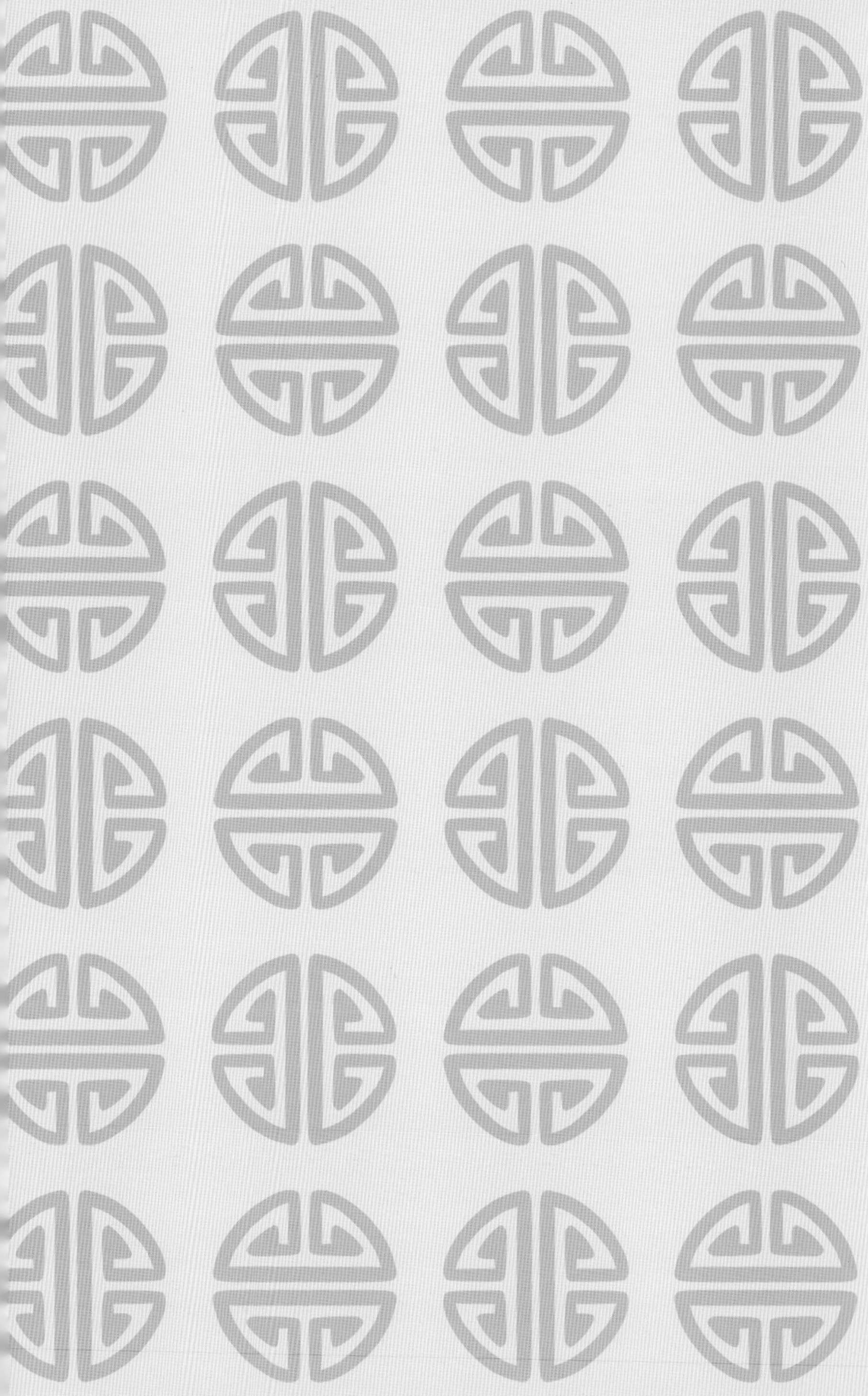

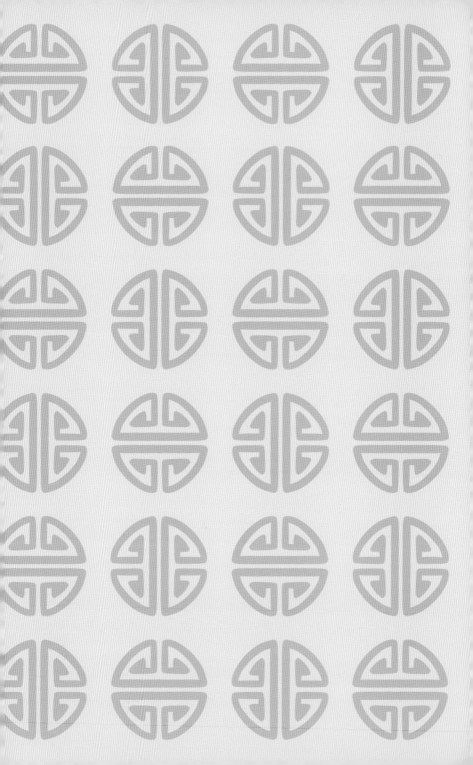

DID YOU KNOW?

ALL THE CHARACTERS IN THIS BOOK ARE INSPIRED BY MYTHOLOGIES FROM ACROSS THE WORLD. YOU CAN LEARN MORE ABOUT THEM BELOW OR BY READING THEIR ORGINAL STORIES!

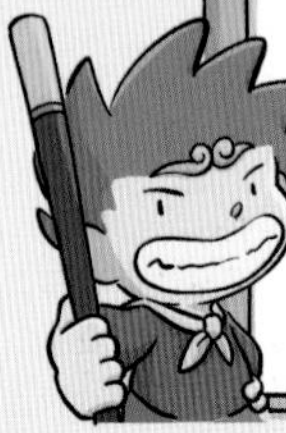

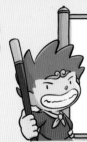

SUN WUKONG

SUN WUKONG IS ONE OF THE MAIN CHARACTERS IN ***JOURNEY TO THE WEST***, A 16TH CENTURY CHINESE CLASSIC WRITTEN BY WU CHENG'EN. SKILLED IN MARTIAL ARTS AND TRANSFORMATION, THIS MISCHIEVOUS MONKEY BEAST IS BEST KNOWN FOR CAUSING CHAOS IN THE HEAVENLY KINGDOM, AS WELL AS BEING ONE OF THREE GUARDIANS FOR A MONK WHO TRAVELED TO THE WEST IN ORDER TO RETRIEVE THE BUDDHIST SUTRAS.

GOD ERLANG

NEPHEW OF THE JADE EMPEROR, GOD ERLANG IS THE SECOND SON OF THE NORTHERN HEAVENLY KING. HIS THIRD EYE COULD SEE THE ULTIMATE TRUTH. AS THE ONLY GOD WHO KNOWS HOW TO TRANSFORM, HIS EPIC BATTLE WITH SUN WUKONG IN ***JOURNEY TO THE WEST*** MAKES GOD ERLANG A MEMORABLE CHARACTER.

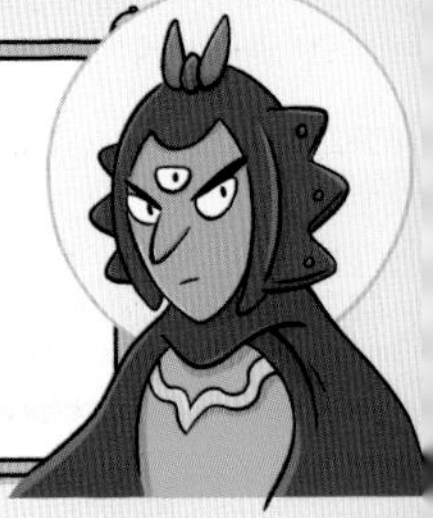

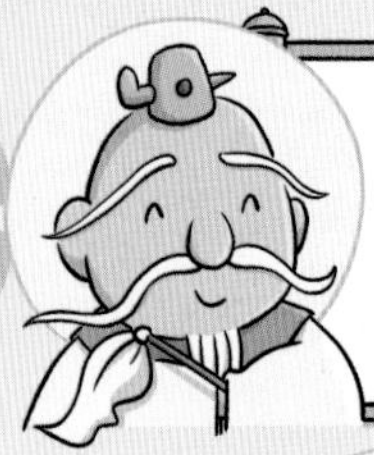

GOD VENUS

ALSO KNOWN AS "THE EVENING STAR," GOD VENUS IS KNOWN TO BE A COMPASSIONATE ELDER. HE SERVES AS A MESSENGER GOD TO THE JADE EMPEROR AND HAS GIVEN A HELPING HAND TO MANY GODS IN VARIOUS LEGENDS, INCLUDING WUKONG IN ***JOURNEY TO THE WEST***.

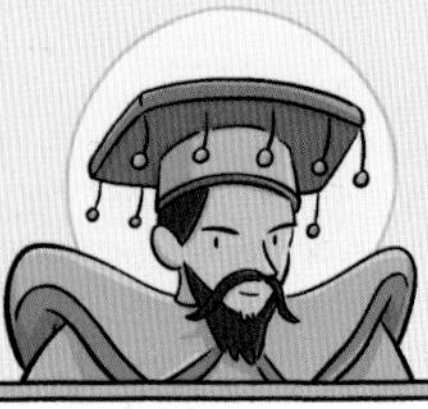

JADE EMPEROR

RULER OF THE HEAVENLY KINGDOM ACCORDING TO TAOISM, THE JADE EMPEROR OVERSEES ALL MATTERS IN THE HEAVENLY COURT.

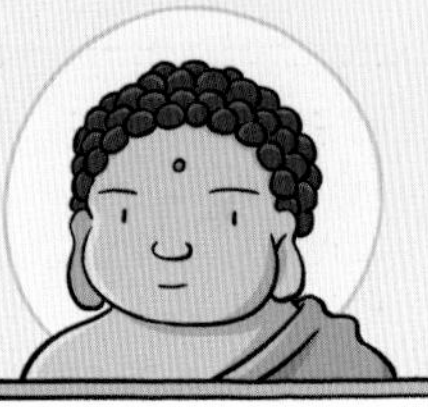

BUDDHA

FOUNDER OF BUDDHISM, THE GREAT, WISE BUDDHA TEACHES PEOPLE KINDNESS AND THE MIDDLE WAY, A PATH TO FREEDOM OF SUFFERING.

CERBERUS

THE THREE-HEADED HOUND HELPS GUARD THE ENTRANCE TO THE UNDERWORLD. HE WAS ONCE CAPTURED BY HERCULES IN HERCULES' FINAL LABORS, BUT WAS LATER RELEASED BACK INTO THE UNDERWORLD TO CONTINUE HIS DUTY.

HADES

KING OF THE UNDERWORLD, HADES IS BROTHER TO ZEUS, KING OF THE GODS, AND POSEIDON, KING OF THE SEA. THE ANCIENT GREEKS BELIEVED THE SOULS OF THE DEAD WOULD GO TO THE UNDERWORLD, WHERE THEY WOULD BE JUDGED FOR THEIR ACTIONS WHEN THEY WERE ALIVE.

THE MINOTAUR

IMPRISONED IN THE LABYRINTH BY KING MINOS, THE HALF-MAN, HALF-BULL BEAST IS RUMORED TO DEVOUR YOUNG ATHENIAN MEN AND WOMEN EVERY YEAR. ULTIMATELY, HE BATTLED AGAINST THESEUS (AS A GROWN MAN, NOT A BABY) AND LOST.

PRINCESS ARIADNE

DAUGHTER OF KING MINOS OF CRETE, THE KINDHEARTED PRINCESS HELPS THESEUS FIND HIS WAY OUT OF THE LABYRINTH AFTER DEFEATING THE MINOTAUR. THEY THEN FALL IN LOVE AND RUN AWAY TOGETHER. BUT THESEUS ULTIMATELY LEAVES HER BEHIND ON THE ISLAND OF NAXOS— A POOR WAY TO REPAY HER KINDNESS.

KING AEGEUS

WHEN KING MINOS OF CRETE DECLARES WAR ON ATHENS, KING AEGEUS FEELS HELPLESS. THE ONLY OTHER WAY TO AVOID WAR IS TO SEND FOURTEEN YOUNG MEN AND WOMEN TO FEED THE MINOTAUR. KING AEGEUS REFUSES TO SACRIFICE HIS PEOPLE. INSTEAD, HIS GROWN-UP SON, THESEUS, VOLUNTEERS TO FIGHT THE MINOTAUR, ALL TO BRING PEACE BETWEEN ATHENS AND CRETE.

A NOTE FROM THE AUTHOR

CHARACTERS IN MYTHOLOGY ARE OFTEN FILLED WITH FLAWS, AS THEY
ARE A REFLECTION OF OURSELVES. PERSONALLY, I LOVE THEM FLAWED—IT
MAKES THEM SO MUCH MORE RELATABLE. LIKE WUKONG IN MY STORY, MANY
MISTAKES WERE MADE, BUT HE LEARNED IN THE PROCESS. DON'T WE ALL?

I HAVE ALWAYS WANTED TO MIX AND MATCH ALL THE WORLD
MYTHOLOGICAL CHARACTERS IN MY OWN STORY. MAYBE THIS, TOO, IS DUE
TO MY MIXED-CULTURE EXPERIENCE, FOR I SPENT THE FIRST ELEVEN YEARS
OF MY LIFE IN HONG KONG BEFORE MOVING TO LOS ANGELES. GROWING UP,
I WAS CONTANTLY TRYING TO JUGGLE AND INTEGRATE BOTH THE CHINESE
AND AMERICAN CULTURE. IN THE END, THE STORY IS A REFLECTION OF MY
OWN JOURNEY AS I GO THROUGH LIFE.

AS JOSEPH CAMPBELL ONCE SAID, "MYTHS ARE STORIES OF OUR SEARCH
THROUGH THE AGES OF TRUTH, FOR MEANING, FOR SIGNIFICANCE."

I HOPE YOU ENJOYED THE JOURNEY JUST AS MUCH AS I ENJOYED
CREATING THIS STORY.

ACKNOWLEDGMENTS

I WOULD LIKE TO THANK MY FAMILY,
MOM, DAD, AND DENISE. THANK YOU
FOR ALWAYS BEING SUPPORTIVE AND
LOVING.

I WANT TO THANK MY EDITOR,
CHRISTOPHER HERNANDEZ, MY AGENT,
JORDAN HAMESSLEY, AND ALL THE
FANTASTIC STAFF AT PENGUIN FOR
THEIR HARD WORK ON MAKING THIS
BOOK A REALITY.